BRANDON SANDERSON

WORDS OF
RADIANCE

PART TWO

Book Two of
THE STORMLIGHT ARCHIVE

Copyright © Dragonsteel Entertainment, LLC 2014
All rights reserved

Illustrations preceding chapters 54, 70, 75, and 77 by Ben McSweeney

Maps and illustrations preceding chapters 60, 65, 80, 83,
and the Endnote by Isaac Stewart

The right of Brandon Sanderson to be identified as the author of this
work has been asserted by him in accordance with the
Copyright, Designs and Patents Act 1988.

First published in Great Britain in 2014
by Gollancz
An imprint of the Orion Publishing Group
Orion House, 5 Upper St Martin's Lane, London WC2H 9EA
An Hachette UK Company

This edition published in Great Britain in 2015 by Gollancz

1 3 5 7 9 10 8 6 4 2

A CIP catalogue record for this book is available
from the British Library

ISBN 978 0 575 09332 4

Typeset by Input Data Services Ltd, Bridgwater, Somerset

Printed and bound in Great Britain by Clays Ltd, St Ives plc

The Orion Publishing Group's policy is to use papers that are natural,
renewable and recyclable products and made from wood grown in sustainable
forests. The logging and manufacturing processes are expected to conform to
the environmental regulations of the country of origin.

www.brandonsanderson.com
www.orionbooks.co.uk
www.gollancz.co.uk

CONTENTS

Part Three: Deadly (continued)   1

Interludes   99

Part Four: The Approach   149

Interludes   342

Part Five: Winds Alight   373

Epilogue: Art and Expectation   551

Endnote   557

Ars Arcanum   559

ILLUSTRATIONS

NOTE: *Many illustrations, titles included contain spoilers for material that comes before them in the book. Look ahead at your own risk.*

Map of Roshar   vi-vii

Shallan's Sketchbook: Walks   34

Map of Stormseat   159

Life Cycle of a Chull   203

Shallan's Sketchbook: Chasm Life   268

Shallan's Sketchbook: Chasmfiend   329

Shallan's Sketchbook: Whitespine   390

Representation of the Shape of the Shattered Plains   418

Navani's Notebook: Battle Map   462

Navani's Notebook: Ketek   557

Roshar

ENDLESS OCEAN

Rall Elorim

RESHI

Kasitor

IRI

Riira

Kurth

Reshi

Eila

The Misted Mountains

BABATHARNAM

Panatham

MARABETHIA

The Purelake

SHINOVAR

JULAY

Fu Nan

DESH

AZIR

ALM

UEZIER

Azimir

EMUL

The Vall

AIMIA

Aimian Sea

LIAFOR

TASHIKK

GREAT
HE

STEEN

Sesemalex Dar

Icewater

TUKAR

MARA

N

LEEWARD

STORMWARD

S

SOUTHERN DEPTHS

STEAMWATER OCEAN

ISLES

Sea

Northgrip

HERDAZ

Mourn's
Vault

AKAK

Varikev

Ru Parat

Elanar

JAH KEVED

Kholinar

ALETHKAR

UNCLAIMED HILLS

TU
BAYLA

Valath

Hornetreats

Shulin

Dawn's
Shadow

BAVLAND

Rathalas

Silnasen

TU
TRIAX

Vedenar

Dumadari

Shattered
Plain

FALLI

Ta rat Sea

Karanak

FROSTLANDS

New Natanan

Kharbranth

Longbrow's

Straits

THAYLENAH

The Shallow Crypts

OCEAN OF ORIGINS

For His Royal Majesty King Gavilar Kholin
By His Royal High Cartographer Isasik Shulin
1167

PART

THREE

CONTINUED

Deadly

KALADIN • SHALLAN • ADOLIN

INTO THE SKY

Now, as the Truthwatchers were esoteric in nature, their order being formed entirely of those who never spoke or wrote of what they did, in this lies frustration for those who would see their exceeding secrecy from the outside; they were not naturally inclined to explanation; and in the case of Corberon's disagreements, their silence was not a sign of an exceeding abundance of disdain, but rather an exceeding abundance of tact.

—From *Words of Radiance,* chapter 11, page 6

K aladin strolled along the Shattered Plains at night, passing tufts of shalebark and vines, lifespren spinning about them as motes. Puddles still lingered in low spots from the previous day's highstorm, fat with crem for the plants to feast upon. To his left, Kaladin heard the sounds of the warcamps, busy with activity. To the right ... silence. Just those endless plateaus.

When he'd been a bridgeman, Sadeas's troops hadn't stopped him from walking this path. What was there for men out here, on the Plains? Instead, Sadeas had posted guards at the edges of the camps and at bridges, so the slaves couldn't escape.

What was there for men out here? Nothing but salvation itself, discovered in the depths of those chasms.

Kaladin turned and strolled out along one of the chasms, passing soldiers on guard duty at bridges, torches shivering in the wind. They saluted him.

There, he thought, picking his way along a particular plateau. The warcamps to his left stained the air with light, enough to see where he was. At the plateau's edge he came to the place where he had met with the King's Wit on that night weeks ago. A night of decision, a night of change.

Kaladin stepped up to the edge of the chasm, looking eastward.

Change and decision. He checked over his shoulder. He'd passed the guard post, and now nobody was close enough to see him. So, belt laden with bags of spheres, Kaladin stepped off into the chasm.

⁂

Shallan did not care for Sadeas's warcamp.

The air was different here than it was in Sebarial's camp. It stank, and it smelled of desperation.

Was desperation even a smell? She thought she could describe it. The scent of sweat, of cheap drink, and of crem that had not been cleaned off the streets. That all churned above roads that were poorly lit. In Sebarial's camp, people walked in groups. Here, they loped along in packs.

Sebarial's camp smelled of spice and industry – of new leather and, sometimes, livestock. Dalinar's camp smelled of polish and oil. Around every second corner in Dalinar's camp, someone was doing something practical. There were too few soldiers in Dalinar's camp these days, but each wore his uniform, as if it were a shield against the chaos of the times.

In Sadeas's camp, the men who wore their uniforms wore them with unbuttoned jackets and wrinkled trousers. She passed tavern after tavern, each spitting forth a racket. The women who idled in front of some in-dicated that not all were simply taverns. Whorehouses were common in every camp, of course, but they seemed more blatant here.

She passed fewer parshmen than she commonly saw in Sebarial's camp. Sadeas preferred traditional slaves: men and women with branded foreheads, scurrying about with backs bowed and shoulders slumped.

This was, honestly, what she'd expected from all of the warcamps. She'd read accounts of men at war – of camp followers and discipline problems. Of tempers flaring, of the attitudes of men who were trained to kill. Perhaps, instead of wondering at the awfulness of Sadeas's camp, she should be marveling that the others weren't the same.

Shallan hurried on her way. She wore the face of a young darkeyed man, her hair pushed up into her cap. She wore a pair of sturdy gloves. Even disguised as a boy, she wasn't about to go around with her safehand exposed.

Before leaving tonight, she had done a series of sketches to use as new faces, if need be. Testing had proven she could draw a sketch in the morning, then use it for an image in the afternoon. If she waited longer than about a day, though, the image she created was blurred and sometimes looked melted. That made perfect sense to Shallan. The process of creation left a picture in her mind that eventually wore thin.

Her current face had been based on the messenger youths who moved in Sadeas's camp. Though her heart thumped every time she passed a pack of soldiers, nobody gave her a second glance.

Amaram was a highlord – a man of third dahn, which made him a full rank higher than Shallan's father had been, two ranks higher than Shallan herself. That entitled him to his own little domain within his liege's warcamp. His manor flew his own banner, and he had his own personal military force occupying nearby buildings. Posts set into the stone and striped with his colors – burgundy and forest green – delineated his sphere of influence. She passed them without pausing.

'Hey, you!'

Shallan froze in place, feeling very small in the darkness. Not small enough. She turned slowly as a pair of patrolling guards walked up. Their uniforms were sharper than any she'd seen in this camp. Even the buttons were polished, though at the waists they wore skirtlike takama instead of trousers. Amaram was a traditionalist, and his uniforms reflected that.

The guards loomed over her, as most Alethi did. 'Messenger?' one asked. 'This time of night?' He was a solid fellow with a greying beard and a thick, wide nose.

'It's not even second moon yet, sir,' Shallan said in what she hoped was a boyish voice.

He frowned at her. What had she said? *Sir*, she realized. *He's not an officer.*

'Report at the guard posts from now on when you visit,' the man said, pointing toward a small, lit area in the distance behind them. 'We're going to start keeping a secure perimeter.'

'Yes, Sergeant.'

'Oh, stop harassing the lad, Hav,' the other soldier said. 'You can't expect him to know rules that half the soldiers don't even know yet.'

'On with you,' Hav said, waving Shallan through. She hastened to obey. A secure perimeter? She didn't envy these men that task. Amaram didn't have a wall to keep people out, just some striped posts.

Amaram's manor was relatively small – two stories, with a handful of rooms on each floor. It might once have been a tavern, and was temporary, as he'd only just arrived at the warcamps. Stacked piles of crembrick and stone nearby indicated some far grander building was being planned. Near the piles stood other buildings that had been appropriated as barracks for Amaram's personal guard, which included only about fifty men. Most of the soldiers he'd brought, recruited from Sadeas's lands and sworn to him, would billet elsewhere.

Once she got close to Amaram's home, she ducked beside an outbuilding and squatted down. She'd spent three evenings scouting this area, wearing a different face each time. Perhaps that had been overly cautious. She wasn't certain. She'd never done anything like this before. Fingers trembling, she took off her cap – that part of the costume was real – and let her hair spill around her shoulders. Then she dug a folded picture out of her pocket and waited.

Minutes passed as she stared at the manor. *Come on . . .* she thought. *Come on . . .*

Finally, a young darkeyed woman stepped out of the manor, arm-in-arm with a tall man in trousers and a loose buttoned shirt. The woman tittered as her friend said something, then she scampered off into the night, the man calling after her and following. The maid – Shallan *still* hadn't been able to learn her name – left every night at this time. Twice with this man. Once with another.

Shallan took a deep breath, drawing in Stormlight, then held up the picture she'd drawn of the girl earlier. About Shallan's height, hair about the same length, similar enough build . . . It would have to do. She breathed out, and became someone else.

She giggles and laughs, Shallan thought, plucking off her masculine gloves and replacing the one on the safehand with a tan feminine one, *and often prances about, walking on her toes. Her voice is higher than mine, and she doesn't have an accent.*

Shallan had practiced sounding right, but hopefully she wouldn't need to find out how believable her voice was. All she had to do was go in the door, up the stairs, and slip into the appropriate room. Easy.

She stood up, holding her breath and living off the Stormlight, and strode toward the building.

．．．

Kaladin hit the bottom of the chasm in a glowing storm of Light. He took off at a jog, spear over his shoulder. It was difficult to stand still with Stormlight in his veins.

He dropped a few of the pouches of spheres to use later. The Stormlight rising from his exposed skin was enough to illuminate the chasm, and it cast shadows on the walls as he ran. Those seemed to become figures, crafted by the bones and branches stretching from the heaps on the ground. Bodies and souls. His movement made the shadows twist, as if turning to regard him.

He ran with a silent audience, then. Syl flew down as a ribbon of light and took up position beside his head, matching his speed. He leaped over obstacles and splashed through puddles, letting his muscles warm to the exercise.

Then he jumped up onto the wall.

He hit awkwardly, tripping and rolling through some frillblooms. He came to rest facedown, lying on the wall. He growled and pushed himself to his feet as Stormlight sealed a small cut on his arm.

Jumping onto the wall felt too unnatural; when he hit, it took time to orient himself.

He started running again, sucking in more Stormlight, accustoming himself to the change of perspective. When he reached the next gap between plateaus, to his eyes it looked as if he'd reached a deep pit. The walls of the chasm were his floor and ceiling.

He hopped off the wall, focused on the floor of the chasm, and blinked – willing that direction to become *down* to him again. He landed in another stumble, and this time tripped into a puddle.

He rolled over onto his back, sighing, lying in the cold water. Crem that had settled to the bottom squished between his fingers as he clenched fists.

Syl landed on his chest, taking the form of a young woman. She put hands on her hips.

'What?' he asked.

'That was pathetic.'

'Agreed.'

'Maybe you're taking it a little too quickly,' she said. 'Why not try to jump onto the wall without a running start?'

'The assassin could do it this way,' Kaladin said. 'I need to be able to fight like he does.'

'I see. And I suppose he started doing all of this the moment he was born, without any practice at all.'

Kaladin exhaled softly. 'You sound like Tukks used to.'

'Oh? Was he brilliant, beautiful, and always right?'

'He was loud, intolerant, and profoundly acerbic,' Kaladin said, standing up. 'But yes, he was basically always right.' He faced the wall and leaned his spear against it. 'Szeth called this "Lashing."'

'A good term,' Syl said, nodding.

'Well, to get this down, I'm going to have to practice some fundamentals.' Just like learning a spear.

That probably meant hopping onto and off the wall a couple hundred times.

Better than dying on that assassin's Shardblade, he thought, and got to it.

⁕

Shallan stepped into Amaram's kitchens, trying to move with the energetic grace of the girl whose face she wore. The large room smelled strongly of the curry simmering over the hearth – the remnants of the night's meal, waiting in case any lighteyes got peckish. The cook browsed a novel in the corner while her girls scrubbed pots. The room was well lit with spheres. Amaram apparently trusted his servants.

A long flight of steps led up to the second floor, providing quick access for servants to bring meals to Amaram. Shallan had drawn a layout of the building from guesses based on window locations. The room with the secrets had been easy to locate – Amaram had the windows shuttered, and never opened them. She'd guessed right about the stairwell in the kitchens, it seemed. She strode toward those steps, humming to herself, as the woman she imitated often did.

'Back already?' the cook said, not looking up from her novel. She was

Herdazian, from the accent. 'His gift tonight wasn't nice enough? Or did the other one spot you two together?'

Shallan said nothing, trying to cover her anxiety with the humming. 'Might as well put you to use,' the cook said. 'Stine wanted someone to polish mirrors for him. He's in the study, cleaning the master's flutes.'

Flutes? A soldier like Amaram had flutes?

What would the cook do if Shallan bolted up the stairs and ignored the order? The woman was probably high ranked for a darkeyes. An important member of the household staff.

The cook didn't look up from her novel, but continued softly. 'Don't think we haven't noticed you sneaking off during midday, child. Just because the master is fond of you doesn't mean you can take advantage. Go to work. Spending your free evening cleaning instead of playing might remind you that you have duties.'

Gritting her teeth, Shallan looked up those steps toward her goal. The cook slowly lowered her novel. Her frown seemed the type that one didn't disobey.

Shallan nodded, moving away from the steps and into the corridor beyond. There would be another set of steps upward in the front hall. She'd just have to make her way in that direction and—

Shallan froze in place as a figure stepped into the hallway from a side room. Tall with a square face and angular nose, the man wore a lighteyed outfit of modern design: an open jacket over a buttoned shirt, stiff trousers, a stock tied in place at his neck.

Storms! Highlord Amaram – fashionable or otherwise – was *not* supposed to be in the building today. Adolin had said that Amaram was dining with Dalinar and the king tonight. Why was he here?

Amaram stood looking over a ledger in his hand, and didn't seem to have noticed her. He turned away from her and strolled down the corridor.

Run. It was her immediate reaction. Escape out the front doors, vanish into the night. The problem was, she'd spoken to the cook. When the woman Shallan was imitating came back later, she'd be in a storm of trouble – and she'd be able to prove, with witnesses, that she hadn't come back into the house earlier. Whatever Shallan did, there was a good chance that once she was gone, Amaram would find out that someone had been sneaking about, imitating one of his maids.

Stormfather! She'd only just stepped into the building, and already she'd messed everything up.

Stairs creaked up ahead. Amaram was going up to his room, the one Shallan was supposed to inspect.

The Ghostbloods will be mad at me for alerting Amaram, Shallan thought, *but they'll be even angrier if I do that and then return with no information.*

She had to get into that room, alone. That meant she couldn't let Amaram enter it.

Shallan scrambled after him, rushing into the entry hall and twisting around the newel post to propel herself up the stairs. Amaram reached the top landing and turned toward the hallway. Maybe he wouldn't go in that room.

She wasn't so lucky. As Shallan scurried up the steps, Amaram turned toward just that door and raised a key, slipping it into the lock and turning it.

'Brightlord Amaram,' Shallan said, out of breath as she reached the top landing.

He turned toward her, frowning. 'Telesh? Weren't you going out tonight?'

Well, at least she knew her name now. Did Amaram really take such an interest in his servants as to be aware of a lowly maid's evening plans?

'I did, Brightlord,' Shallan said, 'but I came back.'

Need a distraction. But not something too suspicious. Think! Was he going to notice that the voice was different?

'Telesh,' Amaram said, shaking his head. 'You still can't choose between them? I promised your good father I'd see you cared for. How can I do that if you won't settle down?'

'It's not that, Brightlord,' Shallan said quickly. 'Hav stopped a messenger on the perimeter coming for you. He sent me back to tell you.'

'Messenger?' Amaram said, slipping the key back out of the lock. 'From whom?'

'Hav didn't say, Brightlord. He seemed to think it was important, though.'

'That man . . .' Amaram said with a sigh. 'He's too protective. He thinks he can keep a tight perimeter in this mess of a camp?' The highlord considered, then stuffed the key back in his pocket. 'Better see what it's about.'

Shallan gave him a bow as he passed her by and trotted down the stairs. She counted to ten once he was out of sight, then scrambled to the door. It was still locked.

'Pattern!' Shallan whispered. 'Where are you?'

He came out from the folds of her skirts, moving across the floor and then up the door until he was just before her, like a raised carving on the wood.

'The lock?' Shallan asked.

'It is a pattern,' he said, then grew very small and moved into the key-hole. She'd had him try a few more times on locks back in her rooms, and he'd been able to unlock those as he had Tyn's trunk.

The lock clicked, and she opened the door and slipped into the dark room. A sphere plucked from her dress pocket lit it for her.

The secret room. The room with shutters always closed, kept locked at all times. A room that the Ghostbloods wanted so desperately to see.

It was filled with maps.

⁂

The trick to jumping between surfaces wasn't the landing, Kaladin discovered. It wasn't about reflexes or timing. It wasn't even about changing perspective.

It was about fear.

It was about that moment when, hanging in the air, his body lurched from being pulled *down* to being pulled *sideways*. His instincts weren't equipped to deal with this shift. A primal part of him panicked every time down stopped being down.

He ran at the wall and jumped, throwing his feet to the side. He couldn't hesitate, couldn't be afraid, couldn't flinch. It was like teaching himself to dive face-first onto a stone surface without raising his hands for protection.

He shifted his perspective and used Stormlight to make the wall become downward. He positioned his feet. Even still, in that brief moment, his instincts rebelled. The body knew, it *knew*, that he was going to fall back to the chasm floor. He would break bones, hit his head.

He landed on the wall without stumbling.

Kaladin stood up straight, surprised, and exhaled a deep breath, puffing with Stormlight.

'Nice!' Syl said, zipping around him.

'It's unnatural,' Kaladin said.

'No. I could never be involved in anything unnatural. It's just … *extra*-natural.'

'You mean supernatural.'

'No I don't.' She laughed and zipped on ahead of him.

It *was* unnatural – as walking wasn't natural for a child who was just learning. It became natural over time. Kaladin was learning to crawl – and unfortunately, he'd soon be required to run. Like a child dropped in a whitespine's lair. Learn quickly or be lunch.

He ran along the wall, hopping over a shalebark outcropping, then jumped to the side and shifted to the floor of the chasm. He landed with only a slight stumble.

Better. He ran after Syl and kept at it.

❖

Maps.

Shallan crept forward, her solitary sphere revealing a room draped with maps and strewn with papers. They were covered in glyphs that had been scribbled quickly, not made to be beautiful. She could barely read most of them.

I've heard of this, she thought. *The stormwarden script. The way they get around the restrictions on writing.*

Amaram was a stormwarden? A chart of times on one wall, listing highstorms and calculations of their next arrival – written in the same hand as the notes on the maps – seemed proof of that. Perhaps this was what the Ghostbloods were seeking: blackmail material. Stormwardens, as male scholars, made most people uncomfortable. Their use of glyphs in a way that was basically the same as writing, their secretive nature … Amaram was one of the most accomplished generals in all of Alethkar. He was respected even by those he fought. Exposing him as a storm-warden could seriously damage his reputation.

Why would he bother with such strange hobbies? All of these maps faintly reminded her of the ones she'd discovered in her father's study, after his death – though those had been of Jah Keved. 'Watch outside, Pattern,' she said. 'Bring me word quickly when Amaram returns to the building.'

'Mmmm,' he buzzed, withdrawing.

Aware that her time was short, Shallan hurried to the wall, holding up her sphere and taking Memories of the maps. The Shattered Plains? This map was far more extensive than any she'd seen before – and that included the Prime Map that she'd studied in the king's Gallery of Maps.

How had Amaram obtained something so extensive? She tried to work out the use of glyphs – there was no grammar to them that she could see. Glyphs weren't meant to be used that way. They conveyed a single idea, not a string of thoughts. She read a few in a row.

Origin . . . direction . . . uncertainty. . . . The place of the center is uncertain? That was probably what it meant.

Other notes were similar, and she translated in her head. *Perhaps pushing this direction will yield results. Warriors spotted watching from here.* Other groupings of glyphs made no sense to her. This script was bizarre. Perhaps Pattern could translate it, but she certainly couldn't.

Aside from the maps, the walls were covered in long sheets of paper filled with writing, figures, and diagrams. Amaram was working on something, something big—

Parshendi! she realized. *That's what those glyphs mean. Parap-shenesh-idi.* The three glyphs individually meant three separate things – but together, their sounds made the word 'Parshendi.' That was why some of the writings seemed like gibberish. Amaram was using some glyphs phonetically. He underlined them when he did this, and that allowed him to write in glyphs things that never should have worked. The stormwardens really *were* turning glyphs into a full script.

Parshendi, she translated, still distracted by the nature of the characters, *must know how to return the Voidbringers.*

What?

Remove secret from them.

Reach center before Alethi armies.

Some of the writings were lists of references. Though they'd been translated to glyphs, she recognized some of the quotes from Jasnah's work. They referred to the Voidbringers. Others were purported sketches of Voidbringers and other creatures of mythology.

This was it, full proof that the Ghostbloods were interested in the same things Jasnah was. As was Amaram, apparently. Heart beating with excitement, Shallan turned around, looking over the room. Was the secret to Urithiru here? Had he found it?

There was too much for Shallan to translate fully at the moment. The script was too difficult, and her thumping heart made her too nervous. Besides, Amaram would likely return very soon. She took Memories so she could sketch this all out later.

As she did, the writings she translated in passing caused a new species of dread to rise within her. It seemed . . . it seemed that Highlord Amaram – paragon of Alethi honor – was *actively* trying to bring about the return of the Voidbringers.

I have to stay a part of this, Shallan thought. *I can't afford to have the Ghostbloods cast me out for making a mess of this incursion. I need to discover what else they know. And I have to know why Amaram is doing what he does.*

She couldn't just run tonight. She couldn't risk leaving Amaram alerted that someone had infiltrated his secret room. She couldn't botch this assignment.

Shallan had to craft better lies.

She pulled a sheet of paper from her pocket and slapped it onto the desk, then began to frantically draw.

⁂

Kaladin jumped off the wall at a careful speed, twisting to the side and landing back on the ground without breaking step. He wasn't going very quickly, but at least he didn't stumble anymore.

With each jump, he shoved the visceral panic farther down. Up, back onto the wall. Down again. Again and again, sucking in Stormlight.

Yes, this was natural. Yes, this was *him*.

He continued running along the chasm bottom, feeling a surge of excitement. Shadows waved him on as he dodged between piles of bone and moss. He leaped over a large pool of water, but misjudged its size. He came down – about to splash into the shallow water.

But by reflex, he looked upward and Lashed himself toward the sky.

For a brief moment, Kaladin stopped falling down and fell up instead. His momentum continued forward, and he cleared the pool, then Lashed himself downward again. He landed in a trot, sweating.

I could Lash myself upward, he thought, *and fall into the sky forever.*

But no, that was how an ordinary person thought. A skyeel didn't fear falling, did it? A fish didn't fear drowning.

Until he began thinking in a new way, he wouldn't control this gift he had been given. And it *was* a gift. He would embrace this.

The sky was now his.

Kaladin shouted, dashing forward. He leaped and Lashed himself to the wall. No pausing, no hesitance, no *fear*. He hit at a dead run, and nearby, Syl laughed for joy.

But that, that was simple. Kaladin jumped off the wall and looked directly above him at the opposite wall. He Lashed himself in that direction, and flung his body into a flip. He landed, going down on one knee upon what had been the ceiling to him a moment before.

'You did it!' Syl said, flitting around him. 'What changed?'

'I did.'

'Well, yeah, but what about you?' Syl asked.

'Everything.'

She frowned at him. He grinned back, then took off at a run along the side of the chasm.

⁜

Shallan strode down the mansion's back steps to the kitchen, thumping each foot down harder than it would normally fall, trying to imitate being heavier than she was. The cook looked up from her novel and dropped it in a wide-eyed panic, moving to stand. 'Brightlord!'

'Remain seated,' Shallan mouthed, scratching at her face to mask her lips. Pattern spoke the words she'd told him to say in a perfect imitation of Amaram's voice.

The cook remained seated, as ordered. Hopefully, from that position, she wouldn't notice that Amaram was shorter than he should be. Even walking on her tiptoes – which was masked by the illusion – she was much shorter than the highlord.

'You spoke to the maid Telesh earlier,' Pattern said as Shallan mouthed the words.

'Yes, Brightlord,' the cook said, speaking softly to match Pattern's tone of voice. 'I sent her off to work with Stine for the evening. I thought the girl needed a little direction.'

'No,' Pattern said. 'Her return was at my command. I have sent her out again, and told her not to speak of what happened tonight.'

The cook frowned. 'What . . . happened tonight?'

'You are not to speak of this event. You interfered with something that is not of your concern. Pretend you did not see Telesh. Never speak of this event to me. If you do, I will pretend none of this happened. Do you understand?'

The cook grew pale, and nodded her head, sinking down in her chair.

Shallan nodded to her curtly, then walked from the kitchens out into the night. There, she ducked to the side of the building, heart pounding. A grin formed on her face anyway.

Out of sight, she exhaled Stormlight in a cloud, then stepped forward. As she passed through it, the image of Amaram vanished, replaced by that of the messenger boy she'd been imitating before. She scrambled back to the front of the building and sat down on the steps, slumping and leaning with her head on her hand.

Amaram and Hav walked up through the night, speaking softly. '. . . I didn't notice that the girl had seen me talking to the messenger, Highlord,' Hav was saying. 'She must have realized . . .' He trailed off as they saw Shallan.

She hopped to her feet and bowed to Amaram.

'It's no matter now, Hav,' Amaram said, waving the soldier back to his rounds.

'Highlord,' Shallan said. 'I bring you a message.'

'Obviously, darkborn,' the man said, stepping up to her. 'What does he want?'

'He?' Shallan asked. 'This is from Shallan Davar.'

Amaram cocked his head. 'Who?'

'Betrothed of Adolin Kholin,' she said. 'She is trying to update the accounting of all of the Shardblades in Alethkar with pictures. She would like to schedule a time to come and do a sketch of yours, if you are willing.'

'Oh,' Amaram said. He seemed to relax. 'Yes, well, that would be fine. I am free most afternoons. Have her send someone to speak with my steward to arrange a meeting.'

'Yes, Highlord. I'll see that it is done.' Shallan moved to leave.

'You came this late?' Amaram asked. 'To ask such a simple question.'

Shallan shrugged. 'I don't question the commands of lighteyes, Highlord. But my mistress, well, she can be distracted at times. I suppose she wanted me on her task while it was fresh in her mind. And she's really interested in Shardblades.'

'Who isn't?' Amaram mused, turning away, speaking softly. 'They're wondrous things, aren't they?'

Was he talking to her, or to himself? Shallan hesitated. A sword formed in his hand, mist coalescing, water beading on its surface. Amaram held it up, looking at himself in the reflection.

'Such beauty,' he said. 'Such art. Why must we kill with our grandest creations? Ah, but I'm babbling, delaying you. I apologize. The Blade is still new to me. I find excuses to summon it.'

Shallan was barely listening. A Blade with the back edge ridged like flowing waves. Or perhaps tongues of fire. Etchings all along its surface. Curved, sinuous.

She knew this Blade.

It belonged to her brother Helaran.

⁂

Kaladin charged through the chasm, and the wind joined him, blowing at his back. Syl soared before him as a ribbon of light.

He reached a boulder in his way and jumped into the air, Lashing himself upward. He soared a good thirty feet upward before Lashing himself to the side and downward at the same time. The downward Lashing slowed his momentum upward; the sideways Lashing brought him to the wall.

He dismissed the downward Lashing and hit the wall with one hand, twisting and throwing himself to his feet. He kept running along the chasm wall. When he reached the end of the plateau, he leaped toward the next one and Lashed himself at its wall instead.

Faster! He held nearly all of the Stormlight he had left, fetched from the pouches he'd dropped earlier. He held so much that he glowed like a bonfire. It encouraged him as he jumped and Lashed himself forward, eastward. This made him fall *through* the chasm. The floor of the chasm whipped along beneath him, plants a blur to his sides.

He had to remember that he was falling. This was not flight, and every second he moved, his speed increased. That didn't stop the feeling of liberty, of ultimate freedom. It just meant this could be dangerous.

The winds picked up and he Lashed himself backward at the last moment, slowing his descent as he crashed against a chasm wall before him.

That direction was down to him now, so he stood and ran along it. He was using the Stormlight at a furious rate, but he didn't need to scrimp. He was paid like a lighteyed officer of the sixth dahn, and his spheres held not tiny chips of gemstone, but broams. A month's pay for him now was more than he had ever seen at a time, and the Stormlight it held was a vast fortune compared to what he'd once known.

He shouted as he jumped a group of frillblooms, their fronds pulling in beneath him. He Lashed himself to the other chasm wall and crossed the chasm, landing on his hands. He threw himself back upward, and somehow Lashed himself only *slightly* in that direction.

Now much lighter, he was able to twist in the air and come down on his feet. He stood on the wall, facing down the chasm, hands in fists and Light pouring off him.

Syl hesitated, flitting around him back and forth. 'What?' she asked.

'More,' he said, then Lashed himself forward again, down the corridor.

Fearless, he fell. This was his ocean to swim, his winds upon which to soar. He fell face-first toward the next plateau. Just before he arrived, he Lashed himself sideways and backward.

His stomach lurched. He felt like someone had tied a rope around him and pushed him off a cliff, then yanked on the rope right as he reached the end of it. The Stormlight inside, however, made the discomfort negligible. He pulled sideways, into another chasm.

Lashings sent him eastward again down another corridor, and he wove around plateaus, keeping to the chasms – like an eel swimming through the waves, swerving around boulders. Onward, faster, still falling . . .

Teeth clenched at both the wonder and the forces twisting him, he tossed caution aside and Lashed himself upward. Once, twice, three times. He let go of all else, and amid the streaming Light, he shot from the chasms out into the open air above.

He Lashed himself back to the east so that he could fall in that direction again, but now no plateau walls got in his way. He soared toward the horizon, distant, lost in the darkness. He gained speed, coat flapping, hair whipping behind him. Air buffeted his face, and he narrowed his eyes, but did not close them.

Beneath, dark chasms passed one after another. Plateau. Pit. Plateau.

Pit. This sensation . . . flying over the land . . . he had felt this before, in dreams. What took bridgemen hours to cross, he passed in minutes. He felt as if something were boosting him from behind, the wind itself carrying him. Syl zipped along to his right.

And to his left? No, those were other windspren. He'd accumulated dozens of them, flying around him as ribbons of light. He could pick out Syl. He didn't know how; she didn't look different, but he could tell. Like you could pick a family member out of a crowd just by their walk.

Syl and her cousins twisted around him in a spiral of light, free and loose, but with a hint of coordination.

How long had it been since he felt this good, this triumphant, this *alive*? Not since before Tien's death. Even after saving Bridge Four, darkness had shadowed him.

That evaporated. He saw a spire of rock ahead on the plateaus, and nudged himself toward it with a careful Lashing to the right. Other Lashings to his rear slowed his fall enough that when he hit the tip of the spire of rock, he could clutch to it and spin around it, fingers on the smooth cremstone.

A hundred windspren broke around him, like the crash of a wave, spraying outward from Kaladin in a fan of light.

He grinned. Then he looked upward, toward the sky.

.•.

Highlord Amaram continued to stare at the Shardblade in the night. He held it up before him in the light spilling from the front of the manor house.

Shallan remembered her father's quiet terror as he looked upon that weapon, leveled toward him. Could it be a coincidence? Two weapons that looked the same? Perhaps her memory was flawed.

No. No, she would *never* forget the look of that Blade. It *was* the one Helaran had held. And no two Blades were the same.

'Brightlord,' Shallan said, drawing Amaram's attention. He seemed startled, as if he'd forgotten she was there.

'Yes?'

'Brightness Shallan,' she said, 'wants to make certain the records are all correct and that the histories of the Blades and Plate in the Alethi army have been properly traced. Your Blade is not in them. She asked if you would mind sharing the origin of your Blade, in the name of scholarship.'

'I've explained this to Dalinar already,' Amaram said. 'I don't know the history of my Shards. Both were in the possession of an assassin who tried to kill me. A younger man. Veden, with red hair. We don't know his name, and his face was ruined in my counterattack. I had to stab him through his faceplate, you see.'

Young man. Red hair.

She stood before her brother's killer.

'I . . .' Shallan stammered, feeling sick. 'Thank you. I will pass the information along.'

She turned, trying not to stumble as she walked away. She finally knew what had happened to Helaran.

You were involved in all of this, weren't you, Helaran? she thought. *Just like Father was. But how, why?*

It seemed that Amaram was trying to bring back the Voidbringers. Helaran had tried to kill him.

But would anyone really *want* to bring back the Voidbringers? Perhaps she was mistaken. She needed to get to her rooms, draw those maps from the Memories she'd taken, and try to figure this all out.

The guards, blessedly, did not give her any further troubles as she slipped away from Amaram's camp and into the anonymity of the darkness. That was well, for if they'd looked closely, they'd have seen the messenger boy with tears in his eyes. Crying for a brother that now, once and for all, Shallan knew was dead.

❖

Upward.

One Lashing, then another, then a third. Kaladin shot up into the sky. Nothing but open expanse, an infinite sea for his delight.

The air grew cold. Still upward he went, reaching for the clouds. Finally, worried about running out of Stormlight before returning to the ground – he had only one infused sphere left, carried in his pocket for an emergency – Kaladin reluctantly Lashed himself downward.

He didn't fall downward immediately; his momentum upward merely slowed. He was still Lashed to the sky; he hadn't dismissed the upward Lashings.

Curious, he Lashed himself downward to slow further, then dismissed all of his Lashings except one up and one down. He eventually came to a stop hanging in midair. The second moon had risen, bathing the Plains in light far below. From here, they looked like a broken plate. *No . . .* he thought, squinting. *It's a pattern.* He'd seen this before. In a dream.

Wind blew against him, causing him to drift like a kite. The windspren he'd attracted scampered away now that he wasn't riding upon the winds. Funny. He'd never realized one could attract windspren as one attracted the spren of emotions.

All you had to do was fall into the sky.

Syl remained, spinning around him in a swirl until finally coming to rest on his shoulder. She sat, then looked down.

'Not many men ever see this view,' she noted. From up here, the warcamps – circles of fire to his right – seemed insignificant. It was cold enough to be uncomfortable. Rock claimed the air was thinner up high, though Kaladin couldn't tell any difference.

'I've been trying to get you to do this for a while now,' Syl said.

'It's like when I first picked up a spear,' Kaladin whispered. 'I was just a child. Were you with me back then? All that time ago?'

'No,' Syl said, 'and yes.'

'It can't be both.'

'It can. I knew I needed to find you. And the winds knew you. They led me to you.'

'So everything I've done,' Kaladin said. 'My skill with the spear, the way I fight. That's not me. It's you.'

'It's *us*.'

'It's cheating. Unearned.'

'Nonsense,' Syl said. 'You practice every day.'

'I have an advantage.'

'The advantage of talent,' Syl said. 'When the master musician first picks up an instrument and finds music in it that nobody else can, is that cheating? Is that art unearned, just because she is naturally more skilled? Or is it genius?'

Kaladin Lashed himself westward, back toward the warcamps. He didn't want to leave himself stranded in the middle of the Shattered Plains without Stormlight. The tempest within had calmed greatly since he started. He fell in that direction for a time – getting as close as he dared before slowing himself – then removed part of the upward Lashing and began to drift downward.

'I'll take it,' Kaladin said. 'Whatever it is that gives me that edge. I'll use it. I'll need it to beat *him*.'

Syl nodded, still sitting on his shoulder.

'You don't think he has a spren,' Kaladin said. 'But how does he do what he does?'

'The weapon,' Syl said, more confidently than she had before. 'It's something special. It was created to give abilities to men, much as our bond does.'

Kaladin nodded, light wind ruffling his jacket as he fell through the night. 'Syl . . .' How to broach this? 'I can't fight him without a Shardblade.'

She looked the other way, squeezing her arms together, hugging herself. Such human gestures.

'I've avoided the training with the Blades that Zahel offers,' Kaladin continued. 'It's hard to justify. I *need* to learn how to use one of those weapons.'

'They're evil,' she said in a small voice.

'Because they're symbols of the knights' broken oaths,' Kaladin said. 'But where did they come from in the first place? How were they forged?'

Syl didn't answer.

'Can a new one be forged? One that doesn't bear the stain of broken promises?'

'Yes.'

'How?'

She didn't reply. They floated downward for a time in silence until gently coming to rest on a dark plateau. Kaladin got his bearings, then walked over and drifted off the edge, going down into the chasms. He wouldn't want to walk back using the bridges. The scouts would find it odd that he was coming back without having gone out.

Storms. They'd have seen him flying out here, wouldn't they? What would they think? Were any close enough to have seen him land?

Well, he couldn't do anything about that now. He reached the bottom of the chasm and started walking back toward the warcamps, his Stormlight slowly dying out, leaving him in darkness. He felt deflated without it, sluggish, tired.

He fished the last infused sphere from his pocket and used it to light his path.

'There's a question you're avoiding,' Syl said, landing on his shoulder. 'It's been two days. When are you going to tell Dalinar about those men that Moash took you to meet?'

'He didn't listen when I told him about Amaram.'

'This is *obviously* different,' Syl said.

It was, and she was right. So why hadn't he told Dalinar?

'Those men didn't seem the type who would wait long,' Syl said.

'I'll do something about them,' Kaladin said. 'I just want to think about it some more. I don't want Moash to get caught in the storm when we bring them down.'

She fell silent as he walked the rest of the way, retrieving his spear, then climbed the ladder up onto the plateaus. The sky overhead had grown cloudy, but the weather had been turning toward spring lately.

Enjoy it while you can, he thought. *The Weeping comes soon.* Weeks of ceaseless rain. No Tien to cheer him up. His brother had always been able to do that.

Amaram had taken that from him. Kaladin lowered his head and started walking. At the warcamps' edge, he turned right and walked northward.

'Kaladin?' Syl asked, flitting in beside him. 'Why are you walking this way?'

He looked up. This was the way toward Sadeas's camp. Dalinar's camp was the other direction.

Kaladin kept walking.

'Kaladin? What are you doing?'

Finally, he stopped in place. Amaram would be there, just ahead, inside Sadeas's camp somewhere. It was late, Nomon inching toward its zenith.

'I *could* end him,' Kaladin said. 'Enter his window in a flash of Storm-light, kill him, and be off before anyone has time to react. So easy. Everyone would blame it on the Assassin in White.'

'Kaladin . . .'

'It's *justice*, Syl,' he said, suddenly angry, turning toward her. 'You tell me that I need to protect. If I kill him, that's what I'm doing! Protecting people, keeping him from ruining them. Like he ruined me.'

23

'I don't like how you get,' she said, seeming small, 'when you think about him. You stop being you. You stop thinking. Please.'

'He killed Tien,' Kaladin said. 'I *will* end him, Syl.'

'But tonight?' Syl asked. 'After what you just discovered, after what you just did?'

He took a deep breath, remembering the thrill of the chasms and the freedom of flight. He'd felt true joy for the first time in what seemed like ages.

Did he want to taint that memory with Amaram? No. Not even with the man's demise, which would surely be a wonderful day.

'All right,' he said, turning back toward Dalinar's camp. 'Not tonight.'

Evening stew was finished by the time Kaladin arrived back at the barracks. He passed the fire, where embers still glowed, and made his way to his room. Syl zipped up into the air. She'd ride the winds overnight, playing with her cousins. So far as he knew, she didn't need sleep.

He stepped into his private room, feeling tired and drained, but in a pleasing way. It—

Someone stirred in the room.

Kaladin spun, leveling his spear, and sucked in the last light of the sphere he'd been using to guide his way. The Light that streamed off him revealed a red and black face. Shen looked disturbingly eerie in those shadows, like an evil spren from the stories.

'Shen,' Kaladin said, lowering his spear. 'What in the—'

'Sir,' Shen said. 'I must leave.'

Kaladin frowned.

'I am sorry,' Shen added speaking in his slow, deliberate way. 'I cannot tell you why.' He seemed to be waiting for something, his hands tense on his spear. The spear Kaladin had given him.

'You're a free man, Shen,' Kaladin said. 'I won't keep you here if you feel you must go, but I don't know that there is another place you can go where you will be able to make good on your freedom.'

Shen nodded, then moved to walk past Kaladin.

'You are leaving tonight?'

'Immediately.'

'The guards at the edges of the Plains might try to stop you.'

Shen shook his head. 'Parshmen do not flee captivity. They will see only a slave doing some assigned task. I will leave your spear beside the fire.' He walked to the door, but then hesitated beside Kaladin, and placed a hand on his shoulder. 'You are a good man, Captain. I have learned much. My name is not Shen. It is Rlain.'

'May the winds treat you well, Rlain.'

'The winds are not what I fear,' Rlain said. He patted Kaladin's shoulder, then took a deep breath as if anticipating something difficult, and stepped from the chamber.

PERFECTION

As to the other orders that were inferior in this visiting of the far realm of spren, the Elsecallers were prodigiously benevolent, allowing others as auxiliary to their visits and interactions; though they did never relinquish their place as prime liaisons with the great ones of the spren; and the Lightweavers and Willshapers both also had an affinity to the same, though neither were the true masters of that realm.

—From *Words of Radiance*, chapter 6, page 2

Adolin slapped away Elit's Shardblade with his forearm. Shard-bearers didn't use shields – each section of Plate was stronger than stone.

He swept in, using Windstance as he moved across the sand of the arena.

Win Shards for me, son.

Adolin flowed through the stance's strikes, one direction then the other, forcing Elit away. The man scrambled, Plate leaking from a dozen places where Adolin had struck him.

Any hope for a peaceful end to the war on the Shattered Plains was gone. Done for. He knew how much his father had wanted that end, and the Parshendi arrogance made him angry. Frustrated.

He kept that down. He could not be consumed by it. He moved

smoothly through the stance, careful, maintaining a calm serenity.

Elit had apparently expected Adolin to be reckless, as in his first duel for Shards. Elit kept backing up, waiting for that moment of recklessness. Adolin didn't give it to him.

Today, he fought with precision – exacting form and stance, nothing out of place. Downplaying his ability in his previous duel had not coaxed anyone powerful into agreeing to a bout. Adolin had barely persuaded Elit.

Time for a different tactic.

Adolin passed where Sadeas, Aladar, and Ruthar watched. The core of the coalition against Father. By now, each of them had gone on plateau runs illicitly, getting to the plateau and stealing the gemheart before those assigned could arrive. Each time, they paid the fines Dalinar levied for their disobedience. Dalinar couldn't do anything more to them without risking open war.

But Adolin could punish them in other ways.

Elit stumbled back, wary, as Adolin swept in. The man tested forward, and Adolin slapped the Blade away, then brought in a backhand and clipped Elit's forearm. It, too, started to leak Stormlight.

The crowd murmured, conversations rising over the arena. Elit came in again, and Adolin slapped away his strikes, but did not counterattack.

Ideal form. Each step in place. The Thrill rose within him, but he shoved it down. He was disgusted by the highprinces and their squabbling, but today he would not show them that fury. Instead, he'd show them *perfection*.

'He's trying to wear you down, Elit!' Ruthar's voice from the stands nearby. In his younger years, he'd been something of a duelist himself, though nowhere near as good as Dalinar or Aladar. 'Don't let him!'

Adolin smiled inside his helm as Elit nodded and dashed forward in Smokestance, thrusting with his Blade. A gamble. Most contests against Plate were won by breaking sections, but at times you could drive the point of your Blade through a joint between plates, cracking them and scoring a hit.

It was also a way to try to wound your opponent, more than just defeat him.

Adolin calmly stepped back and used the proper Windstance sweeps for parrying a thrust. Elit's weapon clanged away, and the crowd grumbled further. First, Adolin had given them a brutal show, which had annoyed them. Then, he'd given them a close fight, with plenty of excitement.

This time, he did something opposite of both, refusing the exciting clashes that were often so much a part of a duel.

He stepped to the side and swung to score a slight hit on Elit's helm. It leaked from a small crack. Not as much as it should, however.

Excellent.

Elit growled audibly from within his helm, then came in with another thrust. Right at Adolin's faceplate.

Trying to kill me, are you? Adolin thought, taking one hand from his Blade and raising it just under Elit's oncoming Blade, letting it slide between his thumb and forefinger.

Elit's Blade ground along Adolin's hand as he lifted upward and to the right. It was a move that you could never perform without Plate – you'd end with your hand sliced in half if you tried that on a regular sword, worse if you tried it on a Shardblade.

With Plate, he easily guided the thrust up past his head, then swept in with his other hand, slamming his Blade against Elit's side.

Some in the crowd cheered at the straight-on blow. Others booed, however. The classical strike there would have been to hit Elit's head, trying to shatter the helm.

Elit stumbled forward, knocked off balance by the missed thrust and subsequent blow. Adolin heaved against him with a shoulder, throwing him to the ground. Then, instead of pouncing, he stepped backward.

More booing.

Elit stood up, then took a step. He lurched slightly, then took another step. Adolin backed up and set his Blade with the point toward the ground, waiting. Overhead, the sky rumbled. It would probably rain later today – not a highstorm, thankfully. Just a mundane rainshower.

'Fight me!' Elit shouted from within his helm.

'I have.' Adolin replied quietly. 'And I've won.'

Elit lurched forward. Adolin backed up. To the boos of the crowd, he waited until Elit locked up completely – his Plate out of Stormlight. The dozens of small cracks Adolin had put in the man's armor had finally added up.

Then, Adolin strolled forward, placed a hand against Elit's chest, and shoved him over. He crashed to the ground.

Adolin looked up at Brightlady Istow, highjudge.

'Judgment,' the highjudge said with a sigh, 'again goes to Adolin Kholin. The victor. Elit Ruthar forfeits his Plate.'

The crowd didn't much like it. Adolin turned to face them, sweeping his Blade a few times before dismissing it to mist. He removed his helm and bowed to their boos. Behind, his armorers – whom he'd prepared for this – rushed out and pushed away those of Elit. They pulled off the Plate, which now belonged to Adolin.

He smiled, and when they were done, followed them into the staging room beneath the seats. Renarin waited by the door, wearing his own Plate, and Aunt Navani sat by the room's brazier.

Renarin peeked out at the dissatisfied crowds. 'Stormfather. The first duel like this you did, you were done in under a minute, and they hated you. Today you were at it for the better part of an hour, and they seem to hate you more.'

Adolin sat down with a sigh on one of the benches. 'I won.'

'You did,' Navani said, stepping up, inspecting him as if for wounds. She was always worried when he dueled. 'But weren't you supposed to do it with great fanfare?'

Renarin nodded. 'That's what Father asked for.'

'This will be remembered,' Adolin said, accepting a cup of water from Peet, one of the bridgeman guards for the day. He nodded thankfully. 'Fanfare is about making everyone pay attention. This will work.'

He hoped. The next part was as important.

'Aunt,' Adolin said as she started writing a prayer of thanks. 'Have you given any thought to what I asked?'

Navani kept drawing.

'Shallan's work really does sound important,' Adolin said. 'I mean—'

A knock came at the door to the chamber.

So quickly? Adolin thought, rising. One of the bridgemen opened the door.

Shallan Davar burst in, wearing a violet dress, red hair flaring as she crossed the room. 'That was incredible!'

'Shallan!' She wasn't the person he'd been expecting – but he wasn't unhappy to see her. 'I checked your seat before the fight and you weren't there.'

'I forgot to burn a prayer,' she said, 'so I stopped to do so. I caught most

29

of the fight, though.' She hesitated right before him, seeming awkward for a moment. Adolin shared that awkwardness. They had only been officially courting for little more than a week, but with the causal in place . . . what *was* their relationship?

Navani cleared her throat. Shallan spun and raised her freehand to her lips, as if having only just noticed the former queen. 'Brightness,' she said, and bowed.

'Shallan,' Navani said. 'I hear only good things from my nephew regarding you.'

'Thank you.'

'I will leave you two, then,' Navani said, walking toward the door, her glyphward unfinished.

'Brightness . . .' Shallan said, raising a hand toward her.

Navani left and pulled the door closed.

Shallan lowered her hand, and Adolin winced. 'Sorry,' Adolin said. 'I've been trying to talk to her about it. I think she needs a few more days, Shallan. She'll come around – she knows that she shouldn't be ignoring you, I can sense it. You just remind her of what happened.'

Shallan nodded, looking disappointed. Adolin's armorers came over to help him remove his Plate, but he waved them away. It was bad enough to show her his sloppy hair, plastered to his head from being in the helm. His clothing underneath – a padded uniform – would look awful.

'So, uh, you liked the duel?' he asked.

'You were *wonderful*,' Shallan said, turning back to him. 'Elit kept jumping at you, and you just brushed him off like an annoying cremling trying to crawl up your leg.'

Adolin grinned. 'The rest of the crowd didn't think it was wonderful.'

'They came to see you get stomped,' she said. 'You were so inconsiderate for not giving that to them.'

'I'm quite stingy in that regard,' Adolin said.

'You almost never lose, from what I've discovered. Awfully boring of you. Maybe you should try for a tie now and then. For variety.'

'I'll consider it,' he said. 'We can discuss it, perhaps over dinner this evening? At my father's warcamp?'

Shallan grimaced. 'I'm busy this evening. Sorry.'

'Oh.'

'But,' she said, stepping closer. 'I might have a gift for you soon. I haven't had much time to study – I've been working hard to reconstruct Sebarial's house ledgers – but I might have stumbled upon something that can help you. With your duels.'

'What?' he asked, frowning.

'I remembered something from King Gavilar's biography. It would require you to win a duel in a spectacular way, though. Something amazing, something that would awe the crowd.'

'Fewer boos, then,' Adolin said, scratching at his head.

'I think everyone would appreciate that,' Renarin noted from beside the door.

'Spectacular . . .' Adolin said.

'I'll explain more tomorrow,' Shallan said.

'What happens tomorrow?'

'You're feeding me dinner.'

'I am?'

'And taking me on a walk,' she said.

'I am?'

'Yes.'

'I'm a lucky man.' He smiled at her. 'All right, then, we can—'

The door slammed open.

Adolin's bridgeman guards jumped, and Renarin cursed, standing up. Adolin just turned, gently moving Shallan to the side so he could see who was standing beyond. Relis, current dueling champion and Highprince Ruthar's eldest son.

As expected.

'What,' Relis demanded, stalking into the room, 'was *that*?' He was followed by a small gaggle of other lighteyes, including Brightlady Istow, the highjudge. 'You insult me and my house, Kholin.'

Adolin clasped his gauntleted hands behind his back as Relis stalked right up to him, shoving his face into Adolin's.

'You didn't like the duel?' Adolin asked casually.

'That was *not* a duel,' Relis snapped. 'You embarrassed my cousin by refusing to fight properly. I *demand* that this farce be invalidated.'

'I've told you, Prince Relis,' Istow said from behind. 'Prince Adolin didn't break any—'

'You want your cousin's Plate back?' Adolin asked quietly, meeting Relis's eyes. 'Fight me for it.'

'I won't be goaded by you,' Relis said, tapping the center of Adolin's breastplate. 'I won't let you pull me into another of your dueling farces.'

'Six Shards, Relis,' Adolin said. 'Mine, those of my brother, Eranniv's Plate, and your cousin's Plate. I wager them all on a single bout. You and me.'

'You are a dunnard if you think I'll agree to that,' Relis snapped.

'Too afraid?' Adolin asked.

'You're beneath me, Kholin. These last two fights prove it. You don't even know how to duel anymore – all you know are tricks.'

'Then you should be able to beat me easily.'

Relis wavered, shifting from one foot to the other. Finally, he pointed at Adolin again. 'You're a bastard, Kholin. I know you fought my cousin to embarrass my father and myself. I refuse to be goaded.' He turned to leave.

Something spectacular, Adolin thought, glancing at Shallan. *Father asked for fanfare. . . .*

'If you're afraid,' Adolin said, looking back to Relis, 'you don't have to duel me alone.'

Relis stopped in place. He looked back. 'Are you saying you'll take me on with anyone else at the *same time*?'

'I am,' Adolin said. 'I'll fight you and whomever you bring, together.'

'You *are* a fool,' Relis breathed.

'Yes or no?'

'Two days,' Relis snapped. 'Here in the arena.' He looked to the highjudge. 'You witness this?'

'I do,' she said.

Relis stormed out. The others trailed after. The highjudge lingered, regarding Adolin. 'You realize what you have done.'

'I know the dueling conventions quite well. Yes. I'm aware.'

She sighed, but nodded, walking out.

Peet closed the door, then looked at Adolin, raising an eyebrow. Great. Now he was getting attitude from the bridgemen. Adolin sank back down on the bench. 'Will that do for spectacular?' he asked Shallan.

'You really think you can beat two at once?' she asked.

Adolin didn't reply. Fighting two men at once was hard, particularly if they were both Shardbearers. They could gang up on you, flank you, blindside you. It was far harder than fighting two in a row.

'I don't know,' he said. 'But you wanted spectacular. So I'll try for spectacular. Now, I hope you *actually* have a plan.'

Shallan sat down next to him. 'What do you know of Highprince Yenev . . . ?'

"A LADY'S PACE"
by BRIGHTNESS AXEFACE

A proper Vorin lady walks
with her safehand covered by
her freehand, both held before her.
She steps with poise and deliberation!

~ Head up!
~ Back straight!
~ Feet level with the floor!
She does NOT swing her arms or
raise her toes like a common darkeyes
at a farm dance!

She does not SLOUCH!

54

VEIL'S LESSON

*There came also sixteen of the order of **Windrunners**, and with them a considerable number of squires, and finding in that place the **Skybreakers** dividing the innocent from the guilty, there ensued a great debate.*

—From *Words of Radiance*, chapter 28, page 3

S hallan stepped from the carriage into a light rainfall. She wore the white coat and trousers of the darkeyed version of herself that she'd named Veil. Rain sprinkled on the brim of her hat. She'd spent too long talking with Adolin after his duel, and had needed to rush to make it to this appointment, which was happening in the Unclaimed Hills a good hour's ride out of the warcamps.

But she was here, in costume, on time. Barely. She strode forward, listening to the rain patter on stone around her. She had always liked rainfalls like these. The younger sisters of highstorms, they brought life without the fury. Even the desolate stormlands here west of the warcamps bloomed with the advent of water. Rockbuds split, and though these didn't have blossoms like the ones back home, they did put out vibrant green vines. Grass rose thirstily from holes and refused to retreat until it was practically stepped on. Some reeds produced flowers to entice cremlings, which would feast upon the petals and in so doing rub themselves with spores that would give rise to the

35

next generation, once mixed with the spores of other plants.

If she'd been at home, there would be far more vines – so many that it would be hard to walk without tripping. Going out in a wooded area would require a machete to move more than a couple of feet. Here, the vegetation became colorful, but not an impediment.

Shallan smiled at the wonderful surroundings, the light rainfall, the beautiful plant life. A little dampness was a small price to pay for the melodious sound of sprinkling rain, for fresh clean air and a beautiful sky full of clouds that varied in every shade of grey.

Shallan walked with a waterproof satchel under her arm, the hired carriage driver – she couldn't use Sebarial's coach for today's activity – awaiting her return as she'd instructed. This coach was pulled by parshmen instead of horses, but they were faster than chulls and had worked well enough.

She hiked toward a hillside ahead of her, the destination indicated on the map she'd received via spanreed. She wore a nice pair of sturdy boots. This clothing of Tyn's might be unusual, but Shallan was glad for it. The coat and hat kept off the rain, and the boots gave her sure footing on the slick rock.

She rounded the hill and found that it was broken on the other side, the rock having cracked and fallen in a small avalanche. The strata of hardened crem were clearly visible on the edges of the chunks of rock, which meant this was a newer fracture. If it had been old, new crem would have obscured that coloring.

The crack made a small valley in the hillside – full of clefts and ridges from the crumbled rock. These had caught spores and windborne stems, and that in turn had created an explosion of life. Wherever sheltered from the wind, plants would find purchase and start to grow.

The snarl of green grew haphazardly – this was not a true lait, where life would be safe over time, but instead a temporary shelter, good for a few years at most. For now, plants grew eagerly, sometimes atop one another, sprouting, blossoming, shaking, twisting, alive. It was an example of raw nature.

The pavilion, however, was not.

It covered four people who sat in chairs too fine for the surroundings. Snacking, they were warmed by a brazier at the center of the open-sided tent. Shallan approached, taking Memories of the people's faces. She'd draw those later, as she had done with the first group of the Ghostbloods she'd met. Two of them were the same as last time. Two were not. The discomforting woman with the mask did not seem to be present.

Mraize, standing tall and proud, inspected his long blowgun. He did not look up as Shallan stepped under the awning.

'I like to learn to use the local weapons,' Mraize said. 'It is a quirk, though I feel it is justified. If you want to understand a people, learn their weapons. The way men kill one another says far more about a culture than any scholar's ethnography.'

He raised his weapon toward Shallan, and she froze in place. Then he turned toward the crack and puffed, blowing a dart into the foliage.

Shallan stepped up beside him. The dart pinned a cremling to one of the plant stems. The small, many-legged creature spasmed and thrashed, trying to get free, though surely having a dart sticking through it would prove lethal.

'This is a Parshendi blowgun,' Mraize noted. 'What does it say about them, do you suppose, little knife?'

'It's obviously not for killing big game,' Shallan said. 'Which makes sense. The only big game I know of in the area are the chasmfiends, which the Parshendi are said to have worshipped as gods.'

She wasn't convinced that they actually did. Early reports – which she'd read in detail at Jasnah's insistence – made the *assumption* that the Parshendi gods were the chasmfiends. It wasn't actually clear.

'They probably used it for stalking small game,' Shallan continued. 'Which means they hunted for food, rather than pleasure.'

'Why do you say this?' Mraize asked.

'Men who glory in the hunt seek grand captures,' Shallan said. 'Trophies. That blowgun is the weapon of a man who simply wants to feed his family.'

'And if he used it against other men?'

'It wouldn't be useful in war,' Shallan said. 'Too short a range, I'd guess, and the Parshendi have bows anyway. Maybe this could be used in assassination, though I'd be very curious to discover if it was.'

'And why is that?' Mraize asked.

A test of some sort. 'Well,' Shallan said, 'most indigenous populations – the Silnasen natives, the Reshi peoples, the runners of the Iri plains – have no real concept of assassination. From what I know, they don't seem to have much use for battle at all. Hunters are too valuable, and so a "war" in these cultures will involve a lot of shouting and posturing, but few deaths. That kind of boastful society doesn't seem the type to have assassins.'

And yet the Parshendi had sent one. Against the Alethi.

Mraize was studying her – watching her with unreadable eyes, long blowgun held lightly in his fingertips. 'I see,' he finally said, 'Tyn chose a *scholar* to be her apprentice this time around? I find that unusual.'

Shallan blushed. It occurred to her that this person she became when she put on the hat and dark hair was not an imitation of someone else, not a different person. It was just a version of Shallan herself.

That could be dangerous.

'So,' Mraize said, fishing another dart from his shirt pocket, 'what excuse did Tyn give you today?'

'Excuse?' Shallan asked.

'For failing in her mission.' Mraize loaded the dart.

Failing? Shallan began to sweat, cold prickles on her forehead. But she'd watched to see if anything out of the ordinary happened at Amaram's camp! This morning, she'd gone back – the real reason she'd been late to Adolin's duel – while wearing the face of a worker. She'd listened to see if anyone spoke of a break-in, or of Amaram being suspicious. She'd found nothing.

Well, obviously Amaram had not made his suspicions public. After all the work she'd done to cover up her incursion, she had failed. She probably shouldn't be surprised, but she was anyway.

'I—' Shallan began.

'I'm beginning to wonder if Tyn really is sick,' Mraize said, raising the blowgun and shooting another dart into the foliage. 'To not even try to carry out the assigned task.'

'Not even try?' Shallan asked, baffled.

'Oh, is that the excuse?' Mraize asked. 'That she made an attempt, and failed? I have people watching that house. If she had . . .'

He trailed off as Shallan shook the water from her satchel, then carefully undid it and lifted out a sheet of paper. It was a representation of Amaram's locked room with its maps on the walls. She'd had to guess at some of the details – it had been dark, and her single sphere hadn't illuminated much – but she figured it was close enough.

Mraize took the picture from her and raised it. He studied it, leaving Shallan to sweat nervously.

'It is rare,' Mraize said, 'that I am proven a fool. Congratulations.'

Was that a good thing?

'Tyn doesn't have this skill,' Mraize continued, still inspecting the sheet. 'You saw this room yourself?'

'There is a reason that she chose a scholar as her assistant. My skills are meant to complement her own.'

Mraize lowered the sheet. 'Surprising. Your mistress might be a brilliant thief, but her choice of associates has always been unenlightened.' He had such a refined way of speaking. It didn't seem to match his scarred face, misaligned lip, and weathered hands. He talked like a man who had spent his days sipping wine and listening to fine music, but he looked like someone who had repeatedly had his bones broken – and likely returned the favor many times over.

'Pity there is not more detail to these maps,' Mraize noted, inspecting the picture again.

Shallan obligingly got out the other five pictures she'd drawn for him. Four were the maps on the walls in detail, the other a closer depiction of the wall scrolls with Amaram's script. In each one, the actual writing was indecipherable, just wiggled lines. Shallan had done this on purpose. Nobody would expect an artist to be able to capture such detail from memory, even though she could.

She would keep the details of the script from them. She intended to gain their trust, to learn what she could, but she would *not* help them more than she had to.

Mraize passed his blowgun to the side. The short, masked girl was there, holding the cremling that Mraize had speared along with a dead mink, a blowgun dart in its neck. No, its leg twitched. It was merely stunned. Some poison on the dart, then?

Shallan shivered. Where had this woman been hiding? Those dark eyes stared at Shallan, unblinking, the rest of the face hidden behind the mask of paint and shell. She took the blowgun.

'Amazing,' Mraize said of Shallan's pictures. 'How *did* you get in? We watched the windows.'

Was that how Tyn would have done it, sneaking in during the dead of night through one of the windows? She hadn't trained Shallan in that sort of thing, only accents and imitation. Perhaps she had spotted that Shallan, who sometimes stumbled over her own feet, would not be best at acrobatic larceny.

'These are masterful,' Mraize said, walking to a table and setting out the pictures. 'A triumph, certainly. Such artistry.'

What had happened to the dangerous, emotionless man who had confronted her at her first meeting with the Ghostbloods? Animated with emotion, he leaned down, studying the pictures one at a time. He even got out a magnifying glass in order to inspect the details.

She did not ask what she wondered. What is Amaram doing? Do you know how he got his Shardblade? How he . . . killed Helaran Davar? Her breath caught in her throat even still as she thought about it, but a part of her had admitted years ago that her brother wasn't coming back.

That didn't stop her from feeling a distinct, and surprising, hatred for the man Meridas Amaram.

'Well?' Mraize asked, glancing at her. 'Come sit down, child. You did this yourself?'

'I did,' Shallan said, shoving down her emotions. Had Mraize just called her 'child'? She'd intentionally made this version of her look older, with a more angular face. What did she need to do? Start adding grey hairs to her head?

She settled into the seat beside the table. The woman with the mask appeared beside her, holding a cup and a kettle of something steaming. Shallan nodded hesitantly, and was rewarded with a cup of mulled orange wine. She sipped it – she probably didn't need to worry about poison, as these people could have killed her at any time. The others under the pavilion spoke with one another in hushed voices, but Shallan couldn't make out any of it. She felt like she was on display before an audience.

'I copied some of the text for you,' Shallan said, fishing out one page of script. These were lines she had specifically chosen to show them – they didn't reveal too much, but might act as a primer to get Mraize talking about the topic. 'We didn't have much time in the room, so I only got a few lines.'

'You spent so long in there drawing the pictures, and so little recording the text?' Mraize asked.

'Oh,' Shallan said. 'No, I did those pictures from memory.'

He looked up at her, jaw lowered a fraction, an expression of genuine surprise crossing his face before he quickly restored his usual confident equanimity.

That ... probably wasn't wise to admit, Shallan realized. How many people could draw so well from memory? Had Shallan publicly demonstrated her skill in the warcamps?

So far as she knew, she hadn't. Now she would have to keep that aspect of her skill secret, lest the Ghostbloods make a connection between Shallan the lighteyed lady and Veil the darkeyed con artist. Storms.

Well, she was bound to make some mistakes. At least this one wasn't life threatening. Probably.

'Jin,' Mraize snapped.

A golden-haired man with a bare chest beneath a flowing outer robe stood up from one of the chairs.

'Look at him,' Mraize said to Shallan.

She took a Memory.

'Jin, leave us. You will draw him, Veil.'

She had no choice but to oblige. As Jin walked off, grumbling to himself at the rain, Shallan started sketching. She did a full sketch – not just his face and shoulders, but an environment study, including the background of fallen boulders. Nervous, she didn't do as good a job as she could have, but Mraize still cooed over her picture like a proud father. She finished and got out her lacquer – this was in charcoal, and would want it – but Mraize plucked it from her fingers first.

'Incredible,' he said, holding the sheet up. 'You are wasted with Tyn. You can't do this with text, however?'

'No,' Shallan lied.

'Pity. Still, this is marvelous. *Marvelous.* There should be ways to use this, yes indeed.' He looked to her. 'What is your goal, child? I might have a place for you in my organization, if you prove reliable.'

Yes! 'I wouldn't have agreed to come in Tyn's place if I hadn't wanted that opportunity.'

Mraize narrowed his eyes at Shallan. 'You killed her, didn't you?'

Oh, blast. Shallan blushed immediately, of course. 'Uh ...'

'Ha!' Mraize exclaimed. 'She finally picked an assistant who was too capable. Delightful. After all of her arrogant posturing, she was brought down by someone she thought to make into a sycophant.'

'Sir,' Shallan said. 'I didn't . . . I mean, I didn't want to. She turned on me.'

'That must be quite the story,' Mraize said, smiling. It was not a pleasant smile. 'Know that what you have done is not forbidden, but it is hardly encouraged. We cannot run an organization properly if subordinates consider hunting their superiors to be a primary method of advancement.'

'Yes, sir.'

'*Your* superior, however, was not a member of our organization. Tyn thought herself to be the hunter, but she was game all along. If you are to join us, you should understand. We are not like others you may have known. We have a greater purpose, and we are . . . protective of one another.'

'Yes, sir.'

'So who are you?' he asked, waving for his servant to bring back the blowgun. 'Who are you *really*, Veil?'

'Someone who wants to be part of things,' Shallan said. 'Things more important than stealing from the odd lighteyes or scamming for a weekend of luxury.'

'So it is a hunt, then,' Mraize said softly, grinning. He turned away from her, walking back to the edge of the pavilion. 'More instructions will follow. Do the task assigned to you. Then we shall see.'

It is a hunt, then. . . .

What kind of hunt? Shallan felt chilled by that statement.

Once again, her dismissal was uncertain, but she did up her satchel and started to leave. As she did so, she glanced at the remaining seated people. Their expressions were cold. Frighteningly so.

Shallan left the pavilion and found that the rain had stopped. She walked away, feeling eyes on her back. *They all know that I can identify them with exactness,* she realized, *and can present accurate pictures of them for any who request.*

They would not like that. Mraize had made it clear that Ghostbloods didn't often kill one another. But he'd *also* made it clear that she wasn't one of them, not yet. He'd said it pointedly, as if granting permission to those listening in.

Talat's hand, what had she gotten herself into?

You're only considering that now? she thought as she rounded the hillside. Her carriage was ahead, the coachman lounging on top, his back to her. Shallan looked anxiously over her shoulder. Nobody had followed yet, at least not that she could see.

'Is anyone watching, Pattern?' she asked.

'Mmm. Me. No people.'

A rock. She'd drawn a boulder in the picture for Mraize. Not thinking – working by instinct and no small amount of panic – she breathed out Stormlight and shaped an image of that boulder before her.

Then, she promptly hid inside of it.

It was dark in there. She curled up in the boulder, sitting with her legs pulled against her. It felt undignified. The other people Mraize worked with probably didn't do silly things like this. They were practiced, smooth, capable. Storms, she probably didn't need to be hiding in the first place.

She sat there anyway. The looks in the eyes of the others . . . the way that Mraize had spoken . . .

Better to be overly cautious than naive. She was tired of people assuming she couldn't care for herself.

'Pattern,' she whispered. 'Go to the carriage driver. Tell him this, in my exact voice. "I have entered the carriage when you weren't looking. Do not look. My exit must be stealthy. Carry me back to the city. Pull up to the warcamps and wait to a count of ten. I will leave. Do not look. You have your payment, and discretion was part of it."'

Pattern hummed and moved off. A short time later, the carriage rattled away, pulled by its parshmen. It didn't take long for hoofbeats to follow. She hadn't seen horses.

Shallan waited, anxious. Would any of the Ghostbloods realize this boulder wasn't supposed to be here? Would they come back, looking for her once they didn't see her leave the carriage at the warcamps?

Perhaps they hadn't even gone after her. Perhaps she was being paranoid. She waited, pained. It started raining again. What would that do to her illusion? The stone she'd drawn had already been wet, so dryness wouldn't give it away – but from the way the rain fell on her, it obviously was passing through the image.

I need to find a way to see the outside while I'm hiding like this, she thought. Eyeholes? Could she make those inside her illusion? Perhaps she—

Voices.

'We will need to find how much he knows.' Mraize's voice. 'You will

43

bring these pages to Master Thaidakar. We are close, but so – it appears – are Restares's cronies.'

The response came in a rasping voice. Shallan couldn't make it out.

'No, I'm not worried about that one. The old fool sows chaos, but does not reach for the power offered by opportunity. He hides in his insignificant city, listening to its songs, thinking he plays in world events. He has no idea. His is not the position of the hunter. This creature in Tukar, however, is different. I'm not convinced he is human. If he is, he's certainly not of the local species. . . .'

Mraize continued speaking, but Shallan heard no more as they moved off. A short time later, she heard more hoofbeats.

She waited, water soaking though her coat and trousers. She shivered, satchel in her lap, and clenched her teeth to keep them from chattering. Weather lately had been warmer, but sitting in the rain belied that. She waited until her spine complained and her muscles screamed at her. She waited until finally, the boulder broke into luminescent smoke and faded away.

Shallan started. What had happened?

Stormlight, she realized, stretching her legs. She checked the pouch in her pocket. She'd drained every sphere, unconsciously, while holding up the illusion of the boulder.

Hours had passed, the sky darkening as evening approached. Maintaining something simple like the boulder didn't take much Light, and she didn't have to consciously think about it to keep it going. That was good to know.

She'd also proven herself a fool again for not even worrying about how much Light she had been using. Sighing, she climbed to her feet. She wobbled, her legs protesting the sudden motion. She took a deep breath, then walked over and peeked around the corner. The pavilion was gone and all signs of the Ghostbloods with it.

'I guess this means I'm walking,' Shallan said, turning back toward the warcamps.

'Did you expect otherwise?' Pattern asked from his place on her coat, sounding genuinely curious.

'No,' Shallan said. 'I'm just talking to myself.'

'Mmm. No, you talk to me.'

She walked on into the evening, cold. However, it wasn't the deadly coldness she'd suffered in the south. This was uncomfortable, but nothing more. If she hadn't been wet, the air probably would have been pleasant, despite the shade. She passed the time practicing her accents with Pattern – she'd speak, then have him repeat back to her exactly what she'd said, in her voice and tone. Being able to hear it that way helped a great deal.

She had the Alethi accent down, she was certain. That was good, since Veil pretended to be Alethi. That one was easy, however, as Veden and Alethi were so similar you could almost understand one by knowing the other.

Her Horneater accent was quite good too, in both Alethi and Veden. She was getting better and not overdoing it, as Tyn had suggested. Her Bav accent in both Veden and Alethi was passable, and through most of the time walking back, she practiced speaking both tongues with a Herdazian accent. Palona gave her a good example of this in Alethi, and Pattern could repeat to her things the woman had said, which was helpful for practice.

'What I need to do,' Shallan said, 'is train you to speak along with my images.'

'You should have them speak themselves,' Pattern said.

'Can I *do* that?'

'Why not?'

'Because ... well, I use Light for the illusion, and so they create an imitation of light. Makes sense. I don't use sound to make them, though.'

'This is a Surge,' Pattern said. 'Sound is a part of it. Mmm ... Cousins of one another. Very similar. It can be done.'

'How?'

'Mmmm. Somehow.'

'You're very helpful.'

'I am glad ...' He trailed off. 'Lie?'

'Yup.' Shallan stuffed her safehand into her pocket, which was also wet, and continued walking through patches of grass that pulled away in front of her. Distant hills showed lavis grain growing in orderly fields of polyps, though she didn't see any farmers at this hour.

At least it had stopped raining. She *did* still like rain, though she hadn't considered how unpleasant it might be to have to walk a long distance in it. And—

What was that?

She pulled up short. A clump of something dark shadowed the ground ahead of her. She approached hesitantly, and found that she could smell smoke. The sodden, wet kind of smoke you smelled after a campfire was doused.

Her carriage. She could make it out now, partially burned in the night. The rains had put out the fire; it hadn't burned long. They'd probably started the blaze on the inside, where it would have been dry.

It was certainly the one she'd hired. She recognized the trim on the wheels. She approached hesitantly. Well, she'd been right in her worry. It was a good thing she'd stayed behind. Something nagged at her. . . .

The coachman!

She ran ahead, fearing the worst. His corpse was there, lying beside the broken carriage, staring up at the sky. His throat had been slit. Beside him, his parshman porters lay dead in a pile.

Shallan sat back on the wet stones, feeling sick, hand to her mouth. 'Oh . . . Almighty above . . .'

'Mmm . . .' Pattern hummed, somehow conveying a morose tone.

'They're dead because of me,' Shallan whispered.

'You did not kill them.'

'I did,' Shallan said. 'As sure as if I'd held the knife. I knew the danger I was going into. The coachman didn't.'

And the parshmen. How did she feel about that? Voidbringers, yes, but it was difficult not to feel sick at what had been done.

You'll cause something far worse than this if you prove what Jasnah claims, part of her said.

Briefly, while watching Mraize's excitement over her art, she'd wanted to like the man. Well, she'd best remember *this* moment. He'd allowed these murders. He might not have been the one to slit the coachman's throat, but he'd all but assured the others it was all right to remove her if they could.

They'd burned the carriage to make it look like bandits had been behind this, but no bandits would come this close to the Shattered Plains.

You poor man, she thought toward the coachman. But if she hadn't arranged a ride, she wouldn't have been able to hide as she did while the coach laid a false trail. Storms! How could she have handled this so nobody died? Would it have been possible?

She eventually forced herself to her feet and, with slumped shoulders, continued to walk back toward the warcamps.

The considerable abilities of the Skybreakers for making such amounted to an almost divine skill, for which no specific Surge or spren grants capacity, but however the order came to such an aptitude, the fact of it was real and acknowledged even by their rivals.

—From *Words of Radiance*, chapter 28, page 3

'Great. You're the one guarding me today?'

Kaladin turned as Adolin came out of his room. The prince wore a sharp uniform, as always. Monogrammed buttons, boots that cost more than some houses, side sword. An odd choice for a Shardbearer, but Adolin probably wore it as an ornament. His hair was a mess of blond sprinkled with black.

'I don't trust her, princeling,' Kaladin said. 'Foreign woman, secret betrothal, and the only person who could vouch for her is dead. She could be an assassin, and that means putting you under the watch of the best I have.'

'Humble, aren't we?' Adolin said, striding down the stone hallway, Kaladin falling into step beside him.

'No.'

'That was a joke, bridgeboy.'

'My mistake. I was under the impression that jokes were supposed to be funny.'

'Only to people with a sense of humor.'

'Ah, of course,' Kaladin said. 'I traded in my sense of humor long ago.'

'And what did you get for it?'

'Scars,' Kaladin said softly.

Adolin's eyes flicked toward the brands on Kaladin's forehead, though most would be obscured by hair. 'This is great,' Adolin said under his breath. 'Just great. I'm so *happy* you're coming along.'

At the end of the hallway, they stepped into daylight. Not much of it, though. The sky was still overcast from the rains of the last few days.

They emerged into the warcamp. 'We collecting any other guards?' Adolin asked. 'Usually there's two of you.'

'Just me today.' Kaladin was short-manned, with the king under his watch and with Teft taking the new recruits out patrolling again. He had two or three men on everyone else, but Adolin he figured he could watch on his own.

A carriage waited, pulled by two mean-looking horses. All horses looked mean, with those too-knowing eyes and sudden movements. Unfortunately, a prince couldn't arrive in a carriage pulled by chulls. A footman opened the door for Adolin, who settled into the confines. The footman closed the door, then climbed into a place at the back of the carriage. Kaladin prepared to swing up into the seat beside the carriage driver, then stopped.

'You!' he said, pointing at the driver.

'Me!' the King's Wit replied from where he sat holding the reins. Blue eyes, black hair, black uniform. What was he doing driving the carriage? He wasn't a servant, was he?

Kaladin clambered cautiously up into his seat, and Wit shook the reins, prodding the horses into motion.

'What are you doing here?' Kaladin asked him.

'Trying to find mischief,' Wit replied cheerfully, as the horses' hooves rang against the stone. 'Have you been practicing with my flute?'

'Uh . . .'

'Don't tell me you left it in Sadeas's camp when you moved out.'

'Well—'

'I said *not* to tell me,' Wit replied. 'You don't need to, since I already know. A shame. If you knew the history of that flute, it would make your brain flip upside-down. And by that, I mean that I would shove you off the carriage for having spied on me.'

'Uh . . .'

'Eloquent today, I see.'

Kaladin *had* left the flute behind. When he had gathered the bridgemen left in Sadeas's camp – the wounded from Bridge Four, and the members of the other bridge crews – he'd been focused on people, not things. He hadn't bothered with his little bundle of possessions, forgetting that the flute was among them.

'I'm a soldier, not a musician,' Kaladin said. 'Besides, music is for women.'

'All people are musicians,' Wit countered. 'The question is whether or not they share their songs. As for music being feminine, it's interesting that the woman who wrote that treatise – the one you all practically *worship* in Alethkar – decided that all of the feminine tasks involve sitting around having fun while all the masculine ones involve finding someone to stick a spear in you. Telling, eh?'

'I guess so.'

'You know, I'm working very hard to come up with engaging, clever, meaningful points of interest to offer you. I can't help thinking you're not upholding your side of the conversation. It's a little like playing music for a deaf man. Which I might try doing, as it sounds fun, if only someone hadn't *lost my flute.*'

'I'm sorry,' Kaladin said. He'd rather be thinking about the new sword stances that Zahel had taught him, but Wit *had* shown him kindness before. The least Kaladin could do was chat with him. 'So, uh, did you keep your job? As King's Wit, I mean. When we met before, you implied you were in danger of losing your title.'

'I haven't checked yet,' Wit said.

'You . . . you haven't . . . Does the king know you're back?'

'Nope! I'm trying to think of a properly dramatic way to inform him. Perhaps a hundred chasmfiends marching in unison, singing an ode to my magnificence.'

'That sounds . . . hard.'

'Yeah, the storming things have real trouble tuning their tonic chords and maintaining just intonation.'

'I have no idea what you just said.'

'Yeah, the storming things have real trouble tuning their tonic chords and maintaining just intonation.'

'That didn't help, Wit.'

'Ah! So you're going deaf, are you? Let me know when the process is complete. I have something I want to try. If I can just remember—'

'Yes, yes,' Kaladin said, sighing. 'You want to play the flute for one.'

'No, that's not it . . . Ah! Yes. I've always wanted to sneak up and poke a deaf man in the back of the head. I think it will be *hilarious*.'

Kaladin sighed. It would take an hour or so, even moving quickly, to reach Sebarial's warcamp. A very *long* hour.

'So you're just here,' Kaladin said, 'to mock me?'

'Well, it's kind of what I *do*. But I'll go easy on you. I wouldn't want you to go flying off on me.'

Kaladin jolted with a start.

'You know,' Wit said, nonchalant, 'flying off in an angry tirade. That kind of thing.'

Kaladin narrowed his eyes at the tall lighteyed man. 'What do you know?'

'Almost everything. That *almost* part can be a real kick in the teeth sometimes.'

'What do you want, then?'

'What I can't have.' Wit turned to him, eyes solemn. 'Same as everyone else, Kaladin Stormblessed.'

Kaladin fidgeted. Wit knew about him and about Surgebinding. Kaladin was sure of it. So, should he expect some kind of demand?

'What do you want,' Kaladin said, trying to speak more precisely, 'from *me*?'

'Ah, so you're thinking. Good. From you, my friend, I want one thing. A story.'

'What kind of story?'

'That is for you to decide.' Wit smiled at him. 'I hope it will be dynamic. If there is one thing I cannot stomach, it is boredom. Kindly avoid being dull. Otherwise I might have to sneak up and poke you in the back of the head.'

'I'm *not* going deaf.'

'It's also hilarious on people who aren't deaf, obviously. What, you think I'd torment someone just because they were deaf? That would be immoral. No, I torment all people equally, thank you very much.'

'Great.' Kaladin settled back, waiting for more. Amazingly, Wit seemed content to let the conversation die.

Kaladin watched the sky, so dull. He hated days like these, which reminded him of the Weeping. Stormfather. Grey skies and miserable weather made him wonder why he'd even bothered to get out of bed. Eventually, the carriage reached Sebarial's warcamp, a place that looked even more like a city than the other warcamps. Kaladin marveled at the fully constructed tenements, the markets, the—

'Farmers?' he asked as they rolled past a group of men hiking toward the gates, carrying worming reeds and buckets of crem.

'Sebarial has them setting up lavis fields on the southwestern hills,' Wit explained.

'The highstorms out here are too powerful for farming.'

'Tell that to the Natan people. They used to farm this entire area. Requires a strain of plant that doesn't grow as large as you're accustomed to.'

'But why?' Kaladin asked. 'Why wouldn't farmers go someplace where it's easier? Like Alethkar proper.'

'You don't know a lot about human nature, do you, Stormblessed?'

'I . . . No, I don't.'

Wit shook his head. 'So frank, so blunt. You and Dalinar are alike, certainly. Someone needs to teach the pair of you how to have a good time now and then.'

'I know full well how to have a good time.'

'Is that so?'

'Yes. It involves being anywhere *you* aren't.'

Wit stared at him, then chuckled, shaking the reins so the horses danced a little. 'So you *do* have some spark of wit in you.'

It came from Kaladin's mother. She'd often said things like that, though never so insulting. *Being around Wit must be corrupting me.*

Eventually, Wit pulled the carriage up to a nice manor home, the likes of which Kaladin would have expected in some fine lait, not here in a warcamp. With those pillars and beautiful glass windows, it was even finer than the citylord's manor back in Hearthstone.

In the carriageway, Wit asked the footman to fetch Adolin's causal betrothed. Adolin climbed out to await her, straightening his jacket, polishing the buttons on one sleeve. He glanced up toward the driver's seat, then started.

'You!' Adolin exclaimed.

'Me!' Wit replied. He swung down from the top of the carriage and performed a flowery bow. 'Ever at your service, Brightlord Kholin.'

'What did you do with my usual carriage driver?'

'Nothing.'

'Wit—'

'What, you're implying that I *hurt* the poor fellow? Does that sound like me, Adolin?'

'Well, no,' Adolin said.

'Exactly. Besides, I'm certain he's gotten the ropes undone by now. Ah, and here's your lovely almost-but-not-quite bride.'

Shallan Davar had emerged from the house. She bobbed down the steps, not gliding down them as most lighteyed ladies would have. *She's certainly an enthusiastic one,* Kaladin thought idly, holding the reins, which he'd picked up after Wit had dropped them.

Something just felt *off* about this Shallan Davar. What was she hiding behind that eager attitude and ready smile? That buttoned sleeve on the safehand of a lighteyed woman's dress, that could hide any number of deadly implements. A simple poisoned needle, stuck through the fabric, would be enough to end Adolin's life.

Unfortunately, he couldn't watch her every moment she was with Adolin. He had to show more initiative than that; could he instead confirm that she was who she said she was? Decide from her past if she was a threat or not?

Kaladin stood up, planning to jump down onto the ground to keep an eye on her as she approached Adolin. She suddenly started, eyes widening. She pointed at Wit with her freehand.

'You!' Shallan exclaimed.

'Yes, yes. People certainly are good at identifying me today. Perhaps I need to wear—'

Wit cut off as Shallan lunged at him. Kaladin dropped to the ground, reaching for his side knife, then hesitated as Shallan grabbed Wit in an embrace, her head against his chest, her eyes squeezed shut.

Kaladin took his hand off his knife, raising an eyebrow at Wit, who looked completely flabbergasted. He stood with his arms at his sides, as if he didn't know what to do with them.

'I always wanted to say thank you,' Shallan whispered. 'I never had a chance.'

Adolin cleared his throat. Finally, Shallan released Wit and looked at the prince.

'You hugged Wit,' Adolin said.

'Is that his name?' Shallan asked.

'One of them,' Wit said, apparently still unsettled. 'There are too many to count, really. Granted, most of them are related to one form of curse or another. . . .'

'You hugged *Wit*,' Adolin said.

Shallan blushed. 'Was that improper?'

'It's not about propriety,' Adolin said. 'It's about common sense. Hugging him is like hugging a whitespine or, or a pile of nails or something. I mean it's Wit. You're not supposed to *like* him.'

'We need to talk,' Shallan said, looking up at Wit. 'I don't remember everything we talked about, but some of it—'

'I'll try to squeeze it into my schedule,' Wit said. 'I'm fairly busy, though. I mean, insulting Adolin alone is going to take until sometime next week.'

Adolin shook his head, waving away the footman and helping Shallan into the carriage himself. After he did so, he leaned in to Wit. 'Hands off.'

'She's *far* too young for me, child,' Wit said.

'That's right,' Adolin said with a nod. 'Stick to women your own age.'

Wit grinned. 'Well, that might be a little harder. I think there's only one of those around these parts, and she and I never did get along.'

'You are so bizarre,' Adolin said, climbing into the carriage.

Kaladin sighed, then moved to follow them in.

'You intend to ride in there?' Wit asked, grin widening.

'Yeah,' Kaladin said. He wanted to watch Shallan. She wasn't likely to try something in the open, while riding in the carriage with Adolin. But Kaladin might learn something by watching her, and he couldn't be *absolutely* certain she wouldn't try to harm him.

'Try not to flirt with the girl,' Wit whispered. 'Young Adolin seems to be growing possessive. Or . . . what am I saying? Flirt with the girl, Kaladin. It might make the prince's eyes bulge.'

Kaladin snorted. 'She's lighteyed.'

'So?' Wit asked. 'You people are too fixated on that.'

'No offense,' Kaladin whispered, 'but I'd sooner flirt with a chasm-fiend.' He left Wit to drive the carriage, hauling himself into it.

Inside, Adolin looked toward the heavens. 'You're kidding.'

'It's my job,' Kaladin said, seating himself next to Adolin.

'Surely I'm safe in here,' Adolin said through gritted teeth, 'with my betrothed.'

'Well, maybe I just want a comfortable seat, then,' Kaladin said, nodding to Shallan Davar.

She ignored him, smiling at Adolin as the carriage started rolling. 'Where are we going today?'

'Well, you said something about a dinner,' Adolin said. 'I know of a new winehouse in the Outer Market, and it actually serves food.'

'You always know the best places,' Shallan said, her smile widening.

Could you be any more obvious with your flattery, woman? Kaladin thought.

Adolin smiled back. 'I just listen.'

'Now if you only paid more attention to what wines were good . . .'

'I don't because it's easy!' He grinned. 'They're *all* good.'

She giggled.

Storms, lighteyes were annoying. Particularly when they fawned over one another. Their conversation continued, and Kaladin found it blatantly obvious how badly this woman wanted a relationship with Adolin. Well, that wasn't surprising. Lighteyes were always looking for chances to get ahead – or to stab one another in the back, if they were in that mood instead. His job wasn't to figure out if this woman was an opportunist. Every lighteyes was an opportunist. He just had to find out if she was an opportunistic fortune hunter or an opportunistic assassin.

They continued talking, and Shallan circled the conversation back toward the day's activity.

'Now, I'm not saying I mind another winehouse,' Shallan said. 'But I *do* wonder if those are becoming a tad too obvious a choice.'

'I know,' Adolin replied. 'But there's storming little to do out here otherwise. No concerts, no art shows, no sculpture contests.'

Is that really what you people spend your time on? Kaladin wondered. *Almighty save you if you don't have* sculpture contests *to watch.*

'There's a menagerie,' Shallan said, eager. 'In the Outer Market.'

'A menagerie,' Adolin said. 'Isn't that a little . . . low?'

'Oh, come on. We could look at all of the animals, and you could tell me which ones you've bravely slaughtered while hunting. It'll be very diverting.' She hesitated, and Kaladin thought he saw something in her eyes. A flash of something deeper. Pain? Worry? 'And I could use some distraction,' Shallan added more softly.

'I actually despise hunting,' Adolin said, as if he hadn't noticed. 'No real contest to it.' He looked to Shallan, who pasted on a smile and nodded eagerly. 'Well, something different could be a pleasant change. All right, I'll tell Wit to take us there instead. Hopefully he'll do it, instead of driving us into a chasm to laugh at our screams of horror.'

Adolin turned to open the small sliding shutter up to the driver's perch and gave the order. Kaladin watched Shallan, who sat back, a self-satisfied smile on her face. She had an ulterior motive for going to the menagerie. What was it?

Adolin turned back around and asked after her day. Kaladin listened with half an ear, studying Shallan, trying to pick out any knives hidden on her person. She blushed at something Adolin said, then laughed. Kaladin didn't really like Adolin, but at least the prince was honest. He had his father's earnest temperament, and had always been straight with Kaladin. Dismissive and spoiled, but straight.

This woman was different. Her movements were calculated. The way she laughed, the way she chose her words. She would giggle and blush, but her eyes were always discerning, always watching. She exemplified what made him sick about lighteyed culture.

You're just in an irritable mood, part of him acknowledged. It happened sometimes, more often when the sky was cloudy. But did they *have* to act nauseatingly cheery?

He kept an eye on Shallan as the ride continued, and eventually decided he was being too suspicious of her. She wasn't an immediate threat to Adolin. He found his mind drifting back toward the night in the chasms. Riding the winds, Light churning inside of him. Freedom.

No, not just freedom. Purpose.

You have a purpose, Kaladin thought, dragging his mind back to the present. *Guard Adolin.* This was an ideal job for a soldier, one others dreamed of. Great pay, his own squad to command, an important task. A dependable commander. It was perfect.

But those winds . . .

'Oh!' Shallan said, reaching for her satchel and digging into it. 'I brought that account for you, Adolin.' She hesitated, glancing at Kaladin.

'You can trust him,' Adolin said, somewhat grudgingly. 'He's saved my life twice, and Father lets him guard us at even the most important meetings.'

Shallan took out several sheets of paper with notes on them in the scribble-like women's script. 'Eighteen years ago, Highprince Yenev was a force in Alethkar, one of the most powerful highprinces who opposed King Gavilar's unification campaign. Yenev wasn't defeated in battle. He was killed in a duel. By *Sadeas.*'

Adolin nodded, leaning forward, eager.

'Here is Brightness Ialai's own account of events,' Shallan said. ' "Bringing down Yenev was an act of inspired simplicity. My husband spoke with Gavilar regarding the Right of Challenge and the King's Boon, ancient traditions that many of the lighteyes knew, but ignored in modern circumstances.

' "As traditions that shared a relationship to the historical crown, invoking them echoed our right of rule. The occasion was a gala of might and renown, and my husband first entered into a duel with another man." '

'A what of might and renown?' Kaladin asked.

Both looked at him, as if surprised to hear him speak. *Keep forgetting I'm here, do you?* Kaladin thought. *You prefer to ignore darkeyes.*

'A gala of might and renown,' Adolin said. 'It's fancy speak for a tournament. They were common back then. Ways for the highprinces who happened to be at peace with one another to show off.'

'We need a way for Adolin to duel, or at least discredit, Sadeas,' Shallan explained. 'While thinking about it, I remembered a reference to the Yenev duel in Jasnah's biography of the old king.'

'All right . . .' Kaladin said, frowning.

' "The purpose," ' Shallan continued, holding up her finger as she read further from the account, ' "of this preliminary duel was to conspicuously awe and impress the highprinces. Though we had plotted this earlier, the first man to be defeated did not know of his role in our ploy. Sadeas defeated him with calculated spectacle. He paused the fighting at several points and raised the stakes, first with money, then with lands.

' "In the end, the victory was dramatic. With the crowd so engaged, King Gavilar stood and offered Sadeas a boon for having pleased him, after the ancient tradition. Sadeas's reply was simple: "I will have no boon other than Yenev's cowardly heart on the end of my sword, Your Majesty!"'

'You're kidding,' Adolin said. 'Blowhard Sadeas said it like that?'

'The event, along with his words, is recorded in several major histories,' Shallan said. 'Sadeas then dueled Yenev, killed the man, and made an opening for an ally – Aladar – to take control of that princedom instead.'

Adolin nodded thoughtfully. 'It *could* work, Shallan. I can try the same thing – make a spectacle of my fight with Relis and the other person he brings, wow the crowd, earn a boon from the king and demand a Right of Challenge to Sadeas himself.'

'It has a certain charm to it,' Shallan agreed. 'Taking a maneuver that Sadeas himself employed, then using it against him.'

'He'd never agree,' Kaladin said. 'Sadeas won't let himself be trapped like that.'

'Perhaps,' Adolin said. 'But I think you underestimate the position he'd be in, if we do this correctly. The Right of Challenge is an ancient tradition – some say the Heralds instituted it. A lighteyed warrior who has proven himself before the Almighty and the king, turning and demanding justice from one who wronged him . . .'

'He'll agree,' Shallan said. 'He'll *have* to. But can you be *spectacular*, Adolin?'

'The crowd expects me to cheat,' Adolin said. 'They won't come thinking much of my recent duels – that should work to my favor. If I can give them a *real* show, they'll be thrilled. Besides, defeating two men at once? That alone should give us the attention we need.'

Kaladin looked from one to the other. They were taking this very seriously. 'You really think this could work?' Kaladin said, growing thoughtful.

'Yes,' Shallan said, 'though, by this tradition, Sadeas could appoint a champion to fight on his behalf, so Adolin might not get to duel him personally. He'd still win Sadeas's Shards, though.'

'It wouldn't be quite as satisfying,' Adolin said. 'But it would be acceptable. Beating his champion in a duel would cut Sadeas off at the knees. He'd lose immense credibility.'

'But it wouldn't *really* mean anything,' Kaladin said. 'Right?'

The other two looked at him.

'It's just a duel,' Kaladin said. 'A game.'

'This would be different,' Adolin said.

'I don't see why. Sure, you might win his Shards, but his title and authority would be the same.'

'It's about perception,' Shallan said. 'Sadeas has formed a coalition against the king. That implies he is stronger than the king. Losing to the king's champion would deflate that.'

'But it's all just *games*,' Kaladin said.

'Yes,' Adolin said – Kaladin hadn't expected him to agree. 'But it's a game that Sadeas is playing. They are rules he's accepted.'

Kaladin sat back, letting it sink in. *This tradition might be an answer*, he thought. *The solution I've been looking for . . .*

'Sadeas used to be such a strong ally,' Adolin said, sounding regretful. 'I'd forgotten things like his defeat of Yenev.'

'So what changed?' Kaladin asked.

'Gavilar died,' Adolin said softly. 'The old king was what kept Father and Sadeas pointed in the same direction.' He leaned forward, looking at Shallan's sheets of notes, though he obviously couldn't read them. 'We *have* to make this happen, Shallan. We have to yank this noose around that eel's throat. This is brilliant. Thank you.'

She blushed, then packed away the notes in an envelope and handed it to him. 'Give this to your aunt. It details what I've found. She and your father will know better if this is a good idea or not.'

Adolin accepted the envelope, and took her hand in his as he did so. The two shared a moment, melting over one another. Yes, Kaladin was increasingly convinced that the woman wasn't going to be of immediate danger to Adolin. If she was some kind of con woman, she wasn't after Adolin's life. Just his dignity.

Too late, Kaladin thought, watching Adolin sit back with a stupid grin on his face. *That's dead and burned already.*

The carriage soon reached the Outer Market, where they passed several groups of men on patrol in Kholin blue. Bridgemen from the various bridges other than Bridge Four. Being guardsmen here was one of the ways Kaladin was training them.

Kaladin climbed out of the carriage first, noting the lines of stormwagons set up in rows nearby. Ropes on posts blocked off the area, ostensibly to keep people from sneaking in, though the men with cudgels lounging beside some of the posts probably did a better job of that.

'Thanks for the ride, Wit,' Kaladin said, turning. 'I'm sorry again about that flute you—'

Wit was gone from the top of the carriage. Another man sat there instead, a younger fellow in brown trousers and a white shirt, a cap on his head. He pulled that off, looking embarrassed.

'Oi'm sorry, sir,' the man said. He had an accent Kaladin didn't recognize. 'He paid me well, he did. Said exactly where Oi was to stand so we could swap places.'

'What's this?' Adolin said, climbing from the carriage and looking up. 'Oh. Wit does this, bridgeboy.'

'This?'

'Likes to vanish mysteriously,' Adolin said.

'It weren't so mysterious, sir,' the lad said, turning and pointing. 'It was joust back there a short ways, where the carriage stopped 'fore turning. Oi was to wait for him, then take over driving this here coach. Oi had to hop on without jostling things. He ran off giggling like a child, he did.'

'He just likes to surprise people,' Adolin said, helping Shallan from the carriage. 'Ignore him.'

The new carriage driver hunched down as if embarrassed. Kaladin didn't recognize him; he wasn't one of Adolin's regular servants. *I'll have to ride up there on the way back. Keep an eye on the man.*

Shallan and Adolin walked off toward the menagerie. Kaladin retrieved his spear from the back of the carriage, then jogged to catch up, eventually falling in a few steps behind them. He listened to them both laughing, and wanted to punch them in the face.

'Wow,' Syl's voice said. 'You're supposed to harness the storms, Kaladin. Not carry them about behind your eyes.'

He glanced at her as she flew over and danced around him in the air, a ribbon of light. He set his spear on his shoulder and kept walking.

'What's wrong?' Syl asked, settling down in the air in front of him. Whichever way he turned his head, she automatically glided that way, as

60

if seated on an invisible shelf, girlish dress fluttering to mist just below her knees.

'Nothing's wrong,' Kaladin said softly. 'I'm just tired of listening to those two.'

Syl looked over her shoulder at the pair just ahead. Adolin paid their way in, thumbing back toward Kaladin, paying for him as well. A pompous-looking Azish man in an odd patterned hat and long coat with an intricate design waved them forward, pointing to the different rows of cages and indicating which animals were where.

'Shallan and Adolin seem happy,' Syl said. 'What's wrong with that?'

'Nothing,' Kaladin said. 'So long as I don't have to listen to it.'

Syl wrinkled her nose. 'It's not them, it's you. You're being sour. I can practically taste it.'

'Taste?' Kaladin asked. 'You don't eat, Syl. I doubt you have a sense of taste.'

'It's a metaphor. And I can imagine it. And you taste sour. And stop arguing, because I'm *right*.' She zipped off to dangle near Shallan and Adolin as they inspected the first cage.

Blasted spren, Kaladin thought, walking up beside Shallan and Adolin. *Arguing with her is like . . . well, arguing with the wind, I guess.*

This stormwagon looked a lot like the slaver cage he'd ridden in on his way to the Shattered Plains, though the animal within looked to have been treated far better than the slaves had. It sat on a rock, and the cage had been covered over with crem on the inside as if to imitate a cave. The creature itself was little more than a lump of flesh with two bulbous eyes and four long tentacles.

'Ooo . . .' Shallan said, eyes wide. She looked like she'd been given a pile of jewelry – only instead, it was a slimy lump of something that Kaladin would have expected to find stuck to the bottom of his boot.

'That,' Adolin said, 'is the ugliest thing I've ever seen. It's like the stuff in the middle of a hasper, only without the shell.'

'It's one of the sarpenthyn,' Shallan said.

'Poor thing,' Adolin said. 'Did its mother give it that name?'

Shallan swatted him on the shoulder. 'It's a family.'

'So the mother *was* behind it.'

'A family of animals, idiot. They have more of them in the west, where the storms aren't as strong. I've only seen a few of them – we've got little ones in Jah Keved, but nothing like this. I don't even know what species this is.' She hesitated, then stuck her fingers through the bars and grabbed one of the tentacle arms.

The thing pulled away immediately, inflating to look bigger, raising two of its arms behind its head in a threatening way. Adolin yelped and pulled Shallan back.

'He said not to touch any of them!' Adolin said. 'What if it's poisonous?'

Shallan ignored him, digging a notebook from her satchel. 'Warm to the touch,' she mumbled to herself. 'Truly warm-blooded. Fascinating. I need a sketch of it.' She squinted at a little plaque on the cage. 'Well, that's useless.'

'What does it say?' Adolin asked.

' "Devil rock captured in Marabethia. The locals claim it is the reborn vengeful spirit of a child who was murdered." Not even a mention of its species. What kind of scholarship is this?'

'It's a menagerie, Shallan,' Adolin said, chuckling. 'Brought all this distance to entertain soldiers and camp followers.'

Indeed, the menagerie was popular. As Shallan sketched, Kaladin kept busy watching those who passed by, making certain they kept their distance. He saw everything from washmaids and tenners to officers, and even some higher lighteyes. Behind them, a lighteyed woman was paraded past in her palanquin, barely even glancing at the cages. It provided quite a contrast to Shallan's eager drawing and Adolin's good-natured gibes.

Kaladin wasn't giving those two enough credit. They might ignore him, but they weren't actively *mean* to him. They were happy and pleasant. Why did that annoy him so?

Eventually, Shallan and Adolin moved on to the next cage, which contained skyeels and a large tub of water for them to dip in. They didn't look as comfortable as the 'devil rock.' There wasn't much room to move in the cage, and they didn't often take to the air. Not very interesting.

Next was a cage with a creature that looked like a small chull, but with larger claws. Shallan wanted a sketch of this one too, so Kaladin found himself lounging beside the cage, watching people pass and listening to Adolin try to crack jokes to amuse his betrothed. He wasn't very good at it, but Shallan laughed anyway.

'Poor thing,' Syl said, landing on the floor of the cage, looking at its crab occupant. 'What kind of life is this?'

'A safe one.' Kaladin shrugged. 'At least it has no need to worry about predators. Always kept fed. I doubt a chull-thing could ask for more than that.'

'Oh?' Syl asked. 'And *you'd* be all right if that were you.'

'Of course not. I'm not a chull-thing. I'm a soldier.'

They moved on, passing cage after cage of animals. Some Shallan wanted to draw, others she concluded didn't need an immediate sketch. The one she found the most fascinating was also the strangest, a kind of colorful chicken with red, blue, and green feathers. She dug out colored pencils to do that sketch. Apparently, she'd missed a chance at sketching one of these a long time ago.

Kaladin had to admit the thing *was* pretty. How did it survive, though? It had shell on the very front of its face, but the rest of it wasn't squishy, so it couldn't hide in cracks like the devil rock. What did this chicken do when a storm came?

Syl landed on Kaladin's shoulder.

'I'm a soldier,' Kaladin repeated, speaking very softly.

'That's what you *were*,' Syl said.

'It's what I want to be again.'

'Are you sure?'

'Mostly.' He folded his arms, spear leaning against his shoulder. 'The only thing is . . . It's crazy, Syl. Insane. My time as a bridgeman was the worst in my life. We suffered death, oppression, indignity. Yet I don't think I've ever felt so alive as I did in those final weeks.'

Next to the work he'd done with Bridge Four, being a simple soldier – even a highly respected one, like captain of a highprince's guard – just felt mundane. Ordinary.

But soaring on the winds – *that* had been anything but ordinary.

'You're almost ready, aren't you?' Syl whispered.

He nodded slowly. 'Yeah. Yeah, I think I am.'

The next cage in line had a large crowd around it, and even a few fear-spren wiggling out of the ground. Kaladin pushed in, though he didn't have to clear a space – the people made room for Dalinar's heir as soon as they realized who he was. Adolin walked past them without a second glance, obviously accustomed to such deference.

This cage was different from the others. The bars were closer together, the wood reinforced. The animal inside didn't seem to deserve the special treatment. The sorry beast lay in front of some rocks, eyes closed. The square face showed sharpened mandibles – like teeth, only somehow more vicious – and a pair of long, toothlike tusks that pointed down from the upper jaw. The stark spikes running from the head along the sinuous back, along with powerful legs, were clues as to what this beast was.

'Whitespine,' Shallan breathed, stepping closer to the cage.

Kaladin had never seen one. He remembered a young man, lying dead on the operating table, blood everywhere. He remembered fear, frustration. And then misery.

'I expected,' Kaladin said, trying to sort through it all, 'the thing to be . . . *more.*'

'They don't do well in captivity,' Shallan said. 'This one probably would have gone dormant in crystal long ago, if it had been allowed. They must keep dousing it to wash away the shell.'

'Don't feel sorry for the thing,' Adolin said. 'I've seen what they can do to a man.'

'Yeah,' Kaladin said softly.

Shallan got out her drawing things, though as she started, people began to move away from the cage. At first, Kaladin thought it was something about the beast itself – but the animal continued to just lie there, eyes closed, occasionally snorting out of its nose holes.

No, people were congregating at the other side of the menagerie. Kaladin caught Adolin's attention, then pointed. *I'm going to go check that out*, the gesture implied. Adolin nodded and rested his hand on his sword. *I'll be on the watch*, that said.

Kaladin jogged off, spear on his shoulder, to investigate. Unfortunately, he soon recognized a familiar face above the crowd. Amaram was a tall man. Dalinar stood at his side, guarded by several of Kaladin's men, who were keeping the gawking crowd back a safe distance.

'. . . heard my son was here,' Dalinar was saying to the well-dressed owner of the menagerie.

'You needn't pay, Highprince!' the menagerie owner said, speaking with a lofty accent similar to Sigzil's. 'Your presence is a grand blessing from the Heralds upon my humble collection. And your distinguished guest.'

Amaram. He wore a strange cloak. Bright yellow-gold, with a black glyph on the back. Oath? Kaladin didn't recognize the shape. It looked familiar, though.

The double eye, he realized. Symbol of . . .

'Is it true?' the menagerie owner asked, inspecting Amaram. 'The rumors around camp are most intriguing. . . .'

Dalinar sighed audibly. 'We were going to announce this at the feast tonight, but as Amaram insists on wearing the cloak, I suppose it needs to be stated. Under the king's direction, I have commanded the refounding of the Knights Radiant. Let it be spoken of in the camps. The ancient oaths are spoken again, and Brightlord Amaram was – at my request – the first to speak them. The Knights Radiant have been reestablished, and he stands at their head.'

WHITESPINE
UNCAGED

Twenty-three cohorts followed behind, that came from the contributions of the King of Makabakam, for though the bond between man and spren was at times inexplicable, the ability for bonded spren to manifest in our world rather than their own grew stronger through the course of the oaths given.

—From *Words of Radiance*, chapter 35, page 9

'Amaram obviously doesn't have any Surgebinding abilities,' Sigzil said softly, standing beside Kaladin.

Dalinar, Navani, the king, and Amaram climbed out of their carriage ahead. The dueling arena rose before them, another of the crater-like formations that rimmed the Shattered Plains. It was much smaller than the ones that held the warcamps, however, and had tiered seats inside.

With both Elhokar and Dalinar in attendance – not to mention Navani and both of Dalinar's sons – Kaladin had brought every guard he could. That included some of the men from Bridge Seventeen and Bridge Two. Those stood proudly, with spears held high, obviously excited to finally be trusted with their first bodyguard assignment. In total, he had forty men on duty.

None of them would be worth a drop of rain if the Assassin in White attacked.

'Can we be certain?' Kaladin asked, nodding toward Amaram, who still wore his yellow-gold cloak with the symbol of the Knights Radiant on the back. 'I haven't shown anyone my powers. There have to be others training as I am. Storms, Syl all but promised me there were.'

'He'd have displayed the abilities if he had them,' Sigzil said. 'Gossip is moving through the ten warcamps like floodwater. Half the people think it's blasphemous and stupid, what Dalinar is doing. The other half are undecided. If Amaram displayed Surgebinding powers, Brightlord Dalinar's move would look a lot less precarious.'

Sigzil was probably right. But ... Amaram? The man walked with such pride, head held high. Kaladin felt his neck growing hot, and for a moment it seemed the only thing he could see was Amaram. Golden cloak. Haughty face.

Bloodstained. That man was *bloodstained*. Kaladin *told* Dalinar about it!

Dalinar wouldn't do anything.

Someone else would have to.

'Kaladin?' Sigzil asked.

Kaladin realized he'd stepped toward Amaram, hands clenched on his spear. He took a deep breath, then pointed. 'Put men up on the rim of the arena there. Skar and Eth are in the preparation room with Adolin, for all the good it will do him out on the field. Put another few down at the arena bottom, just in case. Three men at every door. I'll take six with me to the king's seats.' Kaladin paused, then added, 'Let's also put two men guarding Adolin's betrothed, just in case. She'll be sitting with Sebarial.'

'Will do.'

'Tell the men to keep focused, Sig. This is likely to be a dramatic fight. I want their minds on the possibility of assassins, not on the duel.'

'Is he really going to fight two men at once?'

'Yeah.'

'Can he possibly win that?'

'I don't know, and I don't really care. Our job is to watch for other threats.'

Sigzil nodded, and moved to leave. He hesitated, however, taking Kaladin by the arm. 'You could join them, Kal,' he said softly. 'If the king's refounding the Knights Radiant, you have an excuse to show what you are. Dalinar is trying, but so many think of the Radiants as an evil force, forgetting the good they did before they betrayed mankind. But if you showed your powers, it could change minds.'

Join. Under Amaram. Not likely.

'Go pass my orders,' Kaladin said, gesturing, then pulled his arm free of Sigzil's grip and jogged after the king and his retinue. At least the sun was out today, the spring air warm.

Syl bobbed along behind Kaladin. 'Amaram is ruining you, Kaladin,' she whispered. 'Don't let him.'

He gritted his teeth and didn't reply. Instead, he moved up beside Moash, who was in charge of a team who would watch Brightness Navani – she preferred to watch the duels from down below, in the preparation rooms.

A part of him wondered if he should let Moash guard anyone other than Dalinar, but storm it, Moash had *sworn* to him that he'd take no more actions against the king. Kaladin trusted him on that count. They were Bridge Four.

I'll get you out of this, Moash, Kaladin thought, pulling the man aside. *We'll fix this.*

'Moash,' Kaladin said, speaking softly. 'Starting tomorrow, I'm putting you on patrol duty.'

Moash frowned. 'I thought you always wanted me guarding . . .' His expression grew hard. 'This is about what happened. In the tavern.'

'I want you to take a deep patrol,' Kaladin said. 'Head out toward New Natanan. I don't want you here when we move against Graves and his people.' It had been too long already.

'I'm not leaving.'

'You will, and it's not subject to—'

'What they're doing is *right*, Kal!'

Kaladin frowned. 'Have you still been meeting with them?'

Moash looked away. 'Only once. To assure them that you'd come around.'

'You still disobeyed an order!' Kaladin said. 'Storm it, Moash!'

The noise inside the arena was building.

'Almost time for the match,' Moash said, pulling his arm free of Kaladin's grip. 'We can talk about this later.'

Kaladin ground his teeth, but unfortunately, Moash was right. This wasn't the time.

Should have grabbed him this morning, Kaladin thought. *No, what I should have done was make a decision on this days ago.*

It was his own fault. 'You *will* go on that patrol, Moash,' he said. 'You don't get to be insubordinate just because you're my friend. Go on.'

The man jogged ahead, collecting his squad.

⁖

Adolin knelt beside his sword in the preparation room and found he didn't know what to say.

He looked at his reflection in the Blade. Two Shardbearers at once. He'd never even tried that outside of the practice grounds.

Fighting multiple opponents was tough. In the histories, if you heard of a man fighting six men at once or whatnot, the truth was probably that he managed to take them one at a time somehow. Two at once was hard, if they were prepared and careful. Not impossible, but really hard.

'It comes down to this,' Adolin said. He had to say *something* to the sword. It was tradition. 'Let's go be spectacular. Then let's wipe that smile off Sadeas's face.'

He stood up, dismissing his Blade. He left the small preparation room, walking down the tunnel with carved, painted duelists. In the room beyond, Renarin sat in his Kholin uniform – he wore that to official functions like this, instead of the blasted Bridge Four uniform – waiting anxiously. Aunt Navani was screwing the lid off a jar of paint to do a glyphward.

'No need,' Adolin said, taking one from his pocket. Painted in Kholin blue, it read 'excellence.'

Navani cocked an eyebrow. 'The girl?'

'Yeah,' Adolin said.

'The calligraphy isn't bad,' Navani said, grudgingly.

'She's quite wonderful, Aunt,' Adolin said. 'I wish you'd give her more of a chance. And she *does* want to share her scholarship with you.'

'We'll see,' Navani said. She sounded more thoughtful than she had before, regarding Shallan. A good sign.

Adolin placed the glyphward in the brazier, then bowed his head as it burned. A prayer to the Almighty for aid. His combatants for the day would probably be burning their own prayers. How did the Almighty decide whom to help?

I can't believe, Adolin thought, raising his head from the prayer, *that he'd want those who serve Sadeas, even indirectly, to succeed.*

'I'm worried,' Navani said.

'Father thinks the plan could work, and Elhokar really likes it.'

'Elhokar can be impulsive,' Navani said, folding her arms and watching the remnants of the glyphward burn. 'The terms change things.'

The terms – agreed upon with Relis and spoken in front of the high-judge just earlier – indicated that this duel would go until surrender, not until a certain number of Plate sections were broken. That meant if Adolin did manage to beat one of his foes, making the man give in, the other could keep fighting.

It also meant that Adolin didn't have to stop fighting until he was convinced he was bested.

Or until he was incapacitated.

Renarin walked over, resting a hand on Adolin's shoulder. 'I think the plan is a good one,' he said. 'You can do this.'

'They're going to try to break you,' Navani said. 'That's why they in-sisted this be a match until the surrender. They'll leave you crippled if they can, Adolin.'

'No different from the battlefield,' he said. 'Actually, in this case, they will want to leave me alive. I'll work better as an object lesson with Blade-dead legs than I would as ashes.'

Navani closed her eyes, drawing in a breath. She looked pale. It was a little like having his mother back. A little.

'Make *sure* you don't give Sadeas any outs,' Renarin said to him as the armorers entered with Adolin's Shardplate. 'When you corner him with a challenge, he will look for a way to escape. Don't let him. Bring him down on those sands and beat him bloody, Brother.'

'With pleasure.'

'Now, you ate chicken?' Renarin asked.

'Two plates of the stuff, with curry.'

'Mother's chain?'

Adolin felt in his pocket.

Then he felt in his other one.

'What?' Renarin asked, fingers tightening on Adolin's shoulder.

'I could have *sworn* I slipped it in.'

Renarin cursed.

'Might be back in my rooms,' Adolin said. 'In the warcamps. On my end table.' Assuming he hadn't grabbed it, then lost it on the way. *Storms.*

It was just a good luck charm. It didn't mean anything. He started sweating anyway as Renarin scrambled to send a runner off to search. They wouldn't get back in time. Already he could hear the crowd outside, the growing roar that came before a duel. Adolin reluctantly allowed his armorers to begin putting on his Plate.

By the time they gave him his helm, he had recovered most of his rhythm – the anticipation that was an odd blend of anxiety in his stomach and relaxation in his muscles. You couldn't fight while tense. You could fight while nervous, but not while tense.

He nodded to the servants, and they pushed open the doors, letting him stride out onto the sand. He could tell from their cheering where the darkeyes sat. In contrast, the lighteyes grew softer, instead of louder, when he emerged. It was good that Elhokar reserved space for the darkeyes. Adolin liked the noise. It reminded him of a battlefield.

There was a time, he thought, *when I didn't like the battlefield because it wasn't quiet, like a duel.* Despite his original reluctance, he had become a soldier.

He strode out into the center of the arena. The others hadn't left their preparation room yet. *Take Relis first,* Adolin told himself. *You know his dueling style.* The man preferred Vinestance, slow and steady, but with sudden, quick lunges. Adolin wasn't sure whom he'd bring along to fight with him, though he'd borrowed a full set of the King's Blade and Plate. Perhaps his cousin wanted to try again, for vengeance?

Shallan was there, on the opposite side of the arena, her red hair standing out like blood on stone. She had two bridgeman guards. Adolin found himself nodding in appreciation of that, and raised a fist to her. She waved back.

Adolin danced from one foot to the other, letting the power of the Plate flow through him. He could win, even without Mother's chain. The problem was, he intended to challenge Sadeas after this. So he had to retain enough strength for that duel.

He checked, anxious. Was Sadeas there? Yes; he sat only a little ways from Father and the king. Adolin narrowed his eyes, remembering the crushing moment of realization when he'd seen Sadeas's armies retreating from the Tower.

That steadied him. He'd stewed long about that betrayal. It was time, finally, to do something.

The doors across from him opened.

Four men in Shardplate strode out.

•••

'Four?' Dalinar said, leaping to his feet.

Kaladin took a step downward toward the arena floor. Yes, those were all Shardbearers, entering the sands of the dueling arena below. One wore a set of the King's Plate; the other three wore their own, ornamented and painted.

Down below, the highjudge for the bout turned and cocked her head toward the king.

'What is this?' Dalinar bellowed toward Sadeas, who sat only a short distance away. The lighteyes on the benchlike rows of seats between them hunched down or fled, leaving a direct line of sight between the highprinces.

Sadeas and his wife turned about, lazily. 'Why do you ask me?' Sadeas called back. 'None of those men are mine. I'm just an observer today.'

'Oh, don't be tiresome, Sadeas,' Elhokar called. 'You know full well what is happening. Why are there four? Is Adolin supposed to pick the two he wants to duel?'

'Two?' Sadeas asked. 'When was it said that he would fight two?'

'That's what he said when he set up the duel!' Dalinar shouted. 'Paired disadvantaged duel, two against one, as per the dueling conventions!'

'Actually,' Sadeas replied, 'that is *not* what young Adolin agreed to. Why, I have it on very good authority that he told Prince Relis: "I'll fight you and whomever you bring." I don't hear a specification of a number in there – which subjects Adolin to a *full* disadvantaged duel, not a paired duel. Relis may bring as many as he wishes. I know several scribes who recorded Adolin's precise words, and I hear the highjudge asked him *specifically* if he understood what he was doing, and he said that he did.'

Dalinar growled softly. It was a sound Kaladin had never heard from him, the growl of a beast on a chain. It surprised him. The highprince contained himself, however, sitting down with a curt motion.

'He outthought us,' Dalinar said softly to the king. 'Again. We'll need to retreat and consider our next move. Someone tell Adolin to pull out of the contest.'

'Are you certain?' the king said. 'Pulling out would require that Adolin forfeit, Uncle. That's six Shards, I believe. Everything you own.'

Kaladin could read the conflict in Dalinar's features – the scrunched-up brow, the red fury rising on his cheeks, the indecision in his eyes. Give up? Without a fight? It was probably the right thing to do.

Kaladin doubted he could have done it.

Below, after an extended pause – frozen on the sand – Adolin raised his hand in a sign of agreement. The judge began the duel.

∴

I'm an idiot. I'm an idiot. I'm a storm-cursed idiot!

Adolin jogged backward across the sand-covered circle of the arena. He'd need to put his back to the wall to avoid being completely surrounded. That meant he'd start the duel with no place to retreat, locked in a box. Cornered.

Why hadn't he been more specific? He could see the holes in his challenge – he'd agreed to a full disadvantaged duel without realizing it. He should have stated, specifically, that Relis could bring *one* other. But no, doing so would have been smart. And Adolin was a storming idiot!

He recognized Relis from his Plate and Blade, colored completely a deep black, breakaway cloak bearing his father's glyphpair. The man in King's Plate – judging by his height and the way he walked – would indeed be Elit, Relis's cousin, returned for a rematch. He carried an enormous hammer, rather than a Blade. The two moved across the field carefully, and their two companions took the flanks. One in orange, the other in green.

Adolin recognized the Plate. That would be Abrobadar, a full Shard-bearer from Aladar's camp and . . . and Jakamav, bearing the King's Blade that Relis had borrowed.

Jakamav. Adolin's friend.

Adolin cursed. Those two were among the best duelists in the camp. Jakamav would have won his own Blade years ago if he'd been allowed to risk his Plate. That had apparently changed. Had he, and his house, been bought with a promise of a share in the spoils?

Blade forming in his hand, Adolin backed into the cool shade of the wall around the arena grounds. Just above him, darkeyes roared on their benches. Whether they were thrilled or horrified by what he faced, Adolin could not tell. He'd come here intending to give a spectacular show. They'd get the opposite instead. A quick slaughter.

Well, he'd made this pyre himself. If he was going to burn on it, he'd at least put up a fight first.

Relis and Elit prowled closer – one in slate grey, the other in black – as their allies worked around the sides. Those would hang back to try to make Adolin focus on the two in front of him. Then the others could attack him from the sides.

'One at a time, lad!' One shout from the stands seemed to separate from the others. Was that Zahel's voice? 'You're not cornered!'

Relis stepped forward in a quick motion, testing Adolin. Adolin danced away in Windstance – certainly the best against so many foes – with both hands holding the Blade in front of him, positioned sideways with one foot forward.

You're not cornered! What did Zahel mean? Of course he was cornered! It was the only way to face four. And how could he possibly face them one at a time? They'd never allow that.

Relis tested forward again, making Adolin shuffle sideways along the wall, focused on him. He had to turn somewhat to face Relis, however, and that put Abrobadar – moving up the other way, wearing orange – in his blind spot. Storms!

'They're scared of you.' Zahel's voice, drifting again above the crowd. 'Do you see it in them? Show them *why.*'

Adolin hesitated. Relis stepped forward, making a Stonestance strike. Stonestance, to be immobile. Elit came in next, hammer held wardingly. They backed Adolin along the wall toward Abrobadar.

No. Adolin had demanded this duel. He had wanted it. He would not become a frightened rat.

Show them why.

Adolin attacked. He leaped forward, sweeping with a barrage of strikes at Relis. Elit jumped away with a curse as he did so. They were like men with spears prodding at a whitespine.

And this whitespine was not yet caged.

Adolin shouted, beating against Relis, scoring strikes on his helm and left vambrace, cracking the latter. Stormlight rose from Relis's forearm.

As Elit recovered, Adolin spun on him and struck, leaving Relis dazed from the attack. His assault forced Elit to hold his hammer back and block with his forearm, lest Adolin slice the hammer in two and leave him unarmed.

This was what Zahel meant. Attack with fury. Don't allow them time to respond or assess. Four men. If he could intimidate them into hesitating ... Maybe ...

Adolin stopped thinking. He let the flow of the fight consume him, let the rhythm of his heart guide the beating of his sword. Elit cursed and pulled away, leaking Stormlight from his left shoulder and forearm.

Adolin turned and smashed his shoulder into Relis, who was stepping back into his stance. His shove threw the black-Plated man tumbling to the ground. Then, with a shout, Adolin turned and met Abrobadar headon as the man came dashing up to help. Adolin fell into Stonestance himself, smashing his Blade down again and again against Abrobadar's raised sword until he heard grunts, curses. Until he could *feel* the fear coming off the man in orange like a stench, and could see fearspren on the ground.

Elit approached, wary, as Relis scrambled up to his feet. Adolin fell back into Windstance and swept about himself in a wide, fluid motion. Elit jumped away and Abrobadar stumbled back, gauntleted hand against the wall of the arena.

Adolin turned back toward Relis, who had recovered well, all things considered. Still, Adolin got in a second strike at the champion's breastplate. If this had been a battlefield and these common foes, Relis would be dead, Elit maimed. Adolin was yet untouched.

But they weren't common foes. They were Shardbearers, and a second strike against Relis's breastplate didn't break the armor. Adolin was forced to turn on Abrobadar before he wanted to, and the man was now braced for the fury of the assault, sword raised defensively. Adolin's barrage didn't stun him this time. The man weathered it while Elit and Relis got into position.

Just need to—

Something crashed into Adolin from behind.

Jakamav. Adolin had taken too long, and had allowed the fourth man – his supposed friend – to get into position. Adolin spun about, moving into a puff of Stormlight rising from his back plate. He raised his sword into Jakamav's next attack, but that opened his left flank. Elit swung, hammer crashing into Adolin's side. Plate cracked, and the blow shoved Adolin off balance.

He swept around himself, growing desperate. This time, his foes didn't back away. Instead, Jakamav charged in, head down, not even swinging. Smart man. His green armor was unscored. Even though the move let Adolin slam his sword down and hit the man on the back, it threw Adolin completely out of his stance.

Adolin stumbled backward, barely keeping from being thrown to the ground as Jakamav crashed into him. Adolin shoved the man aside, somehow keeping hold of his Shardblade, but the other three moved in. Blows rained on his shoulders, helm, breastplate. Storms. That hammer hit *hard*.

Adolin's head rang from a blow. He'd almost done it. He let himself grin as they beat on him. Four at once. And he'd almost *done it*.

'I yield,' he said, voice muffled by his helm.

They continued attacking. He said it louder.

Nobody listened.

He raised his hand to signal to the judge to stop the proceedings, but someone slammed his arm downward.

No! Adolin thought, swinging about himself in a panic.

The judge could not end the fight. If he left this duel alive, he would do so as a cripple.

⁙

'That's it,' Dalinar said, watching the four Shardbearers take turns coming in to swing at Adolin, who was obviously disoriented, barely able to fight them off. 'The rules allow Adolin to have help, so long as his side is disadvantaged – one less than Relis's team. Elhokar, I'll need your Shardblade.'

'No,' Elhokar said. The king sat with folded arms beneath the shade. Those around them watched the duel . . . no, the beating . . . in silence.

'Elhokar!' Dalinar said, turning. 'That is my *son*.'

'You're without Plate,' Elhokar said. 'If you take the time to put some on, you'll be too late. If you go down, you won't save Adolin. You'll simply lose *my* Blade as well as all the others.'

Dalinar clenched his teeth. There was a drop of wisdom in that, and he knew it. Adolin was finished. They needed to end the match now and not put more on the line.

'You could help him, you know.' Sadeas's voice.

Dalinar spun toward the man.

'The dueling conventions don't forbid it,' Sadeas said, speaking loudly enough for Dalinar to hear. 'I checked to make sure. Young Adolin can be helped by up to two people. The Blackthorn I once knew would have been down there already, fighting with a *rock* if he had to. I guess you're not that man anymore.'

Dalinar sucked in a breath, then stood. 'Elhokar, I'll pay the fee and borrow your Blade by right of the tradition of the King's Blade. You won't risk it that way. I'm going to fight.'

Elhokar caught him by the arm, standing. 'Don't be a fool, Uncle. Listen to him! Do you see what he's doing? He obviously *wants* you to go down and fight.'

Dalinar turned to meet the king's eyes. Pale green. Like his father's.

'Uncle,' Elhokar said, grip tightening on his arm, '*listen* to me for once. Be a little paranoid. Why would Sadeas want you down there? It's so that an "accident" can occur! He wants you *removed*, Dalinar. I guarantee that if you step onto those sands, all four will attack you straight out. Shardblade or none, you'll be dead before you get into stance.'

Dalinar puffed in and out. Elhokar was right. Storm him, but he was right. Dalinar had to do *something* though.

A murmur rose from the watching crowd, whispers like scratches on paper. Dalinar spun to see that someone else had joined the battle, stepping from the preparation room, Shardblade held nervously in two hands but wearing no Plate.

Renarin.

Oh no . . .

※

One of the attackers moved away, Plated feet crunching on sand. Adolin threw himself in that direction, battering his way out from among the three others. He spun and backed away. His Plate was starting to feel heavy. How much Stormlight had he lost?

No broken sections, he thought, keeping his sword toward the three other men who fanned out to advance on him. He could maybe . . .

No. Time to end this. He felt a fool, but better a live fool than a dead one. He turned toward the highjudge to signal his surrender. Surely she could see him now.

'Adolin,' Relis said, prowling forward, his Plate leaking from small cracks on his chest. 'Now, we wouldn't want to end this prematurely, would we?'

'What glory do you think will come of such a fight?' Adolin spat back, sword held carefully, ready to give the signal. 'You think people will cheer you? For beating a man four against one?'

'This isn't for honor,' Relis said. 'It's simple punishment.'

Adolin snorted. Only then did he notice something on the other side of the arena. Renarin in Kholin blue, holding a wobbly Shardblade and facing down Abrobadar, who stood with sword on his shoulder as if completely unthreatened.

'Renarin!' Adolin shouted. 'What in the storms are you doing! Go back—'

Abrobadar attacked, and Renarin parried awkwardly. Renarin had done all of his sparring in Shardplate so far, but hadn't had the time to fetch his Plate. Abrobadar's blow just about knocked the weapon from Renarin's hands.

'Now,' Relis said, stepping closer to Adolin, 'Abrobadar there is fond of young Renarin, and doesn't want to hurt him. So he'll just keep the young man engaged, make a good fight of it. So long as you're willing to keep up what you promised, and have a good duel with us. Surrender like a coward, or get the king to end the bout, and Abrobadar's sword might just slip.'

Adolin felt a panic rising. He looked toward the highjudge. She could call this on her own, if she felt it had gone too far.

She sat imperiously in her seat, watching him. Adolin thought he saw something behind her calm expression. *They got to her*, he thought. *With a bribe, perhaps.*

Adolin tightened his grip on his Blade and looked back toward his three foes. 'You bastards,' he whispered. 'Jakamav, how *dare* you be a part of this?'

Jakamav didn't reply, and Adolin could not see his face behind his green helm.

'So,' Relis said. 'Shall we?'

Adolin's response was a charge.

∵

Dalinar reached the judge's seat, which sat on its own small, stone dais hanging out a few inches over the dueling grounds.

Brightness Istow was a tall, greying woman who sat with hands in her lap, watching the duel. She did not turn as Dalinar stepped up beside her.

'It is time to end this, Istow,' Dalinar said. 'Call the fight. Award the victory to Relis and his team.'

The woman kept her eyes forward, watching the duel.

'Did you *hear* me?' Dalinar demanded.

She said nothing.

'Fine,' he said. 'I'll end it then.'

'*I* am highprince here, Dalinar,' the woman said. 'In this arena, my word is the only law, granted me by the authority of the king.' She turned to him. 'Your son has not surrendered and he is not incapacitated. The terms of the duel have not been met, and I will not end it until they have been. Have you no respect for the law?'

Dalinar ground his teeth together, then looked back at the arena. Renarin fought one of the men. The lad had barely any training in the sword. In fact, as Dalinar watched, Renarin's shoulder began to twitch, pulling up toward his head violently. One of his fits.

Adolin fought the other three, having cast himself among them again. He fought marvelously, but could not fend off all of them. The three surrounded him and struck.

The pauldron on Adolin's left shoulder exploded into a burst of molten metal, bits trailing smoke through the air, the main chunk of it skidding to the sands a short distance away. That left Adolin's flesh exposed to the air, and to the Blades facing him.

Please . . . Almighty . . .

Dalinar turned upon the stands full of spectating lighteyes. 'You can watch this?' he shouted at them. 'My sons fight alone! There are Shardbearers among you. Is there not one of you who will fight with them?'

He scanned the crowd. The king was looking at his feet. Amaram. What of Amaram? Dalinar found him seated near the king. Dalinar met the man's eyes.

Amaram looked away.

No . . .

'What has happened to us?' Dalinar asked. 'Where is our honor?'

'Honor is dead,' a voice whispered from beside him.

Dalinar turned and looked at Captain Kaladin. He hadn't noticed the bridgeman walking down the steps behind him.

Kaladin took a deep breath, then looked at Dalinar. 'But I'll see what I can do. If this goes poorly, take care of my men.' Spear in hand, he grabbed the edge of the wall and flung himself over, dropping to the sands of the arena floor below.

TO KILL THE WIND

Malchin was stymied, for though he was inferior to none in the arts of war, he was not suitable for the Lightweavers; he wished for his oaths to be elementary and straightforward, and yet their spren were liberal, as to our comprehension, in definitions pertaining to this matter; the process included speaking truths as an approach to a threshold of self-awareness that Malchin could never attain.

—From *Words of Radiance*, chapter 12, page 12

S hallan stood up in her seat, watching Adolin's beating below. Why didn't he surrender? Give up the bout?

Four men. She should have seen that loophole. As his wife, watching for intrigue like this would be her duty. Now, barely betrothed, she'd already failed him disastrously. Beyond that, this fiasco had been her idea.

Adolin seemed about to give in, but then for some reason, he threw himself back into the fight instead.

'Fool man,' Sebarial said, lounging beside her, Palona on his other side. 'Too arrogant to see that he's beaten.'

'No,' Shallan said. 'There's something more.' Her eyes flicked down toward poor Renarin, completely overwhelmed as he tried to fight a Shardbearer.

For the briefest instant, she considered going down to help. Sheer stupidity; she'd be even more useless than Renarin down there. Why didn't anyone else help them? She glared across at the gathered Alethi lighteyes, including Highlord Amaram, the supposed Knight Radiant.

Bastard.

Shocked at how quickly that sentiment rose inside of her, Shallan looked away from him. *Don't think about it.* Well, as nobody was going to help, both princes seemed to stand a good chance of dying.

'Pattern,' she whispered. 'Go see if you can distract that Shardbearer fighting Prince Renarin.' She would not interfere with Adolin's fight, not as he'd obviously decided he needed to keep going for some reason. But she would try to keep Renarin from getting maimed, if she could.

Pattern hummed and slipped from her skirt, moving across the stone of the arena benches. He seemed painfully obvious to her, moving in the open, but everybody was focused on the fighting below.

Don't you get yourself killed on me, Adolin Kholin, she thought, glancing back up at him as he struggled against his three opponents. *Please . . .*

Someone else dropped to the sands.

⁘

Kaladin dashed across the arena floor.

Again, he thought, remembering coming to Amaram's rescue so long ago. 'This had better end differently than it did that time.'

'It will,' Syl promised, zipping along beside his head, a line of light. 'Trust me.'

Trust. He'd trusted her and spoken to Dalinar about Amaram. That had gone wonderfully.

One of the Shardbearers – Relis, the one in black armor – trailed Stormlight from a crack in the vambrace on his left forearm. He glanced at Kaladin as he approached, then turned back away, indifferent. Relis obviously didn't think a simple spearman was a threat.

Kaladin smiled, then sucked in some Stormlight. On this bright day, with the sun blazing white overhead, he could risk more than he normally would. Nobody would see it. Hopefully.

He sped up, then lunged between two of the Shardbearers, ramming his spear into Relis's cracked vambrace. The man let out a shout of pain and Kaladin pulled his spear back, twisting between the attackers and getting close to Adolin. The young man in blue armor glanced at him, then quickly turned to put his back toward Kaladin.

Kaladin put his own back toward Adolin, preventing either of them from being attacked from behind.

'What are you doing here, bridgeboy?' Adolin hissed from within his helmet.

'Playing one of the ten fools.'

Adolin grunted. 'Welcome to the party.'

'I won't be able to get through their armor,' Kaladin said. 'You'll need to crack it for me.' Nearby, Relis shook his arm, cursing. The tip of Kaladin's spear had blood on it. Not much, unfortunately.

'Just keep one of them distracted from me,' Adolin said. 'I can handle two.'

'I— All right.' It was probably the best plan.

'Keep an eye on my brother, if you can,' Adolin said. 'If things go sour for these three, they might decide to use him as leverage against us.'

'Done,' Kaladin said, then pulled away and jumped to the side as the one with a hammer – Dalinar had named him Elit – tried to attack Adolin. Relis came in from the other side, swinging, as if to cut right through Kaladin and hit Adolin.

His heart thumped, but training with Zahel had done its job. He could stare down that Shardblade and feel only a *mild* panic. He twisted around Relis, dodging the Blade.

The black-Plated man glanced at Adolin and took a step in that direction, but Kaladin lunged as if to strike him in the arm again.

Relis turned back, then reluctantly let Kaladin draw him away from the fight with Adolin. The man attacked quickly, using what Kaladin could now identify as Vinestance – a style of fighting that focused on defensive footing and flexibility.

He went more offensive against Kaladin, but Kaladin twisted and spun, always getting *just* out of the way of the attacks. Relis started cursing, then turned back to the fight with Adolin.

Kaladin slapped him on the side of the head with the butt of his spear. It was a terrible weapon for fighting a Shardbearer, but the blow got the man's attention again. Relis turned and swept out with his Blade.

Kaladin pulled back a hair too slowly, and the Blade sheared the pointed end off his spear. A reminder. His own flesh would put up less resistance than that. Severing his spine would kill him, and no amount of Stormlight would undo that.

Careful, he tried to lead Relis farther away from the fight. However, when he pulled back too far, the man just turned and moved toward Adolin.

The prince fought desperately against his two opponents, swinging his Blade back and forth between the men on either side of him. And *storms* he was good. Kaladin had never seen this level of skill from Adolin on the practice grounds – nothing there had ever challenged him this much. Adolin moved between sweeps of his Blade, deflecting the Shardblade of the one in green, then warding away the one with the hammer.

He frequently came within inches of striking his opponents. Two-on-one against Adolin actually seemed an even match.

Three would obviously be too much for him. Kaladin needed to keep Relis distracted. But how? He couldn't get through that Plate with a spear. The only weak points were the eye slit and the small crack on the vambrace. He had to do something. The man was striding back toward Adolin, weapon raised. Gritting his teeth, Kaladin charged.

He crossed the sands in a quick dash and then, right before reaching Relis, Kaladin jumped to put his feet toward the Shardbearer and Lashed himself that direction many times in quick succession. As many as he dared, so many that he burned through all of his Stormlight.

Though Kaladin fell only a short distance – enough that it wouldn't look too unusual to those watching – he hit with the force of having fallen much farther. His feet smashed against the Plate as he *kicked* with everything he had.

Pain shot up his legs like lightning striking, and he heard his bones crack. The kick flung the black-armored Shardbearer forward as if he'd been struck by a boulder. Relis went sprawling on his face, Blade flung from his hands. It vanished to mist.

Kaladin crashed to the sand, groaning, his Stormlight exhausted and the Lashings ended. By reflex, he sucked in more Light from the spheres in his pocket, letting it heal his legs. He'd broken them both, and his feet. The healing process seemed to take forever, and he forced himself to roll over and look at Relis. Incredibly, Kaladin's attack had *cracked* the Shardplate. Not the center of the back plate where he'd hit, but at the shoulders and sides. Relis climbed to his knees, shaking his head. He looked back at Kaladin with what seemed like an attitude of awe.

Beyond the fallen man, Adolin spun and came in at one of his opponents – Elit, the one with the hammer – and slammed his Shardblade two-handed into the man's chest. The breastplate there exploded into molten light. Adolin took a hit on the side of the helm from the man in green to do it.

Adolin was in bad shape. Practically every piece of Plate the young man wore was leaking Stormlight. At this rate, he'd soon have none left, and the Plate would grow too heavy to move in.

For now, fortunately, he'd basically incapacitated one of his adversaries. A Shardbearer could fight with his breastplate broken, but it was supposed to be storming difficult. Indeed, as Elit backed away, his steps were awkward, as if his Plate suddenly weighed a lot more.

Adolin had to turn to fight the other Shardbearer near him. On the other side of the arena, the fourth man – the one who had been 'fighting' Renarin – was waving his sword at the ground for some reason. He looked up and saw how poorly things were going for his allies, then left Renarin and dashed across the arena floor.

'Wait,' Syl said. 'What is *that*?' She zipped away toward Renarin, but Kaladin couldn't spare much thought for her behavior. When the man in orange reached Adolin, he'd again be surrounded.

Kaladin scrambled to his feet. Blessedly, they worked; the bones had reknit enough for him to walk. He charged Elit, kicking up sand as he ran, spear clutched in one hand.

Elit wobbled toward Adolin, intending to continue the fight despite his disabled Plate. Kaladin reached him first, however, ducking under the man's hasty hammer strike. Kaladin came in swinging from the shoulder, holding his broken spear in two hands, giving the attack all he had.

It smashed into Elit's exposed chest, making a satisfying *crunch*. The man let out an enormous gasp, doubling over. Kaladin raised his spear to swing again, but the man lifted a wobbling hand, trying to say something. 'Yield . . .' his weak voice said.

'Louder!' Kaladin snapped at him.

The man tried, out of breath. The hand he raised, however, was enough. The watching judge spoke. 'Brightlord Elit yields the combat,' she said, sounding reluctant.

Kaladin backed away from the cowering man, light on his feet, Stormlight thundering inside of him. The crowd roared, even many of the lighteyes making noise.

Three Shardbearers remained. Relis had now returned to his companion in green, both harrying Adolin. They had the prince backed up against a wall. The final Shardbearer, wearing orange, arrived to join them, having left Renarin behind.

Renarin sat on the sand, head bowed, Shardblade stuck into the ground before him. Had he been defeated? Kaladin had heard no announcement from the judge.

No time to worry. Adolin once again had *three* people to fight. Relis scored a hit on his helm, and the thing exploded, exposing the prince's face. He would not last much longer.

Kaladin charged up to Elit, who was trying to hobble off the field in defeat. 'Remove your helm,' Kaladin shouted at him.

The man turned to him with a shocked posture.

'Your helm!' Kaladin screamed, raising his weapon to strike again.

In the stands, people shouted. Kaladin wasn't sure of the rules, but he had a suspicion that if he struck this man, he would forfeit the duel. Maybe even face criminal charges. Fortunately, he wasn't forced to make good on the threat, as Elit removed his helm. Kaladin snatched it from his hand, then left him and ran toward Adolin.

As he ran, Kaladin dropped his broken spear and shoved his hand into the helm from the bottom. He'd learned something about Shardplate – it attached itself automatically to its bearer. He'd hoped it might work for the helm now, and it did – the inside tightened around his wrist. When he let go, the helm remained on his hand like a very strange glove.

Taking a deep breath, Kaladin yanked out his side knife. He'd started carrying one meant for throwing again, as he had as a spearman before his captivity, though he was out of practice with that. Throwing wouldn't work against that armor anyway; this was a pitiful weapon against Shardbearers. Still, he could not use the spear one-handed. He charged Relis again.

This time, Relis backed away immediately. He watched Kaladin, sword held out. At least Kaladin had managed to worry him.

Kaladin advanced, backing him away. Relis went easily, keeping his distance. Kaladin made a show of it, darting in, backing the man away as if to give the two of them space to fight. The Shardbearer would be eager for this; with his Blade, he would want a good open area around them. Tight quarters would favor Kaladin's knife.

However, once a sufficient distance away, Kaladin turned and dashed back toward Adolin and the two men he was fighting. He left Relis standing there in an anxious pose, momentarily befuddled by Kaladin's retreat.

Adolin glanced at Kaladin, then nodded.

The man in green turned with surprise at Kaladin's advance. He swung, and Kaladin caught the blow on the Shardplate helm he carried, deflecting it. The man grunted as Adolin threw everything he had at the other Shardbearer, the one in orange, slamming his weapon down again and again.

For a short time, Adolin had only one foe to fight. Hopefully he could use that time well, though his steps were lethargic and his Plate's leaking Stormlight had slowed to a trickle. His legs were nearly immobile.

Green Plate attacked Kaladin again, who deflected the blow off the helm, which cracked and began leaking Stormlight. Relis came charging up on the other side, but didn't join the fight against Adolin – instead, he thrust at Kaladin.

Kaladin gritted his teeth, dodging to the side, feeling the Blade pass in the air. He had to buy Adolin time. Moments. He needed moments.

The wind began to blow around him. Syl returned to him, zipping through the air as a ribbon of light.

Kaladin ducked another blow, then slammed his improvised shield against the Blade of the other, throwing it back. Sand flew as Kaladin leaped back, a Shardblade biting the ground before him.

Wind. Motion. Kaladin fought two Shardbearers at once, knocking their Blades aside with the helm. He couldn't attack – didn't dare *try* to attack. He could only survive, and in this, the winds seemed to urge him.

Instinct ... then something deeper ... guided his steps. He danced between those Blades, cool air wrapping around him. And for a moment, he felt – impossibly – that he could have dodged just as well if his eyes had been closed.

The Shardbearers cursed, trying again and again. Kaladin heard the judge say something, but was too absorbed in the fight to pay attention. The crowd was growing louder. He leaped one attack, then stepped just to the side of another.

You could not kill the wind. You could not stop it. It was beyond the touch of men. It was infinite. . . .

His Stormlight ran out.

Kaladin stumbled to a halt. He tried to suck in more, but all of his spheres were drained.

The helm, he realized, noticing that it was *gushing* Stormlight from its numerous cracks, yet hadn't exploded. It had somehow fed upon his Stormlight.

Relis attacked and Kaladin barely scrambled out of the way. His back hit the wall of the arena.

Green Plate saw his opening and raised his Blade.

Someone hopped on him from behind.

Kaladin watched, dumbfounded, as Adolin grappled Green Plate, latching on to him. Adolin's armor hardly leaked at all anymore; his Stormlight was exhausted. It seemed that he could barely move – the sand nearby displayed a set of lurching tracks that led away from Orange Plate, who lay in the sand defeated.

That was what the judge had said just earlier: the man in orange had yielded. Adolin had beaten his foe, then walked slowly – one laborious step after another – over to where Kaladin fought. It looked like he'd used his final bit of energy to hop up on Green Plate's back and grab hold.

Green Plate cursed, swatting at Adolin. The prince held on, and his Plate had locked, as they called it – becoming heavy and almost impossible to move.

The two teetered, then toppled over.

Kaladin looked at Relis, who glanced from the fallen Green Plate to the man in orange, then to Kaladin.

Relis turned and dashed across the sands toward Renarin.

Kaladin cursed, scrambling after him and tossing the helm aside. His body felt sluggish without the Stormlight to help.

'Renarin!' Kaladin yelled. 'Yield!'

The boy looked up. Storms, he'd been crying. Was he hurt? He didn't look it.

'Surrender!' Kaladin said, trying to run faster, summoning every drop of energy from muscles that felt drained, exhausted from being inflated by Stormlight.

The lad focused on Relis, who was bearing down on him, but said nothing. Instead, Renarin dismissed his Blade.

Relis skidded to a stop, raising his Blade high over his head toward the defenseless prince. Renarin closed his eyes, looking upward, as if exposing his throat.

Kaladin wasn't going to arrive in time. He was too slow compared to a man in Plate.

Relis hesitated, fortunately, as if unwilling to strike Renarin.

Kaladin arrived. Relis spun around and swung at him instead.

Kaladin skidded to his knees in the sand, momentum carrying him forward a short distance as the Blade fell. He raised his hands and snapped them together.

Catching the Blade.

Screaming.

Why could he hear *screaming*? Inside his head? Was that *Syl's* voice?

It reverberated through Kaladin. That horrible, awful screech shook him, made his muscles tremble. He released the Shardblade with a gasp, falling backward.

Relis dropped the Blade as if bitten. He backed away, raising his hands to his head. 'What is it? What is it! No, I didn't kill you!' He shrieked as if in great pain, then ran across the sands and pulled open the door to the preparation room, fleeing inside. Kaladin heard his screams echoing inside the hallways there long after the man vanished.

The arena grew still.

'Highlord Relis Ruthar,' the judge finally called, sounding disturbed, 'forfeits by cause of leaving the dueling arena.'

Kaladin climbed, trembling, to his feet. He glanced at Renarin – the lad was fine – then slowly crossed the arena. Even the watching darkeyes had grown silent. Kaladin was pretty sure they hadn't heard that strange scream, though. It had only been audible to him and Relis.

He stepped up to Adolin and Green Plate.

'Stand up and fight me!' Green Plate shouted. He lay faceup on the ground, Adolin buried beneath him and holding on in a wrestling grip.

Kaladin knelt down. Green Plate struggled more as Kaladin retrieved his side knife from the sand, then pressed the tip of it into the opening in Green Plate's armor.

The man grew perfectly still.

'You going to yield?' Kaladin growled. 'Or do I get to kill my second Shardbearer?'

Silence.

'Storms curse you both!' Green Plate finally shouted inside his helm. 'This wasn't a duel, this was a circus! Grappling is the way of the coward!'

Kaladin pressed the knife in farther.

'I yield!' the man yelled, holding up his hand. 'Storm you, I yield!'

'Brightlord Jakamav yields,' the judge said. 'The day goes to Brightlord Adolin.'

The darkeyes in their seats cheered. The lighteyes seemed stunned. Above, Syl spun with the winds, and Kaladin could feel her joy. Adolin released Green Plate, who rolled off him and stomped away. Underneath, the prince lay in a depression in the sand, head and shoulder exposed through broken pieces of Plate.

He was laughing.

Kaladin sat down beside the prince as Adolin laughed himself silly, tears streaming from his eyes.

'That was the most ridiculous thing I've ever done,' Adolin said. 'Oh, wow. . . . Ha! I think I just won three full suits of Plate and two Blades, bridgeboy. Here, help me get this armor off.'

'Your armorer can do that,' Kaladin said.

'No time,' Adolin said, trying to sit up. 'Storms. Completely drained. Hurry, help with this. There's something yet for me to do.'

Challenge Sadeas, Kaladin realized. That was the point of all of this. He reached in under Adolin's gauntlet, helping him undo the strap there. The gauntlet didn't come off automatically, as it was supposed to. Adolin really had completely drained the suit.

They pulled the gauntlet off, then worked on the other one. A few minutes later, Renarin wandered over and helped. Kaladin didn't ask him about what had happened. The lad provided some spheres, and after

Kaladin had tucked those in under Adolin's loosened breastplate, the armor started to function again.

They worked to the roar of the crowd as Adolin finally got free of the Plate and stood up. Ahead, the king had stepped up beside the judge, one foot on the railing around the arena. He looked down at Adolin, who nodded.

This is Adolin's chance, Kaladin realized, *but it can be my chance too.*

The king raised his hands, quieting the crowd.

'Warrior, duelmaster,' the king shouted, 'I am greatly pleased by what you have accomplished today. This was a fight the like of which hasn't been seen in Alethkar for generations. You have pleased your king greatly.'

Cheering.

I could do this, Kaladin thought.

'I offer you a boon,' the king proclaimed, pointing to Adolin as the cheering quieted. 'Name what you wish of me or of this court. It shall be yours. No man, having seen this display, could deny you.'

The Right of Challenge, Kaladin thought.

Adolin sought out Sadeas, who had stood and was making his way up the steps to flee. He understood.

Far to the right, Amaram sat in his golden cloak.

'For my boon,' Adolin shouted to the quiet arena, 'I demand the Right of Challenge. I demand the chance to duel Highprince Sadeas, right here and now, as redress for the crimes he committed against my house!'

Sadeas stopped upon the steps. A murmur ran through the crowd. Adolin looked as if he were going to say something more, but hesitated as Kaladin stepped up beside him.

'And for my boon!' Kaladin shouted, 'I demand the Right of Challenge against the murderer Amaram! He stole from me and slaughtered my friends to cover it up. Amaram branded me a slave! I will duel him here, right now. That is the boon I demand!'

The king's jaw dropped.

The crowd grew very, very still.

Beside him, Adolin groaned.

Kaladin didn't spare either one a thought. Across the distance, he met the eyes of Brightlord Amaram, the murderer.

He saw horror therein.

Amaram stood up, then stumbled back. He hadn't known, hadn't recognized Kaladin, until just then.

You should have killed me, Kaladin thought. The crowd started to shout and yell.

'Arrest him!' the king bellowed over the din.

Perfect. Kaladin grinned.

Until he noticed the soldiers were coming for him and not Amaram.

58

NEVER AGAIN

So Melishi retired to his tent, and resolved to destroy the Voidbringers upon the next day, but that night did present a different stratagem, related to the unique abilities of the Bondsmiths; and being hurried, he could make no specific account of his process; it was related to the very nature of the Heralds and their divine duties, an attribute the Bondsmiths alone could address.

—From *Words of Radiance*, chapter 30, page 18

'Captain Kaladin is a man of honor, Elhokar!' Dalinar shouted, gesturing toward Kaladin, who sat nearby. 'He was the only one who went to help my sons.'

'That's his job!' Elhokar snapped back.

Kaladin listened dully, chained to a seat inside Dalinar's rooms back in the warcamp. They hadn't gone to the palace. Kaladin didn't know why.

The three of them were alone.

'He insulted a highlord in front of the *entire court*,' Elhokar said, pacing beside the wall. 'He *dared* challenge a man so high above his station, the gap between them could hold a kingdom.'

'He was caught up in the moment,' Dalinar said. 'Be reasonable, Elhokar. He'd just helped bring down four Shardbearers!'

'On a dueling ground, where his help was invited,' Elhokar said, throwing his hands into the air. 'I still don't agree with letting a darkeyes duel Shardbearers. If you hadn't held me back . . . Bah! I won't stand for this, Uncle. I *won't*. Common soldiers challenging our highest and most important generals? It is *madness*.'

'What I said was true,' Kaladin whispered.

'Don't you speak!' Elhokar shouted, stopping and leveling a finger at Kaladin. 'You've ruined everything! We lost our chance at Sadeas!'

'Adolin made his challenge,' Kaladin said. 'Surely Sadeas can't ignore it.'

'Of course he can't,' Elhokar shouted. 'He's already responded!'

Kaladin frowned.

'Adolin didn't get a chance to pin down the duel,' Dalinar said, looking at Kaladin. 'As soon as he was free of the arena, Sadeas sent word agreeing to duel Adolin – in one year's time.'

One *year*? Kaladin felt a hollowness in his stomach. By the time a year had passed, chances were the duel wouldn't matter anymore.

'He wiggled out of the noose,' Elhokar said, throwing up his hands. 'We *needed* that moment in the arena to pin him down, to shame him into a fight! You stole that moment, bridgeman.'

Kaladin lowered his head. He'd have stood up to confront them, except for the chains. They were cold around his ankles, locking him to the chair.

He remembered chains like those.

'This is what you get, Uncle,' Elhokar said, 'for putting a slave in charge of our guard. Storms! What were you thinking? What was *I* thinking in allowing you?'

'You saw him fight, Elhokar,' Dalinar said softly. 'He is good.'

'It's not his skill but his discipline that is the problem!' The king folded his arms. 'Execution.'

Kaladin looked up sharply.

'Don't be ridiculous,' Dalinar said, stepping up beside Kaladin's chair.

'It is the punishment for slandering a highlord,' Elhokar said. 'It is the *law*.'

'You can pardon any crime, as king,' Dalinar said. 'Don't tell me you honestly want to see this man hanged after what he did today.'

'Would you stop me?' Elhokar said.

'I wouldn't stand for it, that's certain.'

Elhokar crossed the room, stepping right up to Dalinar. For a moment, Kaladin seemed forgotten.

'Am I king?' Elhokar asked.

'Of course you are.'

'You don't act like it. You're going to have to decide something, *Uncle*. I won't continue letting you rule, making a puppet of me.'

'I'm not—'

'I say the boy is to be executed. What do you say of that?'

'I'd say that in attempting such a thing, you'd make an enemy of me, Elhokar.' Dalinar had grown tense.

Just try to execute me . . . Kaladin thought. *Just try.*

The two stared at each other for a long moment. Finally, Elhokar turned away. 'Prison.'

'How long?' Dalinar said.

'Until I say he's done!' the king said, waving a hand and stalking toward the exit. He stopped there, looking at Dalinar, a challenge in his eyes.

'Very well,' Dalinar said.

The king left.

'Hypocrite,' Kaladin hissed. 'He's the one who insisted you put me in charge of his guard. Now he blames you?'

Dalinar sighed, kneeling down beside Kaladin. 'What you did today was a wonder. In protecting my sons, you justified my faith in you before the entire court. Unfortunately, you then threw it away.'

'He asked me for a boon!' Kaladin snapped, raising his manacled hands. 'I got one, it seems.'

'He asked *Adolin* for a boon. You knew what we were about, soldier. You heard the plan in conference with us this morning. You overshadowed it in the name of your own petty vengeance.'

'Amaram—'

'I don't know where you got this idea about Amaram,' Dalinar said, 'but you have to *stop*. I checked into what you said, after you brought it to my attention the first time. Seventeen witnesses told me that Amaram won his Shardblade only four months ago, long after your ledger says you were made a slave.'

'Lies.'

'Seventeen men,' Dalinar repeated. 'Lighteyed and dark, along with the word of a man I've known for decades. You're wrong about him, soldier. You're just plain *wrong*.'

'If he is so honorable,' Kaladin whispered, 'then why didn't *he* fight to save your sons?'

Dalinar hesitated.

'It doesn't matter,' Kaladin said, looking away. 'You're going to let the king put me in prison.'

'Yes,' Dalinar said, rising. 'Elhokar has a temper. Once he cools down, I'll get you free. For now, it might be best if you had some time to think.'

'They'll have a tough time forcing me to go to prison,' Kaladin said softly.

'Have you even been listening?' Dalinar suddenly roared.

Kaladin sat back, eyes widening, as Dalinar leaned down, red-faced, taking Kaladin by the shoulders as if to shake him. 'Have you not *felt* what is coming? Have you not seen how this kingdom squabbles? We don't have time for this! We don't have time for games! Stop being a child, and start being a *soldier*! You'll go to prison, and you'll go happily. That's an order. Do you *listen* to orders anymore?'

'I . . .' Kaladin found himself stammering.

Dalinar stood up, rubbing his hands on his temples. 'I thought we had Sadeas cornered, there. I thought maybe we'd be able to cut his feet out from under him and save this kingdom. Now I don't know what to do.' He turned and walked to the door. 'Thank you for saving my sons.'

He left Kaladin alone in the cold stone room.

⁘

Torol Sadeas slammed the door to his quarters. He walked to his table and leaned over it, hands flat on the surface, looking down at the slice through the center he'd made with Oathbringer.

A drop of sweat smacked the surface right beside that slot. He'd kept himself from trembling all the way back to the safety of his warcamp – he'd actually managed to paste on a smile. He'd shown no concern, even as he dictated to his wife a response to the challenge.

And all the while, in the back of his mind a voice had laughed at him.

Dalinar. Dalinar had almost *outmaneuvered* him. If that challenge had been sustained, Sadeas would quickly have found himself in the arena with a man who had just defeated not one, but *four* Shardbearers.

He sat down. He did not look for wine. Wine made a man forget, and he didn't want to forget this. He must never forget this.

How satisfying it would be to someday ram Dalinar's own sword into his chest. Storms. To think he'd almost felt pity for his former friend. Now the man pulled something like this. How had he grown so deft?

No, Sadeas told himself. *This was not deftness. It was luck. Pure and simple luck.*

Four Shardbearers. *How?* Even allowing for the help of that slave, it was now obvious that Adolin was at last growing into the man his father had once been. That terrified Sadeas, because the man Dalinar had once been – the Blackthorn – had been a large part of what had conquered this kingdom.

Isn't this what you wanted? Sadeas thought. *To reawaken him?*

No. The deeper truth was that Sadeas *didn't* want Dalinar back. He wanted his old friend out of the way, and it had been such for months now, no matter what he wanted to tell himself.

A while later, the door to his study opened and Ialai slipped in. Seeing him lost in thought, she stopped by the door.

'Organize all of your informants,' Sadeas said, looking up at the ceiling. 'Every spy you have, every source you know. Find me something, Ialai. Something to *hurt* him.'

She nodded.

'And after that,' Sadeas said, 'it will be time to make use of those assassins you've planted.'

He had to ensure that Dalinar was desperate and wounded – had to guarantee that the others viewed him as broken, ruined.

Then he'd end this.

⁂

Soldiers arrived for Kaladin a short time later. Men that Kaladin didn't know. They were respectful as they unchained him from the chair, though they left the chains binding his hands and feet. One gave him a lifted fist, a sign of respect. *Stay strong,* the fist said.

Kaladin bowed his head and shuffled with them, led through camp before the watching eyes of soldiers and scribes alike. He caught a glimpse of Bridge Four uniforms in the crowd.

He reached Dalinar's camp prison, where soldiers did time for fighting or other offenses. It was a small, nearly windowless building with thick walls.

Inside, in an isolated section, Kaladin was placed in a cell with stone walls and a door of steel bars. They left the chains on as they locked him in.

He sat down on a stone bench, waiting, until Syl finally drifted into the room.

'This,' Kaladin said, looking at her, 'is what comes of trusting lighteyes. Never again, Syl.'

'Kaladin . . .'

He closed his eyes, turning and lying down on the cold stone bench.

He was in a cage once again.

THE END OF

Part Three

INTERLUDES

LIFT • SZETH • ESHONAI

I-9

LIFT

Lift had never robbed a palace before. Seemed like a dangerous thing to try. Not because she might get caught, but because once you robbed a starvin' palace, where did you go next?

She climbed up onto the outer wall and looked in at the grounds. Everything inside – trees, rocks, buildings – reflected the starlight in an odd way. A bulbous-looking building stuck up in the middle of it all, like a bubble on a pond. In fact, most of the buildings were that same round shape, often with small protrusions sprouting out of the top. There wasn't a straight line in the whole starvin' place. Just lots and lots of curves.

Lift's companions climbed up to peek over the top of the wall. A scuffling, scrambling, rowdy mess they were. Six men, supposedly master thieves. They couldn't even climb a wall properly.

'The Bronze Palace itself,' Huqin breathed.

'Bronze? Is that what everythin' is made of?' Lift asked, sitting on the wall with one leg over the side. 'Looks like a bunch of breasts.'

The men looked at her, aghast. They were all Azish, with dark skin and hair. She was Reshi, from the islands up north. Her mother had told her that, though Lift had never seen the place.

'What?' Huqin demanded.

'Breasts,' Lift said, pointing. 'See, like a lady layin' on her back. Those points on the tops are nipples. Bloke who built this place musta been single for a *looong* time.'

Huqin turned to one of his companions. Using their ropes, they scuttled back down the outside of the wall to hold a whispered conference.

'Grounds at this end look empty, as my informant indicated would be the case,' Huqin said. He was in charge of the lot of them. Had a nose like someone had taken hold of it when he was a kid and pulled real, *real* hard. Lift was surprised he didn't smack people in the face with it when he turned.

'Everyone's focused on choosing the new Prime Aqasix,' said Maxin. 'We could really do this. Rob the Bronze Palace itself, and right under the nose of the vizierate.'

'Is it . . . um . . . safe?' asked Huqin's nephew. He was in his teens, and puberty hadn't been kind to him. Not with that face, that voice, and those spindly legs.

'Hush,' Huqin snapped.

'No,' Tigzikk said, 'the boy is right to express caution. This will be very dangerous.'

Tigzikk was considered the learned one in the group on account of his being able to cuss in three languages. Downright scholarly, that was. He wore fancy clothing, while most of the others wore black. 'There will be chaos,' Tigzikk continued, 'because so many people move through the palace tonight, but there will also be danger. Many, many bodyguards and a likelihood of suspicion on all sides.'

Tigzikk was an aging fellow, and was the only one of the group Lift knew well. She couldn't say his name. That 'quq' sound on the end of his name sounded like choking when someone pronounced it correctly. She just called him Tig instead.

'Tigzikk,' Huqin said. Yup. Choking. 'You were the one who suggested this. Don't tell me you're getting cold now.'

'I'm not backing down. I'm pleading caution.'

Lift leaned down over the wall toward them. 'Less arguing,' she said. 'Let's move. I'm hungry.'

Huqin looked up. '*Why* did we bring her along?'

'She'll be useful,' Tigzikk said. 'You'll see.'

'She's just a child!'

'She's a youth. She's at least twelve.'

'I *ain't* twelve,' Lift snapped, looming over them.

They turned up toward her.

'I ain't,' she said. 'Twelve's an unlucky number.' She held up her hands. 'I'm only this many.'

'. . . Ten?' Tigzikk asked.

'Is that how many that is? Sure, then. Ten.' She lowered her hands. 'If I can't count it on my fingers, it's unlucky.' And she'd been that many for three years now. So there.

'Seems like there are a lot of unlucky ages,' Huqin said, sounding amused.

'Sure are,' she agreed. She scanned the grounds again, then glanced back the way they had come, into the city.

A man walked down one of the streets leading to the palace. His dark clothing blended into the gloom, but his silver buttons glinted each time he passed a streetlight.

Storms, she thought, a chill running up her spine. *I didn't lose him after all.*

She looked down at the men. 'Are you coming with me or not? 'Cuz I'm *leaving*.' She slipped over the top and dropped into the palace yards. Lift squatted there, feeling the cold ground. Yup, it was metal. Everything was bronze. Rich people, she decided, loved to stick with a theme.

As the boys finally stopped arguing and started climbing, a thin, twisting trail of vines grew out of the darkness and approached Lift. It looked like a little stream of spilled water picking its way across the floor. Here and there, bits of clear crystal peeked out of the vines, like sections of quartz in otherwise dark stone. Those weren't sharp, but smooth like polished glass, and didn't glow with Stormlight.

The vines grew super-fast, curling about one another in a tangle that formed a face.

'Mistress,' the face said. 'Is this *wise*?'

' 'Ello, Voidbringer,' Lift said, scanning the grounds.

'I am *not* a Voidbringer!' he said. 'And you know it. Just . . . just stop saying that!'

Lift grinned. 'You're my pet Voidbringer, and no lies are going to change that. I got you captured. No stealing souls, now. We ain't here for souls. Just a little thievery, the type what never hurt nobody.'

The vine face – he called himself Wyndle – sighed. Lift scuttled across the bronze ground over to a tree that was, of course, also made of bronze. Huqin had chosen the darkest part of night, between moons, for them to slip in – but the starlight was enough to see by on a cloudless night like this.

Wyndle grew up to her, leaving a small trail of vines that people didn't seem to be able to see. The vines hardened after a few moments of sitting, as if briefly becoming solid crystal, then they crumbled to dust. People spotted that on occasion, though they certainly couldn't see Wyndle himself.

'I'm a spren,' Wyndle said to her. 'Part of a proud and noble—'

'Hush,' Lift said, peeking out from behind the bronze tree. An open-topped carriage passed on the drive beyond, carrying some important Azish folk. You could tell by the coats. Big, drooping coats with really wide sleeves and patterns that argued with each other. They all looked like kids who had snuck into their parents' wardrobe. The hats were nifty, though.

The thieves followed behind her, moving with reasonable stealth. They really weren't *that* bad. Even if they didn't know how to climb a wall properly.

They gathered around her, and Tigzikk stood up, straightening his coat – which was an imitation of one of those worn by the rich scribe types who worked in the government. Here in Azir, working for the government was real important. Everyone else was said to be 'discrete,' whatever that meant.

'Ready?' Tigzikk said to Maxin, who was the other one of the thieves dressed in fine clothing.

Maxin nodded, and the two of them moved off to the right, heading toward the palace's sculpture garden. The important people would supposedly be shuffling around in there, speculating about who should be the next Prime.

Dangerous job, that. The last two had gotten their heads chopped off by some bloke in white with a Shardblade. The most recent Prime hadn't lasted two starvin' days!

With Tigzikk and Maxin gone, Lift only had four others to worry about. Huqin, his nephew, and two slender brothers who didn't talk much and kept reaching under their coats for knives. Lift didn't like their type. Thieving shouldn't leave bodies. Leaving bodies was easy. There was no *challenge* to it if you could just kill anyone who spotted you.

'You *can* get us in,' Huqin said to Lift. 'Right?'

Lift pointedly rolled her eyes. Then she scuttled across the bronze grounds toward the main palace structure.

Really does look like a breast . . .

Wyndle curled along the ground beside her, his vine trail sprouting tiny bits of clear crystal here and there. He was as sinuous and speedy as a moving eel, only he *grew* rather than actually moving. Voidbringers were a strange lot.

'You realize that *I* didn't choose you,' he said, a face appearing in the vines as they moved. His speaking left a strange effect, the trail behind him clotted with a sequence of frozen faces. The mouth seemed to move because it was growing so quickly beside her. '*I* wanted to pick a distinguished Iriali matron. A grandmother, an accomplished gardener. But no, the Ring said we should choose you. "She has visited the Old Magic," they said. "Our mother has blessed her," they said. "She will be young, and we can mold her," they said. Well, *they* don't have to put up with—'

'Shut it, Voidbringer,' Lift hissed, drawing up beside the wall of the palace. 'Or I'll bathe in blessed water and go listen to the priests. Maybe get an exorcism.'

Lift edged sideways until she could look around the curve of the wall to spot the guard patrol: men in patterned vests and caps, with long halberds. She looked up the side of the wall. It bulged out just above her, like a rockbud, before tapering up further. It was of smooth bronze, with no handholds.

She waited until the guards had walked farther away. 'All right,' she whispered to Wyndle. 'You gotta do what I say.'

'I do *not*.'

'Sure you do. I captured you, just like in the stories.'

'I came to *you*,' Wyndle said. 'Your powers come from me! Do you even *listen* to—'

'Up the wall,' Lift said, pointing.

Wyndle sighed, but obeyed, creeping up the wall in a wide, looping pattern. Lift hopped up, grabbing the small handholds made by the vine, which stuck to the surface by virtue of thousands of branching stems with sticky discs on them. Wyndle wove ahead of her, making a ladder of sorts.

It wasn't easy. It was starvin' difficult, with that bulge, and Wyndle's handholds weren't very big. But she did it, climbing all the way to the near-top of the building's dome, where windows peeked out at the grounds.

She glanced toward the city. No sign of the man in the black uniform. Maybe she'd lost him.

She turned back to examine the window. Its nice wooden frame held very thick glass, even though it pointed east. It was unfair how well Azimir was protected from highstorms. They should have to live with the wind, like normal folk.

'We need to Voidbring that,' she said, pointing at the window.

'Have you realized,' Wyndle said, 'that while you *claim* to be a master thief, *I* do all of the work in this relationship?'

'You do all the complainin' too,' she said. 'How do we get through this?'

'You have the seeds?'

She nodded, fishing in her pocket. Then in the other one. Then in her back pocket. Ah, there they were. She pulled out a handful of seeds.

'I can't affect the Physical Realm except in minor ways,' Wyndle said. 'This means that you will need to use Investiture to—'

Lift yawned.

'Use Investiture to—'

She yawned *wider*. Starvin' Voidbringers never could catch a hint.

Wyndle sighed. 'Spread the seeds on the frame.'

She did so, throwing the handful of seeds at the window.

'Your bond to me grants two primary classes of ability,' Wyndle said. 'The first, manipulation of friction, you've already – don't yawn at me! – discovered. We have been using that well for many weeks now, and it is time for you to learn the second, the power of Growth. You aren't ready for what was once known as Regrowth, the healing of—'

Lift pressed her hand against the seeds, then summoned her awesomeness.

She wasn't sure how she did it. She just *did*. It had started right around when Wyndle had first appeared.

He hadn't talked then. She kind of missed those days.

Her hand glowed faintly with white light, like vapor coming off the skin. The seeds that saw the light started to grow. Fast. Vines burst from the seeds and wormed into the cracks between the window and its frame.

The vines grew at her will, making constricted, straining sounds. The glass cracked, then the window frame *popped* open.

Lift grinned.

'Well done,' Wyndle said. 'We'll make an Edgedancer out of you yet.' Her stomach grumbled. When had she last eaten? She'd used a lot of her awesomeness practicing earlier. She probably should have stolen something to eat. She wasn't quite so awesome when she was hungry.

She slipped inside the window. Having a Voidbringer was useful, though she wasn't *completely* sure her powers came from him. That seemed the sorta thing a Voidbringer would lie about. She *had* captured him, fair and square. She'd used words. A Voidbringer had no body, not really. To catch something like that, you had to use words. Everybody knew it. Just like curses made evil things come find you.

She had to get out a sphere – a diamond mark, her lucky one – to see properly in here. The small bedroom was decorated after the Azish way with lots of intricate patterns on the rugs and the fabric on the walls, mostly gold and red here. Those patterns were everything to the Azish. They were like words.

She looked out the window. Surely she'd escaped Darkness, the man in the black and silver with the pale crescent birthmark on his cheek. The man with the dead, lifeless stare. Surely he hadn't followed her all the way from Marabethia. That was half a continent away! Well, a quarter one, at the least.

Convinced, she uncoiled the rope that she wore wrapped around her waist and over her shoulders. She tied it to the door of a built-in closet, then fed it out the window. It tightened as the men started climbing. Nearby, Wyndle grew up around one of the bedposts, coiled like a skyeel.

She heard whispered voices below. 'Did you *see* that? She climbed right up it. Not a handhold in sight. How . . . ?'

'Hush.' That was Huqin.

Lift began poking through cabinets and drawers as the boys clambered in the window one at a time. Once inside, the thieves pulled up the rope and shut the window as best they could. Huqin studied the vines she'd grown from seeds on the frame.

Lift stuck her head in the bottom of a wardrobe, groping around. 'Ain't nothing in this room but moldy shoes.'

'You,' Huqin said to her, 'and my nephew will hold this room. The three of us will search the bedrooms nearby. We will be back shortly.'

'You'll probably have a whole *sack* of moldy shoes . . .' Lift said, pulling out of the wardrobe.

'Ignorant child,' Huqin said, pointing at the wardrobe. One of his men grabbed the shoes and outfits inside, stuffing them in a sack. 'This clothing will sell for bundles. It's exactly what we're looking for.'

'What about real riches?' Lift said. 'Spheres, jewelry, art . . .' She had little interest in those things herself, but she'd figured it was what Huqin was after.

'That will all be *far* too well guarded,' Huqin said as his two associates made quick work of the room's clothing. 'The difference between a successful thief and a dead thief is knowing when to escape with your takings. This haul will let us live in luxury for a year or two. That is enough.'

One of the brothers peeked out the door into the hallway. He nodded, and the three of them slipped out. 'Listen for the warning,' Huqin said to his nephew, then eased the door almost closed behind him.

Tigzikk and his accomplice below would listen for any kind of alarm. If anything seemed to be amiss, they'd slip off and blow their whistles. Huqin's nephew crouched by the window to listen, obviously taking his duty very seriously. He looked to be about sixteen. Unlucky age, that.

'How did you climb the wall like that?' the youth asked.

'Gumption,' Lift said. 'And spit.'

He frowned at her.

'I gots magic spit.'

He seemed to believe her. Idiot.

'Is it strange for you here?' he asked. 'Away from your people?'

She stood out. Straight black hair – she wore it down to her waist – tan skin, rounded features. Everyone would immediately mark her as Reshi.

'Don't know,' Lift said, strolling to the door. 'Ain't never been around my people.'

'You're not from the islands?'

'Nope. Grew up in Rall Elorim.'

'The . . . City of Shadows?'

'Yup.'

'Is it—'

'Yup. Just like they say.'

She peeked through the door. Huqin and the others were well out of the way. The hallway was bronze – walls and everything – but a red and blue rug, with lots of little vine patterns, ran down the center. Paintings hung on the walls.

She pulled the door all the way open and stepped out.

'Lift!' The nephew scrambled to the door. 'They told us to wait here!'

'And?'

'And we should *wait here*! We don't want to get Uncle Huqin in trouble!'

'What's the point of sneaking into a palace if not to get into trouble?' She shook her head. Odd men, these. 'This should be an interesting place, what with all of the rich folk hanging around.' There ought to be some *really* good food in here.

She padded out into the hallway, and Wyndle grew along the floor beside her. Interestingly, the nephew followed. She'd expected him to stay in the room.

'We shouldn't be doing this,' he said as they passed a door that was open a crack, shuffles sounding from inside. Huqin and his men, robbing the place silly.

'Then stay,' Lift whispered, reaching a large stairwell. Servants whisked back and forth below, even a few parshmen, but she didn't catch sight of anyone in one of those coats. 'Where are the important folk?'

'Reading forms,' the nephew said from beside her.

'Forms?'

'Sure,' he said. 'With the Prime dead, the viziers, scribes, and arbiters were all given a chance to fill out the proper paperwork to apply to take his place.'

'You *apply* to be emperor?' Lift said.

'Sure,' he said. 'Lots of paperwork involved in that. And an essay. Your essay has to be *really* good to get this job.'

'Storms. You people are crazy.'

'Other nations do it better? With bloody succession wars? This way, everyone has a chance. Even the lowest of clerks can submit the paperwork. You can even be *discrete* and end up on the throne, if you are convincing enough. It happened once.'

'Crazy.'

'Says the girl who talks to herself.'

Lift looked at him sharply.

'Don't pretend you don't,' he said. 'I've seen you doing it. Talking to the air, as if somebody were there.'

'What's your name?' she asked.

'Gawx.'

'Wow. Well then, Gaw. I don't talk to myself because I'm crazy.'

'No?'

'I do it because I'm *awesome*.' She started down the steps, waited for a gap between passing servants, then made for a closet across the way. Gawx cursed, then followed.

Lift was tempted to use her awesomeness to slide across the floor quickly, but she didn't need that yet. Besides, Wyndle kept complaining that she used the awesomeness too often. That she was at risk of malnutrition, whatever that meant.

She slipped up to the closet, using just her normal everyday sneakin' skills, and moved inside. Gawx scrambled into the closet with her just before she pulled it shut. Dinnerware on a serving cart clinked behind them, and they could barely crowd into the space. Gawx moved, causing more clinks, and she elbowed him. He stilled as two parshmen passed, bearing large wine barrels.

'You should go back upstairs,' Lift whispered to him. 'This could be dangerous.'

'Oh, sneaking into the storming *royal palace* is dangerous? Thanks. I hadn't realized.'

'I mean it,' Lift said, peeking out of the closet. 'Go back up, leave when Huqin returns. He'll abandon me in a heartbeat. Probably will you, too.'

Besides, she didn't want to be awesome with Gawx around. That started questions. And rumors. She hated both. For once, she'd like to be able to stay someplace for a while without being forced to run off.

'No,' Gawx said softly. 'If you're going to steal something good, I want a piece of it. Then maybe Huqin will stop making me stay behind, giving me the easy jobs.'

Huh. So he had some spunk to him.

A servant passed carrying a large, plate-filled tray. The food smells wafting from it made Lift's stomach growl. Rich-person food. So *delicious*.

Lift watched the woman go, then broke out of the closet, following after. This was going to get difficult with Gawx in tow. He'd been trained well enough by his uncle, but moving unseen through a populated building wasn't easy.

The serving woman pulled open a door that was hidden in the wall. Servants' hallways. Lift caught it as it closed, waited a few heartbeats, then eased it open and slipped through. The narrow hallway was poorly lit and smelled of the food that had just passed.

Gawx entered behind Lift, then silently pulled the door closed. The serving woman disappeared around a corner ahead – there were probably lots of hallways like this in the palace. Behind Lift, Wyndle grew around the doorframe, a dark green, funguslike creep of vines that covered the door, then the wall beside her.

He formed a face in the vines and spots of crystal, then shook his head.

'Too narrow?' Lift asked.

He nodded.

'It's dark in here. Hard to see us.'

'Vibrations on the floor, mistress. Someone coming this direction.'

She looked longingly after the servant with the food, then shoved past Gawx and pushed open the door, entering the main hallways again.

Gawx cursed. 'Do you even know what you're doing?'

'No,' she said, then scuttled around a corner into a large hallway lined with alternating green and yellow gemstone lamps. Unfortunately, a servant in a stiff, black and white uniform was coming right at her.

Gawx let out a 'meep' of worry, ducking back around the corner. Lift stood up straight, clasped her hands behind her back, and strolled forward.

She passed the man. His uniform marked him as someone important, for a servant.

'You, there!' the man snapped. 'What is this?'

'Mistress wants some cake,' Lift said, jutting out her chin.

'Oh, for Yaezir's sake. Food is served in the gardens! There is cake *there*!'

'Wrong type,' Lift said. 'Mistress wants berry cake.'

The man threw his hands into the air. 'Kitchens are back the other way,' he said. 'Try and persuade the cook, though she'll probably chop your hands off before she takes another special request. Storming country scribes! Special dietary needs are supposed to be sent ahead of time, with the proper forms!' He stalked off, leaving Lift with hands behind her back, watching him.

Gawx slunk around the corner. 'I thought we were dead for sure.'

'Don't be stupid,' Lift said, hurrying down the hallway. 'This ain't the dangerous part yet.'

At the other end, this hallway intersected another one – with the same wide rug down the center, bronze walls, and glowing metal lamps. Across the way was a door with no light shining under it. Lift checked in both directions, then dashed to the door, cracked it, peeked in, then waved for Gawx to join her inside.

'We should go right down that hallway outside,' Gawx whispered as she shut the door all but a crack. 'Down that way, we'll find the vizier quarters. They're probably empty, because everyone will be in the Prime's wing deliberating.'

'You know the palace layout?' she asked, crouching in near darkness beside the door. They were in a small sitting room of some sort, with a couple of shadowed chairs and a small table.

'Yeah,' Gawx said. 'I memorized the palace maps before we came. You didn't?'

She shrugged.

'I've been in here once before,' Gawx said. 'I watched the Prime sleeping.'

'You *what*?'

'He's public,' Gawx said, 'belongs to everyone. You can enter a lottery to come look at him sleeping. They rotate people through every hour.'

'What? On a special day or something?'

'No, every day. You can watch him eat too, or watch him perform his daily rituals. If he loses a hair or cuts off a nail, you might be able to keep it as a relic.'

'Sounds creepy.'

'A little.'

'Which way to his rooms?' Lift asked.

'That way,' Gawx said, pointing left down the hallway outside – the opposite direction from the vizier chambers. 'You don't want to go there, Lift. That's where the viziers and everyone important will be reviewing applications. In the Prime's presence.'

'But he's dead.'

'The new Prime.'

'He ain't been chosen yet!'

'Well, it's kind of strange,' Gawx said. By the dim light of the cracked door, she could see him blushing, as if he knew how starvin' odd this all was. 'There's never *not* a Prime. We just don't know who he is yet. I mean, he's alive, and he's already Prime – right now. We're just catching up. So, those are his quarters, and the scions and viziers want to be in his presence while they decide who he is. Even if the person they decide upon isn't in the room.'

'That makes no sense.'

'Of course it makes sense,' Gawx said. 'It's government. This is all *very* well detailed in the codes and . . .' He trailed off as Lift yawned. Azish could be *real* boring. At least he could take a hint, though.

'Anyway,' Gawx continued, 'everyone outside in the gardens is hoping to be called in for a personal interview. It might not come to that, though. The scions can't be Prime, as they're too busy visiting and blessing villages around the kingdom – but a vizier can, and they tend to have the best applications. Usually, one of their number is chosen.'

'The Prime's quarters,' Lift said. 'That's the direction the food went.'

'What is it with you and food?'

'I'm going to eat their dinner,' she said, soft but intense.

Gawx blinked, startled. 'You're . . . *what*?'

'I'm gonna eat their food,' she said. 'Rich folk have the best food.'

'But . . . there might be spheres in the vizier quarters. . . .'

'Eh,' she said. 'I'd just spend 'em on food.'

Stealing regular stuff was no fun. She wanted a *real* challenge. Over the last two years, she'd picked the most difficult places to enter. Then she'd snuck in.

And eaten their dinners.

'Come on,' she said, moving out of the doorway, then turned left toward the Prime's chambers.

'You really *are* crazy,' Gawx whispered.

'Nah. Just bored.'

He looked the other way. 'I'm going for the vizier quarters.'

'Suit yourself,' she said. 'I'd go back upstairs instead, if I were you. You aren't practiced enough for this kind of thing. You leave me, you're probably going to get into trouble.'

He fidgeted, then slipped off in the direction of the vizier quarters. Lift rolled her eyes.

'Why did you even come with them?' Wyndle asked, creeping out of the room. 'Why not just sneak in on your own?'

'Tigzikk found out about this whole election thing,' she said. 'He told me tonight was a good night for sneaking. I owed it to him. Besides, I wanted to be here in case he got into trouble. I might need to help.'

'Why bother?'

Why indeed? 'Someone has to care,' she said, starting down the hallway. 'Too few people care, these days.'

'You say this while coming in to *rob* people.'

'Sure. Ain't gonna hurt them.'

'You have an odd sense of morality, mistress.'

'Don't be stupid,' she said. 'Every sense of morality is odd.'

'I suppose.'

'Particularly to a Voidbringer.'

'I'm not—'

She grinned and hurried her pace toward the Prime's quarters. She knew she'd found those when she glanced down a side hallway and spotted guards at the end. Yup. That door was so nice, it *had* to belong to an emperor. Only super-rich folk built fancy doors. You needed money coming out your ears before you spent it on a *door*.

Guards were a problem. Lift knelt down, peeking around the corner. The hallway leading to the emperor's rooms was narrow, like an alleyway. Smart. Hard to sneak down something like that. And those two guards, they weren't the bored type. They were the 'we gotta stand here and look real angry' type. They stood so straight, you'd have thought someone had shoved brooms up their backsides.

She glanced upward. The hallway was tall; rich folk liked tall stuff. If they'd been poor, they'd have built another floor up there for their aunts and cousins to live in. Rich people wasted space instead. Proved they had so much money, they could waste it.

Seemed perfectly rational to steal from them.

'There,' Lift whispered, pointing to a small ornamented ledge that ran along the wall up above. It wouldn't be wide enough to walk on, unless you were Lift. Which, fortunately, she was. It was dim up there too. The chandeliers were the dangly kind, and they hung low, with mirrors reflecting their spherelight downward.

'Up we go,' she said.

Wyndle sighed.

'You gotta do what I say or I'll prune you.'

'You'll . . . prune me.'

'Sure.' That sounded threatening, right?

Wyndle grew up the wall, giving her handholds. Already, the vines he'd trailed through the hallway behind them were vanishing, becoming crystal and disintegrating into dust.

'Why don't they notice you?' Lift whispered. She'd never asked him, despite their months together. 'Is it 'cuz only the pure in heart can see you?'

'You're not serious.'

'Sure. That'd fit into legends and stories and stuff.'

'Oh, the theory itself isn't ridiculous,' Wyndle said, speaking out of a bit of vine near her, the various cords of green moving like lips. 'Merely the idea that *you* consider yourself to be pure in heart.'

'I'm pure,' Lift whispered, grunting as she climbed. 'I'm a child and stuff. I'm so storming pure I practically belch rainbows.'

Wyndle sighed again – he liked to do that – as they reached the ledge. Wyndle grew along the side of it, making it slightly wider, and Lift stepped onto it. She balanced carefully, then nodded to Wyndle. He grew further along the ledge, then doubled back and grew up the wall to a point above her head. From there, he grew horizontally to give her a handhold. With the extra inch of vine on the ledge and the handhold above, she managed to sidle along, stomach to the wall. She took a deep breath, then turned the corner into the hallway with the guards.

She moved along it slowly, Wyndle wrapping back and forth, enhancing both footing and handholds for her. The guards didn't cry out. She was *doing* it.

'They can't see me,' Wyndle said, growing up beside her to create another line of handholds, 'because I exist mostly in the Cognitive Realm, even though I've moved my consciousness to this Realm. I can make myself visible to anyone, should I desire, though it's not easy for me. Other spren are more skilled at it, while some have the opposite trouble. Of course, no matter *how* I manifest, nobody can touch me, as I barely have any substance in this Realm.'

'Nobody but me,' Lift whispered, inching down the hallway.

'You shouldn't be able to either,' he said, sounding troubled. 'What did you ask for, when you visited my mother?'

Lift didn't have to answer that, not to a storming Voidbringer. She eventually reached the end of the hallway. Beneath her was the door. Unfortunately, that was exactly where the guards stood.

'This does not seem very well thought out, mistress,' Wyndle noted. 'Had you considered *what* you were going to do once you got here?'

She nodded.

'Well?'

'Wait,' she whispered.

They did, Lift with her front pressed to the wall, her heels hanging out above a fifteen-foot drop onto the guards. She didn't want to fall. She was pretty sure she was awesome enough to survive it, but if they saw her, that would end the game. She'd have to run, and she'd *never* get any dinner.

Fortunately, she'd guessed right, unfortunately. A guard appeared at the other end of the hallway, looking out of breath and not a little annoyed. The other two guards jogged over to him. He turned, pointing the other way.

That was her chance. Wyndle grew a vine downward, and Lift grabbed it. She could feel the crystals jutting out between the tendrils, but they were smooth and faceted – not angular and sharp. She dropped, vine smooth between her fingers, pulling herself to a stop just before the floor.

She only had a few seconds.

'. . . caught a thief trying to ransack the vizier quarters,' said the newer guard. 'Might be more. Keep watch. By Yaezir himself! I can't believe they'd dare. Tonight of all nights!'

Lift cracked open the door to the emperor's rooms and peeked in. Big room. Men and women at a table. Nobody looking her direction. She slipped through the door.

Then became awesome.

She ducked down, kicked herself forward, and for a moment, the floor – the carpet, the wood beneath – had no purchase on her. She glided as if on ice, making no noise as she slid across the ten-foot gap. Nothing could hold her when she got Slick like this. Fingers would slip off her, and she could glide forever. She didn't think she'd ever stop unless she turned off the awesomeness. She'd slide all the way to the storming ocean itself.

Tonight, she stopped herself under the table, using her fingers – which weren't Slick – then removed the Slickness from her legs. Her stomach growled in complaint. She needed food. Real fast, or no more awesomeness for her.

'Somehow, you are partly in the Cognitive Realm,' Wyndle said, coiling beside her and raising a twisting mesh of vines that could make a face. 'Tis is the only answer I can find to why you can touch spren. And you can metabolize food *directly* into Stormlight.'

She shrugged. He was always saying words like those. Trying to confuse her, starvin' Voidbringer. Well, she wouldn't talk back to him, not now. The men and women standing around the table might hear her, even if they couldn't hear Wyndle.

That food was in here somewhere. She could smell it.

'But *why*?' Wyndle said. 'Why did She give you this incredible talent? Why a child? There are soldiers, grand kings, incredible scholars among humankind. Instead she chose you.'

Food, food, food. Smelled *great*. Lift crawled along under the long table. The men and women up above were talking in very concerned voices.

'Your application was *clearly* the best, Dalksi.'

'What! I misspelled three words in the first paragraph alone!'

'I didn't notice.'

'You didn't … Of course you noticed! But this is pointless, because *Axikk's* essay was obviously superior to mine.'

'Don't bring me into this again. We disqualified me. I'm not fit to be Prime. I have a bad back.'

'Ashno of Sages had a bad back. He was one of the greatest Emuli Primes.'

'Bah! My essay was utter rubbish, and you know it.'

Wyndle moved along beside Lift. 'Mother has given up on your kind. I can feel it. She doesn't care any longer. Now that He's gone . . .'

'This arguing does not befit us,' said a commanding female voice. 'We should take our vote. People are waiting.'

'Let it go to one of those fools in the gardens.'

'Their essays were *dreadful*. Just look at what Pandri wrote across the top of hers.'

'My . . . I . . . I don't know what half of that even means, but it *does* seem insulting.'

This finally caught Lift's attention. She looked up toward the table above. Good cusses? *Come on,* she thought. *Read a few of those.*

'We'll have to pick one of them,' the other voice – she sounded very in charge – said. 'Kadasixes and Stars, this is a puzzle. What do we do when *nobody* wants to be Prime?'

Nobody wanted to be Prime? Had the entire country suddenly grown some sense? Lift continued on. Being rich seemed fun and all, but being in charge of that many people? Pure misery, that would be.

'Perhaps we should pick the *worst* application,' one of the voices said. 'In this situation, that would indicate the cleverest applicant.'

'Six different monarchs killed . . .' one of the voices said, a new one. 'In a mere two months. Highprinces slaughtered throughout the East. Religious leaders. And then, two Primes murdered in a matter of a single week. Storms . . . I almost think it's another Desolation come upon us.'

'A Desolation in the form of a single man. Yaezir help the one we choose. It is a death sentence.'

'We have stalled too long as it is. These weeks of waiting with no Prime have been harmful to Azir. Let's just pick the worst application. From this stack.'

'What if we pick someone who is legitimately terrible? Is it not our *duty* to care for the kingdom, regardless of the risk to the one we choose?'

'But in picking the best from among us, we doom our brightest, our best, to die by the sword . . . Yaezir help us. Scion Ethid, a prayer for guidance would be appreciated. We need Yaezir himself to show us his will. Perhaps if we choose the right person, he or she will be protected by his hand.'

Lift reached the end of the table and looked out at a banquet that had been set onto a smaller table at the other side of the room. This place was *very* Azish. Curls of embroidery everywhere. Carpets so fine, they probably drove some poor woman blind weaving them. Dark colors and dim lights. Paintings on the walls.

Huh, Lift thought, *someone scratched a face off of that one.* Who'd ruin a painting like that, and such a fine one, the Heralds all in a row?

Well, nobody seemed to be touching that feast. Her stomach growled, but she waited for a distraction.

It came soon after. The door opened. Likely the guards coming to report about the thief they'd found. Poor Gawx. She'd have to go break him out later.

Right now, it was time for food. Lift shoved herself forward on her knees and used her awesomeness to Slick her legs. She slid across the floor and grabbed the corner leg of the food table. Her momentum smoothly pivoted her around and behind it. She crouched down, the tablecloth neatly hiding her from the people at the room's center, and unSlicked her legs.

Perfect. She reached up a hand and plucked a dinner roll off the table. She took a bite, then hesitated.

Why had everyone grown quiet? She risked a glance over the tabletop.

He had arrived.

The tall Azish man with the white mark on his cheek, like a crescent. Black uniform with a double row of silver buttons down the coat's front, a stiff silver collar poking up from a shirt underneath. His thick gloves had collars of their own that extended halfway back around his forearms.

Dead eyes. This was Darkness himself.

Oh no.

'What is the meaning of this!' demanded one of the viziers, a woman in one of their large coats with the too-big sleeves. Her cap was of a different pattern, and it clashed quite spectacularly with the coat.

'I am here,' Darkness said, 'for a thief.'

'Do you realize where you are? How *dare* you interrupt—'

'I have,' Darkness said, 'the proper forms.' He spoke completely without emotion. No annoyance at being challenged, no arrogance or pomposity. Nothing at all. One of his minions entered behind him, a man in a black and silver uniform, less ornamented. He proffered a neat stack of papers to his master.

'Forms are all well and good,' the vizier said. 'But this is *not* the time, constable, for—'

Lift bolted.

Her instincts finally battered down her surprise and she ran, leaping over a couch on her way to the room's back door. Wyndle moved beside her in a streak.

She tore a hunk off the roll with her teeth; she was going to need the food. Beyond that door would be a bedroom, and a bedroom would have a window. She slammed open the door, dashing through.

Something swung from the shadows on the other side.

A cudgel took her in the chest. Ribs cracked. Lift gasped, dropping face-first to the floor.

Another of Darkness's minions stepped from the shadows inside the bedroom.

'Even the chaotic,' Darkness said, 'can be predictable with proper study.' His feet thumped across the floor behind her.

Lift gritted her teeth, curled up on the floor. *Didn't get enough to eat . . .* So hungry.

The few bites she'd taken earlier worked within her. She felt the familiar feeling, like a storm in her veins. Liquid awesomeness. The pain faded from her chest as she healed.

Wyndle ran around her in a circle, a little lasso of vines sprouting leaves on the floor, looping her again and again. Darkness stepped up close.

Go! She leaped to her hands and knees. He seized her by the shoulder, but she could escape that. She summoned her awesomeness.

Darkness thrust something toward her.

The little animal was like a cremling, but with *wings*. Bound wings, tied-up legs. It had a strange little face, not crabbish like a cremling. More like a tiny axehound, with a snout, mouth, and eyes.

It seemed sickly, and its shimmering eyes were pained. How could she tell that?

The creature sucked the awesomeness from Lift. She actually *saw* it go, a glistening whiteness that streamed from her to the little animal. It opened its mouth, drinking it in.

Suddenly, Lift felt very tired and very, *very* hungry.

Darkness handed the animal to one of his minions, who made it vanish into a black sack he then tucked in his pocket. Lift was certain that the viziers – standing in an outraged cluster at the table – hadn't seen any of this, not with Darkness's back to them and the two minions crowding around.

'Keep all spheres from her,' Darkness said. 'She must not be allowed to Invest.'

Lift felt terror, panicked in a way she hadn't known for years, ever since her days in Rall Elorim. She struggled, thrashing, biting at the hand that held her. Darkness didn't even grunt. He hauled her to her feet, and another minion took her by the arms, wrenching them backward until she gasped at the pain.

No. She'd freed herself! She couldn't be taken like this. Wyndle continued to spin around her on the ground, distressed. He was a good type, for a Voidbringer.

Darkness turned to the viziers. 'I will trouble you no further.'

'Mistress!' Wyndle said. 'Here!'

The half-eaten roll lay on the floor. She'd dropped it when the cudgel hit. Wyndle ran into it, but he couldn't do anything more than make it wobble. Lift thrashed, trying to pull free, but without that storm inside of her, she was just a child in the grip of a trained soldier.

'I am *highly* disturbed by the nature of this incursion, constable,' the lead vizier said, shuffling through the stack of papers that Darkness had dropped. 'Your paperwork is in order, and I see you even included a plea – granted by the arbiters – to search the palace itself for this urchin. Surely you did not need to disturb a holy conclave. For a common thief, no less.'

'Justice waits upon no man or woman,' Darkness said, completely calm. 'And this thief is anything but common. With your leave, we will cease disturbing you.'

He didn't seem to care if they gave him leave or not. He strode toward the door, and his minion pulled Lift along after. She got her foot out to the roll, but only managed to kick it forward, under the long table by the viziers.

'This is a leave of *execution*,' the vizier said with surprise, holding up the last sheet in the stack. 'You will kill the child? For mere thievery?'

Kill? *No. No!*

'That, in addition to trespassing in the Prime's palace,' Darkness said, reaching the door. 'And for interrupting a holy conclave in session.'

The vizier met his gaze. She held it, then *wilted*. 'I . . .' she said. 'Ah, of course . . . er . . . constable.'

Darkness turned from her and pulled open the door. The vizier set one hand on the table and raised her other hand to her head.

The minion dragged Lift up to the door.

'Mistress!' Wyndle said, twisting up nearby. 'Oh . . . oh dear. There is something very wrong with that man! He is not right, not right at all. You must use your powers.'

'Trying,' Lift said, grunting.

'You've let yourself grow too thin,' Wyndle said. 'Not good. You always use up the excess. . . . Low body fat . . . That might be the problem. I don't know *how* this works!'

Darkness hesitated beside the door and looked at the low-hanging chandeliers in the hallway beyond, with their mirrors and sparkling gem-stones. He raised his hand and gestured. The minion not holding Lift moved out into the hallway and found the chandelier ropes. He unwound those and pulled, raising the chandeliers.

Lift tried to summon her awesomeness. Just a little more. She just needed a *little*.

Her body felt exhausted. Drained. She really *had* been overdoing it. She struggled, increasingly panicked. Increasingly desperate.

In the hallway, the minion tied off the chandeliers high in the air. Nearby, the vizier leader glanced from Darkness to Lift.

'Please,' Lift mouthed.

The vizier pointedly *shoved* the table. It clipped the elbow of the minion holding Lift. He cursed, letting go with that hand.

Lift dove for the floor, ripping out of his grip. She squirmed forward, getting underneath the table.

The minion seized her by the ankles.

'What was that?' Darkness asked, his voice cold, emotionless.

'I slipped,' the vizier said.

'Watch yourself.'

'Is that a threat, constable? I am beyond your reach.'

'Nobody is beyond my reach.' Still no emotion.

Lift thrashed underneath the table, kicking at the minion. He cursed softly and hauled Lift out by her legs, then pulled her to her feet. Darkness watched, face emotionless.

She met his gaze, eye to eye, a half-eaten roll in her mouth. She stared him down, chewing quickly and swallowing.

For once, he showed an emotion. Bafflement. 'All that,' he said, 'for a roll?'

Lift said nothing.

Come on . . .

They walked her down the hallway, then around the corner. One of the minions ran ahead and purposefully removed the spheres from the lamps on the walls. Were they *robbing* the place? No, after she passed, the minion ran back and restored the spheres.

Come on . . .

They passed a palace guard in the larger hallway beyond. He noted something about Darkness – perhaps that rope tied around his upper arm, which was threaded with an Azish sequence of colors – and saluted. 'Constable, sir? You found another one?'

Darkness stopped, looking as the guard opened the door beside him. Inside, Gawx sat on a chair, slumped between two other guards.

'So you did have accomplices!' shouted one of the guards in the room. He slapped Gawx across the face.

Wyndle gasped from just behind her. 'That was *certainly* uncalled for!'

Come on . . .

'This one is not your concern,' Darkness said to the guards, waiting as one of his minions did the strange gemstone-moving sequence. Why *did* they worry about that?

Something stirred inside of Lift. Like the little swirls of wind at the advent of a storm.

Darkness looked at her with a sharp motion. 'Something is—'

Awesomeness returned.

Lift became Slick, every part of her but her feet and the palms of her hands. She yanked her arm – it slipped from the minion's fingers – then kicked herself forward and fell to her knees, sliding under Darkness's hand as he reached for her.

Wyndle let out a whoop, zipping along beside her as she began slapping the floor like she was swimming, using each swing of her arms to push herself forward. She skimmed the floor of the palace hallway, knees sliding across it as if it were greased.

The posture wasn't particularly dignified. Dignity was for rich folk who had time to make up games to play with one another.

She got going real fast real quick – so fast it was hard to control herself as she relaxed her awesomeness and tried to leap to her feet. She crashed into the wall at the end of the hallway instead, a sprawling heap of limbs.

She came out of it with a grin. That had gone *way* better than the last few times she'd tried this. Her first attempt had been super embarrassing. She'd been so Slick, she hadn't even been able to stay on her knees.

'Lift!' Wyndle said. 'Behind.'

She glanced down the hallway. She could *swear* he was glowing faintly, and he was certainly running too quickly.

Darkness was awesome too.

'That is *not* fair!' Lift shouted, scrambling to her feet and dashing down a side hallway – the way she'd come when sneaking with Gawx. Her body had already started to feel tired again. One roll didn't get it far.

She sprinted down the lavish hallway, causing a maid to jump back, shrieking as if she'd seen a rat. Lift skidded around a corner, dashed toward the nice scents, and burst into the kitchens.

She ran through the mess of people inside. The door slammed open behind her a second later. Darkness.

Ignoring startled cooks, Lift leaped up onto a long counter, Slicking her leg and riding on it sideways, knocking off bowls and pans, causing a clatter. She came down off the other end of the counter as Darkness shoved his way past cooks in a clump, his Shardblade held up high.

He didn't curse in annoyance. A fellow should curse. Made people feel real when they did that.

But of course, Darkness wasn't a real person. Of that, though little else, she was sure.

Lift snatched a sausage off a steaming plate, then pushed into the servant hallways. She chewed as she ran, Wyndle growing along the wall beside her, leaving a streak of dark green vines.

'Where are we going?' he asked.

'*Away.*'

The door into the servant hallways slammed open behind her. Lift turned a corner, surprising an equerry. She went awesome, and threw herself to the side, easily slipping past him in the narrow hallway.

'What has become of me?' Wyndle asked. 'Thieving in the night, chased by abominations. I was a gardener. A wonderful gardener! Cryptics and honorspren alike came to see the crystals I grew from the minds of your world. Now this. What *have* I become?'

'A whiner,' Lift said, puffing.

'Nonsense.'

'So you were always one of those, then?' She looked over her shoulder. Darkness casually shoved down the equerry, barely breaking stride as he charged over the man.

Lift reached a doorway and slammed her shoulder against it, scrambling out into the rich hallways again.

She needed an exit. A window. Her flight had just looped her around back near the Prime's quarters. She picked a direction by instinct and started running, but one of Darkness's minions appeared around a corner that way. He *also* carried a Shardblade. Some starvin' luck, she had.

Lift turned the other way and passed by Darkness striding out of the servant hallways. She barely dodged a swing of his Blade by diving, Slicking herself, and sliding along the floor. She made it to her feet without stumbling this time. That was something, at least.

'Who *are* these men?' Wyndle asked from beside her.

Lift grunted.

'Why do they care so much about you? There's something about those weapons they carry . . .'

'Shardblades,' Lift said. 'Worth a whole kingdom. Built to kill Voidbringers.' And they had *two* of the things. Crazy.

Built to kill Voidbringers . . .

'You!' she said, still running. 'They're after you!'

'What? Of course they aren't!'

'They *are*. Don't worry. You're mine. I won't lettem have you.'

'That's endearingly loyal,' Wyndle said. 'And not a little insulting. But they are not after—'

The second of Darkness's minions stepped out into the hallway ahead of her. He held Gawx.

He had a knife to the young man's throat.

Lift stumbled to a halt. Gawx, in far over his head, whimpered in the man's hands.

'Don't move,' the minion said, 'or I will kill him.'

'Starvin' bastard,' Lift said. She spat to the side. 'That's dirty.'

Darkness thumped up behind her, the other minion joining him. They penned her in. The entrance to the Prime's quarters was actually just ahead, and the viziers and scions had flooded out into the hallway, where they jabbered to one another in outraged tones.

Gawx was crying. Poor fool.

Well. This sorta thing never ended well. Lift went with her gut – which was basically what she always did – and called the minion's bluff by dashing forward. He was a lawman type. Wouldn't kill a captive in cold—

The minion slit Gawx's throat.

Crimson blood poured out and stained Gawx's clothing. The minion dropped him, then stumbled back, as if startled by what he'd done.

Lift froze. He couldn't— He didn't—

Darkness grabbed her from behind.

'That was poorly done,' Darkness said to the minion, tone emotionless. Lift barely heard him. *So much blood.* 'You will be punished.'

'But . . .' the minion said. 'I had to do as I threatened . . .'

'You have not done the proper paperwork in this kingdom to kill that child,' Darkness said.

'Aren't we above their laws?'

Darkness actually let go of her, striding over to slap the minion across the face. 'Without the law, there is nothing. You will subject yourself to their rules, and accept the dictates of justice. It is all we have, the only sure thing in this world.'

Lift stared at the dying boy, who held his hands to his neck, as if to stop the blood flow. Those tears . . .

The other minion came up behind her.

'Run!' Wyndle said.

She started.

'*Run!*'

Lift ran.

She passed Darkness and pushed through the viziers, who gasped and yelled at the death. She barreled into the Prime's quarters, slid across the table, snatched another roll off the platter, and burst into the bedroom. She was out the window a second later.

'Up,' she said to Wyndle, then stuffed the roll in her mouth. He streaked up the side of the wall, and Lift climbed, sweating. A second later, one of the minions leaped out the window beneath her.

He didn't look up. He charged out onto the grounds, twisting about, searching, his Shardblade flashing in the darkness as it reflected starlight.

Lift safely reached the upper reaches of the palace, hidden in the shadows there. She squatted down, hands around her knees, feeling cold.

'You barely knew him,' Wyndle said. 'Yet you mourn.'

She nodded.

'You've seen much death,' Wyndle said. 'I know it. Aren't you accustomed to it?'

She shook her head.

Below, the minion moved off, hunting farther and farther for her. She was free. Climb across the roof, slip down on the other side, disappear.

Was that motion on the wall at the edge of the grounds? Yes, those moving shadows were men. The other thieves were climbing their wall and disappearing into the night. Huqin had left his nephew, as expected.

Who would cry for Gawx? Nobody. He'd be forgotten, abandoned.

Lift released her legs and crawled across the curved bulb of the roof toward the window she'd entered earlier. Her vines from the seeds, unlike the ones Wyndle grew, were still alive. They'd overgrown the window, leaves quivering in the wind.

Run, her instincts said. *Go.*

'You spoke of something earlier,' she whispered. 'Re . . .'

'Regrowth,' he said. 'Each bond grants power over two Surges. You can influence how things grow.'

'Can I use this to help Gawx?'

'If you were better trained? Yes. As it stands, I doubt it. You aren't very strong, aren't very practiced. And he might be dead already.'

She touched one of the vines.

'Why do you care?' Wyndle asked again. He sounded curious. Not a challenge. An attempt to understand.

'Because someone has to.'

For once, Lift ignored what her gut was telling her and, instead, climbed through the window. She crossed the room in a dash.

Out into the upstairs hallway. Onto the steps. She soared down them, leaping most of the distance. Through a doorway. Turn left. Down the hallway. Left again.

A crowd in the rich corridor. Lift reached them, then wiggled through. She didn't need her awesomeness for that. She'd been slipping through cracks in crowds since she started walking.

Gawx lay in a pool of blood that had darkened the fine carpet. The viziers and guards surrounded him, speaking in hushed tones.

Lift crawled up to him. His body was still warm, but the blood seemed to have stopped flowing. His eyes were closed.

'Too late?' she whispered.

'I don't know,' Wyndle said, curling up beside her.

'What do I do?'

'I . . . I'm not sure. Mistress, the transition to your side was difficult and left holes in my memory, even with the precautions my people took. I . . .'

She set Gawx on his back, face toward the sky. He *wasn't* really anything to her, that was true. They'd barely just met, and he'd been a fool. She'd told him to go back.

But this was who she was, who she had to be.

I will remember those who have been forgotten.

Lift leaned forward, touched her forehead to his, and breathed out. A shimmering something left her lips, a little cloud of glowing light. It hung in front of Gawx's lips.

Come on . . .

It stirred, then drew in through his mouth.

A hand took Lift by the shoulder, pulling her away from Gawx. She sagged, suddenly exhausted. *Real* exhausted, so much so that even standing was difficult.

Darkness pulled her by the shoulder away from the crowd. 'Come,' he said.

Gawx stirred. The viziers gasped, their attention turning toward the youth as he groaned, then sat up.

'It appears that you are an Edgedancer,' Darkness said, steering her down the corridor as the crowd moved in around Gawx, chattering. She stumbled, but he held her upright. 'I had wondered which of the two you would be.'

'Miracle!' one vizier said.

'Yaezir has spoken!' said one of the scions.

'Edgedancer,' Lift said. 'I don't know what that is.'

'They were once a glorious order,' Darkness said, walking her down the hallway. Everyone ignored them, focused instead on Gawx. 'Where you blunder, they were elegant things of beauty. They could ride the thinnest rope at speed, dance across rooftops, move through a battlefield like a ribbon on the wind.'

'That sounds . . . amazing.'

'Yes. It is unfortunate they were always so concerned with small-minded things, while ignoring those of greater import. It appears you share their temperament. You have become one of them.'

'I didn't mean to,' Lift said.

'I realize this.'

'Why . . . why do you hunt me?'

'In the name of justice.'

'There are *tons* of people who do wrong things,' she said. She had to force out every word. Talking was hard. *Thinking* was hard. So tired. 'You . . . you coulda hunted big crime bosses, murderers. You chose me instead. Why?'

'Others may be detestable, but they do not dabble in arts that could return Desolation to this world.' His words were so cold. 'What you are must be stopped.'

Lift felt numb. She tried to summon her awesomeness, but she'd used it all up. And then some, probably.

Darkness turned her and pushed her against the wall. She couldn't stand, and slumped down, sitting. Wyndle moved up beside her, spreading out a starburst of creeping vines.

Darkness knelt next to her. He held out his hand.

'I *saved* him,' Lift said. 'I did something good, didn't I?'

'Goodness is irrelevant,' Darkness said. His Shardblade dropped into his fingers.

'You don't even care, do you?'

'No,' he said. 'I don't.'

'You should,' she said, exhausted. 'You should . . . should try it, I mean. I wanted to be like you, once. Didn't work out. Wasn't . . . even like being alive . . .'

Darkness raised his Blade. Lift closed her eyes.

'She is pardoned!'

Darkness's grip on her shoulder tightened.

Feeling completely drained – like somebody had held her up by the toes and squeezed everything out of her – Lift forced her eyes to open. Gawx stumbled to a stop beside them, breathing heavily. Behind, the viziers and scions moved up as well.

Clothing bloodied, his eyes wide, Gawx clutched a piece of paper in his hand. He thrust this at Darkness. 'I pardon this girl. Release her, constable!'

'Who are you,' Darkness said, 'to do such a thing?'

'I am the Prime Aqasix,' Gawx declared. 'Ruler of Azir!'

'Ridiculous.'

'The Kadasixes have spoken,' said one of the scions.

'The Heralds?' Darkness said. 'They have done no such thing. You are mistaken.'

'We have voted,' said a vizier. 'This young man's application was the best.'

'What application?' Darkness said. 'He is a thief!'

'He performed the miracle of Regrowth,' said one of the older scions. 'He was dead and he returned. What better application could we ask for?'

'A sign has been given,' said the lead vizier. 'We have a Prime who can survive the attacks of the One All White. Praise to Yaezir, Kadasix of Kings, may he lead in wisdom. This youth is Prime. He has *been* Prime always. We have only now realized it, and beg his forgiveness for not seeing the truth sooner.'

'As it always has been done,' the elderly scion said. 'As it will be done again. Stand down, constable. You have been given an order.'

Darkness studied Lift.

She smiled tiredly. Show the starvin' man some teeth. That was the right of it.

His Shardblade vanished to mist. He'd been bested, but he didn't seem to care. Not a curse, not even a tightening of the eyes. He stood up and pulled on his gloves by the cuffs, first one, then the other. 'Praise Yaezir,' he said. 'Herald of Kings. May he lead in wisdom. If he ever stops drooling.'

Darkness bowed to the new Prime, then left with a sure step.

'Does anyone know the name of that constable?' one of the viziers asked. 'When did we start letting officers of the law requisition Shardblades?'

Gawx knelt beside Lift.

'So you're an emperor or something now,' she said, closing her eyes, settling back.

'Yeah. I'm still confused. It seems I performed a miracle or something.'

'Good for you,' Lift said. 'Can I eat your dinner?'

SZETH

S zeth-son-son-Vallano, Truthless of Shinovar, sat atop the highest tower in the world and contemplated the End of All Things.

The souls of the people he had murdered lurked in the shadows. They whispered to him. If he drew close, they screamed.

They also screamed when he shut his eyes. He had taken to blinking as little as possible. His eyes felt dry in his skull. It was what any . . . sane man would do.

The highest tower in the world, hidden in the tops of the mountains, was perfect for his contemplation. If he had not been bound to an Oathstone, if he had been another man entirely, he would have stayed here. The only place in the East where the stones were not cursed, where walking on them was allowed. This place was holy.

Bright sunlight shone down to banish the shadows, which kept those screams to a minimum. The screamers deserved their deaths, of course. They should have killed Szeth. *I hate you. I hate . . . everyone.* Glories within, what a strange emotion.

He did not look up. He would not meet the gaze of the God of Gods. But it *was* good to be in the sunlight. There were no clouds here to bring the darkness. This place was above them all. Urithiru ruled even the clouds.

The massive tower was also empty; that was another reason he liked it. A hundred levels, built in ring shapes, each one beneath larger than the one above it to provide a sunlit balcony. The eastern side, however, was a sheer, flat edge that made the tower look from a distance as if that side had been sliced off by an enormous Shardblade. What a strange shape.

He sat on that edge, right at the top, feet swinging over a drop of a hundred massive stories and a plummet down the mountainside below. Glass sparkled on the smooth surface of the flat side there.

Glass windows. Facing *east*, toward the Origin. The first time he had visited this place – just after being exiled from his homeland – he hadn't understood just how odd those windows were. Back then, he'd still been accustomed to gentle highstorms. Rain, wind, and meditation.

Things were different in these cursed lands of the stonewalkers. These hateful lands. These lands flowing with blood, death, and screams. And . . . And . . .

Breathe. He forced the air in and out and stood up on the rim of the parapet atop the tower.

He had fought an impossibility. A man with Stormlight, a man who knew the storm within. That meant . . . problems. Years ago, Szeth had been banished for raising the alarm. The *false* alarm, it had been said.

The Voidbringers are no more, they had told him.

The spirits of the stones themselves promised it.

The powers of old are no more.

The Knights Radiant are fallen.

We are all that remains.

All that remains. . . . Truthless.

'Have I not been faithful?' Szeth shouted, finally looking up to face the sun. His voice echoed against the mountains and their spirit-souls. 'Have I not obeyed, kept my oath? Have I not done as you *demanded* of me?'

The killing, the murder. He blinked tired eyes.

SCREAMS.

'What does it mean if the Shamanate are wrong? What does it mean if they banished me in error?'

It meant the End of All Things. The end of truth. It would mean that nothing made sense, and that his oath was meaningless.

It would mean he had killed for no reason.

He dropped off the side of the tower, white clothing – now a symbol to him of many things – flapping in the wind. He filled himself with Stormlight and Lashed himself southward. His body lurched in that direction, falling across the sky. He could only travel this way for a short time; his Stormlight did not last long.

Too imperfect a body. The Knights Radiant ... they'd been said ... they'd been said to be better at this ... like the Voidbringers.

He had just enough Light to free himself from the mountains and land in a village in the foothills. They often set out spheres for him there as an offering, considering him some kind of god. He would feed upon that Light, and it would let him go a farther distance until he found another city and more Stormlight.

It would take days to get where he was going, but he *would* find answers. Or, barring that, someone to kill.

Of his own choice, this time.

I-II

NEW RHYTHMS

Eshonai waved her hand as she climbed the central spire of Narak, trying to shoo away the tiny spren. It danced around her head, shedding rings of light from its cometlike form. Horrid thing. Why would it not leave her alone?

Perhaps it could not stay away. She was experiencing something wonderfully new, after all. Something that had not been seen in centuries. Stormform. A form of true power.

A form given of the gods.

She continued up the steps, feet clinking in her Shardplate. It felt good on her.

She had held this form for fifteen days now, fifteen days of hearing new rhythms. At first, she had attuned those often, but this had made some people very nervous. She had backed off, and forced herself to attune the old, familiar ones when speaking.

It was difficult, for those old rhythms were so *dull*. Buried within those new rhythms, the names of which she intuited somehow, she could almost hear voices speaking to her. Advising her. If her people had received such guidance over the centuries, they surely would not have fallen so far.

Eshonai reached the top of the spire, where the other four awaited her. Again, her sister Venli was also there, and she wore the new form as well – with its spiking armor plates, its red eyes, its lithe danger. This meeting would proceed very differently from the previous one. Eshonai cycled through the new rhythms, careful not to hum them. The others weren't ready yet.

She sat down, then gasped.

That rhythm! It sounded like ... like her own voice yelling at her. Screaming in pain. What was *that*? She shook her head, and found that she had reflexively pulled her hand to her chest in anxiety. When she opened it, the cometlike spren shot out.

She attuned Irritation. The others of the Five regarded her with heads cocked, a couple humming to Curiosity. Why did she act as she did?

Eshonai settled herself, Shardplate grinding against stone. This close to the lull – the time called the Weeping by the humans – highstorms were growing more rare. That had created a small impediment in her march to see every listener given stormform. There had only been one storm since Eshonai's own transformation, and during it, Venli and her scholars had taken stormform along with two hundred soldiers chosen by Eshonai. Not officers. Common soldiers. The type she was *sure* would obey.

The next highstorm was mere days away, and Venli had been gathering her spren. They had thousands ready. It was time.

Eshonai regarded the others of the Five. Today's clear sky rained down white sunlight, and a few windspren approached on a breeze. They stopped when they grew near, then zipped away in the opposite direction.

'Why have you called this meeting?' Eshonai asked the others.

'You've been speaking of a plan,' Davim said, broad worker's hands clasped before him. 'You've been telling everyone of it. Shouldn't you have brought it to the Five first?'

'I'm sorry,' Eshonai said. 'I am merely excited. I believe, however, we should now be the Six.'

'That has not been decided,' Abronai said, weak and plump. Mateform was disgusting. 'This moves too quickly.'

'We *must* move quickly,' Eshonai replied to Resolve. 'We have only two highstorms before the lull. You know what the spies report. The humans are planning a final push toward us, toward Narak.'

'It is a pity,' Abronai said to Consideration, 'that your meeting with them went so poorly.'

'They wanted to tell me of the destruction they planned to bring,' Eshonai lied. 'They wanted to gloat. That was the only reason they met with me.'

'We need to be ready to fight them,' Davim said to Anxiety.

Eshonai laughed. A blatant use of emotion, but she truly felt it. 'Fight them? Haven't you been listening? I can summon a *highstorm*.'

'With help,' Chivi said to Curiosity. Nimbleform. Another weak form. They should expunge that one from their ranks. 'You have said you cannot do it alone. How many others would you need? Certainly the two hundred you have now are enough.'

'No, that is not *nearly* enough,' Eshonai replied. 'I feel that the more people we have in this form, the more likely we are to succeed. I would like, therefore, to move that we transform.'

'Yes,' Chivi said. 'But how many of us?'

'All of us.'

Davim hummed to Amusement, thinking it must be a joke. He trailed off as the rest sat in silence.

'We will have just one chance,' Eshonai said to Resolve. 'The humans will leave their warcamps together, in one large army that intends to reach Narak during the lull. They will be completely exposed on the plateaus, with no shelter. A highstorm at that time would *destroy* them.'

'We don't even truly know if you can summon one,' Abronai said to Skepticism.

'That is why we need as many of us in stormform as possible,' Eshonai said. 'If we miss this opportunity, our children will sing us the songs of Cursing, assuming they even live long enough to do so. This is our chance, our one chance. Imagine the ten armies of men, isolated on the plateaus, buffeted and overwhelmed by a tempest they could never have expected! With stormform, we would be immune to its effects. If any survive, we could destroy them easily.'

'It *is* tempting,' Davim said.

'I do not like the look of those who have taken this form,' Chivi said. 'I do not like how people clamor to be given it. Perhaps two hundred are enough.'

'Eshonai,' Davim said, 'how does this form feel?'

He was asking more than he actually said. Each form changed a person in some ways. Warform made you more aggressive, mateform made you easy to distract, nimbleform encouraged focus, and workform made you obedient.

Eshonai attuned Peace.

No. *That* was the screaming voice. How had she spent weeks in this form and not noticed?

'I feel alive,' Eshonai said to Joy. 'I feel strong, and I feel powerful. I feel a connection to the world that I should have always known. Davim, this is like the change from dullform to one of the other forms – it is *that* much of an upgrade. Now that I hold this strength, I realize I wasn't fully alive before.'

She lifted her hand and made a fist. She could feel the energy coursing down her arm as the muscles flexed, though it was hidden beneath the Shardplate.

'Red eyes,' Abronai whispered. 'Have we come to this?'

'If we decide to do this,' Chivi said. 'Perhaps we four should assess it first, then say if the others should join us.' Venli opened her mouth to speak, but Chivi waved her hand, interrupting her. 'You have had your say, Venli. We know what you wish.'

'We cannot wait, unfortunately,' Eshonai said. 'If we want to trap the Alethi armies, we will need time to transform everyone before the Alethi leave to search for Narak.'

'I'm willing to try it,' Abronai said. 'Perhaps we should propose a mass transformation to our people.'

'No.' Zuln spoke to Peace.

The dullform member of the Five sat slouched, looking at the ground before her. She almost never said anything.

Eshonai attuned Annoyance. 'What was that?'

'No,' Zuln repeated. 'It is not right.'

'I would have us all be in agreement,' Davim said. 'Zuln, can you not listen to reason?'

'It is not right,' the dullform said again.

'She is dull,' Eshonai said. 'We should ignore her.'

Davim hummed to Anxiety. 'Zuln represents the past, Eshonai. You shouldn't say such things of her.'

'The past is dead.'

Abronai joined Davim in humming to Anxiety. 'Perhaps this is worth more thought. Eshonai, you . . . do not speak as you used to. I hadn't real- ized the changes were so stark.'

Eshonai attuned one of the new rhythms, the Rhythm of Fury. She held the song inside, and found herself humming. These were so cautious, so weak! They would see her people destroyed.

'We will meet again later today,' Davim said. 'Let us spend time considering. Eshonai, I would speak with you alone during that period, if you are willing.'

'Of course.'

They rose from their places atop the pillar. Eshonai stepped to the edge and looked down as the others filed down. The spire was too high to jump from, even in Shardplate. She so wanted to try.

It seemed that every person in the city had gathered around the base to await the decision. In the weeks since Eshonai's transformation, talk of what had happened to her – then the others – had infused the city with a certain mixture of anxiety and hope. Many had come to her, begging to be given the form. They saw the chance it offered.

'They're not going to agree to it,' Venli said from behind once the others were down. She spoke to Spite, one of the new rhythms. 'You spoke too aggressively, Eshonai.'

'Davim is with us,' Eshonai said to Confidence. 'Chivi will come too, with persuasion.'

'That isn't enough. If the Five do not come to a consensus—'

'Don't worry.'

'Our people *must* take that form, Eshonai,' Venli said. 'It is inevitable.'

Eshonai found herself attuning the new version of Amusement ... Ridicule, it was. She turned to her sister. 'You knew, didn't you? You knew *exactly* what this form would do to me. You knew this before you took the form yourself.'

'I . . . Yes.'

Eshonai grabbed her sister by the front of her robe, then yanked her forward, holding her tightly. With Shardplate it was easy, though Venli resisted more than she should have been able to, and a small spark of red lightning ran across the woman's arms and face. Eshonai was not accustomed to such strength from her scholar of a sister.

'You could have destroyed us,' Eshonai said. 'What if this form had done something terrible?'

Screaming. In her head. Venli smiled.

'How did you discover this?' Eshonai asked. 'It didn't come from the songs. There is more.'

Venli did not speak. She met Eshonai's eyes and hummed to Confidence. 'We must make certain the Five agree to this plan,' she said. 'If we are to survive, and if we are to defeat the humans, we must be in this form – all of us. We *must* summon that storm. It has been . . . waiting, Eshonai. Waiting and building.'

'I will see to it,' Eshonai said, dropping Venli. 'You can gather enough spren for us to transform all of our people?'

'My staff have been working on it these three weeks. We will be ready to transform thousands upon thousands over the course of the final two highstorms before the lull.'

'Good.' Eshonai started down the steps.

'Sister?' Venli asked. 'You are planning something. What is it? How will you persuade the Five?'

Eshonai continued down the steps. With the added balance and strength of Shardplate, she didn't need to bother with the chains to steady herself. As she neared the bottom, where the others of the Five were speaking to the people, she stopped a short distance above the crowd and drew in a deep breath.

Then, as loudly as she could, Eshonai shouted, 'In two days, I will take any who wish to go into the storm and give them this new form.'

The crowd stilled, their humming dropping off.

'The Five seek to deny you this right,' Eshonai bellowed. 'They don't want you to have this form of power. They are frightened, like cremlings hiding in cracks. They *cannot* deny you! It is the right of every person to choose their own form.'

She raised her hands above her head, humming to Resolve, and summoned a storm.

A tiny one, a mere trickle compared to what waited. It grew between her hands, a wind coursing with lightning. A miniature tempest in her palms, light and power, wind spinning in a vortex. It had been centuries since this power had been used, and so – like a river that had been dammed – the energy waited impatiently to be freed.

The tempest grew so that it whipped at her clothing, spinning around her in a swirl of wind, crackling red lightning, and dark mist. Finally, it dissipated. She heard Awe being sung throughout the crowd – full songs, not humming. Their emotions were strong.

'With this power,' Eshonai declared, 'we can destroy the Alethi and protect our people. I have seen your despair. I have heard you sing to Mourning. It need not be so! Come with me into the storms. It is your right, your *duty*, to join with me.'

Behind her on the steps, Venli hummed to Tension. 'This will divide us, Eshonai. Too aggressive, too abrupt!'

'It will work,' Eshonai said to Confidence. 'You do not know them as I do.'

Below, the other members of the Five were glaring up at her, looking betrayed, though she could not hear their songs.

Eshonai marched to the bottom of the spire, then pushed her way through the crowd, being joined by her soldiers in stormform. The people made way for her, many humming to Anxiety. Most who had come were workers or nimbleforms. That made sense. The warforms were too pragmatic for gawking.

Eshonai and her stormform warriors left the town's center ring. She allowed Venli to tag along behind, but paid the woman no heed. Eshonai eventually approached the barracks on the leeward side of the city, a large group of buildings built together to form a community for the soldiers. Though her troops were not required to sleep here, many did so.

The practice grounds one plateau over were busy with the sounds of warriors honing their skills, or – more likely – newly transformed soldiers being trained. The second division, a hundred and twenty-eight in number, were away watching for humans entering the middle plateaus. Scouts in warpairs roamed the Plains. She'd set them on this task soon after obtaining her form, as she had known even then that she would need to change the way this battle worked. She wanted every bit of information about the Alethi and their current tactics that she could get.

Her soldiers would ignore chrysalises for the time being. She would not lose soldiers to that petty game any longer, not when each man and woman under her command represented the potential of stormform.

The other divisions were all here, however. Seventeen thousand soldiers total. A mighty force in some ways, but also so few, compared to what they had once been. She raised her hand in a fist, and her stormform division raised the call for all soldiers in the listener army to gather. Those practicing set down their weapons and jogged over. Others left the barracks. In a short time, all had joined her.

'It is time to end the fight against the Alethi,' Eshonai announced in a loud voice. 'Which of you are willing to follow me in doing so?'

Humming to Resolve moved through the crowd. So far as she could hear, not a one hummed to Skepticism. Excellent.

'This will require each soldier to join me in this form,' Eshonai shouted, her words being relayed through the ranks.

More humming to Resolve.

'I am proud of you,' Eshonai said. 'I am going to have the Storm Division go among you and take your word, each of you, on this transformation. If there are any here who do not wish to change, I would know of it personally. It is your decision, by right, and I will not force you – but I must know.'

She looked to her stormforms, who saluted and broke apart, moving in warpairs. Eshonai stepped back, folding her arms, watching as these visited each other division in turn. The new rhythms thrummed in her skull, though she stayed away from the Rhythm of Peace, with its strange screams. There was no fighting against what she had become. The eyes of the gods were too strongly upon her.

Nearby, some soldiers gathered, familiar faces beneath hardened skullplates, the men bearing bits of gemstone tied to their beards. Her own division, once her friends.

She could not quite explain why she had not chosen them at first for the transformation, instead picking two hundred soldiers from across many divisions. She'd needed soldiers who were obedient, but not known for their brightness.

Thude and the soldiers of Eshonai's former division . . . they knew her too well. They would have questioned.

Soon, she had gotten word. Of her seventeen thousand troops, only a handful refused the required transformation. Those who had declined were gathered on the practice grounds.

As she contemplated her next move, Thude approached. Tall and thicklimbed, he had always worn warform save for two weeks as a mate to Bila. He hummed to Resolve – the way for a soldier to indicate a willingness to obey orders.

'I am worried about this, Eshonai,' he said. 'Do so many need to change?'

'If we do not transform,' Eshonai said, 'we are dead. The humans will ruin us.'

He continued to hum to Resolve, to indicate he trusted her. His eyes seemed to tell another story.

Melu, of her stormforms, returned and saluted. 'The counting is finished, sir.'

'Excellent,' Eshonai said. 'Pass word to the troops. We're going to do the same thing for everyone in the city.'

'*Everyone?*' Thude said to Anxiety.

'Our time is short,' Eshonai said. 'If we do not act, we will miss our opportunity to move against the humans. We have two storms left; I want every willing person in this city ready to take up stormform before those have passed us. Those who will not are given that right, but I want them gathered so we may know where we stand.'

'Yes, General,' Melu said.

'Use a tight scouting formation,' Eshonai said, pointing toward parts of the city. 'Move through the streets, counting every person. Use the nonstormform divisions too, for speed. Tell the common people that we're trying to determine how many soldiers we will have for the coming battle, and have our soldiers be calm and sing to Peace. Put those people who are willing to transform into the central ring. Send those who are unwilling out here. Give them an escort so that they do not get lost.'

Venli stepped up to her as Melu passed the word, sending ranks out to obey. Thude rejoined his division.

Every half year, they did an accounting to determine their numbers and see if the forms were properly balanced. Once in a while, they would need more volunteers to become mates or workers. Most often, they needed more warforms.

That meant this exercise was familiar to the soldiers, and they took easily to the orders. After years of war, they were accustomed to doing as she said. Many had the same depression that the regular people expressed – only for the troops, it manifested as bloodlust. They just wanted to fight. They would probably have charged head-on against the human encampments, and ten times their own numbers, if Eshonai ordered.

The Five all but handed this to me, she thought as the first of the unwilling began to trickle out of the city, guarded by her soldiers. *For years I've been absolute leader of our armies, and every person among us with a hint of aggression has been given to me as a soldier.*

Workers would obey; it was their nature. Many of the nimbles who hadn't transformed yet were loyal to Venli, as the majority of them aspired to be scholars. The mates wouldn't care, and the few dulls would be too numb of brain to object.

The city was hers.

'We'll have to kill them, unfortunately,' Venli said, watching the unwilling be gathered. They huddled together, afraid, despite the soft songs of the soldiers. 'Will your troops be able to do it?'

'No,' Eshonai said, shaking her head. 'Many would resist us if we did this now. We will have to wait for all of my soldiers to be transformed. They will not object then.'

'That's sloppy,' Venli said to Spite. 'I thought you commanded their loyalty.'

'Do not question me,' Eshonai said. 'I control this city, not you.'

Venli quieted, though her humming to Spite continued. She would attempt to seize control from Eshonai. It was an uncomfortable realization, as was the realization of how deeply Eshonai herself wanted to be in control. That didn't feel like her. Not at all.

None of this feels like me. I . . .

The new rhythms' beats surged in her mind. She turned from such thoughts as a group of soldiers approached, towing a shouting figure. Abronai, of the Five. She should have realized that he'd be trouble; he maintained mateform too easily, avoiding its distractions.

Transforming him would have been dangerous, she thought. *He has too much control over himself.*

As the stormform soldiers pulled him to Eshonai, his shouts beat against her. 'This is outrageous! The dictates of the Five rule us, not the will of a single person! Can't you see that the form, the new form is overriding her! You've all lost your minds! Or . . . or *worse.*'

It was discomfortingly close to the truth.

'Put him with the others,' Eshonai said, gesturing toward the group of dissidents. 'What of the rest of the Five?'

'They agreed,' Melu said. 'Some were reluctant, but they agreed.'

'Go and fetch Zuln. Put her with the dissenters. I don't trust her to do what is needed.'

The soldier didn't question as she towed Abronai away. There were perhaps a thousand dissenters there on the large plateau that made up the practice grounds. An acceptably small number.

'Eshonai . . .' The song was sung to Anxiety. She turned as Thude approached. 'I don't like this, what we're doing here.'

Bother. She had worried that he would be difficult. She took him by the arm, leading him a ways off. The new rhythms cycled through her mind as her armored feet crunched on the stones. Once they were far enough away from Venli and the others for some privacy, she turned Thude to look him in the eyes.

'Out with it,' she said to Irritation, picking one of the old, familiar rhythms for him.

'Eshonai,' he said quietly. 'This isn't right. You *know* it's not right. I agreed to change – every soldier did – but it's not right.'

'Do you disagree that we needed new tactics in this war?' Eshonai said to Resolve. 'We were dying slowly, Thude.'

'We did need new tactics,' Thude said. 'But this . . . Something's wrong with you, Eshonai.'

'No, I just needed an excuse for such extreme action. Thude, I've been considering something like this for months.'

'A coup?'

'Not a coup. A refocusing. We are *doomed* if we don't change our methods! My only hope was Venli's research. The only thing she turned up was this form. Well, I've got to try and use it, make one last attempt to save our people. The Five tried to stop me. I've heard you yourself complain about how much they talk instead of acting.'

He hummed to Consideration. She knew him well enough, however, to sense when he was forcing a rhythm. The beat was too obvious, too strong. *I almost convinced him,* she thought. *It's the red eyes. I've instilled in him, and some of the others of my own division, too much of a fear of our gods.*

It was a shame, but she'd probably have to see him, and her other former friends, executed.

'I see you're not convinced,' Eshonai said.

'I just . . . I don't know, Eshonai. This seems bad.'

'I'll talk you through it later,' Eshonai said. 'I don't have time right now.'

'And what are you going to do to those?' Thude asked, nodding toward the dissenters. 'This looks an awful lot like a roundup of people who don't agree with you. Eshonai . . . did you realize your own mother was among them?'

She started, looking and seeing her aging mother being guided to the group by two stormforms. They hadn't even come to her with the question. Did that mean they were extra obedient, following her orders no matter what, or were they worried she would weaken because her mother refused to change?

She could hear her mother singing. One of the old songs, as she was guided.

'You can watch over that group,' Eshonai said to Thude. 'You and soldiers you trust. I'll put my own division in charge of the people there, you at their head. That way, nothing will happen to them without your agreement.'

He hesitated, then nodded, humming to Consideration for real this time. She let him go and he jogged over to Bila and a few others of Eshonai's former division.

Poor, trusting Thude, she thought as he took command of guarding the dissenters. *Thank you for rounding yourself up so neatly.*

'This was handled well,' Venli said as Eshonai walked back to her. 'Can you control the city long enough for the transformation?'

'Easily,' Eshonai said, nodding to the soldiers who came to give her a report. 'Just make certain you can deliver the proper spren and in the proper quantities.'

'I will,' Venli said to Satisfaction.

Eshonai took the reports. Everyone who had agreed was gathered in the center of the city. It was time to speak to them and deliver the lies she'd prepared. That the Five would be reinstated once the humans were dealt with, that there was no reason to worry. That everything was just fine.

Eshonai strode into a city that was now hers, flanked by soldiers in the new form. She summoned her Blade for effect, the last one her people owned, resting it on her shoulder.

She made her way to the center of the city, passing melted buildings and shacks built from carapace. It was a wonder that those things survived the storms. Her people deserved better. With the return of the gods, they would *have* better.

Irritatingly, it took some time to get the people ready for her speech. Some twenty thousand non-warforms gathered together was quite a sight; looking upon them, the city's population did not seem nearly so small. Still, this was a fraction of their original numbers.

Her soldiers seated them all, prepared messengers to deliver her words to those not near enough to hear. As she waited for the preparations, she listened to reports regarding the population. Surprisingly, the majority of those who had dissented were workers. They were supposed to be obedient. Well, the greater number of them were elderly, the ones who had not fought in the war against the Alethi. Those who had not been forced to watch their friends be killed.

She waited by the base of the pillar until everything was ready. She climbed the steps to begin her speech, but stopped as she noticed Varanis, one of her lieutenants, running toward her. He was one she had chosen for stormform.

Suddenly alert, Eshonai attuned the Rhythm of Destruction.

'General,' he said to Anxiety. 'They've escaped!'

'Who?'

'The ones you had us set apart, the ones who did not want to transform. They've fled.'

'Well, chase them down,' Eshonai said to Spite. 'They can't get far. The workers won't be able to jump chasms; they can only go as far as the bridges allow.'

'General! They cut down one of the bridges, then used the ropes to climb down into the chasm itself. They've fled through those.'

'Then they're dead anyway,' Eshonai said. 'There is a storm in two days. They'll be caught in the chasms and killed. Ignore them.'

'What of their guards?' Venli demanded to Spite, shoving her way up beside Eshonai. 'Why weren't they being watched?'

'The guards went with them,' Varanis said. 'Eshonai, Thude was leading those—'

'No matter,' Eshonai said. 'You are dismissed.'

Varanis retreated.

'You aren't surprised,' Venli said to Destruction. 'Who are these guards that are willing to *help* their prisoners escape? What have you done, Eshonai?'

'Do not challenge me.'

'I—'

'Do *not* challenge me,' Eshonai said, grabbing her sister by the neck with a gauntleted hand.

'Kill me, and you'll ruin everything,' Venli said, not a hint of fear in her voice. 'They'll never follow a woman who murdered her own sister in public, and only I can provide the spren you need for this transformation.'

Eshonai hummed to the Rhythm of Derision, but let go. 'I'm going to make my speech.' She turned her back on Venli and stepped up to address the people.

FOUR

The Approach

KALADIN • SHALLAN • DALINAR

I'll address this letter to my 'old friend,' as I have no idea what name you're using currently.

Kaladin had never been in prison before.

Cages, yes. Pits. Pens. Under guard in a room. Never a proper prison.

Perhaps that was because prisons were too nice. He had two blankets, a pillow, and a chamber pot that was changed regularly. They fed him far better than he'd ever been fed as a slave. The stone shelf wasn't the most comfortable bed, but with the blankets, it wasn't too bad. He didn't have any windows, but at least he wasn't out in the storms.

All in all, the room was very nice. And he hated it.

In the past, the only times he'd been stuck in a small space had been to weather a highstorm. Now, being enclosed here for hours on end, with nothing to do but lie on his back and think ... Now he found himself restless, sweating, missing the open spaces. Missing the wind. The solitude didn't bother him. Those walls, though. They felt like they were crushing him.

On the third day of his imprisonment, he heard a disturbance from farther inside the prison, beyond his chamber. He stood up, ignoring Syl, who sat on an invisible bench on his wall. What *was* that shouting? It echoed in from the hallway.

His little cell was in its own room. The only people he'd seen since being locked up were the guards and the servants. Spheres glowed on the walls, keeping the place well lit. Spheres in a room meant for criminals. Were they there to taunt the men locked away? Riches just beyond reach.

He pressed against the cold bars, listening to the indistinct shouts. He imagined Bridge Four having come to break him out. Stormfather send they didn't try something so foolish.

He eyed one of the spheres in its setting on the wall.

'What?' Syl asked him.

'I might be able to get close enough to suck that Light out. It's only a little farther than the Parshendi were when I drew the Light from their gemstones.'

'Then what?' Syl asked, voice small.

Good question. 'Would you help me break out, if I wanted to?'

'Do you want to?'

'I'm not sure.' He turned around, still standing, and rested his back against the bars. 'I might need to. Breaking out would be against the law, though.'

She lifted her chin. 'I'm no highspren. Laws don't matter; what's *right* matters.'

'On that point, we agree.'

'But you came willingly,' Syl said. 'Why would you leave now?'

'I won't let them execute me.'

'They're not going to,' Syl said. 'You heard Dalinar.'

'Dalinar can go rot. He let this happen.'

'He tried to—'

'He let it happen!' Kaladin snapped, turning and slamming his hands against the bars. Another *storming* cage. He was right back where he'd begun! 'He's the same as the others,' Kaladin growled.

Syl zipped over to him, coming to rest between the bars, hands on hips. 'Say that again.'

'He . . .' Kaladin turned away. Lying to her was hard. 'All right, fine. He's not. But the king is. Admit it, Syl. Elhokar is a terrible king. At first he *lauded* me for trying to protect him. Now, at the snap of his fingers, he's willing to execute me. He's a child.'

'Kaladin, you're scaring me.'

'Am I? You told me to trust you, Syl. When I jumped down into the arena, you said this time things would be different. *How* is this different?'

She looked away, seeming suddenly very small.

'Even Dalinar admitted that the king had made a big mistake in letting Sadeas wiggle out of the challenge,' Kaladin said. 'Moash and his friends are right. This kingdom would be better off without Elhokar.'

Syl dropped to the floor, head bowed.

Kaladin walked back to his bench, but was too stirred up to sit. He found himself pacing. How could a man be expected to live trapped in a little room, without fresh air to breathe? He wouldn't let them leave him here.

You'd better keep your word, Dalinar. Get me out. Soon.

The disturbance, whatever it had been, quieted. Kaladin asked the servant about it when she came with his food, pushing it through the small opening at the bottom of the bars. She wouldn't speak to him, and scurried off like a cremling before a storm.

Kaladin sighed, retrieving the food – steamed vegetables, dribbled with a salty black sauce – and flopping back on his bench. They gave him food he could eat with his fingers. No forks or knives for him, just in case.

'Nice place you have here, bridgeboy,' Wit said. 'I considered moving in here myself on several occasions. The rent might be cheap, but the price of admission is quite steep.'

Kaladin scrambled up to his feet. Wit sat on a bench by the far wall, outside the cell and under the spheres, tuning some kind of strange instrument on his lap made of taut strings and polished wood. He hadn't been there a moment ago. Storms . . . had the *bench* even been there before?

'How did you get in?' Kaladin asked.

'Well, there are these things called *doors* . . .'

'The guards let you?'

'Technically?' Wit asked, plucking at a string, then leaning down to listen as he plucked another. 'Yes.'

Kaladin sat back down on the bench in his cell. Wit wore his black-on-black, his thin silver sword undone from his waist and sitting on the bench beside him. A brown sack slumped there as well. Wit leaned down to tune his instrument, one leg crossed over the other. He hummed softly to himself and nodded. 'Perfect pitch,' Wit said, 'makes this all so much easier than it once was. . . .'

Kaladin sat, waiting, as Wit settled back against the wall. Then did nothing.

'Well?' Kaladin asked.

'Yes. Thank you.'

'Are you going to play music for me?'

'No. You wouldn't appreciate it.'

'Then why are you here?'

'I like visiting people in prison. I can say whatever I want to them, and they can't do anything about it.' He looked up at Kaladin, then rested his hands on his instrument, smiling. 'I've come for a story.'

'What story?'

'The one you're going to tell me.'

'Bah,' Kaladin said, lying back down on his bench. 'I'm in no mood for your games today, Wit.'

Wit plucked a note on his instrument. 'Everyone always says that – which, first off, makes it a cliche. I am led to wonder. Is anyone *ever* in the mood for my games? And if they are, would that not defeat the point of my type of game in the first place?'

Kaladin sighed as Wit continued to pluck out notes. 'If I play along today,' Kaladin asked, 'will that get rid of you?'

'I will leave as soon as the story is done.'

'Fine. A man went to jail. He hated it there. The end.'

'Ah . . .' Wit said. 'So it's a story about a child, then.'

'No, it's about—' Kaladin cut off.

Me.

'Perhaps a story *for* a child,' Wit said. 'I will tell you one, to get you in the mood. A bunny rabbit and a chick went frolicking in the grass together on a sunny day.'

'A chick . . . baby chicken?' Kaladin said. 'And a what?'

'Ah, forgot myself for a moment,' Wit said. 'Sorry. Let me make it more appropriate for you. A piece of wet slime and a disgusting crab thing with seventeen legs slunk across the rocks together on an insufferably rainy day. Is that better?'

'I suppose. Is the story over?'

'It hasn't started yet.'

Wit abruptly slapped the strings, then began to play them with ferocious intent. A vibrant, energetic repetition. One punctuated note, then seven in a row, frenzied.

The rhythm got inside of Kaladin. It seemed to shake the entire room. 'What do you see?' Wit demanded.

'I . . .'

'Close your eyes, idiot!'

Kaladin closed his eyes. *This is stupid.*

'What do you see?' Wit repeated.

Wit was playing with him. The man was said to do that. He was supposedly Sigzil's old mentor. Shouldn't Kaladin have earned a reprieve by helping out his apprentice?

There was nothing of humor to those notes. Those powerful notes. Wit added a second melody, complementing the first. Was he playing that with his other hand? Both at the same time? How could one man, one instrument, produce so much music?

Kaladin saw . . . in his mind . . .

A race.

'That's the song of a man who is running,' Kaladin said.

'In the driest part of the brightest day, the man set off from the eastern sea.' Wit said it perfectly to the beat of his music, a chant that was almost a song. 'And where he went or why he ran, the answer comes from you to me.'

'He ran from the storm,' Kaladin said softly.

'The man was Fleet, whose name you know; he's spoken of in song and lore. The fastest man e'er known to live. The surest feet e'er known to roam. In time long past, in times I've known, he raced the Herald Chan-a-rach. He won that race, as he did each one, but now the time for defeat had come.

'For Fleet so sure, and Fleet the quick, to all that heard he yelled his goal: to beat the wind, and race a storm. A claim so brash, a claim too bold. To race the wind? It can't be done. Undaunted, Fleet was set to run. So to the east, there went our Fleet. Upon the shore his mark was set.

'The storm grew strong, the storm grew wild. Who was this man all set to dash? No man should tempt the God of Storms. No fool had ever been so rash.'

How did Wit play this music with only two hands? Surely another hand had joined him. Should Kaladin look?

In his mind's eye, he saw the race. Fleet, a barefooted man. Wit claimed all knew of him, but Kaladin had never heard of such a story. Lanky, tall, with tied-back long hair that went to his waist. Fleet took his mark on the shore, leaning forward in a running posture, waiting as the stormwall thundered and crashed across the sea toward him. Kaladin jumped as Wit hit a burst of notes, signaling the race's start.

Fleet tore off just in front of an angry, violent wall of water, lightning, and wind-blown rocks.

Wit did not speak again until Kaladin prompted him. 'At first,' Kaladin said, 'Fleet did well.'

'O'er rock and grass, our Fleet did run! He leaped the stones and dodged the trees, his feet a blur, his soul a sun! The storm so grand, it raged and spun, but away from it our Fleet did run! The lead was his, the wind behind, did man now prove that storms could *lose*?

'Through land he ran so quick and sure, and Alethkar he left behind. But now the test he saw ahead, for mountains he would have to climb. The storm surged on, released a howl; it saw its chance might now approach.

'To the highest mounts and the coldest peaks, our hero Fleet did make his way. The slopes were steep and paths unsure. Would he maintain his mighty lead?'

'Obviously not,' Kaladin said. 'You can never stay ahead. Not for long.'

'No! The storm grew close, 'til it chewed his heels. Upon his neck, Fleet felt its chill. Its breath of ice was all around, a mouth of night and wings of frost. Its voice was of the breaking rocks; its song was of the crashing rain.' Kaladin could feel it. Icy water seeping through his clothing. Wind buffeting his skin. A roar so loud that soon, he could hear nothing at all.

He'd been there. He'd felt it.

'Then the tip he reached! The point he found! Fleet climbed no more; he crossed the peak. And down the side, his speed returned! Outside the storm, Fleet found the sun. Azir's plains were now his path. He sprinted west, more broad his stride.'

'But he was growing weak,' Kaladin said. 'No man can run that far without getting tired. Even Fleet.'

'Yet soon the race its toll did claim. His feet like bricks, his legs like cloth. In gasps our runner drew his breath. The end approached, the storm outdone, but slowly did our hero run.'

'More mountains,' Kaladin whispered. 'Shinovar.'

'A final challenge raised its head, a final shadow to his dread. The land did rise up once again, the Misted Mountains guarding Shin. To leave the storming winds behind, our Fleet again began to climb.'

'The storm caught up.'

'The storms again came to his back, the winds again did spin around! The time was short, the ending near, as through those mounts our Fleet did dash.'

'It was right upon him. Even going down the other side of the mountains, he was unable to stay very far ahead.'

'He crossed the peaks, but lost his lead. The last paths lay before his feet, but strength he'd spent and might he'd lost. Each step was toil, each breath in pain. A sunken land he crossed with grief, the grass so dead it did not move.

'But here the storm, it too did wilt, with thunder lost and lightning spent. The drops slipped down, now weak as wet. For Shin is not a place for them.

'Ahead the sea, the race's end. Fleet stayed ahead, his muscles raw. Eyes barely saw, legs barely walked, but on he went to destiny. The end you know, the end will live, a shock for men to me you'll give.'

Music, but no words. Wit waited for Kaladin's reply. *Enough of this*, Kaladin thought. 'He died. He didn't make it. The end.'

The music stopped abruptly. Kaladin opened his eyes, looking toward Wit. Would he be mad that Kaladin had made such a poor conclusion to the story?

Wit stared at him, instrument still in his lap. The man didn't seem angry. 'So you *do* know this story,' Wit said.

'What? I thought you were making it up.'

'No, you were.'

'Then what is there to know?'

Wit smiled. 'All stories told have been told before. We tell them to ourselves, as did all men who ever were. And all men who ever will be. The only things new are the names.'

Kaladin sat up. He tapped one finger against his stone block of a bench. 'So . . . Fleet. Was he real?'

'As real as I am,' Wit said.

'And he died?' Kaladin said. 'Before he could finish the race?'

'He died.' Wit smiled.

'What?'

Wit attacked the instrument. Music ripped through the small room. Kaladin rose to his feet as the notes reached new heights.

'Upon that land of dirt and soil,' Wit shouted, 'our hero fell and did not stir! His body spent, his strength undone, Fleet the hero was no more.

'The storm approached and found him there. It stilled and stopped upon its course! The rains they fell, the winds they blew, but forward they could not progress.

'For glory lit, and life alive, for goals unreached and aims to strive. All men must try, the wind did see. It is the test, it is the dream.'

Kaladin stepped slowly up to the bars. Even with eyes open, he could see it. Imagine it.

'So in that land of dirt and soil, our hero stopped the storm itself. And while the rain came down like tears, our Fleet refused to end this race. His body dead, but not his will, within those winds his soul did *rise*.

'It flew upon the day's last song, to win the race and claim the dawn. Past the sea and past the waves, our Fleet no longer lost his breath. Forever strong, forever fast, forever free to race the wind.'

Kaladin rested his hands against the bars of his cage. The music rang in the room, then slowly died.

Kaladin gave it a moment, Wit looking at his instrument, a proud smile on his lips. Finally, he tucked his instrument under his arm, took his bag and sword, and walked toward the doorway out.

'What does it mean?' Kaladin whispered.

'It's your story. You decide.'

'But you already knew it.'

'I know most stories, but I'd never sung this one before.' Wit looked back at him, smiling. 'What *does* it mean, Kaladin of Bridge Four? Kaladin Stormblessed?'

'The storm caught him,' Kaladin said.

'The storm catches everyone, eventually. Does it matter?'

'I don't know.'

'Good.' Wit tipped his sword up toward his forehead, as if in respect. 'Then you have something to think about.'

He left.

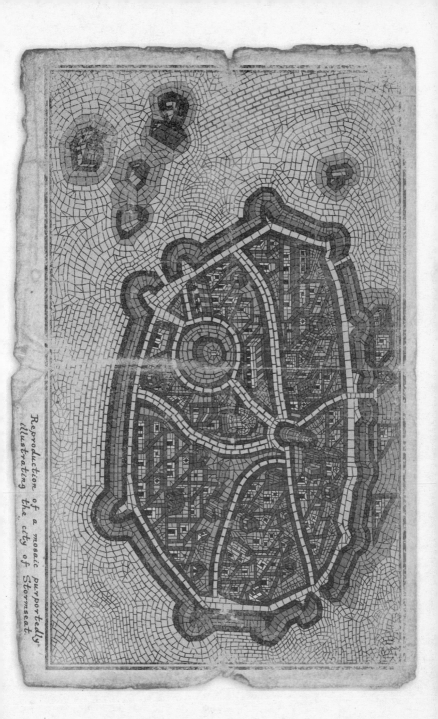

Reproduction of a mosaic purportedly illustrating the city of Stormseat.

Have you given up on the gemstone, now that it is dead? And do you no longer hide behind the name of your old master? I am told that in your current incarnation you've taken a name that references what you presume to be one of your virtues.

'Aha!' Shallan said. She scrambled across her fluffy bed – sinking down practically to her neck with each motion – and leaned precariously over the side. She scrabbled among the stacks of papers on the floor, tossing aside irrelevant sheets.

Finally, she retrieved the one she wanted, holding it up while pushing hair out of her eyes and tucking it behind her ears. The page was a map, one of those ancient ones that Jasnah had talked about. It had taken forever to find a merchant at the Shattered Plains who had a copy.

'Look,' Shallan said, holding the map beside a modern one of the same area, copied by her own hand from Amaram's wall.

Bastard, she noted to herself.

She turned the maps around so that Pattern – who decorated the wall above her headboard – could see them.

'Maps,' he said.

'A pattern!' Shallan exclaimed. 'I see no pattern.'

'Look right here,' she said, edging over beside the wall. 'On this old map, the area is . . .'

'Natanatan,' Pattern read, then hummed softly.

'One of the Epoch Kingdoms,' Shallan said. 'Organized by the Heralds themselves for divine purposes and blah blah. But *look*.' She stabbed the page with her finger. 'The capital of Natanatan, Stormseat. If you were to judge where we'd find the ruins of it, comparing this old map to the one Amaram had . . .'

'It would be in those mountains somewhere,' Pattern said, 'between the words "Dawn's Shadow" and the *U* in "Unclaimed Hills."'

'No, no,' Shallan said. 'Use a little imagination! The old map is wildly inaccurate. Stormseat was *right here*. On the Shattered Plains.'

'That is not what the map says,' Pattern said, humming.

'Close enough.'

'That is *not* a pattern,' he said, sounding offended. 'Humans; you do not understand patterns. Like right now. It is second moon. Each night, you sleep during this time. But not tonight.'

'I can't sleep tonight.'

'More information, please,' Pattern said. 'Why *not* tonight? Is it the day of the week? Do you always not sleep on Jesel? Or is it the weather? Has it grown too warm? The position of the moons relative to—'

'It's none of that,' Shallan said, shrugging. 'I just can't sleep.'

'Your body is capable of it, surely.'

'Probably,' Shallan said. 'But not my head. It surges with too many ideas, like waves against the rocks. Rocks that . . . I guess . . . are also in my head.' She cocked her head. 'I don't think that metaphor makes me sound particularly bright.'

'But—'

'No more complaints,' Shallan said, raising a finger. 'Tonight, I am doing *scholarship*.'

She put the page down on her bed, then leaned over the side, fishing out several others.

'I *wasn't* complaining,' Pattern complained. He moved down onto the bed beside her. 'I do not remember well, but did Jasnah not use a *desk* when . . . "doing scholarship"?'

'Desks are for boring people,' Shallan said. 'And for people who don't have a squishy bed.' Would Dalinar's camp have had such a plush bed for her? Likely, the workload would have been smaller. Though, finally, she'd managed to finish sorting through Sebarial's personal finances and was almost ready to present him with a set of relatively neat books.

In a stroke of insight, she'd slipped a copy of one of her pages of quotes about Urithiru – its potential riches, and its connection to the Shattered Plains – in among the other reports she'd sent Palona. At the bottom, she wrote, 'Among Jasnah Kholin's notes are these indications of something valuable hidden out on the Shattered Plains. Will keep you informed of my discoveries.' If Sebarial thought there was opportunity beyond gem-hearts out on the Plains, she might be able to get him to take her out there with his armies, in case Adolin's promises didn't come through.

Getting all of that ready had left her with little time for studying, un-fortunately. Perhaps that was why she couldn't sleep. *This would be easier,* Shallan thought, *if Navani would agree to meet with me.* She'd written again, and gotten the reply that Navani was busy caring for Dalinar, who had come down with a sickness. Nothing life-threatening, apparently, but he had withdrawn for a few days to recuperate.

Did Adolin's aunt blame her for botching the dueling agreement? After what Adolin had decided to do last week . . . Well, at least his pre-occupation left Shallan with some time to read and think about Urithiru. Anything other than worrying about her brothers, who still hadn't re-sponded to her letters pleading for them to leave Jah Keved and come to her.

'I find sleeping very odd,' Pattern said. 'I know that all beings in the Physical Realm engage in it. Do you find it pleasant? You fear nonexist-ence, but is not unconsciousness the same thing?'

'With sleep, it's only temporary.'

'Ah. It is all right, because in the morning, you each return to sentience.'

'Well, that depends on the person,' Shallan said absently. 'For many of them, "sentience" might be too generous a term. . . .'

Pattern hummed, trying to sort through to the meaning of what she said. Finally, he buzzed an approximation of a laugh.

Shallan cocked an eyebrow at him.

'I have guessed that what you said is humorous,' Pattern said. 'Though I do not know why. It was not a joke. I know of jokes. A soldier came running into camp after going to see the prostitutes. He was white in the face. His friends asked if he had found a good time. He said that he had not. They asked why. He said that when he'd asked how much the woman charged, she'd said one mark plus the tip. He told his friends that he hadn't realized they were charging body parts now.'

Shallan grimaced. 'You heard that from Vathah's men, didn't you?'

'Yes. It is funny because the word "tip" means several different things. A payment made in addition to the sum initially charged, usually given voluntarily, and the top piece of something. In addition, I believe that "the tip" means something in the slang of the soldiers, and so the man in the joke thought she was going to cut off his—'

'Yes, thank you,' Shallan said.

'That is a joke,' Pattern continued. 'I understand why it is funny. Ha ha. Sarcasm is similar. You replace an expected result with one grossly unexpected, and the humor is in the juxtaposition. But why was your earlier comment funny?'

'It's debatable whether it was, at this point....'

'But—'

'Pattern, nothing is *less* funny than explaining humor,' Shallan said. 'We have more important things to discuss.'

'Mmm . . . Such as why you have forgotten how to make your images produce sound? You did it once, long ago.'

. . .

Shallan blinked, then held up the modern map. 'The capital of Natanatan *was* here, on the Shattered Plains. The old maps are misleading. Amaram notes that the Parshendi use weapons of masterly design, far beyond their skill in craftsmanship. Where would they have gotten those? From the ruins of the city that once was here.'

Shallan dug in her stacks of papers, getting out a map of the city itself. It didn't show the surrounding area – it was just a city map, and a rather vague one, taken from a book she'd purchased. She thought it was the one that Jasnah referenced in her notes.

The merchant she'd bought it from claimed it was ancient – that it was a copy of a copy from a book in Azir that claimed to be a drawing of a tile mosaic depiction of the city of Stormseat. The mosaic no longer existed – so much of what they had of the shadowdays came from fragments like these.

'Scholars reject the idea that Stormseat was here on the Plains,' Shallan said. 'They say that the craters of the warcamps don't match the descriptions of the city. Instead, they propose that the ruins must be hidden up in the highlands, where you indicated. But Jasnah didn't agree with them. She points out that few of the scholars have actually been here, and that this area in general is poorly explored.'

'Mmm,' Pattern said. 'Shallan . . .'

'I agree with Jasnah,' Shallan said, turning from him. 'Stormseat wasn't a large city. It could have been in the middle of the Plains, and these craters something else. . . . Amaram says here he thinks they might once have been domes. I wonder if that is even possible. . . . They'd be so large. . . . Anyway, this might have been a satellite city of some sort.'

Shallan felt like she was getting close to something. Amaram's notes spoke mostly of trying to meet with the Parshendi, to ask them about the Voidbringers and how to return them. He did mention Urithiru, however, and seemed to have come to the same conclusion as Jasnah – that the ancient city of Stormseat would have contained a path to Urithiru. Ten of them had once connected the ten capitals of the Epoch Kingdoms to Urithiru, which had some kind of conference room for the ten monarchs of the Epoch Kingdoms – and a throne for each one.

That was why none of the maps placed the holy city in the same location. It was ridiculous to walk there; instead, you made for the nearest city with an Oathgate and used that.

He's searching for the information there, Shallan thought. *Same as I am. But he wants to return the Voidbringers, not fight them. Why?*

She held up the antique map of Stormseat, the copy from the mosaic. It had artistic stylings instead of specific indications of things like distance and location. While she appreciated the former, the latter was truly frustrating.

Are you on here? she thought. *The secret, the Oathgate? Are you here, on this dais, as Jasnah thought?*

'The Shattered Plains haven't always been shattered,' Shallan whispered to herself. 'That's what the scholars, all but Jasnah, are missing. Stormseat was destroyed during the Last Desolation, but it was so long ago, nobody talks about *how*. Fire? Earthquake? No. Something more terrible. The city was broken, like a piece of fine dinnerware hit with a hammer.'

'Shallan,' Pattern said, moving closer to her. 'I know that you have forgotten much of what once was. Those lies attracted me. But you cannot continue like this; you must admit the truth about me. About what I can do, and what we have done. Mmm ... More, you *must* know yourself. And remember.'

She sat cross-legged on the too-nice bed. Memories tried to claw their way out of the boxes inside her head. Those memories all pointed one way, toward carpet bloodied. And carpet ... not.

'You wish to help,' Pattern said. 'You wish to prepare for the Everstorm, the spren of the unnatural one. You must become something. I did not come to you merely to teach you tricks of light.'

'You came to learn,' Shallan said, staring at her map. 'That's what you said.'

'I came to learn. We became to do something greater.'

'Would you have me unable to laugh?' she demanded, suddenly holding back tears. 'Would you have me crippled? That is what those memories would do to me. I can *be* what I *am* because I cut them off.'

An image formed in front of her, born of Stormlight, created by instinct. She hadn't needed to draw this image first, for she knew it too well.

The image was of herself. Shallan, as she *should* be. Curled in a huddle on the bed, unable to weep for she had long since run out of tears. This girl ... not a woman, a girl ... flinched whenever spoken to. She expected everyone to shout at her. She could not laugh, for laughter had been squeezed from her by a childhood of darkness and pain.

That was the real Shallan. She knew it as surely as she knew her own name. The person she had become instead was a lie, one she had fabricated in the name of survival. To remember herself as a child, discovering Light in the gardens, Patterns in the stonework, and dreams that became real ...

...

'Mmmm ... Such a deep lie,' Pattern whispered. 'A deep lie indeed. But still, you must obtain your abilities. Learn again, if you have to.'

'Very well,' Shallan said. 'But if we did this before, can't you just tell me how it is done?'

'My memory is weak,' Pattern said. 'I was dumb so long, nearly dead. Mmm. I could not speak.'

'Yeah,' Shallan said, remembering him spinning on the ground and running into the wall. 'You were kind of cute, though.' She banished the image of the frightened, huddled, whimpering girl, then got out her drawing implements. She tapped a pencil against her lips, then did something simple, a drawing of Veil, the darkeyed con woman.

Veil was not Shallan. Her features were different enough that the two of them would be distinct individuals to anyone who happened to see them both. Still, Veil did bear echoes of Shallan. She was a darkeyed, tanskinned, Alethi version of Shallan – a Shallan that was a few years older and had a pointier nose and chin.

Finished with the drawing, Shallan breathed out Stormlight and created the image. It stood beside the bed, arms folded, looking as confident as a master duelist facing a child with a stick.

Sound. How would she do sound? Pattern had called it a force, part of the Surge of Illumination – or at least similar to it. She situated herself on the bed, one leg folded beneath her, inspecting Veil. Over the next hour, Shallan tried everything she could think of, from straining herself and concentrating, to trying to *draw* sounds to make them appear. Nothing worked.

Finally, she climbed off the bed and walked to get herself a drink from the bottle chilling in the bucket in the next room. As she approached it, however, she felt a *tugging* inside of her. She looked over her shoulder into the bedroom, and saw that the image of Veil had started to blur, like smudged pencil lines.

Blast, but that was inconvenient. Sustaining the illusion required Shallan to provide a constant source of Stormlight. She walked back into the bedroom and set a sphere on the floor inside of Veil's foot. When she walked away, the illusion still grew indistinct, like a bubble preparing to pop. Shallan turned and put her hands on her hips, staring at the version of Veil that had gone all fuzzy.

'Annoying!' she snapped.

Pattern hummed. 'I'm sorry that your mystical, godlike powers do not instantly work as you would like them to.'

She raised an eyebrow at him. 'I thought you didn't understand humor.'

'I do. I just explained ...' He paused for a moment. 'Was I being funny? Sarcasm. I was *sarcastic*. By accident!' He seemed surprised, even gleeful.

'I guess you're learning.'

'It is the bond,' he explained. 'In Shadesmar, I do not communicate this way, this ... human way. My connection to you gives me the means by which I can manifest in the Physical Realm as more than a mindless glimmer. Mmmm. It links me to you, helps me communicate as you do. Fascinating. Mmmm.'

He settled down like a trumping axehound, perfectly content. And then Shallan noticed something.

'I'm not glowing,' Shallan said. 'I'm holding a lot of Stormlight, but I'm not glowing.'

'Mmm ...' Pattern said. 'Large illusion transforms the Surge into another. Feeds off your Stormlight.'

She nodded. The Stormlight she held fed the illusion, drawing the excess from her that would normally float above her skin. That could be useful. As Pattern moved up onto the bed, Veil's elbow – which was closest to him – grew more distinct.

Shallan frowned. 'Pattern, move closer to the image.'

He obliged, crossing the cover of her bed toward where Veil stood. She unfuzzed. Not completely, but his presence made a noticeable difference.

Shallan walked over, her proximity making the illusion snap back to full clarity.

'Can you hold Stormlight?' Shallan asked Pattern.

'I don't ... I mean ... Investiture is the means by which I ...'

'Here,' Shallan said, pressing her hand down on him, muffling his words to an annoyed buzzing. It was an odd sensation, as if she'd trapped an angry cremling under the bedsheets. She pushed some Stormlight into him. When she lifted her hand, he was trailing wisps of it, like steam off a hotplate fabrial.

'We're bonded,' she said. 'My illusion is your illusion. I'm going to get a drink. See if you can keep the image from breaking apart.' She backed to the sitting room and smiled. Pattern, still buzzing with annoyance, moved down off the bed. She couldn't see him – the bed was in the way – but she guessed he'd gone to Veil's feet.

It worked. The illusion stayed. 'Ha!' Shallan said, getting herself a cup of wine. She walked back and eased onto the bed – flopping down with a cup of red wine did not seem prudent – and looked over the side at the floor, where Pattern sat beneath Veil. He was visible because of the Stormlight.

I'll need to take that into account, Shallan thought. *Build illusions so that he can hide in them.*

'It worked?' Pattern said. 'How did you know it would work?'

'I didn't.' Shallan took a sip of wine. 'I guessed.'

She drank another sip as Pattern hummed. Jasnah would not have approved. *Scholarship requires a sharp mind and alert senses. These do not mix with alcohol.* Shallan drank the rest of the wine in a gulp.

'Here,' Shallan said, reaching down. She did the next bit by instinct. She had a connection to the illusion, and she had a connection to Pattern, so . . .

With a *push* of Stormlight, she attached the illusion to Pattern as she often attached them to herself. His glow subsided. 'Walk around,' she said.

'I don't walk . . .' Pattern said.

'You know what I mean,' Shallan said.

Pattern moved, and the image moved with him. It didn't walk, unfortunately. The image just kind of glided. Like light reflected onto the wall from a spoon you idly turned in your hands. She cheered to herself anyway. After so long failing to get sounds from one of her creations, this different discovery seemed a major victory.

Could she get it to move more naturally? She settled down with her sketchpad and started drawing.

61

OBEDIENCE

ONE AND A HALF YEARS AGO

Shallan became the perfect daughter.

She kept quiet, particularly in Father's presence. She spent most days in her room, sitting by the window, reading the same books over and over or sketching the same objects again and again. He had proven several times by this point that he would not touch her if she angered him.

Instead, he would beat others in her name.

The only times she allowed herself to drop the mask was when she was with her brothers, times when her father couldn't hear. Her three brothers often cajoled her – with an edge of desperation – to tell them stories from her books. For their hearing only, she made jokes, poked fun at Father's visitors, and invented extravagant tales by the hearth.

Such an insignificant way to fight back. She felt a coward for not doing more. But surely . . . surely things would get better now. Indeed, as Shallan was involved more by the ardents in accounts, she noted a shrewdness to the way her father stopped being bullied by other lighteyes and started playing them against each other. He impressed her, but frightened her, in how he seized for power. Father's fortunes changed further when a new marble deposit was discovered on his lands – providing resources to keep up with his promises, bribes, and deals.

Surely that would make him start laughing again. Surely that would drive the darkness from his eyes.

It did not.

⁖

'She is too low for you to marry,' Father said, setting down his mug. 'I won't have it, Balat. You will break off contact with that woman.'

'She belongs to a good family!' Balat said, standing, palms on the table. It was lunch, and so Shallan was expected to be here, rather than remaining shut up in her room. She sat to the side, at her private table. Balat stood facing Father across the high table.

'Father, they're your vassals!' Balat snapped. 'You yourself have invited them to dine with us.'

'My axehounds dine at my feet,' Father said. 'I do not allow my sons to court them. House Tavinar is not nearly ambitious enough for us. Now, Sudi Valam, that might be worth considering.'

Balat frowned. 'The highprince's daughter? You can't be serious. She's in her fifties!'

'She is single.'

'Because her husband died in a duel! Anyway, the highprince would never approve it.'

'His perception of us will change,' Father said. 'We are a wealthy family now, with much influence.'

'Yet still headed by a murderer,' Balat snapped.

Too far! Shallan thought. On Father's other side, Luesh laced his fingers in front of him. The new house steward had a face like a well-worn glove, leathery and wrinkled in the places most used – notably the frown lines.

Father stood up slowly. This new anger of his, the cold anger, terrified Shallan. 'Your new axehound pups,' he said to Balat. 'Terrible that they caught a sickness during the latest highstorm. Tragic. It is unfortunate they need to be put down.' He gestured, and one of his new guards – a man Shallan did not know well – stepped outside, pulling his sword from its sheath.

Shallan grew very cold. Even Luesh grew concerned, placing a hand on Father's arm.

'You bastard,' Balat said, growing pale. 'I'll—'

'You'll *what*, Balat?' Father asked, shaking off Luesh's touch, leaning toward Balat. 'Come on. Say it. Will you challenge me? Don't think I wouldn't kill you if you did. Wikim may be a pathetic wreck, but he will serve just as well as you for what this house needs.'

'Helaran is back,' Balat said.

Father froze, hands on the table, unmoving.

'I saw him two days ago,' Balat said. 'He sent for me, and I rode out to meet him in the city. Helaran—'

'That name is *not* to be spoken in this house!' Father said. 'I mean it, *Nan* Balat! Never.'

Balat met his father's gaze, and Shallan counted ten beats of her thumping heart before Balat broke the stare and looked away.

Father sat down, looking exhausted as Balat stalked out of the room. The hall fell completely silent, Shallan too frightened to speak. Father eventually stood up, shoving his chair back and leaving. Luesh trailed soon after.

That left Shallan alone with the servants. Timidly she stood up, then went after Balat.

He was in the kennel. The guard had worked swiftly. Balat's new pod of pups lay dead in a pool of violet blood on the stone floor.

She'd encouraged Balat to breed these. He'd been making progress with his demons, over the years. He rarely hurt anything larger than a cremling. Now he sat on a box, looking down at the small corpses, horrified. Painspren cluttered the ground near him.

The metal gate into the kennel rattled as Shallan pushed it open. She raised her safehand to her mouth as she drew closer to the pitiful remains. 'Father's guards,' Balat said. 'It's like they were *waiting* for a chance to do something like this. I don't like the new group he has. That Levrin, with the angry eyes, and Rin . . . that one frightens me. What ever happened to Ten and Beal? Soldiers that you could joke with. Almost friends . . .'

She rested a hand on his shoulder. 'Balat. Did you really see Helaran?'

'Yes. He said I wasn't to tell anyone. He warned me that this time when he left, he might not be coming back for a long time. He told me . . . told me to watch over the family.' Balat buried his head in his hands. 'I can't be him, Shallan.'

'You don't need to be.'

'He's brave. He's strong.'

'He abandoned us.'

Balat looked up, tears running down his cheeks. 'Maybe he was right. Maybe that's the only way, Shallan.'

'Leave our house?'

'What of it?' Balat asked. 'You spend every day locked away, brought out only for Father to display. Jushu has gone back to his gambling – you know he has, even if he's smarter about it. Wikim talks about becoming an ardent, but I don't know if Father will ever let go of him. He's insurance.'

It was, unfortunately, a good argument. 'Where would we go?' Shallan asked. 'We have nothing.'

'I have nothing here either,' Balat said. 'I'm not going to give up on Eylita, Shallan. She's the only beautiful thing that has happened in my life. If she and I have to go live in Vedenar as tenth dahn, with me working as a house guard or something like that, we'll do it. Doesn't that seem a better life than this?' He gestured toward the dead pups.

'Perhaps.'

'Would you go with me? If I took Eylita and left? You could be a scribe. Earn your own way, be free of Father.'

'I . . . No. I need to stay.'

'Why?'

'Something has hold of Father, something awful. If we all leave, we give him to it. Someone has to help him.'

'Why do you defend him so? You know what he did.'

'He didn't do it.'

'You can't remember,' Balat said. 'You've told me over and over that your mind blanks. You saw him kill her, but you don't want to admit that you witnessed it. Storms, Shallan. You're as broken as Wikim and Jushu. As . . . as I am sometimes . . .'

She shook off her numbness.

'It doesn't matter,' she said. 'If you go, are you going to take Wikim and Jushu with you?'

'I couldn't afford to,' Balat said. 'Jushu in particular. We'd have to live lean, and I couldn't trust that he'd . . . you know. But if you came, it might be easier for one of us to find work. You're better at writing and art than Eylita.'

'No, Balat,' Shallan said, frightened of how eager a part of her was to say yes to him. 'I *can't*. Particularly if Jushu and Wikim remain here.'

'I see,' he said. 'Maybe . . . maybe there's another way out. I'll think.'

She left him in the kennel, worried that Father would find her there and that it would upset him. She entered the manor, but couldn't help feeling that she was trying to hold together a carpet as dozens of people pulled out threads from the sides.

What would happen if Balat left? He backed down from fights with Father, but at least he resisted. Wikim merely did what he was told, and Jushu was still a mess. *We have to just weather this*, Shallan thought. *Stop provoking Father, let him relax. Then he'll come back. . . .*

She climbed the steps and passed Father's door. It was open a crack; she could hear him inside.

'. . . find him in Valath,' Father said. 'Nan Balat claims to have met him in the city, and that is what he must have meant.'

'It will be done, Brightlord.' That voice. It was Rin, captain of Father's new guards. Shallan backed up, peeking into the room. Father's strongbox shone behind the picture on the back wall, bright light bursting through the canvas. To her it was almost blinding, though the men in the room didn't seem able to see it.

Rin bowed before Father, hand on sword.

'Bring me his head, Rin,' Father said. 'I want to see it with my own eyes. He is the one who could ruin all of this. Surprise him, kill him before he can summon his Shardblade. That weapon will be yours in payment so long as you serve House Davar.'

Shallan stumbled back from the door before Father could look up and see her. Helaran. Father had just ordered *Helaran's* assassination.

I have to do something. I have to warn him. How? Could Balat contact him again? Shallan—

'How dare you,' said a feminine voice within.

Stunned silence followed. Shallan edged back to look into the room. Malise, her stepmother, stood in the doorway between the bedroom and the sitting room. The small, plump woman had never seemed threatening to Shallan before. But the storm on her face today could have frightened a whitespine.

'Your own *son*,' Malise said. 'Have you no morals left? Have you no compassion?'

'He is no longer my son,' Father growled.

'I believed your story about the woman before me,' Malise said. 'I've supported you. I've lived with this cloud over the house. Now I hear *this*? It is one thing to beat the servants, but to kill your *son*?'

Father whispered something to Rin. Shallan jumped, and barely got down the hallway to her room before the man slipped out of the room, then closed Father's door with a *click*.

Shallan shut herself in her room as the shouting started, a violent, angry back-and-forth between Malise and her father. Shallan huddled up beside the bed, tried to use a pillow to keep out the sounds. When she thought it was over, she removed the pillow.

Her father stormed out into the hallway. 'Why will nobody in this house *obey*?' he shouted, thumping down the stairs. 'This wouldn't happen if you all just obeyed.'

62

THE ONE WHO
KILLED PROMISES

This is, I suspect, a little like a skunk naming itself for its stench.

Life continued in Kaladin's cell. Though the accommodations were nice for a dungeon, he found himself wishing he were back in the slave wagon. At least then he'd been able to watch the scenery. Fresh air, wind, an occasional rinse in the highstorm's last rains. Life certainly hadn't been good, but it had been better than being locked away and forgotten.

They took the spheres away at night, abandoning him to blackness. In the dark, he found himself imagining that he was someplace deep, with miles of stone above him and no pathway out, no hope of rescue. He could not conceive a worse death. Better to be gutted on the battlefield, looking up at the open sky as your life leaked away.

❖

Light awoke him. He sighed, watching the ceiling as the guards – light-eyed soldiers he didn't know – replaced the lamp spheres. Day after day, everything was the storming *same* in here. Waking to the frail light of spheres, which only made him wish for the sun. The servant arrived to give him his breakfast. He'd placed his chamber pot in reach of the opening at the bottom of the bars, and it scraped stone as she pulled it out and replaced it with a fresh one.

She scurried away. He frightened her. With a groan at stiff muscles, Kaladin sat up and regarded his meal. Flatbread stuffed with bean paste. He stood, waving away some strange spren like taut wires crossing before him, then forced himself to do a set of push-ups. Keeping his strength up would be difficult if the imprisonment continued too long. Perhaps he could ask for some stones to use for training.

Was this what happened to Moash's grandparents? Kaladin wondered, taking the food. *Waiting for a trial until they died in prison?*

Kaladin sat back on his bench, nibbling on the flatbread. There'd been a highstorm yesterday, but he'd barely been able to hear it, locked away in this room.

He heard Syl humming nearby, but couldn't find where she'd gone. 'Syl?' he asked. She kept hiding from him.

'There was a Cryptic at the fight,' her voice said softly.

'You mentioned those before, didn't you? A type of spren?'

'A revolting type.' She paused. 'But not evil, I don't think.' She sounded begrudging. 'I was going to follow it, as it fled, but you needed me. When I went back to look, it had hidden from me.'

'What does it mean?' Kaladin asked, frowning.

'Cryptics like to plan,' Syl said slowly, as if recalling something long lost. 'Yes . . . I remember. They debate and watch and never *do* anything. But . . .'

'What?' Kaladin asked, rising.

'They're looking for someone,' Syl said. 'I've seen the signs. Soon, you might not be alone, Kaladin.'

Looking for someone. To choose, like him, as a Surgebinder. What kind of Knight Radiant had been made by a group of spren Syl so obviously detested? It didn't seem like someone he'd want to get to know.

Oh, storms, Kaladin thought, sitting back down. *If they choose Adolin . . .*

The thought should have made him sick. Instead, he found Syl's revelation oddly comforting. Not being alone, even if it *did* turn out to be Adolin, made him feel better and drove away some small measure of his gloom.

As he was finishing his meal, a thump came from the hallway. The door opening? Only lighteyes could visit him, though so far none had. Unless you counted Wit.

The storm catches everyone, eventually. . . .

Dalinar Kholin stepped into the room.

Despite his sour thoughts, Kaladin's immediate reaction – drilled into him over the years – was to stand and salute, hand to breast. This was his commanding officer. He felt an idiot as soon as he did it. He stood behind bars and saluted the man who'd put him here?

'At ease,' Dalinar said with a nod. The wide-shouldered man stood with hands clasped behind his back. Something about Dalinar was imposing, even when he was relaxed.

He looks like the generals from the stories, Kaladin thought. Thick of face and greying of hair, solid in the same way that a brick was. He didn't wear a uniform, the uniform wore *him.* Dalinar Kholin represented an ideal that Kaladin had long since decided was a mere fancy.

'How are your accommodations?' Dalinar asked.

'Sir? I'm in storming *prison.*'

A smile cracked Dalinar's face. 'So I see. Calm yourself, soldier. If I'd ordered you to guard a room for a week, would you have done it?'

'Yes.'

'Then consider this your duty. Guard this room.'

'I'll make sure nobody unauthorized runs off with the chamber pot, sir.'

'Elhokar is coming around. He's finished cooling off, and now only worries that releasing you too quickly will make him look weak. I'll need you to stay here a few more days, then we'll draft a formal pardon for your crime and have you reinstated to your position.'

'I don't see that I have any choice, sir.'

Dalinar stepped closer to the bars. 'This is hard for you.'

Kaladin nodded.

'You are well cared for, as are your men. Two of your bridgemen guard the way into the building at all times. There is nothing to worry you, soldier. If it's your reputation with me—'

'Sir,' Kaladin said. 'I guess I'm just not convinced that the king will ever let me go. He has a history of letting inconvenient people rot in dungeons until they die.'

As soon as he said the words, Kaladin couldn't believe they'd come from his lips. They sounded insubordinate, even treasonous. But they'd been sitting there, in his mouth, *demanding* to be spoken.

Dalinar remained in his posture with hands clasped behind his back. 'You speak of the silversmiths back in Kholinar?'

So he did know. Stormfather . . . had Dalinar been involved? Kaladin nodded.

'How did you hear of that incident?'

'From one of my men,' Kaladin said. 'He knew the imprisoned people.'

'I had hoped we could escape those rumors,' Dalinar said. 'But of course, rumor grows like lichen, crusted on and impossible to completely scrub free. What happened with those people was a mistake, soldier. I'll admit that freely. The same won't happen to you.'

'Are the rumors about them true, then?'

'I would really rather not speak of the Roshone affair.'

Roshone.

Kaladin remembered screams. Blood on the floor of his father's surgery room. A dying boy.

A day in the rain. A day when one man tried to steal away Kaladin's light. He eventually succeeded.

'Roshone?' Kaladin whispered.

'Yes, a minor lighteyes,' Dalinar said, sighing.

'Sir, it's important that I know of this. For my own peace of mind.'

Dalinar looked him up and down. Kaladin just stared straight ahead, mind . . . numb. Roshone. Everything had started to go wrong when Roshone had arrived in Hearthstone to be the new citylord. Before then, Kaladin's father had been respected.

When that horrid man had arrived, dragging petty jealousy behind him like a cloak, the world had twisted upon itself. Roshone had infected Hearthstone like rotspren on an unclean wound. He was the reason Tien had gone to war. He was the reason Kaladin had followed.

'I suppose I owe you this,' Dalinar said. 'But it is not to be spread around. Roshone was a petty man who gained Elhokar's ear. Elhokar was crown prince then, commanded to rule over Kholinar and watch the kingdom while his father organized our first camps here in the Shattered Plains. I was . . . away at the time.

'Anyway, do not blame Elhokar. He was taking the advice of someone he trusted. Roshone, however, sought his own interests instead of those of the Throne. He owned several silversmith shops . . . well, the details are not important. Suffice it to say that Roshone led the prince to make some errors. I cleared it up when I returned.'

'You saw this Roshone punished?' Kaladin asked, voice soft, feeling numb.

'Exiled,' Dalinar said, nodding. 'Elhokar moved the man to a place where he couldn't do any more harm.'

A place he couldn't do any more harm. Kaladin almost laughed.

'You have something to say?'

'You don't want to know what I think, sir.'

'Perhaps I don't. I probably need to hear it anyway.'

Dalinar *was* a good man. Blinded in some ways, but a good man. 'Well, sir,' Kaladin said, controlling his emotions with difficulty, 'I find it ... troubling that a man like this Roshone could be responsible for the deaths of innocent people, yet escape prison.'

'It was complicated, soldier. Roshone was one of Highprince Sadeas's sworn liegemen, cousin to important men whose support we needed. I originally argued that Roshone should be stripped of station and made a tenner, forced to live his life in squalor. But this would have alienated allies, and could have undermined the kingdom. Elhokar argued for leniency toward Roshone, and his father agreed via spanreed. I relented, figuring that mercy was not an attribute I should discourage in Elhokar.'

'Of course not,' Kaladin said, clenching his teeth. 'Though it seems that such mercy often ends up serving the cousins of powerful lighteyes, and rarely someone lowly.' He stared through the bars between himself and Dalinar.

'Soldier,' Dalinar asked, voice cool. 'Do you think I've been unfair toward you or your men?'

'You. No, sir. But this isn't about you.'

Dalinar exhaled softly, as if in frustration. 'Captain, you and your men are in a unique position. You spend your daily lives around the king. You don't see the face that is presented to the world, you see the *man*. It has ever been so for close bodyguards.

'So your loyalty needs to be extra firm and generous. Yes, the man you guard has flaws. Every man does. He is still your king, and I *will* have your respect.'

'I can and do respect the Throne, sir,' Kaladin said. Not the man sitting in it, perhaps. But he did respect the office. Somebody needed to rule.

'Son,' Dalinar said after a moment's thought, 'do you know why I put you into the position that I did?'

'You said it was because you needed someone you could trust not to be a spy for Sadeas.'

'That's the rationale,' Dalinar said, stepping up closer to the bars, only inches from Kaladin. 'But it's not the *reason*. I did it because it felt right.'

Kaladin frowned.

'I trust my hunches,' Dalinar said. 'My gut said you were a man who could help change this kingdom. A man who could live through Damnation itself in Sadeas's camp and still somehow inspire others was a man I wanted under my command.' His expression grew harder. 'I gave you a position no darkeyes has ever held in this army. I let you into conferences with the king, and I listened when you spoke. Do *not* make me regret those decisions, soldier.'

'You don't already?' Kaladin asked.

'I've come close,' Dalinar said. 'I understand, though. If you truly believe what you told me about Amaram . . . well, if I'd been in your place, I'd have been hard pressed not to do the same thing you did. But storm it, man, you're still a *darkeyes*.'

'It shouldn't matter.'

'Maybe it shouldn't, but it *does*. You want to change that? Well, you're not going to do it by screaming like a lunatic and challenging men like Amaram to duels. You'll do it by distinguishing yourself in the position I gave you. Be the kind of man that others admire, whether they be light-eyed or dark. Convince Elhokar that a darkeyes can lead. *That* will change the world.'

Dalinar turned and walked away. Kaladin couldn't help thinking that the man's shoulders seemed more bowed than when he'd entered.

After Dalinar left, Kaladin sat back on his bench, letting out a long, annoyed breath. 'Stay calm,' he whispered. 'Do as you're told, Kaladin. Stay in your cage.'

'He's trying to help,' Syl said.

Kaladin glanced to the side. Where *was* she hiding? 'You heard about Roshone.'

Silence.

'Yes,' Syl finally said, voice sounding small.

'My family's poverty,' Kaladin said, 'the way the town ostracized us,

Tien being forced into the army, these things were all Roshone's fault. Elhokar sent him to us.'

Syl didn't respond. Kaladin fished a bit of flatbread from his bowl, chewing on it. Stormfather – Moash really *was* right. This kingdom would be better off without Elhokar. Dalinar tried his best, but he had an enormous blind spot regarding his nephew.

It was time someone stepped in and cut the ties binding Dalinar's hands. For the good of the kingdom, for the good of Dalinar Kholin himself, the king had to die.

Some people – like a festering finger or a leg shattered beyond repair – just needed to be removed.

*Now, look what you've made me say. You've always been able to bring
out the most extreme in me, old friend. And I do still name you a friend,
for all that you weary me.*

W hat are you doing? the spanreed wrote to Shallan.
        Nothing much, she wrote back by spherelight, *just working
on Sebarial's income ledgers.* She peeked out through the hole
in her illusion, regarding the street far below. People flowed through the
city as if marching to some strange rhythm. A dribble, then a burst, then
back to a dribble. Rarely a constant flow. What caused that?

You want to come visit? the pen wrote. *This is getting really boring.*

Sorry, she wrote back to Adolin, *I really need to get this work done. It
might be nice to have a spanreed conversation to keep me company, though.*

Pattern hummed softly beside her at the lie. Shallan had used an illusion to expand the size of the shed atop this tenement in Sebarial's
warcamp, providing a hidden place to sit and watch the street below. Five
hours of waiting – comfortable enough, with the stool and spheres for
light – had revealed nothing. Nobody had approached the lone stone-
barked tree growing beside the pathway.

She didn't know the species. It was too old to have been planted there
recently; it must predate Sebarial's arrival. The gnarled, sturdy bark made
her think it was some variety of dendrolith, but the tree also had long

fronds that rose into the air like streamers, twisting and fluttering in the wind. Those were reminiscent of a dalewillow. She'd already done a sketch; she would look it up in her books later.

The tree was used to people, and didn't pull in its fronds as they passed it. If someone had approached carefully enough to avoid brushing the fronds, Shallan would have spotted them. If, instead, they'd moved quickly, the fronds would have felt the vibrations and withdrawn – which she also would have spotted. She was reasonably certain that if anyone had tried to fetch the item in the tree, she'd have known it, even if she'd been looking away for a moment.

I suppose, the pen wrote, *I can continue to keep you company. Shoren isn't doing anything else.*

Shoren was the ardent who wrote for Adolin today, come to visit by Adolin's order. The prince had pointedly noted that he was using an ardent, rather than one of his father's scribes. Did he think she'd grow jealous if he used another woman for scribing duties?

He did seem surprised that she didn't get jealous. Were the women of the court so petty? Or was Shallan the odd one, too relaxed? His eyes *did* wander, and she had to admit that wasn't something that pleased her. And there was his reputation to consider. Adolin was said to have, in the past, changed relationships as frequently as other men changed coats.

Perhaps she should cling more firmly, but the thought of it nauseated her. Such behavior reminded her of Father, holding so tightly to everything that he eventually broke it all.

Yes, she wrote back to Adolin, using the board set on a box beside her, *I'm certain the good ardent has nothing at all better to do than transcribe notes between two courting lighteyes.*

He's an ardent, Adolin sent. *He likes to serve. It's what they do.*

I thought, she wrote, *that saving souls was what they did.*

He's tired of that, Adolin sent. *He told me that he already saved three this morning.*

She smiled, checking on the tree – still no change. *He did, did he?* she wrote. *Has them tucked away in his back pocket for safekeeping, I assume?*

No, Father's way was not right. If she wanted to keep Adolin, she had to try something far more difficult than just clinging to him. She'd have to be so irresistible that he didn't want to let go. Unfortunately, this was one area where neither Jasnah's training nor Tyn's would help. Jasnah had been indifferent toward men, while Tyn had not talked about keeping men, only distracting them for a quick con.

Is your father feeling better? she wrote.

Yes, actually. He's been up and about since yesterday, looking as strong as ever.

Good to hear, she wrote. The two continued exchanging idle comments, Shallan watching the tree. Mraize's note had instructed her to come at sunrise and search the hole in the tree trunk for her instructions. So she'd come four hours early, while the sky was still dark, and sneaked up to the top of this building to watch.

Apparently, she hadn't come early enough. She'd really wanted to get a view of them placing the instructions. 'I don't like this,' Shallan said, whispering to Pattern and ignoring the pen, which scribed Adolin's next line to her. 'Why didn't Mraize just give me the instructions via spanreed? Why make me come here?'

'Mmm . . .' Pattern said from the floor beneath her.

The sun had long since risen. She needed to go get the instructions, but still she hesitated, tapping her finger against the paper-covered board beside her.

'They're watching,' she realized.

'What?' Pattern said.

'They are doing exactly what I did. They are hiding somewhere, and want to watch me pick up the instructions.'

'Why? What does it accomplish?'

'It gives them information,' Shallan said. 'And that is the sort of thing these people thrive upon.' She leaned to the side, peering out of her hole, which would appear from the outside as a gap between two of the bricks.

She didn't think Mraize wanted her dead, despite the sickening incident with the poor carriage driver. He'd given leave for the others around him to kill her, if they feared her, but that – like so much about Mraize – had been a test. *If you really are strong and clever enough to join us,* that incident implied, *then you'll avoid being assassinated by these people.*

This was another test. How did she pass it in a way that didn't leave anyone dead this time?

They'd be watching for her to come get her instructions, but there weren't many good places to keep an eye on the tree. If she were Mraize and his people, where would she go to observe?

She felt silly thinking it. 'Pattern,' she whispered, 'go look in the windows of this building that face the street. See if anyone is sitting in one of them, watching as we are.'

'Very well,' he said, sliding out of her illusion.

She was suddenly conscious of the fact that Mraize's people might be hiding somewhere very close, but shoved aside her nervousness, reading Adolin's reply.

Good news, by the way, the pen wrote. *Father visited last night, and we talked at length. He's preparing his expedition out onto the Plains to fight the Parshendi, once and for all. Part of getting ready involves some scouting missions in the coming days. I got him to agree to bring you out onto the plateaus during one of them.*

And we can find a chrysalis? Shallan asked.

Well, the pen wrote, *even if the Parshendi aren't fighting over those anymore, Father doesn't take risks. I can't bring you on a run when there is a chance they might come and contest us. But, I've been thinking we can probably arrange the scouting mission so it passes by a plateau with a chrysalis a day or so after it was harvested.*

Shallan frowned. *A dead, harvested chrysalis?* she wrote. *I don't know how much that will tell me.*

Well, Adolin replied, *it's better than not seeing one at all, right? And you did say you wanted the chance to cut one up. This is almost the same thing.*

He was right. Besides, getting out onto the Plains was the real goal. *Let's do it. When? In a few days.* 'Shallan!'

She jumped, but it was only Pattern, buzzing with excitement. 'You were right,' he said. 'Mmmm. She watches below. Only one level down, second room.'

'She?'

'Mmm. The one with the mask.'

Shallan shivered. Now what? Go back to her rooms, then write to Mraize and say that she didn't appreciate being spied upon?

It wouldn't accomplish anything useful. Looking down at her pad of paper, she realized that her relationship with Mraize was similar to her relationship with Adolin. In both cases, she couldn't just do as expected. She needed to excite, exceed.

I'll need to go, she wrote to Adolin. *Sebarial is asking for me. It might take me a while.*

She clicked off the spanreed and tucked it and the board away in her satchel. Not her usual one, but a rugged bag with a leather strap that went over her shoulder, like Veil would carry. Then, before she could lose her nerve, she ducked out of her illusory hiding place. She put her back to the wall of the shed, facing away from the street, then touched the side of the illusion and withdrew the Stormlight.

That made the illusory section of wall vanish, quickly breaking down and streaming into her hand. Hopefully, nobody had been looking at the shed at that moment. If they had been, though, they would probably just think the change a trick of the eyes.

Next, she knelt and used Stormlight to infuse Pattern and bind to him an image of Veil from a drawing she'd done earlier. Shallan nodded for him to move, and as he did, the image of Veil walked.

She looked good. A confident stride, a swishing coat, peaked hat shading her face against the sun. The illusion even blinked and turned her head on occasion, as prescribed by the drawing sequence Shallan had done earlier.

She watched, hesitating. Was that actually how she looked while wearing Veil's face and clothing? She didn't feel nearly that poised, and the clothing always seemed exaggerated, even silly, to her. On this image, it looked appropriate.

'Go down,' Shallan whispered to Pattern, 'and walk to the tree. Try to approach carefully, slowly, and buzz loudly to get the tree's leaves to pull back. Stand at the trunk for a moment, as if retrieving the thing inside, then walk to the alleyway between this building and the next.'

'Yes!' Pattern said. He zipped off toward the stairs, excited to be part of the lie.

'Slower!' Shallan said, wincing to see Veil's pace not matching her speed. 'As we practiced!'

Pattern slowed and reached the steps. Veil's image moved down them. Awkwardly. The illusion could walk and stand still on flat ground, but other terrain – such as steps – wasn't accommodated. To anyone watching, it would seem like Veil was stepping on nothing and gliding down the stairs.

Well, it was the best they could do for the moment. Shallan took a deep breath and pulled on her hat, breathing out a second image, one that covered her over and transformed her into Veil. The one on Pattern would remain so long as he had Stormlight. That Stormlight drained from him a lot faster than it did from Shallan, though. She didn't know why.

She went down the steps, but only one level, walking as quietly as she could. She counted over two doors in the dim hallway. The masked woman was inside that one. Shallan left it alone, instead ducking into an alcove by the stairwell, where she would be hidden from anyone in the hallway.

She waited.

A door eventually clicked open, and clothing rustled in the hallway. The masked woman passed Shallan's hiding place, amazingly quiet as she moved down the steps.

'What is your name?' Shallan asked.

The woman froze on the steps. She spun – gloved safehand on the knife at her side – and saw Shallan standing in the alcove. The woman's masked eyes flicked back toward the room she'd left.

'I sent a double,' Shallan said, 'wearing my clothing. That's what you saw.'

The woman did not move, still crouched on the steps.

'Why did he want you to follow me?' Shallan asked. 'He's that interested in finding out where I'm staying?'

'No,' the woman finally said. 'The instructions in the tree call for you to set about a task immediately, with no time to waste.'

Shallan frowned, considering. 'So your job wasn't to follow me home, but to follow me on the mission. To watch how I accomplished it?'

The woman said nothing.

Shallan strolled forward and seated herself on the top step, crossing her arms on her legs. 'So what is the job?'

'The instructions are in—'

'I'd rather hear it from you,' Shallan said. 'Call me lazy.'

'How did you find me?' the woman asked.

'A sharp-eyed ally,' Shallan said. 'I told him to watch the windows, then send me word of where you were. I was waiting up above.' She grimaced. 'I was hoping to catch one of you placing the instructions.'

'We placed them before even contacting you,' the woman said. She hesitated, then took a few steps upward. 'Iyatil.'

Shallan cocked her head.

'My name,' the woman said. 'Iyatil.'

'I've never heard one like it.'

'Unsurprising. Your task today was to investigate a certain new arrival into Dalinar's camp. We wish to know about this person, and Dalinar's allegiances are uncertain.'

'He's loyal to the king and the Throne.'

'Outwardly,' the woman said. 'His brother knew things of an extraordinary nature. We are uncertain if Dalinar was told of these things or not, and his interactions with Amaram worry us. This newcomer is linked.'

'Amaram is making maps of the Shattered Plains,' Shallan said. 'Why? What is out there that he wants?' *And why would he want to return the Voidbringers?*

Iyatil didn't answer.

'Well,' Shallan said, rising, 'let's get to it, then. Shall we?'

'Together?' Iyatil said.

Shallan shrugged. 'You can sneak along behind, or you can just go with me.' She extended her hand.

Iyatil inspected the hand, then clasped it with her own gloved freehand in acceptance. She kept her other hand on the dagger at her side the entire time, though.

◆

Shallan flipped through the instructions Mraize had left, as the oversized palanquin lurched along toward Dalinar's warcamp. Iyatil sat across from Shallan, legs tucked beneath her, watching with beady, masked eyes. The woman wore simple trousers and a shirt, such that Shallan had originally mistaken her for a boy that first time.

Her presence was *thoroughly* unsettling.

'A madman,' Shallan said, flipping to the next page of instructions. 'Mraize is this interested in a simple madman?'

'Dalinar and the king are interested,' Iyatil said. 'So, then, are we.'

There *did* seem to be some sort of cover-up involved. The madman had arrived in the custody of a man named Bordin, a servant whom Dalinar had stationed in Kholinar years ago. Mraize's information indicated that this Bordin was no simple messenger, but instead one of Dalinar's most trusted footmen. He had been left behind in Alethkar to spy on the queen, or so the Ghostbloods inferred. But why would someone need to keep an eye on the queen? The briefing didn't say.

This Bordin had come to the Shattered Plains in haste a few weeks ago, bearing the madman and other mysterious cargo. Shallan's charge was to find out who this madman was and why Dalinar had hidden him away in a monastery with strict instructions that nobody was to be allowed access save specific ardents.

'Your master knows more about this,' Shallan said, 'than he is telling me.'

'My master?' Iyatil asked.

'Mraize.'

The woman laughed. 'You mistake. He is not my master. He is my student.'

'In what?' Shallan asked.

Iyatil stared at her with a level gaze and gave no reply.

'Why the mask?' Shallan asked, leaning forward. 'What does it mean? Why do you hide?'

'I have many times asked myself,' Iyatil said, 'why those of you here go about so brazenly with features exposed to all who would see them. My mask reserves my self. Besides, it gives me the ability to adapt.'

Shallan sat back, thoughtful.

'You are willing to ponder,' Iyatil said. 'Rather than asking question after question. This is good. Your instincts, however, must be judged. Are you the hunter, or are you the quarry?'

'Neither,' Shallan said immediately.

'All are one or the other.'

The palanquin's porters slowed. Shallan peeked out the curtains and found that they had finally reached the edge of Dalinar's warcamp. Here, soldiers at the gates stopped each person in line waiting to enter.

'How will you get us in?' Iyatil asked as Shallan closed the curtains. 'Highprince Kholin has grown cautious of late, with assassins appearing in the night. What lie will gain us access to his realm?'

Delightful, she thought, revising her list of tasks. Shallan not only had to infiltrate the monastery and discover information about this madman, she had to do it without revealing too much about herself – or what she could do – to Iyatil.

She had to think quickly. The soldiers at the front called for the palanquin to approach – lighteyes wouldn't be required to wait in the ordinary line, and the soldiers would assume this nice a vehicle had someone rich inside. Taking a deep breath, Shallan removed her hat, pulled her hair forward over her shoulder, then pushed her face out of the curtains so that her hair hung down before her outside the palanquin. At the same moment, she withdrew her illusion and pulled the curtains closed behind her head, tight against her neck, to prevent Iyatil from seeing the transformation.

The porters were parshmen, and she doubted the parshmen would say anything about what they saw her do. Their lighteyed master was turned away, fortunately. Her palanquin wobbled up to the front of the line, and the guards started when they saw her. They waved her through immediately. The face of Adolin's betrothed was well known by this point.

Now, how to get Veil's appearance back on? There were people on the street here; she wasn't about to breathe Stormlight while hanging out the window.

'Pattern,' she whispered. 'Go make a noise at the window on the other side of the palanquin.'

Tyn had drilled into her the need to make a distracting motion with one hand while palming an object with the other. The same principle might work here.

A sharp yelp sounded from the other window. Shallan moved her head back into the palanquin with a quick motion, breathing out Stormlight. She flipped the curtains in a diverting way and obscured her face with the hat as she put it on.

Iyatil looked back toward her from the window where the yelp had sounded, but Shallan was Veil again. She settled back, meeting Iyatil's gaze. Had the smaller woman seen?

They rode in silence for a moment.

'You bribed the guards ahead of time,' Iyatil finally guessed. 'I would know how you did this. Kholin's men are difficult to bribe. You got to one of the supervisors, perhaps?'

Shallan smiled in what she hoped was a frustrating way.

The palanquin continued on toward the warcamp's temple, a part of Dalinar's camp that she'd never visited. Actually, she hadn't been to visit Sebarial's ardents very often either – though when she had gone, she'd found them surprisingly devout, considering who owned them.

She peeked out the window as they approached. Dalinar's temple grounds were as plain as she would have expected. Grey-robed ardents passed the palanquin in pairs or small groups, mixing among people of all stations. Those had come for prayers, instruction, or advice – a good temple, properly equipped, could provide each of these things and more. Darkeyes from almost any nahn could come to be taught a trade, exercising their divine Right to Learn, as mandated by the Heralds. Lesser lighteyes came to learn trades as well, and the higher dahns came to learn the arts or progress in their Callings to please the Almighty.

A large population of ardents like this one would have true masters in every art and trade. Perhaps she should come and seek Dalinar's artists for training.

She winced, wondering where she would find time for such a thing. What with courting Adolin, infiltrating the Ghostbloods, researching the Shattered Plains, and doing Sebarial's ledgers, it was a wonder she had time to sleep. Still, it felt impious of her to expect success in her duties while ignoring the Almighty. She did need to have more concern for such things.

And what is the Almighty to think of you? she wondered. *And the lies you're growing so proficient at producing.* Honesty was among the divine attributes of the Almighty, after all, which everyone was supposed to seek.

The temple complex here included more than one building, though most people would only visit the main structure. Mraize's instructions had included a map, so she knew the specific building she needed – one near the back, where the ardent healers saw to the sick and cared for people with long-term illnesses.

'It will not be easy to enter,' Iyatil said. 'The ardents are protective of their charges, and have them locked away in the back, kept from the eyes of other men. They will not welcome an attempt at intrusion.'

'The instructions indicated that today was the perfect time to sneak in,' Shallan said. 'I was to make haste to not miss the opportunity.'

'Once a month,' Iyatil said, 'all may come to the temple to ask questions or see a physician with no offering requested. Today will be a busy day, a day of confusion. That will make for an easier time infiltrating, but it does not mean they will simply let you saunter in.'

Shallan nodded.

'If you would rather do this at night,' Iyatil said, 'perhaps I can persuade Mraize that the matter can wait until then.'

Shallan shook her head. She had no experience sneaking about in the darkness. She'd just make a fool of herself.

But how to get in . . .

'Porter,' she commanded, sticking her head out the window and pointing, 'take us to that building there, then set us down. Send one of your number to seek the master healers. Tell them I need their aid.'

The tenner who led the parshmen – hired with Shallan's spheres – nodded brusquely. Tenners were a strange lot. This one didn't own the parshmen; he just worked for the woman who rented them out. Veil, with dark eyes, would be beneath him socially, but was also the one paying his wage, and so he just treated her as he would any other master.

The palanquin settled down and one of the parshmen walked off to deliver her request.

'Going to feign sickness?' Iyatil asked.

'Something like that,' Shallan said as footsteps arrived outside. She climbed out to meet a pair of square-bearded ardents, conferring as the parshmen led them in her direction. They looked her over, noting her dark eyes and her clothing – which was well-made but obviously intended for rugged use. Likely, they placed her in one of the upper-middle nahns, a citizen, but not a particularly important one.

'What is the problem, young woman?' asked the older of the two ardents.

'It is my sister,' Shallan said. 'She has put on this strange mask and refuses to remove it.'

A soft groan rose from inside the palanquin.

'Child,' said the lead ardent, his tone suffering, 'a stubborn sister is not a matter for the ardents.'

'I understand, good brother,' Shallan said, raising her hands before her. 'But this is no simple stubbornness. I think . . . I think one of the Voidbringers has inhabited her!'

She pushed aside the curtains of the palanquin, revealing Iyatil inside. Her strange mask made the ardents pull back and break off their objections. The younger of the two men peered in at Iyatil with wide eyes.

Iyatil turned to Shallan, and with an almost inaudible sigh, started rocking back and forth in place. 'Should we kill them?' she muttered. 'No. No, we shouldn't. But someone will see! No, do not say these things. No. I will not listen to you.' She started humming.

The younger ardent turned to look back at the senior.

'This is dire,' the ardent said, nodding. 'Porter, come. Have your parsh-men bring the palanquin.'

◆◆

A short time later, Shallan waited in the corner of a small monastery room, watching Iyatil sit and resist the ministration of several ardents. She kept warning them that if they removed her mask, she would have to kill them.

That did not seem to be part of the act.

Fortunately, she otherwise played her part well. Her ravings, mixed with her hidden face, gave even Shallan shivers. The ardents seemed alternately fascinated and horrified.

Concentrate on the drawing, Shallan thought to herself. It was a sketch of one of the ardents, a portly man about her own height. The drawing was rushed but capable. She idly found herself wondering what a beard would feel like. Would it itch? But no, hair on your head didn't itch, so why should hair on your face? How did they keep food out of the things?

She finished with a few quick marks, then rose quietly. Iyatil kept the ardents' attention with a new bout of raving. Shallan nodded to her in thanks, then slipped out of the door, entering the hallway. After glancing to the sides to see that she was alone, she used a cloud of Stormlight to transform into the ardent. That done, she reached up and tucked her straight red hair – the only part of her that threatened to pop out of the illusion – inside the back of her coat.

'Pattern,' she whispered, turning and walking down the hallway with a relaxed demeanor.

'Mmm?'

'Find him,' she said, removing from her satchel a sketch of the madman that Mraize had left in the tree. The sketch had been done at a distance, and wasn't terribly good. Hopefully . . .

'Second hallway on the left,' Pattern said.

Shallan looked down at him, though her new costume – an ardent's robe – obscured him where he sat on her coat. 'How do you know?'

'You were distracted by your drawing,' he said. 'I peeked about. There is a very interesting woman four doors down. She appears to be rubbing excrement on the wall.'

193

'Ew.' Shallan thought she could smell it.

'Patterns . . .' he said as they walked. 'I did not get a good look at what she was writing, but it seemed very interesting. I think I shall go and—'

'No,' Shallan whispered, 'stay with me.' She smiled, nodding to several ardents who strolled past. They didn't speak to her, fortunately, merely nodding back.

The monastery building, like most everything in Dalinar's warcamp, was sliced through with dull, unornamented hallways. Shallan followed Pattern's instructions to a thick door set into the stone. The lock clicked open with Pattern's help, and Shallan quietly slipped inside.

A single small window – more of a slit – proved insufficient to fully illuminate the large figure sitting on the bed. Dark-skinned, like a man from the Makabaki kingdoms, he had dark, ragged hair and hulking arms. Those were the arms of either a laborer or a soldier. The man sat slumped, back bowed, head down, frail light from the window cutting a slice across his back in white. It made for a grim, powerful silhouette.

The man was whispering. Shallan couldn't make out the words. She shivered, her back to the door, and held up the sketch Mraize had given her. This seemed to be the same person – at least, the skin color and stout build were the same, though this man was far more muscled than the picture indicated. Storms . . . those hands of his looked as if they could crush her like a cremling.

The man did not move. He did not look up, did not shift. He was like a boulder that had rolled to a stop here.

'Why is it kept so dark in this room?' Pattern asked, perfectly cheerful.

The madman didn't react to the comment, or even Shallan, as she stepped forward.

'Modern theory for helping the mad suggests dim confines,' Shallan whispered. 'Too much light stimulates them, and can reduce the effectiveness of treatment.' That was what she remembered, at least. She hadn't read much on this subject. The room *was* dark. That window couldn't be more than a few fingers wide.

What was he whispering? Shallan cautiously continued forward. 'Sir?' she asked. Then she hesitated, realizing that she was projecting a young woman's voice from an old, fat ardent's body. Would that startle the man? He wasn't looking, so she withdrew the illusion.

'He doesn't seem angry,' Pattern said. 'But you call him mad.'

' "Mad" has two definitions,' Shallan said. 'One means to be angry. The other means broken in the head.'

'Ah,' Pattern said, 'like a spren who has lost his bond.'

'Not exactly, I'd guess,' Shallan said, stepping up to the madman. 'But similar.' She knelt down by the man, trying to figure out what he was saying.

'The time of the Return, the Desolation, is at hand,' he whispered. She would have expected an Azish accent from him, considering the skin color, but he spoke perfect Alethi. 'We must prepare. You will have forgotten much, following the destruction of times past.'

She looked over at Pattern, lost in the shadows at the side of the room, then back at the man. Light glinted off his dark brown eyes, two bright pinpricks on an otherwise shadowed visage. That slumped posture seemed so morose. He whispered on, about bronze and steel, about preparations and training.

'Who are you?' Shallan whispered.

'Talenel'Elin. The one you call Stonesinew.'

She felt a chill. Then the madman continued, whispering the same things he had before, repeated exactly. She couldn't even be certain if his comment had been a reply to her question, or just a part of his recitation. He did not answer further questions.

Shallan stepped back, folding her arms, satchel over her shoulder.

'Talenel,' Pattern said. 'I know that name.'

'Talenelat'Elin is the name of one of the Heralds,' Shallan said. 'This is almost the same.'

'Ah.' Pattern paused. 'Lie?'

'Undoubtedly,' Shallan said. 'It defies reason that Dalinar Kholin would have one of the *Heralds of the Almighty* locked away in a temple's back rooms. Many madmen think themselves someone else.'

Of course, many said that Dalinar himself was mad. And he *was* trying to refound the Knights Radiant. Scooping up a madman who thought he was one of the Heralds could be in line with that.

'Madman,' Shallan said, 'where do you come from?'

He continued ranting.

'Do you know what Dalinar Kholin wishes of you?'

More ranting.

Shallan sighed, but knelt and wrote his exact words to deliver to Mraize. She got the entire sequence down, and listened to it twice through to make sure he wasn't going to say anything new. He didn't say his supposed name this time, though. So that was one deviation.

He couldn't *actually* be one of the Heralds, could he?

Don't be silly, she thought, tucking away her writing implements. *The Heralds glow like the sun, wield the Honorblades, and speak with the voices of a thousand trumpets.* They could cast down buildings with a command, force the storms to obey, and heal with a touch.

Shallan walked to the door. By now, her absence in the other room would have been noticed. She should get back and give her lie, of seeking a drink for her parched throat. First, though, she'd want to put back on the ardent disguise. She sucked in some Stormlight, then breathed out, using the still-fresh memory of the ardent to create—

'Aaaaaaaah!'

The madman leaped to his feet, screaming. He lurched for her, moving with incredible speed. As Shallan yelped in surprise, he grabbed her and shoved her out of her cloud of Stormlight. The image fell apart, evaporating, and the madman smashed her up against the wall, his eyes wide, his breathing ragged. He searched her face with frantic eyes, pupils darting back and forth.

Shallan trembled, breath catching.

Ten heartbeats.

'One of Ishar's Knights,' the madman whispered. His eyes narrowed. 'I remember . . . He founded them? Yes. Several Desolations ago. No longer just talk. It hasn't been talk for thousands of years. But . . . When . . .'

He stumbled back from her, hand to his head. Her Shardblade dropped into her hands, but she no longer appeared to need it. The man turned his back to her, walked to his bed, then lay down and curled up.

Shallan inched forward, and found he was back to whispering the same things as before. She dismissed the Blade.

Mother's soul . . .

'Shallan?' Pattern asked. 'Shallan, are you mad?'

She shook herself. How much time had passed? 'Yes,' she said, walking hurriedly for the door. She peeked outside. She couldn't risk using Stormlight again in this room. She'd just have to slip out—

Blast. Several people approached down the hallway. She would have to wait for them to pass. Except, they seemed to be heading right to this very door.

One of those men was Highlord Amaram.

Yes, I'm disappointed. Perpetually, as you put it.

Kaladin lay on his bench, ignoring the afternoon bowl of steamed, spiced tallew on the floor.

He had begun to imagine himself as that whitespine in the menagerie. A predator in a cage. Storms send that he didn't end up like that poor beast. Wilted, hungry, confused. *They don't do well in captivity*, Shallan had said.

How many days had it been? Kaladin found himself not caring. That worried him. During his time as a slave, he'd also stopped caring about the date. He wasn't so far removed from that wretch he'd once been. He felt himself slipping back toward that same mindset, like a man climbing a cliff covered in crem and slime. Each time he tried to pull himself higher, he slid back. Eventually he'd fall.

Old ways of thinking . . . a slave's ways of thinking . . . churned within him. Stop caring. Worry only about the next meal, and keeping it away from the others. Don't think too much. Thinking is dangerous. Thinking makes you hope, makes you want.

Kaladin shouted, throwing himself off his bench and pacing in the small room, hands to his head. He'd thought himself so strong. A fighter. But all they had to do to take that away was stuff him in a box for a few weeks, and the truth returned! He slammed himself against the bars and stretched a hand between them, toward one of the lamps on the wall. He sucked in a breath.

Nothing happened. No Stormlight. The sphere continued to glow, even and steady.

Kaladin cried out, reaching farther, pushing his fingertips toward that distant light. *Don't let the darkness take me*, he thought. He ... prayed. How long had it been since he'd done that? He didn't have someone to properly write and burn the words, but the Almighty listened to hearts, didn't he? *Please. Not again. I can't go back to that.*

Please.

He strained for that sphere, breathing in. The Light seemed to *resist*, then gloriously streamed out into his fingertips. The storm pulsed in his veins.

Kaladin held his breath, eyes shut, savoring it. The power strained against him, trying to escape. He pushed off the bars and started pacing again, eyes closed, not so frantic as before.

'I'm worried about you.' Syl's voice. 'You're growing dark.'

Kaladin opened his eyes and finally found her, sitting between two of the bars as if on a swing.

'I'll be all right,' Kaladin said, letting Stormlight rise from his lips like smoke. 'I just need to get out of this cage.'

'It's worse than that. It's the darkness ... the darkness ...' She looked to the side, then giggled suddenly, streaking off to inspect something on the floor. A little cremling that was creeping along the edge of the room. She stood over it, eyes widening at the stark red and violet color of its shell.

Kaladin smiled. She was still a spren. Childlike. The world was a place of wonder to Syl. What would that be like?

He sat down and ate his meal, feeling as if he'd pushed aside the gloom for a time. Eventually, one of the guards checked on him and found the dun sphere. He pulled it out, frowning, shaking his head before replacing it and moving on.

⁜

Amaram was coming into this room.

Hide!

Shallan was proud of how quickly she spat out the rest of her

Stormlight, wreathing herself in it. She didn't even give thought to how the madman had reacted to her Lightweaving before, though perhaps she should have. Regardless, this time he didn't seem to notice.

Should she become an ardent? No. Something much simpler, something faster.

Darkness.

Her clothing turned black. Her skin, her hat, her hair – everything pure black. She scrambled back away from the door into the corner of the room, farthest from the slot of a window, stilling herself. With her illusion in place, the Lightweaving consumed the trails of Stormlight that would normally rise from her skin, further masking her presence.

The door opened. Her heart thundered within her. She wished she'd had time to create a false wall. Amaram entered the room with a young darkeyed man, obviously Alethi, with short dark hair and prominent eyebrows. He wore Kholin livery. They shut the door quietly behind themselves, Amaram pocketing a key.

Shallan felt an immediate anger at seeing her brother's murderer here, but found that it had quieted somewhat. A smoldering loathing instead of an intense hatred. It had been a long time since she'd seen Helaran, now. And Balat had a point in that her older brother had abandoned them.

To try to kill this man, apparently – or so she'd been able to put together from what she'd read of Amaram and his Shardblade. Why had Helaran gone to kill this man? And could she really blame Amaram when, in truth, he'd probably just been defending himself?

She felt like she knew so little. Though Amaram was still a bastard, of course.

Together, Amaram and the Alethi darkeyes turned to the madman. Shallan couldn't make out much of their features in the mostly dark room. 'I don't know why you need to hear it for yourself, Brightlord,' the servant said. 'I told you what he said.'

'Hush, Bordin,' Amaram said, crossing the room. 'Listen at the door.'

Shallan stood stiff, pressed back in the corner. They'd see her, wouldn't they?

Amaram knelt beside the bed. 'Great Prince,' he whispered, hand to the madman's shoulder. 'Turn. Let me see you.'

The madman looked up, still muttering.

'Ah ...' Amaram said, breathing out. 'Almighty above, ten names, all true. You are beautiful. Gavilar, we have done it. We have finally *done it*.'

'Brightlord?' Bordin said from the door. 'I don't like being here. If we're discovered, people might ask questions. The treasure ...'

'He truly spoke of Shardblades?'

'Yes,' Bordin said. 'A whole cache of them.'

'The Honorblades,' Amaram whispered. 'Great Prince, please, give me the same words you spoke to this one.'

The madman muttered on, the same as Shallan had heard. Amaram continued kneeling, but eventually he turned toward the nervous Bordin. 'Well?'

'He repeated those words every day,' Bordin said, 'but he only spoke of the Blades once.'

'I would hear of them for myself.'

'Brightlord ... We could wait here days and not hear those words. Please. We must go. The ardents will eventually come by on their rounds.'

Amaram stood up with obvious reluctance. 'Great Prince,' he said to the huddled figure of the madman, 'I go to recover your treasures. Speak not of them to the others. I will put the Blades to good use.' He turned to Bordin. 'Come. Let us search out this place.'

'Today?'

'You said it was close.'

'Yes, well, that was why I brought him all the way out here. But—'

'If he accidentally speaks of this to others, I would have them go to the place and find it empty of treasures. Come, quickly. You will be rewarded.'

Amaram strode out. Bordin lingered at the door, looking at the madman, then trailed out and shut the door with a *click*.

Shallan breathed out a long, deep breath, slumping down to the floor. 'It's like that sea of spheres.'

'Shallan?' Pattern asked.

'I've fallen in,' she said, 'and it isn't that the water is over my head – it's that the stuff isn't even water, and I have no idea how to swim in it.'

'I do not understand this lie,' Pattern said.

She shook her head, the color bleeding back into her skin and clothing. She made herself look like Veil again, then walked to the door, accompanied by the sound of the madman's rambling. *Herald of War. The time of the Return is near at hand. . . .*

Outside, she found her way back to the room with Iyatil, then apologized profusely to the ardents there who were looking for her. She pled that she had gotten lost, but said she'd accept an escort to take her back to her palanquin.

Before going, however, she leaned down to hug Iyatil, as if to wish her sister farewell.

'You can escape?' Shallan whispered.

'Don't be stupid. Of course I can.'

'Take this,' Shallan said, pressing a sheet of paper into Iyatil's gloved freehand. 'I wrote upon it the ramblings of the madman. They repeat without change. I saw Amaram sneak into the room; he seems to think these words are authentic, and he seeks a treasure the madman spoke of earlier. I will write a thorough report via spanreed to you and the others tonight.'

Shallan moved to pull back, but Iyatil held on. 'Who are you really, Veil?' the woman asked. 'You caught me in stealth spying upon you, and you can lose me in the streets. This is not easily accomplished. Your clever drawings fascinate Mraize, another near-impossible task, considering all that he has seen. Now what you have done today.'

Shallan felt a thrill. Why should she feel so excited to have the respect of these people? They were murderers.

But storms take her, she had *earned* that respect.

'I seek the truth,' Shallan said. 'Wherever it may be, whoever may hold it. That's who I am.' She nodded to Iyatil, then pulled away and escaped the monastery.

Later on that night, after sending in a full report of the day's events – as well as promising drawings of the madman, Amaram, and Bordin for good measure – she received back a simple message from Mraize.

The truth destroys more people than it saves, Veil. But you have proven yourself. You no longer need fear our other members; they have been instructed not to touch you. You are required to get a specific tattoo, a symbol of your loyalty. I will send a drawing. You may add it to your person wherever you wish, but must prove it to me when we next meet.

Welcome to the Ghostbloods.

recollection of the metamorphosis, and training will have to resume as if with a new beast. There's no guarantee that a docile grub will pupate into

To encourage pupation of the mature larvae, feed them a consistent diet of rocklily leaves. To discourage pupation of your adult chulls, add drops of shalebark oil to the drinking water and feed chulls crushed shelltick before a storm. Sheltering your livestock during a highstorm remains the most-proven method to keep your chulls from pupating.

FIG. 38 -- METAMORPHOSIS OF THE CHULL: LARVA (THE CHULL CREMLING), FIRST PUPATION, ADULT CHULL, SECOND PUPATION, SENESCENCE.

THE ONE WHO
DESERVES IT

ONE AND A HALF YEARS AGO

What is a woman's place in this modern world? Jasnah Kholin's words read. *I rebel against this question, though so many of my peers ask it. The inherent bias in the inquiry seems invisible to so many of them. They consider themselves progressive because they are willing to challenge many of the assumptions of the past.*

They ignore the greater assumption – that a 'place' for women must be defined and set forth to begin with. Half of the population must somehow be reduced to the role arrived at by a single conversation. No matter how broad that role is, it will be – by nature – a reduction from the infinite variety that is womanhood.

I say that there is no role for women – there is, instead, a role for each woman, and she must make it for herself. For some, it will be the role of scholar; for others, it will be the role of wife. For others, it will be both. For yet others, it will be neither.

Do not mistake me in assuming I value one woman's role above another. My point is not to stratify our society – we have done that far too well already – my point is to diversify our discourse.

A woman's strength should not be in her role, whatever she chooses it to be, but in the power to choose that role. It is amazing to me that I even have to make this point, as I see it as the very foundation of our conversation.

Shallan closed the book. Not two hours had passed since Father had ordered Helaran's assassination. After Shallan had retreated to her room, a pair of Father's guards had appeared in the hallway outside. Probably not to watch her – she doubted that Father knew that she'd overheard his order for Helaran to be killed. The guards were to see that Malise, Shallan's stepmother, did not try to flee.

That could be a mistaken assumption. Shallan didn't even know if Malise was still alive, following her screaming and Father's cold, angry ranting.

Shallan wanted to hide, to hunker down in her closet with blankets wrapped around her, eyes squeezed shut. The words in Jasnah Kholin's book strengthened her, though in some ways it seemed laughable for Shallan to even be reading it. Highlady Kholin talked about the nobility of choice, as if every woman had such opportunity. The decision between being a mother or a scholar seemed a difficult decision in Jasnah's estimation. That wasn't a difficult choice at all! That seemed like a *grand* place to be! Either would be delightful when compared to a life of fear in a house seething with anger, depression, and hopelessness.

She imagined what Highlady Kholin must be, a capable woman who did not do as others insisted she must. A woman with power, authority. A woman who had the luxury of seeking her dreams.

What would that be like?

Shallan stood up. She walked to the door, then cracked it open. Though the evening had grown late, the two guards still stood at the other end of the hallway. Shallan's heart thumped, and she cursed her timidity. Why couldn't she be like women who acted, instead of being someone who hid in her room with a pillow around her head?

Shaking, she slipped from the room. She padded toward the soldiers, feeling their eyes on her. One raised his hand. She didn't know the man's name. Once, she'd known all of the guards' names. Those men, whom she'd grown up with, had been replaced now.

'My father will need me,' she said, not stopping at the guard's gesture. Though he was lighteyed, she did not need to obey him. She might spend most of every day in her rooms, but she was still of a much higher rank than he.

She walked by the men, trembling hands clenched tight. They let her go. When she passed her father's door, she heard soft weeping inside. Malise still lived, thankfully.

She found Father in the feast hall, sitting alone with both firepits roaring, full of flames. He slumped at the high table, lit by harsh light, staring at the tabletop.

Shallan slipped into the kitchen before he noticed her, and mixed his favorite. Deep violet wine, spiced with cinnamon and warmed against the chill day. He looked up as she walked back into the feast hall. She set the cup before him, looking into his eyes. No darkness there today. Just him. That was very rare, these days.

'They won't *listen*, Shallan,' he whispered. 'Nobody will listen. I hate that I have to fight my own house. They should support me.' He took the drink. 'Wikim just stares at the wall half the time. Jushu is worthless, and Balat fights me every step. Now Malise too.'

'I will speak to them,' Shallan said.

He drank the wine, then nodded. 'Yes. Yes, that would be good. Balat is still out with those cursed axehound corpses. I'm glad they're dead. That litter was full of runts. He didn't need them anyway. . . .'

Shallan stepped into the chill air. The sun had set, but lanterns hung on the eaves of the manor house. She had rarely seen the gardens at night, and they took on a mysterious cast in the darkness. Vines looked like fingers reaching from the void, seeking something to grab and pull away into the night.

Balat lay on one of the benches. Shallan's feet crunched on something as she stepped up to him. Claws from cremlings, pulled free of their bodies one after another, then tossed to the ground. She shivered.

'You should go,' she said to Balat.

He sat up. 'What?'

'Father can no longer control himself,' Shallan said softly. 'You need to leave, while you can. I want you to take Malise with you.'

Balat ran his hand through his mess of curly dark hair. 'Malise? Father will never let her go. He'd hunt us down.'

'He'll hunt you anyway,' Shallan said. 'He hunts Helaran. Earlier today, he ordered one of his men to find our brother and assassinate him.'

'What!' Balat stood. 'That bastard! I'll . . . I . . .' He looked to Shallan in the darkness, face lit by starlight. Then he crumpled, sitting back down, holding his head in his hands. 'I'm a coward, Shallan,' he whispered. 'Oh, Stormfather, I'm a coward. I won't face him. I can't.'

'Go to Helaran,' Shallan said. 'Could you find him, if you needed to?'

'He ... Yes, he left me the name of a contact in Valath who could put me in touch with him.'

'Take Malise and Eylita. Go to Helaran.'

'I won't have time to find Helaran before Father catches up.'

'Then we will contact Helaran,' Shallan said. 'We will make plans for you to meet him, and you can schedule your flight for a time when Father is away. He is planning another trip to Vedenar a few months from now. Leave when he's gone, get a head start.'

Balat nodded. 'Yes ... Yes, that is good.'

'I will draft a letter to Helaran,' Shallan said. 'We need to warn him about Father's assassins, and we can ask him to take the three of you in.'

'You shouldn't have to do this, small one,' Balat said, head down. 'I'm the eldest after Helaran. I should have been able to stop Father by now. Somehow.'

'Take Malise away,' Shallan said. 'That will be doing enough.'

He nodded.

Shallan returned to the house, passing Father mulling over his disobedient family, and fetched some things from the kitchen. Then she returned to the steps and looked upward. Taking a few deep breaths, she went over what she would say to the guards if they stopped her. Then she raced up them and opened the door into her father's sitting room.

'Wait,' the hallway guard said. 'He left orders. Nobody in or out.'

Shallan's throat tightened, and even with her practice, she stammered as she spoke. 'I just talked to him. He wants me to speak with her.'

The guard inspected her, chewing on something. Shallan felt her confidence wilt, heart racing. Confrontation. She was as much a coward as Balat.

He gestured to the other guard, who went downstairs to check. He eventually returned, nodding, and the first man reluctantly waved for her to continue. Shallan entered.

Into the Place.

She had not entered this room in years. Not since ...

Not since ...

She raised a hand, shading her eyes against the light coming from behind the painting. How could Father sleep in here? How was it that nobody else looked, nobody else cared? That light was *blinding*.

Fortunately, Malise was curled in an easy chair facing that wall, so Shallan could put her back to the painting and obstruct the light. She rested a hand on her stepmother's arm.

She didn't feel that she knew Malise, despite years living together. Who was this woman who would marry a man everyone whispered had killed his previous wife? Malise oversaw Shallan's education – meaning she searched for new tutors each time the women fled – but Malise herself couldn't do much to teach Shallan. One could not teach what one did not know.

'Mother?' Shallan asked. She used the word.

Malise looked. Despite the blazing light of the room, Shallan saw the woman's lip was split and bleeding. She cradled her left arm. Yes, it was broken.

Shallan took out the gauze and cloth she had fetched from the kitchen, then began to wipe down the wounds. She would have to find something to use as a splint for that arm.

'Why doesn't he hate you?' Malise said harshly. 'He hates everyone else but you.'

Shallan dabbed at the woman's lip.

'Stormfather, why did I come to this cursed household?' Malise shuddered. 'He'll kill us all. One by one, he'll break us and kill us. There's a darkness inside of him. I've seen it, behind his eyes. A beast . . .'

'You're going to leave,' Shallan said softly.

Malise barked a laugh. 'He'll never let me go. He never lets go of anything.'

'You're not going to ask,' Shallan whispered. 'Balat is going to run and join Helaran, who has powerful friends. He's a Shardbearer. He'll protect the both of you.'

'We'll never reach him,' Malise said. 'And if we do, why would Helaran take us in? We have nothing.'

'Helaran is a good man.'

Malise twisted in her seat, staring away from Shallan, who continued her ministrations. The woman whimpered when Shallan bound her arm, but wouldn't respond to questions. Finally, Shallan gathered up the bloodied cloths to throw away.

'If I go,' Malise whispered, 'and Balat with me, who will he hate? Who will he hit? Maybe you, finally? The one who actually deserves it?'

'Maybe,' Shallan whispered, then left.

Is not the destruction we have wrought enough? The worlds you now tread bear the touch and design of Adonalsium. Our interference so far has brought nothing but pain.

Feet scraped on the stone outside of Kaladin's cage. One of the jailers checking on him again. Kaladin continued to lie motionless with closed eyes, and did not look.

In order to keep the darkness at bay, he had begun planning. What would he do when he got out? *When* he got out. He had to tell himself that forcibly. It wasn't that he didn't trust Dalinar. His mind, though ... his mind betrayed him, and whispered things that were not true.

Distortions. In his state, he could believe that Dalinar lied. He could believe that the highprince secretly wanted Kaladin in prison. Kaladin was a terrible guard, after all. He'd failed to do anything about the mysterious countdowns scrawled on walls, and he'd failed to stop the Assassin in White.

With his mind whispering lies, Kaladin could believe that Bridge Four was happy to be rid of him – that they pretended they wanted to be guards, just to make him happy. They secretly wanted to go on with their lives, lives they'd enjoy, without Kaladin spoiling them.

These untruths *should* have seemed ridiculous to him. They didn't.

Clink.

Kaladin snapped his eyes open, growing tense. Had they come to take him, to execute him, as the king wished? He leaped to his feet, coming down in a battle stance, the empty bowl from his meal held to throw.

The jailer at the cell door stepped back, eyes widening. 'Storms, man,' he said. 'I thought you were asleep. Well, your time is served. King signed a pardon today. They didn't even strip your rank or position.' The man rubbed his chin, then pulled the cell door open. 'Guess you're lucky.'

Lucky. People always said that about Kaladin. Still, the prospect of freedom forced away the darkness inside of him, and Kaladin approached the door. Wary. He stepped out, the guard backing away.

'You are a distrustful one, aren't you?' the jailer said. A lighteyes of low rank. 'Guess that makes you a good bodyguard.' The man gestured for Kaladin to leave the room first.

Kaladin waited.

Finally, the guard sighed. 'Right, then.' He walked out the doorway into the hall beyond.

Kaladin followed, and with each step felt himself traveling back a few days in time. Shut the darkness away. He wasn't a slave. He was a soldier. Captain Kaladin. He'd survived this ... what had it been? Two, three weeks? This short time back in a cage.

He was free now. He could return to his life as a bodyguard. But one thing ... one thing had changed.

Nobody will ever, ever, do this to me again. Not king or general, not brightlord or brightlady.

He would die first.

They passed a leeward window, and Kaladin stopped to breathe in the cool, fresh scent of open air. The window gave an ordinary, mundane view of the camp outside, but it seemed glorious. A small breeze stirred his hair, and he let himself smile, reaching a hand to his chin. Several weeks' growth. He'd have to let Rock shave that.

'Here,' the jailer said. 'He's free. Can we finally be done with this farce, Your Highness?'

'Your Highness'? Kaladin turned down the hallway to where the guard had stopped at another cell – one of the larger ones set into the hallway itself. Kaladin had been put in the deepest cell, away from the windows.

The jailer twisted a key in the lock of the wooden door, then pulled it open. Adolin Kholin – wearing a simple tight uniform – stepped out. He also had several weeks of growth on his face, though the beard was blond, speckled black. The princeling took a deep breath, then turned toward Kaladin and nodded.

'He locked *you* away?' Kaladin said, baffled. 'How . . . ? What . . . ?'

Adolin turned to the jailer. 'Were my orders followed?'

'They wait in the room just beyond, Brightlord,' the jailer said, sounding nervous.

Adolin nodded, moving in that direction.

Kaladin reached the jailer, taking him by the arm. 'What is happening? The king put Dinar's *heir* in here?'

'The king didn't have anything to do with it,' the jailer said. 'Brightlord Adolin insisted. So long as you were in here, he wouldn't leave. We tried to stop him, but the man's a prince. We can't storming make him do anything, not even leave. He locked himself away in the cell and we just had to live with it.'

Impossible. Kaladin glanced at Adolin, who walked slowly down the hallway. The prince looked a lot better than Kaladin felt – Adolin had obviously seen a few baths, and his prison cell had been much larger, with more privacy.

It had still been a cell.

That was the disturbance I heard, Kaladin thought, *on that day, early after I was imprisoned. Adolin came and shut himself in.*

Kaladin jogged up to the man. 'Why?'

'Didn't seem right, you in here,' Adolin said, eyes forward.

'I ruined your chance to duel Sadeas.'

'I'd be crippled or dead without you,' Adolin said. 'So I wouldn't have had the chance to fight Sadeas anyway.' The prince stopped in the hallway, and looked at Kaladin. 'Besides. You saved Renarin.'

'It's my job,' Kaladin said.

'Then we need to pay you more, bridgeboy,' Adolin said. 'Because I don't know if I've ever met another man who would jump, unarmored, into a fight among six Shardbearers.'

Kaladin frowned. 'Wait. Are you wearing cologne? In *prison*?'

'Well, there was no need to be barbaric, just because I was incarcerated.'

'Storms, you're spoiled,' Kaladin said, smiling.

'I'm refined, you insolent farmer,' Adolin said. Then he grinned.

'Besides, I'll have you know that I had to use *cold* water for my baths while here.'

'Poor boy.'

'I know.' Adolin hesitated, then held out a hand.

Kaladin clasped it. 'I'm sorry,' he said. 'For ruining the plan.'

'Bah, you didn't ruin it,' Adolin said. 'Elhokar did that. You think he couldn't have simply ignored your request and proceeded, letting me expand on my challenge to Sadeas? He threw a tantrum instead of taking control of the crowd and pushing forward. Storming man.'

Kaladin blinked at the audacious tone, then glanced toward the jailer, who stood a distance behind, obviously trying to look inconspicuous.

'The things you said about Amaram,' Adolin said. 'Were they true?'

'Every one.'

Adolin nodded. 'I've always wondered what that man was hiding.' He continued walking.

'Wait,' Kaladin said, jogging to catch up, 'you *believe* me?'

'My father,' Adolin said, 'is the best man I know, perhaps the best man *alive*. Even he loses his temper, makes bad judgment calls, and has a troubled past. Amaram never seems to do anything wrong. If you listen to the stories about him, it's like everyone expects him to glow in the dark and piss nectar. That stinks, to me, of someone who works too hard to maintain his reputation.'

'Your father says I shouldn't have tried to duel him.'

'Yeah,' Adolin said, reaching the door at the end of the hallway. 'Dueling is formalized in a way I suspect you just don't get. A darkeyes can't challenge a man like Amaram, and you certainly shouldn't have done it like you did. It embarrassed the king, like spitting on a gift he'd given you.' Adolin hesitated. 'Of course, that shouldn't matter to you anymore. Not after today.'

Adolin pushed open the door. Beyond, most of the men of Bridge Four crowded into a small room where the jailers obviously spent their days. A table and chairs had been shoved to the corner to make room for the twentysomething men who saluted Kaladin as the door opened. Their salutes dissolved immediately as they started to cheer.

That sound ... that sound quashed the darkness until it vanished completely. Kaladin found himself smiling as he stepped out to meet them, taking hands, listening to Rock make a wisecrack about his beard.

Renarin was there in his Bridge Four uniform, and he immediately joined his brother, speaking to him quietly in a jovial way, though he had out his little box that he liked to fidget with.

Kaladin glanced to the side. Who were those men beside the wall? Members of Adolin's retinue. Was that one of Adolin's armorers? They carried some items draped with sheets. Adolin stepped into the room and loudly clapped his hands, quieting Bridge Four.

'It turns out,' Adolin said, 'that I'm in possession of not one, but *two* new Shardblades and *three* sets of Plate. The Kholin princedom now owns a quarter of the Shards in all of Alethkar, and I've been named dueling champion. Not surprising, considering Relis was on a caravan back to Alethkar the night after our duel, sent by his father in an attempt to hide the shame of being beaten so soundly.

'One complete set of those Shards is going to General Khal, and I've ordered two of the sets of Plate given to appropriate lighteyes of rank in my father's army.' Adolin nodded toward the sheets. 'That leaves one full set. Personally, I'm curious to know if the stories are true. If a darkeyes bonds a Shardblade, will his eyes change color?'

Kaladin felt a moment of sheer panic. Again. It was happening again.

The armorers removed the sheets, revealing a shimmering silvery Blade. Edged on both sides, a pattern of twisting vines ran up its center. At their feet, the armorers uncovered a set of Plate, painted orange, taken from one of the men Kaladin had helped defeat.

Take these Shards, and everything changed. Kaladin immediately felt sick, almost cripplingly so. He turned back to Adolin. 'I can do with these as I wish?'

'Take them,' Adolin said, nodding. 'They are yours.'

'Not anymore,' Kaladin said, pointing toward one of the members of Bridge Four. 'Moash. Take these. You're now a Shardbearer.'

All of the color drained from Moash's face. Kaladin prepared himself. Last time . . . He flinched as Adolin grabbed him by the shoulder, but the tragedy of Amaram's army did not repeat. Instead, Adolin yanked Kaladin back into the hallway, holding up a hand to stop the bridgemen from talking.

'Just a second,' Adolin said. 'Nobody move.' Then, in a quieter voice, he hissed to Kaladin. 'I'm *giving* you a *Shardblade* and *Shardplate*.'

'Thank you,' Kaladin said. 'Moash will use them well. He's been training with Zahel.'

'I didn't give them to him. I gave them to you.'

'If they're really mine, then I can do with them as I wish. Or are they not really mine?'

'What's *wrong* with you?' Adolin said. 'This is the dream of every soldier, darkeyed or light. Is this out of spite? Or . . . is it . . .' Adolin seemed completely baffled.

'It's not out of spite,' Kaladin said, speaking softly. 'Adolin, those Blades have killed too many people I love. I can't look at them, can't *touch* them, without seeing blood.'

'You'd be lighteyed,' Adolin whispered. 'Even if it didn't change your eye color, you'd count as one. Shardbearers are immediately of the fourth dahn. You could challenge Amaram. Your whole life would change.'

'I don't want my life to change because I've become a lighteyes,' Kaladin said. 'I want the lives of people like me . . . like I am now . . . to change. This gift is not for me, Adolin. I'm not trying to spite you or anyone else. I just don't want a Shardblade.'

'That assassin is going to come back,' Adolin said. 'We both know it. I'd rather have you there with Shards to back me up.'

'I'll be more useful without them.'

Adolin frowned.

'Let me give the Shards to Moash,' Kaladin said. 'You saw, on that field, that I can handle myself fine without a Blade and Plate. If we Shardup one of my best men, there will be three of us to fight him, not just two.'

Adolin looked into the room, then skeptically back at Kaladin. 'You *are* crazy, you realize.'

'I'll accept that.'

'Fine,' Adolin said, striding back into the room. 'You. Moash, was it? I guess those Shards are yours, now. Congratulations. You now outrank ninety percent of Alethkar. Pick yourself a family name and ask to join one of the houses under Dalinar's banner, or start your own if you are inclined.'

Moash glanced at Kaladin for confirmation. Kaladin nodded.

The tall bridgeman walked to the side of the room, reaching out a hand to rest his fingers on the Shardblade. He ran those fingers all the way down to the hilt, then seized it, lifting the Blade in awe. Like most, it was enormous, but Moash held it easily in one hand. The heliodor set into the pommel flashed with a burst of light.

Moash looked to the others of Bridge Four, a sea of wide eyes and speechless mouths. Gloryspren rose around him, a spinning mass of at least two dozen spheres of light.

'His eyes,' Lopen said. 'Shouldn't they be changing?'

'If it happens,' Adolin said, 'it might not be until he's bonded the thing. That takes a week.'

'Put the Plate on me,' Moash said to the armorers. Urgent, as if he feared it would be taken from him.

'Enough of this!' Rock said as the armorers began to work, his voice filling the room like captive thunder. 'We have party to give! Great Captain Kaladin, Stormblessed and dweller in prisons, you will come eat my stew now. Ha! I have been cooking it as long as you were locked away.'

Kaladin let the bridgemen usher him out into the sunlight, where a crowd of soldiers waited – including many of the bridgemen from other crews. These cheered, and Kaladin caught sight of Dalinar waiting off to the side. Adolin moved to join his father, but Dalinar watched Kaladin. What did that look mean? So pensive. Kaladin looked away, accepting the greetings of bridgemen as they clasped his hand and clapped him on the back.

'What did you say, Rock?' Kaladin said. 'You cooked a stew for each day I was locked in prison?'

'No,' Teft said, scratching his beard. 'The storming Horneater has been cooking a single pot, letting it simmer for weeks now. He won't let us try it, and insists on getting up at night and tending it.'

'Is celebratory stew,' Rock said, folding his arms. 'Must simmer long time.'

'Well, let's get to it, then,' Kaladin said. 'I could certainly use something better than prison food.'

The men cheered, piling off toward their barrack. As they moved, Kaladin grabbed Teft by the arm. 'How did the men take it?' he asked. 'My imprisonment?'

'There was talk of breaking you out,' Teft admitted softly. 'I beat some sense into them. Ain't no good soldier who hasn't spent a day or two locked up. It's part of the job. They didn't demote you, so they just wanted to slap your wrist a little. The men saw the truth of it.'

Kaladin nodded.

Teft glanced at the others. 'There's quite a lot of anger among them about this Amaram fellow. And a lot of interest. Anything about your past gets them talking, you know.'

'Lead them back to the barrack,' Kaladin said. 'I'll join you in a moment.'

'Don't take too long,' Teft said. 'The lads have been guarding this doorway for three weeks now. You owe them their celebration.'

'I'll be along,' Kaladin said. 'I just want to say a few things to Moash.'

Teft nodded and jogged off to wrangle the others. The prison's front room felt empty when Kaladin walked back in. Only Moash and the armorers remained. Kaladin walked up to them, watching Moash make a fist with his gauntlet.

'I'm still having trouble believing this, Kal,' Moash said as the armorers fit on his breastplate. 'Storms ... I'm now worth more than some *kingdoms*.'

'I wouldn't suggest selling the Shards, at least not to a foreigner,' Kaladin said. 'That sort of thing can be considered treason.'

'Sell?' Moash said, looking up sharply. He made another fist. 'Never.' He smiled, a grin of pure joy as the breastplate locked into place.

'I'll help him with the rest,' Kaladin said to the armorers. They withdrew reluctantly, leaving Kaladin and Moash alone.

He helped Moash fit one of the pauldrons to his shoulder. 'I had a lot of time to think, in there,' Kaladin said.

'I can imagine.'

'The time led me to a few decisions,' Kaladin said as the section of Plate locked into place. 'One is that your friends are right.'

Moash turned to him sharply. 'So ...'

'So tell them I agree with their plan,' Kaladin said. 'I'll do what they want me to in order to help them ... accomplish their task.'

The room grew strangely still.

Moash took him by the arm. 'I told them you'd see.' He gestured to the Plate he wore. 'This will help too, with what we must do. And once we've finished, I think a certain man you challenged might need the same treatment.'

'I only agree,' Kaladin said, 'because it's for the best. For you, Moash, this is about revenge – and don't try to deny it. *I* really think it is what Alethkar needs. Maybe what the world needs.'

'Oh, I know,' Moash said, putting on the helmet, visor up. He took a deep breath, then took a step and stumbled, nearly crashing to the ground. He steadied himself by grabbing a table, which he crunched beneath his fingers, the wood splitting.

He stared at what he'd done, then laughed. 'This ... this is going to change *everything*. Thank you, Kaladin. Thank you.'

'Let's get those armorers and help you take it off,' Kaladin said.

'*No*. You go to Rock's storming feast. I'm going to the sparring grounds to practice! I won't take this off until I can move in it naturally.'

Having seen how much work Renarin was putting into learning his Plate, Kaladin suspected that might take longer than Moash wanted. He didn't say anything, instead stepping back out into the sunlight. He enjoyed that for a moment, eyes closed, head toward the sky.

Then, he jogged off to rejoin Bridge Four.

My path has been chosen very deliberately. Yes, I agree with everything you have said about Rayse, including the severe danger he presents.

Dalinar stopped on the switchbacks down from the Pinnacle, Navani at his side. In the waning light, they watched a river of men flowing back into the warcamps from the Shattered Plains. The armies of Bethab and Thanadal were returning from their plateau run, following their highprinces, who had probably gotten back somewhat earlier. Down below, a rider approached the Pinnacle, likely with news for the king on the runs. Dalinar looked to one of his guards – he had four tonight, two for him, two for Navani – and gestured.

'You want the details, Brightlord?' asked the bridgeman.

'Please.'

The man jogged off down the switchbacks. Dalinar watched him go, thoughtful. These men were remarkably disciplined, considering their origin – but they were not career soldiers. They did not like what he had done in throwing their captain into prison.

He suspected they wouldn't let it become a problem. Captain Kaladin led them well – he was the exact type of officer Dalinar looked for. The kind that showed initiative not because of a desire for advancement, but because of the satisfaction of a job well done. Those kinds of soldiers often had rocky starts until they learned to keep their heads. Storms.

Dalinar himself had needed similar lessons pounded into him at various points in his life.

He continued with Navani down the switchbacks, walking slowly. She looked radiant tonight, hair done with sapphires that glowed softly in the light. Navani liked these strolls together, and they were in no hurry to arrive at the feast.

'I keep thinking,' Navani said, continuing their previous conversation, 'that there should be a way to use fabrials as *pumps*. You have seen the gemstones built to attract certain substances, but not others – it is most useful with something like smoke above a fire. Could we make this work with water?'

Dalinar grunted, nodding.

'More and more buildings in the warcamps are plumbed,' she continued, 'after the Kharbranthian manner – but those use gravity itself as a way to conduct the liquid through their piping. I imagine true motion, with gemstones at the ends of piping segments to pull water through at a flow, against the pull of the earth. . . .'

He grunted again.

'We made a breakthrough in the design of new Shardblades the other day.'

'What, really?' he asked. 'What happened? How soon will you have one ready?'

She smiled, arm around his.

'What?'

'Just seeing if you are still you,' she said. 'Our breakthrough was realizing that the gemstones in the Blades – used to bond them – might not have originally been part of the weapons.'

He frowned. 'That's important?'

'Yes. If this is true, it means the Blades aren't powered by the stones. Credit goes to Rushu, who asked why a Shardblade can be summoned and dismissed even if its gemstone has gone dun. We had no answers, and she spent the last few weeks in contact with Kharbranth, using one of those new information stations. She came up with a scrap from several decades after the Recreance which talks about men learning to summon and dismiss Blades by adding gemstones to them, an accident of ornamentation it seems.'

He frowned as they passed a shalebark outcropping where a gardener was working late, carefully filing away and humming to himself. The sun had set; Salas had just risen in the east.

'If this is true,' Navani said, sounding happy, 'we're back to knowing absolutely nothing about how Shardblades were crafted.'

'I don't see why that's a breakthrough at all.'

She smiled, patting him on the arm. 'Imagine you had spent the last five years believing an enemy had been following Dialectur's *War* as a model for tactics, but then heard it reported they instead had never heard of the treatise.'

'Ah . . .'

'We had been assuming that somehow, the strength and lightness of the Blades was a fabrial construct powered by the gemstone,' Navani said. 'This might not be the case. It seems the gemstone's purpose is *only* used in initially bonding the Blade – something that the Radiants didn't need to do.'

'Wait. They didn't?'

'Not if this fragment is correct. The implication is that the Radiants could always dismiss and summon Blades – but for a time the ability was lost. It was only recovered when someone added a gemstone to his Blade. The fragment says the weapons actually shifted *shape* to adopt the stones, but I'm not certain if I trust that.

'Either way, after the Radiants fell but before men learned to put gem-stones into their Blades and bond them, the weapons were apparently *still* supernaturally sharp and light, though bonding was impossible. This would explain several other fragments of records I've read and found confusing. . . .'

She continued, and he found her voice pleasant. The details of fabrial construction, however, were not pressing to him at the moment. He did care. He had to care. Both for her, and for the needs of the kingdom.

He just couldn't care *right now*. In his head, he went over prepara-tions for the expedition out onto the Shattered Plains. How to protect the Soulcasters from sight, as they preferred. Sanitation shouldn't be an issue, and water would be plentiful. How many scribes would he need to bring? Horses? Only one week remained, and he had the majority of the preparations in place, such as mobile bridge construction and supply estimations. There was always more to plan, however.

Unfortunately, the biggest variable was one he couldn't plan for, not specifically. He didn't know how many troops he'd have. It depended on which of the highprinces, if any, agreed to go with him. Less than a week out, and he still wasn't certain if *any* of them would.

I could use Hatham most, Dalinar thought. *He runs a tight army. If only Aladar hadn't sided with Sadeas so vigorously; I can't figure that man out. Thanadal and Bethab ... storms, will I bring their mercenaries if either of those two agree to come? Is that the kind of force I want? Dare I refuse any spear that comes to me?*

'I'm not going to get a good conversation out of you tonight, am I?' Navani asked.

'No,' he admitted as they reached the base of the Pinnacle and turned south. 'I'm sorry.'

She nodded, and he could see the mask cracking. She talked about her work because it was something to talk about. He stopped beside her. 'I know it hurts,' he said softly. 'But it will get better.'

'She wouldn't let me be a mother to her, Dalinar,' Navani said, staring into the distance. 'Do you know that? It was almost like ... like once Jasnah climbed into adolescence, she no longer *needed* a mother. I would try to get close to her, and there was this *coldness*, like even being near me reminded her that she had once been a child. What happened to my little girl, so full of questions?'

Dalinar pulled her close; propriety could seek Damnation. Nearby, the three guards shuffled, looking the other way.

'They'll take my son too,' Navani whispered. 'They're trying.'

'I will protect him,' Dalinar promised.

'And who will protect you?'

He had no answer to that. Answering that his guards would do it sounded trite. That wasn't the question she'd asked. *Who will protect you when that assassin returns?*

'I almost wish that you would fail,' she said. 'In holding this kingdom together, you make a target of yourself. If everything just collapsed, and we fractured back to princedoms, perhaps he'd leave us alone.'

'And then the storm would come,' Dalinar replied softly. Eleven days.

Navani eventually pulled back, nodding, composing herself. 'You're right, of course. I just ... this is the first time, for me. Dealing with this. How did you manage it, when *Shshshsh* died? I know you loved her, Dalinar. You don't have to deny it for my ego.'

He hesitated. *The first time;* an implication that when Gavilar had died, she had not been broken up about it. She had never stated so outright an implication of the . . . difficulties the two had been having.

'I'm sorry,' she said. 'Was that too difficult a question, considering its source?' She tucked away her kerchief, which she'd used to dab her eyes dry. 'I apologize; I know that you don't like to talk about her.'

It wasn't that it was a difficult question. It was that Dalinar didn't remember his wife. How odd, that he could go weeks without even noticing this hole in his memories, this change that had ripped out a piece of him and left him patched over. Without even a prick of emotion when her name, which he could not hear, was mentioned.

Best to move to some other topic. 'I cannot help but assume that the assassin is involved in all of this, Navani. The storm that comes, the secrets of the Shattered Plains, even Gavilar. My brother knew something, something he never shared with any of us.' *You must find the most important words a man can say.* 'I would give almost anything to know what it was.'

'I suppose,' Navani said. 'I will go back to my journals of the time. Perhaps he said something that would give us clues – though I warn you, I've pored over those accounts dozens of times.'

Dalinar nodded. 'Regardless, that isn't a worry for today. Today, *they* are our goal.'

They turned, looking as coaches clattered past, making their way to the nearby feasting basin, where lights glowed a soft violet in the night. He narrowed his eyes and found Ruthar's coach approaching. The highprince had been stripped of Shards, all but his own Blade. They had cut off Sadeas's right hand in this mess, but the head remained. And it was venomous.

The other highprinces were almost as big a problem as Sadeas. They resisted him because they wanted things to be easy, as they had been. They glutted themselves on their riches and their games. Feasts manifested that all too much, with their exotic food, their rich costumes.

The world itself seemed close to ending, and the Alethi threw a party.

'You must not despise them,' Navani said.

Dalinar's frown deepened. She could read him too well.

'Listen to me, Dalinar,' she said, turning him to meet her eyes. 'Has any good ever come from a father hating his children?'

'I don't hate them.'

'You loathe their excess,' she said, 'and you are close to applying that emotion to them as well. They live the lives they have known, the lives that society has taught them are proper. You won't change them with contempt. You aren't Wit; it isn't your job to scorn them. Your job is to enfold them, encourage them. Lead them, Dalinar.'

He drew a deep breath, and nodded.

'I will go to the women's island,' she said, noticing the bridgeman guard returning with news on the plateau assault. 'They consider me an eccentric vestige of things better left in the past, but I think they still listen to me. Sometimes. I'll do what I can.'

They parted, Navani hurrying to the feast, Dalinar idling as the bridgeman passed his news. The plateau run had been successful, a gemheart captured. It had taken quite a long time to reach the target plateau, which was deep into the Plains – almost to the edge of the scouted area. The Parshendi had not appeared to contest the gemheart, though their scouts had watched from a distance.

Again they decide not to fight, Dalinar thought, walking the last distance to the feast. *What does the change mean? What are they planning?*

The feast basin was made up of a series of Soulcast islands beside the Pinnacle complex. It had been flooded, as it often was, in a way that made the Soulcast mounds rise between small rivers. The water glowed. Spheres, and a lot of them, must have been dumped into the water to give it that ethereal cast. Purple, to match the moon that was just rising, violet and frail on the horizon.

Lanterns were placed intermittently, but with dim spheres, perhaps to not distract from the glowing water. Dalinar crossed the bridges to the farthest island – the king's island, where the genders mixed and only the most powerful were invited. This was where he knew he'd find the highprinces. Even Bethab, who had just returned from his plateau run, was already in attendance – though, as he preferred to use mercenary companies for the bulk of his army, it wasn't surprising he had returned so quickly from the run. Once they captured the gemheart, he'd often ride back quickly with the prize, letting them sort out how to return.

Dalinar passed Wit – who had arrived back at the warcamps with characteristic mystery – insulting everyone who passed. He had no wish to fence words with the man today. Instead, he sought out Vamah; the highprince seemed to have actually listened to Dalinar's pleas during their most recent dinner. Perhaps with more nudging, he would commit to joining Dalinar's assault on the Parshendi.

Eyes followed Dalinar as he crossed the island, and whispered conversations broke out like rashes as he passed. He expected those looks by now, though they still unnerved him. Were they more plentiful this night? More lingering? He couldn't move in Alethi society these days without catching a smile on the lips of too many people, as if they were all part of some grand joke that he had not been told.

He found Vamah speaking with a group of three older women. One was Sivi, a highlady from Ruthar's court who – contrary to custom – had left her husband at home to see to their lands, coming to the Shattered Plains herself. She eyed Dalinar with a smile and eyes like daggers. The plot to undermine Sadeas had to a large extent failed – but that was in part because the damage and shame had been deflected to Ruthar and Aladar, who had suffered the loss of Shardbearers in the men who had dueled Adolin.

Well, those two were never going to have been Dalinar's – they were Sadeas's strongest supporters.

The four people grew silent as Dalinar stepped up to them. Highprince Vamah squinted in the dim light, looking Dalinar up and down. The round-faced man had a cupbearer standing behind him with a bottle of some exotic liquor or another. Vamah often brought his own spirits to feasts, regardless of who hosted them; being engaging enough a conversationalist to earn a sip of what he'd managed to import was considered a political triumph by many attendees.

'Vamah,' Dalinar said.

'Dalinar.'

'There's a matter I've been wanting to discuss with you,' Dalinar said. 'I find it impressive what you've been able to do with light cavalry on your plateau runs. Tell me, how do you decide when to risk an all-out assault with your riders? The loss of horses could easily overwhelm your earnings from gemhearts, but you have managed to balance this with clever stratagems.'

'I . . .' Vamah sighed, looking to the side. A group of young men nearby was snickering as they looked toward Dalinar. 'It is a matter of . . .'

Another sound, louder, came from the opposite side of the island.

Vamah started again, but his eyes flicked in that direction, and a round of laughter burst out more loudly. Dalinar forced himself to look, noting women with hands to mouths, men covering their exclamations with coughs. A halfhearted attempt at maintaining Alethi propriety.

Dalinar looked back at Vamah. 'What is happening?'

'I'm sorry, Dalinar.'

Beside him, Sivi tucked some sheets of paper under her arm. She met Dalinar's gaze with a forced nonchalance.

'Excuse me,' Dalinar said. Hands forming fists, he crossed the island toward the source of the disturbance. As he neared, they quieted and people broke up into smaller groups, moving off. It almost seemed *planned* how quickly they dispersed, leaving him to face Sadeas and Aladar, standing side by side.

'What are you doing?' Dalinar demanded of the two of them.

'Feasting,' Sadeas said, then shoved a piece of fruit into his mouth. 'Obviously.'

Dalinar drew in a deep breath. He glanced at Aladar, long-necked and bald, with his mustache and tuft of hair on his bottom lip. 'You should be ashamed,' Dalinar growled at him. 'My brother once called you a friend.'

'And not me?' Sadeas said.

'What have you done?' Dalinar demanded. 'What is everyone talking about, snickering about behind their hands?'

'You always assume it's me,' Sadeas said.

'That's because any time I think it *isn't* you, I'm wrong.'

Sadeas gave him a thin-lipped smile. He started to reply, but then thought a moment, and finally just stuffed another chunk of fruit in his mouth. He chewed and smiled.

'Tastes good,' was all he said. He turned to walk away.

Aladar hesitated. Then he shook his head and followed.

'I never figured you for a pup to follow at a master's heels, Aladar,' Dalinar called after him.

No reply.

Dalinar growled, moving back across the island, looking for someone from his own warcamp who might have heard what was happening. Elhokar was late to his own feast, it seemed, though Dalinar did see him approaching outside now. No sign of Teshav or Khal yet – they would undoubtedly make an appearance, now that he was a Shardbearer.

Dalinar might have to move to one of the other islands, where lesser lighteyes would be mingling. He started that way, but stopped as he heard something.

'Why, Brightlord Amaram,' Wit cried. 'I was *hoping* I'd be able to see you tonight. I've spent my life learning to make others feel miserable, and so it's a true joy to meet someone so innately talented in that very skill as you are.'

Dalinar turned, noticing Amaram, who had just arrived. He wore his cape of the Knights Radiant and carried a sheaf of papers stuck under his arm. He stopped beside Wit's chair, the nearby water casting a lavender tone across their skin.

'Do I know you?' Amaram asked.

'No,' Wit said lightly, 'but fortunately, you can add it to the list of many, many things of which you are ignorant.'

'But now I've met you,' Amaram said, holding out a hand. 'So the list is one smaller.'

'Please,' Wit said, refusing the hand. 'I wouldn't want it to rub off on me.'

'It?'

'Whatever you've been using to make your hands look clean, Brightlord Amaram. It must be powerful stuff indeed.'

Dalinar hurried over.

'Dalinar,' Wit said, nodding.

'Wit. Amaram, what are those papers?'

'One of your clerks seized them and brought them to me,' Amaram said. 'Copies were being passed around the feast before your arrival. Your clerk thought Brightness Navani might want to see them if she hasn't already. Where is she?'

'Staying away from you, obviously,' Wit noted. 'Lucky woman.'

'Wit,' Dalinar said sternly, 'do you mind?'

'Rarely.'

Dalinar sighed, looking back to Amaram and taking the papers. 'Brightness Navani is on another island. Do you know what these say?'

Amaram's expression grew grim. 'I wish I didn't.'

'I could hit you in the head with a hammer,' Wit said happily. 'A good bludgeoning would make you forget *and* do wonders for that face of yours.'

'Wit,' Dalinar said flatly.

'I'm only joking.'

'Good.'

'A hammer would hardly dent that thick skull of his.'

Amaram turned to Wit, a look of bafflement on his face.

'You're *very* good at that expression,' Wit noted. 'A great deal of practice, I assume?'

'*This* is the new Wit?' Amaram asked.

'I mean,' Wit said, 'I wouldn't want to call Amaram an imbecile . . .'

Dalinar nodded.

'. . . because then I'd have to explain to him what the word means, and I'm not certain any of us have the requisite time.'

Amaram sighed. 'Why hasn't anyone killed him yet?'

'Dumb luck,' Wit said. 'In that I'm lucky you're all so dumb.'

'Thank you, Wit,' Dalinar said, taking Amaram by the arm and towing him to the side.

'One more, Dalinar!' Wit said. 'Just one last insult, and I leave him alone.'

They continued walking.

'Lord Amaram,' Wit called, standing to bow, his voice growing solemn. 'I salute you. You *are* what lesser cretins like Sadeas can only aspire to be.'

'The papers?' Dalinar said to Amaram, pointedly ignoring Wit.

'They are accounts of your . . . experiences, Brightlord,' Amaram said softly. 'The ones you have during the storms. Written by Brightness Navani herself.'

Dalinar took the papers. His visions. He looked up and saw groups of people collecting on the island, chatting and laughing, shooting glances at him.

'I see,' he said softly. It made sense now, the hidden snickering. 'Find Brightness Navani for me, if you would.'

'As you request,' Amaram said, but stopped short, pointing. Navani stalked across the next island over, heading toward them with a tempestuous air about her.

'What do you think, Amaram?' Dalinar said. 'Of the things that are being said of me?'

Amaram met his eyes. 'They are obviously visions from the Almighty himself, given to us in a time of great need. I wish I had known their contents earlier. They give me great confidence in my position, and in your appointment as prophet of the Almighty.'

'A dead god can have no prophets.'

'Dead . . . No, Dalinar! You obviously misinterpret that comment from your visions. He speaks of being dead in the minds of men, that they no longer listen to his commands. God cannot die.'

Amaram seemed so earnest. *Why didn't he help your sons?* Kaladin's voice rang in Dalinar's mind. Amaram had come to him that day, of course, professing his apologies and explaining that – with his appointment as a Radiant – he couldn't possibly have helped one faction against another. He said he needed to be above the squabbles between highprinces, even when it pained him.

'And the supposed Herald?' Dalinar asked. 'The thing I asked you about?'

'I am still investigating.'

Dalinar nodded.

'I was surprised,' Amaram noted, 'that you left the slave as head of your guard.' He glanced to the side, to where Dalinar's guards for the night stood, just off the island in their own area, waiting with the other bodyguards and attendants, including many of the wards of the highladies present.

There had been a time not too long ago when few had felt the need to bring their guards with them to a feast. Now, the place was crowded. Captain Kaladin wasn't there; he was resting, after his imprisonment.

'He's a good soldier,' Dalinar said softly. 'He just carries a few scars that are having trouble healing.' *Vedeledev knows*, Dalinar thought, *I have a few of those myself.*

'I merely worry that he is incapable of properly protecting you,' Amaram said. 'Your life is important, Dalinar. We *need* your visions, your leadership. Still, if you trust the slave, then so be it – though I certainly wouldn't mind hearing an apology from him. Not for my own ego, but to know that he's put aside this misconception of his.'

Dalinar gave no reply as Navani strode across the short bridge onto their island. Wit started to proclaim an insult, but she swatted him in the face with a stack of papers, giving him barely a glance as she continued on toward Dalinar. Wit watched after, rubbing his cheek, and grinned.

She noted the papers in his hand as she joined the two of them, who seemed to stand among a sea of amused eyes and hushed laughter.

'They added words,' Navani hissed.

'What?' Dalinar demanded.

She shook the papers. 'These! You've heard what they contain?'

He nodded.

'They aren't as I wrote them,' Navani said. 'They've changed the tone, some of my words, to imply a ridiculousness to the entire experience – and to make it sound as if I am merely indulging you. What's worse, they added a commentary in another handwriting that pokes fun at what you say and do.' She took a deep breath, as if to calm herself. 'Dalinar, they're trying to destroy any shred of credibility left to your name.'

'I see.'

'How did they get these?' Amaram asked.

'Through theft, I do not doubt,' Dalinar said, realizing something. 'Navani and my sons always have guards – but when they leave their rooms, those are relatively unprotected. We may have been too lax in that regard. I misunderstood. I thought his attacks would be physical.'

Navani looked out at the sea of lighteyes, many congregating in groups around the various highprinces in the soft, violet light. She stepped closer to Dalinar, and though her eyes were fierce, he knew her well enough to guess what she was feeling. Betrayal. Invasion. That which was private to them, opened up, mocked and then displayed for the world.

'Dalinar, I'm sorry,' Amaram said.

'They did not change the visions themselves?' Dalinar asked. 'They copied them accurately.'

'So far as I can tell, yes,' Navani said. 'But the tone is different, and that *mockery*. Storms. It's nauseating. When I find the woman who did this . . .'

'Peace, Navani,' Dalinar said, resting his hand on her shoulder.

'How can you say that?'

'Because this is the act of childish men who assume that I can be embarrassed by the truth.'

'But the commentary! The changes. They've done everything they can to discredit you. They even managed to undermine the part where you offer a translation of the Dawnchant. It—'

' "As I fear not a child with a weapon he cannot lift, I will never fear the mind of a man who does not think."'

Navani frowned at him.

'It's from *The Way of Kings*,' Dalinar said. 'I am not a youth, nervous at his first feast. Sadeas makes a mistake in believing I will respond to this as he would. Unlike a sword, scorn has only the bite you give it.'

'This *does* hurt you,' Navani said, meeting his eyes. 'I can see it, Dalinar.'

Hopefully, the others would not know him well enough to see what she did. Yes, it did hurt. It hurt because these visions were *his*, entrusted to him – to be shared for the good of men, not to be held up for mockery. It was not the laughter itself that pained him, but the loss of what could have been.

He stepped away from her, passing through the crowd. Some of those eyes he now interpreted as being sorrowful, not just amused. Perhaps he was imagining it, but he thought some pitied him more than scorned him.

He wasn't certain which emotion was more damaging.

Dalinar reached the food table at the back of the island. There, he picked up a large pan and handed it to a bewildered serving woman, then hauled himself up onto the table. He set one hand on the lantern pole beside the table and looked out over the small crowd. They were the most important people in Alethkar.

Those who hadn't already been watching him turned with shock to see him up there. In the distance, he noticed Adolin and Brightness Shallan rushing onto the island. They'd likely only just arrived, and heard the talk.

Dalinar looked to the crowd. 'What you have read,' he bellowed, 'is true.'

Stunned silence. Making a spectacle of oneself in this way was not done in Alethkar. He, however, had *already been* this evening's spectacle.

'Commentary has been added to discredit me,' Dalinar said, 'and the tone of Navani's writing has been changed. But I will not hide what has been happening to me. I see visions from the Almighty. They come with almost every storm. This should not surprise you. There have been rumors circulating about my experiences for weeks now. Perhaps I should have released these visions already. In the future, each one I receive will be published, so that scholars around the world can investigate what I have seen.'

He sought out Sadeas, who stood with Aladar and Ruthar. Dalinar gripped the lantern pole, looking back at the Alethi crowd. 'I do not blame you for thinking I am mad. It is natural. But in the coming nights, when rain washes your walls and the wind howls, you will wonder. You will question. And soon, when I offer you proof, you will know. This attempt to destroy me will then vindicate me instead.'

He looked over their faces, some aghast, some sympathetic, others amused.

'There are those among you who assume I will flee, or be broken, because of this attack,' he said. 'They do not know me as well as they presume. Let the feast continue, for I wish to speak with each and every one of you. The words you hold may mock, but if you must laugh, do it while looking me in the eyes.'

He stepped down from the table.

Then he went to work.

❖

Hours later, Dalinar eventually let himself sit down in a seat beside a table at the feast, exhaustionspren swirling around him. He'd spent the rest of the evening moving through the crowd, forcing his way into conversations, drumming up support for his excursion onto the Plains.

He had pointedly ignored the pages with his visions on them, except when asked direct questions about what he'd seen. Instead, he had presented them with a forceful, confident man – the Blackthorn turned politician. Let them chew on that and compare him to the frail madman the falsified transcripts would make him out to be.

Outside, past the small rivers – they now glowed blue, the spheres having been changed to match the second moon – the king's carriage rolled away, bearing Elhokar and Navani the short distance to the Pinnacle, where porters would carry them in a palanquin up to the top. Adolin had already retired, escorting Shallan back to Sebarial's warcamp, which was a fair ride away.

Adolin seemed to be fonder of the young Veden woman than of any woman in the recent past. For that reason alone, Dalinar was increasingly inclined to encourage the relationship, assuming he could ever get some straight answers out of Jah Keved about her family. That kingdom was a mess.

Most of the other lighteyes had retired, leaving him on an island populated by servants and parshmen who cleared away food. A few masterservants, trusted for such duties, began to scoop the spheres out of the river with nets on long poles. Dalinar's bridgemen, at his suggestion, were attacking the feast's leftovers with the voracious appetite exclusive to soldiers who had been offered an unexpected meal.

A servant strolled by, then stopped, resting his hand on his side sword. Dalinar started, realizing he'd mistaken Wit's black military uniform for that of a master-servant in training.

Dalinar put on a firm face, though inwardly he groaned. Wit? Now? Dalinar felt as if he'd been fighting on the battlefield for ten hours straight. Odd, how a few hours of delicate conversation could feel so similar to that.

'What you did tonight was clever,' Wit said. 'You turned an attack into a promise. The wisest of men know that to render an insult powerless, you often need only to embrace it.'

'Thank you,' Dalinar said.

Wit nodded curtly, following the king's coach with his eyes as it vanished. 'I found myself without much to do tonight. Elhokar was not in need of Wit, as few sought to speak to him. All came to you instead.'

Dalinar sighed, his strength seeming to drain away. Wit hadn't said it, but he hadn't needed to. Dalinar read the implication.

They came to you, instead of the king. Because essentially, you are king.

'Wit,' Dalinar found himself asking, 'am I a tyrant?'

Wit cocked an eyebrow, and seemed to be looking for a clever quip. A moment later, he discarded the thought. 'Yes, Dalinar Kholin,' he said softly, consolingly, as one might speak to a tearful child. 'You are.'

'I do not wish to be.'

'With all due respect, Brightlord, that is not *quite* the truth. You seek for power. You take hold, and let go only with great difficulty.'

Dalinar bowed his head.

'Do not sorrow,' Wit said. 'It is an era for tyrants. I doubt this place is ready for anything more, and a benevolent tyrant is preferable to the disaster of weak rule. Perhaps in another place and time, I'd have denounced you with spit and bile. Here, today, I praise you as what this world needs.'

Dalinar shook his head. 'I should have allowed Elhokar his right of rule, and not interfered as I did.'

'Why?'

'Because he is king.'

'And that position is something sacrosanct? Divine?'

'No,' Dalinar admitted. 'The Almighty, or the one claiming to be him, is dead. Even if he hadn't been, the kingship didn't come to our family naturally. We claimed it, and forced it upon the other highprinces.'

'So then why?'

'Because we were wrong,' Dalinar said, narrowing his eyes. 'Gavilar, Sadeas, and I were wrong to do as we did all those years ago.'

Wit seemed genuinely surprised. 'You unified the kingdom, Dalinar. You did a good work, something that was sorely needed.'

'*This* is unity?' Dalinar asked, waving a hand back toward the scattered remnants of the feast, the departing lighteyes. 'No, Wit. We failed. We crushed, we killed, and we have *failed miserably*.' He looked up. 'I receive, in Alethkar, only what I have demanded. In taking the throne by force, we implied – no we *screamed* – that strength is the right of rule. If Sadeas thinks he is stronger than I am, then it is his *duty* to try to take the throne from me. These are the fruits of my youth, Wit. It is why we need more than tyranny, even the benevolent kind, to transform this kingdom. That is what Nohadon was teaching. And *that* is what I've been missing all along.'

Wit nodded, looking thoughtful. 'I need to read that book of yours again, it seems. I wanted to warn you, however. I'll be leaving soon.'

'Leave?' Dalinar said. 'You only just arrived.'

'I know. It's incredibly frustrating, I must admit. I have discovered a place that I must be, though to be honest I'm not *exactly* sure why I need to be there. This doesn't always work as well as I'd like it to.'

Dalinar frowned at him. Wit smiled back affably.

'Are you one of them?' Dalinar asked.

'Excuse me?'

'A Herald.'

Wit laughed. 'No. Thank you, but no.'

'Are you what I've been looking for, then?' Dalinar asked. 'Radiant?'

Wit smiled. 'I am but a man, Dalinar, so much as I wish it were not true at times. I am no Radiant. And while I *am* your friend, please understand that our goals do not completely align. You must not trust yourself with me. If I have to watch this world crumble and burn to get what I need, I will do so. With tears, yes, but I would let it happen.'

Dalinar frowned.

'I will do what I can to help,' Wit said, 'and for that reason, I must go. I cannot risk too much, because if *he* finds me, then I become nothing – a soul shredded and broken into pieces that cannot be reassembled. What I do here is more dangerous than you could ever know.'

He turned to go.

'Wit,' Dalinar called.

'Yes?'

'If who finds you?'

'The one you fight, Dalinar Kholin. The father of hatred.' Wit saluted, then jogged off.

68
BRIDGES

*However, it seems to me that all things have been set up for a purpose,
and if we – as infants – stumble through the workshop, we risk exacerbat-
ing, not preventing, a problem.*

The Shattered Plains.

Kaladin did not claim these lands as he did the chasms, where
his men had found safety. Kaladin remembered all too well
the pain of bloodied feet on his first run, battered by this broken stone
wasteland. Barely anything grew out here, only the occasional patch of
rockbuds or set of enterprising vines draping down into a chasm on the
leeward side of a plateau. The bottoms of the cracks were clogged with
life, but up here it was barren.

The aching feet and burning shoulders from running a bridge had been
nothing compared to the slaughter that had awaited his men at the end
of a bridge run. Storms . . . even looking across the Plains made Kaladin
flinch. He could hear the hiss of arrows in the air, the screams of terrified
bridgemen, the song of the Parshendi.

I should have been able to save more of Bridge Four, Kaladin thought. *If I'd
been faster to accept my powers, could I have done so?*

He breathed in Stormlight to reassure himself. Only it didn't come.
He stood, dumbfounded, while soldiers marched across one of Dalinar's
enormous mechanical bridges. He tried again. Nothing.

He fished a sphere from his pouch. The firemark glowed with its customary light, tinting his fingers red. Something was wrong. Kaladin couldn't *feel* the Stormlight inside as he once had.

Syl flitted across the chasm high in the air with a group of windspren. Her giggling laughter rained down upon him, and he looked up. 'Syl?' he asked quietly. Storms. He didn't want to look like an idiot, but something deep within him was panicking like a rat caught by its tail. 'Syl!'

Several marching soldiers glanced at Kaladin, then up toward the air. Kaladin ignored them as Syl zipped down in the form of a ribbon of light. She swirled around him, still giggling.

The Stormlight returned to him. He could feel it again, and he greedily sucked it from the sphere – though he did have the presence of mind to clutch the sphere in a fist and hold it to his chest to make the process less obvious. The Light of one mark wasn't enough to expose him, but he felt far, far better with that Stormlight raging inside of him.

'What happened?' Kaladin whispered to Syl. 'Is something wrong with our bond? Is it because I haven't found the Words soon enough?'

She landed on his wrist and took the form of a young woman. She peered at his hand, cocking her head. 'What's inside?' she asked with a conspiratorial whisper.

'You know what this is, Syl,' Kaladin said, feeling chilled, as if he'd been hit by a wave of stormwater. 'A sphere. Didn't you see it just now?'

She looked at him, face innocent. 'You are making bad choices. Naughty.' Her features mimicked his for a moment and she jumped forward, as if to startle him. She laughed and zipped away.

Bad choices. Naughty. So, this was because of his promise to Moash that he'd help assassinate the king. Kaladin sighed, continuing forward.

Syl couldn't see why his decision was the right one. She was a spren, and had a stupid, simplistic morality. To be human was often to be forced to choose between distasteful options. Life wasn't clean and neat like she wanted it to be. It was messy, coated with crem. No man walked through life without getting covered in it, not even Dalinar.

'You want too much of me,' he snapped at her as he reached the other side of the chasm. 'I'm not some glorious knight of ancient days. I'm a broken man. Do you hear me, Syl? I'm *broken*.'

She zipped up to him and whispered, 'That's what they *all* were, silly.' She streaked away.

Kaladin watched as the soldiers filed across the bridge. They weren't doing a plateau run, but Dalinar had brought plenty of soldiers anyway. Going out onto the Shattered Plains was entering a war zone, and the Parshendi were ever a threat.

Bridge Four tromped across the mechanical bridge, carrying their smaller one. Kaladin wasn't *about* to leave the camps without that. These mechanisms Dalinar employed – the massive, chull-pulled bridges that could be ratcheted down into place – were amazing, but Kaladin didn't trust them. Not nearly as much as he did a good bridge on his shoulders.

Syl flitted by again. Did she really expect him to live according to *her* perception of what was right and wrong? Was she going to yank his powers away every time he did something that risked offending her?

That would be like living with a noose around his neck.

Determined to not let his worries ruin the day, he went to check on Bridge Four. *Look at the open sky,* he told himself. *Breathe the wind. Enjoy the freedom.* After so much time in captivity, these things were wonders.

He found Bridge Four beside their bridge at parade rest. It was odd to see them with their old padded-shoulder leather vests on over their new uniforms. It transformed them into a weird mix of what they had been and what they were now. They saluted him together, and he saluted back.

'At ease,' he told them, and they broke formation, laughing and joking with one another as Lopen and his assistants distributed waterskins.

'Ha!' Rock said, settling down on the side of the bridge to drink. 'This thing, it is not so hard as I remember it being.'

'It's because we're going slower,' Kaladin said, pointing at Dalinar's mechanical bridge. 'And because you're remembering the early days of bridge carries, not the later ones when we were well-fed and well-trained. It got easier then.'

'No,' Rock said. 'The bridge is light because we have defeated Sadeas. Is the proper way of things.'

'That makes no sense.'

'Ha! Perfect sense.' He took a drink. 'Airsick lowlander.'

Kaladin shook his head, but let himself find a smile at Rock's familiar voice. After slaking his own thirst, he jogged across the plateau toward where Dalinar had just finished crossing. Nearby, a tall rock formation surmounted the plateau, and atop it was a wooden structure like a small fort. Sunlight glinted off one of the spyglasses fitted there.

No permanent bridge led to this plateau, which was just outside the secure area closest to the warcamp. These scouts positioned here were vaulters, who leaped chasms at narrow points with the use of long poles. It seemed like a job that would require a special brand of craziness – and because of that, Kaladin had always felt respect for these men.

One of the vaulters was speaking with Dalinar. Kaladin would have expected the man to be tall and limber, but he was short and compact, with thick forearms. He wore a Kholin uniform with white stripes edging the coat.

'We *did* see something out here, Brightlord,' the vaulter said to Dalinar. 'I saw it with my own two eyes, and recorded the date and time in glyphs on my ledger. It was a man, a glowing one, who flew around in the sky back and forth over the Plains.'

Dalinar grunted.

'I'm not crazy, sir,' the vaulter said, shuffling from one foot to the other. 'The other lads saw it too, once I—'

'I believe you, soldier,' Dalinar said. 'It was the Assassin in White. He looked like that when he came for the king.'

The man relaxed. 'Brightlord, sir, that's what I thought. Some of the men back at camp told me I was just seeing what I wanted.'

'Nobody wants to see that one,' Dalinar said. 'But why would he spend his time out here? Why hasn't he come back to attack, if he's this close?'

Kaladin cleared his throat, uncomfortable, and pointed at the watchman's post. 'That fort up there, is it wood?'

'Yes,' the vaulter said, then noticed the knots on Kaladin's shoulders. 'Uh, sir.'

'That can't possibly withstand a highstorm,' Kaladin said.

'We break it down, sir.'

'And carry it back to camp?' Kaladin asked, frowning. 'Or do you leave it out here for the storm?'

'Leave it, sir?' the short man said. 'We stay here with it.' He pointed toward a burrowed-out section of rock, cut with hammers or a Shardblade, at the base of the stone formation. It didn't look very large – just a cubby, really. It looked like they took the wooden floor of the platform up above, then locked it into place with clasps at the side of the cubby to form a kind of door.

A special kind of crazy indeed.

'Brightlord, sir,' the vaulter said to Dalinar, 'the one in white might be out here somewhere. Waiting.'

'Thank you, soldier,' Dalinar said, nodding his dismissal. 'Keep an eye out for us while we travel. We've had reports of a chasmfiend moving in close to the camps.'

'Yes, sir,' the man said, saluting and then jogging back toward the rope ladder leading up to his post.

'What if the assassin does come for you?' Kaladin asked softly.

'I don't see how it would be any different out here,' Dalinar said. 'He'll be back eventually. On the Plains or in the palace, we'll have to fight him.'

Kaladin grunted. 'I wish you'd accept one of those Shardblades that Adolin has been winning, sir. I'd feel more comfortable if you could defend yourself.'

'I think you'd be surprised,' Dalinar said, shading his eyes, turning toward the warcamp. 'I do feel wrong leaving Elhokar alone back there, though.'

'The assassin said he wanted you, sir,' Kaladin said. 'If you're apart from the king, that will only serve to protect him.'

'I suppose,' Dalinar said. 'Unless the assassin's comments were misdirection.' He shook his head. 'I might order you to stay with him next time. I can't help but feel I'm missing something important, something right in front of me.'

Kaladin set his jaw, trying to ignore the chill he felt. *Order you to stay with him next time. . . .* It was almost like fate itself was pushing Kaladin to be in a position to betray the king.

'About your imprisonment,' the highprince said.

'Already forgotten, sir,' Kaladin said. Dalinar's part in it, at least. 'I appreciate not being demoted.'

'You're a good soldier,' Dalinar said. 'Most of the time.' His eyes flicked toward Bridge Four, picking up their bridge. One of the men at the side drew his attention in particular: Renarin, wearing his Bridge Four uniform, hefting the bridge into place. Nearby, Leyten laughed and gave him pointers on how to hold the thing.

'He's actually starting to fit in, sir,' Kaladin said. 'The men like him. I never thought I'd see the day.'

Dalinar nodded.

'How was he?' Kaladin asked softly. 'After what happened in the arena?'

'He refused to go practice with Zahel,' Dalinar said. 'So far as I know, he hasn't summoned his Shardblade in weeks.' He watched for a moment longer. 'I can't decide if his time with your men is good for him – helping him think like a soldier – or if it's just encouraging him to avoid his greater responsibilities.'

'Sir,' Kaladin said. 'If I may say so, your son seems like kind of a misfit. Out of place. Awkward, alone.'

Dalinar nodded.

'Then, I can say with confidence that Bridge Four is probably the *best* place he could find himself.' It felt odd to be saying it of a lighteyes, but it was true.

Dalinar grunted. 'I'll trust your judgment. Go. Make sure those men of yours are on the watch for the assassin, in case he does come today.'

Kaladin nodded, leaving the highprince behind. He'd heard about Dalinar's visions before – and had had an inkling of their contents. He didn't know what he thought, but he intended to get a copy of the vision records in their entirety so he could have Ka read it to him.

Perhaps these visions were why Syl was always so determined to trust Dalinar.

As the day passed, the army moved across the Plains like the flow of some viscous liquid – mud dribbling down a shallow incline. All of this so Shallan could see a chasmfiend chrysalis. Kaladin shook his head, crossing a plateau. Adolin was certainly smitten; he'd managed to roll out an entire strike force, his father included, just to sate the girl's whims.

'Walking, Kaladin?' Adolin said, trotting up. The prince rode that white beast of a horse, the thing with the hooves like hammers. Adolin wore his full suit of blue Shardplate, helm tied to a knob on the back of the saddle. 'I thought you had full requisition right from my father's stables.'

'I have full requisition right from the quartermasters too,' Kaladin said, 'but you don't see me hiking out here with a cauldron on my back just because I *can*.'

Adolin chuckled. 'You should try riding more. You have to admit that there are advantages. The speed of the gallop, the height of attack.' He patted his horse on the neck.

'I guess I just trust my own feet too much.'

Adolin nodded, as if that had been the wisest thing a man had ever said, before riding back to check on Shallan in her palanquin. Feeling a little fatigued, Kaladin fished in his pocket for another sphere, just a diamond chip this time, and held it to his chest. He breathed in.

Again, nothing happened. Storm it! He looked about for Syl, but couldn't find her. She'd been so playful lately, he was starting to wonder if this was all some kind of trick. He actually hoped it was that, and not something more. Despite his inward grousing and complaints, he desperately wanted this power. He had claimed the sky, the winds themselves. Giving them up would be like giving up his own hands.

He eventually reached the edge of their current plateau, where Dalinar's mechanical bridge was setting up. Here, blessedly, he found Syl inspecting a cremling crawling across the rocks toward the safety of a nearby crack.

Kaladin sat down on a rock beside her. 'So you're punishing me,' he said. 'For agreeing to help Moash. That's why I'm having trouble with the Stormlight.'

Syl followed along behind the cremling, which was a kind of beetle with a round, iridescent shell.

'Syl?' Kaladin asked. 'Are you all right? You seem . . .'

Like you were before. When we first met. It made a feeling of dread rise within him to acknowledge it. If his powers were withdrawing, was it because the bond itself was weakening?

She looked up at him, and her eyes became more focused, her expression like that of her normal self. 'You have to decide what you want, Kaladin,' she said.

'You don't like Moash's plan,' Kaladin said. 'Are you trying to force me to change my mind regarding him?'

She scrunched up her face. 'I don't want to *force* you to do anything. You have to do what you think is right.'

'That's what I'm trying to do!'

'No. I don't think you are.'

'Fine. I'll tell Moash and his friends that I'm out, that I'm not going to help them.'

'But you gave Moash your word!'

'I gave my word to Dalinar too. . . .'

She drew her lips to a line, meeting his eyes.

'That's the problem, isn't it,' Kaladin whispered. 'I've made two promises, and I can't keep my word to both.' Oh, storms. Was this the sort of thing that had destroyed the Knights Radiant?

What happened to your honorspren when you confronted them with a choice like this? A broken vow either way.

Idiot, Kaladin thought at himself. It seemed he couldn't make any right choices these days.

'What do I do, Syl?' he whispered.

She flitted up until she was standing in the air just before him, eyes meeting his. 'You must speak the Words.'

'I don't know them.'

'Find them.' She looked toward the sky. 'Find them soon, Kaladin. And no, simply telling Moash you won't help isn't going to work. We've gone too far for that. You need to do what your heart needs to do.' She rose upward toward the sky.

'Stay with me, Syl,' he whispered after her, standing. 'I'll figure this out. Just . . . don't lose yourself. Please. I need you.'

Nearby, gears on Dalinar's bridge mechanism turned as soldiers twisted levers, and the entire thing started to unfold.

'Stop, stop, *stop*!' Shallan Davar jogged up, a flurry of red hair and blue silk, a large floppy hat on her head to keep off the sun. Two of her guards jogged after her, but neither was Gaz.

Kaladin spun about, alarmed at her tone, searching for signs of the Assassin in White.

Shallan, puffing, raised her safehand to her chest. 'Storms, what is wrong with palanquin porters? They absolutely refuse to move quickly. "It's not stately," they say. Well, I don't really *do* stately. All right, give me a minute, then you can continue.'

She settled down on a rock near the bridge. The baffled soldiers regarded her as she dug out her drawing pad, then started sketching. 'All right,' she said. 'Continue. I've been trying all *day* to get a progressive sketch of that bridge as it unfolds. Storming porters.'

What a bizarre woman.

The soldiers hesitantly continued positioning the bridge, unfolding it beneath the watchful eyes of three of Dalinar's engineers – widowed wives of his fallen officers. Several carpenters were also on hand to work at their orders if the bridge got stuck or a piece snapped.

Kaladin gripped his spear, trying to sort through his emotions regarding Syl, and the promises he'd made. Surely he could work this out somehow. Couldn't he?

Seeing this bridge intruded on his mind with thoughts of bridge runs, and he found that a welcome distraction. He could see why Sadeas had preferred the simple, if brutal, method of the bridge crews. Those bridges were faster, cheaper, and less prone to problems. These massive things were ponderous, like big ships trying to maneuver in a bay.

Armored bridge runners is the natural solution, Kaladin thought. *Men with shields, with full support from the army to get them into position. You could have fast, mobile bridges, but also not leave men to be slaughtered.*

Of course, Sadeas had wanted the bridgemen killed, as bait to keep arrows away from his soldiers.

One of the carpenters helping with the bridge – examining one of the wooden steadying pins and talking about carving a new one – was familiar to Kaladin. The stout man had a birthmark across his forehead, shaded by the carpenter's cap he wore.

Kaladin knew that face. Had the man been one of Dalinar's soldiers, one of those who had lost the will to fight following the slaughter on the Tower? Some of those had switched to other duties in camp.

He was distracted as Moash walked over, raising a hand toward Bridge Four, who cheered him. Moash's brilliant Shardplate – which he'd had repainted blue with red accents at the points – looked surprisingly natural on him. It hadn't even been a week yet, but Moash walked in the armor easily.

He stepped up to Kaladin, then knelt down on one knee, Plate clinking. He saluted, arm across chest.

His eyes ... they *were* lighter in color; tan instead of deep brown as they'd once been. He wore his Shardblade strapped across his back in a guarded sheath. Only one more day until he had it bonded.

'You don't need to salute me, Moash,' Kaladin said. 'You're lighteyed now. You outrank me by a mile or two.'

'I'll never outrank you, Kal,' Moash said, faceplate of his helm up. 'You're my captain. Forever.' He grinned. 'But I can't tell you how much storming *fun* it is to watch the lighteyes try to figure out how to deal with me.'

'Your eyes are really changing.'

'Yeah,' Moash said. 'But I'm not one of them, you hear me? I'm one of us. Bridge Four. I'm our . . . secret weapon.'

'Secret?' Kaladin asked, raising an eyebrow. 'They've probably heard about you all the way in *Iri* by now, Moash. You're the first darkeyed man to be given a Blade and Plate in over a lifetime.'

Dalinar had even granted Moash lands and a stipend from them, a lavish sum, and not just by bridgeman standards. Moash still stopped by for stew some nights, but not all. He was too busy arranging his new quarters.

There was nothing wrong with that. It was natural. It was also part of why Kaladin had turned down the Blade himself – and perhaps why he'd always been worried about showing his powers to the lighteyes. Even if they didn't find a way to take the abilities from him – he knew that fear was irrational, though he felt it all the same – they might find a way to take Bridge Four from him. His men . . . his very self.

They might not be the ones who take it from you, Kaladin thought. *You might be doing it to yourself, better than any lighteyes could.*

The thought nauseated him.

'We're getting close,' Moash said softly as Kaladin took out his waterskin.

'Close?' Kaladin asked. He lowered the waterskin and looked over his shoulder across the plateaus. 'I thought we still had a few hours to go before we reached the dead chrysalis.'

It was far out, almost as far out as the armies went on bridge runs. Bethab and Thanadal had claimed it yesterday.

'Not *that*,' Moash said, looking to the side. 'Other things.'

'Oh. Moash, are you . . . I mean . . .'

'Kal,' Moash said. 'You're with us, right? You said it.'

Two promises. Syl told him to follow his heart.

'Kaladin,' Moash said, more solemnly. 'You gave me these Shards, even after you were angry with me for disobeying you. There's a reason. You know, deep down, that what I'm doing is right. It's the only solution.'

Kaladin nodded.

Moash glanced around, then stood up, Plate clinking. He leaned in to whisper. 'Don't worry. Graves says you aren't going to have to do much. We just need an opening.'

Kaladin felt sick. 'We can't do it when Dalinar is in the warcamp,' he whispered. 'I won't risk him being hurt.'

'No problem,' Moash said. 'We feel the same way. We'll wait for the right moment. The newest plan is to hit the king with an arrow, so there's no risk of implicating you or anyone else. You lead him to the right spot, and Graves will fell the king with his own bow. He's an excellent shot.'

An arrow. It felt so cowardly.

It needed to be done. It *needed* to be.

Moash patted him on the shoulder, stepping off in his clinking Shard-plate. Storms. All Kaladin had to do was lead the king into a specific spot . . . that, and betray Dalinar's trust in him.

And if I don't help kill the king, won't I be betraying justice and honor? The king had murdered – or as good as murdered – many people, some through indifference, others through incompetence. And storms, Dalinar wasn't innocent either. If he'd been as noble as he pretended, wouldn't he have seen Roshone imprisoned, rather than shipped off somewhere where he 'couldn't do any more harm'?

Kaladin walked over to the bridge, watching the men march across. Shallan Davar sat primly on a rock, continuing her sketches of the bridge mechanism. Adolin had climbed off his horse and handed it to some grooms for watering. He waved Kaladin over.

'Princeling?' Kaladin asked, stepping up.

'The assassin has been seen out here,' Adolin said. 'On the Plains at night.'

'Yes. I heard the scout telling your father about it.'

'We need a plan. What if he attacks out here?'

'I hope he does.'

Adolin looked to him, frowning.

'From what I saw,' Kaladin said, 'and from what I've learned about the assassin's initial attack on the old king, he depends on confusion in his victims. He jumps off walls and onto ceilings; he sends men falling the wrong direction. Well, there aren't any walls or ceilings out here.'

'So he can just full-on fly,' Adolin said with a grimace.

'Yes,' Kaladin said, pointing with a smile, 'since we have, what is it, *three hundred* archers with us?'

Kaladin had used his abilities effectively against Parshendi arrows, and so perhaps archers wouldn't be able to kill the assassin. But he imagined it would be hard for the man to fight with wave after wave of arrows flying at him.

Adolin nodded slowly. 'I'll talk to them, get them ready for the possibility.' He started walking toward the bridge, so Kaladin joined him. They passed Shallan, who was still absorbed in her sketching. She didn't even notice Adolin waving at her. Lighteyed women and their diversions. Kaladin shook his head.

'Do you know anything about women, bridgeboy?' Adolin asked, looking over his shoulder and watching Shallan as the two of them crossed the bridge.

'Lighteyed women?' Kaladin asked. 'Nothing. Thankfully.'

'People think I know a lot about women,' Adolin said. 'The truth is, I know how to get them – how to make them laugh, how to make them interested. I don't know how to keep them.' He hesitated. 'I really want to keep this one.'

'So . . . tell her that, maybe?' Kaladin said, thinking back to Tarah, and the mistakes he'd made.

'Do such things work on darkeyed women?'

'You're asking the wrong man,' Kaladin said. 'I haven't had much time for women lately. I was too busy trying to avoid being killed.'

Adolin seemed to be barely listening. 'Perhaps I could say something like that to her. . . . Seems too simple, and she's anything but simple. . . .' He turned back to Kaladin. 'Anyway. Assassin in White. We need more of a plan than just telling the archers to be ready.'

'Do you have any ideas?' Kaladin said.

'You won't have a Shardblade, but won't need one, because of . . . you know.'

'I know?' Kaladin felt a spike of alarm.

'Yeah . . . you know.' Adolin glanced away and shrugged, as if trying to act nonchalant. 'That thing.'

'What thing?'

'The thing . . . with the . . . um, stuff?'

He doesn't know, Kaladin realized. *He's just fishing, trying to figure out why I can fight so well.*

And he's doing a really, really bad job of it.

Kaladin relaxed, and even found himself smiling at Adolin's awkward attempt. It was nice to feel an emotion other than panic or worry. 'I don't think you have any idea what you're talking about.'

Adolin scowled. 'There's something odd about you, bridgeboy,' he said. 'Admit it.'

'I admit nothing.'

'You survived that fall with the assassin,' Adolin said. 'And at first, I worried you were working with him. Now . . .'

'Now what?'

'Well, I've decided that whatever you are, you're on my side.' Adolin sighed. 'Anyway, the assassin. My instincts say the best plan is the one we used when fighting together in the arena. You distract him while I kill him.'

'That could work, though I worry that he's not the type to let himself get distracted.'

'Neither was Relis,' Adolin said. 'We'll do it, bridgeboy. You and I. We're going to bring that monster down.'

'We'll need to be fast,' Kaladin said. 'He'll win a drawn-out fight. And Adolin, strike for the spine or the head. Don't try a weakening blow first. Go right for the kill.'

Adolin frowned at him. 'Why?'

'I saw something when the two of us fell together,' Kaladin said. 'I cut him, but he healed the wound somehow.'

'I have a Blade. He won't be able to heal from *that* . . . right?'

'Best to not find out. Strike to kill. Trust me.'

Adolin met his eyes. 'Oddly, I do. Trust you, I mean. It's a very strange sensation.'

'Yeah, well, I'll try to hold myself back from going skipping across the plateau in joy.'

Adolin grinned. 'I'd pay to see that.'

'Me skipping?'

'You happy,' Adolin said, laughing. 'You've got a face like a storm! I half think you could *frighten off* a storm.'

Kaladin grunted.

Adolin laughed again, slapping him on the shoulder, then turned as Shallan finally crossed the bridge, her sketching apparently done. She looked to Adolin fondly, and as he reached out to take her hand, she rose up on her toes and gave him a kiss on the cheek. Adolin drew back, startled. Alethi were more reserved than that in public.

Shallan grinned at him. Then she turned and gasped, raising a hand to her mouth. Kaladin jumped, *again*, looking for danger – but Shallan just went dashing off to a nearby clump of rocks.

Adolin raised his hand to his cheek, then looked to Kaladin with a grin. 'She probably saw an interesting bug.'

'No, it's moss!' Shallan called back.

'Ah, of course,' Adolin said, strolling over, Kaladin following. 'Moss. So *exciting*.'

'Hush, you,' Shallan said, wagging her pencil at him as she bent down, inspecting the rocks. 'The moss grows in a strange pattern here. What could cause that?'

'Alcohol,' Adolin said.

She glanced at him.

He shrugged. 'Makes *me* do crazy things.' He looked at Kaladin, who shook his head. 'That was *funny*,' Adolin said. 'It was a joke! Well, kind of.'

'Oh hush,' Shallan said. 'This looks almost like the same pattern as a flowering rockbud, the kind common here on the Plains. . . .' She started sketching.

Kaladin folded his arms. Then he sighed.

'What does that sigh mean?' Adolin asked him.

'Boredom,' Kaladin said, glancing back at the army, still crossing the bridge. With a force of three thousand – that was about half of Dalinar's current army, following heavy recruitment – moving out here took time. On bridge runs, these crossings had felt so quick. Kaladin had always been exhausted, savoring the chance to rest. 'I guess out here, it's so barren that there's not much to get excited about other than moss.'

'You hush too,' Shallan told him. 'Go polish your bridge or something.' She leaned in, then poked her pencil at a bug that was crawling across the moss. 'Ah . . .' she said, then hurriedly scribbled some notes. 'Anyway, you're wrong. There's a *lot* out here to get excited about, if you look in the right places. Some of the soldiers said a chasmfiend has been spotted. Do you think it might attack us?'

'You sound entirely too hopeful saying that, Shallan,' Adolin said.

'Well, I *do* still need a good sketch of one.'

'We'll get you to the chrysalis. That will have to be enough.'

Shallan's scholarship was an excuse; the truth was obvious to Kaladin. Dalinar had brought an unusual number of scouts with him today, and Kaladin suspected once they reached the chrysalis – which was on the border of unexplored lands – they'd range ahead and gather information. This was all preparation for Dalinar's expedition.

'I don't understand why we need so many soldiers,' Shallan said, noticing Kaladin's gaze as he studied the army. 'Didn't you say the Parshendi haven't been showing up to fight over chrysalises lately?'

'No, they haven't,' Adolin said. 'That's precisely *what* makes us worried.'

Kaladin nodded. 'Whenever your enemy changes established tactics, you need to worry. It could mean they're getting desperate. Desperation is very, very dangerous.'

'You're good at military thinking, for a bridgeboy,' Adolin said.

'Coincidentally,' Kaladin said, 'you're good at not being unobnoxious, for a prince.'

'Thanks,' Adolin said.

'That was an insult, dear,' Shallan said.

'What?' Adolin said. 'It was?'

She nodded, still sketching, though she glanced up to eye Kaladin. He met the expression calmly.

'Adolin,' Shallan said, turning back to the small rock formation in front of her, 'would you slay this moss for me, please?'

'Slay . . . the moss.' He looked at Kaladin, who just shrugged. How was he to know what a lighteyed woman meant? They were a strange breed.

'Yes,' Shallan said, standing up. 'Give that moss, and the rock behind it, a good chop. As a favor for your betrothed.'

Adolin looked baffled, but he did as she asked, summoning his Shardblade and hacking at the moss and rock. The top of the small pile of stones slipped free, cut with ease, and clattered to the floor of the plateau.

Shallan stepped up eagerly, crouching down beside the perfectly flat top of the sliced stone. 'Mmm,' she said, nodding to herself. She started sketching.

Adolin dismissed his Blade. 'Women!' he said, shrugging at Kaladin. Then he went jogging off to get a drink without asking her for an explanation.

Kaladin took a step after him, but then hesitated. What *did* Shallan find so interesting here? This woman was a puzzle, and he knew he wouldn't be completely comfortable until he understood her. She had too much access to Adolin, and therefore Dalinar, to leave uninvestigated.

He stepped closer, looking over her shoulder as she drew. 'Strata,' he said. 'You're counting the strata of crem to guess how old the rock is.'

'Good guess,' she said, 'but this is a bad location for strata dating. The wind blows across the plateaus too strongly, and the crem doesn't collect in pools evenly. So the strata here are erratic and inaccurate.'

Kaladin frowned, narrowing his eyes. The cross section of rock was normal cremstone on the outside, some strata visible as different shades of brown. The center of the stone, though, was white. You didn't see white rock like that often; it had to be quarried. Which meant this was either a very strange occurrence, or ...

'There was a structure here once,' Kaladin said. 'A long time ago. It must have taken centuries for the crem to get that thick on something sticking out of the ground.'

She glanced at him. 'You're smarter than you look.' Then, turning back to her drawing, she added, 'Good thing ...'

He grunted. 'Why does everything you say have to include some quip? Are you that desperate to prove how clever you are?'

'Perhaps I'm merely annoyed at you for taking advantage of Adolin.'

'Advantage?' Kaladin asked. 'Because I called him obnoxious?'

'You deliberately said it in a way you expected he wouldn't understand. To make him look like a fool. He's trying very hard to be nice to you.'

'Yes,' Kaladin said. 'He's always so munificent to all of the little dark-eyes who flock around to worship him.'

Shallan snapped her pencil against the page. 'You really are a hateful man, aren't you? Underneath the mock boredom, the dangerous glares, the growls – you just hate people, is that it?'

'What? No, I—'

'Adolin is *trying*. He feels bad for what happened to you, and he's doing what he can to make up for it. He is a *good man*. Is it too much for you to stop provoking him?'

'He calls me bridgeboy,' Kaladin said, feeling stubborn. 'He's been provoking *me*.'

'Yes, because *he* is the one storming around with alternating scowls and insults,' Shallan said. 'Adolin Kholin, the most difficult man to get along with on the Shattered Plains. I mean *look* at him! He's so unlikable!'

She gestured with the pencil toward where Adolin was laughing with the darkeyed water boys. The groom walked up with Adolin's horse, and Adolin took his Shardplate helm off the carrying post, handing it over, letting one of the water boys try it on. It was ridiculously large on the lad.

Kaladin flushed as the boy took a Shardbearer's pose, and they all laughed again. Kaladin looked back to Shallan, who folded her arms, drawing pad resting on the flat-topped cut rock before her. She smirked at him.

Insufferable woman. *Bah!*

Kaladin left her and hiked across the rough ground to join Bridge Four, where he insisted on taking a turn hauling the bridge, despite Teft's protests that he was 'above that sort of thing' now. He was no storming lighteyes. He'd never be above doing an honest day's work.

The familiar weight of the bridge settled onto his shoulders. Rock was right. It *did* feel lighter than it once had. He smiled as he heard cursing from Lopen's cousins, who – like Renarin – were being initiated on this run into their first bridge carry.

They hiked the bridge over a chasm – crossing on one of Dalinar's larger, less mobile ones – and started across the plateau. For a time, marching at the front of Bridge Four, Kaladin could imagine that his life was simple. No plateau assaults, no arrows, no assassins or bodyguarding. Just him, his team, and a bridge.

Unfortunately, as they neared the other side of the large plateau, he started to feel weary and – by reflex – tried to suck in some Stormlight to bolster him. It wouldn't come.

Life was not simple. It never *had* been, certainly not while running bridges. To pretend otherwise was to paint over the past.

He helped set the bridge down, then – noticing the vanguard moving out in front of the army – he and the bridgemen shoved their bridge into place across the chasm. The vanguard cheerfully welcomed the chance to get ahead, marching over the bridge and securing the next plateau.

Kaladin and the others followed, then – a half hour later – they let the vanguard onto the next plateau. They continued like that for a time, waiting for Dalinar's bridge to arrive before crossing, then leading the vanguard onto the next plateau. Hours passed – sweaty, muscle-straining hours. Good hours. Kaladin didn't come to any realizations about the king, or his place in the man's potential assassination. But for the moment, he carried his bridge and enjoyed the progress of an army moving toward their goal beneath an open sky.

As the day grew long, they approached the target plateau, where the hollowed-out chrysalis awaited Shallan's study. Kaladin and Bridge Four let the vanguard across as they'd been doing, then settled in to wait. Eventually, the bulk of the army approached, and Dalinar's lumbering bridges moved into position, ratcheting down to span the chasm.

Kaladin gulped deeply of warm water as he watched. He washed his face with the water, then wiped his brow. They were getting close. This plateau was far out onto the Plains, almost to the Tower itself. Getting back would take hours, assuming they moved at the same relaxed speed they had taken getting out here. It would be well after dark when they returned to the warcamps.

If Dalinar does want to assault the center of the Shattered Plains, Kaladin thought, *it will take days of marching, all the while exposed on the plateaus, with the potential of being surrounded and cut off from the warcamps.*

The Weeping *would* make a great chance for that. Four straight weeks of rain, but no highstorms. This was the off year, when there wouldn't even be a highstorm on Lightday in the middle – part of the thousand-day cycle of two years that made up a full storm rotation. Still, he knew that many Alethi patrols had tried exploring eastward before. They'd all been destroyed by highstorms, chasmfiends, or Parshendi assault teams.

Nothing short of an all-out, full-on movement of resources toward the center would work. An assault that would leave Dalinar, and whoever came with him, isolated.

Dalinar's bridge thumped down into place. Kaladin's men traversed their own bridge and prepared to pull it across to go move the vanguard. Kaladin crossed, then waved them on ahead of him. He walked over to where the larger bridge had settled down.

Dalinar was crossing it while walking with some of his scouts, all vaulters, with servants behind carrying long poles. 'I want you to spread out,' the highprince said to them. 'We won't have much time before we need to head back. I want a survey of as many plateaus as you can see from here. The more of our route we can plan now, the less time we'll have to waste during the actual assault.'

The scouts nodded, saluting as he dismissed them. He stepped off the bridge and nodded to Kaladin. Behind them, Dalinar's generals, scribes, and engineers crossed the bridge. They'd be followed by the bulk of the army, and finally the rearguard.

'I hear you've been building mobile bridges, sir,' Kaladin said. 'You realize those mechanical ones are too slow for your assault, I assume.'

Dalinar nodded. 'But I will have soldiers carry them. No need for your men to do so.'

'Sir, that is thoughtful of you, but I don't think you have to worry. The bridge crews will carry for you, if ordered. Many of them will probably welcome the familiarity.'

'I thought you and your men considered assignment to those bridge crews a death sentence, soldier,' Dalinar said.

'The way Sadeas ran them, it was. You could do a better job. Armored men, trained in formations, running the bridges. Soldiers marching in front with shields. Archers with instructions to defend the bridge crews. Besides, the danger is only for an assault.'

Dalinar nodded. 'Prepare the crews, then. Having your men on the bridges will free the soldiers in case we get attacked.' He started to walk across the plateau, but one of the carpenters on the other side of the chasm called to him. Dalinar turned and started to cross the bridge again.

He passed officers and scribes crossing the bridge, including Adolin and Shallan, who walked side by side. She'd given up on the palanquin and he had given up on his horse, and she seemed to be explaining to him about the hidden remnants of a structure she'd found inside that rock earlier.

Behind them, on the other side of the chasm, stood the worker who had called Dalinar back across.

It's that same carpenter, Kaladin thought. The stout man with the cap and the birthmark. *Where* have *I seen him . . . ?*

It clicked. Sadeas's lumberyards. The man had been one of the carpenters there, overseeing the construction of bridges.

Kaladin started running.

He was charging toward the bridge before the connection fully solidified in his mind. Ahead of him, Adolin spun immediately and started running, searching for whatever danger Kaladin had spotted. He left a bewildered Shallan standing in the bridge's center. Kaladin approached her in a rush.

The carpenter grabbed a lever on the side of the bridge contraption.

'The carpenter, Adolin!' Kaladin screamed. 'Stop that man!'

Dalinar still stood on the bridge. The highprince had been distracted by something else. What? Kaladin realized he had heard something too. Horns, the call that the enemy had been spotted.

It happened all in an instant. Dalinar turning toward the horns. The carpenter pulling the lever, Adolin in his glimmering Shardplate reaching Dalinar.

The bridge lurched.

Then it collapsed.

69

NOTHING

Rayse is captive. He cannot leave the system he now inhabits. His destructive potential is, therefore, inhibited.

As the bridge fell out from beneath him, Kaladin reached for Stormlight.

Nothing.

Panic surged through him. His stomach dropped and he tumbled into the air.

The fall into the darkness of the chasm was a brief moment, but also an eternity. He caught a glimpse of Shallan and several men in blue uniforms falling and flailing in terror.

Like a drowning man struggling toward the surface, Kaladin thrashed for the Stormlight. He would *not* die this way! The sky was his! The winds were his. The chasms were his.

He would not!

Syl screamed, a terrified, painful sound that vibrated Kaladin's very bones. In that moment, he got a breath of Stormlight, life itself.

He crashed into the ground at the bottom of the chasm and all went black.

⁂

Swimming through pain.

The pain washed over him, a liquid, but did not get *inside*. His skin kept it out.

WHAT HAVE YOU DONE? The distant voice sounded like rumbling thunder.

Kaladin gasped and opened his eyes, and the pain crawled inside. Suddenly, his entire body hurt.

He lay on his back, staring upward at a streak of light in the air. Syl? No . . . no, that was sunlight. The opening at the top of the chasm, high above him. This far out onto the Shattered Plains, the chasms here were hundreds of feet deep.

Kaladin groaned and sat up. That strip of light seemed impossibly distant. He'd been swallowed by the darkness, and the chasm nearby was shadowed, obscure. He put a hand to his head.

I got some Stormlight right at the end, he thought. *I survived. But that scream!* It haunted him, echoing in his mind. It had sounded too much like the scream he'd heard when touching the duelist's Shardblade in the arena.

Check for wounds, his father's teachings whispered from the back of his mind. The body could go into shock with a bad break or wound, and not notice the damage that had been done. He went through the motions of checking his limbs for breaks, and did not reach for any of the spheres in his pouch. He didn't want to light the gloom, and potentially face the dead around him.

Was Dalinar among them? Adolin had been running toward his father. Had the prince managed to get to Dalinar before the bridge collapsed? He'd been wearing Plate, and had jumped at the end.

Kaladin felt at his legs, then his ribs. He found aches and scrapes, but nothing broken or ripped. That Stormlight he'd held at the end . . . it had protected him, perhaps even healed him, before running out. He finally reached into his pouch and fished out spheres, but found those all drained. He tried his pocket, then froze as he heard something scraping nearby.

He leaped to his feet and spun, wishing he had a weapon. The chasm bottom grew *brighter*. A steady glow revealed fanlike frillblooms and draping vines on the walls, gathered twigs and moss on the floor in patches. Was that a voice? He felt a surreal moment of confusion as shadows moved on the wall ahead of him.

Then someone wandered around the corner, wearing a silk dress and carrying a pack over her shoulder. Shallan Davar.

She screamed when she saw him, throwing the pack to the ground and stumbling backward, hands to her sides. She even dropped her sphere.

Rolling his arm in its socket, Kaladin stepped closer into the light. 'Calm down,' he said. 'It's me.'

'Stormfather!' Shallan said, scrambling to grab the sphere off the ground again. She stepped forward, thrusting the light toward him. 'It *is* you . . . the bridgeman. How . . . ?'

'I don't know,' he lied, looking upward. 'I've got a wicked crick in my neck and my elbow hurts like thunder. What happened?'

'Someone threw the emergency latch on the bridge.'

'What emergency latch?'

'It topples the bridge into the chasm.'

'Sounds like a storming *stupid* thing to have,' Kaladin said, fishing in his pocket for his other spheres. He glanced at them covertly. Also drained. Storms. He'd used them all?

'Depends,' Shallan said. 'What if your men have retreated over the bridge and enemies are pouring across it after you? The emergency latch is supposed to have some kind of safety lock so it can't be thrown by accident, but you can release it in a hurry if you need to.'

He grunted as Shallan shone her sphere past him toward where the two halves of the bridge had smashed into the ground of the chasm. There were the bodies he'd expected.

He looked. He *had* to. No sign of Dalinar, though several of the officers and lighteyed ladies who had been crossing the bridge lay in twisted, broken heaps on the ground. A drop of two hundred feet or more did not leave survivors.

Except Shallan. Kaladin didn't remember grabbing her as he fell, but he didn't remember much of that fall beyond Syl's scream. That *scream* . . .

Well, he must have managed to grab Shallan by reflex, infusing her with Stormlight to slow her fall. She looked disheveled, her blue dress scuffed and her hair a mess, but she was apparently otherwise unharmed.

'I woke up down here in the darkness,' Shallan said. 'It's been a while since we fell.'

'How can you tell?'

'It's almost dark up there,' Shallan said. 'It will be night soon. When I woke I heard echoes of yelling. Fighting. I saw something glowing from around that corner. Turned out to be a soldier who had fallen, his sphere pouch ripped.' She shivered visibly. 'He'd been killed by something before the fall.'

'Parshendi,' Kaladin said. 'Just before the bridge collapsed, I heard horns from the vanguard. We got attacked.' Damnation. That probably meant that Dalinar had retreated, assuming he'd actually survived. There was nothing worth fighting for out here.

'Give me one of those spheres,' Kaladin said.

She handed one over, and Kaladin went searching among the fallen. For pulses, ostensibly, but really for any equipment or spheres.

'You think any of these might be alive?' Shallan asked, voice sounding small in the otherwise silent chasm.

'Well, *we* survived somehow.'

'How do you think that happened?' Shallan said, looking upward toward the gap far, far above.

'I saw some windspren just before we fell,' Kaladin said. 'I've heard folktales of them protecting a person as he falls. Perhaps that's what happened.'

Shallan went silent as he searched the bodies. 'Yes,' she finally said. 'That sounds logical.'

She seemed convinced. Good. So long as she didn't start wondering about the stories told of 'Kaladin Stormblessed.'

Nobody else was alive, but he verified for certain that neither Dalinar nor Adolin were among the corpses.

I was a fool not to spot that an assassination attempt was coming, Kaladin thought. Sadeas had tried hard to undermine Dalinar at the feast a few days back, with the revelation of the visions. It was a classic ploy. Discredit your enemy, *then* kill him, to make certain he didn't become a martyr.

The corpses had little of value. A handful of spheres, some writing implements that Shallan greedily snatched up and stuffed into her satchel. No maps. Kaladin had no specific idea where they were. And with night imminent ...

'What do we do?' Shallan asked softly, staring at the darkened realm, with its unexpected shadows, its gently moving frills, vines, polyplike staccatos, their tendrils out and wafting in the air.

Kaladin remembered his first times down in this place, which always felt too green, too muggy, too alien. Nearby, two skulls peeked out from beneath the moss, watching. Splashing sounded from a distant pool, which made Shallan spin wildly. Though the chasms were a home to Kaladin now, he did not deny that at times they were distinctly unnerving.

'It's safer down here than it seems,' Kaladin said. 'During my time in Sadeas's army, I spent days upon days in the chasms, gathering salvage from the fallen. Just watch for rotspren.'

'And the chasmfiends?' Shallan asked, spinning to look in another direction as a cremling scuttled along the wall.

'I never saw one.' Which was true, though he *had* seen a shadow of one once, scraping its way down a distant chasm. Even thinking of that day gave him chills. 'They aren't as common as people claim. The real danger is highstorms. You see, if it rains, even far away from here—'

'Yes, flash flooding,' Shallan said. 'Very dangerous in a slot canyon. I've read about them.'

'I'm sure that will be very helpful,' Kaladin said. 'You mentioned some dead soldiers nearby?'

She pointed, and he strode in that direction. She followed, sticking close to his light. He found a few dead spearmen who had been shoved off the plateau above. The wounds were fresh. Just beyond them was a dead Parshendi, also fresh.

The Parshendi man had uncut gems in his beard. Kaladin touched one, hesitated, then tried to draw the Stormlight out. Nothing happened. He sighed, then bowed his head for the fallen, before finally pulling a spear from underneath one of the bodies and standing up. The light above had faded to a deep blue. Night.

'So, we wait?' Shallan asked.

'For what?' Kaladin asked, raising the spear to his shoulder.

'For them to come back . . .' She trailed off. 'They're not coming back for us, are they?'

'They'll assume we're dead. Storms, we *should* be dead. We're too far out for a corpse-recovery operation, I'd guess. That's doubly true since the Parshendi attacked.' He rubbed his chin. 'I suppose we could wait for Dalinar's major expedition. He was indicating he'd come this way, searching for the center. It's only a few days away, right?'

Shallan paled. Well, she paled *further*. That light skin of hers was so strange. It and the red hair made her look like a very small Horneater. 'Dalinar is planning to march just after the final highstorm before the Weeping. That storm is close. And it will involve lots, and lots, and *lots* of rain.'

'Bad idea, then.'

'You could say so.'

He'd tried to imagine what a highstorm would be like down here. He had seen the aftereffects when salvaging with Bridge Four. The twisted, broken corpses. The piles of refuse crushed against walls and into cracks. Boulders as tall as a man casually washed through chasms until they got wedged between two walls, sometimes fifty feet up in the air.

'When?' he asked. '*When* is that highstorm?'

She stared at him, then dug into her satchel, flipping through sheets of paper with her freehand while holding the satchel through the fabric of her safehand. She waved him over with his sphere, as she had to tuck hers away.

He held it up for her as she looked over a page with lines of script. 'Tomorrow night,' she said softly. 'Just after first moonset.'

Kaladin grunted, holding up his sphere and inspecting the chasm. *We're just to the north of the chasm we fell from,* he thought. *So the way back should be . . . that way?*

'All right then,' Shallan said. She took a deep breath, then snapped her satchel closed. 'We walk back, and we start immediately.'

'You don't want to sit for a moment and catch your breath?'

'My breath is quite well caught,' Shallan said. 'If it's all the same to you, I'd rather be moving. Once back, we can sit sipping mulled wine and laugh about how silly it was of us to hurry all that way, since we had so much time to spare. I'd like very much to feel that foolish. You?'

'Yeah.' He liked the chasms. It didn't mean he wanted to risk a highstorm in one of them. 'You don't have a map in that satchel, do you?'

'No,' Shallan said with a grimace. 'I didn't bring my own. Brightness Velat has the maps. I was using hers. But I might be able to remember some of what I've seen.'

'Then I think we should go this way,' Kaladin said, pointing. He started walking.

The bridgeman started walking off in the direction he'd pointed, not even giving her a chance to state her opinion on the matter. Shallan kept a huff to herself, snatching up her pack – she'd found some waterskins on the soldiers – and satchel. She hurried after him, her dress catching on something she *hoped* was a very white stick.

The tall bridgeman deftly stepped over and around debris, eyes forward. Why did *he* have to be the one who survived? Though to be honest, she was pleased to find anyone. Walking down here alone would not have been pleasant. At least he was superstitious enough to believe that he'd been saved by some twist of fate and spren. She had no idea how she'd saved herself, let alone him. Pattern rode on her skirts, and before she'd found the bridgeman, he'd been speculating that the Stormlight had kept her alive.

Alive after a fall of at least two hundred feet? It only proved how little she knew about her abilities. Stormfather! She'd saved this man too. She was sure of it; he'd been falling right beside her as they plummeted.

But *how*? And could she figure out how to do it again?

She hurried to keep up with him. Blasted Alethi and their freakishly long legs. He marched like a soldier, giving no thought to how she had to pick her way more carefully than he did. She didn't want to get her skirt caught on *every* branch they passed.

They reached a pool of water on the chasm floor, and he hopped up onto a log that bridged the water, barely breaking stride as he crossed. She stopped at the edge.

He looked back at her, holding up a sphere. 'You aren't going to demand I give you my boots again, are you?'

She raised a foot, revealing the military-style boots she wore underneath her dress. That got him to cock an eyebrow.

'I wasn't *about* to come out onto the Shattered Plains in slippers,' she said, blushing. 'Besides, nobody can see your shoes under a dress this long.' She regarded the log.

'You want me to help you across?' he asked.

'Actually, I'm wondering how the trunk of a stumpweight tree got here,' she confessed. 'They can't possibly be native to this area of the Shattered Plains. Too cold out here. It might have grown along the coast, but a highstorm really carried it that far? Four hundred miles?'

'You're not going to demand we stop for you to sketch a picture, are you?'

'Oh please,' Shallan said, stepping up onto the log and picking her way across. 'Do you know how many sketches I have of stumpweights?'

The other things down here were a different matter entirely. As they continued on their way, Shallan used her sphere – which she had to juggle in her freehand, trying to manage it along with the satchel in her safehand and the pack over her shoulder – to illuminate her surroundings. They were stunning. Dozens of different varieties of vines, frillblooms of red, orange, and violet. Tiny rockbuds on the walls, and haspers in little clusters, opening and closing their shells as if breathing.

Motes of lifespren drifted around a patch of shalebark that grew in knobby patterns like fingers. You almost never saw that formation above. The tiny glowing specks of green light drifted through the chasm toward an entire wall of fist-size tube plants with little feelers wiggling out the top. As Shallan passed, the feelers retracted in a wave running up the wall. She gasped softly and took a Memory.

The bridgeman stopped ahead of her, turning. 'Well?'

'Don't you even notice how beautiful it is?'

He looked up at the wall of tube plants. She was certain she'd read about those somewhere, but the name escaped her.

The bridgeman continued on his way.

Shallan jogged after him, pack thumping against her back. She almost tripped over a snarled pile of dead vines and sticks as she reached him. She cursed, hopping on one foot to stay upright before steadying herself.

He reached out and took the pack from her.

Finally, she thought. 'Thank you.'

He grunted, slipping it over his shoulder before continuing on without another word. They reached a crossroads in the chasms, a path going right and another going left. They'd have to weave around the next plateau before them to continue westward. Shallan looked up at the rift – getting a good picture in her mind of how this side of the plateau looked – as Kaladin chose one of the paths.

'This is going to take a while,' he said. 'Even longer than it took to get out here. We had to wait upon the whole army then, but we could also cut through the centers of the plateaus. Having to go around every one of them will add a lot to the trip.'

'Well, at least the companionship is pleasant.'

He eyed her.

'For you, I mean,' she added.

'Am I going to have to listen to you prattle all the way back?'

'Of course not,' she said. 'I also intend to do some blathering, a little nattering, and the occasional gibber. But not too much, lest I overdo a good thing.'

'Great.'

'I've been practicing my burble,' she added.

'I just can't wait to hear.'

'Oh, well, that was it, actually.'

He studied her, those severe eyes of his boring into her own. She turned away from him. He didn't trust her, obviously. He was a bodyguard; she doubted that he trusted many people.

They reached another intersection, and Kaladin took longer to make this decision. She could see why – down here, it was difficult to determine which way was which. The plateau formations were varied and erratic. Some were long and thin, others almost perfectly round. They had knobs and peninsulas off to their sides, and that made a maze of the twisted paths between them. It should have been easy – there were few dead ends, after all, and so they really just had to keep moving westward.

But which direction was westward? It would be very, very easy to get lost down here.

'You're not picking our course at random, are you?' she asked.

'No.'

'You seem to know a lot about these chasms.'

'I do.'

'Because the gloomy atmosphere matches your disposition, I assume.'

He kept his eyes forward, walking without comment.

'Storms,' she said, hurrying to catch up. 'That was supposed to be light-hearted. What would it take to make you relax, bridgeboy?'

'I guess I'm just a . . . what was it again? A "hateful man"?'

'I haven't seen any proof to the contrary.'

'That's because you don't care to look, lighteyes. Everyone beneath you is just a plaything.'

'What?' she said, taking it like a slap to the face. 'Where would you get that idea?'

'It's obvious.'

'To *whom*? To you only? *When* have you seen me treat someone of a lesser station like a plaything? Give me one example.'

'When I was imprisoned,' he said immediately, 'for doing what any lighteyes would have been applauded for doing.'

'And that was *my* fault?' she demanded.

'It's the fault of your entire class. Each time one of us is defrauded, enslaved, beaten, or broken, the blame rests upon all of you who support it. Even indirectly.'

'Oh please,' she said. 'The world isn't fair? What a huge revelation! Some people in power abuse those they have power over? Amazing! When did this start happening?'

He gave no reply. He'd tied his spheres to the top of his spear with a pouch formed from the white handkerchief he'd found on one of the scribes. Held high, it lit the chasm nicely for them.

'I think,' she said, tucking away her own sphere for convenience, 'that you're just looking for excuses. Yes, you've been mistreated. I admit it. But I think *you're* the one who cares about eye color, that it's just easier for you to pretend that every lighteyes is abusing you because of your status. Have you ever asked yourself if there's a simpler explanation? Could it be that people don't like you, not because you're darkeyed, but because you're just a *huge pain in the neck*?'

He snorted, then moved on more quickly.

'No,' Shallan said, practically running to keep even with him and his long stride. 'You're not wiggling out of this. You don't get to imply that I'm abusing my station, then walk off without a response. You did this earlier, with Adolin. Now with me. What is your *problem*?'

'You want a better example of you playing with people beneath you?' Kaladin asked, dodging her question. 'Fine. You stole my boots. You pretended to be someone you weren't and bullied a darkeyed guard you'd barely met. Is that a good enough example of you playing with someone you saw as beneath you?'

She stopped in her tracks. He was right, there. She wanted to blame Tyn's influence, but his comment cut the bite out of her argument.

He stopped ahead of her, looking back. Finally, he sighed. 'Look,' he said. 'I'm not holding a grudge about the boots. From what I've seen lately, you're not as bad as the others. So let's just leave it at that.'

'Not as bad as the others?' Shallan said, walking forward. 'What a delightful compliment. Well, let's say you're right. Perhaps I *am* an insensitive rich woman. That doesn't change the fact that you can be downright mean and offensive, Kaladin Stormblessed.'

He shrugged.

'That's it?' she asked. 'I apologize, and all I get in return is a shrug?'

'I am what the lighteyes have made me to be.'

'So you're not culpable at all,' she said flatly. 'For the way you act.'

'I'd say not.'

'Stormfather. I can't say anything to change the way you treat me, can I? You're just going to continue to be an intolerant, odious man, full of spite. Incapable of being pleasant around others. Your life must be very lonely.'

That seemed to get under his skin, as his face turned red in the sphere-light. 'I'm starting to revise my opinion,' he said, 'of you not being as bad as the others.'

'Don't lie,' she said. 'You've never liked me. Right from the start. And not just because of the boots. I see how you watch me.'

'That's because,' he said, 'I know you're lying through your smile at everyone you meet. The only time you seem honest is when you're insulting someone!'

'The only honest things I can say to you *are* insults.'

'Bah!' he said. 'I just … Bah! Why is it that being around you makes me want to claw my face off, woman?'

'I have special training,' she said, glancing to the side. 'And I collect faces.' What was that?

'You can't just—'

He cut off as the scraping noise, echoing from one of the chasms, grew louder.

Kaladin immediately put his hand over his improvised sphere lantern, plunging them into darkness. In Shallan's estimation, that did *not* help. She stumbled toward him in the darkness, grabbing his arm with her freehand. He was annoying, but he was also *there*.

The scraping continued. A sound like rock on rock. Or … carapace on rock.

'I guess,' she whispered nervously, 'having a shouting match in an echoing network of chasms was not terribly wise.'

'Yeah.'

'It's getting closer, isn't it?' she whispered. 'Yeah.'

'So . . . run?'

The scraping seemed just beyond the next turn.

'Yeah,' Kaladin said, pulling his hand off his spheres and charging away from the noise.

A variety of vinebud that
is unknown to me.

It is difficult to study,
as it mostly clings to the stone
above the waterline.
It blooms a tremendous flower
of bright leaves, and the vines
grow to be dozens of feet long!

The vines appear to seek not
just water, but others of their
own kind, creating the occasional
tangle in the chasms above.

The volume seems incredibly
elastic! When withdrawn, both
the length and diameter visibly
compress more than any
variety I've ever seen.

A standard, though
very large variety of
frillbloom grows here.

70

FROM A NIGHTMARE

Whether this was Tanavast's design or not, millennia have passed without Rayse taking the life of another of the sixteen. While I mourn for the great suffering Rayse has caused, I do not believe we could hope for a better outcome than this.

Kaladin scrambled down the chasm, leaping branches and refuse, splashing through puddles. The girl kept up better than he'd expected, but – hampered by her dress – she was nowhere near as swift as he was.

He held himself back, matching her pace. Exasperating though she might be, he wasn't going to abandon Adolin's betrothed to be eaten by a chasmfiend.

They reached an intersection and chose a path at random. At the next intersection, he only paused long enough to check to see if they were being followed.

They were. Thumping from behind them, claws on stone. Scraping. He grabbed the girl's satchel – he was already carrying her pack – as they ran down another corridor. Either Shallan was in excellent shape, or the panic got to her, because she didn't even seem winded when they reached the next intersection.

No time for hesitation. He barreled down a pathway, ears full of the sound of grinding carapace. A sudden four-voiced trump echoed through the chasm, as loud as a thousand horns being blown. Shallan screamed, though Kaladin barely heard her over the horrible sound.

The chasm plants withdrew in large waves. In moments, the entire place went from fecund to barren, like the world preparing for a highstorm. They hit another intersection, and Shallan hesitated, looking back toward the sounds. She held her hands out, as if preparing to embrace the thing. Storming woman! He grabbed her and pulled her after him. They ran down two chasms without stopping.

It was still chasing, though he could only hear it. He had no idea how close it was, but it had their scent. Or their sound? He had no idea how they hunted.

Need a plan! Can't just—

At the next intersection, Shallan turned the opposite way from the one he had picked. Kaladin cursed, pounding to a stop and running after her.

'This is no time,' he said, puffing, 'to argue about—'

'Shut it,' she said. 'Follow.'

She led them to an intersection, then another. Kaladin was feeling winded, his lungs protesting. Shallan stopped, then pointed and ran down a chasm. He followed, looking over his shoulder.

He could see only blackness. Moonlight was too distant, too choked, to illuminate these depths. They wouldn't know if the beast was upon them until it entered the light of his spheres. But *Stormfather*, it sounded close.

Kaladin turned his attention back to his running. He nearly tripped over something on the ground. A corpse? He leaped it, catching up to Shallan. The hem of her dress was snarled and ripped from the running, her hair a mess, her face flushed. She led them down another corridor, then slowed to a stop, hand to the wall of the chasm, puffing.

Kaladin closed his eyes, breathing in and out. *Can't rest long. It will be coming.* He felt as if he were going to collapse.

'Cover that light,' Shallan hissed.

He frowned at her, but did so. 'We can't rest long,' he hissed back.

'Quiet.'

The darkness was complete save for the thin light escaping between his fingers. The scraping seemed almost on top of them. Storms! Could he fight one of these monsters? Without Stormlight? Desperate, he tried to suck in the Light he held in his palm.

No Stormlight came, and he hadn't seen Syl since the fall. The scraping continued. He prepared to run, but . . .

The sounds didn't seem to be getting closer anymore. Kaladin frowned. The body he'd stumbled over, it had been one of the fallen from the fight earlier. Shallan had led them back to where they'd started.

And . . . to food for the beast.

He waited, tense, listening to his heartbeat thumping in his chest. Scraping echoed in the chasm. Oddly, some light flashed in the chasm behind. What was that?

'Stay here,' Shallan whispered.

Then, incredibly, she started to move *toward* the sounds. Still holding the spheres awkwardly with one hand, he reached out with the other and snatched her.

She turned back to him, then looked down. Inadvertently, he'd grabbed her by the safehand. He let go immediately.

'I have to see it,' Shallan whispered to him. 'We're so close.'

'Are you *insane?*'

'Probably.' She continued toward the beast.

Kaladin debated, cursing her in his mind. Finally, he put his spear down and dropped her pack and satchel over its spheres to muffle the light. Then he followed. What else could he do? Explain to Adolin? *Yes, princeling. I let your betrothed wander off alone in the darkness to get eaten by a chasmfiend. No, I didn't go with her. Yes, I'm a coward.*

There *was* light ahead. It showed Shallan – her outline, at least – crouching beside a turn in the chasm, peeking around. Kaladin stepped up to her, crouching down and taking a look.

There it was.

The beast filled the chasm. Long and narrow, it wasn't bulbous or bulky, like some small cremlings. It was sinuous, sleek, with that arrowlike face and sharp mandibles.

It was also *wrong*. Wrong in a way difficult to describe. Big creatures were supposed to be slow and docile, like chulls. Yet this enormous beast moved with ease, its legs up on the sides of the chasm, holding it so that its body barely touched the ground. It ate the corpse of a fallen soldier, grasping the body in smaller claws by its mouth, then ripping it in half with a gruesome bite.

That face was like something from a nightmare. Evil, powerful, almost *intelligent*.

'Those spren,' Shallan whispered, so soft he could barely hear. 'I've seen those . . .'

They danced around the chasmfiend, and were the source of the light. They looked like small glowing arrows, and they surrounded the beast in schools, though occasionally one would drift away from the others and then vanish like a small plume of smoke rising into the air.

'Skyeels,' Shallan whispered. 'They follow skyeels too. The chasmfiend likes corpses. Could its kind be carrion feeders by nature? No, those claws, they look like they're meant for breaking shells. I suspect we'd find herds of wild chulls near where these things live naturally. But they come to the Shattered Plains to pupate, and here there's very little food, which is why they attack men. Why has this one remained after pupating?'

The chasmfiend was almost done with its meal. Kaladin took her by the shoulder, and she allowed him – with obvious reluctance – to pull her away.

They returned to their things, gathered them up, and – as silently as possible – retreated farther into the darkness.

⁂

They walked for hours, going in a completely different direction from the one they'd taken before. Shallan allowed Kaladin to lead again, though she tried her best to keep track of the chasms. She'd need to draw it out to be certain of their location.

Images of the chasmfiend tumbled in her head. What a majestic animal! Her fingers practically *itched* to sketch it from the Memory she'd taken. The legs were larger than she'd imagined; not like a legger, with spindly little spinelike legs holding up a thick body. This creature had exuded power. Like the whitespine, only enormous and more alien.

They were far from it now. Hopefully that meant they were safe. The night was dragging on her, after she'd risen early to get moving on the expedition.

She covertly checked the spheres in her pouch. She'd drained them all dun in their flight. Bless the Almighty for the Stormlight – she would need to make a glyphward in thanks. Without the strength and endurance it lent, she'd never have been able to keep up with Kaladin longlegs.

Now, however, she was *storming* exhausted. As if the Light had inflated her capacity, but now left her deflated and worn out.

At the next intersection, Kaladin paused and looked her over.

She gave him a weak smile.

'We'll need to stop for the night,' he said.

'Sorry.'

'It's not just you,' he said, looking up at the sky. 'I honestly have no idea if we're going the right direction or not. I'm all turned around. If we can get an idea in the morning of where the sun is rising, it will tell us which direction to walk.'

She nodded.

'We should still be able to get back in plenty of time,' he added. 'No need to worry.'

The way he said it immediately made her start worrying. Still, she helped him find a relatively dry portion of ground, and they settled down, spheres in the center like a little mock fire. Kaladin dug in the pack she'd found – she'd taken it off a dead soldier – and came out with some rations of flatbread and dried chull jerky. Not the most appetizing of food by any stretch, but it was something.

She sat with her back to the wall and ate, looking upward. The flat-bread was from Soulcast grain – that stale taste was obvious. Clouds above prevented her from seeing the stars, but some starspren moved in front of those, forming distant patterns.

'It's strange,' she whispered as Kaladin ate. 'I've only been down here half a night, but it feels like so much longer. The tops of the plateaus seem so distant, don't they?'

He grunted.

'Ah yes,' she said. 'The bridgeman grunt. A language unto itself. I'll need to go over the morphemes and tones with you; I'm not quite fluent yet.'

'You'd make a terrible bridgeman.'

'Too short?'

'Well, yes. And too female. I doubt you'd look good in the traditional short trousers and open vest. Or, rather, you'd probably look *too* good. It might be a little distracting for the other bridgemen.'

She smiled at that, digging into her satchel and pulling out her sketch-book and pencils. At least she had fallen with those. She started sketching, humming softly to herself and stealing one of the spheres for light. Pattern still lay on her skirts, content to be silent in Kaladin's presence.

'Storms,' Kaladin said. 'You're not drawing a *picture* of you wearing one of those outfits . . .'

'Yes, of course,' she said. 'I'm drawing salacious pictures of myself for you after only a few hours together in the chasm.' She scratched at a line. 'You have quite the imagination, bridgeboy.'

'Well it's what we were talking about,' he grumbled, rising and walking over to look at what she was doing. 'I thought you were tired.'

'I'm exhausted,' she said. 'So I need to relax.' Obviously. This first sketch wouldn't be the chasmfiend. She needed a warm-up.

So she drew their path through the chasms. A map, kind of, but more a picture of the chasms as if she could see them from above. It was imaginative enough to be interesting, though she was certain she got a few of the ridges and corners wrong.

'What *is* that?' Kaladin asked. 'A picture of the Plains?'

'Something of a map,' she said, though she grimaced. What did it say about her that she couldn't just draw a few lines giving their location, like a regular person? She had to do it like a picture. 'I don't know the full shapes of the plateaus we walked around, just the chasm pathways we used.'

'You remember it that well?'

Stormwinds. Hadn't she intended to keep her visual memory more secret than this? 'Uh . . . No, not really. I'm guessing at a lot of this.'

She felt foolish for revealing her skill. Veil would have had words with her. It was too bad Veil wasn't down here, actually. She would be better at this whole surviving-in-the-wilderness thing.

Kaladin took the picture from her fingers, standing up and using his sphere to light it. 'Well, if your map is correct, we've been making our way southward instead of westward. I need light to navigate better.'

'Perhaps,' she said, taking out another sheet to begin her sketch of the chasmfiend.

'We'll wait for the sun tomorrow,' he said. 'That will tell me which way to go.'

She nodded, beginning her sketch as he made a place for himself and settled down, coat folded into a pillow. She wanted to turn in herself, but this sketch would *not* wait. She at least had to get something down.

She only lasted about a half hour – finishing perhaps a quarter of the sketch – before she had to put it away, curl up on the hard ground with the pack as a pillow, and fall asleep.

.·.

It was still dark when Kaladin nudged her awake with the butt of his spear. Shallan groaned, rolling over on the chasm floor, and drowsily tried to put her pillow over her head.

Which, of course, spilled dried chull meat onto her. Kaladin chuckled.

Sure, *that* got a laugh out of him. Storming man. How long had she been able to sleep? She blinked bleary eyes and focused on the open crack of the chasm far above.

Nope, not a single glimmer of light. Two, perhaps three hours of sleep, then? Or, rather, 'sleep.' The definition of what she'd done was debatable. She'd probably have called it 'tossing and turning on the rocky ground, occasionally waking with a start to find that she'd drooled a small puddle.' That didn't really roll off the tongue, though. Unlike the aforementioned drool.

She sat up and stretched sore limbs, checking to make sure her sleeve hadn't come unbuttoned in the night or anything equally embarrassing. 'I need a bath,' she grumbled.

'A bath?' Kaladin asked. 'You have only been away from civilization for *one day*.'

She sniffed. 'Just because you're accustomed to the stench of unwashed bridgeman does not mean I need to join in.'

He smirked, taking a piece of dried chull meat from her shoulder and popping it in his mouth. 'In my home town growing up, bath day was once a week. I think even the local lighteyes would have found it strange that everyone out here, even the common soldiers, finds a bath more frequently.'

How *dare* he be this chipper in the morning? Or, rather, the 'morning.' She threw another piece of chull meat at him when he wasn't looking. The storming man caught it.

I hate him.

'We didn't get eaten by that chasmfiend while we slept,' he said, refilling the pack save for a single waterskin. 'I'd say that was about as much a blessing as we could expect, under the circumstances. Come on, up on your toes. Your map gives me an idea of which way to go, and we can watch for sunlight to make certain we're on the right path. We want to beat that highstorm, right?'

'You're the one I want to beat,' she grumbled. 'With a stick.'

'What was that?'

'Nothing,' she said, standing up and trying to make something of her frazzled hair. Storms. She must look like the aftereffect of a lightning bolt hitting a jar of red ink. She sighed. She didn't have a brush, and he didn't look like he was going to give her time for a proper braid, so she put on her boots – wearing the same pair of socks two days in a row was the least of her indignities – and picked up her satchel. Kaladin carried the pack.

She trailed after him as he led the way through the chasm, her stomach complaining about how little she'd eaten the night before. Food didn't sound good, so she let it growl. *Serves it right,* she thought. Whatever that meant.

Eventually, the sky did start to brighten, and from a direction that indicated that they were going the right way. Kaladin fell into his customary quiet, and his chipper mien from earlier in the morning evaporated. Instead, he looked like he was consumed by difficult thoughts.

She yawned, pulling up beside him. 'What are you thinking about?'

'I was considering how nice it was to have a little silence,' he said. 'With nobody bothering me.'

'Liar. Why do you try so hard to put people off?'

'Maybe I just don't want to have another argument.'

'You won't,' she said, yawning again. 'It's far too early for arguments. Try it. Give me an insult.'

'I don't—'

'Insult! Now!'

'I'd rather walk these chasms with a compulsive murderer than you. At least then, when the conversation got tedious, I'd have an easy way out.'

'And your feet stink,' she said. 'See? Too early. I can't possibly be witty at this hour. So no arguments.' She hesitated, then continued more softly. 'Besides, no murderer would agree to accompany you. Everyone needs to have *some* standards, after all.'

Kaladin snorted, lips tugging up to the sides.

'Be careful,' she said, hopping over a fallen log. 'That was *almost* like a smile – and earlier this morning, I could swear that you were cheerful.

Well, mildly content. Anyway, if you start to be in a better mood, it will destroy the whole variety of this trip.'

'Variety?' he asked.

'Yes. If we're both pleasant, there's no artistry to it. You see, great art is a matter of contrast. Some lights and some darks. The happy, smiling, radiant lady and the dark, brooding, malodorous bridgeman.'

'That—' He stopped. 'Malodorous?'

'A great figure painting,' she said, 'shows the hero with inherent contrast – strong, yet hinting at vulnerability, so that the viewer can relate to him. Your little problem would make for a dynamic contrast.'

'How would you even convey that in a painting?' Kaladin said, frowning. 'Besides, I'm *not* malodorous.'

'Oh, so you're getting better? Yay!'

He looked at her, dumbfounded.

'Confusion,' she said. 'I will graciously take that as a sign that you're amazed that I can be so humorous at such an early hour.' She leaned in conspiratorially, whispering. 'I'm really not very witty. You just happen to be stupid, so it *seems* that way. Contrast, remember?'

She smiled at him, then continued on her way, humming to herself. Actually, the day was looking much better. Why had she been in a bad mood earlier?

Kaladin jogged to catch up with her. 'Storms, woman,' he said. 'I don't know what to make of you.'

'Preferably not a corpse.'

'I'm surprised someone hasn't already done that.' He shook his head. 'Give me an honest answer. Why are you here?'

'Well, there was this bridge that collapsed, and I fell . . .'

He sighed.

'Sorry,' Shallan said. 'Something about you encourages me to crack wise, bridgeboy. Even in the *morning*. Anyway, why did I come here? You mean to the Shattered Plains in the first place?'

He nodded. There *was* a sort of rugged handsomeness to the fellow. Like the beauty of a natural rock formation, as opposed to a fine sculpture like Adolin.

But Kaladin's *intensity*, that frightened her. He seemed like a man who constantly had his teeth clenched, a man who couldn't let himself – or anyone else – just sit down and take a nice rest.

'I came here,' Shallan said, 'because of Jasnah Kholin's work. The scholarship she left behind must not be abandoned.'

'And Adolin?'

'Adolin is a delightful surprise.'

They passed an entire wall covered in draping vines that were rooted in a broken section of rock above. They wriggled and pulled up as Shallan passed. *Very alert,* she noted. *Faster than most vines.* These were the opposite of those in the gardens back home, where the plants had been sheltered for so long. She tried to snatch one for a cutting, but it moved too quickly.

Drat. She needed a bit of one so that when they got back, she could grow a plant for experimentation. Pretending she was here to explore and record new species helped push back the gloom. She heard Pattern humming softly from her skirt, as if he realized what she was doing, distracting herself from the predicament and the danger. She swatted at him. What would the bridgeman think if he heard her clothing buzz?

'Just a moment,' she said, finally snatching one of the vines. Kaladin watched, leaning on his spear, as she cut the tip off the vine with the small knife from her satchel.

'Jasnah's research,' he said. 'It had something to do with structures hidden out here, beneath the crem?'

'What makes you say that?' She tucked the tip of the vine away in an empty ink jar she'd kept for specimens.

'You made too much of an effort to get out here,' he said. 'Ostensibly all to investigate a chasmfiend's chrysalis. A dead one, even. There has to be more.'

'You don't understand the compulsive nature of scholarship, I see.' She shook the jar.

He snorted. 'If you'd really wanted to see a chrysalis, you could have just had them tow one back for you. They have those chull sleds for the wounded; one of those might have worked. There was no need for you to come all the way out here yourself.'

Blast. A solid argument. It was a good thing Adolin hadn't thought of that. The prince *was* wonderful, and he certainly wasn't stupid, but he was also . . . mentally direct.

This bridgeman was proving himself different. The way he watched her, the way he thought. Even, she realized, the way he spoke. He talked like an educated lighteyes. But what of those *slave brands* on his forehead? The hair got in the way, but she thought that one of them was a *shash* brand.

Perhaps she should spend as much time wondering about this man's motives as he apparently fretted about hers.

'Riches,' he said, as they continued on. He held back some dead branches sticking from a crack so she could pass. 'There's a treasure of some sort out here, and that's what you seek? But . . . no. You could have wealth easily enough by marriage.'

She didn't say anything, stepping through the gap he made for her.

'Nobody had heard of you before this,' he continued. 'The Davar house really does have a daughter your age, and you match the description. You could be an impostor, but you're actually lighteyed, and that Veden house isn't particularly significant. If you were going to bother to impersonate someone, wouldn't you pick someone more important?'

'You seem to have thought about this a great deal.'

'It's my job.'

'I'm being truthful with you – Jasnah's research *is* why I came to the Shattered Plains. I think the world itself could be in danger.'

'That's why you talked to Adolin about the parshmen.'

'Wait. How do you . . . Your guards were there on that terrace with us. They told you? I didn't realize they were close enough to listen.'

'I made a point of telling them to stay close,' Kaladin said. 'At the time, I was half convinced you were here to assassinate Adolin.'

Well, he was nothing if not honest. And blunt.

'My men said,' Kaladin continued, 'that you seemed to want to get the parshmen murdered.'

'I said nothing of the sort,' she said. 'Though I am worried that they might betray us. It's a moot point, as I doubt I'll persuade the highprinces without more evidence.'

'If you got your way, though,' Kaladin said, sounding curious, 'what would you do? About the parshmen.'

'Have them exiled,' Shallan said.

'And who will replace them?' Kaladin said. 'Darkeyes?'

'I'm not saying it would be easy,' Shallan said.

'They'd need more slaves,' Kaladin said, contemplative. 'A lot of honest men might find themselves with brands.'

'Still sore about what happened to you, I assume.'

'Wouldn't you be?'

'Yes, I suppose I would. I *am* sorry that you were treated in such a way, but it could have been worse. You could have been hanged.'

'I wouldn't have wanted to be the executioner who tried that.' He said it with a quiet intensity.

'Me neither,' Shallan said. 'I think hanging people is a poor choice of professions for an executioner. Better to be the guy with an axe.'

He frowned at her.

'You see,' she said, 'with the axe, it's easier to get ahead. . . .'

He stared. Then, after a moment, he winced. 'Oh, storms. That was awful.'

'No, it was *funny*. You seem to get those two mixed up a lot. Don't worry. I'm here to help.'

He shook his head. 'It's not that you aren't witty, Shallan. I just feel like you try too hard. The world is not a sunny place, and frantically trying to turn everything into a joke is not going to change that.'

'Technically,' she said, 'it *is* a sunny place. Half the time.'

'To people like you, perhaps,' Kaladin said.

'What does that mean?'

He grimaced. 'Look, I don't want to fight again, all right? I just . . . Please. Let's let the topic drop.'

'What if I promise not to get angry?'

'Are you capable of that?'

'Of course. I spend most of my time not being angry. I'm terribly proficient at it. Most of those times aren't around you, granted, but I think I'll be all right.'

'You're doing it again,' he said.

'Sorry.'

They walked in silence for a moment, passing plants in bloom with a shockingly well-preserved skeleton underneath them, somehow barely disturbed by the flowing of water in the chasm.

'All right,' Kaladin said. 'Here it is. I can imagine how the world must appear to someone like you. Growing up pampered, with everything you want. To someone like you, life is wonderful and sunny and worth laughing over. That's not your fault, and I shouldn't blame you. You haven't had to deal with pain or death like I have. Sorrow is not your companion.'

Silence. Shallan didn't reply. How *could* she reply to that?

'What?' Kaladin finally asked.

'I'm trying to decide how to react,' Shallan said. 'You see, you just said something very, very funny.'

'Then why aren't you laughing?'

'Well, it isn't that kind of funny.' She handed him her satchel and stepped onto a small dry rise of rock running through the middle of a deep pond on the chasm floor. The ground was usually flat – all of that crem settling – but the water in this pool looked a good two or three feet deep.

She crossed with hands out to the sides, balancing. 'So, let me see,' she said as she stepped carefully. 'You think I've lived a simple, happy life full of sunshine and joy. But you also imply that I've got dark, evil secrets, so you're suspicious of and even hostile to me. You tell me I'm arrogant and assume that I consider darkeyes to be playthings, but when I tell you what I'm trying to do to protect them – and everyone else – you imply I'm meddling and should just leave well enough alone.'

She reached the other side and turned about. 'Would you say that's an accurate summary of our conversations up to this point, Kaladin Stormblessed?'

He grimaced. 'Yes. I suppose.'

'Wow,' she said, 'you sure do seem to know me well. Particularly considering that you started this conversation by professing that you don't know what to make of me. An odd statement from someone who seems, from my perspective, to have figured it all out. Next time I'm trying to decide what to do, I'll just ask you, since you appear to understand me better than I understand myself.'

He crossed the same ridge of rock in the path, and she watched anxiously, as he was carrying her satchel. She trusted him better with it over the water than she trusted herself, though. She reached for it when he arrived on the other side, but found herself taking his arm to draw his attention.

'How about this?' she said, holding his eyes. 'I promise, solemnly and by the tenth name of the Almighty, that I mean no harm to Adolin or his family. I mean to prevent a disaster. I might be wrong, and I might be misguided, but I vow to you that I'm sincere.'

He stared into her eyes. So *intense*. She felt a shiver meeting that expression. This was a man of passion.

'I believe you,' he said. 'And I guess that will do.' He looked upward, then cursed.

'What?' she asked, looking toward the distant light above. The sun was peeking out over the lip of the ridge there.

The wrong ridge. They weren't going west any longer. They'd strayed again, pointing southward.

'Blast,' Shallan said. 'Give me that satchel. I need to draw this out.'

71

VIGIL

He bears the weight of God's own divine hatred, separated from the virtues that gave it context. He is what we made him to be, old friend. And that is what he, unfortunately, wished to become.

'I was young,' Teft said, 'so I didn't hear much. Kelek, I didn't *want* to hear much. The things my family did, they weren't the sort of things you want your parents doing, all right? I didn't want to know. So it's not surprising I can't remember.'

Sigzil nodded in that mild, yet infuriating way of his. The Azish man just *knew* things. And he made you tell him things too. Unfair, that was. Terribly. Why did Teft have to end up with him on watch duty?

The two sat on rocks near the chasms just east of Dalinar's warcamp. A cold wind blew in. Highstorm tonight.

He'll be back before then. Surely by then.

A cremling scuttled past. Teft threw a rock at it, driving it toward a nearby crack. 'I don't know why you want to hear all of these things anyway. They aren't any use.'

Sigzil nodded. Storming foreigner.

'All right, fine,' Teft said. 'It was some kind of cult, you see, called the Envisagers. They ... well, they thought if they could find a way to return the Voidbringers, then the Knights Radiant would return as well. Stupid, right? Only, they knew things. Things they shouldn't, things like what Kaladin can do.'

'I see this is hard for you,' Sigzil said. 'Want to play another hand of michim to pass the time instead?'

'You just want my storming spheres,' Teft snapped, wagging his finger at the Azish man. 'And don't call it by that name.'

'Michim is the game's actual name.'

'That's a holy word, and ain't no *game* named a holy word.'

'The word isn't holy where it came from,' Sigzil said, obviously annoyed.

'We ain't there now, are we? Call it something else.'

'I thought you'd like it,' Sigzil said, picking up the colored rocks that were used in the game. You bet them, in a pile, while trying to guess the ones your opponent had hidden. 'It's a game of skill, not chance, so it doesn't offend Vorin sensibilities.'

Teft watched him pick up the rocks. Maybe it would be better if he just lost all of his spheres in that storming game. It wasn't good for him to have money again. He couldn't be trusted with money.

'They thought,' Teft said, 'that people were more likely to manifest powers if their lives were in danger. So . . . they'd put lives in danger. Members of their own group – never an innocent outsider, bless the winds. But that was bad enough. I watched people let themselves be pushed off cliffs, watched them tied in place with a candle slowly burning a rope until it snapped and dropped a rock to crush them. It was bad, Sigzil. Awful. The sort of thing nobody should have to watch, especially a boy of six.'

'So what did you do?' Sigzil asked softly, pulling tight the string on his little bag of rocks.

'Ain't none of your business,' Teft said. 'Don't know why I'm even talking to you.'

'It's all right,' Sigzil said. 'I can see—'

'I turned them in,' Teft blurted out. 'To the citylord. He held a trial for them, a big one. Had them all executed in the end. Never did understand that. They were only a danger to themselves. Their punishment for threatening suicide was to be killed. Nonsense, that is. Should have found a way to help them . . .'

'Your parents?'

'Mother died in that rock–string contraption,' Teft said. 'She really believed, Sig. That she had it in her, you know? The powers? That if she were about to die, they'd come out in her, and she'd save herself . . .'

'And you watched?'

'Storms, no! You think they'd let her son watch that? Are you mad?'

'But—'

'Did watch my father die, though,' Teft said, looking out over the Plains. 'Hanged.' He shook his head, digging in his pocket. Where had he put that flask? As he turned, however, he caught sight of that other lad sitting back there, fiddling with his little box as he often did. Renarin.

Teft wasn't one for all that nonsense like Moash had talked about, wanting to overturn lighteyes. The Almighty had put them in their place, and who had business questioning him? Not spearmen, that's for certain. But in a way, Prince Renarin was as bad as Moash. Neither one knew their place. A lighteyes wanting to join Bridge Four was as bad as a dark-eyes talking stupid and lofty to the king. It didn't fit, even if the other bridgemen seemed to like the lad.

And, of course, Moash was one of them now. Storms. Had he left his flask back at the barrack?

'Heads up, Teft,' Sigzil said, rising.

Teft turned around and saw men in uniform approaching. He scrambled to his feet, grabbing his spear. It was Dalinar Kholin, accompanied by several of his lighteyed advisors, along with Drehy and Skar from Bridge Four, the day's guards. With Moash promoted away and Kaladin . . . well, not there . . . Teft had taken over daily assignments. Nobody else would storming do it. They said he was in command now. Idiots.

'Brightlord,' Teft said, slapping his chest in salute.

'Adolin told me you men were coming here,' the highprince said. He spared a glance for Prince Renarin, who had also stood and saluted, as if this weren't his own father. 'A rotation, I understand?'

'Yes, sir,' Teft said, looking toward Sigzil. It *was* a rotation. Teft was just on nearly every shift.

'You really think he's alive out there, soldier?' Dalinar asked.

'He is, sir,' Teft said. 'It's not about what I or anyone thinks.'

'He fell hundreds of feet,' Dalinar said.

Teft continued to stand at attention. The highprince hadn't asked a question, so Teft didn't give a reply.

He did have to banish a few terrible images in his head. Kaladin having knocked his head while falling. Kaladin having been crushed by the falling bridge. Kaladin lying with a broken leg, unable to find spheres to heal himself. The fool boy thought he was immortal, sometimes.

Kelek. They all thought he was.

'He *is* going to come back, sir,' Sigzil said to Dalinar. 'He's going to come climbing right up out of that chasm right there. It will be well if we're here to meet him. Uniforms on, spears polished.'

'We wait on our own time, sir,' Teft said. 'Neither of us three are supposed to be anywhere else.' He blushed as soon as he said it. And here he'd been thinking about how *Moash* talked back to his betters.

'I didn't come to order you away from your chosen task, soldier,' Dalinar said. 'I came to make certain you were caring for yourselves. No men are to skip meals to wait here, and I don't want you getting any ideas about waiting during a highstorm.'

'Er, yes, sir,' Teft said. He had used his morning meal break to put in duty here. How had Dalinar known?

'Good luck, soldier,' Dalinar said, then continued on his way, flanked by attendants, apparently off to inspect the battalion that was nearest to the eastern edge of camp. Soldiers there scurried like cremlings after a storm, carrying supply bags and piling them inside their barracks. The time for Dalinar's full expedition onto the Plains was quickly approaching.

'Sir,' Teft called after the highprince.

Dalinar turned back toward him, his attendants pausing mid-sentence.

'You don't believe us,' Teft said. 'That he'll come back, I mean.'

'He's dead, soldier. But I understand that you need to be here anyway.' The highprince touched his hand to his shoulder, a salute to the dead, then continued on his way.

Well, Teft supposed that was all right, Dalinar not believing. He'd just be that much more surprised when Kaladin *did* return.

Highstorm tonight, Teft thought, settling back down on his rock. *Come on, lad. What are you doing out there?*

⁘

Kaladin felt like one of the ten fools.

Actually, he felt like all of them. Ten times an idiot. But most specifically Eshu, who spoke of things he did not understand in front of those who did. Navigation this deep in the chasms was hard, but he could usually read directions by the way that the debris was deposited. Water blew in from the east to the west, but then it drained out the other way – so cracks on walls where debris was smashed in tight usually marked a western direction, but places where debris had been deposited more naturally – as water drained – marked where water had flowed east.

His instincts told him which way to go. They'd been wrong. He shouldn't have been so confident. This far from the warcamps, the waterflows must be different.

Annoyed at himself, he left Shallan drawing and walked out a ways. 'Syl?' he asked.

No response.

'Sylphrena!' he said, louder.

He sighed and walked back to Shallan, who knelt on the mossy ground – she'd obviously given up on protecting the once-fine dress from stains and rips – drawing on her sketchpad. She was another reason he felt like a fool. He shouldn't let her provoke him so. He could hold in the retorts against other, far more annoying lighteyes. Why did he lose control when talking with her?

Should have learned my lesson, he thought as she sketched, her expression growing intense. *She's won every argument so far, hands down.*

He leaned against a section of the chasm wall, spear in the crook of his arm, light shining from the spheres tied tightly at its head. He *had* made invalid assumptions about her, as she had so poignantly noted. Again and again. It was like a part of him frantically *wanted* to dislike her.

If only he could find Syl. Everything would be better if he could see her again, if he could know that she was all right. That scream . . .

To distract himself, he moved over to Shallan, then leaned down to see her sketch. Her map was more of a picture, one that looked eerily like the view Kaladin had had, nights ago, when flying above the Shattered Plains.

'Is all that necessary?' he asked as she shaded in the sides of a plateau.

'Yes.'

'But—'

'Yes.'

It took longer than he'd have preferred. The sun passed through the crack overhead, vanishing from sight. Already past noon. They had seven

hours until the highstorm, assuming the timing prediction was right –
even the best stormwardens got the calculations wrong sometimes.

Seven hours. *The hike out here*, he thought, *took about that long*. But
surely they'd made some progress toward the warcamps. They'd been
walking all morning.

Well, no use rushing Shallan. He left her to it, walking back along the
chasm, looking up at the shape of the rift up above and comparing it to
her drawing. From what he could see, her map was dead on. She was
drawing, from memory, their entire path as if seen from above – and she
did it perfectly, every little knob and ledge accounted for.

'Stormfather,' he whispered, jogging back. He'd known she had skill in
drawing, but this was something entirely different.

Who was this woman?

She was still drawing when he arrived. 'Your picture is amazingly accurate,' he said.

'I may have ... underplayed my skill a little last night,' Shallan said.
'I can remember things pretty well, though to be honest, I didn't realize
how far off our path was until I drew it. A lot of these plateau shapes are
unfamiliar to me; we might be into the areas that haven't been mapped
yet.'

He looked to her. 'You remember the shapes of *all* of the plateaus on
the maps?'

'Uh ... yes?'

'That's incredible.'

She sat back on her knees, holding up her sketch. She brushed aside an
unruly lock of red hair. 'Maybe not. Something's very odd here.'

'What?'

'I think my sketch must be off.' She stood up, looking troubled. 'I need
more information. I'm going to walk around one of the plateaus here.'

'All right ...'

She started walking, still focused on her sketch, barely paying attention
to where she was going as she stumbled over rocks and sticks. He kept
up with ease, but didn't bother her as she turned her eyes toward the rift
ahead. She walked them all the way around the base of the plateau to
their right.

It took a painfully long time, even walking quickly. They were losing
minutes. Did she know where they were or not?

'Now that plateau,' she said, pointing to the next wall. She began walking around the base of *that* plateau.

'Shallan,' Kaladin said. 'We don't have—'

'This is important.'

'So is not getting crushed in a highstorm.'

'If we don't find out where we are, we won't ever escape,' she said, handing him the sheet of paper. 'Wait here. I'll be right back.' She jogged off, skirt swishing.

Kaladin stared at the paper, inspecting the path she'd drawn. Though they'd started the morning going the right way, it was as he'd feared – Kaladin had eventually wound them around until they were going directly south again. He'd even somehow turned them back going *east* for a while!

That put them even farther from Dalinar's camp than when they'd begun the night before.

Please let her be wrong, he thought, going around the plateau the other direction to meet her halfway.

But if she *was* wrong, they wouldn't know where they were at all. Which option was worse?

He got a short distance down the chasm before freezing. The walls here were scraped free of moss, the debris on the floor pushed around and scratched. Storms, this was fresh. Since the last highstorm at least. The chasmfiend had come this way.

Maybe ... maybe it had gone past on its way farther out into the chasms. Shallan, distracted and muttering to herself, appeared around the other side of the plateau. She walked, still staring at the sky, muttering to herself. '... I know I said that I saw these patterns, but this is too grand a scale for me to know instinctively. You should have said something. I—'

She cut off abruptly, jumping as she saw Kaladin. He found himself narrowing his eyes. That had sounded like ...

Don't be silly. She's no warrior. The Knights Radiant had been soldiers, hadn't they? He didn't really know much about them.

Still, Syl *had* seen several strange spren about.

Shallan gave a glance to the wall of the chasm and the scrapes. 'Is that what I think it is?'

'Yeah,' he said.

'Delightful. Here, give me that paper.'

He handed it back and she slipped a pencil out of her sleeve. He gave her the satchel, which she set on the floor, using the stiff side as a place to sketch. She filled in the two plateaus closest to them, the ones she'd walked around to get a full view.

'So is your drawing off or not?' Kaladin asked.

'It's accurate,' Shallan said as she drew, 'it's just strange. From my memory of the maps, this set of plateaus nearest to us should be farther to the north. There is another group of them up there that are *exactly* the same shape, only mirrored.'

'You can remember the maps that well?'

'Yes.'

He didn't press further. From what he'd seen, maybe she could do just that.

She shook her head. 'What are the chances that a series of plateaus would take the exact same shape as those on another part of the Plains? Not just one, but an entire sequence . . .'

'The Plains are symmetrical,' Kaladin said.

She froze. 'How do you know that?'

'I . . . it was a dream. I saw the plateaus arrayed in a wide symmetrical formation.'

She looked back at her map, then gasped. She began scribbling notes on the side. 'Cymatics.'

'What?'

'I know where the Parshendi are.' Her eyes widened. 'And the Oathgate. The center of the Shattered Plains. I can see it all – I can map almost the entire thing.'

He shivered. 'You . . . what?'

She looked up sharply, meeting his eyes. 'We have to get back.'

'Yes, I know. The highstorm.'

'More than that,' she said, standing. 'I know too much now to die out here. The Shattered Plains *are* a pattern. This isn't a natural rock formation.' Her eyes widened further. 'At the center of these Plains was a city. Something broke it apart. A weapon . . . Vibrations? Like sand on a plate? An earthquake that could break rock . . . Stone became sand, and at the blowing of the highstorms, the cracks full of sand were hollowed out.'

Her eyes seemed eerily distant, and Kaladin didn't understand half of what she'd said.

'We need to reach the center,' Shallan said. 'I can find it, the heart of these Plains, by following the pattern. And there will be . . . things there . . .'

'The secret you're searching for,' Kaladin said. What had she said just earlier? 'Oathgate?'

She blushed deeply. 'Let's keep moving. Didn't you mention how little time we had? Honestly, if *one* of us weren't chatting away all the time and distracting everyone, I'm half certain we'd be back already.'

He cocked an eyebrow at her, and she grinned, then pointed the direction for them to go. 'I'm leading now, by the way.'

'Probably for the best.'

'Though,' she said, 'as I consider, it might be better to let you lead. That way, we might find our way to the center by accident. Assuming we don't end up in Azir.'

He gave her a chuckle at that because it seemed the right thing to do. Inside, however, it ripped him apart. He'd failed.

The next few hours were excruciating. After walking the length of two plateaus, Shallan had to stop and update her map. It was correct to do so – they *couldn't* risk getting off track again.

It just took so much time. Even moving as quickly as they could between drawing sessions, practically running the entire way, their progress was too slow.

Kaladin shuffled from foot to foot, watching the sky as Shallan filled in her map again. She cursed and grumbled, and he noticed her brushing away a drop of sweat that had fallen from her brow onto the increasingly crumpled paper.

Maybe four hours left until the storm, Kaladin thought. *We aren't going to make it.*

'I'll try for scouts again,' he said.

Shallan nodded. They had entered the territory where Dalinar's pole-wielding scouts watched for new chrysalises. Shouting to them was a slim hope – even if they were lucky enough to find one of those groups, he doubted they had enough rope handy to reach to the bottom of the chasm. But it was a chance. So he moved away – so as to not disturb her drawing – cupped his mouth, and began shouting. 'Hello! Please reply! We're trapped in the chasms! Please reply!'

He walked for a time, shouting, then stopped to listen. Nothing came back. No questioning shouts echoing down from above, no signs of life.

They've probably all withdrawn into their cubbies by now, Kaladin thought. *They've broken down their watchposts and are waiting for the highstorm.*

He stared up with frustration at that slot of attenuated sky. So distant. He remembered this feeling, being down here with Teft and the others, longing to climb out and escape the horrible life of a bridgeman.

For the hundredth time, he tried drawing in the Stormlight of those spheres. He clutched the sphere until his hand and the glass were sweaty, but the Stormlight – the power within – did not flow to him. He couldn't feel the Light anymore.

'Syl!' he yelled, tucking away the sphere, cupping his hands around his mouth. 'Syl! Please! Are you there, anywhere . . . ?' He trailed off. 'I still don't know,' he said more softly. 'Is this a punishment? Or is it something more? What is wrong?'

No reply. Surely if she were watching him, she wouldn't let him die down here. Assuming she could think to notice. He had a horrible image of her riding the winds, mingling with the windspren, having forgotten herself and him – becoming terribly, blissfully ignorant of what she truly was.

She'd feared that. She'd been terrified of it.

Shallan's boots scratched the ground as she walked up. 'No luck?'

He shook his head.

'Well, onward, then.' She took a deep breath. 'Through soreness and exhaustion we go. You wouldn't be willing to carry me a little ways . . .'

He glared at her.

She shrugged with a smile. 'Think how grand it would be! I could even get a reed to whip you with. You'd be able to go back and tell all the other guards what an awful person I am. It'll be a wonderful opportunity for griping. No? Well, all right then. Off we go.'

'You're a strange woman.'

'Thank you.'

He fell into step beside her.

'My,' she noted, 'you've brewed another storm over your head, I see.'

'I've killed us,' he whispered. 'I took the lead, and I got us lost.'

'Well, I didn't notice we were going the wrong way either. I wouldn't have done any better.'

'I should have thought to have you map our progress from the start today. I was too confident.'

'It's done,' she said. 'If I'd been more clear with you about how well I could draw these plateaus, then you'd probably have made better use of my maps. I didn't, and you didn't know, so here we are. You can't blame yourself for everything, right?'

He walked in silence.

'Uh, right?'

'It's my fault.'

She rolled her eyes exaggeratedly. 'You are really intent on beating yourself up, aren't you?'

His father had said the same thing time and time again. It was who Kaladin was. Did they expect him to change?

'We'll be fine,' Shallan said. 'You'll see.'

That darkened his mood further.

'You still think I'm too optimistic, don't you?' Shallan said.

'It's not your fault,' Kaladin said. 'I'd rather be like you. I'd rather not have lived the life I have. I would that the world was only full of people like you, Shallan Davar.'

'People who don't understand pain.'

'Oh, all people understand pain,' Kaladin said. 'That's not what I'm talking about. It's . . .'

'The sorrow,' Shallan said softly, 'of watching a life crumble? Of struggling to grab it and hold on, but feeling hope become stringy sinew and blood beneath your fingers as everything collapses?'

'Yes.'

'The sensation – it's not sorrow, but something deeper – of being broken. Of being crushed so often, and so hatefully, that emotion becomes something you can only *wish* for. If only you could cry, because then you'd feel *something*. Instead, you feel nothing. Just . . . haze and smoke inside. Like you're already dead.'

He stopped in the chasm.

She turned and looked to him. 'The crushing guilt,' she said, 'of being powerless. Of wishing they'd hurt *you* instead of those around you. Of screaming and scrambling and hating as those you love are ruined, popped like a boil. And you have to watch their joy seeping away while you *can't do anything.* They break the ones you love, and not you. And you plead. Can't you just beat me instead?'

'Yes,' he whispered.

Shallan nodded, holding his eyes. 'Yes. It would be nice if nobody in the world knew of those things, Kaladin Stormblessed. I agree. With everything I have.'

He saw it in her eyes. The anguish, the frustration. The terrible nothing that clawed inside and sought to smother her. She knew. It was there, inside. She had been broken.

Then she smiled. Oh, storms. She smiled *anyway*.

It was the single most beautiful thing he'd seen in his entire life.

'How?' he asked.

She shrugged lightly. 'Helps if you're crazy. Come on. I do believe we're under a slight time constraint . . .'

She started down the chasm. He stood behind, feeling drained. And oddly brightened.

He should feel like a fool. He'd done it again – he'd been telling her how easy her life was, while she'd had *that* hiding inside of her all along. This time, though, he didn't feel like an idiot. He felt like he understood. Something. He didn't know what. The chasm just seemed a little brighter.

Tien always did that to me . . . he thought. *Even on the darkest day.*

He stood still long enough that frillblooms opened around him, their wide, fanlike fronds displaying veined patterns of orange, red, and violet. He eventually jogged after Shallan, shocking the plants closed.

'I think,' she said, 'we need to focus on the *positive* side of being down here in this terrible chasm.'

She eyed him. He didn't say anything.

'Come on,' she said.

'I . . . have the sense that it would be better not to encourage you.'

'What's the fun in that?'

'Well, we *are* about to get hit by a highstorm's flood.'

'So our clothing will get washed,' she said with a grin. 'See! Positive.'

He snorted.

'Ah, that bridgeman grunt dialect again,' she noted.

'That grunt meant,' he said, 'that at least if the waters come, it will wash away some of your stench.'

'Ha! Mildly amusing, but no points to you. I already established that you're the malodorous one. Reuse of jokes is strictly forbidden on pain of getting dunked in a highstorm.'

'All right then,' he said. 'It's a good thing we're down here because I had guard duty tonight. Now I'm going to miss it. That is practically like getting the day off.'

'To go swimming, no less!' He smiled.

'I,' she proclaimed, 'am glad we are down here because the sun is far too bright up above, and it tends to give me a sunburn unless I wear a hat. It is much better to be down in the dank, dark, smelly, moldy, potentially lifethreatening depths. No sunburns. Just monsters.'

'I'm glad to be down here,' he said, 'because at least it was me, and not one of my men, who fell.'

She hopped over a puddle, then eyed him. 'You're not very good at this.'

'Sorry. I meant that I'm glad to be down here because when we get out, everyone will cheer me for being a hero for rescuing you.'

'Better,' Shallan said. 'Except for the fact that I *do* believe that I am the one rescuing *you*.'

He glanced at her map. 'Point.'

'I,' she said, 'am glad to be down here because I've always wondered what it's like to be a chunk of meat traveling through a digestive system, and these chasms remind me of the intestines.'

'I hope you're not serious.'

'What?' She looked shocked. 'Of *course* I'm not. Ew.'

'You really *do* try too hard.'

'It's what keeps me insane.'

He scrambled up a large pile of debris, then offered a hand to help her. 'I,' he said, 'am happy to be here because it reminds me of how lucky I am to be free of Sadeas's army.'

'Ah,' she said, stepping up to the top with him.

'His lighteyes sent us down here to gather,' Kaladin said, sliding down the other side. 'And didn't pay us much at all for the effort.'

'Tragic.'

'You could say,' he told her as she stepped down off the pile, 'that we were given only a pittance.'

He grinned at her.

She cocked her head.

'Pit-tance,' he said, gesturing toward the depth of the hole they were in. 'You know. We're in a pit . . .'

'Oh, *storms*,' she said. 'You don't actually expect that to count. That was terrible!'

'I know. I'm sorry. My mother would be disappointed.'

'She didn't like wordplay?'

'No, she loved it. She'd just be mad I tried to do it when she wasn't around to laugh at me.'

Shallan smiled, and they continued on, keeping a brisk pace. 'I am glad we're down here,' she said, 'because by now, Adolin will be worried sick about me – so when we get back, he'll be *ecstatic*. He might even let me kiss him in public.'

Adolin. Right. That dampened his mood.

'We probably need to stop so I can draw out our map,' Shallan said, frowning at the sky. 'And so that you can yell some more for our potential salvation.'

'I suppose,' he said as she settled down to get out her map. He cupped his hands. 'Hey, up there? Anyone? We're down here, and we're making bad puns. Please save us from ourselves!'

Shallan chuckled.

Kaladin smiled, then started as he actually heard something echoing back. Was that a voice? Or ... Wait ...

A trumping sound – like a horn's call, but overlapping itself. It grew louder, washing over them.

Then an enormous, skittering mass of carapace and claws crashed around the corner.

Chasmfiend.

Kaladin's mind panicked, but his body simply *moved*. He snatched Shallan by the arm, hauling her to her feet and pulling her into a run. She shouted, dropping her satchel.

Kaladin pulled her after him and did not look back. He could *feel* the thing, too close, the walls of the chasm shaking from its pursuit. Bones, twigs, shell, and plants cracked and snapped.

The monster trumped again, a deafening sound.

It was almost upon them. Storms, but it could move. He'd never have imagined something so large being so quick. There was no distracting it this time. It was almost upon them; he could *feel* it right behind ...

There.

He whipped Shallan in front of him and thrust her into a fissure in the wall. As a shadow loomed over him, he threw himself into the fissure, shoving Shallan backward. She grunted as he pressed her against some of the refuse of twigs and leaves that had been packed into this crack by floodwaters.

The chasm fell silent. Kaladin could hear only Shallan's panting and his own heartbeat. They'd left most of their spheres on the ground, where Shallan had been preparing to draw. He still had his spear, his improvised lantern.

Slowly, Kaladin twisted about, putting his back to Shallan. She held him from behind, and he could feel her tremble. Stormfather. He trembled himself. He twisted his spear to give light, peering out at the chasm. This fissure was shallow, and only a few feet stood between him and the opening.

The frail, washed-out light of his diamond spheres twinkled off the wet floor. It illuminated broken frillblooms on the walls and several writhing vines on the ground, severed from their plants. They twisted and flopped, like men arching their backs. The chasmfiend . . . Where was it?

Shallan gasped, arms tightening around his waist. He looked up. There, higher up the crack, a large, inhuman eye watched them. He couldn't see the bulk of the chasmfiend's head; just part of the face and jaw, with that terrible glassy green eye. A large claw slammed against the side of the hole, trying to force its way in, but the crack was too small.

The claw dug at the hole, and then the head withdrew. Scraping rock and chitin sounded in the chasm, but the thing didn't go far before stopping.

Silence. A steady drip somewhere fell into a pool. But otherwise, silence.

'It's *waiting*,' Shallan whispered, head near his shoulder.

'You sound proud of it!' Kaladin snapped.

'A little.' She paused. 'How long, do you suppose, until . . .'

He looked upward, but couldn't see the sky. The crack didn't run all the way up the side of the chasm, and was barely ten or fifteen feet tall. He leaned forward to look at the slot high above, not extending all the way out of the crack, just getting a little closer to the lip so he could see the sky. It was getting dark. Not sunset yet, but getting close.

'Two hours, maybe,' he said. 'I—'

A crashing tempest of carapace charged down the chasm. Kaladin jumped back, pressing Shallan against the refuse again as the chasmfiend tried – without success – to get one of its legs into the fissure. The leg was still too large, and though the chasmfiend could shove the tip in toward them – getting close enough to brush Kaladin – it wasn't enough to hurt them.

That eye returned, reflecting the image of Kaladin and Shallan – tattered and dirtied from their time in the chasm. Kaladin looked less frightened than he felt, staring that thing in the eye, spear held up wardingly. Shallan, rather than looking terrified, seemed fascinated.

Crazy woman.

The chasmfiend withdrew again. It stopped just down the chasm. He could hear it settling down to watch.

'So . . .' Shallan said, 'we wait?'

Sweat trickled down the sides of Kaladin's face. Wait. How long? He could imagine staying in here, like a frightened rockbud trapped in its shell, until the waters came crashing through the chasms.

He'd survived a storm once. Barely, and only then with the aid of Stormlight. In here, it would be far different. The waters would whip them in a surge through the chasms, smashing them into walls, boulders, churning them with the dead until they drowned or were ripped limb from limb . . .

It would be a very, very bad way to die.

His grip tightened on his spear. He waited, sweating, worrying. The chasmfiend didn't leave. Minutes passed.

Finally, Kaladin made his decision. He moved to step forward.

'What are you doing!' Shallan hissed, sounding terrified. She tried to hold him back.

'When I'm out,' he said, 'run the other way.'

'Don't be stupid!'

'I'll distract it,' he said. 'Once you're free, I'll lead it away from you, then escape. We can meet back up.'

'Liar,' she whispered.

He twisted about, meeting her eyes. 'You can get back to the warcamps on your own,' he said. 'I can't. You have information that needs to get to Dalinar. I don't. I have combat training. I might be able to get away from the thing after distracting it. You couldn't. If we wait here, we both die. Do you need more logic than that?'

'I hate logic,' she whispered. 'Always have.'

'We don't have time to talk about it,' Kaladin said, twisting around, his back to her.

'You can't do this.'

'I can.' He took a deep breath. 'Who knows,' he said more softly, 'maybe I'll get in a lucky hit.' He reached up and ripped the spheres off his spearhead, then tossed them out into the chasm. He'd need a steadier light. 'Get ready.'

'Please,' she whispered, sounding more frantic. 'Don't leave me down in these chasms alone.'

He smiled wryly. 'Is it really this hard for you to let me win one single argument?'

'Yes!' she said. 'No, I mean . . . Storms! Kaladin, it *will* kill you.'

He gripped his spear. The way things had been going with him lately, perhaps that was what he deserved. 'Apologize to Adolin for me. I actually kind of like him. He's a good man. Not just for a lighteyes. Just . . . a good person. I've never given him the credit he deserves.'

'Kaladin . . .'

'It has to happen, Shallan.'

'At least,' she said, reaching her hand over his shoulder and past his head, 'take this.'

'Take what?'

'*This*,' Shallan said.

Then she summoned a Shardblade.

72

SELFISH REASONS

I suspect that he is more a force than an individual now, despite your insistence to the contrary. That force is contained, and an equilibrium reached.

Kaladin stared at the glistening length of metal, which dripped with condensation from its summoning. It glowed softly the color of garnet along several faint lines down its length.

Shallan had a Shardblade.

He twisted his head toward her, and in so doing, his cheek brushed the flat of the blade. No screams. He froze, then cautiously raised a finger and touched the cold metal.

Nothing happened. The screech he had heard in his mind when fighting alongside Adolin did not recur. It seemed a very bad sign to him. Though he did not know the meaning of that terrible sound, it *was* related to his bond with Syl.

'How?' he asked.

'It's not important.'

'I rather think it *is*.'

'Not at the moment! Look, are you going to take this thing? Holding it this way is awkward. If I drop it by accident and cut off your foot, it's going to be your fault.'

He hesitated, regarding his face reflected in its metal. He saw corpses, friends with burning eyes. He'd refused these weapons each time one was offered to him.

But always before, it had been after the fight, or at least on the practice grounds. This was different. Besides, he wasn't choosing to become a Shardbearer; he would only use this weapon to protect someone's life.

Making a decision, he reached up and seized the Shardblade by the hilt. At least this told him one thing – Shallan wasn't likely to be a Surgebinder. Otherwise, he suspected she'd hate this Blade as much as he did.

'You're not supposed to let people use your Blade,' Kaladin said. 'By tradition, only the king and the highprinces do that.'

'Great,' she said. 'You can report me to Brightness Navani for being wildly indecent and ignorant of protocol. For now, can we just survive, please?'

'Yeah,' he said, hefting the Blade. 'That sounds wonderful.' He barely knew how to use one of these. Training with a practice sword did not make you an expert with the real thing. Unfortunately, a spear was going to be of little use against a creature so large and so well armored.

'Also . . .' Shallan said. 'Could you not do that "reporting me" thing I mentioned? That was a joke. I don't think I'm supposed to have that Blade.'

'Nobody would believe me anyway,' Kaladin said. 'You *are* going to run, right? As I instructed?'

'Yes. But if you could, please lead the monster to the left.'

'That's toward the warcamps,' Kaladin said, frowning. 'I was planning to lead it deeper into the chasms, so that you—'

'I need to get back to my satchel,' Shallan said.

Crazy woman. 'We're fighting for our *lives,* Shallan. The satchel is unimportant.'

'No, it's *very* important,' she said. 'I need it to . . . Well, the sketches in there show the pattern of the Shattered Plains. I'll need that to help Dalinar. Please, just do it.'

'Fine. If I can.'

'Good. And, um, please don't die, all right?'

He was suddenly aware of her pressed against his back. Holding him, breath warm on his neck. She trembled, and he thought he could hear in her voice both terror and fascination at their situation.

'I'll do my best,' he said. 'Get ready.'

She nodded, letting go of him.

One.

Two.

Three.

He leaped out into the chasm, then turned and dashed left, *toward* the chasmfiend. Storming woman. The beast lurked in the shadows in that direction. No, it *was* a shadow. An enormous, looming shadow, long and eel-like, lifted above the floor of the chasm and gripping the walls with its legs.

It trumped and surged forward, carapace scraping on rock. Holding tightly to the Shardblade, Kaladin threw himself to the ground and ducked underneath the monster. The ground *heaved* as the beast smashed claws toward him, but Kaladin came up unscathed. He swung wildly with the Shardblade, carving a line in the rock wall beside him but missing the chasmfiend.

It curled in the chasm, twisting underneath itself, then turning about. The maneuver went far more smoothly for the monster than Kaladin would have hoped.

How do I even kill something like this? Kaladin wondered, backing up as the chasmfiend settled on the floor of the chasm to inspect him. Hacking at that enormous body was unlikely to kill it quickly enough. Did it have a heart? Not the stone gemheart, but a real one? He'd have to try to get underneath it again.

Kaladin continued to back down the chasm, trying to lead the creature away from Shallan. It moved more carefully than Kaladin would have expected. He was relieved to catch sight of Shallan escaping the crack and scrambling away down the passage.

'Come on, you,' Kaladin said, waving the Shardblade at the chasmfiend. It reared up in the chasm, but did not strike at him. It watched, eyes hidden in its darkened face. The only light came from the distant slit high above and the spheres he'd tossed out into the chasm, which now were behind the monster.

Shallan's Blade glowed softly too, from a strange pattern along its length. Kaladin had never seen one do that before, but then, he'd never seen a Shardblade in the dark before.

Looking up at the rearing, alien silhouette before him – with its too many legs, its twisted head, its segmented armor – Kaladin thought he must know what a Voidbringer looked like. Surely nothing more terrible than this could exist.

Stepping backward, Kaladin stumbled on an outcropping of shalebark sprouting from the floor.

The chasmfiend struck.

Kaladin regained his balance easily, but had to throw himself into a roll – which required dropping the Shardblade, lest he slice himself. Shadowy claws smashed around him as he came out of his roll and sprang one way, then the other. He ended up pressed against the slimy side of the chasm just in front of the monster, puffing. He was too close for the claws to get him, perhaps, and—

The head snapped down, mandibles gaping. Kaladin cursed, hurling himself to the side again. He grunted, rolling to his feet and scooping up the discarded Shardblade. It hadn't vanished – he knew enough about them to understand that once Shallan instructed it to remain, it would stay until she summoned it back.

Kaladin turned around as a claw came down where he had just been. He got a swipe at it, cutting through the claw's tip as it crashed into rock.

His cut didn't seem to do much. The Blade scored the carapace and killed the flesh inside – prompting a trump of anger – but the claw was enormous. He'd done the equivalent of cutting off the tip of an enemy soldier's big toe. Storms. He wasn't fighting the beast; he was just annoying it.

It came more aggressively, sweeping at him with a claw. Fortunately, the confines of the chasm made it difficult for the creature to swing; its arms brushed the walls, and it couldn't pull back for full leverage. That was probably why Kaladin was still alive. He got out of the way of the sweep, barely, but tripped in the darkness again. He could hardly see.

As another claw crashed toward him, Kaladin got to his feet and dashed away – running farther down the corridor, farther from the light, passing plants and flotsam. The chasmfiend trumped and charged after him, clacking and scraping.

Kaladin felt so *slow* without Stormlight. So clumsy and awkward.

The chasmfiend was close. He judged his next move by instinct. *Now!* He stopped with a lurch, then sprinted back toward the creature. It slowed with great difficulty, carapace grinding on the walls, and Kaladin ducked and ran beneath it. He slammed the Shardblade upward, sinking it deep into the creature's underside.

The beast trumped more frantically. He seemed to have actually hurt it, for it immediately lifted upward to pull itself off the sword. Then it twisted down upon itself in an eyeblink, and Kaladin found those frightful jaws coming at him. He threw himself forward, but the snapping jaws caught his leg.

Blinding pain ran up the limb, and he struck out with the Blade even as the beast flung him about. He thought he hit its face, though he couldn't be certain.

The world spun.

He hit the ground and rolled.

No time to be dizzy. With everything still spinning, he groaned and turned over. He'd lost the Shardblade – he didn't know where it was. His leg. He couldn't feel it.

He looked down, expecting to see nothing but a ragged stump. It wasn't quite so bad. Bloodied, the trousers ripped, but he couldn't see bone. The numbness was from shock.

His mind had gone analytical and focused on the wounds. That wasn't good. He needed the soldier at the moment, not the surgeon. The chasmfiend was righting itself in the chasm, and a chunk of its facial carapace was missing.

Get. Away.

Kaladin turned over and climbed to hands and knees, then lurched to his feet. The leg worked, kind of. His boot squished as he stepped.

Where was the Shardblade? There, ahead. It had flown far, embedding itself in the ground near the spheres he'd tossed from the rift. Kaladin hobbled toward it, but had trouble walking, let alone running. He was halfway there when his leg gave out. He hit hard, scraping his arm on shalebark.

The chasmfiend trumped and—

'Hey! Hey!'

Kaladin twisted about. Shallan? What was that fool woman doing, standing in the chasm, waving her hands like a maniac? How had she even gotten past him?

She yelled again, getting the chasmfiend's attention. Her voice echoed oddly.

The chasmfiend turned from Kaladin to Shallan, then began to smash at her.

'No!' Kaladin yelled. But what was the use in shouting? He needed his weapon. Gritting his teeth, he twisted about and scrambled – as best he could – to the Shardblade. Storms. Shallan . . .

He ripped the sword from the rock, but then he collapsed again. The leg just wouldn't hold him. He twisted back, holding out the Blade, searching the chasm. The monster continued to swipe about, trumping, the terrible sound echoing and reverberating in the narrow confines. Kaladin couldn't see a corpse. Had Shallan escaped?

Stabbing the blasted thing through the chest only seemed to have made it angrier. The head. His only chance was the head.

Kaladin struggled to his feet. The monster stopped smashing against the ground and with a trump surged toward him. Kaladin gripped the sword in two hands, then wavered. His leg buckled beneath him. He tried to go down on one knee, but the leg gave out completely, and he slumped to the side and narrowly avoided slicing himself with the Shardblade.

He splashed into a pool of water. In front of him, one of the spheres he'd tossed shone with a bright white light.

He reached into the water, snatching it, clutching the chilled glass. He needed that Light. Storms, his life depended on it.

Please.

The chasmfiend loomed above.

Kaladin sucked in a breath, straining, like a man gasping for air. He heard . . . as if distantly . . .

Weeping.

No power entered him.

The chasmfiend swung and Kaladin twisted, and strangely found *himself*. The other version of him stood above him, sword raised, larger than life. It was bigger than him by half.

What in the Almighty's own eyes . . . ? Kaladin thought, dumbfounded, as the chasmfiend smashed an arm down onto the figure beside Kaladin. That not-him shattered into a puff of Stormlight.

What had he done? How had he done it?

No matter. He lived. With a cry of desperation, he threw himself back to his feet and lurched toward the chasmfiend. He needed to get close, as he had before, too close for the claws to swing in these confines.

So close that . . .

The chasmfiend reared, then snapped down for a bite, mandibles extending, terrible eyes bearing down.

Kaladin thrust upward.

⁘

The chasmfiend crashed down, chitin snapping, legs spasming. Shallan cried out, freehand to mouth, from where she hid behind a boulder, her skin and clothing turned deep black.

The chasmfiend had fallen on Kaladin.

Shallan dropped her paper – it bore a drawing of her and another of Kaladin – and scrambled across the rocks, dismissing the blackness around her. She'd needed to be close to the fighting for the illusions to work. Better if she'd been able to send them on Pattern, but that was problematic because—

She stopped in front of the still-twitching beast, a heap of flesh and carapace like a fallen avalanche of stone. She shifted from one foot to another, uncertain what to do. 'Kaladin?' she called out. Her voice was frail in the darkness.

Stop it, she told herself. *No timidity. You're past that.* Taking a deep breath, she moved forward, picking her way over the huge armored legs. She tried to shove aside a claw, but it was far too heavy for her, so she climbed over it and skidded down the other side.

She froze as she heard something. The chasmfiend's head lay nearby, massive eyes cloudy. Spren started to rise from it, like trails of smoke. The same ones as before, only . . . leaving? She held her light closer.

The bottom half of Kaladin's body protruded from the chasmfiend's mouth. Almighty above! Shallan gasped, then scrambled forward. She tried, with difficulty, to pull Kaladin from the closed maw before summoning her Shardblade and cutting away at several mandibles.

'Kaladin?' she asked, nervously peering into the thing's mouth from the side, where she'd removed a mandible.

'Ow,' a weak voice trailed back to her.

Alive! 'Hang on!' she said, hacking at the thing's head, careful not to cut too close to Kaladin. Violet ichor spurted out, coating her arms, smelling like wet mold.

'This is kind of uncomfortable . . .' Kaladin said.

'You're alive,' Shallan said. 'Stop complaining.'

He was alive. Oh, Stormfather. Alive. She would have a whole *heap* of prayers to burn when they got back.

'Smells awful in here,' Kaladin said weakly. 'Almost as bad as you do.'

'Be glad,' Shallan said as she worked. 'Here, I have a reasonably perfect specimen of a chasmfiend – with only a minor case of being dead – and I'm chopping it apart for you instead of studying it.'

'I'm eternally grateful.'

'How did you get in its mouth, anyway?' Shallan asked, prying off a piece of carapace with a sickening sound. She tossed it aside.

'Stabbed it through the roof of its mouth,' Kaladin said, 'into the brain. Only way I could figure to kill the blasted thing.'

She leaned down, reaching her hand through the large hole she'd opened. With some work – and with a little cutting at the front mandibles – she managed to help Kaladin wiggle out the side of the mouth. Covered in ichor and blood, face pale from apparent blood loss, he looked like death itself.

'Storms,' she whispered, as he lay back on the rocks.

'Bind my leg,' Kaladin said weakly. 'The rest of me should be fine. Heal right up . . .'

She looked at the mess of his leg, and shivered. It looked like . . . Like . . . Balat . . .

Kaladin wouldn't be walking on that leg anytime soon. *Oh, Stormfather,* she thought, cutting off the skirt of her dress at the knees. She wrapped his leg tightly, as he instructed. He seemed to think he didn't need a tourniquet. She listened to him; he'd probably bound far more wounds than she had.

She cut the sleeve off her right arm and used that to bind a second wound on his side, where the chasmfiend had started to rip him in half as it bit. Then she settled down next to him, feeling drained and cold, legs and arm now exposed to the chill air of the chasm bottom.

Kaladin took a deep breath, resting on the rock ground, eyes closed. 'Two hours until the highstorm,' he whispered.

Shallan checked the sky. It was almost dark. 'If that long,' she whispered. 'We beat it, but we're dead anyway, aren't we?'

'Seems unfair,' he said. Then he groaned, sitting up.

'Shouldn't you—'

'Bah. I've had far worse wounds than this.'

She raised an eyebrow at him as he opened his eyes. He looked dizzy.

'I have,' he insisted. 'That's not just soldier bravado.'

'This bad?' she asked. 'How often?'

'Twice,' he admitted. He looked over the hulking form of the chasmfiend. 'We actually killed the thing.'

'Sad, I know,' she said, feeling depressed. 'It was beautiful.'

'It would be more beautiful if it hadn't tried to eat me.'

'From my perspective,' Shallan noted, 'it didn't try, it succeeded.'

'Nonsense,' Kaladin said. 'It didn't manage to swallow me. Doesn't count.' He held his hand out to her, as if for help getting to his feet.

'You want to try to keep going?'

'You expect me to just lie here in the chasm until the waters come?'

'No, but . . .' She looked up. The chasmfiend was big. Maybe twenty feet tall, as it lay on its side. 'What if we climbed up that thing, then tried to scale up to the top of the plateau?' The farther westward they'd gone, the shallower the chasms had grown.

Kaladin looked up. 'That's still a good eighty feet of climbing, Shallan. And what would we do on the top of the plateau? The storm would blow us off.'

'We could at least try to find some kind of shelter . . .' she said. 'Storms, it really is hopeless, isn't it?'

Oddly, he cocked his head. 'Probably.'

'Only "probably"?'

'Shelter . . . You have a Shardblade.'

'And?' she asked. 'I can't cut away a wall of water.'

'No, but you *can* cut stone.' He looked up, toward the wall of the chasm.

Shallan's breath caught in her throat. 'We can carve out a cubby! Like the scouts use.'

'High up the wall,' he said. 'You can see the water line up there. If we can get above that . . .'

It still meant climbing. She wouldn't have to go all the way to where the chasm got narrow at the top, but it wouldn't be an easy climb, by any means. And she had very little time.

But it was a chance.

'You're going to have to do it,' Kaladin said. 'I might be able to stand, with help. But climbing while wielding a Shardblade . . .'

'Right,' Shallan said, standing up. She took a deep breath. 'Right.'

She started by scaling the back of the chasmfiend. The smooth carapace made for slippery climbing, but she found footholds between plates. Once on its back, she looked up toward the water line. It seemed much higher than it had from below.

'Cut handholds,' Kaladin called.

Right. She kept forgetting about the Shardblade. She didn't want to think about it . . .

No. No time for that now. She summoned the Blade and cut out a series of long strips of rock, sending chunks falling to bounce off the carapace. She tucked her hair behind her ear, working in the dim light to create a ladderlike series of handholds up the side of the wall.

She started climbing them. Standing on one and clinging to the highest one, she summoned the Blade again and tried to cut a step even higher, but the thing was just so blasted long.

Obligingly, it shrank in her hand to the size of a much shorter sword, really a big knife.

Thank you, she thought, then cut out the next line of rock.

Up she went, handhold after handhold. It was sweaty work, and she periodically had to climb back down and rest her hands from clinging. Eventually, she got about as high as she figured she could, just over the water line. She hung there awkwardly, then began hacking out sections of rock, trying to cut them so they wouldn't tumble backward onto her head.

Falling stone made a beating sound on the dead chasmfiend's armor. 'You're doing great!' Kaladin called up to her. 'Keep at it!'

'When did you get so peppy?' she shouted.

'Ever since I assumed I was dead, then I suddenly wasn't.'

'Then remind me to try to kill you once in a while,' she snapped. 'If I succeed, it will make me feel better, and if I fail, it will make you feel better. Everyone wins!'

She heard him chuckling as she dug deeper into the stone. It was more difficult than she'd have imagined. Yes, the Blade cut the rock easily, but she kept cutting sections that just *wouldn't* fall out. She had to chop them to pieces, then dismiss the Blade and grab chunks to pull them out.

After over an hour of frantic work, however, she managed to craft a semblance of a refuge. She didn't get the cubby hollowed out as deeply as she wanted, but it would have to do. Drained, she crawled back down her improvised ladder one last time and flopped on the chasmfiend's back amid the rubble. Her arms felt like she'd been lifting something heavy – and technically she probably had, since climbing meant lifting herself.

'Done?' Kaladin called up from the chasm floor.

'No,' Shallan said, 'but close enough. I think we might fit.'

Kaladin was silent.

'You *are* coming up into the hole I just cut, Kaladin bridgeboy, chasmfiend-slayer and gloombringer.' She leaned over the side of the chasmfiend to look at him. 'We are *not* having another stupid conversation about you dying in here while I bravely continue on. Understand?'

'I'm not sure if I can walk, Shallan,' Kaladin said with a sigh. 'Let alone climb.'

'You're going,' Shallan said, 'if I have to *carry* you.'

He looked up, then grinned, face covered in dried violet ichor that he'd wiped away as best he could. 'I'd like to see that.'

'Come on,' Shallan said, rising with some difficulty herself. Storms, she was tired. She used the Blade to hack a vine off the wall. It took two hits to get it free, amusingly. The first severed its soul. Then, dead, it could actually be cut by the sword.

The upper part withdrew, curling like a corkscrew to get height. She tossed down one side of the length she'd cut free. Kaladin took it with one hand, and – favoring his bad leg – carefully made his way up to the top of the chasmfiend. Once up, he flopped down beside her, sweat making trails through the grime on his face. He looked up at the ladder cut into the rock. 'You're really going to make me climb that.'

'Yes,' she said. 'For perfectly selfish reasons.'

He looked to her.

'I'm not going to have your last sight in life be a view of me standing in half a filthy dress, covered in purple blood, my hair an utter mess. It's undignified. On your feet, bridgeboy.'

In the distance, she heard a rumbling. *Not good* . . .

'Climb up,' he said.

'I'm not—'

'Climb up,' he said more firmly, 'and lie down in the cubby, then reach your hand over the edge. Once I near the top, you can help me the last few feet.'

She fretted for a moment, then fetched her satchel and made the climb. Storms, those handholds were slick. Once up, she crawled into the shallow cubby and perched precariously, reaching down with one hand as she braced herself with the other. He looked up at her, then set his jaw and started climbing.

He mostly pulled himself with his hands, wounded leg dangling, the other one steadying him. Heavily muscled, his soldier's arms slowly pulled him up slot by slot.

Below, water trickled down the chasm. Then it started to gush.

'Come on!' she said.

Wind howled through the chasms, a haunting, eerie sound that called through the many rifts. Like the moaning of spirits long dead. The high sound was accompanied by a low, rumbling roar.

All around, plants withdrew, vines twisting and pulling tight, rockbuds closing, frillblooms folding away. The chasm hid.

Kaladin grunted, sweating, his face tense with pain and exertion, his fingers trembling. He pulled himself up another rung, then reached his hand up toward hers.

The stormwall hit.

ONE YEAR AGO

Shallan slipped into Balat's room, holding a short note between her fingers.

Balat spun, standing. He relaxed. 'Shallan! You nearly killed me with fright.'

The small room, like many in the manor house, had open windows with simple reed shutters – those were closed and latched today, as a highstorm was approaching. The last one before the Weeping. Servants outside pounded on the walls as they affixed sturdy stormshutters over the reed ones.

Shallan wore one of her new dresses, the expensive kind that Father bought for her, after the Vorin style, straight and slim-waisted with a pocket on the sleeve. A woman's dress. She also wore the necklace he had given her. He liked it when she did that.

Jushu lounged on a chair nearby, rubbing some kind of plant between his fingers, his face distant. He had lost weight during the two years since his creditors had dragged him from the house, though with those sunken eyes and the scars on his wrists, he still didn't look much like his twin.

Shallan eyed the bundles Balat had been preparing. 'Good thing Father never checks in on you, Balat. Those bundles look so fishy, we could make a stew out of them.'

Jushu chuckled, rubbing the scar on one wrist with the other hand. 'Doesn't help that he jumps every time a servant so much as sneezes out in the hallway.'

'Quiet, both of you,' Balat said, eyeing the window where workers locked a stormshutter in place. 'This is not a time for levity. Damnation. If he discovers that I'm planning to leave . . .'

'He won't,' Shallan said, unfolding the letter. 'He's too busy getting ready to parade himself in front of the highprince.'

'Does it feel odd to anyone else,' Jushu said, 'to be this rich? How many deposits of valuable stone are there on our lands?'

Balat turned back to packing his bundles. 'So long as it keeps Father happy, I don't care.'

The problem was, it hadn't made Father happy. Yes, House Davar was now wealthy – the new quarries provided a fantastic income. Yet, the better off they were, the darker Father grew. Walking the hallways grumbling. Lashing out at servants.

Shallan scanned the letter's contents.

'That's not a pleased face,' Balat said. 'They still haven't been able to find him?'

Shallan shook her head. Helaran had vanished. Really vanished. No more contact, no more letters; even the people he'd been in touch with earlier had no idea where he'd gone.

Balat sat down on one of his bundles. 'So what do we do?'

'You will need to decide,' Shallan said.

'I have to get out. I *have* to.' He ran his hand through his hair. 'Eylita is ready to go with me. Her parents are away for the month, visiting Alethkar. It's the perfect time.'

'If you can't find Helaran, then what?'

'I'll go to the highprince. His bastard said that he'd listen to anyone willing to speak against Father.'

'That was years ago,' Jushu said, leaning back. 'Father's in favor now. Besides, the highprince is nearly dead; everyone knows it.'

'It's our only chance,' Balat said. He stood up. 'I'm going to leave. To-night, after the storm.'

'But Father—' Shallan began.

'Father wants me to ride out and check on some of the villages along the eastern valley. I'll tell him I'm doing that, but instead I'll pick up

Eylita and we'll ride for Vedenar and go straight to the highprince. By the time Father arrives a week later, I'll have had my say. It might be enough.'

'And Malise?' Shallan asked. The plan was still for him to take their stepmother to safety.

'I don't know,' Balat said. 'He's not going to let her go. Maybe once he leaves to visit the highprince, you can send her away someplace safe? I don't know. Either way, I *have* to go. Tonight.'

Shallan stepped forward, laying a hand on his arm.

'I'm tired of the fear,' Balat said to her. 'I'm tired of being a coward. If Helaran has vanished, then I really am eldest. Time to show it. I won't just run, spending my life wondering if Father's minions are hunting us. This way . . . this way it will be over. Decided.'

The door slammed open.

For all her complaints that Balat was acting suspicious, Shallan jumped just as high as he did, letting out a squeak of surprise. It was only Wikim.

'Storms, Wikim!' Balat said. 'You could at least knock or—'

'Eylita is here,' Wikim said.

'*What?*' Balat leaped forward, grabbing his brother. 'She wasn't to come! I was going to pick her up.'

'Father summoned her,' Wikim said. 'She arrived with her handmaid just now. He's speaking with her in the feast hall.'

'Oh *no*,' Balat said, shoving Wikim aside, barreling through the door.

Shallan followed, but stopped in the doorway. 'Don't do anything foolish!' she called after him. 'Balat, the plan!'

He didn't appear to have heard her.

'This could be bad,' Wikim said.

'Or it could be wonderful,' Jushu said from behind them, still lounging. 'If Father pushes Balat too far, maybe he'll stop whining and do something.'

Shallan felt cold as she stepped into the hallway. That coldness . . . was that panic? Overwhelming panic, so sharp and strong it washed away everything else.

This had been coming. She'd *known* this had been coming. They tried to hide, they tried to flee. Of course that wouldn't work.

It hadn't worked with Mother either.

Wikim passed her, running. She stepped slowly. Not because she was calm, but because she felt *pulled* forward. A slow pace resisted the inevitability.

She turned up the steps instead of going down to the feast hall. She needed to fetch something.

It took only a minute. She soon returned, the pouch given to her long ago tucked into the safepouch in her sleeve. She walked down the steps and to the doorway of the feast hall. Jushu and Wikim waited just outside of it, watching tensely.

They made way for her.

Inside the feast hall, there was shouting, of course.

'You shouldn't have done this without talking to me!' Balat said. He stood before the high table, Eylita at his side, holding to his arm.

Father stood on the other side of the table, half-eaten meal before him. 'Talking to you is useless, Balat. You don't hear.'

'I *love* her!'

'You're a child,' Father said. 'A foolish child without regard for your house.'

Bad, bad, bad, Shallan thought. Father's voice was soft. He was most dangerous when his voice was soft.

'You think,' Father continued, leaning forward, palms on the tabletop, 'I don't know about your plan to leave?'

Balat stumbled back. *'How?'*

Shallan stepped into the room. *What is that on the floor?* she thought, walking along the wall toward the door into the kitchens. Something blocked the door from closing.

Rain began to pelt the rooftop outside. The storm had come. The guards were in their guardhouse, the servants in their quarters to wait the storm's passing. The family was alone.

With the windows closed, the only light in the room was the cool illumination of spheres. Father did not have a fire burning in the hearth.

'Helaran is dead,' Father said. 'Did you know that? You can't find him because he's been killed. I didn't even have to do it. He found his own death on a battlefield in Alethkar. Idiot.'

The words threatened Shallan's cold calm.

'How did you find out I was leaving?' Balat demanded. He stepped forward, but Eylita held him back. 'Who told you?'

Shallan knelt by the obstruction in the kitchen doorway. Thunder rumbled, making the building vibrate. The obstruction was a body.

Malise. Dead from several blows to the head. Fresh blood. Warm corpse. He had killed her recently. Storms. He'd found out about the plan, had sent for Eylita and waited for her to arrive, *then* killed his wife.

Not a crime of the moment. He'd murdered her as punishment.

So it has come to this, Shallan thought, feeling a strange, detached calm. *The lie becomes the truth.*

This was Shallan's fault. She stood up and rounded the room toward where servants had left a pitcher of wine, with cups, for Father.

'Malise,' Balat said. He hadn't looked toward Shallan; he was just guessing. 'She broke down and told you, didn't she? Damnation. We shouldn't have trusted her.'

'Yes,' Father said. 'She talked. Eventually.'

Balat's sword made a whispering rasp as he pulled it from its leather sheath. Father's sword followed.

'Finally,' Father said. 'You show hints of a backbone.'

'Balat, no,' Eylita said, clinging to him.

'I won't fear him any longer, Eylita! I *won't!*'

Shallan poured wine.

They clashed, Father leaping over the high table, swinging in a two-handed blow. Eylita screamed and scrambled back while Balat swung at his father.

Shallan did not know much of swordplay. She had watched Balat and the others spar, but the only real fights she'd seen were duels at the fair.

This was different. This was *brutal*. Father bashing his sword down again and again toward Balat, who blocked as best he could with his own sword. The *clang* of metal on metal, and above it all the storm. Each blow seemed to shake the room. Or was that the thunder?

Balat stumbled before the onslaught, falling on one knee. Father batted the sword out of Balat's fingers.

Could it really be over that quickly? Only seconds had passed. Not like the duels at all.

Father loomed over his son. 'I've always despised you,' Father said. 'The coward. Helaran was noble. He resisted me, but he had *passion*. You . . . you crawl about, whining and complaining.'

Shallan moved up to him. 'Father?' She handed the wine toward him. 'He's down. You've won.'

'I always wanted sons,' Father said. 'And I got four. All worthless! A coward, a drunkard, and a weakling.' He blinked. 'Only Helaran . . . Only Helaran . . .'

'Father?' Shallan said. *'Here.'*

He took the wine, gulping it down.

Balat grabbed his sword. Still on one knee, he struck with a lunge. Shallan screamed, and the sword made a strange *clang* as it barely missed Father, stabbing through his coat and out the back, connecting with something metallic.

Father dropped the cup. It smashed, empty, to the ground. He grunted, feeling at his side. Balat pulled the sword back and stared upward at his father in horror.

Father's hand came back with a touch of blood on it, but not much. 'That's the best you have?' Father demanded. 'Fifteen years of sword training, and that's your best attack? Strike at me! Hit me!' He held his sword out to the side, raising his other hand.

Balat started to blubber, sword slipping from his fingers.

'Bah!' Father said. 'Useless.' He tossed his sword onto the high table, then stepped over to the hearth. He grabbed an iron poker, then walked back. 'Useless.'

He slammed the poker down on Balat's thigh.

'Father!' Shallan screamed, trying to take his arm. He shoved her aside as he struck again, smashing his poker against Balat's leg.

Balat screamed.

Shallan hit the ground hard, knocking her head against the floor. She could only hear what happened next. Shouts. The poker connecting with a sound like a dull thump. The storm raging above.

'Why.' *Smack.* 'Can't.' *Smack.* 'You.' *Smack.* 'Do.' *Smack.* 'Anything.' *Smack.* 'Right?'

Shallan's vision cleared. Father drew deep breaths. Blood had splattered his face. Balat whimpered on the floor. Eylita held to him, face buried in his hair. Balat's leg was a bloody mess.

Wikim and Jushu still stood in the doorway to the hall, looking horrified.

Father looked to Eylita, murder in his eyes. He raised his poker to strike. But then the weapon slipped from his fingers and clanged to the ground. He looked at his hand as if surprised, then stumbled. He grabbed the table for support, but fell to his knees, then slumped to the side.

Rain pelted the roof. It sounded like a thousand scurrying creatures looking for a way into the building.

Shallan forced herself to her feet. Coldness. Yes, she recognized that coldness inside of her now. She'd felt it before, on the day when she'd lost her mother.

'Bind Balat's wounds,' she said, approaching the weeping Eylita. 'Use his shirt.'

The woman nodded through her tears and began working with trembling fingers.

Shallan knelt beside her father. He lay motionless, eyes open and dead, staring at the ceiling.

'What . . . what happened?' Wikim asked. She hadn't noticed him and Jushu timidly entering the room, rounding the table and joining her. Wikim peered over her shoulder. 'Did Balat's strike to the side . . .'

Father was bleeding there; Shallan could feel it through the clothing. It wasn't nearly bad enough to have caused this though. She shook her head.

'You gave me something a few years ago,' she said. 'A pouch. I kept it. You said it grows more potent over time.'

'Oh, *Stormfather*,' Wikim said, raising his hand to his mouth. 'The blackbane? You . . .'

'In his wine,' Shallan said. 'Malise is dead by the kitchen. He went too far.'

'You've killed him,' Wikim said, staring at their father's corpse. 'You've *killed* him!'

'Yes,' Shallan said, feeling exhausted. She stumbled over to Balat, then began helping Eylita with the bandages. Balat was conscious and grunting at the pain. Shallan nodded to Eylita, who fetched him some wine. Unpoisoned, of course.

Father was dead. She'd killed him.

'What is this?' Jushu asked.

'Don't do that!' Wikim said. 'Storms! You're going through his pockets already?'

Shallan glanced over to see Jushu pulling something silvery from Father's coat pocket. It was shrouded in a small black bag, mildly wet with blood, only pieces of it showing from where Balat's sword had struck.

'Oh, *Stormfather*,' Jushu said, pulling it out. The device consisted of several chains of silvery metal connecting three large gemstones, one of which was cracked, its glow lost. 'Is this what I think it is?'

'A *Soulcaster*,' Shallan said.

'Prop me up,' Balat said as Eylita returned with the wine. 'Please.'

Reluctantly the girl helped him sit. His leg . . . his leg was not in good shape. They would need to get him a surgeon.

Shallan stood, wiping bloodied hands on her dress, and took the Soulcaster from Jushu. The delicate metal was broken where the sword had struck it.

'I don't understand,' Jushu said. 'Isn't that blasphemy? Don't those belong to the king, only to be used by ardents?'

Shallan rubbed her thumb across the metal. She couldn't think. Numbness . . . shock. That was it. Shock.

I killed Father.

Wikim yelped suddenly, jumping back. 'His leg twitched.'

Shallan spun on the body. Father's fingers spasmed.

'Voidbringers!' Jushu said. He looked up at the ceiling, and at the raging storm. 'They're here. They're inside of him. It—'

Shallan knelt next to the body. The eyes trembled, then focused on her. 'It wasn't enough,' she whispered. 'The poison wasn't strong enough.'

'Oh, storms!' Wikim said, kneeling next to her. 'He's still breathing. It didn't kill him, it just paralyzed him.' His eyes widened. 'And he's waking.'

'We need to finish the job, then,' Shallan said. She looked to her brothers.

Jushu and Wikim stumbled away, shaking their heads. Balat, dazed, was barely conscious.

She turned back to her father. He was looking at her, his eyes moving easily now. His leg twitched.

'I'm sorry,' she whispered, unhooking her necklace. 'Thank you for what you did for me.' She wrapped the necklace around his neck.

Then she began to twist.

She used the handle of one of the forks that had fallen from the table as her father tried to steady himself. She looped one side of the closed necklace around it, and in twisting, pulled the chain very tight around Father's throat.

'Now go to sleep,' she whispered, 'in chasms deep, with darkness all around you . . .'

A lullaby. Shallan spoke the song through her tears – the song he'd sung for her as a child, when she was frightened. Red blood speckled his face and covered her hands.

'Though rock and dread may be your bed, so sleep my baby dear.'

She felt his eyes on her. Her skin squirmed as she held the necklace tight.

'Now comes the storm,' she whispered, 'but you'll be warm, the wind will rock your basket . . .'

Shallan had to watch as his eyes bulged out, his face turning colors. His body trembling, straining, trying to move. The eyes looked to her, demanding, *betrayed*.

Almost, Shallan could imagine that the storm's howls were part of a nightmare. That soon she would awaken in terror, and Father would sing to her. As he'd done when she was a child . . .

'The crystals fine . . . will glow sublime . . .'

Father stopped moving.

'And with a song . . . you'll sleep . . . my baby dear.'

You, however, have never been a force for equilibrium. You tow chaos behind you like a corpse dragged by one leg through the snow. Please, hearken to my plea. Leave that place and join me in my oath of nonintervention.

Kaladin caught Shallan's hand.

Boulders crashed above, smashing against the plateaus, breaking off chunks and tossing them down around him. Wind raged. Water swelled below, rising toward him. He clung to Shallan, but their wet hands started to slip.

And then, in a sudden *surge,* her grip tightened. With a strength that seemed to belie her smaller form, she heaved. Kaladin shoved with his good leg as water washed over it, and forced himself up the remaining distance to join her in the rocky alcove.

The hollow was barely three or four feet deep, shallower than the crack they'd hid in. Fortunately, it faced westward. Though icy wind twisted about and sprayed water on them, the brunt of the storm was broken by the plateau.

Puffing, Kaladin pulled against the wall of the alcove, his injured leg smarting like nothing else, Shallan clinging to him. She was a warmth in his arms, and he held to her as much as she did him, both of them sitting hunched against the rock, his head brushing the top of the hollowed hole.

The plateau shuddered, quivering like a frightened man. He couldn't see much; the blackness was absolute except when lightning came. And the *sound*. Thunder crashing, seemingly disconnected from the sprays of lightning. Water roared like an angry beast, and the flashes illuminated a frothing, churning, raging river in the chasm.

Damnation . . . it was almost up to their alcove. It had risen fifty or more feet in moments. The dirty water was filled with branches, broken plants, vines ripped from their mountings.

'The sphere?' Kaladin asked in the blackness. 'You had a sphere with you for light.'

'Gone,' she shouted over the roar. 'I must have dropped it when I grabbed you!'

'I didn't—'

A *crash* of thunder, accompanied by a blinding flash of light, sent him stuttering. Shallan pulled more tightly against him, fingers digging into his arm. The light left an afterimage in his eyes.

Storms. He could swear that afterimage was a face, horribly twisted, the mouth pulled open. The next lightning bolt lit the flood just outside with a sequence of crackling light, and it showed water bobbing with corpses. Dozens of them pulled past in the current, dead eyes toward the sky, many just empty sockets. Men and Parshendi.

The water surged upward, and a few inches of it flooded the chamber. The water of dead men. The storm went dark again, as black as a cavern beneath the ground. Just Kaladin, Shallan, and the bodies.

'That was,' Shallan said, her head near his, 'the most surreal thing I've ever seen.'

'Storms are strange.'

'You speak from experience?'

'Sadeas hung me out in one,' he said. 'I was supposed to die.'

That tempest had tried to rip the skin, then muscles, from his skeleton. Rain like knives. Lightning like a cauterizing iron.

And a small figure, all white, standing before him with hands forward, as if to part the tempest for him. Tiny and frail, yet as strong as the winds themselves.

Syl . . . what have I done to you?

'I need to hear the story,' Shallan said.

'I'll tell it to you sometime.'

Water washed up over them again. For a moment, they became lighter, floating in the sudden burst of water. The current pulled with unexpected strength, as if eager to tow them out into the river. Shallan screamed and Kaladin gripped the rock on either side, holding on in a panic. The river retreated, though he could still hear it rushing. They settled back into the alcove.

Light came from above, too steady to be lightning. Something was *glowing* on the plateau. Something that moved. It was hard to see, since water streamed off the side of the plateau above, falling in a sheet before their refuge. He *swore* he saw an enormous figure walking up there, a glowing inhuman form, followed by another, alien and sleek. Striding the storm. Leg after leg, until the glow passed.

'Please,' Shallan said. 'I need to hear something other than *that*. Tell me.'

He shivered, but nodded. Voices. Voices would help. 'It started when Amaram betrayed me,' he said, tone hushed, just loud enough for her – pressed close – to hear. 'He made me a slave for knowing the truth, that he'd killed my men in his lust to get a Shardblade. That it mattered more to him than his own soldiers, more to him than honor . . .'

He continued on, talking of his days as a slave, of his attempts to escape. Of the men he'd gotten killed for trusting him. It gushed from him, a story he'd never told. Who would he have told it to? Bridge Four had lived most of it with him.

He told her of the wagon and of Tvlakv – that name earned a gasp. She apparently knew him. He spoke of the numbness, the . . . *nothing*. The thinking he should kill himself, but the trouble believing that it was worth the effort.

And then, Bridge Four. He didn't talk about Syl. Too much pain there right now. Instead, he talked of bridge runs, of terror, of death, and of decision.

Rain washed over them, blown in swirls, and he swore he could hear chanting out there somewhere. Some kind of strange spren zipped past their enclosure, red and violet and reminiscent of lightning. Was that what Syl had seen?

Shallan listened. He would have expected questions from her, but she didn't ask a single one. No pestering for details, no chattering. She apparently *did* know how to be quiet.

He got through it all, amazingly. The last bridge run. Rescuing Dalinar. He wanted to spill it all out. He talked about facing the Parshendi Shardbearer, about how he'd offended Adolin, about holding the bridgehead on his own . . .

When he finished, they both let the silence settle on them, and shared warmth. Together, they stared out at the rushing water just out of reach and lit by flashing.

'I killed my father,' Shallan whispered.

Kaladin looked toward her. In a flash of light, he saw her eyes as she looked up from where her head had been resting against his chest, beads of water on her eyelashes. With his hands around her waist, hers around him, it was as close as he'd held a woman since Tarah.

'My father was a violent, angry man,' Shallan said. 'A murderer. I loved him. And I strangled him as he lay on the floor, watching me, unable to move. I killed my own father . . .'

He didn't prod her, though he wanted to know. *Needed* to know.

She went on, fortunately, speaking of her youth and the terrors she had known. Kaladin had thought his life terrible, but there was one thing he'd had, and perhaps not cherished enough: parents who loved him. Roshone had brought Damnation itself to Hearthstone, but at least Kaladin's mother and father had always been there to rely upon.

What would he have done, if his father had been like the abusive, hateful man Shallan described? If his mother had died before his own eyes? What would *he* have done if, instead of living off Tien's light, *he* had been required to bring light to the family?

He listened with wonder. Storms. Why wasn't this woman broken, truly broken? She described herself that way, but she was no more broken than a spear with a chipped blade – and a spear like that could still be as sharp a weapon as any. He preferred one with a score or two on the blade, a worn handle. A spearhead that had known fighting was just . . . better than a new one. You could know it had been used by a man fighting for his life, and that it had remained sure and not broken. Marks like those were signs of strength.

He did feel a chill as she mentioned her brother Helaran's death, anger in her voice.

Helaran had been killed in Alethkar. At Amaram's hands.

Storms ... I killed him, didn't I? Kaladin thought. *The brother she loved.* Had he told her about that?

No. No, he hadn't mentioned that he'd killed the Shardbearer, only that Amaram had killed Kaladin's men to cover up his lust for the weapon. He'd gotten used to, over the years, referencing the event without mentioning that he'd killed a Shardbearer. His first few months as a slave had beaten into him the dangers of talking about an event like that. He hadn't even realized he'd fallen into that habit of speaking here.

Did she realize? Had she inferred that Kaladin, not Amaram, had been the one to actually kill the Shardbearer? She didn't seem to have made that connection. She continued talking, speaking of the night – also during a storm – when she'd poisoned, then murdered her father.

Almighty above. This woman was stronger than he'd ever been.

'And so,' she continued, pressing her head back against his chest, 'we decided that I would find Jasnah. She ... had a Soulcaster, you see.'

'You wanted to see if she could fix yours?'

'That would have been too rational.' He couldn't see her scowl at herself, but he heard it, somehow. 'My plan – being stupid and naive – was to *swap* mine for hers and bring back a working one to make money for the family.'

'You had never left your family's lands before.'

'Yes.'

'And you went to *rob* one of the smartest women in the world?'

'Er ... yes. Remember that bit about "stupid and naive"? Anyway, Jasnah found out. Fortunately, I intrigued her and she agreed to take me on as a ward. The marriage to Adolin was her idea, a way to protect my family while I trained.'

'Huh,' he said. Lightning flashed outside. The winds seemed to be building even further, if that was possible, and he had to raise his voice even though Shallan was right there. 'Generous, for a woman you intended to rob.'

'I think she saw something in me that—' Silence.

Kaladin blinked. Shallan was gone. He panicked for a moment, searching about himself, until he realized that his leg no longer hurt and the fuzziness in his head – from blood loss, shock, and possible hypothermia – was gone too.

Ah, he thought. *This again.*

He took a deep breath and stood up, stepping out of the blackness to the lip of the opening. The stream below had stopped, as if frozen solid, and the opening of the alcove – which Shallan had made far too low to stand up in – could now hold him standing at full height.

He looked out and met the gaze of a face as wide as eternity itself. 'Stormfather,' Kaladin said. Some named him Jezerezeh, Herald. This didn't fit what Kaladin had heard of any Herald, however. Was the Stormfather a spren, perhaps? A god? It seemed to stretch forever, yet he could see it, make out the face in its infinite expanse.

The winds had stopped. Kaladin could hear his own heartbeat.

CHILD OF HONOR. It spoke to him this time. Last time, in the middle of the storm, it had not – though it had done so in dreams.

Kaladin looked to the side, again checking to see if Shallan was there, but he couldn't see her any longer. She wasn't part of this vision, whatever it was.

'She's one of them, isn't she?' he asked. 'Of the Knights Radiant, or at least a Surgebinder. That's what happened when fighting the chasm-fiend, that's how she survived the fall. It wasn't me either time. It was her.'

The Stormfather rumbled.

'Syl,' Kaladin said, looking back to the face. The plateaus in front of him had vanished. It was just him and the face. He had to ask. It hurt him, but he *had* to. 'What have I done to her?'

YOU HAVE KILLED HER. The voice shook everything. It was as if . . . as if the shaking of the plateau and his own body *made* the sounds for the voice.

'No,' Kaladin whispered. 'No!'

IT HAPPENED AS IT ONCE DID, the Stormfather said, angry. A human emotion. Kaladin recognized it. MEN CANNOT BE TRUSTED, CHILD OF TANAVAST. YOU HAVE TAKEN HER FROM ME. MY BELOVED ONE.

The face seemed to withdraw, fading.

'Please!' Kaladin screamed. 'How can I fix it? What can I do?'

IT CANNOT BE FIXED. SHE IS BROKEN. YOU ARE LIKE THE ONES WHO CAME BEFORE, THE ONES WHO KILLED SO MANY OF THOSE I LOVE. FAREWELL, SON OF HONOR. YOU WILL NOT RIDE MY WINDS AGAIN.

'No, I—'

The storm returned. Kaladin collapsed back into the alcove, gasping at the sudden restoration of pain and cold.

'Kelek's breath!' Shallan said. 'What was *that*?'

'You saw the face?' Kaladin asked.

'Yes. So vast ... I could see stars in it, stars upon stars, infinity ...'

'The Stormfather,' Kaladin said, tired. He reached around beneath him for something that was suddenly glowing. A sphere, the one Shallan had dropped earlier. It had gone dun, but was now renewed.

'That was amazing,' she whispered. 'I need to draw it.'

'Good luck,' Kaladin said, 'in this rain.' As if to punctuate his point, another wave of it washed over them. It would swirl in between the chasms, twisting about and sometimes blowing back at them. They sat in water a few inches deep, but it didn't threaten to pull them away again.

'My poor drawings,' Shallan said, pulling her satchel to her breast with her safehand as she held to him – the only thing *to* hold to – with her other. 'The satchel is waterproof, but ... I don't know that it's highstormproof.'

Kaladin grunted, staring out at the rushing water. There was a mesmerizing pattern to it, surging with broken plants and leaves. No corpses, not anymore. The flowing water rose in a large bump before them, as if rushing over something large beneath. The chasmfiend's carcass, he realized, was still wedged down there. It was too heavy for even the flood to budge.

They fell silent. With light, the need to speak had passed, and though he considered confronting her about what he was increasingly sure she was, he said nothing. Once they were free, there would be time.

For now, he wanted to think – though he was still glad for her presence. And aware of it in more ways than one, pushed against him and wearing the wet, increasingly tattered dress.

His conversation with the Stormfather, however, drew his attention away from that sort of thought.

Syl. Had he really ... killed her? He had heard her weeping earlier, hadn't he?

He tried, just out of futile experimentation, to pull in some Stormlight. He kind of wanted Shallan to see, to gauge her reaction. It didn't work, of course.

The storm slowly passed, the floodwaters receding bit by bit. After the rains slackened to the level of an ordinary storm, the waters started flowing in the other direction. It was as he'd always assumed, though never seen. Now rain was falling more on the ground west of the Plains than on the Plains themselves, and the drainage was all to the east. The river churned – far more lethargically – back out the way it had come.

The chasmfiend's corpse emerged from the river. Then, finally, the flood was done – the river reduced to a trickle, the rain a drizzle. The drops that dripped from the plateaus above were far larger and heavier than the rain itself.

He shifted to move to climb down, but realized that Shallan, curled up against him, had fallen asleep. She snored softly.

'You must be the only person,' he whispered, 'to ever fall asleep while outside in a highstorm.'

Uncomfortable though he was, he realized he *really* didn't fancy the idea of climbing down with this wounded leg. Strength sapped, feeling a crushing darkness at what the Stormfather had said about Syl, he let himself succumb to the numbness, and fell asleep.

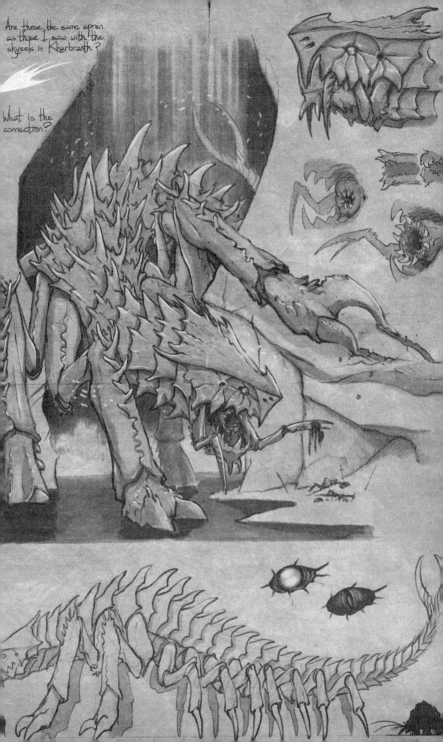

Are these the same spren as those I saw with the skyeels in Kharbranth?

What is the connection?

TRUE GLORY

The cosmere itself may depend upon our restraint.

'A t least speak with him, Dalinar,' Amaram said. The man walked quickly to match Dalinar's pace, his cloak of the Knights Radiant billowing behind him, as they inspected the lines of troops loading up wagons with supplies for the trip out onto the Shattered Plains. 'Come to an accommodation with Sadeas before you leave. Please.'

Dalinar, Navani, and Amaram passed a group of spearmen running to get into place with their battalion, which was counting ranks. Just beyond them, the men and women of the camp acted similarly excited. Cremlings scuttled this way and that, moving through pools of water left by the storm.

Last night's highstorm was the final one of the season. Sometime tomorrow, the Weeping would begin. Wet though it would be, it provided a window. Safety from storms, time to strike out. He planned to leave by midday.

'Dalinar?' Amaram asked. 'Will you talk to him?'

Careful, Dalinar thought. *Don't make any judgments just yet.* This had to be done with precision. At his side, Navani eyed him. He'd shared his plans regarding Amaram with her.

'I—' Dalinar began.

A series of horns interrupted him, blaring above through the camp.

They seemed more urgent than usual. A chrysalis had been spotted. Dalinar counted the rhythms, placing the plateau location.

'Too far,' he said, pointing to one of his scribes, a tall, lanky woman that often helped Navani with her experiments. 'Who is on the schedule for today's runs?'

'Highprinces Sebarial and Roion, sir,' the scribe said, consulting her ledger.

Dalinar grimaced. Sebarial never sent troops, even when commanded. Roion was slow. 'Send the signal flags to tell those two the gemheart is too far out to try for. We'll be marching for the Parshendi camp later today, and I can't have some of our troops splitting off and running for a gemheart.'

He made the order as if either man would commit any troops to his march. He had hopes for Roion. Almighty send that the man didn't get frightened at the last minute and refuse to go on the expedition.

The attendant rushed away to call off the plateau run. Navani pointed to a group of scribes who were tabulating supply lists, and he nodded, stopping while she walked over to talk to the women and get an estimate on readiness.

'Sadeas won't like a gemheart being left unharvested,' Amaram said as the two of them waited. 'When he hears you called off the run, he'll send his own troops for it.'

'Sadeas will do as he wishes, regardless of my intervention.'

'Each time you allow him to disobey openly,' Amaram said, 'it drives a wedge between him and the Throne.' Amaram took Dalinar by the arm. 'We have bigger problems than you and Sadeas, my friend. Yes, he betrayed you. Yes, he likely will again. But we can't afford to let the two of you go to war. The Voidbringers *are* coming.'

'How can you be certain of that, Amaram?' Dalinar asked.

'Instinct. You gave me this title, this position, Dalinar. I can feel something from the Stormfather himself. I know that a disaster is coming. Alethkar needs to be strong. That means you and Sadeas working together.'

Dalinar shook his head slowly. 'No. The opportunity for Sadeas to work with me has long since passed. The road to unity in Alethkar is not at the table of negotiation, it's out there.'

Across the plateaus, to the Parshendi camp, wherever it was. An end to this war. Closure for both him and his brother.

Unite them.

'Sadeas *wants* you to try this expedition,' Amaram said. 'He's certain you will fail.'

'And when I do not,' Dalinar said, 'he will lose all credibility.'

'You don't even know where you'll find the Parshendi!' Amaram said, throwing his hands into the air. 'What are you going to do, just wander out there until you run across them?'

'Yes.'

'Madness. Dalinar, you appointed me to this position – an impossible position, mind you – with the charge to be a light to all nations. I'm finding it hard to even get *you* to listen to me. Why should anyone else?'

Dalinar shook his head, looking eastward, over those broken plains. 'I have to go, Amaram. The answers are out there, not here. It's like we walked all the way to the shore, then huddled there for years, peering out at the waters but afraid to get wet.'

'But—'

'Enough.'

'Eventually, you're going to have to give away authority and let it stay *given*, Dalinar,' Amaram said softly. 'You can't hold it all, pretending you aren't in charge, but then ignore orders and advice as if you were.'

The words, problematically truthful, slapped him hard. He did not react, not outwardly.

'What of the matter I assigned you?' Dalinar asked him.

'Bordin?' Amaram said. 'So far as I can tell, his story checks out. I really think that the madman is only raving about having had a Shardblade. It's patently ridiculous that he might have actually had one. I—'

'Brightlord!' A breathless young woman in a messenger uniform – narrow skirt slit up the sides, with silk leggings beneath – scrambled up to him. 'The plateau!'

'Yes,' Dalinar said, sighing. 'Sadeas is sending out troops?'

'No, sir,' the woman said, flush in the cheeks from her run. 'Not . . . I mean . . . He came *out* of the chasms.'

Dalinar frowned, looking sharply toward her. 'Who?'

'Stormblessed.'

❖

Dalinar ran the entire way.

When he drew close to the triage pavilion at the edge of camp – normally reserved for tending to the wounded who came back from plateau runs – he had trouble seeing because of the crowd of men in cobalt blue uniforms blocking the path. A surgeon was yelling for them to back up and give him room.

Some of the men saw Dalinar and saluted, hastily pulling out of the way. The blue parted like waters blown in a storm.

And there he was. Ragged, hair matted in snarls, face scratched and leg wrapped in an improvised bandage. He sat on a triage table and had removed his uniform coat, which sat on the table beside him, tied into a round bundle with what looked like a vine wrapping it.

Kaladin looked up as Dalinar approached, and then moved to pull himself to his feet.

'Soldier, don't—' Dalinar began, but Kaladin didn't listen. He hauled himself up tall, using a spear to support his bad leg. Then he raised hand to breast, a slow motion, as if the arm were tied with weights. It was, Dalinar figured, the most tired salute he'd ever seen.

'Sir,' Kaladin said. Exhaustionspren puffed around Kaladin like little jets of dust.

'How . . .' Dalinar said. 'You fell *into* a chasm!'

'I fell face-first, sir,' Kaladin said, 'and fortunately, I'm particularly hard-headed.'

'But . . .'

Kaladin sighed, leaning on his spear. 'I'm sorry, sir. I don't really know how I survived. Some spren were involved, we think. Anyway, I hiked back through the chasms. I had a duty to see to.' He nodded to the side.

Farther into the triage tent, Dalinar saw something he hadn't originally noticed. Shallan Davar – a tangle of red hair and ripped clothing – sat amid a pack of surgeons.

'One future daughter-in-law,' Kaladin said, 'delivered safe and sound. Sorry about the damage done to the packaging.'

'But there was a highstorm!' Dalinar said.

'We really wanted to get back before that,' Kaladin said. 'Ran into some troubles along the way, I'm afraid.' With lethargic movements, he took out his side knife and cut the vines off the package beside him. 'You know how everyone kept saying there was a chasmfiend prowling about in the nearby chasms?'

'Yes . . .'

Kaladin lifted the remnants of his coat away from the table, revealing a massive green gemstone. Though bulbous and uncut, the gemheart shone with a powerful inner light.

'Yeah,' Kaladin said, taking the gemheart in one hand and tossing it to the ground before Dalinar. 'We took care of that for you, sir.' In the blink of an eye, gloryspren replaced his exhaustionspren.

Dalinar stared mutely at the gemheart as it rolled and tapped against the front of his boot, its light almost blinding.

'Oh, don't be so melodramatic, bridgeman,' Shallan called. 'Brightlord Dalinar, we found the beast already dead and rotting in the chasm. We survived the highstorm by climbing up its back to a crack in the side of the plateau, where we waited out the rains. We could only get the gem-heart out because the thing was half-rotted already.'

Kaladin looked to her, frowning. He turned back to Dalinar almost immediately. 'Yes,' Kaladin said. 'That's what happened.'

He was a far worse liar than Shallan was.

Amaram and Navani finally arrived, the former having remained behind to escort the latter. Navani gasped when she saw Shallan, then ran to her, snapping angrily at the surgeons. She fussed and bustled around Shallan, who seemed far less the worse for wear than Kaladin, despite the terrible state of her dress and hair. In moments, Navani had Shallan wrapped in a blanket to cover her exposed skin, then she sent a runner back to prepare a warm bath and meal at Dalinar's complex, to be had in whichever order Shallan wished.

Dalinar found himself smiling. Navani pointedly ignored Shallan's protests that none of this was necessary. The mother axehound had finally emerged. Shallan was apparently no longer an outsider, but one of Navani's clutch – and Chana help the man or woman who stood between Navani and one of her own.

'Sir,' Kaladin said, finally letting the surgeons settle him back on the table. 'The soldiers are gathering supplies. The battalions forming up. Your expedition?'

'You needn't worry, soldier,' Dalinar said. 'I could hardly expect you to guard me in your state.'

'Sir,' Kaladin said, more softly, 'Brightness Shallan found something out there. Something you need to know. Talk to her before you set out.'

'I'll do so,' Dalinar said. He waited for a moment, then waved the surgeons aside. Kaladin seemed to be in no immediate danger. Dalinar stepped closer, leaning in. 'Your men waited for you, Stormblessed. They skipped meals, pulled triple shifts. I half think they'd have sat out here, at the head of the chasms, through the highstorm itself if I hadn't intervened.'

'They are good men,' Kaladin said.

'It's more than that. They *knew* you would return. What is it they understand about you that I don't?'

Kaladin met his eyes.

'I've been searching for you, haven't I?' Dalinar said. 'All this time, without seeing it.'

Kaladin looked away. 'No, sir. Maybe once, but . . . I'm just what you see, and not what you think. I'm sorry.'

Dalinar grunted, inspecting Kaladin's face. He had almost thought . . . But perhaps not.

'Give him anything he wants or needs,' Dalinar said to the surgeons, letting them approach. 'This man is a hero. Again.'

He withdrew, letting the bridgemen crowd around – which, of course, started the surgeons cursing at them again. Where *had* Amaram gone? The man had been here just a few minutes ago. As the palanquin arrived for Shallan, Dalinar decided to follow and find out just what it was that Kaladin said the girl knew.

❖

One hour later, Shallan snuggled into a nest of warm blankets, wet hair on her neck, smelling of flowered perfume. She wore one of Navani's dresses – which was too big for her. She felt like a child in her mother's clothing. That was, perhaps, exactly what she was. Navani's sudden affection was unexpected, but Shallan would certainly accept it.

The bath had been glorious. Shallan wanted to curl up on this couch and sleep for ten days. For the moment, however, she let herself revel in the distinctive feeling of being clean, warm, and safe for the first time in what seemed like an eternity.

'You can't take her, Dalinar.' Navani's voice came from Pattern on the table beside Shallan's couch. She didn't feel a moment's guilt for sending him to spy on the two of them while she bathed. After all, they had been talking about her.

'This map . . .' Dalinar's voice said.

'She can draw you a better map and you can take it.'

'She can't draw what she hasn't seen, Navani. She'll need to be there, with us, to draw out the center of the pattern on the Plains once we penetrate in that direction.'

'Someone else—'

'Nobody else has been able to do this,' Dalinar said, sounding awed. 'Four years, and none of our scouts or cartographers saw the pattern. If we're going to find the Parshendi, I'm going to need her. I'm sorry.'

Shallan winced. She was *not* doing a very good job of keeping her drawing ability hidden.

'She just got *back* from that terrible place,' Navani's voice said.

'I won't let a similar accident occur. She will be safe.'

'Unless you all die,' Navani snapped. 'Unless this entire expedition is a disaster. Then everything will be taken from me. Again.' Pattern stopped, then spoke further in his own voice. 'He held her at this point, and whispered some things I did not hear. From there, they got *very* close and made some interesting noises. I can reproduce—'

'No,' Shallan said, blushing. 'Too private.'

'Very well.'

'I need to go with them,' Shallan said. 'I need to complete that map of the Shattered Plains and find some way to correlate it with the ancient ones of Stormseat.'

It was the only way to find the Oathgate. *Assuming it wasn't destroyed in whatever shattered the Plains*, Shallan thought. *And, if I do find it, will I even be able to open it?* Only one of the Knights Radiant was said to be able to open the pathway.

'Pattern,' she said softly, clutching a mug of warmed wine, 'I'm not a Radiant, right?'

'I do not think so,' he said. 'Not yet. There is more to do, I believe, though I cannot be certain.'

'How can you not know?'

'I was not me when the Knights Radiant existed. It is complex to explain. I have always existed. We are not "born" as men are, and we cannot truly die as men do. Patterns are eternal, as is fire, as is the wind.

As are all spren. Yet, I was not in this state. I was not . . . aware.'

'You were a mindless spren?' Shallan said. 'Like the ones that gather around me when I draw?'

'Less than that,' Pattern said. 'I was . . . everything. In everything. I cannot explain it. Language is insufficient. I would need numbers.'

'Surely there are others among you, though,' Shallan said. 'Older Cryptics? Who *were* alive back then?'

'No,' Pattern said softly. 'None who experienced the bond.'

'Not a single one?'

'All dead,' Pattern said. 'To us, this means they are mindless – as a force cannot truly be destroyed. These old ones are patterns in nature now, like Cryptics unborn. We have tried to restore them. It does not work. Mmmm. Perhaps if their knights still lived, something could be done . . .'

Stormfather. Shallan pulled the blanket around her closer. 'An entire people, all killed?'

'Not just one people,' Pattern said, solemn. 'Many. Spren with minds were less plentiful then, and the majorities of several spren peoples were all bonded. There were very few survivors. The one you call Stormfather lived. Some others. The rest, thousands of us, were killed when the *event* happened. You call it the Recreance.'

'No wonder you're certain I will kill you.'

'It is inevitable,' Pattern said. 'You will eventually betray your oaths, breaking my mind, leaving me dead – but the opportunity is worth the cost. My kind is too static. We always change, yes, but we change in the same way. Over and over. It is difficult to explain. You, though, you are *vibrant*. Coming to this place, this world of yours, I had to give up many things. The transition was . . . traumatic. My memory returns slowly, but I am pleased at the chance. Yes. Mmm.'

'Only a Radiant can open the pathway,' Shallan said, then took a sip of her wine. She liked the warmth it built inside of her. 'But we don't know why, or how. Maybe I'll count as enough of a Radiant to make it work.'

'Perhaps,' Pattern said. 'Or you could progress. Become more. There *is* something more you must do.'

'Words?' Shallan said.

'You have said the Words,' Pattern said. 'You said them long ago. No . . . it is not words that you lack. It is truth.'

'You prefer lies.'

337

'Mmm. Yes, and you are a lie. A powerful one. However, what you do is not *just* lie. It is truth and lie mixed. You must understand both.'

Shallan sat in thought, finishing her wine, until the door to the sitting room burst open, letting in Adolin. He stopped, wild-eyed, regarding her.

Shallan stood up, smiling. 'It appears that I have failed at properly—'

She cut off as he grabbed her in an embrace. Drat. She'd had a perfectly clever quip prepared too. She'd worked on it during the entire bath.

Still, it was nice to be held. This was the most physically forward he'd ever been. Surviving an impossible journey did have its benefits. She let herself wrap her arms around him, feel the muscles on his back through his uniform, breathe in his cologne. He held her for several heartbeats. Not enough. She twisted her head and forced a kiss, her mouth enclosing his, firm in his embrace.

Adolin melted into the kiss, and did not pull back. Eventually, though, the perfect moment ended. Adolin took her head in his hands, looking into her eyes, and smiled. Then he grabbed her in another hug and laughed that barking, exuberant laugh of his. A *real* laugh, the one of which she was so fond.

'Where were you?' she asked.

'Visiting the other highprinces,' Adolin said, 'one at a time and delivering Father's final ultimatum – to join us in this assault, or forever be known as those who refused to see the Vengeance Pact fulfilled. Father thought giving me something to do would help distract me from . . . well, you.'

He leaned back, holding her by the arms, and gave her a silly grin.

'I have pictures to draw for you,' Shallan said, grinning back. 'I saw a chasmfiend.'

'A dead one, right?'

'Poor thing.'

'Poor thing?' Adolin said, laughing. 'Shallan, if you'd seen a live one, you'd have surely been killed!'

'Almost surely.'

'I still can't believe . . . I mean, you fell. I should have saved you. Shallan, I'm sorry. I ran for Father first—'

'You did what you should have,' she said. 'No person on that bridge would have had you rescue one of us instead of your father.'

He embraced her once more. 'Well, I won't let it happen again. Nothing like it. I'll protect you, Shallan.'

She stiffened.

'I will make *sure* you aren't ever hurt,' Adolin said fiercely. 'I should have realized that you could be caught in an assassination attempt intended for Father. We'll have to make it so that you aren't ever in that kind of position again.'

She pulled away from him.

'Shallan?' Adolin said. 'Don't worry, they won't get to you. I'll protect you. I—'

'Don't say things like that,' she hissed.

'What?' He ran his hand through his hair.

'Just *don't*,' Shallan said, shivering.

'The man who did this, who threw that lever, is dead now,' Adolin said. 'Is that what you're worried about? He was poisoned before we could get answers – though we're sure he belonged to Sadeas – but you don't need to worry about him.'

'I will worry about what I wish to worry about,' Shallan said. 'I don't need to be protected.'

'But—'

'I don't!' Shallan said. She breathed in and out, calming herself. She reached out and took him by the hand. 'I won't be locked away again, Adolin.'

'Again?'

'It's not important.' Shallan raised his hand and wove his fingers between her own. 'I appreciate the concern. That's all that matters.'

But I won't let you, or anyone else, treat me like a thing to be hidden away. Never, never again.

Dalinar opened the door into his study, letting Navani pass through first, then followed her into the room. Navani looked serene, her face a mask.

'Child,' Dalinar said to Shallan, 'I have a somewhat difficult request to make of you.'

'Anything you wish, Brightlord,' Shallan said, bowing. 'But I do wish to make a request of you in turn.'

'What is it?'

'I need to accompany you on your expedition.'

Dalinar smiled, shooting a glance at Navani. The older woman did not react. *She can be so good with her emotions*, Shallan thought. *I can't even read what she's thinking*. That would be a useful skill to learn.

'I believe,' Shallan said, looking back to Dalinar, 'that the ruins of an ancient city are hidden on the Shattered Plains. Jasnah was searching for them. So, then, must I.'

'This expedition will be dangerous,' Navani said. 'You understand the risks, child?'

'Yes.'

'One would think,' Navani continued, 'that considering your recent ordeal, you would wish for a time of shelter.'

'Uh, I wouldn't say things like that to her, Aunt,' Adolin said, scratching at his head. 'She's kind of funny about them.'

'It is not a matter of humor,' Shallan said, lifting her head high. 'I have a duty.'

'Then I shall allow it,' Dalinar said. He liked anything having to do with duty.

'And your request of me?' Shallan asked him.

'This map,' Dalinar said, crossing the room and holding up the crinkled map detailing her path back through the chasms. 'Navani's scholars say this is as accurate as any map we have. You can truly expand this? Deliver a map of the entire Shattered Plains?'

'Yes.' Particularly if she used what she remembered of Amaram's map to fill in some details. 'But Brightlord, might I make a suggestion?'

'Speak.'

'Leave your parshmen behind in the warcamp,' she said.

He frowned.

'I cannot accurately explain why,' Shallan said, 'but Jasnah felt that they were dangerous. Particularly to bring out onto the Plains. If you wish my help, if you trust me to create this map for you, then trust me on this one single point. Leave the parshmen. Conduct this expedition without them.'

Dalinar looked to Navani, who shrugged. 'Once our things are packed, they won't be *needed* really. The only ones inconvenienced will be the officers, who will have to set up their own tents.'

Dalinar considered, chewing on her request. 'This comes from Jasnah's notes?' Dalinar asked.

Shallan nodded. To the side, blessedly, Adolin piped in. 'She's told me some of it, Father. You should listen to her.'

Shallan shot him a grateful smile.

'Then it shall be done,' Dalinar said. 'Gather your things and send word to your uncle Sebarial, Brightness. We're leaving within the hour. Without parshmen.'

THE END OF

Part Four

INTERLUDES

LHAN • ESHONAI • TARAVANGIAN

LHAN

'Congratulations,' Brother Lhan said. 'You have found your way to the easiest job in the world.'

The young ardent pursed her lips, looking him up and down. She had obviously not expected her new mentor to be rotund, slightly drunk, and yawning.

'You are the . . . *senior* ardent I've been assigned to?'

' "To whom I've been assigned," ' Brother Lhan corrected, putting an arm around the young woman's shoulders. 'You're going to have to learn how to speak punctiliously. Queen Aesudan likes to feel that those around her are refined. It makes her feel refined by association. My job is to mentor you on these items.'

'I have been an ardent here in Kholinar for over a year,' the woman said. 'I hardly think that I need mentoring at all—'

'Yes, yes,' Brother Lhan said, guiding her out of the monastery's entryway. 'It's just that, you see, your superiors say you might need a little extra direction. Being assigned to the queen's own retinue is a marvelous privilege! One, I understand, you have requested with some measure of . . . ah . . . persistence.'

She walked with him, and each step revealed her reluctance. Or perhaps confusion. They passed into the Circle of Memories, a round room with ten lamps on the walls, one for each of the ancient Epoch Kingdoms. An eleventh lamp represented the Tranquiline Halls, and a large ceremonial keyhole set into the wall represented the need for ardents to ignore borders, and look only at the hearts of men . . . or something like that. He wasn't sure, honestly.

Outside the Circle of Memories, they entered one of the covered walkways between monastery buildings, a light rain sprinkling the rooftops. The last leg of the walkways, the sunwalk, gave a wonderful view of Kholinar – at least on a clear day. Even today, Lhan could see much of the city, as both the temple and the high palace occupied a flat-topped hill.

Some said that the Almighty himself had drawn Kholinar in rock, scooping out sections of ground with a fluent finger. Lhan wondered how drunk he'd been at the time. Oh, the city was beautiful, but it was the beauty of an artist who wasn't quite right in the mind. The rock took the shape of rolling hills and steeply sloping valleys, and when the stone was cut into, it exposed thousands of brilliant strata of red, white, yellow, and orange.

The most majestic formations were the windblades – enormous, curving spines of rock that cut through the city. Beautifully lined with colorful strata on the sides, they curved, curled, rose, and fell unpredictably, like fish leaping from the ocean. Supposedly, this all had to do with how the winds blew through the area. He *did* mean to get around to studying why that was. One of these days.

Slippered feet fell softly on glossy marble, accompanying the sound of the rains, as Lhan escorted the girl – what was her name again? 'Look at that city,' he said. 'Everyone out there has to work, even the lighteyes. Bread to bake, lands to oversee, cobblestones to . . . ah . . . cobble? No, that's shoes. Damnation. What do you call people who cobble, but don't *actually* cobble?'

'I don't know,' the young woman said softly.

'Well, it's no matter to us. You see, we have only one job, and it's an easy one. To serve the queen.'

'That is not easy work.'

'But it is!' Lhan said. 'So long as we're all serving the same way. In a very . . . ah . . . careful way.'

'We are sycophants,' the young woman said, staring out over the city. 'The queen's ardents tell her only what she wants to hear.'

'Ah, and here we are, at the point of the matter.' Lhan patted her on the arm. What *was* her name again? They'd told it to him. . . .

Pai. Not a very Alethi name; she'd probably chosen it upon being made an ardent. It happened. A new life, a new name, often a simple one.

'You see, Pai,' he said, watching to notice if she reacted. Yes, it did seem he'd gotten the name right. His memory must be improving. 'This is what your superiors wanted me to talk to you about. They fear that if you're not properly instructed, you might cause a bit of a storm here in Kholinar. Nobody wants that.'

He and Pai passed other ardents along the sunwalk, and Lhan nodded to them. The queen had a lot of ardents. A *lot* of ardents.

'Here's the thing,' Lhan said. 'The queen . . . she sometimes worries that maybe the Almighty isn't pleased with her.'

'Rightly so,' Pai said. 'She—'

'Hush, now,' Lhan said, wincing. 'Just . . . hush. Listen. The queen figures that if she treats her ardents well, it will buy her favor with the One who makes the storms, so to speak. Nice food. Nice robes. Fantastic quarters. Lots of free time to do whatever we want. We get these things as long as she thinks she's on the right path.'

'Our duty is to give her the truth.'

'We do!' Lhan said. 'She's the Almighty's chosen, isn't she? Wife of King Elhokar, ruler while he's off fighting a holy war of retribution against the regicides on the Shattered Plains. Her life is very hard.'

'She throws feasts every night,' Pai whispered. 'She engages in debauchery and excess. She wastes money while Alethkar languishes. People in outer towns starve as they send food here, with the understanding that it will be passed on to soldiers who need it. It rots because the queen can't be bothered.'

'They have plenty of food on the Shattered Plains,' Lhan said. 'They've got gemstones coming out of their ears there. And nobody is starving here either. You're exaggerating. Life is good.'

'It is if you're the queen or one of her lackeys. She even canceled the Beggars' Feasts. It is reprehensible.'

Lhan groaned inside. This one . . . this one was going to be hard. How to persuade her? He wouldn't want the child to do anything that endangered her. Or, well, him. Mostly him.

They entered the palace's grand eastern hall. The carved pillars here were considered one of the greatest artworks of all time, and one could trace their history back to before the shadowdays. The gilding on the floor was ingenious – a lustrous gold that had been placed beneath Soulcast ribbons of crystal. It ran like rivulets between floor mosaics. The ceiling had been decorated by Oolelen himself, the great ardent painter, and depicted a storm blowing in from the east.

All of this could have been crem in the gutter for the reverence Pai gave it. She seemed to see only the ardents strolling about, contemplating the beauty. And eating. And composing new poems for Her Majesty – though honestly, Lhan avoided that sort of thing. It seemed like work.

Perhaps Pai's attitude came from a residual jealousy. Some ardents were envious of the queen's personal chosen. He tried to explain some of the luxuries that were now hers: warm baths, horseback riding using the queen's personal stables, music and art . . .

Pai's expression grew darker with each item. Bother. This wasn't working.

New plan.

'Here,' Lhan said, steering her toward the steps. 'There's something I want to show you.'

The steps twisted down through the palace complex. He loved this place, every bit of it. White stone walls, golden sphere lamps, and an *age*. Kholinar had never been sacked. It was one of the few eastern cities that hadn't suffered that fate in the chaos after the Hierocracy's fall. The palace had burned once, but that fire had died out after consuming the eastern wing. Rener's miracle, it was called. The arrival of a highstorm to put out the fire. Lhan swore the place still smelled of smoke, three hundred years later. And . . .

Oh, right. The girl. They continued down the steps and eventually entered the palace kitchens. Lunch had ended, though that didn't stop Lhan from snatching a plate of fried bread, Herdazian style, from the counter as they passed. Plenty was laid out for the queen's favorites, who might find themselves peckish at any time. Being a proper sycophant could work up an appetite.

'Trying to lure me with exotic foods?' Pai asked. 'For the past five years, I have eaten only a bowl of boiled tallew for each meal, with a piece of fruit on special occasions. This will not tempt me.'

Lhan stopped in place. 'You're not serious, are you?'

She nodded.

'What is *wrong* with you?'

She blushed. 'I am of the Devotary of Denial. I wished to experience separation from the physical needs of my—'

'This is worse than I thought,' Lhan said, taking her by the hand and pulling her through the kitchens. Near the back, they found the door leading out to the service yard, where supplies were delivered and refuse taken away. There, shaded from the rain by an awning, they found piles of uneaten food.

Pai gasped. 'Such waste! You bring me here to convince me *not* to make a storm? You are doing quite the opposite!'

'There used to be an ardent who took all of this and distributed it to the poor,' Lhan said. 'She died a few years back. Since then, the others have made some effort to take care of it. Not much, but some. The food does get taken away eventually, usually dumped into the square to be picked through by beggars. It's mostly rotten by then.'

Storms. He could almost *feel* the heat of her anger.

'Now,' Lhan said, 'if there were an ardent among us whose only hunger was to do good, think how much she could accomplish. Why, she could feed hundreds just from what is wasted.'

Pai eyed the piles of rotting fruit, the sacks of open grain, now ruined in the rain.

'Now,' Lhan said, 'let us contemplate the opposite. If some ardent tried to take away that which we have . . . well, what might happen to her?'

'Is that a threat?' she asked softly. 'I do not fear physical harm.'

'Storms,' Lhan said. 'You think we'd – Girl, I have someone else put my *slippers* on for me in the morning. Don't be dense. We're not going to hurt you. Too much work.' He shivered. 'You'd get sent away, quickly and quietly.'

'I do not fear that either.'

'I doubt you fear anything,' Lhan said, 'except maybe having a little fun. But what good would it do anyone if you were sent away? Our lives wouldn't change, the queen would remain the same, and that food out there would still spoil. But if you *stay,* you can do good. Who knows, maybe your example will help all of us reform, eh?'

He patted her on the shoulder. 'Think about it for a few minutes. I want to go finish my bread.' He wandered off, checking over his shoulder a few times. Pai settled down beside the heaps of rotting food and stared at them. She didn't seem bothered by the ripe odor.

Lhan watched her from inside until he got bored. When he got back from his afternoon massage, she was still there. He ate dinner in the kitchen, which wasn't terribly luxurious. The girl was entirely too interested in those heaps of garbage.

Finally, as evening fell, he ambled back to her.

'Don't you even wonder?' she asked, staring at those piles of refuse, rain pattering just beyond. 'Don't you stop to think about the cost of your gluttony?'

'Cost?' he asked. 'I told you nobody starves because we—'

'I don't mean the monetary cost,' she whispered. 'I mean the spiritual cost. To you, to those around you. Everything's wrong.'

'Oh, it's not that bad,' he said, settling down.

'It *is*. Lhan, it's bigger than the queen, and her wasteful feasts. It wasn't much better before that, with King Gavilar's hunts and the wars, princedom against princedom. The people hear of the glory of the battle on the Shattered Plains, of the riches there, but none of it ever materializes here.

'Does anyone among the Alethi elite *care* about the Almighty anymore? Sure, they curse by his name. Sure, they talk about the Heralds, burn glyphwards. But what do they *do*? Do they change their lives? Do they listen to the Arguments? Do they transform, recasting their souls into something greater, something better?'

'They have Callings,' Lhan said, fidgeting with his fingers. Digiting, then? 'The devotaries help.'

She shook her head. 'Why don't we hear from Him, Lhan? The Heralds said we defeated the Voidbringers, that Aharietiam was the great victory for mankind. But shouldn't He have sent them to speak with us, to counsel us? Why didn't they come during the Hierocracy and denounce us? If what the Church had been doing was so evil, where was the word of the Almighty against it?'

'I . . . Surely you're not suggesting we *return* to that?' He pulled out his handkerchief and dabbed at his neck and head. This conversation was getting worse and worse.

'I don't know what I'm suggesting,' she whispered. 'Only that something is wrong. All of this is just so very wrong.' She looked to him, then climbed to her feet. 'I have accepted your proposal.'

'You have?'

'I will not leave Kholinar,' she said. 'I will stay here and do what good I can.'

'You won't get the other ardents into trouble?'

'My problem is not with the ardents,' she said, offering a hand to help him to his feet. 'I will simply try to be a good example for all to follow.'

'Well, then. That seems like a fine choice.'

She walked off, and he dabbed his head. She hadn't promised, not exactly. He wasn't certain how worried he should be about that.

Turned out, he should have been *very* worried.

The next morning, he stumbled into the People's Hall – a large, open building in the shadow of the palace where the king or queen addressed the concerns of the masses. A murmuring crowd of horrified ardents stood just inside the perimeter.

Lhan had already heard, but he had to see for himself. He forced his way to the front. Pai knelt on the floor here, head bowed. She'd painted all night, apparently, writing glyphs on the floor by spherelight. Nobody had noticed. The place was usually locked up tight when not in use, and she'd started working well after everyone was either asleep or drunk.

Ten large glyphs, written directly on the stone of the floor running up to the dais with the king's Common Throne. The glyphs listed the ten foolish attributes, as represented by the ten fools. Beside each glyph was a written paragraph in women's script explaining how the queen exemplified each of the fools.

Lhan read with horror. This ... this didn't just chastise. It was a condemnation of the entire government, of the lighteyes, and of the Throne itself!

Pai was executed the very next morning.

The riots started that evening.

A PART TO PLAY

That voice deep within Eshonai still screamed. Even when she didn't attune the old Rhythm of Peace. She kept herself busy to quiet it, walking the perfectly circular plateau just outside of Narak, the one where her soldiers often practiced.

Her people had become something old, yet something new. Something powerful. They stood in lines on this plateau, humming to Fury. She divided them by combat experience. A new form would not a soldier make; many of these had been workers all their lives.

They would have a part to play. They would bring about something grand.

'The Alethi will come,' Venli said, strolling at Eshonai's side and absently bringing energy to her fingers and letting it play between two of them. Venli smiled often while wearing this new form. Otherwise, it didn't seem to have changed her at all.

Eshonai knew that she herself had changed. But Venli . . . Venli acted the same.

Something felt wrong about that.

'The agent who sent this report is certain of it,' Venli continued. 'Your visit to the Blackthorn seems to have encouraged them to action, and the humans intend to strike toward Narak in force. Of course, this could still turn into a disaster.'

'No,' Eshonai said. 'No. It is perfect.'

Venli looked to her, stopping on the rock field. 'We need no more training. We should act, right now, to bring a highstorm.'

'We will do it when the humans near,' Eshonai said.

'Why? Let us do it tonight.'

'Foolishness,' Eshonai said. 'This is a tool to use in battle. If we produce an unexpected storm now, the Alethi won't come, and we won't win this war. We *must* wait.'

Venli seemed thoughtful. Finally, she smiled, then nodded.

'What do you know that you aren't telling me?' Eshonai demanded, taking her sister by the shoulder.

Venli smiled more broadly. 'I'm simply persuaded. We must wait. The storm will blow the wrong way, after all. Or is it all other storms that have blown the wrong way, and this one will be the first to blow the right way?'

The wrong way? 'How do you know? About the direction?'

'The songs.'

The songs. But . . . they said nothing about . . .

Something deep within Eshonai nudged her to move on. 'If that is true,' she said, 'we'll have to wait until the humans are practically on top of us to catch them in it.'

'Then that is what we do,' Venli said. 'I will set to the teaching. Our weapon will be ready.'

She spoke to the Rhythm of Craving, a rhythm like the old Rhythm of Anticipation, but more violent.

Venli walked away, joined by her once-mate and many of her scholars. They seemed comfortable in these forms. Too comfortable. They couldn't have held these forms before . . . could they?

Eshonai shoved down the screams and went to prepare another battalion of new soldiers. She had always hated being a general. How ironic, then, that she would be recorded in their songs as the warleader who had finally crushed the Alethi.

TARAVANGIAN

T aravangian, king of Kharbranth, awoke to stiff muscles and an ache in his back. He didn't feel stupid. That was a good sign.

He sat up with a groan. Those aches were perpetual now, and his best healers could only shake their heads and promise him that he was fit for his age. Fit. His joints cracked like logs on the fire and he couldn't stand quickly, lest he lose his balance and topple to the floor. To age truly was to suffer the ultimate treason, that of one's body against oneself.

He sat up in his cot. Water lapped quietly against the hull of his cabin, and the air smelled of salt. He heard shouts in the near distance, however. The ship had arrived on schedule. Excellent.

As he settled himself, one servant approached with a table and another with a warm, wet cloth for wiping his eyes and hands. Behind them waited the King's Testers. How long had it been since Taravangian had been alone, truly alone? Not since before the aches had come upon him.

Maben knocked on the open door, bearing his morning meal on a tray, stewed and spiced grain mush. It was supposed to be good for his constitution. Tasted like dishwater. Bland dishwater. Maben stepped forward to set out the meal, but Mrall – a Thaylen man in a black leather cuirass who wore both his head and eyebrows shaved – stopped her with a hand to the arm.

'Tests first,' Mrall said.

Taravangian looked up, meeting the large man's gaze. Mrall could loom over a mountain and intimidate the wind itself. Everyone assumed he was Taravangian's head bodyguard. The truth was more disturbing.

Mrall was the one who got to decide whether Taravangian would spend the day as king or as a prisoner.

'Surely you can let him eat first!' Maben said.

'This is an important day,' Mrall said, voice low. 'I would know the result of the testing.'

'But—'

'It is his right to demand this, Maben,' Taravangian said. 'Let us be on with it.'

Mrall stepped back, and the testers approached, a group of three storm-wardens in deliberately esoteric robes and caps. They presented a series of pages covered in figures and glyphs. They were today's variation on a sequence of increasingly challenging mathematical problems devised by Taravangian himself on one of his better days.

He picked up his pen with hesitant fingers. He did not *feel* stupid, but he rarely did. Only on the worst of days did he immediately recognize the difference. On those days, his mind was thick as tar, and he felt like a prisoner in his own mind, aware that something was profoundly wrong.

Today wasn't one of those, fortunately. He wasn't a complete idiot. At worst, he'd just be very stupid.

He set to his task, solving what mathematical problems he could. It took the better part of an hour, but during the process, he was able to gauge his capacity. As he had suspected, he was not terribly smart – but he was not stupid, either. Today . . . he was average.

That would do.

He turned over the problems to the stormwardens, who consulted in low voices. They turned to Mrall. 'He is fit to serve,' one proclaimed. 'He may not offer binding commentary on the Diagram, but he may inter-act outside of supervision. He may change government policy so long as there is a three-day delay before the changes take effect, and he may also freely pass judgment in trials.'

Mrall nodded, looking to Taravangian. 'Do you accept this assessment and these restrictions, Your Majesty?'

'I do.'

Mrall nodded, then stepped back, allowing Maben to set out Taravangian's morning meal.

The trio of stormwardens tucked away the papers he'd filled out, then they retreated to their own cabins. The testing was an extravagant procedure, and consumed valuable time each morning. Still, it was the best way he had found to deal with his condition.

Life could be tricky for a man who awoke each morning with a different level of intelligence. Particularly when the entire world might depend upon his genius, or might come crashing down upon his idiocy.

'How is it out there?' Taravangian asked softly, picking at his meal, which had gone cold during the testing.

'Horrible,' Mrall said with a grin. 'Just as we wanted it.'

'Do not take pleasure in suffering,' Taravangian replied. 'Even when it is a work of our hands.' He took a bite of the mush. '*Particularly* when it is a work of our hands.'

'As you wish. I will do so no more.'

'Can you really change that easily?' Taravangian asked. 'Turn off your emotions on a whim?'

'Of course,' Mrall said.

Something about that tickled at Taravangian, some thread of interest. If he had been in one of his more brilliant states, he might have seized upon it – but today, he sensed thought seeping away like water between fingers. Once, he had fretted about these missed opportunities, but he had eventually made his peace. Days of brilliance – he had come to learn – brought their own problems.

'Let me see the Diagram,' he said. Anything to distract from this slop they insisted on feeding him.

Mrall stepped aside, allowing Adrotagia – head of Taravangian's scholars – to approach, bearing a thick, leatherbound volume. She set it onto the table before Taravangian, then bowed.

Taravangian rested his fingers upon the leatherbound cover, feeling a moment of . . . reverence? Was that right? Did he revere anything anymore? God was dead, after all, and Vorinism therefore a sham.

This book, though, *was* holy. He opened it to one of the pages marked with a reed. Inside were scribbles.

Frenetic, bombastic, majestic scribbles that had been painstakingly copied from the walls of his former bedroom. Sketches laid atop one another, lists of numbers that seemed to make no sense, lines upon lines upon lines of script written in a cramped hand.

Madness. And genius.

Here and there, Taravangian could find hints that this writing was his own. The way he wiggled a line, the way he wrote along the edge of a wall, much like how he would write along the side of a page when he was running out of room. He didn't remember any of this. It was the product of twenty hours of lucid insanity, the most brilliant he had ever been.

'Does it strike you as odd, Adro,' Taravangian asked the scholar, 'that genius and idiocy are so similar?'

'Similar?' Adrotagia asked. 'Vargo, I do not see them as similar at all.' He and Adrotagia had grown up together, and she still used Taravangian's boyhood nickname. He liked that. It reminded him of days before all of this.

'On both my most stupid days and my most incredible,' Taravangian said, 'I am unable to interact with those around me in a meaningful way. It is like . . . like I become a gear that cannot fit those turning beside it. Too small or too large, it does not matter. The clock will not work.'

'I had not considered that,' Adrotagia said.

When Taravangian was at his stupidest, he was not allowed from his room. Those were the days he spent drooling in a corner. When he was merely dull-minded, he was allowed out under supervision. He spent those nights crying for what he had done, knowing that the atrocities he committed were important, but not understanding why.

When he was dull, he could not change policy. Interestingly, he had decided that when he was too brilliant, he was *also* not allowed to change policy. He'd made this decision after a day of genius where he'd thought to fix all of Kharbranth's problems with a series of very rational edicts – such as requiring people to take an intelligence test of his own devising before being allowed to breed.

So brilliant on one hand. So stupid on another. *Is that your joke here, Nightwatcher?* he wondered. *Is that the lesson I'm to learn? Do you even care about lessons, or is what you do to us merely for your own amusement?*

He turned his attention back to the book, the Diagram. That grand plan he had devised on his singular day of unparalleled brilliance. Then, too, he'd spent the day staring at a wall. He'd *written* on it. Babbling the whole time, making connections no man had ever before made, he had scribbled all over his walls, floor, even parts of the ceiling he could reach. Most of it had been written in an alien script – a language he himself had devised, for the scripts he had known had been unable to convey ideas precisely enough. Fortunately, he'd thought to carve a key on the top of his bedside table, otherwise they wouldn't have been able to make sense of his masterpiece.

They could barely make sense of it anyway. He flipped through several pages, copied exactly from his room. Adrotagia and her scholars had made notations here and there, offering theories on what various drawings and lists might mean. They wrote those in the women's script, which Taravangian had learned years ago.

Adrotagia's notes on one page indicated that a picture there appeared to be a sketch of the mosaic on the floor of the Veden palace. He paused on that page. It might have relevance to this day's activities. Unfortunately, he wasn't smart enough today to make much sense of the book or its secrets. He had to trust that his smarter self was correct in his interpretations of his even *smarter* self's genius.

He shut the book and put down his spoon. 'Let us be on with it.' He stood up and left the cabin, Mrall on one side of him and Adrotagia on the other. He emerged into sunlight and to the sight of a smoldering coastal city, complete with enormous terraced formations – like plates, or sections of shalebark, the remnants of city covering them and practically spilling over the sides. Once, this sight had been wondrous. Now, it was black, the buildings – even the palace – destroyed.

Vedenar, one of the great cities of the world, was now little more than a heap of rubble and ash.

Taravangian idled by the rail. When his ship had sailed into the harbor the night before, the city had been dotted with the red glow of burning buildings. Those had seemed alive. More alive than this. The wind was blowing in off the ocean, pushing at him from behind. It swept the smoke inland, away from the ship, so that Taravangian could barely smell it. An entire city burned just beyond his fingertips, and yet the stench vanished into the wind.

The Weeping would come soon. Perhaps it would wash away some of this destruction.

'Come, Vargo,' Adrotagia said. 'They are waiting.'

He nodded, joining her in climbing into the rowboat for tendering to shore. There had once been grand docks for this city. No more. One faction had destroyed them in an attempt to keep out the others.

'It's amazing,' Mrall said, settling down into the tender beside him.

'I thought you said you weren't going to be pleased any longer,' Taravangian said, stomach turning as he saw one of the heaps at the edge of the city. Bodies.

'I am not pleased,' Mrall said, 'but in awe. Do you realize that the Eighty's War between Emul and Tukar has lasted six years, and hasn't produced nearly this level of desolation? Jah Keved *ate* itself in a matter of months!'

'Soulcasters,' Adrotagia whispered.

It was more than that. Even in his painfully normal state, Taravangian could see it was so. Yes, with Soulcasters to provide food and water, armies could march at speed – no carts or supply lines to slow them – and commence a slaughter in almost no time at all. But Emul and Tukar had their share of Soulcasters as well.

Sailors started rowing them toward shore.

'There was more,' Mrall said. 'Each highprince sought to seize the capital. That made them converge. It was almost like the wars of some Northern savages, with a time and place appointed for the shaking of spears and chanting of threats. Only here, it depopulated a kingdom.'

'Let us hope, Mrall, that you make an overstatement,' Taravangian said. 'We will need this kingdom's people.' He turned away, stifling a moment of emotion as he saw bodies upon the rocks of the shore, men who had died by being shoved over the side of a nearby cliff into the ocean. That ridge normally sheltered the dock from highstorms. In war, it had been used to kill, one army pressing the other back off the drop.

Adrotagia saw his tears, and though she said nothing, she pursed her lips in disapproval. She did not like how emotional he became when he was low of intellect. And yet, he knew for a fact that the old woman still burned a glyphward each morning as a prayer for her deceased husband. A strangely devout action for blasphemers such as they.

'What is the day's news from home?' Taravangian asked to draw attention from the tears he wiped away.

'Dova reports that the number of Death Rattles we're finding has dropped even further. She didn't find a single one yesterday, and only two the day before.'

'Moelach moves, then,' Taravangian said. 'It is certain now. The creature must have been drawn by something westward.' What now? Did Taravangian suspend the murders? His heart yearned to – but if they could discover even one more glimmer about the future, one fact that could save hundreds of thousands, would it not be worth the lives of the few now?

'Tell Dova to continue the work,' he said. He had not anticipated that their covenant would attract the loyalty of an ardent, of all things. The Diagram, and its members, knew no boundaries. Dova had discovered their work on her own, and they'd needed to either induct her or assassinate her.

'It will be done,' Adrotagia said.

The boatmen moved them up alongside some smoother rocks at the harbor's edge, then hopped out into the water. The men were servants of his, and were part of the Diagram. He trusted them, for he needed to trust some people.

'Have you researched that other matter I requested?' Taravangian asked.

'It is a difficult matter to answer,' Adrotagia said. 'The exact intelligence of a man is impossible to measure; even your tests only give us an approximation. The speed at which you answer questions and the *way* you answer them . . . well, it lets us make a judgment, but it is a crude one.'

The boatmen hauled them up onto the stony beach with ropes. Wood scraped stone with an awful sound. At least it covered up the moans in the near distance.

Adrotagia took a sheet from her pocket and unfolded it. Upon it was a graph, with dots plotted in a kind of hump shape, a small trail to the left rising to a mountain in the center, then falling off in a similar curve to the right.

'I took your last five hundred days' test results and assigned each one a number between zero and ten,' Adrotagia said. 'A representation of how intelligent you were that day, though as I said, it is not exact.'

'The hump near the middle?' Taravangian asked, pointing.

'When you were average intelligence,' Adrotagia said. 'You spend most of your time near there, as you can see. Days of pure intelligence and days of ultimate stupidity are both rare. I had to extrapolate from what we had, but I think this graph is somewhat accurate.'

Taravangian nodded, then allowed one of the boatmen to help him debark. He had known that he spent more days average than he did otherwise. What he had asked her to figure out, however, was when he could expect another day like the one during which he'd created the Diagram. It had been years now since that day of transcendent mastery.

She climbed out of the boat and Mrall followed. She stepped up to him with her sheet.

'So this is where I was most intelligent,' Taravangian said, pointing at the last point on the chart. It was far to the right, and very close to the bottom. A representation of high intelligence and a low frequency of occurrence. 'This was that day, that day of perfection.'

'No,' Adrotagia said.

'What?'

'That was the time you were the most intelligent during the last five hundred days,' Adrotagia explained. 'This point represents the day you finished the most complex problems you'd left for yourself, and the day you devised new ones for use in future tests.'

'I remember that day,' he said. 'It was when I solved Fabrisan's Conundrum.'

'Yes,' she said. 'The world may thank you for that, someday, if it survives.'

'I was smart on that day,' he said. Smart enough that Mrall had declared he needed to be locked in the palace, lest he reveal his nature. He'd been convinced that if he could just explain his condition to the city, they would all listen to reason and let him control their lives perfectly. He'd drafted a law requiring that all people of less than average intellect be required to commit suicide for the good of the city. It had seemed reasonable. He had considered they might resist, but thought that the brilliance of the argument would sway them.

Yes, he had been smart on that day. But not nearly as smart as the day of the Diagram. He frowned, inspecting the paper.

'This is why I can't answer your question, Vargo,' Adrotagia said. 'That graph, it's what we call a logarithmic scale. Each step from that center point is not equal – they compound on one another the farther out you get. How smart *were* you on the day of the Diagram? Ten times smarter than your smartest otherwise?'

'A hundred,' Taravangian said, looking at the graph. 'Maybe more. Let me do the calculations. . . .'

'Aren't you stupid today?'

'Not stupid. Average. I can figure this much. Each step to the side is . . .'

'A measureable change in intelligence,' she said. 'You might say that each step sideways is a doubling of your intelligence, though that is hard to quantify. The steps upward are easier; they measure how frequently you have days of the given intelligence. So if you start at the center of the peak, you can see that for every five days you spend being average, you spend one day being mildly stupid and one day mildly smart. For every five of those, you spend one day moderately stupid and one day moderately genius. For every five days like that . . .'

Taravangian stood on the rocks, his soldiers waiting above, as he counted on the graph. He moved sideways off the graph until he reached the point where he guessed the day of the Diagram might have been. Even that seemed conservative to him.

'Almighty above . . .' he whispered. Thousands of days. Thousands upon thousands. 'It should never have happened.'

'Of course it should have,' she said.

'But it's so unlikely as to be impossible!'

'It's perfectly possible,' she said. 'The likelihood of it having happened is one, as it *already occurred*. That is the oddity of outliers and probability, Taravangian. A day like that could happen again tomorrow. Nothing forbids it. It's all pure chance, so far as I can determine. But if you want to know the likelihood of it happening again . . .'

He nodded.

'If you were to live another *two thousand years*, Vargo,' she said, 'you'd maybe have one single day like this among them. Maybe. Even odds, I'd say.'

Mrall snorted. 'So it was luck.'

'No, it was simple probability.'

'Either way,' Taravangian said, folding the paper. 'This was not the answer I wanted.'

'Since when has it mattered what we want?'

'Never,' he said. 'And it never will.' He tucked the sheet into his pocket.

They picked their way up the rocks, passing corpses bloated from too long in the sun, and joined a small group of soldiers at the top of the beach. They wore the burnt-orange crest of Kharbranth. He had few soldiers to his name. The Diagram called for his nation to be unthreatening.

The Diagram was not perfect, however. They caught errors in it now and then. Or ... not truly errors, just missed guesses. Taravangian had been supremely brilliant that day, but he had *not* been able to see the future. He had made educated guesses – very educated – and had been right an eerie amount of the time. But the farther they went from that day and the knowledge he'd had then, the more the Diagram needed tending and cultivation to stay on course.

That was why he'd hoped for another such day soon, a day to revamp the Diagram. That would not come, most likely. They would have to continue, trusting in that man that he had once been, trusting his vision and understanding.

Better that than anything else in this world. Gods and religion had failed them. Kings and highlords were selfish, petty things. If he was going to trust one thing to believe in, it would be himself and the raw genius of a human mind unfettered.

It *was* difficult at times, though, to stay the course. Particularly when he faced the consequences of his actions.

They entered the battlefield.

Most of the fighting had apparently moved outside of the city, once the fire began. The men had continued warring even as their capital burned. Seven factions. The Diagram had guessed six. Would that matter?

A soldier handed him a scented handkerchief to hold over his face as they passed the dead and dying. Blood and smoke. Scents he would come to know all too well before this was through.

Men and women in the burnt-orange livery of Kharbranth picked through the dead and wounded. Throughout the East, the color had become synonymous with healing. Indeed, tents flying his banner – the banner of the surgeon – dotted the battlefield. Taravangian's healers had arrived just before the battle, and had started ministering to the wounded immediately.

As he left the fields of the dead, Veden soldiers began to stand up from where they sat in a dull-eyed stupor at the edges of the battlefield. Then they started to cheer him.

'Pali's mind,' Adrotagia said, watching them rise. 'I don't believe it.'

The soldiers sat separated in groups by banner, being tended to by Taravangian's surgeons, water-bearers, and comforters. Wounded and unwounded alike, any who could stand rose for the king of Kharbranth and cheered him.

'The Diagram said it would happen,' Taravangian said.

'I thought for certain that was an error,' she replied, shaking her head.

'They know,' Mrall said. 'We are the only victors this day. Our healers, who earned the respect of all sides. Our comforters who helped the dying pass. Their highlords brought them only misery. You brought them life and hope.'

'I brought them death,' Taravangian whispered.

He had ordered the execution of their king, along with specific high-princes the Diagram indicated. In doing so, he had pushed the various factions into war with one another. He had brought this kingdom to its knees.

Now they cheered him for it. He forced himself to stop with one of the groups, asking after their health, seeing if there was anything he could do for them. It was important to be seen by the people as a compassionate man. The Diagram explained this in casual sterility, as if compassion were something one could measure in a cup next to a pint of blood.

He visited another group of soldiers, then a third. Many stepped up to him, touching his arms or his robe, weeping tears of thanks and joy. Many more of the Veden soldiers remained sitting in the tents, however, staring out over the fields of dead. Numb of mind.

'The Thrill?' he whispered to Adrotagia as they left the latest group of men. 'They fought through the night as their capital burned. It must have been in force.'

'I agree,' she said. 'It gives us a further reference point. The Thrill is at least as strong here as it is in Alethkar. Maybe stronger. I will speak to our scholars. Perhaps this will help pinpoint Nergaoul.'

'Do not spend too much effort on that,' Taravangian said, approaching another group of Veden soldiers. 'I'm not sure what we would even do if we found the thing.' An ancient, evil spren was not something he had the resources to tackle. Not yet at least. 'I would rather know where Moelach is moving.'

Hopefully, Moelach hadn't decided to slumber again. The Death Rattles had, so far, offered them the best way that they'd found to augment the Diagram.

There was one answer, however, he'd never been able to determine. One he'd give almost anything to know.

Would all of this be enough?

He met with the soldiers, and adopted the air of a kindly – if not bright – old man. Caring and helpful. He was almost that man in truth, today. He tried to do an imitation of himself when he was a little dumber. People accepted that man, and when he was of that intellect, he did not need to feign compassion nearly as much as he did when smarter.

Blessed with intelligence, cursed with compassion to feel pain for what he had done. They came inversely. Why couldn't he have both at once? He did not think that in other people, intelligence and compassion were tied in such a way. The Nightwatcher's motives behind her boons and curses were unfathomable.

Taravangian moved through the crowd of men, listening to them beg for more relief and for drugs to ease their pain. Listening to their thanks. These soldiers had suffered a fight that – even yet – seemed to have no victor. They wanted *something* to hold to, and Taravangian was neutral, supposedly. It was shocking how easily they bared their souls to him.

He came to the next soldier in line, a cloaked man clutching an apparently broken arm. Taravangian looked into the man's hooded eyes.

It was Szeth-son-son-Vallano.

Taravangian felt a moment of sheer panic.

'We need to speak,' the Shin man said.

Taravangian grabbed the assassin by the arm, hauling him away from the crowd of Veden soldiers. With his other hand, Taravangian felt in his pocket for the Oathstone he carried on his person at all times. He pulled it out just to see. Yes, it was no fake. Damnation, seeing Szeth there had made him think that he'd been bested somehow, the stone stolen and Szeth sent to kill him.

Szeth let himself be pulled away. What had he said? *That he needed to talk, you fool,* Taravangian thought to himself. *If he'd come to kill you, you would be dead.*

Had Szeth been seen here? What would people say if they saw Taravangian interacting with a bald Shin man? Rumors had started from less.

If anyone got even a *hint* that Taravangian had been involved with the infamous Assassin in White . . .

Mrall noticed immediately that something was wrong. He barked orders to the guards, separating Taravangian from the Veden soldiers. Adrotagia – who had been sitting with crossed arms nearby, watching and tapping her foot – leaped to stride over. She peeked at the person under the hood, then gasped, the color draining from her face.

'How *dare* you come here?' Taravangian said to Szeth, speaking under his breath while maintaining a cheerful pose and expression. He was of only average intelligence today, but he was still a king, raised and trained to the court. He could maintain his composure.

'A problem has arisen,' Szeth said, face hooded, voice emotionless. Speaking to this creature was like speaking to one of the dead themselves.

'Why have you failed to kill Dalinar Kholin?' Adrotagia demanded with quiet urgency. 'We know you fled. Return and do the job!'

Szeth glanced at her, but did not reply. She did not hold his Oathstone. He did seem to note her, however, with those too-blank eyes of his.

Damnation. Their plan had been to keep Szeth from meeting or knowing of Adrotagia, just in case he decided to turn against Taravangian and kill him. The Diagram hypothesized this possibility.

'Kholin has a Surgebinder,' Szeth said.

So, Szeth knew about Jasnah. Had she faked her death, then, as he'd suspected? Damnation.

The battlefield seemed to grow still. To Taravangian, the moans of the wounded faded away. Everything narrowed to just him and Szeth. Those eyes. The tone of the man's voice. A dangerous tone. What—

He spoke with emotion, Taravangian realized. *That last sentence was said with passion.* It had sounded like a plea. As if Szeth's voice were being squeezed on the sides.

This man was not sane. Szeth-son-son-Vallano was the most dangerous weapon on all of Roshar, and he was broken.

Storms, why couldn't this have happened on a day when Taravangian had more than half a wit?

'What makes you say this?' Taravangian said, trying to buy time for his mind to lumber through the implications. He held Szeth's Oathstone before him, almost as if it could chase away problems like a superstitious woman's glyphward.

'I fought him,' Szeth said. 'He protected Kholin.'

'Ah, yes,' Taravangian said, thinking furiously. Szeth had been banished from Shinovar, made Truthless for something relating to a claim that the Voidbringers had returned. If he discovered that he wasn't wrong about that claim, then what—

Him?

'You fought a Surgebinder?' Adrotagia said, glancing at Taravangian.

'Yes,' Szeth said. 'An Alethi man who fed upon Stormlight. He healed a Blade-severed arm. He is . . . Radiant . . .' That strain in his voice did not sound safe. Taravangian glanced at Szeth's hands. They were clenching into fists time and time again, like hearts beating.

'No, no,' Taravangian said. 'I have learned this only recently. Yes, it makes sense now. One of the Honorblades has vanished.'

Szeth blinked, and he focused on Taravangian, as if returning from a distant place. 'One of the other seven?'

'Yes,' Taravangian said. 'I have heard only hints. Your people are secretive. But yes . . . I see, it is one of the two that allow Regrowth. Kholin must have it.'

Szeth swayed back and forth, though he did not seem conscious of the motion. Even now, he moved with a fighter's grace. *Storms.*

'This man I fought,' Szeth said, 'he summoned no Blade.'

'But he used Stormlight,' Taravangian said.

'Yes.'

'So he must have an Honorblade.'

'I . . .'

'It is the *only* explanation.'

'It . . .' Szeth's voice grew colder. 'Yes, the only explanation. I will kill him and retrieve it.'

'No,' Taravangian said firmly. 'You are to return to Dalinar Kholin and do the task assigned you. Do not fight this other man. Attack when he is not present.'

'But—'

'Have I your Oathstone?' Taravangian demanded. 'Is my word to be questioned?'

Szeth stopped swaying. His gaze locked with Taravangian's. 'I am Truthless. I do as my master requires, and I do not ask for an explanation.'

'Stay away from the man with the Honorblade,' Taravangian repeated. 'Kill Dalinar.'

'It will be done.' Szeth turned and strode away. Taravangian wanted to yell further instructions. *Don't be seen! Don't* ever *come to me in public again!*

Instead, he sat right there on the path, composure crumbling. He gasped, trembling, sweat streaming down his brow.

'Stormfather,' Adrotagia said, settling on the ground beside him. 'I thought we were dead.'

Servants brought Taravangian a chair while Mrall made excuses for him. *The king is overcome with grief at the deaths of so many. He is old, you know. And so caring . . .*

Taravangian breathed in and out, struggling to regain control. He looked to Adrotagia, who sat in the middle of a circle of servants and soldiers, all sworn to the Diagram. 'Who is it?' he asked softly. 'Who is this Surgebinder?'

'Jasnah's ward?' Adrotagia said.

They had been startled when that one arrived on the Shattered Plains. Already they hypothesized that the girl had been trained. If not by Jasnah, then by the girl's brother, before his death.

'No,' Taravangian said. 'A male. One of Dalinar's family members?' He thought for a time. 'We need the Diagram itself.'

She went to fetch it from the ship. Nothing else – his visits to the soldiers, more important meetings with Veden leaders – mattered right now. The Diagram was off. They strayed into dangerous territory.

She returned with it, and with the stormwardens, who set up a tent around Taravangian right there on the path. Excuses continued. *The king is weak from the sun. He must rest and burn glyphwards to the Almighty for the preservation of your nation. Taravangian cares while your own lighteyes sent you to the slaughter . . .*

By the light of spheres, Taravangian picked through the tome, poring over translations of his own words written in a language he had invented and then forgotten. Answers. He *needed* answers.

'Did ever I tell you, Adro, what I asked for?' he whispered as he read.

'Yes.'

He was barely listening. 'Capacity,' he whispered, turning a page. 'Capacity to stop what was coming. The capacity to save humankind.'

He searched. He was not brilliant today, but he had spent many days reading these pages, going over, and over, and over passages. He knew them.

The answers would be here. They *would*. Taravangian worshipped only one god now. It was the man he had been on that day.

There.

He found it on a reproduction of one corner of his room, where he'd written in tiny script sentences over the top of one another because he'd run out of space. In his clarity of genius, the sentences had looked easy to separate, but it had taken his scholars years to piece together what this said.

They will come. You cannot stop their oaths. Look for those who survive when they should not. That pattern will be your clue.

'The bridgemen,' Taravangian whispered.

'What?' Adrotagia asked.

Taravangian looked up, blinking bleary eyes. 'Dalinar's bridgemen, the ones he took from Sadeas. Did you read the account of their survival?'

'I didn't think it important. Just another game of power between Sadeas and Dalinar.'

'No. It's more.' They had survived. Taravangian stood up. 'Wake every Alethi sleeper we have; send every agent in the area. There will be stories told of one of these bridgemen. Miraculous survival. Favored of the winds. One is among them. He might not know yet exactly what he's doing, but he has bonded a spren and sworn at least the First Ideal.'

'If we find him?' Adrotagia asked.

'We keep him away from Szeth at all costs.' Taravangian handed her the Diagram. 'Our lives depend upon it. Szeth is a beast who gnaws at his leg to escape his bonds. If he gets free . . .'

She nodded, moving off to do as he commanded. She hesitated at the flaps to their temporary tent. 'We might have to reassess our methods of determining your intelligence. What I have seen in the last hour makes me question whether "average" can be applied to you today.'

'The assessments are not inaccurate,' he said. 'You simply underestimate the average man.'

Besides, in dealing with the Diagram, he might not remember what he had written or why – but there were *echoes* sometimes.

She left, making way as Mrall stepped in. 'Your Majesty,' he said. 'Time runs short. The highprince is dying.'

'He's been dying for years.' Still, Taravangian did hasten his step – as much as he was capable of doing these days – as he resumed his hike. He didn't stop with any more of the soldiers, and gave only brief waves toward the cheers he received.

Eventually, Mrall led him over a hillside away from the immediate stench of the battle and the smoldering city. A series of stormwagons here flew an optimistic flag, that of the king of Jah Keved. The guards there let Taravangian enter their ring of wagons, and he approached the largest one, an enormous vehicle almost like a mobile building on wheels.

They found Highprince Valam ... *King* Valam ... in bed coughing. His hair had fallen out since Taravangian had last seen him, and his cheeks were so sunken that rainwater would have pooled in them. Redin, the king's bastard son, stood at the foot of the bed, head bowed. With the three guards who stood in the room, there wasn't room for Taravangian, so he stopped in the doorway.

'Taravangian,' Valam said, then coughed into his handkerchief. The cloth came back bloodied. 'You've come for my kingdom, have you?'

'I don't know what you mean, Your Majesty,' Taravangian said.

'Don't play coy,' Valam snapped. 'I can't stand it in women or in rivals. Stormfather ... I don't know what they're going to make of you. I half think they'll have you assassinated by the end of the week.' He waved with a sickly hand, all draped in cloth, and the guards made way for Taravangian to enter the small bedchamber.

'Clever ploy,' the king said. 'Sending that food, those healers. The soldiers love you, I've heard. What would you have done if one side had won decisively?'

'I'd have had a new ally,' Taravangian said. 'Grateful for my aid.'

'You helped all sides.'

'But the winner the most, Your Majesty,' Taravangian said. 'We can minister to survivors, but not the dead.'

Valam coughed again, a great hacking mess. His bastard stepped up, concerned, but the king waved him back. 'Would have figured,' the king said to him between wheezes, 'you'd be the only one of my children to live, bastard.' He turned to Taravangian. 'Turns out, you have a legitimate claim on the throne, Taravangian. Through your mother's side, I think? A marriage to a Veden princess some three generations back?'

'I am not aware,' Taravangian said.

'Didn't you hear me about being coy?'

'We both have a role to play in this production, Your Majesty,' Taravangian said. 'I am merely speaking the lines as they were written.'

'You talk like a woman,' Valam said. He spat blood to the side. 'I know what you're up to. In a week or so, after caring for my people, your scribes will "discover" your claim on the throne. You'll reluctantly step in to save the kingdom, as urged by my own storming people.'

'I see you've had the script read to you,' Taravangian said softly.

'That assassin will come for you.'

'He very well might.' That was the truth.

'Don't know why I even storming tried for this throne,' Valam said. 'At least I'll die as king.' He heaved a deep breath, then raised his hand, gesturing impatiently at the scribes huddled outside the room. The women perked up, peeking around Taravangian.

'I'm making this idiot my heir,' Valam said, waving at Taravangian. 'Ha! Let the other highprinces chew on that.'

'They're dead, Your Majesty,' Taravangian said.

'What? All of them?'

'Yes.'

'Even Boriar?'

'Yes.'

'Huh,' Valam said. 'Bastard.'

At first, Taravangian thought that was a reference to one of the deceased. Then, however, he noticed the king waving at his illegitimate son. Redin stepped up, going onto one knee beside the bed as Taravangian made room.

Valam struggled with something beneath his blankets; his side knife. Redin helped him get it out, then held the knife awkwardly.

Taravangian inspected this Redin, curious. This was the king's ruthless executioner that he had read about? This concerned, helpless-looking man?

'Through my heart,' Valam said.

'Father, no . . .' Redin said.

'Through my storming heart!' Valam shouted, spraying bloody spittle

across his sheet. 'I won't lie here and let Taravangian coax my own servants into poisoning me. Do it, boy! Or can't you do a single thing
that—'

Redin slammed the knife down into his father's chest with such force,
it made Taravangian jump. Redin then stood, saluted, and shoved his way
out of the room.

The king heaved a final gasp, eyes glazing over. 'So the night will reign,
for the choice of honor is life . . .'

Taravangian raised an eyebrow. A Death Rattle? Here, now? Blast, and
he wasn't in a position where he could write down the exact phrasing.
He'd have to remember it.

Valam's life faded away until he was simply meat. A Shardblade appeared from vapor beside the bed, then thumped to the wooden floor
of the wagon. Nobody reached for it, and the soldiers in the room and
scribes outside it looked to Taravangian, then knelt.

'Cruel, what Valam did to that one,' Mrall said, nodding toward the
bastard, who shoved his way out of the stormwagon and into the light.

'More than you know,' Taravangian said, reaching out to touch the
knife protruding through blanket and clothing from the old king's chest.
He hesitated, fingers inches from the handle. 'The bastard will be known
as a patricide on the official records. If he had interest in the throne, this
will make it . . . difficult for him, even more so than his parentage.' Taravangian pulled his fingers away from the knife. 'Might I have a moment
with the fallen king? I would speak a prayer for him.'

The others left him, even Mrall. They shut the small door, and Taravangian sat down on the stool beside the corpse. He had no intention
of saying any sort of prayer, but he did want a moment. Alone. To
think.

It had worked. Just as the Diagram instructed, Taravangian was king
of Jah Keved. He had taken the first major step toward unifying the
world, as Gavilar had insisted would need to happen if they were to
survive.

That was, at least, what the visions had proclaimed. Visions Gavilar
had confided in him six years ago, the night of the Alethi king's death.
Gavilar had seen visions of the Almighty, who was also now dead, and of
a coming storm.

Unite them.

'I am doing my best, Gavilar,' Taravangian whispered. 'I *am* sorry that I need to kill your brother.'

That would not be the only sin upon his head when this was done. Not by a faint breeze or a stormwind.

He wished, once again, that this day had been a day of brilliance. Then he wouldn't have felt so guilty.

FIVE

Winds Alight

KALADIN • SHALLAN • DALINAR •
ADOLIN • WIT

*They will come you cannot stop their oaths look for those who survive
when they should not that pattern will be your clue.*

—From the Diagram, Coda of the
Northwest Bottom Corner: paragraph 3

You have killed her....

Kaladin couldn't sleep.

He knew he *should* sleep. He lay in his dark barrack room, surrounded by familiar stone, comfortable for the first time in days. A soft
pillow, a mattress as good as the one he'd had back home in Hearthstone.
His body felt wrung out, like a rag after the washing was done. He'd
survived the chasms and brought Shallan home safely. Now he needed
to sleep and heal.

You have killed her....

He sat up in his bed, and felt a wave of dizziness. He gritted his teeth
and let it pass. His leg wound throbbed inside his bandage. The camp
surgeons had done a good job with that; his father would have been
pleased.

The camp outside felt too quiet. After showering him with praise and
enthusiasm, the men of Bridge Four had gone to join the army for its expedition, along with all of the other bridge crews, who would be carrying

bridges for the army. Only a small force from Bridge Four would remain behind to guard the king.

Kaladin reached out in the darkness, feeling beside the wall until he found his spear. He took hold, then propped himself up and stood. The leg flared with immediate pain, and he gritted his teeth, but it wasn't so bad. He'd taken fathom bark for the pain, and it was working. He'd refused the firemoss the surgeons had tried to give him. His father had hated using the addictive stuff.

Kaladin forced his way to the door of his small room, then shoved it open and stepped into the sunlight. He shaded his eyes and scanned the sky. No clouds yet. The Weeping, the worst part of the year, would roll in sometime tomorrow. Four weeks of ceaseless rain and gloom. It was a Light Year, so not even a highstorm in the middle. Misery.

Kaladin longed for the storm within. That would have awakened his mind, made him feel like moving.

'Hey, gancho?' Lopen said, popping up from where he sat beside the firepit. 'You need something?'

'Let's go watch the army leave.'

'You're not supposed to be walking, I think. . . .'

'I'll be fine,' Kaladin said, hobbling with difficulty.

Lopen rushed over to help him, getting up under Kaladin's arm, lifting weight off the bad leg. 'Why don't you glow a bit, gon?' Lopen asked softly. 'Heal that problem?'

He'd prepared a lie: something about not wanting to alert the surgeons by healing too quickly. He couldn't force it out. Not to a member of Bridge Four.

'I've lost the ability, Lopen,' he said softly. 'Syl has left me.'

The lean Herdazian fell unusually silent. 'Well,' he finally said, 'maybe you should buy her something nice.'

'Buy something nice? For a *spren*?'

'Yeah. Like . . . I don't know. A nice plant, maybe, or a new hat. Yes, a hat. Might be cheap. She's small. If a tailor tries to charge you full price for a hat that small, you thump him real good.'

'That's the most ridiculous piece of advice I've ever been given.'

'You should rub yourself with curry and go prancing through the camp singing Horneater lullabies.'

Kaladin looked at Lopen, incredulous. '*What?*'

'See? Now the bit about the hat is only the *second* most ridiculous piece of advice you've ever been given, so you should try it. Women like hats. I have this cousin who makes them. I can ask her. You might not even need the actual hat. Just the spren of the hat. That'll make it even cheaper.'

'You're a very special kind of weird, Lopen.'

'Of course I am, gon. There's only *one* of *me*.'

They continued through the empty camp. Storms, the place seemed hollow. They passed empty barrack after empty barrack. Kaladin walked with care, glad for Lopen's help, but even this was draining. He shouldn't be moving on the leg. Father's words, the words of a surgeon, floated up from the depths of his mind.

Torn muscles. Bind the leg, ward against infection, and keep the subject from putting weight on it. Further tearing could lead to a permanent limp, or worse.

'You want to get a palanquin?' Lopen asked.

'Those are for women.'

'Ain't nothing wrong with being a woman, gancho,' Lopen said. 'Some of my relatives are women.'

'Of course they . . .' He trailed off at Lopen's grin. Storming Herdazian. How much of what he said was to deliberately sound obtuse? Well, Kaladin had heard men telling jokes about how stupid Herdazians were, but Lopen could talk rings around those men. Of course, half of Lopen's own jokes were about Herdazians. He seemed to find those extra funny.

As they approached the plateaus, the dead silence gave way to the low roar of thousands of people assembled in a limited area. Kaladin and Lopen finally broke free of the barrack rows, emerging onto the natural terrace just above the parade grounds that debouched onto the Shattered Plains. Thousands of soldiers were gathered there. Spearmen in huge blocks, lighteyed archers in thinner ranks, officers prancing on horseback in gleaming armor.

Kaladin gasped softly.

'What?' Lopen asked.

'It's what I always thought I'd find.'

'What? Today?'

'As a young man in Alethkar,' Kaladin said, unexpectedly emotional. 'When I dreamed of the glory of war, this is what I imagined.' He hadn't pictured the greenvines and barely capable soldiers that Amaram had trained in Alethkar. Neither had he pictured the crude, if effective, brutes of Sadeas's army – or even the quick strike teams of Dalinar's plateau runs.

He'd imagined *this*. A full army, arrayed for a grand march. Spears held high, banners fluttering, drummers and trumpeters, messengers in livery, scribes on horses, even the king's Soulcasters in their own sectioned-off square, hidden from sight by walls of cloth carried on poles.

Kaladin knew the truth of battle now. Fighting was not about glory, but about men lying on the ground screaming and thrashing, tangled in their own viscera. It was about bridgemen thrown against a wall of arrows, or of Parshendi cut down while they sang.

Yet in this moment, Kaladin let himself dream again. He gave his youthful self – still there deep inside him – the spectacle he'd always imagined. He pretended that these soldiers were about something wonderful, instead of just another pointless slaughter.

'Hey, someone else is actually coming,' Lopen said, pointing. 'Look at that.'

By the banners, Dalinar had been joined by only a single highprince: Roion. However, as Lopen pointed out, another force – not quite as large or as well organized – was flowing northward up the wide, open pathway along the eastern rim of the warcamps. At least one other highprince had responded to Dalinar's call.

'Let's find Bridge Four,' Kaladin said. 'I want to see the men off.'

∴

'Sebarial?' Dalinar asked. '*Sebarial's* troops are joining us?'

Roion grunted, wringing his hands – as if wishing to wash them – as he sat in the saddle. 'I guess we should be glad for any support at all.'

'Sebarial,' Dalinar said, dumbfounded. 'He wouldn't even send troops on close plateau runs, where there was no risk of Parshendi. Why would he send men now?'

Roion shook his head and shrugged.

Dalinar turned Gallant and trotted the horse toward the oncoming group, as did Roion. They passed Adolin, who rode just behind with Shallan, side by side, her guards and his following. Renarin was over with the bridgemen, of course.

Shallan was riding one of Adolin's own horses, a petite gelding over which Sureblood towered. Shallan wore a traveling dress of the kind messenger women preferred, with the front and back slit all the way to the waist. She wore leggings – basically silk trousers, but women preferred other names – underneath.

Behind them rode a large group of Navani's scholars and cartographers, including Isasik, the ardent who was the royal cartographer. These passed around the map Shallan had drawn, Isasik riding to the side, chin raised, as if pointedly ignoring the praise the women were giving Shallan's map. Dalinar needed all these scholars, though he wished he didn't. Each scribe he brought was another life he risked. That was made worse by Navani herself coming. He couldn't dismiss her argument. *If you think it's safe enough for you to bring the girl, then it's safe enough for me.*

As Dalinar made his way toward Sebarial's oncoming procession, Amaram rode up, wearing his Shardplate, his golden cloak trailing behind. He had a fine warhorse, the hulking breed used in Shinovar to pull heavy carts. It still looked like a pony beside Gallant.

'Is that *Sebarial?*' Amaram asked, pointing at the oncoming force.

'Apparently.'

'Should we send him away?'

'Why would we do that?'

'He's untrustworthy,' Amaram said.

'He keeps his word, so far as I know,' Dalinar said. 'That is more than I can say for most.'

'He keeps his word because he never promises anything.'

Dalinar, Roion, and Amaram trotted up to Sebarial, who stepped out of a carriage at the front of the army. A carriage. For a war procession. Well, it wouldn't slow Dalinar any more than all of these scribes. In fact, he should probably have a few more carriages made ready. It would be nice for Navani to have a way to ride in comfort once the days wore long.

'Sebarial?' Dalinar asked.

'Dalinar!' the plump man said, shading his eyes. 'You look surprised.'

'I am.'

'Ha! That's reason enough to have come. Wouldn't you say, Palona?' Dalinar could barely make out the woman sitting in the carriage, wearing an enormous fashionable hat and a sleek gown.

'You brought your mistress?' Dalinar asked.

'Sure. Why not? If we fail out there, I'll be dead and she'll be out on her ear. She insisted, anyway. Storming woman.' Sebarial walked up right beside Gallant. 'I've got a feeling about you, Dalinar old man. I think it's wise to stay close to you. Something's going to happen out there on the Plains, and opportunity rises like the dawn.'

Roion sniffed.

'Roion,' Sebarial said, 'shouldn't you be hiding under a table somewhere?'

'Perhaps I should, if only to get away from you.'

Sebarial laughed. 'Well said, you old turtle! Maybe this trip won't be a complete bore. Onward, then! To glory and some such nonsense. If we find riches, remember that I get my part! I got here before Aladar. That has to count for something.'

'Before . . .' Dalinar said with a start. He twisted around, looking back toward the warcamp bordering his own to the north.

There, an army wearing Aladar's colors of white and dark green spilled out onto the Shattered Plains.

'Now *that*,' Amaram said, 'I *really* didn't expect.'

⁂

'We could try a coup,' Ialai said.

Sadeas turned in his saddle toward his wife. Their guards scattered the hills around them, distant enough to be out of earshot as the high-prince and his wife enjoyed a gentle 'ride through the hills.' In reality, the two of them had wanted a closer look at Sebarial's expansions out here west of the warcamps, where he was setting up full-scale farming operations.

Ialai rode with eyes forward. 'Dalinar will be gone from the camp, and with him Roion, his only supporter. We could seize the Pinnacle, execute the king, and take the throne.'

Sadeas turned his horse, looking eastward over the warcamps. He could just barely make out Dalinar's army gathering distantly on the Shattered Plains.

A coup. One last step, a slap in the face of old Gavilar. He'd do it. Storm it, he would.

Except for the fact that he didn't need to.

'Dalinar has committed to this foolish expedition,' Sadeas said. 'He'll be dead soon, surrounded and destroyed on those Plains. We don't need a coup; if I'd known that he would actually *do* this, we wouldn't have even needed your assassin.'

Ialai looked away. Her assassin had failed. She considered it a strong fault on her part, though the plan had been executed with exactness. These things were never certain. Unfortunately, now that they'd tried and failed, they'd need to be careful about . . .

Sadeas turned his horse, frowning as a messenger approached on horseback. The youth was allowed to pass the guards and proffered a letter to Ialai.

She read it, and her disposition darkened.

'You aren't going to like this,' she said, looking up.

·❖·

Dalinar kicked Gallant into motion, tearing across the landscape, startling plants into their dens. He passed his army in a few minutes of hard riding and approached the new force.

Aladar sat on horseback here, surveying his army. He wore a fashionable uniform, black with maroon stripes on the sleeves and a matching stock at the neck. Soldiers swarmed around him. He had one of the largest forces on the Plains – storms, with Dalinar's numbers reduced, Aladar's army might be *the* largest.

He was also one of Sadeas's greatest supporters.

'How are we going to do this, Dalinar?' Aladar asked as Dalinar trotted up. 'Do we all go out on our own, crossing different plateaus but meeting back up, or do we march in an enormous column?'

'Why?' Dalinar asked. 'Why have you come?'

'You made such passionate arguments all along, and now you act surprised that someone listened?'

'Not someone. You.'

Aladar pressed his lips to a line, finally turning to meet Dalinar's eyes. 'Roion and Sebarial, the two biggest cowards in our midst, are marching to war. Am I to stay behind and let them seek the fulfillment of the Vengeance Pact without me?'

'The other highprinces seem content to do so.'

'I suspect they are better at lying to themselves than I am.'

Suddenly, all of Aladar's vehement arguments – at the forefront of the faction against Dalinar – took on a different cast. *He was arguing to convince himself,* Dalinar thought. *He was worried all along that I was right.*

'Sadeas will not be pleased,' Dalinar said.

'Sadeas can storm off. He doesn't own me.' Aladar fiddled with his reins for a moment. 'He wants to, though. I can feel it in the deals he forces me to make, the knives he slowly places at everyone's throats. He'd have us all as his slaves by the end of this.'

'Aladar,' Dalinar said, moving his horse right up alongside the other man's so the two of them faced each other directly. He held Aladar's eyes. 'Tell me Sadeas didn't put you up to this. Tell me this isn't part of another plot to abandon or betray me.'

Aladar smiled. 'You think I'd just tell you if it were?'

'I would hear a promise from your own lips.'

'And you'll trust that promise? How well did that serve you, Dalinar, when Sadeas professed his friendship?'

'A promise, Aladar.'

Aladar met his eyes. 'I think the things you say about Alethkar are naive at best, and undoubtedly impossible. Those delusions of yours aren't a sign of madness, as Sadeas wants us to think – they're just the dreams of a man who wants desperately to believe in something, something foolish. "Honor" is a word applied to the actions of men from the past who have had their lives scrubbed clean by historians.' He hesitated. 'But . . . storm me for a fool, Dalinar, I wish they *could* be true. I came for myself, not Sadeas. I won't betray you. Even if Alethkar can't ever be what you want, we *can* at least crush the Parshendi and avenge old Gavilar. It's just the right thing to do.'

Dalinar nodded.

'I could be lying,' Aladar said.

'But you aren't.'

'How do you know?'

'Honestly? I don't. But if this is all going to work, I am going to have to trust some of you.' To an extent. He would never put himself in another position like the Tower.

Either way, Aladar's presence meant this incursion was actually possible. Together, the four of them would likely outnumber the Parshendi – though he wasn't certain how trustworthy the scribes' counts of their numbers were.

It was not the grand coalition of all highprinces that Dalinar had wanted, but even with the chasms favoring the Parshendi, this could be enough.

'We march together,' Dalinar said, pointing. 'I don't want us spread out. We keep to plateaus next to one another, or the same plateau when possible. And you'll need to leave your parshmen behind.'

'That's an unusual requirement,' Aladar said with a frown.

'We're marching against their cousins,' Dalinar said. 'Best to not risk the possibility of them turning against us.'

'But they'd never . . . Bah, whatever. It can be done.'

Dalinar nodded, extending a hand to Aladar as, behind, Roion and Amaram finally trotted up; Dalinar had outstripped them on Gallant.

'Thank you,' Dalinar said to Aladar.

'You really do believe in all of this, don't you?'

'Yes.'

Aladar extended his hand, but hesitated. 'You realize that I'm stained through and through. I've got blood on these hands, Dalinar. I'm not some perfect, honorable knight as you seem to want to pretend.'

'I know you're not,' Dalinar said, taking the hand. 'I'm not either. We will have to do.'

They shared a nod, then Dalinar turned Gallant and began to trot back toward his own army. Roion groaned, complaining about his thighs after having galloped all the way over. The ride today was not going to be pleasant for him.

Amaram fell in beside Dalinar. 'First Sebarial, then Aladar? Your trust seems to come cheaply today, Dalinar.'

'Would you have me turn them away?'

'Think how spectacular this victory would be if we did it on our own.'

'I hope we're above such vainglory, old friend,' Dalinar said. They rode for a time, passing Adolin and Shallan again. Dalinar scanned his force and noticed something. A tall man in blue sat on a stone in the midst of Bridge Four's bodyguards.

Speaking of fools . . .

'Come with me,' Dalinar said to Amaram.

Amaram let his horse lag behind. 'I think I should go see to—'

'Come,' Dalinar said sharply. 'I want you to speak to that young man so we can put a stop to the rumors and the things he's been saying about you. Those don't do anyone any good.'

'Very well,' Amaram said, catching up.

∴

Kaladin found himself standing up amid the bridgemen, despite the pain of his leg, as he noticed Adolin and Shallan riding past. He followed the pair with his eyes. Adolin, astride his thick-hooved Ryshadium, and Shallan on a more modestly sized brown animal.

She looked gorgeous. Kaladin was willing to admit it, if only to himself. Brilliant red hair, ready smile. She said something clever; Kaladin could almost hear the words. He waited, hoping that she'd look toward him, meet his eyes across the short distance.

She didn't. She rode on, and Kaladin felt like an utter fool. A part of him wanted to hate Adolin for holding her attention, but he found that he couldn't. The truth was, he *liked* Adolin. And those two were good for one another. They *fit*.

Perhaps Kaladin could hate that.

He settled back down on a rock, bowing his head. The bridgemen crowded in around him. Hopefully they hadn't seen Kaladin following Shallan with his eyes, straining to hear her voice. Renarin stood, like a shade, at the back of the group. The bridgemen were coming to accept him, but he still seemed very awkward around them. Of course, he seemed awkward around most people.

I need to talk to him more about his condition, Kaladin thought. Something seemed off to him about that man and his explanation of the epilepsy.

'Why are you here, sir?' Bisig asked, drawing Kaladin's attention back to the other bridgemen.

'I wanted to see you off,' Kaladin said, sighing. 'I assumed you'd be happy to see me.'

'You are like child,' Rock said, wagging a thick finger at Kaladin. 'What would you do, great Captain Stormblessed, if you caught one of *these* men walking about with hurt leg? You would have that man beaten! Once he healed, of course.'

'I thought,' Kaladin noted, 'that I was your *commander*.'

'Nah, can't be,' Teft said, 'because our commander would be smart enough to stay in bed.'

'And eat much stew,' Rock said. 'I left you stew to eat while I am gone.'

'You're going on the expedition?' Kaladin asked, looking up at the large Horneater. 'I thought you were just seeing the men off. You aren't willing to fight. What will you do out there?'

'Someone must fix food for them,' Rock said. 'This expedition, it will take days. I will not leave my friends to the mercy of camp chefs. Ha! The food they cook will all be from Soulcast grain and meat. Tastes like crem! Someone must come with proper spices.'

Kaladin looked up at the group of frowning men. 'Fine,' he said. 'I'll go back. Storms, I . . .'

Why were the bridgemen parting? Rock looked over his shoulder, then laughed, backing away. 'Now we shall see real trouble.'

Behind them, Dalinar Kholin was climbing from his saddle. Kaladin sighed, then waved for Lopen to help him to his feet so he could salute properly. He got upright – earning a glare from Teft – before noticing that Dalinar was not alone.

Amaram. Kaladin stiffened, straining to keep his face expressionless.

Dalinar and Amaram approached. The pain in Kaladin's leg seemed to fade, and for the moment he could only see that man. That *monster* of a man. Wearing Plate Kaladin had earned, a golden cloak billowing out behind, bearing the symbol of the Knights Radiant.

Control yourself, Kaladin thought. He managed to swallow his rage. Last time it had gotten the better of him, he'd earned himself weeks in prison.

'You should be resting, soldier,' Dalinar said.

'Yes, sir,' Kaladin replied. 'My men have already made that abundantly clear.'

'Then you trained them well. I'm proud to have them along with me on this expedition.'

Teft saluted. 'If there is danger to you, Brightlord, it will be out there on the Plains. We can't protect you if we wait back here.'

Kaladin frowned, realizing something. 'Skar is here . . . Teft . . . so who is watching the king?'

'We've seen to it, sir,' Teft said. 'Brightlord Dalinar asked me leave our best man behind with a team of his own selection. They'll watch the king.'

Their best man . . .

Coldness. Moash. *Moash* had been left in charge of the king's safety, and had a team of his own choosing.

Storms.

'Amaram,' Dalinar said, waving for the highlord to step up. 'You told me that you'd never seen this man before arriving here on the Shattered Plains. Is that true?'

Kaladin met the eyes of a murderer. 'Yes,' Amaram said.

'What of his claim that you took your Blade and Plate from him?' Dalinar asked.

'Brightlord,' Amaram said, taking Dalinar by the arm, 'I don't know if the lad is touched in the head or merely starved for attention. Perhaps he served in my army, as he claims – he certainly bears the correct slave brand. But his allegations regarding me are *obviously* preposterous.'

Dalinar nodded to himself, as if this were all expected. 'I believe an apology is due.'

Kaladin struggled to remain upright, his leg feeling weak. So this would be his final punishment. Apologizing to Amaram in public. A humiliation above all others.

'I—' Kaladin began.

'Not you, son,' Dalinar said softly.

Amaram turned, posture suddenly more alert – like that of a man preparing for a fight. 'Surely you don't believe these allegations, Dalinar!'

'A few weeks ago,' Dalinar said, 'I received two special visitors in camp. One was a trusted servant who had come from Kholinar in secret, bringing a precious cargo. The other was that cargo: a madman who had arrived at the gates of Kholinar carrying a Shardblade.'

Amaram paled and stepped back, hand going to his side.

'I told my servant,' Dalinar said calmly, 'to go drinking with your personal guard – he knew many of them – and talk of a treasure that the madman said had been hidden for years outside the warcamp. By my order, he then placed the madman's Shardblade in a nearby cavern. After that, we waited.'

He's summoning his Blade, Kaladin thought, looking at Amaram's hand. Kaladin reached for his side knife, but Dalinar was already raising his own hand.

White mist coalesced in Dalinar's fingers, and a Shardblade appeared, tip to Amaram's throat. Wider than most, it was almost cleaverlike in appearance.

A Blade formed in Amaram's hand a second later – a second too late.

His eyes went wide as he stared at the silvery Blade held to his throat.

Dalinar had a Shardblade.

'I thought,' Dalinar said, 'that if you *had* been willing to murder for one Blade, you would certainly be willing to lie for a second. And so, after I knew you'd sneaked in to see the madman on your own, I asked you to investigate his claims for me. I gave your conscience plenty of time to come clean, out of respect for our friendship. When you told me you'd found nothing – but in fact you had actually recovered the Shardblade – I knew the truth.'

'How?' Amaram hissed, looking at the Blade Dalinar held. 'How did you get it back? I removed it from the cave. My men had it safe!'

'I wasn't about to risk it just to prove a point,' Dalinar said, cold. 'I bonded this Blade before we hid it away.'

'That week you spent ill,' Amaram said.

'Yes.'

'Damnation.'

Dalinar exhaled, a hissing sound through his teeth. 'Why, Amaram? Of all people, I thought that you ... Bah!' Dalinar's grip on the weapon tightened, knuckles white. Amaram raised his chin, as if thrusting his neck toward the point of the Shardblade.

'I did it,' Amaram said, 'and I would do it again. The Voidbringers will soon return, and we must be strong enough to face them. That means practiced, accomplished Shardbearers. In sacrificing a few of my soldiers, I planned to save many more.'

'Lies!' Kaladin said, stumbling forward. 'You just wanted the Blade for yourself!'

Amaram looked Kaladin in the eyes. 'I am sorry for what I did to you and yours. Sometimes, good men must die so that greater goals may be accomplished.'

Kaladin felt a gathering chill, a numbness that spread from his heart outward.

He's telling the truth, he thought. *He ... honestly believes that he did the right thing.*

Amaram dismissed his Blade, turning back to Dalinar. 'What now?'

'You are guilty of murder – of killing men for personal wealth.'

'And what is it,' Amaram said, 'when you send thousands of men to their deaths so that you may secure gemhearts, Dalinar? Is that different somehow? We all know that sometimes lives must be spent for the greater good.'

'Take off that cloak,' Dalinar growled. 'You are no Radiant.'

Amaram reached up and undid it, then dropped it to the rock. He turned and started to walk away.

'No!' Kaladin said, stumbling after him.

'Let him go, son,' Dalinar said, sighing. 'His reputation is broken.'

'He is still a murderer.'

'And we will try him fairly,' Dalinar said, 'once I return. I can't imprison him – Shardbearers are above that, and he'd cut his way out anyway. Either you execute a Shardbearer or you leave him free.'

Kaladin sagged, and Lopen appeared on one side, holding him up while Teft got under his other arm. He felt drained.

Sometimes lives must be spent for the greater good....

'Thank you,' Kaladin said to Dalinar, 'for believing me.'

'I *do* listen sometimes, soldier,' Dalinar said. 'Now go back to camp and *get some rest.*'

Kaladin nodded. 'Sir? Stay safe out there.'

Dalinar smiled grimly. 'If possible. At least now I've got a way to fight that assassin, if he arrives. With all of these Shardblades flying around lately, I figured having one myself made too much sense to ignore.' He narrowed his eyes, turning eastward. 'Even if it feels ... wrong somehow to hold one. Strange, that. Why should it feel wrong? Perhaps I just miss my old Blade.'

Dalinar dismissed the Blade. 'Go,' he said, walking back toward his horse, where Highprince Roion – looking stunned – was watching Amaram stalk away, his personal guard of fifty joining him.

❖

Yes, that *was* Aladar's banner, joining Dalinar's. Sadeas could make it out through the spyglass.

He lowered it, and sat quietly for a long, long time. So long that his guards, and even his wife, started to fidget and looked nervous. But there was no reason.

He quelled his annoyance.

'Let them die out there,' he said. 'All four. Ialai, make a report for me. I would like to know ... Ialai?'

His wife started, looking toward him.

'Is all well?'

'I was merely thinking,' she said, seeming distant. 'About the future. And what it is going to bring. For us.'

'It is going to bring Alethkar new highprinces,' Sadeas said. 'Make a report of which among our sworn highlords would be appropriate to take the place of those who will fall on Dalinar's trip.' He tossed the spyglass back to the messenger. 'We do nothing until they're dead. This will end, it appears, with Dalinar killed by the Parshendi after all. Aladar can go with him, and to Damnation with the lot of them.'

He turned his horse and continued the day's ride, his back pointedly toward the Shattered Plains.

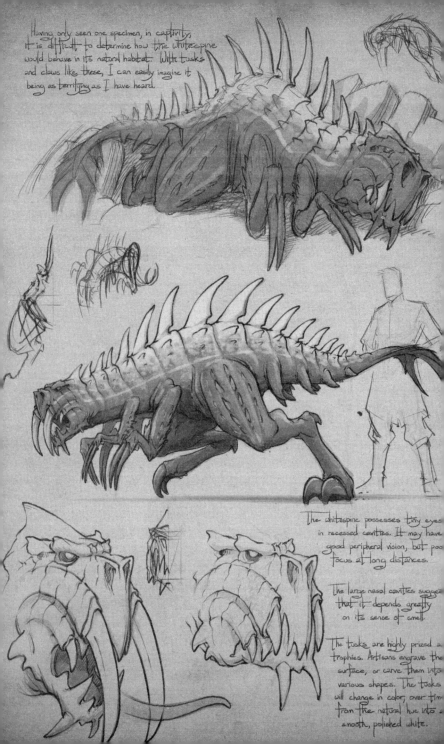

Having only seen one specimen, in captivity,
it is difficult to determine how the whitespine
would behave in its natural habitat. With tusks
and claws like these, I can easily imagine it
being as terrifying as I have heard.

The whitespine possesses tiny eyes
in recessed cavities. It may have
good peripheral vision, but poor
focus at long distances.

The large nasal cavities suggest
that it depends greatly
on its sense of smell.

The tusks are highly prized as
trophies. Artisans engrave the
surface, or carve them into
various shapes. The tusks
will change in color, over time
from the natural hue into a
smooth, polished white.

TRUST

One danger in deploying such a potent weapon will be the potential en-couragement of those exploring the Nahel bond. Care must be taken to avoid placing these subjects in situations of powerful stress unless you accept the consequences of their potential Investiture.

—From the Diagram, Floorboard 27: paragraph 6

Like a river suddenly undammed, the four armies flooded out onto the plateaus. Shallan watched from horseback, excited, anxious. Her little part of the convoy included Vathah and her soldiers, along with Marri, her lady's maid. Gaz, notably, hadn't arrived yet, and Vathah claimed to not know where he was. Perhaps she should have looked more into the nature of his debts. She'd been so busy with other things . . . storms, if the man vanished, how would she feel about that?

She would have to deal with that later. Today, she was part of something extremely important – a story that had begun with Gavilar and Dalinar's first hunting expedition into the Unclaimed Hills years ago. Now came the final chapter, the mission that would unearth the truth and determine the future of the Shattered Plains, the Parshendi, and perhaps Alethkar itself.

Shallan kicked her horse forward, eager. The gelding started to walk, placid despite Shallan's prodding.

Storming animal.

Adolin trotted up beside her on Sureblood. The beautiful animal was pure white – not dusty grey, like some horses she'd seen, but actually white. That Adolin should have the larger horse was patently unfair. She was shorter than he was, so she should be on the taller horse.

'You purposely gave me a slow one,' Shallan complained, 'didn't you?'

'Sure did.'

'I'd smack you. If I could reach you up there.'

He chuckled. 'You said you don't have a lot of experience riding, so I picked a horse that had a lot of experience being ridden. Trust me, you'll be thankful.'

'I want to ride in a majestic charge as we begin our expedition!'

'And you can do so.'

'Slowly.'

'Technically, slow speeds can be very majestic.'

'Technically,' she said, 'a man doesn't need all of his toes. Shall we remove a few of yours and prove it?'

He laughed. 'As long as you don't hurt my face, I suppose.'

'Don't be ridiculous. I like your face.'

He grinned, Shardplate helm hanging from his saddle so as to not mess up his hair. She waited for him to add a quip to hers, but he didn't.

That was all right. She liked Adolin as he was. He was kind, noble, and *genuine*. It didn't matter that he wasn't brilliant or . . . or whatever else Kaladin was. She couldn't even define it. So there.

Passionate, with an intense, smoldering resolve. A leashed anger that he used, because he had dominated it. And a certain tempting arrogance. Not the haughty pride of a highlord. Instead, the secure, stable sense of determination that whispered that no matter who you were – or what you did – you could not hurt him. Could not change him.

He was. Like the wind and rocks were.

Shallan completely missed what Adolin said next. She blushed. 'What was that?'

'I said that Sebarial has a carriage. You might want to travel with him.'

'Because I'm too delicate for riding?' Shallan said. 'Did you miss that I *walked* back through the chasms in the middle of a *highstorm*?'

'Um, no. But walking and riding are different. I mean, the soreness . . .'

'Soreness?' Shallan asked. 'Why would I be sore? Doesn't the horse do all of the work?'

Adolin looked at her, eyes widening.

'Um,' she said. 'Dumb question?'

'You said you'd ridden before.'

'Ponies,' she said, 'on my father's estates. Around in circles . . . All right, from that expression, I'm led to believe I'm being an idiot. When I get sore, I'll go ride with Sebarial.'

'*Before* you get sore,' Adolin said. 'We'll give it an hour.'

As annoyed as she was at this turn, she couldn't deny his expertise. Jasnah had once defined a fool as a person who ignored information because it disagreed with desired results.

She determined to not be bothered, and instead enjoy the ride. The army as a whole moved slowly, considering that each piece seemed to be so efficient. Spearmen in blocks, scribes on horseback, scouts roving outward. Dalinar had six of the massive mechanical bridges, but he had also brought all of the former bridgemen and their simpler, man-carried bridges, designed as copies of the ones they'd left in Sadeas's camp. That was good, since Sebarial only had a couple of bridge crews.

She allowed herself a moment of personal satisfaction at the fact that he'd come on the expedition. As she was thinking on that, she noticed someone running up the line of troops behind her. A short man, with an eye patch, who drew glares from Adolin's bridgeman guards for the day.

'Gaz?' Shallan said with relief as he hustled up, carrying a package under his arm. Her fears that he'd been knifed in an alley somewhere were unfounded.

'Sorry, sorry,' he said. 'It came. You owe the merchant two sapphire broams, Brightness.'

'It?' Shallan asked, accepting the package.

'Yeah. You asked me to find one for you. I storming did.' He seemed proud of himself.

She unwrapped the cloth around the rectangular object, and found inside a book. *Words of Radiance,* the cover said. The sides were worn, and the pages faded – one patch across the top was even stained from spilled ink sometime in the past.

Rarely had she been as pleased to receive something so damaged. 'Gaz!' she said. 'You're wonderful!'

He grinned, shooting Vathah a triumphant smile. The taller man rolled his eyes, muttering something Shallan didn't hear.

'Thank you,' Shallan said. 'Thank you truly, Gaz.'

⁘

As the time passed and one day led into another, Shallan found the distraction of the book extremely welcome. The armies moved about as fast as a herd of sleepy chulls, and the scenery was actually quite boring, though she'd never admit that to Kaladin or Adolin, considering what she'd told them last time she was out here.

The book, though. The book was wonderful. And frustrating.

But what was the 'wicked thing of eminence' that led to the Recreance? she thought, writing the quote in her notebook. It was the second day of their travels on the Plains, and she had agreed to ride in the coach Adolin had provided – alone, though it baffled Adolin why she wouldn't want her lady's maid with her. Shallan did not want to explain Pattern to the girl.

The book had a chapter for each order of Knights Radiant, with talk of their traditions, their abilities, and their attitudes. The author admitted that a lot of it was hearsay – the book had been written two hundred years after the Recreance, and by then facts, lore, and superstition had mixed freely. Beyond that, it was in an old dialect of Alethi, using the proto-script, a precursor to the true women's script of modern day. She spent a lot of her time sorting out meanings, occasionally calling over some of Navani's scholars to provide definitions or interpretation.

Still, she had learned a great deal. For example, each order had different Ideals, or standards, to determine advancement. Some were specific, others left to the interpretation of the spren. Also, some orders were individualistic, while others – like the Windrunners – functioned in teams, with a specific hierarchy.

She settled back, thinking about the powers described. Would the others be appearing, then? As she and Jasnah had? Men who could glide elegantly across the ground as if they weighed nothing, women who could melt stone with a touch. Pattern had offered some few insights, but mostly he had been of use telling her what sounded likely to have been real, and what from the book was a mistake based on hearsay. His memory was spotty, but growing much better, and hearing what the book said often made him remember more.

Right now, he buzzed on the seat beside her in a contented way. The carriage hit a bump – it was rough out here – but at least in the coach, she could read and reference other books at the same time. That would have been practically impossible while riding.

The coach did make her feel shut away, though. *Not everyone who tries to take care of you is trying to do what your father did,* she told herself firmly.

Adolin's warned-of soreness had never manifested, of course. Originally, she'd felt a small amount of pain in her thighs from holding herself in place in the saddle, but Stormlight had made it vanish.

'Mmm,' Pattern said, climbing onto the door of the carriage. 'It comes.'

Shallan looked out the window and felt a drop of water sprinkle against her face. Rock darkened as rain coated it. Soon, the air filled with a steady drizzle, light and pleasant. Though colder, it reminded her of some of the rainfalls back in Jah Keved. Here in the stormlands, it seemed that rain was rarely this soft.

She pulled down the shades and scooted to the center of the seat so she wouldn't get rained on. She soon found that the pleasing sound of water muffled the soldiers' voices and the monotonous sound of marching feet, making it a nice accompaniment to reading. A quote sparked her interest, and so she dug out her sketch of the Shattered Plains and her old maps of Stormseat.

I need to find out how these maps relate, she thought. *Multiple points of reference, preferably.* If she could identify two places on the Shattered Plains that matched points on her map of Stormseat, she could judge how large Stormseat had been – the old map had no scale – and then overlay it on the map of the Shattered Plains. That would give them some context.

What really drew her attention was the Oathgate. On the map of Stormseat, Jasnah thought it was represented by a round disc, like a dais, on the southwestern side of the city. Was there a doorway there on that dais somewhere? A magical portal to Urithiru? How did one of the knights operate it?

'Mmm,' Pattern said.

Shallan's carriage started to slow. She frowned, scooting to the door, meaning to peek out the window. The door opened, however, to reveal Highlady Navani standing outside, Dalinar himself holding up an umbrella for her.

'Would you mind company?' Navani asked.

'Not at all, Brightness,' Shallan said, scrambling to pick up her papers and books, which she'd spread about on all of the seats. Navani patted Dalinar fondly on the arm, then climbed into the coach, using a towel to dry her feet and legs. She sat once Dalinar shut the door.

They started rolling again, and Shallan fidgeted with her papers. What was her relationship with Navani? She was Adolin's aunt, but she was romantically involved with his father. So she was kind of Shallan's future mother-in-law, though by Vorin tradition Dalinar would never be allowed to marry her.

Shallan had tried for weeks to get this woman to listen to her, and had failed. Now, she seemed to have been forgiven for bearing the news of Jasnah's death. Did that mean Navani . . . liked her?

'So,' Shallan said, feeling awkward, 'did Dalinar exile you to the coach to protect you from getting sore, as Adolin did to me?'

'Sore? Heavens no. If anyone should be riding in the coach, it's Dalinar. When there is fighting to be done, we'll need him rested and ready. I came because it's rather difficult to read while riding in the rain.'

'Oh.' Shallan shifted in her seat.

Navani studied her, then finally sighed. 'I have been ignoring things,' the older woman said, 'that I should not. Because they bring me pain.'

'I am sorry.'

'You have nothing to apologize for.' Navani held out her hand toward Shallan. 'May I?'

Shallan looked at her handful of notes, diagrams, and maps. She hesitated.

'You are engaged in work you obviously think very important,' Navani said softly. 'This city Jasnah was searching for, according to the notes you sent me? Perhaps I can help you interpret my daughter's intentions.'

Was there anything in these pages that would incriminate Shallan and reveal her powers? Her activities as Veil?

She didn't think so. She'd been studying the Knights Radiant as part of it, but she was searching for their center of power, so that made sense. Hesitant, she handed over the papers.

Navani leafed through them, reading by spherelight. 'The organization of these notes is . . . interesting.'

Shallan blushed. The organization made sense to her. As Navani continued to look through the notes, Shallan found herself growing oddly anxious. She'd wanted Navani's help – she'd all but begged for it. Now, however, she found herself feeling like this woman was intruding. This had become Shallan's project, her duty and her quest. Now that Navani had apparently overcome her grief, would she insist on taking over completely?

'You think like an artist,' Navani said. 'I can see it in the way you put the notes together. Well, I suppose I can't expect everything you do to be annotated precisely as I'd wish. A magical portal to another city? Jasnah actually believed in this?'

'Yes.'

'Hmm,' Navani said. 'Then it's probably true. That girl never did have the decency to be *wrong* an appropriate amount of the time.'

Shallan nodded, glancing at the notes, feeling anxious.

'Oh, don't get so touchy,' Navani said. 'I'm not going to steal the project from you.'

'I'm that transparent?' Shallan said.

'This research is obviously very important to you. I assume Jasnah persuaded you that the fate of the world itself rested upon the answers you find?'

'She did.'

'Damnation,' Navani said, flipping to the next page. 'I shouldn't have ignored you. It was petty.'

'It was the act of a grieving mother.'

'Scholars don't have time for such nonsense.' Navani blinked, and Shallan caught a tear in the woman's eye.

'You're still human,' Shallan said, reaching across, putting her hand on Navani's knee. 'We can't all be emotionless chunks of rock like Jasnah.'

Navani smiled. 'She sometimes had the empathy of a corpse, didn't she?'

'Comes from being too brilliant,' Shallan said. 'You grow accustomed to everyone else being something of an idiot, trying to keep up with you.'

'Chana knows, I wondered sometimes how I raised that child without strangling her. By age six, she was pointing out my logical fallacies as I tried to get her to go to bed on time.'

Shallan grinned. 'I always just assumed she was born in her thirties.'

'Oh, she was. It just took thirty-some years for her body to catch up.'

Navani smiled. 'I won't take this from you, but neither should I allow you to attempt a project so important on your own. I would be part. Figuring out the puzzles that captivated her . . . it will be like having her again. My little Jasnah, insufferable and wonderful.'

How surreal it was to imagine Jasnah as a child being held by a mother. 'It would be an honor to have your aid, Brightness Navani.'

Navani held up the page. 'You're trying to overlay Stormseat with the Shattered Plains. It's not going to work unless you have a point of reference.'

'Preferably two,' Shallan said.

'It's been centuries since that city fell. It was destroyed during Ahari-etiam itself, I believe. We're going to have trouble finding clues out here, though your list of descriptions will help.' She tapped her finger against the papers. 'This isn't my area of expertise, but I have several archaeologists among Dalinar's scribes. I should show them these pages.'

Shallan nodded.

'We'll want copies of everything here,' Navani said. 'I don't want to lose originals to all of this rain. I could have the scribes work on it tonight, after we camp.'

'If you wish.'

Navani looked up at her, then frowned. 'It is your decision.'

'You're serious?' Shallan asked.

'Absolutely. Think of me as an additional resource.'

All right then. 'Yes, have them make copies,' Shallan said, digging in her satchel. 'And copies of this too – it's my attempt at re-creating one of the murals described as being on the outer wall of the temple to Chanaranach in Stormseat. It faced leeward, and was supposedly shaded, so we might be able to find hints of it.

'Also, I need a surveyor to measure each new plateau we cross, once we get farther in. I can draw them out, but my spatial reasoning can be off. I want exact sizes to make the map more accurate. I'll need guards and scribes to ride out with me ahead of the army to visit plateaus parallel to our course. It would really help if you could convince Dalinar to allow this.

'I'd like a team to study the quotes on that page underneath the map. They talk about methods for opening the Oathgate, which was supposed to be the duty of the Knights Radiant. Hopefully we can discover another method. Also, alert Dalinar that we'll be trying to open the portal if we find it. I do not expect there to be anything dangerous on the other side, but he'll undoubtedly want to send soldiers through first.'

Navani raised an eyebrow at her. 'You've done a touch of thinking about this, I see.'

Shallan nodded, blushing.

'I'll see it done,' Navani said. 'I myself will head the research team studying those quotes you mention.' She hesitated. 'Do you know *why* Jasnah thought this city, Urithiru, was so important?'

'Because it was the seat of the Knights Radiant, and she expected to find information on them – and the Voidbringers – there.'

'So she was like Dalinar,' Navani said, 'trying to bring back powers that – perhaps – we should leave alone.'

Shallan felt a sudden spike of anxiety. *I need to say it. Say something.* 'She wasn't trying. She succeeded.'

'Succeeded?'

Shallan took a deep breath. 'I don't know what she said regarding the origin of her Soulcaster, but the truth was that it was a fake. Jasnah could Soulcast on her own, without any fabrial. I saw her do it. She knew secrets from the past, secrets I don't think anyone else knows. Brightness Navani . . . your daughter *was* one of the Knights Radiant.' Or as close to one as the world was going to have again.

Navani raised an eyebrow, obviously skeptical.

'I swear this is true,' Shallan said, 'on the tenth name of the Almighty.'

'That is disturbing. Radiants, Heralds, and Voidbringers alike are supposed to be gone. We won that war.'

'I know.'

'I will go get to work on this,' Navani said, knocking for the carriage driver to halt the vehicle.

⁑

The Weeping began.

A steady stream of rain. Kaladin could hear it inside his room, like a whisper in the background. Weak, miserable rain, without the fury and passion of a true highstorm.

He lay in the darkness, listening to the patter, feeling his leg throb. Wet, cold air leaked into his room, and he dug for the extra blankets that the quartermaster had delivered. He curled up and tried to sleep, but after sleeping most of the day yesterday – the day that Dalinar's army had left – he found himself wide awake.

He hated being wounded. Bed rest wasn't supposed to happen to him. Not anymore.

Syl . . .

The Weeping was a bad time for him. Days spent trapped indoors. A perpetual gloom in the sky that seemed to affect him more than it did others, leaving him lethargic and uncaring.

A knock came at his door. Kaladin raised his head in the darkness, then sat up and settled himself on his bench of a bed. 'Come,' he said.

The door opened and let in the sound of rain, like a thousand little footsteps scrambling about. Very little light accompanied the sounds. The overcast sky of the Weeping left the land in perpetual twilight.

Moash stepped in. He wore his Shardplate, as always. 'Storms, Kal. Were you asleep? I'm sorry!'

'No, I was awake.'

'In the darkness?'

Kaladin shrugged. Moash clicked the door shut behind him, but took off his gauntlet and hung it from a clip at the waist of his Shardplate. He reached beneath a fold in the metal and pulled out a handful of spheres to light his way. Riches that would have seemed incredible to bridgemen were now pocket change to Moash.

'Aren't you supposed to be guarding the king?' Kaladin asked.

'On and off,' Moash said, sounding eager. 'They quartered the five of us guards up by his rooms. In the palace itself! Kaladin, it's *perfect*.'

'When?' Kaladin asked softly.

'We don't want to ruin Dalinar's expedition,' Moash said, 'so we're going to wait until he's out there some distance, maybe until he's engaged the enemy. That way, he'll be committed and won't turn back when he gets news. Better for Alethkar if he succeeds at defeating the Parshendi. He will return a hero . . . and a king.'

Kaladin nodded, feeling sick.

'We have everything planned out,' Moash said. 'We'll raise an alert in the palace that the Assassin in White has been seen. Then we'll do what was done last time – send all of the servants into hiding in their rooms.

Nobody will be around to see what we do, nobody will get hurt, and they'll all believe that the Shin assassin was behind this. We couldn't have *asked* for this to play out better! And you won't have to do anything, Kal. Graves says that we won't need your help after all.'

'So why are you here?' Kaladin asked.

'I just wanted to check on you,' Moash said. He stepped in closer. 'Is it true, what Lopen says? About your . . . abilities?'

Storming Herdazian. Lopen had stayed behind – with Dabbid and Hobber – to take care of the barrack and watch over Kaladin. They'd been talking to Moash, it seemed.

'Yes,' Kaladin said.

'What happened?'

'I'm not sure,' he lied. 'I offended Syl. I haven't seen her in days. Without her, I can't draw in Stormlight.'

'We'll have to fix that somehow,' Moash said. 'Either that, or get you Plate and Blade of your own.'

Kaladin looked up at his friend. 'I think she left because of the plot to kill the king, Moash. I don't think a Radiant could be involved in something like this.'

'Shouldn't a Radiant care about doing what is right? Even if it means a difficult decision?'

'Sometimes lives must be spent for the greater good,' Kaladin said.

'Yes, exactly!'

'That's what Amaram said. In regards to my friends, whom he murdered to cover up his secrets.'

'Well, that's different, obviously. He's a lighteyes.'

Kaladin looked to Moash, whose eyes had turned as light a tan as those of any Brightlord. Same color as Amaram's, actually. 'So are you.'

'Kal,' Moash said. 'You're worrying me. Don't say things like that.'

Kaladin looked away.

'The king wanted me to deliver a message,' Moash said. 'That's my excuse for being here. He wants you to come talk to him.'

'What? Why?'

'I don't know. He's been dipping into the wine, now that Dalinar is gone. Not the orange stuff, either. I'll tell him you're too wounded to come.'

Kaladin nodded.

'Kal,' Moash said. 'We can trust you, right? You're not having second thoughts?'

'You said it yourself,' Kaladin said. 'I don't have to do anything. I just have to stay away.' *What could I do, anyway? Wounded, with no spren?*

Everything was in motion. It was too far along for him to stop.

'Great,' Moash said. 'You heal up, all right?'

Moash walked out, leaving Kaladin in the darkness again.

Ahbuttheywereleftbehind Itisobviousfromthenatureofthebond
Butwherewherewherewhere Setoff Obvious Realizationlikeapricity
Theyarewiththe Shin Wemustfindone Canwemaketousea Truthless Can
wecraftaweapon

—From the Diagram, Floorboard 17: paragraph 2,
every second letter starting with the first

I n the darkness, Shallan's violet spheres gave life to the rain. Without the spheres, she couldn't see the drops, only hear their deaths upon the stones and the cloth of her pavilion. With the light, each falling speck of water flashed briefly, like starspren.

She sat at the edge of the pavilion, as she liked to watch the rainfall between bouts of sketching, while the other scholars sat closer to the center. So did Vathah and a couple of his soldiers, watching over her like nesting skyeels with a single pup. It amused her that they'd grown so protective; they seemed actively *proud* to be her soldiers. She'd honestly expected them to run off after gaining their clemency.

Four days into the Weeping, and she still enjoyed the weather. Why did the soft sound of gentle rain make her feel more imaginative? Around her, creationspren slowly vanished, most having taken the shapes of things about the camp. Swords that sheathed and unsheathed repeatedly, tiny tents that untied and blew in unseen wind. Her picture was of Jasnah as she'd been on that night just over a month ago, when Shallan had last seen her. Leaning upon the desk of a darkened ship's cabin, hand pushing back hair freed from its customary twists and braids. Exhausted, overwhelmed, terrified.

The drawing didn't depict a single faithful Memory, not as Shallan usually did them. This was a re-creation of what she remembered, an interpretation that was not exact. Shallan was proud of it, as she'd captured Jasnah's contradictions.

Contradictions. Those were what made people real. Jasnah exhausted, yet somehow still strong – stronger, even, because of the vulnerability she revealed. Jasnah terrified, yet also brave, for one allowed the other to exist. Jasnah overwhelmed, yet powerful.

Shallan had recently been trying to do more drawings like this – ones synthesized from her own imaginings. Her illusions would suffer if she could only reproduce what she'd experienced. She needed to be able to create, not just copy.

The last creationspren faded away, this one imitating a puddle that was being splashed by a boot. Her sheet of paper dimpled as Pattern moved up onto it.

He sniffed. 'Useless things.'

'The creationspren?'

'They don't *do* anything. They flit around and watch, admire. Most spren have a purpose. These are merely attracted by someone *else's* purpose.'

Shallan sat back, thinking on that, as Jasnah had taught her. Nearby, the scholars and ardents argued about how large Stormseat had been. Navani had done her part well – better than Shallan could have hoped. The army's scholars now worked at Shallan's command.

Around her in the night, an uncountable array of lights both near and far indicated the breadth of the army. The rain continued to sprinkle down, catching the purple spherelight. She had chosen all spheres of one color.

'The artist Eleseth,' Shallan observed to Pattern, 'once did an experiment. She set out only ruby spheres, in their strength, to light her studio. She wanted to see what effect the all-red light would have upon her art.'

'Mmmm,' Pattern said. 'To what result?'

'At first, during a painting session, the color of light affected her strongly. She would use too little red, and fields of blossoms would look washed out.'

'Not unexpected.'

'The interesting thing, however, was what happened if she continued working,' Shallan said. 'If she painted for hours by that light, the effects diminished. The colors of her reproductions grew more balanced, the pictures of flowers more vivid. She eventually concluded that her mind *compensated* for the colors she saw. Indeed, if she switched the color of the light during a session, she'd continue for a time to paint as if the room were still red, reacting against the new color.'

'Mmmmmm ...' Pattern said, content. 'Humans can see the world as it is not. It is why your lies can be so strong. You are able to *not* admit that they are lies.'

'It frightens me.'

'Why? It is wonderful.'

To him, she was a subject of study. For a moment, she understood how Kaladin must have seen Shallan as she spoke of the chasmfiend. Admiring its beauty, the form of its creation, oblivious to the present reality of its danger.

'It frightens me,' Shallan said, 'because we all see the world by some kind of light personal to us, and that light changes our perception. I don't see clearly. I want to, but I don't know if I ever truly can.'

Eventually, a pattern broke through the sound of rain, and Dalinar Kholin entered the tent. Straight-backed and greying, he looked more like a general than a king. She had no sketches of him. It seemed a gross omission on her part, so she took a Memory of him walking into the pavilion, an aide holding an umbrella for him.

He strode up to Shallan. 'Ah, here you are. The one who has taken command of this expedition.'

Shallan belatedly scrambled to her feet and bowed. 'Highprince?'

'You have co-opted my scribes and cartographers,' Dalinar said, sounding amused. 'They hum of it like the rainfall. Urithiru. Stormseat. How did you do it?'

'I didn't. Brightness Navani did.'

'She says you convinced her.'

'I ...' Shallan blushed. 'I was really just there, and she changed her mind ...'

Dalinar nodded curtly to the side, and his aide stepped over to the debating scholars. The aide spoke with them softly, and they rose – some quickly, others with reluctance – and departed into the rain, leaving their papers. The aide followed them, and Vathah looked to Shallan. She nodded, excusing him and the other guards.

Soon Shallan and Dalinar were alone in the pavilion.

'You told Navani that Jasnah had discovered the secrets of the Knights Radiant,' Dalinar said.

'I did.'

'You're certain that Jasnah didn't mislead you somehow,' Dalinar said, 'or allow you to mislead yourself – that would be far more like her.'

'Brightlord, I . . . I don't think that is . . .' She took a breath. 'No. She did not mislead me.'

'How can you be sure?'

'I saw it,' Shallan said. 'I witnessed what she did, and we spoke of it. Jasnah Kholin did not *use* a Soulcaster. She was one.'

Dalinar folded his arms, looking past Shallan into the night. 'I think I'm supposed to refound the Knights Radiant. The first man I thought I could trust for the job turned out to be a murderer and a liar. Now you tell me that Jasnah might have had actual power. If that is true, then I am a fool.'

'I don't understand.'

'In naming Amaram,' Dalinar said. 'I did what I thought was my task. I wonder now if I was mistaken all along, and that refounding them was never my duty. They might be refounding themselves, and I am an arrogant meddler. You have given me a great deal to think upon. Thank you.'

He did not smile as he said it; in fact, he looked severely troubled. He turned to leave, clasping his hands behind his back.

'Brightlord Dalinar?' Shallan said. 'What if your task *wasn't* to refound the Knights Radiant?'

'That is what I just said,' Dalinar replied.

'What if instead, your task was to *gather* them?'

He looked back to her, waiting. Shallan felt a cold sweat. What was she doing?

I have to tell someone sometime, she thought. *I can't do as Jasnah did, holding it all. This is too important.* Was Dalinar Kholin the right person?

Well, she certainly couldn't think of anyone better.

Shallan held out her palm, then breathed in, draining one of her spheres. Then she breathed back out, sending a cloud of shimmering Stormlight into the air between herself and Dalinar. She formed it into a small image of Jasnah, the one she'd just drawn, on top of her palm.

'Almighty above,' Dalinar whispered. A single awespren, like a ring of blue smoke, burst out above him, spreading like the ripple from a stone dropped in a pond. Shallan had seen such a spren only a handful of times in her life.

Dalinar stepped closer, reverent, leaning down to inspect Shallan's image. 'Can I?' he asked, reaching out a hand.

'Yes.'

He touched the image, causing it to fuzz back into shifting light. When he withdrew his finger, the image re-formed.

'It's just an illusion,' Shallan said. 'I can't create anything real.'

'It's amazing,' Dalinar said, his voice so soft she could barely hear it over the pattering rain. 'It is wonderful.' He looked up at her, and there were – shockingly – tears in his eyes. 'You're one of them.'

'Maybe, kind of?' Shallan said, feeling awkward. This man, so commanding, so much larger than life, should not be crying in front of her.

'I'm not mad,' he said, more to himself, it seemed. 'I had decided that I wasn't, but that's not the same as knowing. It's all true. They're returning.' He tapped at the image again. 'Jasnah taught you this?'

'I more stumbled into it on my own,' Shallan said. 'I think I was led to her so she could teach me. We didn't have much time for that, unfortunately.' She grimaced, withdrawing the Stormlight, heart beating quickly because of what she'd done.

'I need to give *you* the golden cape,' Dalinar said, standing up straight, wiping his eyes and growing firm of voice again. 'Put you in charge of them. So we—'

'*Me?*' Shallan yelped, thinking of what that would mean to her alternate identity. 'No, I can't! I mean, Brightlord, sir, what I can do is mostly useful if nobody knows it's possible. I mean, if everyone is *looking* for my illusions, I'll never fool them.'

'Fool them?' Dalinar said.

Perhaps the not best choice of words for Dalinar.

'Brightlord Dalinar!'

Shallan spun, alert, suddenly worried that someone had seen what she did. A lithe messenger approached the tent, dripping wet, locks of hair undone from her braids and sticking to her face. 'Brightlord Dalinar! Parshendi spotted, sir!'

'Where?'

'Eastern side of this plateau,' the messenger said, panting. 'Scouting party, we think.'

Dalinar looked from the messenger to Shallan, then cursed and started out into the rain.

Shallan tossed her sketchpad onto her chair and followed.

'This could be dangerous,' Dalinar said.

'I appreciate the concern, Brightlord,' she said softly. 'But I think I could actually take a spear through the stomach, and my abilities would heal me up without a scar. I'm probably the most difficult person to kill in this entire camp.'

Dalinar strode in silence for a moment. 'The fall into the chasm?' he asked softly.

'Yes. I think I must have rescued Captain Kaladin too, though I don't know how I managed that.'

He grunted. They moved quickly through the rain, the water wetting Shallan's hair and clothing. She practically had to jog to keep pace with Dalinar. Storming Alethi and their long legs. Guards ran up, members of Bridge Four, and fell in around them.

She heard shouting in the distance. Dalinar sent the guards into a wider perimeter to give himself and Shallan a measure of privacy.

'Can you Soulcast?' Dalinar asked softly. 'Like Jasnah did?'

'Yes,' Shallan said. 'But I haven't practiced it much.'

'It could prove very useful.'

'It's also very dangerous. Jasnah didn't want me practicing without her, though now that she's gone . . . Well, I will do more with it, eventually. Sir, please don't tell anyone about this. For now, at least.'

'This was why Jasnah took you on as a ward,' Dalinar said. 'It's why she wanted you marrying Adolin, isn't it? To bind you to us?'

'Yes,' Shallan said, blushing in the darkness.

'A great many things make more sense now. I will tell Navani about you, but nobody else, and I will swear her to secrecy. She *can* keep a secret, if she has to.'

She opened her mouth to say yes, but stopped herself. Was that what Jasnah would have said?

'We'll send you back to the warcamps,' Dalinar continued, eyes forward, speaking softly. 'Immediately, with an escort. I don't care how hard you are to kill. You're too valuable to risk on this expedition.'

'Brightlord,' Shallan said, splashing through a pool of water, glad she was wearing boots and leggings under the skirt, 'you are not my king, nor are you my highprince. You have no authority over me. My duty is to find Urithiru, so you will *not* be sending me back. And, by your honor, I will have your promise not to tell a soul what I can do unless I give leave. That includes Brightness Navani.'

He stopped in place, and stared at her in surprise. Then he grunted, his face barely visible. 'I see Jasnah in you.'

Rarely had Shallan been given such a compliment.

Lights bobbed and approached in the rain, soldiers bearing sphere lanterns. Vathah and his men jogged up, having been left behind, and Bridge Four held them back for the moment.

'Very well, Brightness,' Dalinar said to Shallan. 'Your secret will remain one, for now. We *will* consult further, once this expedition is done. You have read of the things I have been seeing?'

She nodded.

'The world is about to change,' Dalinar said. He took a deep breath. 'You give me hope, true hope, that we can change it in the right way.'

The approaching scouts saluted, and Bridge Four parted to allow their leader access to Dalinar. He was a portly man with a brown hat that reminded her of the one Veil wore, except it was wide-brimmed. The scout wore soldier's trousers, but a leather jacket over them, and certainly didn't seem in fighting shape.

'Bashin,' Dalinar said.

'Parshendi on that plateau next to us, sir,' Bashin said, pointing. 'The Parshendi stumbled over one of my scouting teams. The lads raised the alarm quickly, but we lost all three men.'

Dalinar cursed softly, then turned toward Highlord Teleb, who had approached from the other direction, wearing his Shardplate, which he'd painted silver. 'Wake the army, Teleb. Everyone on alert.'

'Yes, Brightlord,' Teleb said.

'Brightlord Dalinar,' Bashin said, 'the lads took down one of those shellheads before being killed themselves. Sir . . . you need to see this. Something has changed.'

Shallan shivered, feeling sodden and cold. She'd brought clothing that would last well in the rain, of course, but that didn't mean standing out here was *comfortable*. Though they wore coats, nobody else seemed to pay much heed. Likely, they took it for granted that during the Weeping, you were going to get soaked. That was something else for which her sheltered childhood had not prepared her.

Dalinar did not object as Shallan joined him in walking toward a nearby bridge – one of the more mobile ones run by Kaladin's bridge teams, who wore raincoats and front-brimmed caps. A group of soldiers on the other side of the bridge dragged something across, pushing a little wave of water before it. A Parshendi corpse.

Shallan had only seen the one that she'd found with Kaladin in the chasm. She'd done a sketch of that earlier, and this one looked very different. It had hair – well, a kind of hair. Leaning down, she found that it was thicker than human hair, and felt too . . . slick. Was that the right word? The face was marbled, like that of a parshman, this one with prominent red streaks through the black. The body was lean and strong, and something seemed to grow *under* the skin of the exposed arms, peeking out. Shallan prodded at it, and found it hard and ridged, like a crab shell. In fact, the face was crusted with a kind of thin, bumpy carapace just above the cheeks and running back around the sides of the head.

'This isn't a type we've seen before, sir,' Bashin said to Dalinar. 'Look at those ridges. Sir . . . some of the lads that were killed, they had *burn marks* on them. In the rain. Shakiest thing I've ever seen . . .'

Shallan looked up at them. 'What do you mean by a "type," Bashin?'

'Some Parshendi have hair,' the man said – he was a darkeyes, but clearly well respected, though he didn't bear an obvious military rank. 'Others have carapace. The ones we met with King Gavilar long ago, they were . . . *shaped* different from the ones we fight.'

'They have specialized subspecies?' Shallan said. Some cremlings were like that, working in a hive, with different specializations and varied forms.

'We might be depleting their numbers,' Dalinar said to Bashin. 'Forcing them to send out their equivalent of lighteyes to fight.'

'And the burns, Dalinar?' Bashin said, scratching his head under his hat.

Shallan reached out to check the Parshendi's eye color. Did they have lighteyes and dark, like humans? She lifted the eyelid.

The eye beneath was completely red.

She screamed, jumping back, pulling her hand up to her chest. The soldiers cursed, looking around, and Dalinar's Shardblade appeared in his hand a few seconds later.

'Red eyes,' Shallan whispered. 'It's happening.'

'The red eyes are just a legend.'

'Jasnah had an entire notebook of references to this, Brightlord,' Shallan said, shivering. 'The Voidbringers are here. Time is short.'

'Throw the body into the chasm,' Dalinar said to his men. 'I doubt we'd be able to easily burn it. Keep everyone alert. Be prepared for an attack tonight. They—'

'Brightlord!'

Shallan spun as a hulking armored figure came up, rainwater trailing down his silvery Plate. 'We've found another one, sir,' Teleb said.

'Dead?' Dalinar said.

'No, sir,' the Shardbearer said, pointing. 'He walked right up to us, sir. He's sitting on a rock over there.'

Dalinar looked to Shallan, who shrugged. Dalinar started off in the direction Teleb had pointed.

'Sir?' Teleb said, voice resonating inside his helm. 'Should you . . .'

Dalinar ignored the warning, and Shallan hastened after him, collecting Vathah and his two guards.

'Should you head back?' Vathah said under his breath to her. Storms, but that face of his looked dangerous in the dim light, even if his voice was respectful. She couldn't help but still see him as the man who had almost killed her, back in the Unclaimed Hills.

'I will be safe,' Shallan replied softly.

'You might have a Blade, Brightness, but you could still die to an arrow in the back.'

'Unlikely, in this rain,' she said.

He fell in behind her, offering no further objection. He was trying to do the job she had assigned him. Unfortunately, she was discovering that she didn't much like being guarded.

They found the Parshendi after a hike through the rain. The rock he sat on was about as high as a man was tall. He seemed to have no weapons, and about a hundred Alethi soldiers stood around the base of his seat, spears pointed upward. Shallan couldn't make out much more, as he sat across the chasm from them, a portable bridge in place to his plateau.

'Has he said anything?' Dalinar asked softly as Teleb stepped up.

'Not that I know of,' the Shardbearer said. 'He just sits there.'

Shallan peered across the chasm toward the solitary Parshendi man. He stood up, and shaded his eyes against the rain. The soldiers below shuffled, spears rising into more threatening positions.

'Skar?' the Parshendi's voice called. 'Skar, is that you? And Leyten?'

Nearby, one of Dalinar's bridgeman guards cursed. He ran across the bridge, and several other bridgemen followed.

They returned a moment later. Shallan crowded in closely to hear what their leader whispered to Dalinar.

'It's him, sir,' Skar said. 'He's changed, but storm me for a fool if I'm wrong – it's *him*. Shen. He ran bridges with us for months, then vanished. Now he's here. He says he wants to surrender to you.'

*Q: For what essential must we strive? A: The essential of preservation,
to shelter a seed of humanity through the coming storm. Q: What cost
must we bear? A: The cost is irrelevant. Mankind must survive. Our
burden is that of the species, and all other considerations are but dust
by comparison.*

—From the Diagram, Catechism of the
Back of the Flowered Painting: paragraph 1

Dalinar stood with hands behind his back, waiting in his command tent and listening to the patter of rain on the cloth. The
floor of the tent was wet. You couldn't avoid that, in the Weeping. He knew that from miserable experience – he'd been out on more
than one military excursion during this time of year.

It was the day after they'd discovered the Parshendi on the Plains –
both the dead one and the one the bridgemen called Shen, or Rlain, as
he had said his name was. Dalinar himself had allowed the man to be
armed.

Shallan claimed that all parshmen were Voidbringers in embryo. He
had ample reason to believe her word, considering what she'd shown him.
But what was he to *do*? The Radiants had returned, the Parshendi had
manifested red eyes. Dalinar felt as if he were trying to stop a dam from

breaking, all the while not knowing where the leaks were actually coming from.

The tent flaps parted and Adolin ducked in, escorting Navani. She hung her stormcoat on the rack beside the flap, and Adolin grabbed a towel and began drying his hair and face.

Adolin was betrothed to a member of the Knights Radiant. *She says she's not one yet,* Dalinar reminded himself. That made sense. One could be a trained spearman without being a soldier. One implied skill, the other a position.

'They are bringing the Parshendi man?' Dalinar asked.

'Yes,' Navani said, sitting down in one of the room's chairs. Adolin didn't take his seat, but found a pitcher of filtered rainwater and poured himself a cup. He tapped the side of the tin cup as he drank.

They were restless, all of them, following the discovery of red-eyed Parshendi. After no attack had come that night, Dalinar had pushed the four armies into another day of marching.

Slowly, they approached the middle of the Plains, at least as Shallan's projections indicated. They were already well beyond the regions that scouts had explored. Now, they had to rely on the young woman's maps.

The flaps opened again, and Teleb marched in with the prisoner. Dalinar had put the highlord and his personal guard in charge of this 'Rlain,' as he didn't like how defensive the bridgemen were about him. He did invite their lieutenants – Skar and the Horneater cook they called Rock – to come to the interrogation, and those two entered after Teleb and his men. General Khal and Renarin were in another tent with Aladar and Roion, going over tactics for when they approached the Parshendi encampment.

Navani sat up, leaning forward, narrowing her eyes at the prisoner. Shallan had wanted to attend, but Dalinar had promised to have everything written down for her. The Stormfather had given her some sense, fortunately, and she hadn't insisted. Having too many of them near this spy felt dangerous to Dalinar.

He had a vague recollection of the parshman guard who had occasionally joined the men of Bridge Four. Parshmen were practically invisible, but once this one had started carrying a spear, he had become instantly noticeable. Not that there had been anything else distinctive about him – same squat parshman body, marbled skin, dull eyes.

This creature before him was nothing like that. He was a full Parshendi warrior, complete with orange-red skullplate and armored carapace at the chest, thighs, and outer arms. He was as tall as an Alethi, and more muscular.

Though he carried no weapon, the guards still treated him as if he were the most dangerous thing on this plateau – and perhaps he was just that. As he stepped up, he saluted Dalinar, hand to chest. Like the other bridgemen. He bore their tattoo on his forehead, reaching up and blending into his skullplate.

'Sit,' Dalinar ordered, nodding toward a stool at the center of the room.

Rlain obeyed.

'I'm told,' Dalinar said, 'that you refuse to tell us anything about the Parshendi plans.'

'I don't know them,' Rlain said. He had the rhythmic intonations common to the Parshendi, but he spoke Alethi very well. Better than any parshman Dalinar had heard.

'You were a spy,' Dalinar said, hands clasped behind his back, trying to loom over the Parshendi – but staying far enough away that the man could not grab him without Adolin getting in the way first.

'Yes, sir.'

'For how long?'

'About three years,' Rlain said. 'In various warcamps.'

Nearby, Teleb – faceplate up – turned and raised an eyebrow at Dalinar.

'You answer me when I ask,' Dalinar said. 'But not the others. Why?'

'You're my commanding officer,' Rlain said.

'You're Parshendi.'

'I . . .' The man looked down at the ground, shoulders bowing. He raised a hand to his head, feeling at the ridge of skin just where his skullplate ended. 'Something is very wrong, sir. Eshonai's voice . . . on the plateau that day, when she came to meet with Prince Adolin . . .'

'Eshonai,' Dalinar prompted. 'The Parshendi Shardbearer?' Nearby, Navani scribbled on a pad of paper, writing down each word spoken.

'Yes. She was my commander. But now . . .' He looked up, and despite the alien skin and the strange way of speaking, Dalinar recognized grief in this man's face. Terrible grief. 'Sir, I have reason to believe that everyone I know . . . everyone I loved . . . has been destroyed, monsters left in

415

their place. The listeners, the Parshendi, may be no more. I have nothing left . . .'

'Yes you do,' Skar said from outside the ring of guards. 'You're Bridge Four.'

Rlain looked at him. 'I'm a traitor.'

'Ha!' Rock said. 'Is little problem. Can be fixed.'

Dalinar gestured to quiet the bridgemen. He glanced at Navani, who nodded for him to continue.

'Tell me,' Dalinar said, 'how you hid among the parshmen.'

'I . . .'

'Soldier,' Dalinar barked. 'That was an order.'

Rlain sat up. Amazingly, he seemed to want to obey – as if he needed something to lend him strength. 'Sir,' Rlain said, 'it's just something my people can do. We choose a form based on what we need, the job required of us. Dullform, one of those forms, looks a lot like a parshman. Hiding among them is easy.'

'We account our parshmen with precision,' Navani said.

'Yes,' Rlain replied, 'and we are noticed – but rarely questioned. Who questions when you find an extra sphere lying on the ground? It's not something suspicious. It's merely fortune.'

Dangerous territory, Dalinar thought, noticing the change in Rlain's voice – the beat to which he was speaking. This man did not like how the parshmen were treated.

'You spoke of the Parshendi,' Dalinar said. 'This has to do with the red eyes?'

Rlain nodded.

'What does it mean, soldier?' Dalinar asked.

'It means our gods have returned,' Rlain whispered.

'Who are your gods?'

'They are the souls of those ancient. Those who gave of themselves to destroy.' A different rhythm to his words this time, slow and reverent. He looked up at Dalinar. 'They hate you and your kind, sir. This new form they have given my people . . . it is something terrible. It will *bring* something terrible.'

'Can you lead us to the Parshendi city?' Dalinar asked.

Rlain's voice changed again. A different rhythm. 'My people . . .'

'You said they are gone,' Dalinar said.

'They might be,' Rlain said. 'I got close enough to see an army, tens of thousands. But surely they left some in other forms. The elderly? The young? Who watches our children?'

Dalinar stepped up to Rlain, waving back Adolin, who raised an anxious hand. He stooped down, laying an arm on the Parshendi man's shoulder.

'Soldier,' Dalinar said, 'if what you're telling me is correct, then the most important thing you can do is lead us to your people. I will see that the noncombatants are protected, my word of honor on it. If something terrible is happening to your people, you need to help me stop it.'

'I . . .' Rlain took a deep breath. 'Yes, sir,' he said to a different rhythm.

'Meet with Shallan Davar,' Dalinar said. 'Describe the route to her, and get us a map. Teleb, you may release the prisoner into the custody of Bridge Four.'

The Oldblood Shardbearer nodded. As the group of them left, letting in a gust of rainy wind, Dalinar sighed and sat down beside Navani.

'You trust his word?'

'I don't know,' Dalinar said. 'But something *did* shake that man, Navani. Soundly.'

'He's Parshendi,' she said. 'You may be misreading his body language.'

Dalinar leaned forward, clasping his hands before him. 'The countdown?' he asked.

'Three days away,' Navani said. 'Three days before Lightday.'

So little time. 'We hasten our pace,' he said.

Inward. Toward the center.

And destiny.

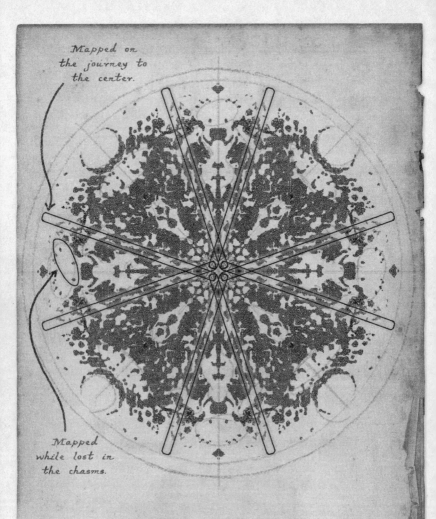

Mapped on
the journey to
the center.

Mapped
while lost in
the chasms.

Note: Eastern side of the Plains is much more eroded
than this. Light areas are plateaus packed closely together.
Dark areas represent plateaus less densely packed.

I know you wanted me to draw every plateau, but shadows,
woman! Even I'm not THAT crazy.

TO FIGHT THE RAIN

You must become king. Of Everything.

—From the Diagram, Tenets of Instruction,
Back of the Footboard: paragraph 1

S hallan fought against the wind, pulling her stormcoat – stolen
from a soldier – close around her as she struggled up the slick
incline.

'Brightness?' Gaz asked. He grabbed his cap to keep it from blowing
free. 'Are you certain you want to do this?'

'Of course I am,' Shallan said. 'Whether or not what I'm doing is wise
... well, that's another story.'

These winds were unusual for the Weeping, which was supposed to
be a period of placid rainfall, a time for contemplating the Almighty, a
respite from highstorms.

Maybe things were different out here in the stormlands. She pulled
herself up the rocks. The Shattered Plains had grown increasingly rough
as the armies traveled inward – now on their eighth day of the expedition – following Shallan's map, created with the help of Rlain, the former
bridgeman.

Shallan crested the rock formation and found the view that the scouts
had described. Vathah and Gaz stomped up behind her, muttering about

the cold. The heart of the Shattered Plains extended before Shallan. The inner plateaus, never explored by men.

'It's here,' she said.

Gaz scratched at the socket beneath his eye patch. 'Rocks?'

'Yes, guardsman Gaz,' Shallan said. 'Rocks. Beautiful, wonderful rocks.'

In the distance, she saw shadows draped in a veil of misty rain. Seen together in a group like this, it was unmistakable. This *was* a city. A city covered over with centuries' worth of crem, like children's blocks dribbled with many coats of melted wax. To the innocent eye, it undoubtedly looked much like the rest of the Shattered Plains. But it was oh so much more.

It was proof. Even this formation Shallan stood upon had probably once been a building. Weathered on the stormward side, dribbled with crem down the leeward side to create the bulbous, uneven slope they had climbed.

'Brightness!'

She ignored the voices from down below, instead waving impatiently for the spyglass. Gaz handed it to her, and she raised it to inspect the plateaus ahead. Unfortunately, the thing had fogged up on one end. She tried to rub it clean, rain washing over her, but the fog was on the inside. Blasted device.

'Brightness?' Gaz asked. 'Shouldn't we, uh, listen to what they're saying down below?'

'More twisted Parshendi spotted,' Shallan said, raising the spyglass again. Wouldn't the designer of the thing have built it to be sealed on the inside, to prevent moisture from getting in?

Gaz and Vathah stepped back as several members of Bridge Four reached the top of the incline.

'Brightness,' one of the bridgemen said, 'Highprince Dalinar has withdrawn the vanguard and ordered a secure perimeter on the plateau behind us.' He was a tall, handsome man whose arms seemed entirely too long for his body. Shallan looked with dissatisfaction at the inner plateaus.

'Brightness,' the bridgeman continued reluctantly, 'he did say that if you wouldn't come, he would send Adolin to ... um ... cart you back over his shoulder.'

'I would like to see him do that,' Shallan said. It *did* sound kind of romantic, the sort of thing you'd read of in a novel. 'He's that worried about the Parshendi?'

'Shen ... er, Rlain ... says we're practically to their home plateau, Brightness. Too many of their patrols have been spotted. Please.'

'We need to get in there,' Shallan said, pointing. 'That's where the secrets are.'

'Brightness ...'

'Very well,' she said, turning and hiking down the incline. She slipped, which did not help her dignity, but Vathah caught her arm before she tumbled onto her face.

Once down, they quickly crossed this smaller plateau, joining scouts who were jogging back toward the bulk of the army. Rlain claimed to know nothing himself of the Oathgate – or even really much about the city, which he called 'Narak' instead of Stormseat. He said his people had only taken up permanent residence here following the Alethi invasion.

During the push inward, Dalinar's soldiers had spotted an increasing number of Parshendi and had clashed with them in brief skirmishes. General Khal thought that the forays had been intended to draw the army off course, though how they would figure that, Shallan didn't know – but she *did* know she was growing tired of feeling damp all the time. They had been out here nearly two weeks now, and some of the soldiers had begun to mutter that the army would need to return to the warcamps soon, or risk not getting back before the highstorms resumed.

Shallan stalked across the bridge and passed several lines of spearmen setting up behind short, wavelike ridges in the stone – likely the footings of old walls. She found Dalinar and the other highprinces in a tent set up at the center of camp. It was one of six identical tents, and it wasn't immediately obvious which one held the four highprinces. A safety precaution of some sort, she assumed. As Shallan stepped in out of the rain, she intruded upon their conversation.

'The current plateau does have very favorable defensible positions,' Aladar said, gesturing toward a map set out on the travel table before them. 'I prefer our chances against an assault here to moving deeper.'

'And if we move deeper,' Dalinar said with a grunt, 'we'll be in danger of getting split during an attack, half on one plateau, half on the other.'

'But do they even *need* to attack?' Roion said. 'If I were them, I'd just form up out there as if to prepare for an attack – but then I wouldn't. I'd stall, forcing my enemy to get stuck out here waiting for an attack until the highstorms returned!'

'He makes a valid point,' Aladar admitted.

'Trust a coward,' Sebarial said, 'to know the smartest way to stay out of fighting.' He sat with Palona beside the table, eating fruit and smiling pleasantly.

'I am *not* a coward,' Roion said, forming fists at his sides.

'I didn't mean it as an insult,' Sebarial said. 'My insults are far more pithy. *That* was a compliment. If I had my way, I'd hire you to run all wars, Roion. I suspect there would be far fewer casualties, and the price of undergarments would double once soldiers were told that you were in charge. I'd make a fortune.'

Shallan handed her dripping coat to a servant, then took off her cap and began drying her hair with a towel. 'We need to press closer to the center of the Plains,' she said. 'Roion is right. I refuse to let us bivouac. The Parshendi will just wait us out.'

The others looked to her.

'I wasn't aware,' Dalinar said, 'that you decided our tactics, Brightness Shallan.'

'It's our own fault, Dalinar,' Sebarial said, 'for giving her so much leeway. We probably should have tossed her off the Pinnacle weeks ago, the moment she arrived at that meeting.'

Shallan was stirring up a retort as the tent flaps parted and Adolin trudged in, Shardplate streaming. He pushed up his faceplate. Storms . . . he looked so good, even when you could see only half his face. She smiled.

'They are *definitely* agitated,' Adolin said. He saw her, and gave her a quick smile before clinking up to the table. 'There are at least ten thousand of those twisted Parshendi out there, moving in groups around the plateaus.'

'Ten thousand,' Aladar said with a grunt. 'We can take ten thousand. Even with them having the terrain advantage, even if we have to assault rather than defend, we should handle that many with ease. We have over thirty thousand.'

'This *is* what we came to do,' Dalinar said. He looked at Shallan, who blushed at her forwardness earlier. 'Your portal, the one you think is out here. Where would it be?'

'Closer to the city,' Shallan said.

'What of those red eyes?' Roion asked. He looked very uncomfortable. 'And the flashes of light they cause when they fight? Storms, when I spoke earlier, I didn't mean that I wanted us to go farther. I was just worried at what the Parshendi would do. I ... there's no easy way to do this, is there?'

'So far as Rlain has said,' Navani said from her seated position at the side of the room, 'only their soldiers can jump between plateaus, but we can assume the new form capable of it as well. They can flee us if we push forward.'

Dalinar shook his head. 'They set up on the Plains, rather than fleeing all those years ago, because they knew it was their best chance for survival. On the open, unbroken rock of the stormlands, they could be hunted and destroyed. Out here they have the advantage. They won't abandon it now. Not if they think they can fight us.'

'If we want to make them fight, then,' Aladar said, 'we need to threaten their homes. I guess we really should press toward the city.'

Shallan relaxed. Each step closer to the center – by Rlain's explanations, they were but half a day away – got her closer to the Oathgate.

Dalinar leaned forward, spreading his hands to the sides, his shadow falling on the battle maps. 'Very well. I did not come all this way to timidly wait upon Parshendi whims. We'll march inward tomorrow, threaten their city, and force them to engage.'

'The closer we get,' Sebarial noted, 'the more likely we are to become cut off without hope of retreat.'

Dalinar didn't respond, but Shallan knew what he was thinking. *We gave up hope of retreat days ago.* A flight across days and days of plateaus would be a disaster if the Parshendi decided to harry. The Alethi fought here, and they won, seizing the shelter of Narak.

That was their only option.

Dalinar adjourned the meeting, and the highprinces left, surrounded by groups of aides holding umbrellas. Shallan waited as Dalinar caught her eye. In moments only she, Dalinar, Adolin, and Navani remained.

Navani walked up to Dalinar, taking his arm with both of hers. An intimate posture.

'This portal of yours,' Dalinar said.

'Yes?' Shallan asked.

Dalinar looked up and met her eyes. 'How real is it?'

'Jasnah was convinced it was completely real. She was never wrong.'

'This would be a storming *bad* time for her to break her record,' he said softly. 'I agreed to press forward, in part, because of your exploration.'

'Thank you.'

'I did not do it for scholarship,' Dalinar said. 'From what Navani tells me, this portal offers a unique opportunity for retreat. I had hoped to defeat the Parshendi before danger overtook us, whatever it was. Judging by what we've seen, danger has arrived early.'

Shallan nodded.

'Tomorrow is the last day of the countdown,' Dalinar said. 'Scribbled on the walls during highstorms. Whatever it is, whatever it was, we meet it tomorrow – and you are my backup plan, Shallan Davar. You will find this portal, and you will make it work. If the evil overwhelms us, your pathway will be our escape. You may be the only chance that our armies – and indeed, Alethkar itself – have for survival.'

⁘

Days passed, and Kaladin refused to let the rain overcome him.

He limped through the camp, using a crutch that Lopen had fetched for him despite objecting that it was too soon for Kaladin to be up and about.

The place was still empty, save for the occasional parshmen lugging wood from the forests outside or carrying sacks of grain. The camp didn't get any news about the expedition. The king was probably being sent word via spanreed, but he didn't share it with everyone else.

Storms, this place feels eerie, Kaladin thought, limping past deserted barracks, rain pattering against the umbrella that Lopen had tied to Kaladin's crutch. It worked. Kind of. He passed rainspren, like blue candles sprouting from the ground, each with a single eye in the center of its top. Creepy things. Kaladin had always disliked them.

He fought the rain. Did that make any sense? It seemed that the rain wanted him to stay inside, so he went out. The rain wanted him to give in to the despair, so he forced himself to think. Growing up, he'd had Tien to help lighten the gloom. Now, even thinking of Tien increased that gloom instead – though he couldn't avoid it. The Weeping reminded him of his brother. Of laughter when the darkness threatened, of cheerful joy and carefree optimism.

Those images warred with ones of Tien's death. Kaladin squeezed his eyes shut, trying to banish that memory. Of the frail young man, barely trained, being cut down. Tien's own company of soldiers had put him at the front as a distraction, a sacrifice to slow the enemy.

Kaladin set his jaw, opening his eyes. No more moping. He would not whine or wallow. Yes, he'd lost Syl. He'd lost many loved ones during his life. He would survive this agony as he had survived the others.

He continued his limping circuit of the barracks. He did this four times a day. Sometimes Lopen came with him, but today Kaladin was alone. He splashed through puddles of water, and found himself smiling because he wore the boots Shallan had stolen from him.

I never did believe she was a Horneater, he thought. *I need to make sure she knows that.*

He stopped, leaning on the crutch and looking out through the rain toward the Shattered Plains. He couldn't see far. The haze of rainfall prevented that.

You come back safely, he thought to those out there. *All of you. This time, I can't help you if something goes wrong.*

Rock, Teft, Dalinar, Adolin, Shallan, everyone in Bridge Four – all out on their own. How different a place would the world be if Kaladin had been a better man? If he'd used his powers and had returned to the warcamp with Shallan full of Stormlight? He had been so close to revealing what he could do . . .

You'd been thinking that for weeks, he thought to himself. *You'd never have done it. You were too scared.*

He hated admitting it, but it was true.

Well, if his suspicions about Shallan were true, perhaps Dalinar would have his Radiant anyway. May she make a better run of it than Kaladin had.

He continued on his limping way, rounding back to Bridge Four's barrack. He stopped when he saw a fine carriage, pulled by horses bearing the king's livery, waiting in front of it.

Kaladin cursed, hobbling forward. Lopen ran out to meet him, not carrying an umbrella. A lot of people gave up on trying to stay dry during the Weeping.

'Lopen!' Kaladin said. 'What?'

'He's waiting for you, gancho,' Lopen said, gesturing urgently. 'The king himself.'

Kaladin limped more quickly toward his room. The door was open, and Kaladin peeked in to find King Elhokar standing inside, looking about the small chamber. Moash guarded the door, and Taka – a former member of the King's Guard – stood nearer to the king.

'Your Majesty?' Kaladin asked.

'Ah,' the king said, 'bridgeman.' Elhokar's cheeks were flushed. He'd been drinking, though he didn't appear drunk. Kaladin understood. With Dalinar and that disapproving glare of his gone for a time, it was probably nice to relax with a bottle.

When Kaladin had first met the king, he'd thought Elhokar lacked regality. Now, oddly, he thought Elhokar did look like a king. It wasn't that the king had changed – the man still had his imperious features, with that overly large nose and condescending manner. The change was in Kaladin. The things he'd once associated with kingship – honor, strength of arms, nobility – had been replaced with Elhokar's less inspiring attributes.

'This is really all that Dalinar assigns one of his officers?' Elhokar asked, gesturing around the room. 'That man. He expects everyone to live with his own austerity. It is as if he's completely forgotten how to enjoy himself.'

Kaladin looked to Moash, who shrugged, Shardplate clinking.

The king cleared his throat. 'I was told you were too weak to make the trip to see me. I see that might not be the case.'

'I'm sorry, Your Majesty,' Kaladin said. 'I'm not well, but I walk the camp each day to rebuild my strength. I feared that my weakness and appearance might be offensive to the Throne.'

'You've learned to speak politically, I see,' the king said, folding his arms. 'The truth is that my command is meaningless, even to a darkeyes. I no longer have authority in the eyes of men.'

Great. Here we go again.

The king waved curtly. 'Out, you other two. I'd speak to this man alone.'

Moash glanced at Kaladin, looking concerned, but Kaladin nodded. With reluctance, Moash and Taka walked out, shutting the door, leaving them to the light of a few dwindling spheres that the king set out. Soon, those wouldn't have any Stormlight to them at all – it had been too long without a highstorm. They'd need to break out candles and oil lamps.

'How did you know,' the king asked him, 'how to be a hero?'

'Your Majesty?' Kaladin asked, sagging against his crutch.

'A hero,' the king said, waving flippantly. 'Everyone loves you, bridge-man. You saved Dalinar, you fought Shardbearers, you came back after falling into the storming chasms! How do you do it? How do you know?'

'It's really just luck, Your Majesty.'

'No, no,' the king said. He began pacing. 'It's a pattern, though I can't figure it out. When I try to be strong, I make a fool of myself. When I try to be merciful, people walk all over me. When I try to listen to counsel, it turns out I've picked the wrong men! When I try to do everything on my own, Dalinar has to take over lest I ruin the kingdom.

'How do people know what to do? Why don't *I* know what to do? I was born to this office, given the throne by the Almighty himself! Why would he give me the title, but not the capacity? It defies reason. And yet, everyone seems to know things that I do not. My father could rule even the likes of Sadeas – men loved Gavilar, feared him, and served him all at once. I can't even get a darkeyes to obey a command to come visit the palace! Why doesn't this work? What do I have to *do?*'

Kaladin stepped back, shocked at the frankness. 'Why are you asking me this, Your Majesty?'

'Because you know the secret,' the king said, still pacing. 'I've seen how your men regard you; I've heard how people speak of you. You're a *hero*, bridgeman.' He stopped, then walked up to Kaladin, taking him by the arms. 'Can you teach me?'

Kaladin regarded him, baffled.

'I want to be a king like my father was,' Elhokar said. 'I want to lead men, and I want them to respect me.'

'I don't . . .' Kaladin swallowed. 'I don't know if that's possible, Your Majesty.'

Elhokar narrowed his eyes at Kaladin. 'So you do still speak your mind. Even after the trouble it brought you. Tell me. Do you think me a bad king, bridgeman?'

'Yes.'

The king drew in a sharp breath, still holding Kaladin by the arms.

I could do it right here, Kaladin realized. *Strike the king down. Put*

Dalinar on the throne. No hiding, no secrets, no cowardly assassination. A fight, him and me.

That seemed a more honest way to be about it. Sure, Kaladin would probably be executed, but he found that didn't bother him. Should he do it, for the good of the kingdom?

He could imagine Dalinar's anger. Dalinar's disappointment. Death didn't bother Kaladin, but failing Dalinar . . . *Storms.*

The king let go and stalked away. 'Well, I did ask,' he muttered to himself. 'I merely have to win you over as well. I *will* figure this out. I will be a king to be remembered.'

'Or you could do what is best for Alethkar,' Kaladin said, 'and step down.'

The king stopped in place. He turned on Kaladin, expression darkening. 'Do *not* overstep yourself, bridgeman. Bah. I should never have come here.'

'I agree,' Kaladin said. He found this entire experience surreal.

Elhokar made to leave. He stopped at the door, not looking at Kaladin. 'When you came, the shadows went away.'

'The . . . shadows?'

'I saw them in mirrors, in the corners of my eyes. I could swear I even heard them whispering, but you frightened them. I haven't seen them since. There's something about you. Don't try to deny it.' The king looked to him. 'I am sorry for what I did to you. I watched you fight to help Adolin, and then I saw you defend Renarin . . . and I grew jealous. There you were, such a champion, so loved. And everyone hates me. I should have gone to fight myself.

'Instead, I overreacted to your challenge of Amaram. You weren't the one who ruined our chance against Sadeas. It was me. Dalinar was right. Again. I'm so tired of him being right, and me being wrong. In light of that, I am not at all surprised that you find me a bad king.'

Elhokar pushed open the door and left.

The Unmade are a deviation, a flair, a conundrum that may not be worth your time. You cannot help but think of them. They are fascinating. Many are mindless. Like the spren of human emotions, only much more nasty. I do believe a few can think, however.

—From the Diagram, Book of the 2nd Desk Drawer: paragraph 14

D alinar strode from the tent into a subtle rain, joined by Navani and Shallan. The rain sounded softer out here than it had inside the tent, where the drops had drummed upon the fabric.

They had marched farther inward all that morning, bringing them to the very heart of the ruined plateaus. They were close now. So close, they had the Parshendi's full attention.

It was happening.

An attendant offered an umbrella to each person leaving the tent, but Dalinar waved his away. If his men had to stand in this, he'd join them. He'd be soaked by the end of this day anyway.

He strode through the ranks, following bridgemen in stormcoats who led the way with sapphire lanterns. It was still day, but the thick cloud cover rendered everything dim. He used blue light to identify himself. Roion and Aladar, seeing that Dalinar had eschewed an umbrella, stepped out into the rain with him. Sebarial, of course, stayed underneath his.

They reached the edge of the mass of troops who had formed up in a large oval, facing outward. He knew his soldiers well enough to sense their anxiety. They stood too stiffly, with no shuffling or stretching. They were also silent, not chattering to distract themselves – not even griping. The only voices he heard were occasional barked orders as officers trimmed the lines. Dalinar soon saw what was causing the uneasiness.

Glowing red eyes amassed on the next plateau.

They hadn't glowed before. Red eyes yes, but not with those uncanny glows. In the dim light, the Parshendi bodies were indistinct, no more than shadows. The crimson eyes hovered like Taln's Scar – like spheres in the darkness, deeper in color than any ruby. Parshendi beards often bore bits of gemstone woven into them in patterns, but today those didn't glow.

Too long without a highstorm, Dalinar thought. Even the gems in Alethi spheres – cut with facets and so able to hold light longer – had almost all failed by this point of the Weeping, though larger gemstones might last another week or so.

They had entered the darkest part of the year. The time when Stormlight did not shine.

'Oh, Almighty!' Roion whispered, looking at those red eyes. 'Oh, by the names of God himself. What have you brought us to, Dalinar?'

'Can you do anything to help?' Dalinar asked softly, looking to Shallan, who stood beneath her umbrella at his side, her guards just behind.

Face pale, she shook her head. 'I'm sorry.'

'The Knights Radiant were warriors,' Dalinar said, very softly.

'If they were, then I've got a long way to go. . . .'

'Go, then,' Dalinar told the girl. 'When there is an opening in the fighting, find that pathway to Urithiru, if it exists. You're my only contingency plan, Brightness.'

She nodded.

'Dalinar,' Aladar said, sounding horrified as he watched the red eyes, which were forming into ordered ranks on the other side of the chasm, 'tell me straight. When you brought us on this march, did you *expect* to find these horrors?'

'Yes.' It was true enough. He didn't know what horrors he'd find, but he had known that something was coming.

'You came anyway?' Aladar demanded. 'You hauled us all the way out onto these cursed plains, you let us be surrounded by monsters, to be slaughtered and—'

Dalinar grabbed Aladar by the front of the jacket and hauled him forward. The move caught the other man completely off guard, and he quieted, eyes widening.

'Those are *Voidbringers* out there,' Dalinar hissed, rain dribbling down his face. 'They've returned. Yes, it is true. And we, Aladar, *we* have a chance to stop them. I don't know if we can prevent another Desolation, but I'd do *anything* – including sacrificing myself and this entire army – to protect Alethkar from those things. Do you understand?'

Aladar nodded, wide-eyed.

'I hoped to get here before this happened,' Dalinar said, 'but I didn't. So now we're going to fight. And storm it, we're going to destroy those things. We're going to stop them, and we're going to hope that will stop this evil from spreading to the world's parshmen, as my niece feared. If you survive this day, you'll be known as one of the greatest men of our generation.'

He released Aladar, letting the highprince stumble back. 'Go to your men, Aladar. Go lead them. Be a champion.'

Aladar stared at Dalinar, mouth gaping. Then, he straightened. He slapped his arm to his chest, giving a salute as crisp as any Dalinar had seen. 'It will be done, Brightlord,' Aladar said. 'Highprince of War.' Aladar barked to his attendants – including Mintez, the highlord that Aladar usually had use his Shardplate in battle – then put his hand to his sidesword and dashed away in the rain.

'Huh,' Sebarial said from beneath his umbrella. 'He's actually buying into it. He thinks he's going to be a storming hero.'

'He now knows I was right about the need to unify Alethkar. He's a good soldier. Most of the highprinces are . . . or were, at some point.'

'Pity you ended up with us two instead of them,' Sebarial said, nodding toward Roion, who still stared out at the shifting red eyes. There were thousands now, still increasing as more Parshendi arrived. Scouts reported that they were gathering on all three plateaus bordering the large one that the Alethi occupied.

'I'm useless in a battle,' Sebarial continued, 'and Roion's archers will be wasted in this rain. Besides, he's a coward.'

'Roion is not a coward,' Dalinar said, laying a hand on the shorter highprince's arm. 'He's careful. That did not serve him well in the squabbling over gemhearts, where men like Sadeas threw away lives in exchange for prestige. But out here, care is an attribute I'd choose over recklessness.'

Roion turned to Dalinar, blinking away water. 'Is this really happening?'

'Yes,' Dalinar said. 'I want you with your men, Roion. They need to see you. This is going to terrify them, but not you. You're careful, in control.'

'Yeah,' Roion said. 'Yes. You ... you're going to get us out of this, right?'

'No, I'm not,' Dalinar said.

Roion frowned.

'We're all going to get ourselves out of it *together*.'

Roion nodded, and didn't object. He saluted as Aladar had, if less crisply, then headed toward his army on the northern flank, calling for his aides to give him the numbers of his reserves.

'Damnation,' Sebarial said, watching Roion go. 'Dam*nation*. What about me? Where's my impassioned speech?'

'You,' Dalinar said, 'are to go back to the command tent and not get in the way.'

Sebarial laughed. 'All right. That I can do.'

'I want Teleb in command of your army,' Dalinar said. 'And I'm sending both Serugiadis and Rust to join him. Your men will fight better against these things with a few Shardbearers at their head.' All three were men who had been given Shards following Adolin's dueling spree.

'I'll give the order that Teleb is to be obeyed.'

'And Sebarial?' Dalinar asked.

'Yes?'

'If you have a mind for it, burn some prayers. I don't know if anyone up there is listening anymore, but it can't hurt.' Dalinar turned toward the sea of red eyes. Why were they just standing there watching?

Sebarial hesitated. 'Not as confident as you acted to the other two, eh?' He smiled, as if that comforted him, then sauntered off. What a strange man. Dalinar nodded to one of his aides, who went to give the orders to the three Kholin Shardbearers, first picking Serugiadis – a lanky young man whose sister Adolin had once courted – out of his command post along the ranks, then running off to fetch Teleb and explain Dalinar's orders.

That seen to, Dalinar stepped up to Navani. 'I need to know you're safe in the command tent. As safe as anyone can be.'

'Then pretend I'm there,' she said.

'But—'

'You want my help with fabrials?' Navani said. 'I can't set up that sort of thing remotely, Dalinar.'

He ground his teeth, but what could he say? He was going to need every edge he could get. He looked out at the red eyes again.

'Campfire tales come alive,' said Rock, the massive Horneater bridge-man. Dalinar had never seen that one guarding him or his sons; he was a quartermaster, Dalinar believed. 'These things should not be. Why do they not move?'

'I don't know,' Dalinar said. 'Send a few of your men to fetch Rlain. I want to see if he can provide any explanations.' As two bridgemen ran off, Dalinar turned to Navani. 'Gather your scribes to write my words. I will speak to the soldiers.'

Within moments, she had a pair of scribes – shivering as they stood under umbrellas with pencils out to write – ready to record his words. They'd send women down the lines and read his message to all the men.

Dalinar climbed into Gallant's saddle to get a little height. He turned toward the ranks of men nearby. 'Yes,' he shouted over the sound of the rain, 'these are Voidbringers. Yes, we're going to fight them. I don't know what they can do. I don't know why they've returned. But we came here to *stop them*.

'I know you're scared, but you have heard of my visions in the high-storms. In the warcamps, the lighteyes mocked me and dismissed what I'd seen as delusions.' He thrust his arm to the side, pointing at the sea of red eyes. 'Well out there, you see proof that my visions were true! Out there, you see what I have been told would come!'

Dalinar licked wet lips. He had given many battlefield speeches in his life, but never had he said anything like what came to him now. 'I,' he shouted, 'have been sent by the Almighty himself to save this land from another Desolation. I have *seen* what those things can do; I have lived lives broken by the Voidbringers. I've seen kingdoms shattered, peoples ruined, technology forgotten. I've seen civilization itself brought to the trembling edge of collapse.

'*We will prevent this!* Today you fight not for the wealth of a lighteyes, or even for the honor of your king. Today, you fight for the good of all men. You will not fight alone! Trust in what I have seen, trust in my words. If those *things* have returned, then so must the forces that once defeated them. We will see miracles before this day is out, men! We merely have to be strong enough to deserve them.'

He looked across a sea of hopeful eyes. Storms. Were those glory-spren about his head, spinning like golden spheres in the rain? His scribes finished writing down the short speech, then hurriedly started making copies to send with runners. Dalinar watched them go, hoping to the Tranquiline Halls that he hadn't just lied to everyone.

His force seemed small in this darkness, surrounded by enemies. Soon, he heard his own words being spoken in the distance, read out to the troops. Dalinar remained seated, Shallan beside his horse, though Navani moved off to see to several of her contraptions.

The battle plan called for them to wait a little longer, and Dalinar was content to do so. With these chasms to cross, it was far better to be assaulted than to assault. Perhaps the separate armies forming up would encourage the Parshendi to start the battle by coming to him. Fortunately, the rain meant no arrows. The bowstrings wouldn't stand the dampness, nor would the animal glue in the Parshendi recurve bows.

The Parshendi started singing.

It came in a sudden roar over the rains, startling his men, making them shy backward in a wave. The song wasn't one Dalinar had ever heard during plateau runs. This was more staccato, more frenetic. It rose all around, coming from the three surrounding plateaus, shouted like thrown axes at the Alethi in the center.

Dalinar shivered. Wind blew against him, stronger than was normal during the Weeping. The gust drove raindrops against the side of his face. Cold bit his skin.

'Brightlord!'

Dalinar turned in his saddle, noting four bridgemen approaching along with Rlain – he still had the man under guard at all times. He waved for his guards to part, allowing the Parshendi bridgeman to scramble up to his horse.

'That song!' Rlain said. 'That *song.*'

'What is it, man?'

'It is death,' Rlain whispered. 'Brightlord, I have never heard it before, but the rhythm is one of destruction. Of power.'

Across the chasm, the Parshendi started to glow. Tiny lines of red sparked around their arms, blinking and shaking, like lightning.

'What is *that*?' Shallan asked.

Dalinar narrowed his eyes, and another burst of wind washed over him.

'You have to stop it,' Rlain said. 'Please. Even if you have to kill them. *Do not let them finish that song.*'

It was the day of the countdown he had scribbled on the walls without knowing. The last day.

Dalinar made his decision based on instinct. He called for a messenger, and one jogged up – Teshav's ward, a girl in her fifteenth year. 'Pass the word,' he commanded her. 'Send to General Khal at the command tent, the battalionlords, my son, Teleb, and the other highprinces. We're changing strategies.'

'Brightlord?' the messenger asked. 'What change?'

'We attack. *Now!*'

⁂

Kaladin stopped at the entrance to the lighteyed training grounds, rainwater streaming off his umbrella's waxed cloth, surprised at what he saw. In preparation for a storm, the ardents normally swept and shoveled the sand into covered trenches at the edges of the ground to keep it from being blown away.

He had expected to see something similar during the Weeping. Instead, they had left the sand out, but had then placed a short wooden barrier across the gateway in. It plugged the front of the sparring grounds, allowing them to fill up with water. A small cascade of rainwater poured over the lip of the barrier and into the roadway.

Kaladin regarded the small lake that now filled the courtyard, then sighed and reached down, undoing his laces, then pulling off both boots and socks. When he stepped in, the cold water came up to his calves.

Soft sand squished between his toes. What was the purpose of this? He crossed the courtyard, crutch under his arm, boots joined by the laces and slung over his shoulder. The chill water numbed his wounded foot, which actually felt nice, though his leg still hurt with each step. It seemed that the two weeks of healing hadn't done much for his wounds. His continued insistence that he walk so much probably wasn't helping.

He'd been spoiled by his abilities; a soldier with such a wound normally would take months to recover. Without Stormlight, he'd just have to be patient and heal like everyone else.

He had expected to find the training grounds as abandoned as most of the camp. Even the markets were relatively empty, people preferring to remain indoors during the Weeping. Here, however, he found the ardents laughing and chatting as they sat in chairs in the raised arcades framing the sparring grounds. They sewed leather practice jerkins, cups of auburn wine on tables at their sides. That area rose enough above the yard floor to stay dry.

Kaladin walked along, searching among them, but didn't find Zahel. He even peeked in the man's room, but it was empty.

'Up above, bridgeman!' one of the ardents called. The bald woman pointed toward the stairwell at the corner, where Kaladin had often sent guards to secure the roof when Adolin and Renarin practiced.

Kaladin waved in thanks, then hobbled over and awkwardly made his way up the steps. He had to close his umbrella to fit. Rain fell on his head as he poked it out of the opening in the roof, where the stairwell ended. The roof was made of tile set into hardened crem, and Zahel lay there in a hammock he'd strung between two poles. Kaladin thought they might be lightning rods, which didn't strike him as safe. A tarp hung above the hammock and kept Zahel almost dry.

The ardent swung gently, eyes closed, holding a square bottle of hard honu, a type of lavis grain liquor. Kaladin inspected the rooftop, judging his ability to cross those sloped tiles without toppling off and breaking his neck.

'Ever been to the Purelake, bridgeman?' Zahel asked.

'No,' Kaladin said. 'One of my men talks about it, though.'

'What have you heard?'

'It's an ocean that's so shallow, you can wade across it.'

'It's ridiculously shallow,' Zahel said. 'Like an endless bay, mere feet deep. Warm water. Calm breezes. Reminds me of home. Not like this cold, damp, godsforsaken place.'

'So why aren't you there instead of here?'

'Because I can't stand being reminded of home, idiot.'

Oh. 'Why are we talking about it, then?'

'Because you were wondering why we made our own little Purelake down below.'

'I was?'

'Of course you were. Damnation boy. I know you well enough by now to know that questions bother you. You don't think like a spearman.'

'Spearmen can't be curious?'

'No. Because if they are, they either get killed or they end up showing someone in charge how smart they are. Then they get put somewhere more useful.'

Kaladin raised an eyebrow, waiting for more explanation. Finally, he sighed, and asked, 'Why have you blocked off the courtyard below?'

'Why do you think?'

'You are a really annoying person, Zahel. Do you realize that?'

'Sure do.' He took a drink of his honu.

'I assume,' Kaladin said, 'that you blocked off the front of the practice grounds so that the rain wouldn't wash the sand away.'

'Excellent deduction,' Zahel said. 'Like fresh blue paint on a wall.'

'Whatever that means. The problem is, why is it necessary to keep the sand in the courtyard? Why not just put it away, like you do before highstorms?'

'Did you know,' Zahel said, 'that rains during the Weeping don't drop crem?'

'I . . .' Did he know that? Did it matter?

'Good thing too,' Zahel said, 'or our entire camp here would end up clogged with the stuff. Anyway, rain like this, it's great for washing.'

'You're telling me that you've turned the floor of the dueling grounds into a *bath*?'

'Sure did.'

'You wash in that?'

'Sure do. Not ourselves, of course.'

'Then what?'

'Sand.'

Kaladin frowned, then peered over the side, looking at the pool below.

'Every day,' Zahel said, 'we go in there and stir it up. The sand settles back down to the bottom, and all the yuck floats away, carried by the rain in little streams out of the camp. Did you ever consider that sand might need washing?'

'No, actually.'

'Well it does. After a year's worth of being kicked by stinky bridgeman feet and equally stinky – but far more refined – lighteyes feet, after a year of having people like me spill food on it, or having animals find their way in here to do business, the sand needs cleaning.'

'Why are we talking about this?'

'Because it's important,' Zahel said, taking a drink. 'Or something. I don't know. You came to me, kid, interrupting my vacation. That means you have to listen to me blab.'

'You're supposed to say something profound.'

'Did you miss the part about me being on vacation?'

Kaladin stood in the rain. 'Do you know where the King's Wit is?'

'That fool, Dust? Not here, blessedly. Why?'

Kaladin needed someone to talk to, and had spent the better part of the day searching for Wit. He hadn't found the man, though he had broken down and bought some chouta from a lonely street vendor.

It had tasted good. That hadn't helped his mood.

So, he'd given up on finding Wit and had come to Zahel instead. That appeared to have been a mistake. Kaladin sighed, turning back down the stairs.

'What was it you wanted?' Zahel called to him. The man had cracked an eye, looking toward Kaladin.

'Have you ever had to choose between two equally distasteful choices?'

'Every day I choose to keep breathing.'

'I worry something awful is going to happen,' Kaladin said. 'I can prevent it, but the awful thing ... it might be best for everyone if it *does* happen.'

'Huh,' Zahel said.

'No advice?' Kaladin asked.

'Choose the option,' Zahel said, rearranging his pillow, 'that makes it easiest for you to sleep at night.' The old ardent closed his eyes and settled back. 'That's what I wish I'd done.'

Kaladin continued down the steps. Below, he didn't get out his umbrella. He was already soaked anyway. Instead, he poked through the racks at the side of the practice grounds until he found a spear – real, not practice. Then he set down his crutch and hobbled out into the water.

There, he fell into a spearman's stance and closed his eyes. Rain fell around him. It splattered in the water of the pool, sprinkled the rooftop, pattered the streets outside. Kaladin felt drained, like his blood had been sucked from him. The gloom made him want to sit still.

Instead, he started dancing with the rain. He went through spear forms, doing his best to avoid putting weight on his wounded leg. He splashed in the waters. He sought peace and purpose in the comfortable forms.

He didn't find either.

His balance was off, and his leg screamed. The rain didn't accompany him; it just annoyed him. Worse, the wind didn't blow. The air felt *stale*.

Kaladin stumbled over his own feet. He twisted the spear about him, then dropped it clumsily. It spun away to splash into the pool. As he fetched it, he noticed the ardents watching him with looks ranging from befuddled to amused.

He tried again. Simple spear forms. No spinning the weapon, no showing off. Step step thrust.

The spear's shaft felt wrong in his fingers. Off balance. Storms. He'd come here seeking solace, but he only grew more and more frustrated as he tried to practice.

How much of his ability with the spear had come from his powers? Was he nothing without them?

He dropped the spear again after trying a simple twist and thrust. He reached for it, and found a rainspren sitting next to it in the water, looking upward, unblinking.

He snatched the spear with a growl, then looked up toward the sky. 'He deserves it!' he bellowed at those clouds.

Rain pelted him.

'Give me a reason why he doesn't!' Kaladin yelled, uncaring if the ardents heard. 'It might not be his fault, and he might be trying, but he's still *failing*.'

Silence.

'It's right to remove the wounded limb,' Kaladin whispered. 'This is what we have to do. To . . . To . . .'

To stay alive.

Where had those words come from?

Gotta do what you can to stay alive, son. Turn a liability into an advantage whenever you can.

Tien's death.

That moment, that horrible moment, when he watched unable to do anything as his brother died. Tien's own squadleader had sacrificed the untrained to gain a moment's advantage.

That squadleader had spoken to Kaladin after it was all over. *Gotta do what you can to stay alive. . . .*

It made a twisted, horrible kind of sense.

It hadn't been Tien's fault. Tien had tried. He'd still failed. So they'd killed him.

Kaladin fell to his knees in the water. 'Almighty, oh Almighty.'

The king . . .

The king was Dalinar's Tien.

⬦

'Attack?' Adolin asked. 'Are you certain that is what my father said?'

The young woman who had run the message nodded a rain-slicked head, looking miserable in her slitted dress and runner's sash. 'You're to stop that singing, if you can, Brightlord. Your father indicated it was important.'

Adolin looked over his battalions, which held the southern flank. Just beyond them, on one of the three plateaus that surrounded their army, the Parshendi sang a horrible song. Sureblood danced, snorting.

'I don't like it either,' Adolin said softly, patting the horse on the neck. That song put him on edge. And those threads of red light on their arms, in their hands. What were those?

'Perel,' he said to one of his field commanders, 'tell the men to get ready for the mark. We're going to charge across those bridges onto the southern plateau. Heavy infantry first, shortspears behind, longspears at the ready in case we're overrun. I want the men ready to form blocks on the other side until we're sure where the Parshendi lines will fall. Storms, I wish we had archers. Go!'

The word spread, and Adolin nudged Sureblood up beside one of the bridges, which had already been set. His bridgeman guards for the day followed, a pair named Skar and Drehy.

'You two going to sit out?' Adolin asked the bridgemen, his eyes forward. 'Your captain doesn't like you going into battle against Parshendi.'

'To Damnation with that!' Drehy said. 'We'll fight, sir. Those aren't Parshendi anyway. Not anymore.'

'Good answer. They'll advance once we start our assault. We need to hold the bridgehead for the rest of our army. Try to keep up with me, if you can.' He glanced over his shoulder, waiting. Watching until . . .

A large blue gemstone rose into the air, hoisted high on a distant pole near the command tent.

'Go!' Adolin kicked Sureblood into motion, thundering across the bridge and splashing through a pool on the other side. Rainspren wavered. His two bridgemen followed at a run. Behind them, the heavy infantry in thick armor with hammers and axes – perfect for splitting Parshendi carapace – surged into motion.

The bulk of the Parshendi continued their chanting. A smaller group broke off, perhaps two thousand in number, and moved to intercept Adolin. He growled, leaning low, Shardblade appearing in his hand. If they—

A flash of light.

The world lurched, and Adolin found himself skidding on the ground, his Shardplate grinding against stones. The armor absorbed the blow of the fall, but could do nothing for Adolin's own shock. The world spun, and a spray of water spurted in through the slits in his helm, washing over his face.

As he came to rest, he heaved himself backward, up to his feet. He stumbled, clanking, thrashing about in case any Parshendi had gotten close. He blinked away water inside his helm, then oriented himself on a change in the landscape in front of him. White amid the brown and grey. What was that . . .

He finally blinked his eyes clear enough to get a good look. The whiteness was a horse, fallen to the ground.

Adolin screamed something raw, a sound that echoed in his helm. He ignored the shouts of soldiers, the sound of rain, the sudden and unnatural *crack* behind him. He ran to the body on the ground. Sureblood.

'No, no, no,' Adolin said, skidding to his knees beside the horse. The animal bore a strange, branching burn all down the side of his white coat. Wide, jagged. Sureblood's dark eyes, open to the rain, did not blink.

Adolin raised his hands, suddenly hesitant to touch the animal.

A youth on an unfamiliar field.

Sureblood wasn't moving.

More nervous that day than during the duel that won his Blade.

Shouts. Another *crack* in the air, sharp, immediate.

They pick their rider, son. We fixate on Shards, but any man – courageous or coward – can bond a Blade. Not so here, on this ground. Only the worthy win here . . .

Move.

Grieve later.

Move!

Adolin roared, leaping to his feet and charging past the two bridgemen who nervously stood guard over him with spears. He started the process of summoning his Blade and ran toward the fighting up ahead. Only moments had passed, but already the Alethi lines were collapsing. Some infantry advanced in clusters while others had hunkered down, stunned and confused.

Another flash, accompanied by a *crack*ing of the air. Lightning. Red lightning. It appeared in flashes from groups of Parshendi, then was gone in the blink of an eye. It left a bright afterimage – glowing, forked – that briefly obscured Adolin's sight.

Ahead of him, men dropped, fried in their armor. Adolin shouted as he charged, bellowing for the men to hold their lines.

More *crack*s sounded, but the strikes didn't seem well aimed. They'd sometimes flash backward or would follow strange paths, rarely going straight toward the Alethi. As he ran, he saw a blast come from a pair of Parshendi, but it arced immediately down into the ground.

The Parshendi stared downward, befuddled. It was as if the lightning worked . . . well, like lightning from the sky, not following any sort of predictable path.

'Charge them, you cremlings!' Adolin shouted, running through the middle of the soldiers. 'Back into your lines! It's just like advancing on archers! Keep your heads. Tighten up. If we break, we're dead!'

He wasn't certain how much of that they heard, but the image of him yelling, crashing into the line of Parshendi, did something. Shouts rose from officers, lines re-formed.

Lightning flashed right at Adolin.

The sound was incredible, and the *light*. He stood in place, blinded. When it faded, he found himself completely unharmed. He looked down at the armor, which was *vibrating* softly – a hum that rattled his skin in a strangely comforting way. Nearby, another crack of lightning left a small group of Parshendi, but it didn't blind him. His helm – which as always was partially translucent from the inside – darkened in a jagged streak, perfectly overlaying the lightning.

Adolin grinned with clenched teeth, feeling a savage satisfaction as he pushed into the Parshendi and swung his Shardblade through their necks. By the old stories, the suit he wore had been created to fight these very monsters.

Though these Parshendi soldiers were sleeker and more ferocious-looking than the ones he'd previously fought, their eyes burned just as easily. Then they dropped dead and something wiggled out of their chests – small red spren, like tiny lightning, that zipped into the air and vanished.

'They *can* be killed!' one of the soldiers yelled nearby. 'They can die!'

Others raised the call, passing it down the lines. Obvious though the revelation seemed, it bolstered his troops, and they surged forward.

They can die.

∵

Shallan drew. Frantic.

A map in ink. Each line precise. The large sheet, crafted at her order, covered a wide board on the floor. It was the largest drawing she'd ever done; she'd filled it in, section by section, as they traveled.

She listened with half an ear to the other scholars in the tent. They were a distraction, but an important one.

Another line, rippled on the sides, forming a thin plateau. It was a copy of the one she'd drawn in seven other places on the map. The Plains were a fourfold radial pattern mirrored down the center of each quadrant, and so anything she drew in one quadrant she could repeat in the others, mirrored as appropriate. The eastern side was worn down, yes, so her map wouldn't be accurate in that area – but for cohesion, she needed to finish those parts. So she could see the whole pattern.

'Scout reporting in,' a messenger woman said, bursting into the tent, letting in a gust of the wet wind. This unexpected wind . . . it almost felt like the wind before a highstorm.

'What is the report?' Inadara asked. The severe woman was supposed to be a great scholar. She reminded Shallan of her father's ardents. In the corner of the room, Prince Renarin stood in his Shardplate, arms folded.

443

He had orders to protect them all, should the Parshendi try to break onto the command plateau.

'The large center plateau is just as the parshman told us,' the scout said, breathless. 'It's only one plateau over, to the east.' Lyn was a solid-looking woman with long black hair and keen eyes. 'It's obviously inhabited, though there doesn't seem to be anyone there right now.'

'And the plateaus surrounding it?' Inadara asked.

'Shim and Felt are scouting those,' Lyn said. 'Felt should be back soon. I can do a rough drawing of what I saw of the center plateau for you.'

'Do it,' Inadara said. 'We need to find that Oathgate.'

Shallan wiped a stray drop of water – fallen from Lyn's coat – off her map, then continued drawing. The army's path from the warcamps inward had allowed her to extrapolate and draw eight chains of plateaus, two each – mirrored – starting from the four 'sides' of the Plains and working inward.

She had almost completed the last of the eight arms reaching toward the center. This close, earlier scout reports – and what Shallan had seen herself – allowed her to fill in everything around the center. Rlain's explanations had helped, but he hadn't been able to draw out the center plateaus for her. He'd never paid attention to their shapes, and Shallan needed precision.

Fortunately, earlier reports had almost been enough. She didn't need much more. She was almost done.

'What do you think?' Lyn asked.

'Show it to Brightness Shallan.' Inadara sounded displeased, which seemed her normal state.

Shallan glanced over Lyn's hastily sketched map, then nodded, turning back to her drawing. It would be better if she could see the center plateau herself, but the corner this woman had drawn gave Shallan an idea.

'Not going to say anything?' Inadara asked.

'Not done yet,' Shallan said, dipping her pen in the ink.

'We have been given an order by the highprince himself to find the Oathgate.'

'I will.'

Something crashed outside, like distant lightning.

'Mmm . . .' Pattern said. 'Bad. Very bad.'

Inadara looked at Pattern, who dimpled the floor near Shallan. 'I do not like this thing. Spren should not speak. It may be of *them*, a Voidbringer.'

'I am *not* a Voidspren,' Pattern said.

'Brightness Shallan—'

'He's not a Voidspren,' Shallan said absently.

'We should study it,' Inadara said. 'How long did you say it has been following you?'

A heavy footstep sounded on the floor, Renarin stepping forward. Shallan would have preferred to keep Pattern secret, but when the winds had started picking up, he'd started buzzing loudly. There was no avoiding it now that he'd drawn the scholars' attention. Renarin leaned down. He seemed fascinated by Pattern.

He wasn't the only one. 'It is likely involved,' Inadara said. 'You should not dismiss one of my theories so quickly. I still think it might be related to the Voidbringers.'

'Know you nothing of Patterns, old human?' Pattern said, huffing. When had he picked up how to huff? 'Voidbringers have no pattern. Besides, I have read of them in your lore. They speak of spindly arms like bone, and horrific faces. I should think, if you wish to find one, the mirror might be a location where you can begin your search.'

Inadara recoiled. Then she stomped away, moving to chat with Brightness Velat and the ardent Isasik about their interpretation of Shallan's map.

Shallan smiled as she drew. 'That was clever.'

'I am trying to learn,' Pattern replied. 'Insults in particular will be of great use to my people, as they are truths and lies combined in a quite interesting manner.'

The pops continued outside. 'What is that?' she asked softly, finishing another plateau.

'Stormspren,' Pattern said. 'They *are* a variety of Voidspren. It is not good. I feel something very dangerous brewing. Draw more quickly.'

'The Oathgate must be in that center plateau somewhere,' Inadara said to her group of scholars.

'We will never search the entire thing in time,' said one of the ardents, a man who seemed to be constantly removing his spectacles and wiping them down. He put them back on. 'That plateau is by far the largest we've found on the Plains.'

It *was* a problem. How to find the Oathgate? It could be anywhere. *No*, Shallan thought, drawing with precise motions, *the old maps placed what Jasnah thought was the Oathgate southwest of the city center*. Unfortunately, she still didn't have a scale for reference. The city was too ancient, and all the maps were copies of copies of copies or re-creations from descriptions. She was certain by now that Stormseat hadn't made up the entire Shattered Plains – the city hadn't been nearly so huge. Structures like the warcamps had been outbuildings, or satellite cities.

But that was just a guess. She needed something concrete. Some sign.

The tent flaps opened again. It had grown cold outside. Was the rain harder than it had been?

'Damnation!' the newcomer swore, a thin man in a scout's uniform. 'Have you *seen* what is happening out there? Why are we split across the plateaus? Wasn't the plan to fight a defensive battle?'

'Your report?' Inadara asked.

'Get me a towel and some paper,' the scout said. 'I rounded the southern side of the central plateau. I'll draw what I saw ... but *Damnation*! They're throwing lightning, Brightness. Throwing it! It's insane. How do we fight such things?'

Shallan finished the last plateau on her drawing. She settled back on her heels, lowering her pen. The Shattered Plains, drawn almost in their entirety. But what was she doing? What was the point?

'We will make an expedition into the central plateau,' Inadara said. 'Brightlord Renarin, we will need your protection. Perhaps in the Parshendi city we will find the elderly or the workers, and we can protect them, as Brightlord Dalinar has instructed. They might know about the Oathgate. If not, we can begin breaking into buildings and searching for clues.'

Too slow, Shallan thought.

The newly arrived scout stepped up to Shallan's large map. He leaned over, inspecting it as he dried himself off with a towel. Shallan gave him a glare. If he dripped water on this after all she'd done ...

'That's wrong,' he said.

Wrong? Her art? Of *course* it wasn't wrong. 'Where?' she asked, exhausted.

'That plateau there,' the man said, pointing. 'It's not long and thin, as

446

you drew it. It's a perfect circle, with big gaps between it and the plateaus on its east and west.'

'That's unlikely,' Shallan said. 'If it were that way—' She blinked.

If it were that way, it wouldn't match the pattern.

⁂

'Well then, find Brightness Shallan a squad of soldiers and do as she says!' Dalinar said, turning and raising his arm against the wind.

Renarin nodded. Blessedly, he'd agreed to put on his Plate for the battle, rather than continuing on with Bridge Four. Dalinar barely understood the lad these days. . . . *Storms.* Dalinar had never known a man who could look awkward in Shardplate, but his son managed it. The sheet of wind-driven rain passed. Light from blue lanterns reflected from Renarin's wet armor.

'Go,' Dalinar said. 'Protect the scholars on their mission.'

'I . . .' Renarin said. 'Father, I don't know . . .'

'It wasn't a request, Renarin!' Dalinar shouted. 'Do as you're told, or give that storming Plate to someone who will!'

The boy stumbled back, then saluted with a metallic slap. Dalinar pointed at Gaval, who barked orders, gathering a squad of soldiers. Renarin followed Gaval as the two of them moved off.

Stormfather. The sky had grown darker and darker. They'd need Navani's fabrials soon. That wind came in bursts, blowing rain that was entirely too strong for the Weeping. 'We have to interrupt that singing!' Dalinar shouted against the rain, making his way to the edge of the plateau, joined by officers and messengers, including Rlain and several members of Bridge Four. 'Parshman. Is this storm their doing?'

'I believe so, Brightlord Dalinar!'

On the other side of the chasm, Aladar's army fought a desperate battle against the Parshendi. Red lightning came in bursts, but according to field reports, the Parshendi didn't know how to control it. It could be very dangerous to those who stood close by, but was not the terrible weapon it had first seemed.

In direct combat, unfortunately, these new Parshendi were another thing entirely. A group of them prowled close to the chasm, where they ripped through a squad of spearmen like a whitespine through a patch of ferns. They fought with a ferocity beyond what the Parshendi had ever shown on the plateau runs, and their weapons connected with flashes of red.

It was difficult to watch, but Dalinar's place was not out there fighting. Not today.

'Aladar's eastern flank needs reinforcement,' Dalinar said. 'What do we have?'

'Light infantry reserves,' General Khal said, wearing only his uniform. His son wore his Shards, fighting with Roion's army. 'Fifteenth spear division from Sebarial's army. But those were supposed to support Brightlord Adolin. . . .'

'He'll survive without them. Get those men over here and see Aladar reinforced. Tell him to punch through to those Parshendi in the back, engage the ones singing at all costs. What's Navani's status?'

'She is ready with the devices, Brightlord,' a messenger said. 'She wants to know where she should begin.'

'Roion's flank,' Dalinar said immediately. He sensed a disaster brewing there. Speeches were all well and good, but even with Khal's son fighting on that front, Roion's troops were the worst he had. Teleb was supporting them with some of Sebarial's troops, who were surprisingly good. The man himself was practically useless in a battle, but he knew how to hire the right people – and that had always been his genius. Sebarial probably assumed that Dalinar didn't know that.

He'd kept many of Sebarial's troops as a reserve up until now. With them on the field, they'd committed almost every soldier they had.

Dalinar hiked back toward the command tent, passing Shallan, Inadara, some bridgemen, and a squad of soldiers – Renarin included – crossing the plateau at a trot, heading out on their mission. They'd have to skirt across the southern plateau, near the fighting, to get where they were going. Kelek speed their way.

Dalinar himself pushed through the rain, soaked to the very bones, reading the battle through what he could see of the flanks. His force had the size advantage, as anticipated. But now, this red lightning, this wind . . . The Parshendi moved through the darkness and the gusts of wind with ease while the humans slipped, squinted, and were battered.

Still, the Alethi were holding their own. The problem was that this was only half of the Parshendi. If the other half attacked, his people would be in serious trouble – but they didn't attack, so they must consider that singing to be important. They saw the wind they were creating as more damaging, more deadly to the humans, than simply joining the battle.

That terrified him. What was coming would be worse.

'I am sorry that you have to die this way.'

Dalinar stood still. Rain streamed down. He looked to the flock of messengers, aides, bodyguards, and officers who attended him. 'Who spoke?'

They looked at one another.

Wait . . . He recognized that voice, didn't he? It was familiar to him.

Yes. He'd heard it many times. In his visions.

It was the voice of the Almighty.

There is one you will watch. Though all of them have some relevance to precognition, Moelach is one of the most powerful in this regard. His touch seeps into a soul as it breaks apart from the body, creating manifestations powered by the spark of death itself. But no, this is a distraction. Deviation. Kingship. We must discuss the nature of kingship.

—From the Diagram, Book of the 2nd Desk Drawer: paragraph 15

K aladin limped up the switchbacks to the palace, his leg a knotted mass of pain. Almost falling as he reached the doors, he slumped against them, gasping, his crutch under one arm, spear in the other hand. As if he could do anything with that.

Have . . . to get . . . to the king. . . .

How would he get Elhokar away? Moash would be watching. Storms. The assassination could happen any day . . . any *hour* now. Surely Dalinar was already far enough from the warcamps.

Keep. Moving.

Kaladin stumbled into the entryway. No guards at the doors. Bad sign. Should he have raised the alarm? There weren't any soldiers in camp to help, and if he'd come in force, Graves and his men would know something was wrong. Alone, Kaladin might be able to see the king. His best hope was to get Elhokar to safety quietly.

Fool, Kaladin thought to himself. *You change your mind now? After all of this? What are you doing?*

But storm it . . . the king tried. He actually tried. The man was arrogant, perhaps incapable, but he *tried.* He was sincere.

Kaladin stopped, exhausted, leg screaming, and leaned against the wall. Shouldn't this be easier? Now that he'd made the decision, shouldn't he be focused, confident, energized? He felt none of that. He felt wrung out, confused, and uncertain.

He pushed himself forward. *Keep going.* Almighty send that he wasn't too late.

Was he back to praying now?

He picked through darkened corridors. Shouldn't there be more light? With some difficulty, he reached the king's upper rooms, with the conference chamber and its balcony to the side. Two men in Bridge Four uniforms guarded the door, but Kaladin didn't recognize either of them. They weren't Bridge Four – they weren't even members of the old King's Guard. Storms.

Kaladin hobbled up to them, knowing he must look a sight, soaked through and through, limping on a leg that – he noticed – was trailing blood. He'd split the sutures on his wounds.

'Stop,' said one of the men. The fellow had a chin so cleft, it looked like he'd taken an axe to the face as a baby. He looked Kaladin up and down. 'You're the one they call Stormblessed.'

'You're Graves's men.'

The two looked at each other.

'It's all right,' Kaladin said. 'I'm with you. Is Moash here?'

'He's off for the moment,' the soldier said. 'Getting some sleep. It's an important day.'

I'm not too late, Kaladin thought. Luck was with him. 'I want to be part of what you're doing.'

'It's taken care of, bridgeman,' the guard said. 'Go back to your barrack and pretend nothing is happening.'

Kaladin leaned in close, as if to whisper something. The guard leaned forward.

So Kaladin dropped his crutch and slammed his spear up between the man's legs. Kaladin immediately turned, spinning on his good leg and dragging the other one, whipping his spear toward the other man.

The man got his spear up to block, and tried to shout. 'To arms! To—'

Kaladin slammed against him, knocking aside his spear. Kaladin dropped his own spear and grabbed the man by the neck with numb, wet fingers and cracked his head against the wall. Then he twisted and dropped, bringing his elbow down onto Cleft-chin's head, driving it down into the floor.

Both men fell still. Light-headed from the sudden exertion, Kaladin slammed himself back against the door. The world spun. At least he knew he could still fight without Stormlight.

He found himself laughing, though it turned into a cough. Had he really just attacked those men? He was committed now. Storms, he didn't even really know why he was doing this. The king's sincerity was part of it, but that wasn't the true reason, not deep down. He knew this was what he should do, but *why?* The thought of the king dying for no good reason made him sick. It reminded him of what had been done to Tien.

But that wasn't the full reason either. Storms, he wasn't making any sense, not even to himself.

Neither guard moved save for a few twitches. Kaladin coughed and coughed, gasping for breath. No time for weakness. He reached up a clawlike hand and twisted the door handle, forcing it open. He half fell into the room, then stumbled to his feet.

'Your Majesty?' he called, propping himself up on his spear and dragging his bad leg. He reached the back of a couch and used it to pull himself fully upright. Where was the—

The king lay on the couch, unmoving.

⁜

Adolin swept broadly with his Blade, maintaining perfect Windstance, the sword's point spraying water as he sheared through the neck of a Parshendi soldier. Red lightning crackled from the corpse in a bright flare, connecting the soldier to the ground as he died. Nearby Alethi were careful not to step in puddles beside the corpse. They had learned the hard way that this strange lightning could kill quickly via water.

Raising his sword and charging, Adolin led a rush against the nearest Parshendi group. Curse this storm and the winds that had brought it! Fortunately, the darkness had been pushed back somewhat, as Navani had sent fabrials to bathe the battlefield in an extraordinarily even white light.

Adolin and his team clashed again with the Parshendi. However, as soon as he got among the enemy, he felt something tug on his left arm. A loop of rope? He jerked back. No rope could hold Shardplate. He growled and yanked the rope free of the hands holding it. Then he jerked as another rope looped his neck and pulled him backward.

He shouted, spinning and sweeping his Blade through the rope, severing it. Three more loops leaped from the darkness for him; the Parshendi had sent an entire team. Adolin turned to defensive sweeps, as he'd been trained by Zahel to resist a dedicated rope strike. They'd have strung other ropes across the ground in front of him, expecting that he'd charge them . . . Yes, there they were.

Adolin backed away, slicing free the ropes that reached him. Unfortunately, his men had been depending on him to break the Parshendi line. As he backed away instead, the enemy pressed against the Alethi line in force. As always, they didn't use traditional battle formations, instead attacking in squads and pairs. That was frightfully effective on this chaotic, rainsoaked battlefield, with cracks of lightning and bursts of wind.

Perel, the field commander that he'd put in charge near the lights, called the retreat for Adolin's flank. Adolin let out a series of curses, cutting loose one final rope and stepping backward, sword out in case the Parshendi pursued.

They didn't. Two figures, however, shadowed him as he joined the retreat.

'Still alive, bridgemen?' Adolin asked.

'Still alive,' Skar said.

'You've got some loops of rope stuck to you still, sir,' Drehy said.

Adolin held out his arm and let Drehy cut them free with his side knife. Over his shoulder, Adolin watched the Parshendi re-form their lines. From farther back, the sound of that harsh chanting reached him between crashes of lightning and bursts of wind.

'They keep sending teams to engage and distract me,' Adolin said. 'They don't intend to defeat me; they just want to keep me out of the battle.'

'They'll have to really fight you sooner or later,' Drehy said, cutting off another of the ropes. Drehy reached up and ran his hand over his bald head, wiping the rain off. 'They can't just leave a Shardbearer alone.'

'Actually,' Adolin said, narrowing his eyes, listening to that chanting. 'That's exactly what they're doing.'

Through sheets of windborne rain, Adolin jogged in a clanking run up to the command position, near the lights. Perel – wrapped in a large stormcoat – stood there bellowing orders. He gave Adolin a quick salute.

'Status?' Adolin asked.

'Treading water, Brightlord.'

'I have no idea what that means,' Adolin said.

'Swimming term, sir,' Perel said. 'We're fighting back and forth, but we're not making any headway. We're fairly evenly matched; each side is looking for an edge. I'm most worried about those Parshendi reserves. They should have committed those by now.'

'The reserves?' Adolin asked, peering across the dim plateau. 'You mean the singers.' To both right and left, Alethi troops engaged other Parshendi units. Men shouted and screamed, weapons clashed, the familiar deadly sounds of a battlefield.

'Yes, sir,' Perel said. 'They're up against that rock formation at the middle of the plateau, singing their storming hearts out.'

Adolin remembered that rock outcropping, looming in the dim light. It was easily large enough for a battalion on top. 'Could we climb it from behind?'

'In this rain, Brightlord?' Perel asked. 'Not likely. Maybe *you* could, but would you really want to go alone?'

Adolin waited for the familiar eagerness to urge him forward, the desire to rush into the fight without concern for the consequences. He'd trained himself to resist that urge, and was surprised to find it . . . gone. Nothing.

He frowned. He was tired. Was that the reason? He considered the situation, thinking to the sound of rain on his helmet.

We need to get to those Parshendi at the back, he thought. *Father wants the reserves engaged, the song broken off . . .*

What had Shallan said about these inner plateaus? And the rock formations on them?

'Gather me a battalion,' Adolin said. 'A thousand men, heavy infantry. Once I've been gone with them for a half hour, send the rest of the men in a full assault against the Parshendi. I'm going to try something, and I want you to provide a distraction.'

'You're dead,' Dalinar shouted toward the sky. He spun about, still on the central plateau between the three battlefields, startling the aides and attendants near him. 'You told me you had been killed!'

Rain pelted his face. Were his ears playing tricks on him in this havoc of rain and shouting?

'I am not the Almighty,' the voice said. Dalinar turned, searching among his startled companions. Four bridgemen in stormcoats stepped back, as if frightened. His captains watched the clouds unsteadily, holding hands on swords.

'Did any of you hear that voice?' Dalinar asked.

Women and men alike shook heads.

'Are you ... hearing the Almighty?' asked one of the messenger women.

'Yes.' It was the simplest answer, though he wasn't sure what was happening. He continued to cross the central plateau, intending to check on Adolin's battlefront.

'I am sorry,' the voice repeated. Unlike in the visions, Dalinar could find no avatar speaking the words. They came out of nowhere. 'You have striven hard. But I can do nothing for you.'

'Who are you?' Dalinar hissed.

'I am the one left behind,' the voice said. It wasn't exactly as he'd heard it in the visions; this voice had a depth to it. A density. 'I am the sliver of Him that remains. I saw His corpse, saw Him die when Odium murdered Him. And I ... I fled. To continue as I always have. The piece of God left in this world, the winds that men must feel.'

Was he responding to Dalinar's question, or speaking a mere monologue? In the visions, Dalinar had originally assumed he was having conversations with this voice, only to find that its half of the seeming dialogue had been preset. He could not tell if this was the same or not.

Storms ... was he in the middle of a vision now? He froze in place, suddenly imagining a horrible picture of himself, sprawled on the floor of the palace, having imagined everything leading up to this battle in the rain.

No, he thought forcefully. *I will not travel down that path.* He had always recognized when he was in a vision before; he had no reason to believe that had changed.

The reserves he'd ordered for Aladar trotted past, spearmen with points toward the sky. That would be storming dangerous if real lightning came, but they didn't have much choice.

Dalinar waited for the voice to say more, but nothing happened. He proceeded, and soon approached Adolin's plateau.

Was that thunder?

No. Dalinar turned and picked out a horse galloping across the plateau toward him, a messenger on its back. He held up a hand, interrupting a tactical report by Captain Javih.

'Brightlord!' the messenger shouted. She reared the horse. 'Brightlord Teleb has fallen! Highprince Roion has been routed. His lines are broken, his remaining men surrounded by Parshendi! He's trapped on the northern plateau!'

'Damnation! Captain Khal?'

'Still up, fighting toward where Roion was last seen. He's nearly overwhelmed.'

Dalinar spun to Javih. 'Reserves?'

'I don't know what we have left,' the man said, face pale in the dim light. 'Depends on if any have rotated out.'

'Find out and bring them here!' Dalinar said, running to the messenger. 'Off,' he told her.

'Sir?'

'Off!'

The woman scrambled from the saddle as Dalinar placed foot into stirrup and swung into position. He turned the horse – thankful, for once, he didn't have on any Shardplate. This light horse wouldn't have been able to carry him.

'Gather whatever you can and follow!' he shouted. 'I need men, even if you have to pull that battalion of spearmen back from Aladar.'

Captain Javih's reply was lost in the rain as Dalinar leaned low and cued the horse with his heels. The animal snorted, and Dalinar had to fight it before getting it to move. The pops of lightning in the distance had the creature skittish.

Once pointed the right direction, he gave the horse its head, and it galloped eagerly. Dalinar crossed the plateau in a rush, triage tents, command posts, and food stations passing in a blur. As he neared the northern plateau, he reined in the horse and scanned the area for Navani.

No sign of her, though he did see several large tarps laid on the ground here – expansive squares of black cloth. She'd been at work. He called a question to an engineer, and she pointed, so Dalinar rode along the chasm in that direction. He passed a succession of other tarps that had been arranged on the stone.

Across the chasm to his left, men died with shouts and screams. He saw firsthand how terribly Roion's battle was progressing. The danger was manifest in broken groups of men flying beleaguered banners, split into vulnerable small bunches by red-eyed enemies. The Alethi would fight on, but with their line fragmenting, their prospects were grim.

Dalinar remembered fighting like that himself two months ago, surrounded by a sea of enemies, without hope for salvation. Dalinar pushed his horse faster, and soon spotted Navani. She stood beneath an umbrella directing a group of workers with another large tarp.

'Navani!' Dalinar shouted, pulling his horse to a slippery stop across the tarp from her. 'I need a miracle!'

'Working on it,' she shouted back.

'No time for working. Execute your plan. *Now*.'

He was too distant to see her glare, but he felt it. Fortunately, she waved workers away from her current tarp and began shouting orders to her engineers. The women ran up to the chasm, where a line of rocks was arrayed. They were attached to ropes, Dalinar thought, though he wasn't sure how this process worked. Navani shouted instructions.

Too much time, Dalinar thought, anxious, watching across the chasm. Had they recovered Teleb's Plate and the King's Blade he was wielding? He couldn't spare grief for the man, not now. They *needed* those Shards.

Behind Dalinar, soldiers gathered. Roion's archers, finest in the warcamps, had been useless in this rain. The engineers backed up at a barked order from Navani, and the workers shoved the line of some forty rocks into the chasm.

As the rocks fell, tarps jumped fifty feet into the air, pulled at the front corners and centers. In an instant, a long line of improvised pavilions flanked the chasm.

'Move!' Dalinar said, urging his horse between two of the pavilions. 'Archers forward!'

Men dashed into the protected areas under the tarps, some muttering at the lack of any visible poles holding them in the air. Navani had pulled up only the fronts, so the tarps slanted backward, away from the chasm. The rain streamed down in that direction. They also had sides, like tents, so only the open faces were toward Roion's battlefront.

Dalinar swung from the horse and handed the reins to a worker. He jogged under one of the pavilions to where archers were forming ranks. Navani entered, carrying a large sack over her shoulder. She opened it to reveal a large glowing garnet suspended within a delicate wire lacework fabrial.

She fiddled with it for a moment, then stepped back.

'We really should have had more time to test this,' she warned to Dalinar, folding her arms. 'Attractors are new inventions. I'm still half afraid this thing will suck the blood out of anyone who touches it.'

It didn't. Instead, water quickly started to pool around the thing. Storms, it worked! The fabrial was pulling moisture from the air. Roion's archers removed bowstrings from protected pockets, bending bows and stringing them at the orders of their lieutenants. Many of the men here were lighteyes – archery was seen as an acceptable Calling for a lighteyed man of modest means. Not everyone could be an officer.

The archers began loosing waves of arrows across the chasm into the Parshendi who had surrounded Roion's forces. 'Good,' Dalinar said, watching the arrows fly. 'Very good.'

'The rain and wind are still going to make aiming the arrows difficult,' Navani said. 'And I don't know how well the fabrials will work; with the front of the pavilions open, humidity is going to flood in constantly. We might run out of Stormlight after just a short time.'

'It's enough,' Dalinar said. The arrows made an almost immediate difference, drawing Parshendi attention away from the beleaguered men. It wasn't a maneuver to try unless you were desperate – the risk of hitting allies was great – but Roion's archers proved deserving of their reputation.

He pulled Navani close with one arm. 'You did well.' Then he called for his horse – *his* horse, not that wild messenger beast – as he charged out of the pavilion. Those archers would give him an opening. Hopefully it wasn't too late for Roion.

No! Kaladin thought, rounding the couch to the king's side. Was he dead? There was no obvious wound.

The king shifted, then groaned in a lazy way and sat upright. Kaladin let out a deep breath. An empty wine bottle rested on the end table, and Kaladin could smell the spilled wine now that he was closer.

'Bridgeman?' Elhokar's speech was slurred. 'Have you come to gloat over me?'

'Storms, Elhokar,' Kaladin said. 'How much have you had?'

'They all . . . they *all* talk about me,' Elhokar said, flopping down on the couch. 'My own guards . . . every one. Bad king, they say. Everyone hates him, they say.'

Kaladin felt a chill. 'They wanted you to drink, Elhokar. Makes their job easier.'

'Huh?'

Storms. The man was barely conscious.

'Come on,' Kaladin said. 'Assassins are coming for you. We're getting out of here.'

'Assassins?' Elhokar leapt to his feet, then wobbled. 'He wears white. I knew he'd come . . . but then . . . he only cared about Dalinar . . . Not even the assassin thinks I'm worthy of the throne. . . .'

Kaladin managed to get under Elhokar's arm, holding his spear for support with one hand. The king slumped against him, and Kaladin's leg cried out. 'Please, Your Majesty,' Kaladin said, almost collapsing, 'I need you to try to walk.'

'Assassins probably want you, bridgeman,' the king muttered. 'You're more a leader than I am. I wish . . . wish you'd teach me . . .'

Thankfully, Elhokar then did support himself to an extent. It was a struggle to walk the two of them to the doorway, where the guard's body still lay—

Body? Where was the other one?

Kaladin twisted out of the king's grip as a blur with a knife lunged at him. By instinct, Kaladin snapped his spear haft back – bringing his hands up near to the head for a close-quarters fight – then thrust. The spearhead sank in deep into Cleft-chin's stomach. The man grunted.

But he *hadn't* been lunging for Kaladin.

He'd plunged his knife into the king's side.

Cleft-chin flopped to the floor, falling off Kaladin's spear and dropping his knife. Elhokar reached – a stunned expression on his face – to his side. The hand came away bloody. 'I'm dead,' Elhokar whispered, regarding the blood.

In that moment, Kaladin's pain and weakness seemed to fade. The moment of panic was a moment of strength, and he used it to rip at Elhokar's clothing while kneeling on his good leg. The knife had glanced off a rib. The king was bleeding heavily, but it was a very survivable wound, with medical attention.

'Keep pressure on that,' Kaladin said, pushing a cut section of the king's shirt against the wound, then placing the king's hand over it. 'We need to get out of the palace. Find safety somewhere.' The dueling grounds, maybe? The ardents could be relied upon, and they could fight too. But would that be too obvious?

Well, first they had to actually get out of the palace. Kaladin grabbed his spear and turned to lead the way out, but his leg nearly betrayed him. He managed to catch himself, but it left him gasping in pain, clinging to his spear to keep from falling.

Storms. Was that pool of blood at his feet *his*? He'd ripped his sutures out, and then some.

'I was wrong,' the king said. 'We're both dead.'

'Fleet kept running,' Kaladin growled, getting back under Elhokar's arm.

'What?'

'He couldn't win, but he kept running. And when the storm caught him, it didn't matter that he'd died, because he'd run for all he had.'

'Sure. All right.' The king sounded groggy, though Kaladin couldn't tell if it was the alcohol or the blood loss.

'We all die in the end, you see,' Kaladin said. The two of them walked down the corridor, Kaladin leaning on his spear to keep them upright. 'So I guess what truly matters is just how well you've run. And Elhokar, you've kept running since your father was killed, even if you screw up all the *storming* time.'

'Thank you?' the king said, drowsy.

They reached an intersection, and Kaladin decided on escaping through the bowels of the palace complex, rather than the front gates. It was equally fast, but might not be the first place the plotters would look.

The palace was empty. Moash had done as he'd said, sending the servants away into hiding, using the precedent of the Assassin in White's attack. It *was* a perfect plan.

'Why?' the king whispered. 'Shouldn't you hate me?'

'I don't like you, Elhokar,' Kaladin said. 'But that doesn't mean it's right to let you die.'

'You said I should step down. Why, bridgeman? Why help me?'

I don't know.

They turned down a hallway, but only made it about halfway before the king stopped walking and slumped to the ground. Kaladin cursed, kneeling beside Elhokar, checking his pulse and the wound.

This is the wine, Kaladin decided. That, plus the blood loss, left the king too light-headed.

Bad. Kaladin worked to rebind the wound as best he could, but then what? Try to pull the king out on a litter? Go for help, and risk leaving him alone?

'Kaladin?'

Kaladin froze, still kneeling over the king.

'Kaladin, what are you *doing*?' Moash's voice demanded from behind. 'We found the men at the door to the king's room. Storms, did *you* kill them?'

Kaladin rose and turned, putting his weight on his good leg. Moash stood at the other end of the corridor, resplendent in his blue and red Shardplate. Another Shardbearer accompanied him, Blade up on the shoulder of his Plate, faceplate down. Graves.

The assassins had arrived.

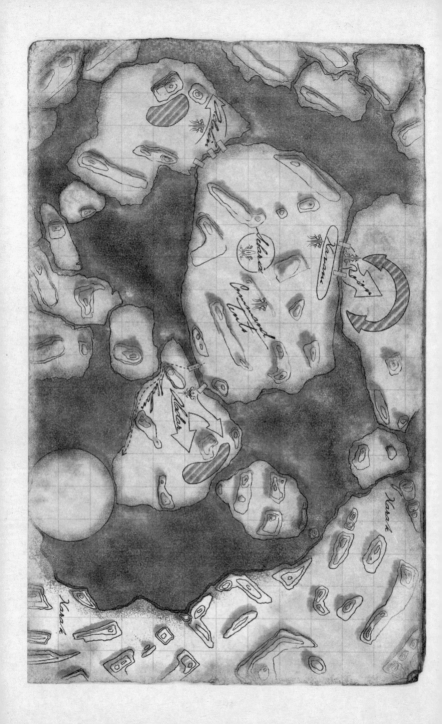

83

TIME'S ILLUSION

Obviously they are fools The Desolation needs no usher It can and will sit where it wishes and the signs are obvious that the spren anticipate it doing so soon The Ancient of Stones must finally begin to crack It is a wonder that upon his will rested the prosperity and peace of a world for over four millennia

—From the Diagram, Book of the 2nd Ceiling Rotation: pattern 1

S hallan stepped off the bridge onto a deserted plateau.

The rain muffled the sounds of warfare, making the area feel even more isolated. Darkness like dusk. Rainfall like hushed whispers.

This plateau was higher than most, so she could see Stormseat's center arrayed around her. Pillars with crem accreting at their bases, transforming them to stalagmites. Buildings that had become mounds, overgrown with stone like snow covering a fallen log. In the darkness and rain, the ancient city presented a sketch of skyline for the imagination to fill in.

This city hid beneath time's own illusion.

The others followed her across the bridge. They'd skirted the fighting on Aladar's battlefront, slipping along the Alethi lines to attain this farther plateau. Getting up here had taken time, as the bridgemen had needed to locate a usable landing. They'd had to climb a slope on the adjoining plateau and place their bridge there to get across the chasm.

'How can you be sure this is the right place?' Renarin asked, clinking down onto the plateau beside her. Shallan had opted for an umbrella, but Renarin stood in the rain, helm under his arm, letting the water stream down his face. Didn't he wear spectacles? She hadn't seen them on him much lately.

'It is the right place,' Shallan said, 'because it's deviant.'

'That's hardly a logical conclusion,' Inadara said, joining the two of them as soldiers and bridgemen crossed to the empty plateau. 'A portal of this nature would be kept hidden; it would not be deviant.'

'The Oathgates were not hidden,' Shallan said. 'That is beside the point, however. This plateau is a circle.'

'Many are circular.'

'Not *this* circular,' Shallan said, striding forward. Now that she was here, she could see just how irregularly . . . well, *regular* the plateau was. 'I was looking for a dais on a plateau, but didn't realize the scale of what I was searching for. This entire *plateau* is the dais upon which the Oathgate sat.

'Don't you see? The other plateaus were created by some kind of disaster – they are jagged, broken. This place is not. That's because it was *already here* when the shattering happened. On the old maps it was a raised section, like a giant pedestal. When the Plains were broken, it remained this way.'

'Yes . . .' Renarin said, nodding. 'Imagine a plate with a circle etched into the center . . . if a force shattered the plate, it might break along the already weakened lines.'

'Leaving you with a bunch of irregular pieces,' Shallan agreed, 'and one shaped like a circle.'

'Perhaps,' Inadara said. 'But I find it odd that something so tactically important would be exposed.'

'The Oathgates were a symbol,' Shallan said, continuing to walk. 'The Vorin Right of Travel, given to all citizens of sufficient rank, is based on the Heralds' declaration that all borders should be open. If you were going to create a symbol of that unity – a portal that connected all of the Silver Kingdoms together – where would you put it? Hidden in a locked room? Or on a stage that rose above the city? It was out here because they were proud of it.'

They continued through the blowing rain. There was a hallowed quality to this place, and honestly, that was part of how she knew she was right.

'Mmmm,' Pattern said softly. 'They are raising a storm.'

'The Voidspren?' Shallan whispered.

'The bonded ones. They craft a storm.'

Right. Her task was urgent; she didn't have time to stand around thinking. She was about to order the search begun, but paused as she noticed Renarin staring westward, his eyes distant.

'Prince Renarin?' she asked.

'The wrong way,' he whispered. 'The wind is blowing from the *wrong direction*. West to east . . . Oh, Almighty above. It's terrible.'

She followed his gaze, but could see nothing.

'It's actually real,' Renarin said. 'The Everstorm.'

'What are you talking about?' Shallan asked, feeling a chill at the tone of his voice.

'I . . .' He looked to her and wiped the water from his eyes, gauntlet hanging from his waist. 'I should be with my father. I should be able to fight. Only I'm useless.'

Great. He was creepy *and* whiny. 'Well, your father ordered you to help me, so deal with your issues. Everyone, let's search this place.'

'What are we looking for, cousin?' asked Rock, one of the bridgemen.

Cousin, she thought. *Cute*. Because of the red hair. 'I don't know,' she said. 'Anything strange, out of the ordinary.'

They split up and spread out across the plateau. Along with Inadara, Shallan had a small group of ardents and scholars to help her, including one of Dalinar's stormwardens. She sent teams of several scholars, one bridgeman, and one soldier each in different directions.

Renarin and the majority of the bridgemen insisted on going with her. She couldn't complain about that – this *was* a war zone. Shallan passed a lump on the ground, part of a large ring. Perhaps once a low ornamental wall. How would this place have looked? She pictured it in her mind, and wished she could have drawn it. That would certainly have helped her visualize.

Where would the portal be? Most likely at the center, so that was the direction she went. There she found a large stone mound.

'This is all?' Rock asked. 'He is just more rock.'

'That is exactly what I was hoping to find,' Shallan said. 'Anything exposed to the air would have weathered away or become immured with crem. If we're to discover anything useful, it will have to be inside.'

'Inside?' asked one of the bridgemen. 'Inside what?'

'The buildings,' Shallan said, feeling at the wall until she found a ripple in the back of the rock. She turned to Renarin. 'Prince Renarin, would you kindly slay this rock for me?'

．•．

Adolin raised his sphere in the dark chamber, shining light on the wall. After so long outdoors in the Weeping, it felt strange *not* to have rain tapping against his helm. The musty air in this place was already growing humid, and even with the shuffling of soldiers and men coughing, Adolin felt like it was too silent. Within this rocky tomb, they may as well have been miles away from the battlefield just outside.

'How did you know, sir?' asked Skar, the bridgeman. 'How'd you guess that this rock mound would be hollow?'

'Because a clever woman,' Adolin said, 'once asked me to attack a boulder for her.'

Together, he and these men had circled to the other side of the large rock formation that the chanting Parshendi were using to guard their backs. With a few twists of the Shardblade, Adolin had cut an entrance into the mound, which had proven to be hollow as he'd hoped.

He picked his way through the dusty chambers, passing bones and dried debris that might once have been furniture. Presumably it had rotted away before the crem had finished sealing the building. Had it been a kind of communal dwelling, long ago? Or perhaps a market? It did have a lot of rooms; many doorways still bore rusted hinges that had once held doors.

A thousand men moved through the building with him, holding lanterns that carried large cut gems – five times bigger than broams, though even some of those were starting to fail, as it had been so long since a highstorm.

A thousand men was a large number to navigate through these eerie confines. But, unless he was completely off, they should now be approaching the opposite wall – the one just behind the Parshendi. Some of his men scouted nearby rooms, and came back with the confirmation. The building ended here. Adolin now saw the outlines of windows, sealed up with crem that had spilled in through gaps over the years, dribbling down the wall and piling on the floor.

'All right,' he called out to the company commanders and their captains. 'Let's gather everyone we can in this room here and the hall right outside. I'll cut an exit hole. As soon as it's open, we need to spill out and attack those singing Parshendi.

'First Company, you split to either side and secure this exit. Don't get pushed back! I'll charge and try to draw attention. Everyone else move through and join the assault as quickly as you can manage.'

The men nodded. Adolin took a deep breath, then closed his faceplate and stepped up to the wall. They were on the second floor of the building, but he estimated the buildup of crem outside would place that at about ground level. Indeed, from outside he heard a faint sound. Humming, resonating through the wall.

Storms, the Parshendi were *right there*. He summoned his Blade, waited until the company commanders passed the word back that their men were ready, then hacked at the wall in several long ribbons. He sliced it the other way with sweeping blows, then slammed his Plate shoulder into it.

The wall broke down and fell out, stone blocks cascading away from him. The rain returned in force. He was only a few feet off the ground, and he eagerly pushed his way out onto the slick wet rocks. Just to his left, Parshendi reserves stood in rows facing away from him, absorbed in their chanting. The clamor of battle was nearly inaudible here, all but drowned out by the spine-tingling sound of that inhuman singing.

Perfect. The rain and chanting had covered the noise of the hole opening. He hacked open another hole as men spilled out from the first one, bearing lights. He began to open a third exit, but heard a shout. One of the Parshendi had finally noticed him. She was female – with this new form of theirs, that was more obvious than it had been before.

He charged the short distance to the Parshendi and launched himself into their ranks, sweeping lethally with his Blade. Bodies fell dead with burned eyes. Five, then ten. His soldiers joined him, thrusting spears into the Parshendi, cutting off their awful song.

It was shockingly easy. These Parshendi abandoned their song reluctantly, coming out of their trance disoriented and confused. Those who fought did so without coordination, and Adolin's swift attack didn't allow time for them to summon their strange sparking energy.

It was like killing sleeping men. Adolin had done dirty work with his Shards before. Damnation, any time you took the field with Plate and Blade against ordinary men, you did dirty work – slaughtering those who might as well have been children with sticks. This was worse though. Often they'd come to just before he killed them – blinking to consciousness, shaking themselves awake, only to find themselves face-to-face with a full Shardbearer in the rain, murdering their friends. Those looks of horror haunted Adolin as he sent corpse after corpse to the ground.

Where was the Thrill that usually propelled him through this kind of butchery? He needed it. Instead, he felt only nausea. Standing amid a field of the newly dead – the acrid smoke of burned-out eyes curling up through the rain – he trembled and dropped his Blade in disgust. It vanished to mist.

Something crashed into him from behind.

He lurched over a corpse – stumbling but keeping his feet – and spun about. A Shardblade smashed against his chest, spreading a glowing web of cracks across his breastplate. He deflected the next blow with his forearm and stepped back, taking a battle stance.

She stood before him, rain streaming from her armor. What had she named herself? Eshonai.

Inside his helm, Adolin grinned at the Shardbearer. *This* he could do. An honest fight. He raised his hands, the Shardblade forming from mist as he swung upward and deflected her attack in a sweeping parry.

Thank you, he thought.

❖

Dalinar rode Gallant back across the bridge from Roion's plateau, nursing a bloody wound at his side. Stupid. He should have seen that spear. He'd been too focused on that red lightning and the quickly shifting Parshendi fighting pairs.

The truth, Dalinar thought, sliding from his horse so a surgeon could inspect the wound, *is that you're an old man now.* Perhaps not by the measuring of lifespans, as he was only in his fifties, but by the yardstick of soldiers he was *certainly* old. Without Shardplate to assist, he was getting slow, getting weak. Killing was a young man's game, if only because the old men fell first.

That cursed rain kept coming, so he escaped it under one of Navani's pavilions. The archers kept the Parshendi from following across the chasm to harry Roion's beleaguered retreat. With the help of the bowmen, Dalinar had successfully saved the highprince's army, half of it at least – but they'd lost the entire northern plateau. Roion rode across to safety, followed by an exhausted Captain Khal on foot – General Khal's son wore his own Plate and bore the King's Blade that he'd blessedly recovered from Teleb's corpse after the other man had fallen.

They'd been forced to leave the body, and the Plate. Just as bad, the Parshendi singing continued unabated. Despite the soldiers saved, this was a terrible defeat.

Dalinar undid his breastplate and sat down with a grunt as the surgeon ordered him a stool. He suffered the woman's ministration, though he knew the wound was not terrible. It was bad – any wound was bad on the battlefield, particularly if it impaired the sword arm – but it wouldn't kill him.

'Storms,' the surgeon said. 'Highprince, you're all scars under here. How many times have you been wounded in the shoulder?'

'Can't remember.'

'How can you still use your arm?'

'Training and practice.'

'That's not how it works ...' she whispered, eyes wide. 'I mean ... storms ...'

'Just sew the thing up,' he said. 'Yes, I'll stay off the battlefield today. No, I won't stress it. Yes, I've heard all the lectures before.'

He shouldn't have been out there in the first place. He'd told himself he wouldn't ride into battle anymore. He was supposed to be a politician now, not a warlord.

But once in a while, the Blackthorn needed to come out. The men needed it. Storms, *he* needed it. The—

Navani thundered into the tent.

Too late. He sighed as she stalked up to him, passing this tent's fabrial – which glowed on a little pedestal, collecting water around it in a shimmering globe. That water streamed off along two metal rods at the sides of the fabrial, spilling onto the ground, then running out of the tent and over the plateau's edge.

He looked up at Navani grimly, expecting to be dressed down like a recruit who had forgotten his whetstone. Instead, she took him by his good side, then pulled him close.

'No reprimand?' Dalinar asked.

'We're at war,' she whispered. 'And we're losing, aren't we?'

Dalinar glanced at the archers, who were running low on arrows. He didn't speak too loudly, lest they hear. 'Yes.' The surgeon glanced at him, then lowered her head and kept sewing.

'You rode to battle when someone needed you,' Navani said. 'You saved the lives of a highprince and his soldiers. Why would you expect anger from me?'

'Because you're you.' He reached up with his good hand and ran his fingers through her hair.

'Adolin has won his plateau,' Navani said. 'The Parshendi there are scattered and routed. Aladar holds. Roion has failed, but we're still evenly matched. So how are we losing? I can sense that we are, from your face, but I don't see it.'

'An even match is a loss for us,' Dalinar said. He could *feel* it building. Distant, to the west. 'If they complete that song, then as Rlain warned, that is the end.'

The surgeon finished as best she could, wrapping the wound and giving Dalinar leave to replace his shirt and coat, which would hold the bandage tight. Once dressed, he climbed to his feet, intending to go to the command tent and get an update on the situation from General Khal. He was interrupted as Roion burst into the pavilion.

'Dalinar!' the tall, balding man rushed in, grabbing him by the arm. The bad one. Dalinar winced. 'It's a storming bloodbath out there! We're dead. Storms, we're dead!'

Nearby archers shuffled, their arrows spent. A sea of red eyes gathered on the plateau across the chasm, smoldering coals in the darkness.

For all that Dalinar wanted to slap Roion, that wasn't the sort of thing you did to a highprince, even a hysterical one. Instead, he towed Roion out of the pavilion. The rain – now a full-blown storm – felt icy as it washed over his soaked uniform.

'Control yourself, Brightlord,' Dalinar said sternly. 'Adolin has won his plateau. Not all is as bad as it seems.'

'It should not end this way,' the Almighty said.

Storm it! Dalinar shoved Roion away and strode out into the center of the plateau, looking up toward the sky. 'Answer me! Let me know if you can hear me!'

'I can.'

Finally. Some progress. 'Are you the Almighty?'

'I said I am not, child of Honor.'

'Then what are you?'

I AM THAT WHICH BRINGS LIGHT AND DARKNESS. The voice took on more of a rumbling, distant quality.

'The Stormfather,' Dalinar said. 'Are you a Herald?'

No.

'Then are you a spren or a god?'

BOTH.

'What is the point of talking to me?' Dalinar shouted at the sky. 'What is happening?'

THEY CALL FOR A STORM. MY OPPOSITE. DEADLY.

'How do we stop it?'

YOU DON'T.

'There has to be a way!'

I BRING YOU A STORM OF CLEANSING. IT WILL CARRY AWAY YOUR CORPSES. THIS IS ALL I CAN DO.

'No! Don't you *dare* abandon us!'

YOU MAKE DEMANDS OF ME, YOUR GOD?

'You aren't my god. You were *never* my god! You are a shadow, a lie!'

Distant thunder rumbled ominously. The rain beat harder against Dalinar's face.

I AM CALLED. I MUST GO. A DAUGHTER DISOBEYS. YOU WILL SEE NO FURTHER VISIONS, CHILD OF HONOR. THIS IS THE END.

FAREWELL.

'Stormfather!' Dalinar yelled. 'There has to be a way! I will not die here!'

Silence. Not even thunder. People had gathered around Dalinar: soldiers, scribes, messengers, Roion and Navani. Frightened people.

'Don't abandon us,' Dalinar said, voice trailing off. 'Please . . .'

⁂

Moash stepped forward, his faceplate up, his face pained. 'Kaladin?'

'I had to make the choice that would let me sleep at night, Moash,'

Kaladin said wearily, standing before the unconscious form of the king. Blood pooled around Kaladin's boot from the wounds he'd reopened. Light-headed, he had to lean on his spear to keep on his feet.

'You said he was trustworthy,' Graves said, turning toward Moash, his voice ringing inside his Shardplate helm. 'You promised me, Moash!'

'Kaladin *is* trustworthy,' Moash said. It was just the three of them – four, if you counted the king – standing in a lonely hallway of the palace.

This would be a sad place to die. A place away from the wind.

'He's just a little confused,' Moash said, stepping forward. 'This will still work. You didn't tell anyone, right, Kal?'

I recognize this hallway, Kaladin realized. *It's the very place we fought the Assassin in White.* To his left, windows lined the wall, though shutters kept out the light rainfall. Yes ... there. He spotted where planks had been installed over the hole that the assassin had cut through the wall. The place where Kaladin had fallen into blackness.

Back here again. He took a deep breath and steadied himself as best he could on his good leg, then raised the spear, point toward Moash.

Storms, his leg hurt.

'Kal, the king is obviously wounded,' Moash said. 'We followed your trail of blood here. He's practically dead already.'

Trail of blood. Kaladin blinked bleary eyes. Of course. His thoughts were coming slowly. He should have caught that.

Moash stopped a few feet from Kaladin, just out of easy striking range with the spear. 'What are you going to do, Kal?' Moash demanded, looking at the spear pointed toward him. 'Would you really attack a member of Bridge Four?'

'You left Bridge Four the moment you turned against our duty,' Kaladin whispered.

'And you're different?'

'No, I'm not,' Kaladin said, feeling a hollowness in his stomach. 'But I'm trying to change that.'

Moash took another step forward, but Kaladin pushed the spear point upward, toward Moash's face. His friend hesitated, raising his gauntleted hands in a warding gesture.

Graves moved forward, but Moash shooed him away, then turned to Kaladin. 'What do you think this will accomplish, Kal? If you get in our way, you'll just get yourself killed, and the king will still be dead. You want me to know you don't agree with this? Fine. You tried. Now you're over-matched, and there is no point in fighting. Put down the spear.'

Kaladin glanced over his shoulder. The king was still breathing.

Moash's armor clinked. Kaladin turned back, raising the spear again. Storms . . . his head was really throbbing now.

'I mean it, Kal,' Moash said.

'You'd attack me?' Kaladin said. 'Your captain? Your *friend*?'

'Don't turn this around on me.'

'Why not? Which is more important to you? Me or petty vengeance?'

'He *murdered* them, Kaladin,' Moash snapped. 'That sorry excuse for a king killed the only family I ever had.'

'I know.'

'Then why are you protecting him?'

'It wasn't his fault.'

'That's a load of—'

'It *wasn't his fault*,' Kaladin said. 'But I'd be here even if it had been, Moash! We have to be better than this, you and I. It's . . . I can't explain it, not perfectly. You have to trust me. Back down. The king hasn't yet seen you or Graves. We'll go to Dalinar, and I'll see that you get justice against the *right* man, Roshone, the one truly behind your grandparents' deaths.

'But Moash, we're *not* going to be this kind of men. Murders in dark corridors, killing a drunk man because we find him distasteful, telling ourselves it's for the good of the kingdom. If I kill a man, I'm going to do it in the sunlight, and I'm going to do it only because there is no other way.'

Moash hesitated. Graves clinked up beside him, but again Moash raised a hand, stopping him. Moash met Kaladin's eyes, then shook his head. 'Sorry, Kal. It's too late.'

'You won't have him. I won't back down.'

'I guess I wouldn't want you to.' Moash slammed his faceplate down, the sides misting as it sealed.

84

THE ONE WHO SAVES

11182510111271249151210101114102151171121011121713448311107151425414 3410
91614914934121225410101251271015191011123412551152512157551112341011 12
91512106 1534

—From the Diagram, Book of the 2nd Ceiling Rotation: pattern 15

The stone block slid inward, confirming Shallan's deduction. They had opened a building that hadn't been entered, or even seen, for centuries. Renarin stepped back from the hole he'd made, giving Shallan a chance to step forward. The air from inside smelled stale, musty. Renarin dismissed his Blade, and oddly, as he did so, he let out a relieved sigh and relaxed against the outer wall of the building. Shallan moved to enter, but the bridgemen slipped in front of her to check the building's safety first, raising sapphire lanterns.

The light revealed majesty.

Shallan's breath caught in her throat. The large, circular room was a space worthy of a palace or temple. A mosaic mural covered the wall and floor with majestic images and dazzling color. Knights in armor stood before swirling skies of red and blue. People from all walks of life were depicted in all manner of settings, each crafted from vivid colors of every kind of stone – a masterwork that brought the whole world into one room.

Worried she'd damage the portal somehow, she'd placed Renarin's cuts near a ripple that she had hoped indicated a doorway, and it seemed that she'd been correct. She entered through the hole and walked a curving path through the circular chamber, silently counting the divisions in the floor mural. There were ten main ones, just as there had been ten orders of knights, ten kingdoms, ten peoples. And then – between the segments representing the first and tenth kingdoms – was a narrower eleventh section. It depicted a tall tower. Urithiru.

She'd found it, the portal. And this artwork! Such beauty. It was breathtaking.

No, there wasn't time to admire art right now. The large floor mosaic swirled around the center, but the swords of each knight pointed toward the same area of the wall, so Shallan walked in that direction. Everything in here seemed perfectly preserved, even the lamps on the walls, which appeared to still hold dun gemstones.

On the wall, she found a metal disc set into the stone. Was this steel? It hadn't rusted or even tarnished despite its long abandonment.

'It's coming,' Renarin announced from the other side of the room, his quiet voice echoing across the domed chamber. Storms, that boy was disturbing, particularly when accompanied by a howling storm and the sound of rain pelting the plateau outside.

Brightness Inadara and several scholars arrived. Stepping into the chamber, they gasped and then began talking over one another as they rushed to examine the mural.

Shallan studied the strange disc set into the wall. It was shaped like a ten-pointed star and had a thin slot directly in the center. *The Radiants could operate this place,* she thought. *And what did the Radiants have that nobody else did?* Many things, but the shape of that slot in the metal gave her a pretty good guess why only they could make the Oathgate work.

'Renarin, get over here,' Shallan said.

The boy clomped in her direction.

'Shallan,' Pattern said warningly. 'Time is very short. They have summoned the Everstorm. And . . . and there's something else, coming from the other direction. A highstorm?'

'It's the Weeping,' Shallan said, looking to Pattern, who dimpled the wall just beside the steel disc. 'No highstorms.'

'One is coming anyway. Shallan, they're going to hit together. Two storms coming, one from each direction. They will crash into one another *right here.*'

'I don't suppose they'll just, you know, cancel each other out?'

'They will feed one another,' Pattern said. 'It will be like two waves hitting with their peaks coinciding ... it will create a storm like none the world has ever seen. Stone will shatter, plateaus themselves might collapse. It's going to be bad. Very, *very* bad.'

Shallan looked to Inadara, who had walked up beside her. 'Thoughts?'

'I don't know what to think, Brightness,' Inadara said. 'You were right about this place. I ... I no longer trust myself to judge what is correct and what is false.'

'We need to move the armies to this plateau,' Shallan said. 'Even if they defeat the Parshendi, they're doomed unless we can make this portal work.'

'It doesn't *look* like a portal at all,' Inadara said. 'What will it do? Open a doorway in the wall?'

'I don't know,' Shallan said, looking to Renarin. 'Summon your Shardblade.'

He did so, wincing as it appeared. Shallan pointed at the slot like a keyhole in the wall – acting on a hunch. 'See if you can scratch that metal with your Blade. Be *very* careful. We don't want to ruin the Oathgate, in case I'm wrong.'

Renarin stepped up and carefully – using his hand to pinch the weapon from above – placed the tip of the blade on the metal around the keyhole. He grunted as the Blade wouldn't cut. He tried a little harder, and the metal resisted the Blade.

'Made of the same stuff!' Shallan said, growing excited. 'And that slot is shaped like it might fit a Blade. Try sliding the weapon in, very slowly.'

He did so, and as the point moved into the hole, the entire *shape* of the keyhole shifted, the metal flowing to match the shape of Renarin's Shardblade. It was working! He got the weapon placed, and they turned around, looking over the chamber. Nothing appeared to have changed.

'Did that do anything?' Renarin asked.

'It has to have,' Shallan said. They'd unlocked a door, perhaps. But how to turn the equivalent of the doorknob?

'We need Highlady Navani to help,' Shallan said. 'More importantly, we need to bring everyone here. Go, soldiers, bridgemen! Run and tell

Dalinar to gather his armies on this plateau. Tell him that if he doesn't, they are doomed. The rest of you scholars, we're going to put our heads together and figure out how this storming thing works.'

·◦·

Adolin danced through the storm, trading blows with Eshonai. She was good, though she didn't use stances he recognized. She dodged back and forth, feeling him out with her Blade, bursting through the storm like a crackling thunderbolt.

Adolin kept after her, sweeping with his Shardblade, forcing her away. A duel. He could win a duel. Even in the middle of a storm, even against a monster, this was something he could *do*. He backed her away across the battlefield, closer to where his armies had crossed the chasm to join this battle.

She was difficult to maneuver. He had only met this Eshonai twice, but he felt he knew her through the way she fought. He sensed her eagerness for blood. Her eagerness to kill. The Thrill. He did not feel it himself. He sensed it in her.

Around him, Parshendi fled or fought in pockets as his men harried them. He passed a Parshendi, forced to the ground by soldiers, being gutted in the rain as he tried to crawl away. Water and blood splashed on the plateau, frantic yells sounding amid the thunder.

Thunder. Distant thunder from the west. Adolin glanced in that direction, and nearly lost his concentration. He could *see* it building, wind and rain spinning in a gigantic pillar, flashing red.

Eshonai swung for him, and Adolin turned back, blocking the blow with his forearm. That section of his Plate was getting weak, the cracks leaking Stormlight. He stepped into the blow and swung his own Blade, one-handed, into Eshonai's side. He was rewarded by a grunt. She didn't fold, though. She didn't even step back. She raised her Blade and smashed it down against his forearm yet again.

The Plate there exploded in a flash of light and molten metal. Storms. Adolin was forced to pull the arm back and release the gauntlet – now too heavy, without the connecting Plate to help it – letting it drop off his hand. The wind that blew against his exposed skin was startlingly powerful.

A little more, Adolin thought, not backing away despite the lost section of Plate. He grabbed his Shardblade in two hands – one metal, the other flesh – and battered forward with a series of strikes. He transitioned out of Windstance. No sweeping majesty for him. He needed the frantic fury of Flamestance. Not just for the power, but because of what he needed to convey to Eshonai.

Eshonai growled, forced backward. 'Your day has ended, destroyer,' she said inside her helm. 'Today, your brutality turns against you. Today, extinction turns from us to you.'

A little more.

Adolin pressed her with a burst of swordplay, then he flagged, presenting her with an opening. She took it immediately, swinging for his helm, which leaked from an earlier blow. Yes, she was fully caught up in the Thrill. That lent her energy and strength, but it drove her to recklessness. To ignore her surroundings.

Adolin took the hit to the head and stumbled. Eshonai laughed with glee and moved to swing again.

Adolin lunged forward and slammed his shoulder and head into her chest. His helm exploded from the force of it, but his gambit succeeded.

Eshonai had not noticed how close they were to the chasm.

His shove threw her over the plateau's edge. He felt Eshonai's panic, heard her shout, as she was dropped into the open blackness.

Unfortunately, the exploding helm left Adolin momentarily blinded. He stumbled, and when he put a foot down, it landed only on empty air. He lurched, then fell toward the void of the chasm.

For a timeless moment, all he felt was panic and fright, a frozen eternity before he realized he wasn't falling. His vision cleared, and he looked down into the maw before him, rain falling in curtains all around. Then he looked back over his shoulder.

To where two bridgemen had grabbed hold of the steel link skirt of his Plate and were struggling to hold him back from the brink. Grunting, they clung to the slick metal, holding tight with feet thrust against stones to keep from being pulled off with him.

Other soldiers materialized, rushing to help. Hands grabbed Adolin around the waist and shoulders, and together they hauled him back from the brink of the void – to the point that he was able to get his balance again and stumble away from the chasm.

Soldiers cheered, and Adolin let out an exhausted laugh. He turned to the bridgemen, Skar and Drehy. 'I guess,' Adolin said, 'I don't need to wonder if you two can keep up with me or not.'

'This was nothing,' Skar said.

'Yeah,' Drehy added. 'Lifting fat lighteyes is easy. You should try a bridge sometime.'

Adolin grinned, then wiped water from his face with his exposed hand. 'See if you can find a chunk of my helm or forearm piece. Regrowing the armor will go faster if we've got a seed. Collect my gauntlet too, if you would.'

The two nodded. That red lightning in the sky was building, and that spinning column of dark rain was expanding, growing outward. That ... that did *not* seem like a good sign.

He needed a better grasp on what was happening in the rest of the army. He jogged across the bridge to the central plateau. Where was his father? What was happening on Aladar's and Roion's fronts? Had Shallan returned from her expedition?

Everything seemed chaotic here on the central plateau. The rising winds tore at tents, and some of them had collapsed. People ran this way and that. Adolin spotted a figure in a thick cloak, striding purposefully through the rain. That person looked like he knew what he was doing. Adolin caught his arm as he passed.

'Where's my father?' he asked. 'What orders are you delivering?'

The hood of the cloak fell down and the man turned to regard Adolin with eyes that were slightly too large, too rounded. A bald head. Filmy, loose clothing beneath the cloak.

The Assassin in White.

❖

Moash stepped forward, but did not summon his Shardblade.

Kaladin struck with his spear, but it was futile. He'd used what strength he had to merely remain upright. His spear glanced off Moash's helm, and the former bridgeman slapped a fist down on the weapon, shattering the wood.

Kaladin lurched to a stop, but Moash wasn't done. He stepped forward and slammed an armored fist into Kaladin's gut.

Kaladin gasped, folding as things *broke* inside of him. Ribs snapped like twigs before that impossibly strong fist. Kaladin coughed, spraying blood across Moash's armor, then groaned as his friend stepped back, removing his fist.

Kaladin collapsed to the cold stone floor, everything shaking. His eyes felt like they'd pop from his face, and he curled around his broken chest, trembling.

'Storms.' Moash's voice was distant. 'That was a harder blow than I intended.'

'You did what you had to.' Graves.

Oh . . . Stormfather . . . the pain . . .

'Now what?' Moash.

'We end this. Kill the king with a Shardblade. It will still look like the assassin, hopefully. Those blood trails are frustrating. They might make people ask questions. Here, let me cut down these boards, so it looks like he came in through the wall, like last time.'

Cold air. Rain.

Yelling? Very distant? He knew that voice. . . .

'Syl?' Kaladin whispered, blood on his lips. 'Syl?'

Nothing.

'I ran until . . . until I couldn't any longer,' Kaladin whispered. 'End of . . . the race.'

Life before death.

'I will do it.' Graves. 'I will bear this burden.'

'It is my right!' Moash said.

He blinked, eyes resting on the king's unconscious body just beside him. Still breathing.

I will protect those who cannot protect themselves.

It made sense, now, why he'd had to make this choice. Kaladin rolled to his knees. Graves and Moash were arguing.

'I have to protect him,' Kaladin whispered.

Why?

'If I protect . . .' He coughed. 'If I protect . . . only the people I like, it means that I don't care about doing what is right.' If he did that, he only cared about what was convenient for himself.

That wasn't protecting. That was selfishness.

Straining, agonized, Kaladin raised one foot. The good foot. Coughing blood, he shoved himself upward and stumbled to his feet between El-hokar and the assassins. Fingers trembling, he felt at his belt, and – after two tries – got his side knife out. He squeezed out tears of pain, and through blurry vision, saw the two Shardbearers looking at him.

Moash slowly raised his faceplate, revealing a stunned expression. 'Stormfather . . . Kal, how are you standing?'

It made sense now.

That was why he'd come back. It was about Tien, it was about Dalinar, and it was about what was right – but most of all, it was about protecting people.

This was the man he wanted to be.

Kaladin moved one foot back, touching his heel to the king, forming a battle stance. Then raised his hand before him, knife out. His hand shook like a roof rattling from thunder. He met Moash's eyes.

Strength before weakness.

'You. Will. Not. *Have. Him.*'

'Finish this, Moash,' Graves said.

'Storms,' Moash said. 'There's no need. Look at him. He can't fight back.'

Kaladin felt exhausted. At least he'd stood up.

It was the end. The journey had come and gone.

Shouting. Kaladin heard it now, as if it were closer.

He is mine! a feminine voice said. *I claim him.*

He betrayed his oath.

'He has seen too much,' Graves said to Moash. 'If he lives this day, he'll betray us. You know my words are true, Moash. Kill him.'

The knife slipped from Kaladin's fingers, clanging to the ground. He was too weak to hold it. His arm flopped back to his side, and he stared down at the knife, dazed.

I don't care.

He will kill you.

'I'm sorry, Kal,' Moash said, stepping forward. 'I should have made it quick at the start.'

The Words, Kaladin. That was Syl's voice. *You have to speak the Words!*

I forbid this.

Your will matters not! Syl shouted. You cannot hold me back if he speaks the Words! The Words, Kaladin! Say them!

'I will protect even those I hate,' Kaladin whispered through bloody lips. 'So long as it is right.'

A Shardblade appeared in Moash's hands.

A distant rumbling. Thunder.

THE WORDS ARE ACCEPTED, the Stormfather said reluctantly.

'Kaladin!' Syl's voice. 'Stretch forth thy hand!' She zipped around him, suddenly visible as a ribbon of light.

'I can't . . .' Kaladin said, drained.

'*Stretch forth thy hand!*'

He reached out a trembling hand. Moash hesitated.

Wind blew in the opening in the wall, and Syl's ribbon of light became mist, a form she often took. Silver mist, which grew larger, coalesced before Kaladin, extending into his hand.

Glowing, brilliant, a Shardblade emerged from the mist, vivid blue light shining from swirling patterns along its length.

Kaladin gasped a deep breath as if coming fully awake for the first time. The entire hallway went black as the Stormlight in every lamp down the length of the hall winked out.

For a moment, they stood in darkness.

Then Kaladin *exploded* with Light.

It erupted from his body, making him shine like a blazing white sun in the darkness. Moash backed away, face pale in the white brilliance, throwing up a hand to shade his eyes.

Pain evaporated like mist on a hot day. Kaladin's grip firmed upon the glowing Shardblade, a weapon beside which those of Graves and Moash looked dull. One after another, shutters burst open up and down the hallway, wind screaming into the corridor. Behind Kaladin, frost crystalized on the ground, growing backward away from him. A glyph formed in the frost, almost in the shape of wings.

Graves screamed, falling in his haste to get away. Moash backed up, staring at Kaladin.

'The Knights Radiant,' Kaladin said softly, 'have returned.'

'Too late!' Graves shouted.

Kaladin frowned, then glanced at the king.

'The Diagram spoke of this,' Graves said, scuttling back along the corridor. 'We missed it. We missed it completely! We focused on making certain you were separated from Dalinar, and not on what our actions might push you to become!'

Moash looked from Graves back at Kaladin. Then he ran, Plate clinking as he turned and dashed down the corridor and disappeared.

Kaladin, Syl's voice spoke in his head. *Something is still very wrong. I feel it on the winds.*

Graves laughed like a madman.

'Separating me,' Kaladin whispered. 'From Dalinar? Why would they care?'

He turned, looking eastward.

Oh no . . .

But who is the wanderer, the wild piece, the one who makes no sense?
I glimpse at his implications, and the world opens to me. I shy back.
Impossible. Is it?

—From the Diagram, West Wall Psalm of Wonders: paragraph 8
(Note by Adrotagia: Could this refer to Mraize?)

'She didn't say if she could even open the pathway?' Dalinar asked as he stalked toward the command tent. Rain pummeled the ground around him, so dense that it was no longer possible to distinguish separate windblown sheets in the glare of Navani's fabrial floodlights. It was long past when he should have found cover.

'No, Brightlord,' said Peet, the bridgeman. 'But she was insistent that we couldn't face what was coming at us. Two highstorms.'

'How could there be *two*?' Navani asked. She wore a stout cloak but was soaked clear through anyway, her umbrella having blown away long ago. Roion walked on Dalinar's other side, his beard and mustache limp with water.

'I don't know, Brightness,' Peet said. 'But that's what she said. A highstorm and something else. She called it an Everstorm. She expects they're going to collide right here.'

Dalinar considered, frowning. The command tent was just ahead. Inside, he'd talk to his field commanders, and—

The command tent shuddered, then ripped free in a burst of wind. Trailing ropes and spikes, it blew right past Dalinar, almost close enough to touch. Dalinar cursed as the light of a dozen lanterns – once contained in the tent – spilled onto the plateau. Scribes and soldiers scrambled, trying to grab maps and sheets of paper as rain and wind claimed them.

'Storm it!' Dalinar said, turning his back to the powerful wind. 'I need an update!'

'Sir!' Commander Cael, head of the field command, jogged over, his wife – Apara – following. Cael's clothing was mostly dry, though that was quickly changing. 'Aladar has *won* his plateau! Apara was just composing you a message.'

'Really?' Almighty bless that man. He'd done it.

'Yes, sir,' Cael said. He had to shout against the wind and rain. 'High-prince Aladar said the singing Parshendi went right down, letting him slaughter them. The rest broke and fled. Even with Roion's plateau fallen, we've won the day!'

'Doesn't feel like it,' Dalinar shouted back. Just minutes ago, the rainfall had been light. The situation was degrading quickly. 'Send orders immediately to Aladar, my son, and General Khal. There's a plateau just to the southeast, perfectly round. I want all of our forces to move there to brace for an oncoming storm.'

'Yes, sir!' Cael said with a salute, fist to coat. With the other hand, however, he pointed over Dalinar's shoulder. 'Sir, have you seen *that*?'

He turned, looking back toward the west. Red light flashed, lightning coursing down in repeated blasts. The sky itself seemed to spasm as something built there, swirling in an enormous storm cell that was rapidly expanding outward.

'Almighty above . . .' Navani whispered.

Nearby another tent shook, its stakes coming undone. 'Leave the tents, Cael,' Dalinar said. 'Get everyone moving. *Now.* Navani, go to Brightness Shallan. Help her if you can.'

The officer leaped away and began shouting orders. Navani went with him, vanishing into the night, and a squad of soldiers chased after her to provide protection.

'And me, Dalinar?' Roion asked.

'We'll need you to take command of your men and lead them to safety,' Dalinar said. 'If such a thing can be found.'

That tent nearby shook again. Dalinar frowned. It didn't seem to be moving along with the wind. And was that . . . shouting?

Adolin crashed through the tent's fabric and skidded along the stones on his back, his armor leaking Light.

'Adolin!' Dalinar shouted, dashing to his son.

The young man was missing several segments of his armor. He looked up with gritted teeth, blood streaming from his nose. He said something, but it was lost to the wind. No helm, no left vambrace, the breastplate cracked just short of shattering, his right leg exposed. Who could have done such a thing to a Shardbearer?

Dalinar knew the answer immediately. He cradled Adolin, but looked up past the collapsed tent. It whipped in the storm and tore away as a man strode past it, glowing with spinning trails of Stormlight. Those foreign features, clothing all of white plastered to his body by the rain, a bowed, hairless head, shadows hiding eyes that glowed with Stormlight.

Gavilar's murderer. Szeth, the Assassin in White.

⁘

Shallan worked through the inscriptions on the wall of the round chamber, frantically searching for some way to make the Oathgate function.

This had to work. It *had* to.

'This is all in the Dawnchant,' Inadara said. 'I can't make sense of any of it.'

The Knights Radiant are the key.

Shouldn't Renarin's sword have been enough? 'What's the pattern?' she whispered.

'Mmm . . .' Pattern said. 'Perhaps you cannot see it because you are too close? Like the Shattered Plains?'

Shallan hesitated, then stood and walked to the center of the room, where the depictions of the Knights Radiant and their kingdoms met at a central point.

'Brightlord Renarin?' Inadara asked. 'Is something wrong?' The young prince had fallen to his knees and was huddled next to the wall.

'I can see it,' Renarin answered feverishly, his voice echoing in the chamber. Ardents who had been studying part of the murals looked up at him. 'I can see the future itself. Why? Why, Almighty? Why have you cursed me so?' He screamed a pleading cry, then stood and cracked something against the wall. A rock? Where had he gotten it? He gripped the thing in a gauntleted hand and began to write.

Shocked, Shallan took a step toward him. A sequence of numbers?

All zeros.

'It's come,' Renarin whispered. 'It's come, it's come, it's come. We're dead. We're dead. We're dead. . . .'

⁘

Dalinar knelt beneath a fracturing sky, holding his son. Rainwater washed the blood from Adolin's face, and the boy blinked, dazed from his thrashing.

'Father . . .' Adolin said.

The assassin stepped forward quietly, with no apparent urgency. The man seemed to glide through the rain.

'When you take the princedom, son,' Dalinar said, 'don't let them corrupt you. Don't play their games. Lead. Don't follow.'

'Father!' Adolin said, his eyes focusing.

Dalinar stood up. Adolin lurched over onto all fours and tried to get to his feet, but the assassin had broken one of Adolin's greaves, which made it almost impossible to rise. The boy slipped back into the pooling water.

'You've been taught well, Adolin,' Dalinar said, eyes on that assassin. 'You're a better man than I am. I was always a tyrant who had to learn to be something else. But you, you've been a good man from the start. Lead them, Adolin. Unite them.'

'Father!'

Dalinar walked away from Adolin. Nearby, scribes and attendants, captains and enlisted men all shouted and scrambled, trying to find order in the chaos of the storm. They followed Dalinar's order to evacuate, and most had yet to notice the figure in white.

The assassin stopped ten paces from Dalinar. Roion, pale-faced and stammering, backed away from the two of them and began shouting. 'Assassin! Assassin!'

The rainfall was actually letting up a little. That didn't bring Dalinar much hope; not with that red lightning on the horizon. Was that . . . a

487

stormwall building at the front of the new storm? His efforts to disrupt the Parshendi had fallen short.

The Shin man didn't strike. He stood opposite Dalinar, motionless, expressionless, water dripping down his face. Unnaturally calm.

Dalinar was far taller and broader. This small man in white, with his pale skin, seemed almost a youth, a stripling by comparison.

Behind him, Roion's cries were lost in the confusion. However, Bridge Four did run up to surround Dalinar, spears in hand. Dalinar waved them back. 'There's nothing you can do here, lads,' Dalinar said. 'Let me face him.'

Ten heartbeats.

'Why?' Dalinar asked the assassin, who still stood there in the rain. 'Why kill my brother? Did they explain the reasoning behind your orders?'

'I am Szeth-son-son-Vallano,' the man said. Harshly. 'Truthless of Shinovar. I do as my masters demand, and I do not ask for explanations.'

Dalinar revised his assessment. This man was not calm. He seemed that way, but when he spoke, he did it through clenched teeth, his eyes open too wide.

He's mad, Dalinar thought. *Storms.*

'You don't have to do this,' Dalinar said. 'If it's about pay . . .'

'What I am owed,' the assassin shouted, rainwater spraying from his face and Stormlight rising from his lips, 'will come to me eventually! Every bit of it. I will drown in it, stonewalker!'

Szeth put his hand to the side, Shardblade appearing. Then, with a curt, deprecatory motion – like he was merely trimming a bit of gristle from his meat – he strode forward and swung at Dalinar.

Dalinar caught the Blade with his own, which appeared in his hand as he raised it.

The assassin spared a glance for Dalinar's weapon, then smiled, lips drawn thin, showing only a hint of teeth. That eager smile matched with haunted eyes was one of the most evil things Dalinar had ever seen.

'Thank you,' the assassin said, 'for extending my agony by not dying easily.' He stepped back and burst *afire* with white light.

He came at Dalinar again, inhumanly quick.

٭

Adolin cursed, shaking out of his daze. Storms, his head hurt. He'd smacked it something good when the assassin tossed him to the ground.

Father was fighting Szeth. Bless the man for listening to reason and bonding that madman's Blade. Adolin gritted his teeth and struggled to get to his feet, something that was difficult with a broken greave. Though the rain was letting up, the sky remained dark. To the west, lightning plunged downward like red waterfalls, almost constant.

At the same time, wind gusted from the east. Something was building out there too, from the Origin. This was very bad.

Those things Father said to me . . .

Adolin stumbled, almost falling to the ground, but hands appeared to assist him. He glanced to the side to find those two bridgemen from before, Skar and Drehy, helping him to his feet.

'You two,' Adolin said, 'are getting a storming raise. Help me get this armor off.' He frantically began removing sections of armor. The entire suit was so battered it was nearly useless.

Metal clanged nearby as Dalinar fought. If he could hold a little longer, Adolin would be able to help. He would *not* let that creature get the better of him again. Not again!

He spared a glance for what Dalinar was doing, and froze, hands on the straps for his breastplate.

His father . . . his father moved beautifully.

⁎

Dalinar did not fight for his life. His life hadn't been his own for years.

He fought for Gavilar. He fought as he wished he had all those years ago, for the chance he had missed. In that moment between storms – when the rain stilled and the winds drew in their breaths to blow – he danced with the slayer of kings, and somehow held his own.

The assassin moved like a shadow. His step seemed too quick to be human. When he jumped, he soared into the air. He swung his Shard-blade like flashes of lightning, and would occasionally stretch forward with his other hand, as if to grab Dalinar.

Recalling their previous encounter, Dalinar recognized that as the more dangerous of Szeth's weapons. Each time, Dalinar managed to bring his Blade around and force the assassin away. The man attacked from different directions, but Dalinar didn't think. Thoughts could get jumbled, the mind disoriented.

His instincts knew what to do.

Duck when Szeth leaped over Dalinar's head. Step backward, avoiding a strike that should have severed his spine. Lash out, forcing the assassin away. Three quick steps backward, sword up wardingly, strike for the assassin's palm as it tried to touch him.

It worked. For this brief time, he fought this creature. Bridge Four remained back, as he'd commanded. They'd only have interfered.

He survived.

But he did not win.

Finally, Dalinar twisted away from a strike but was unable to move quickly enough. The assassin rounded on him and thrust a fist into his side.

Dalinar's ribs cracked. He grunted, stumbling, almost falling. He swung his Blade toward Szeth, warding the man back, but it didn't matter. The damage was done. He sank to his knees, barely able to remain upright for the pain.

In that instant he knew a truth he should always have known.

If I'd been there, on that night, awake instead of drunk and asleep . . . Gavilar would still have died.

I couldn't have beaten this creature. I can't do it now, and I couldn't have done it then.

I couldn't have saved him.

It brought peace, and Dalinar finally set down that boulder, the one he'd been carrying for over six years.

The assassin stalked toward him, glowing with terrible Stormlight, but a figure lunged for him from behind.

Dalinar expected it to be Adolin, perhaps one of the bridgemen.

Instead, it was Roion.

⁘

Adolin tossed aside the last bit of armor and went running for his father. He wasn't too late. Dalinar knelt before the assassin, defeated, but not dead.

Adolin shouted, drawing close, and an unexpected figure leapt out of the wreckage of a tent. Highprince Roion – incongruously holding a side sword and leading a small force of soldiers – rushed the assassin.

Rats had a better chance fighting a chasmfiend.

Adolin barely had time to shout as the assassin – moving at blinding speed – spun and cut the blade from the hilt of Roion's sword. Szeth's hand shot out and slammed against Roion's chest.

Roion shot into the air, trailing a wisp of Stormlight. He screamed as the sky swallowed him.

He lasted longer than his men. The assassin swept between them, deftly avoiding spears, moving with uncanny grace. A dozen soldiers fell in an instant, eyes burning.

Adolin jumped over one of the bodies as it collapsed. Storms. He could still hear Roion screaming up above somewhere.

Adolin thrust at the assassin, but the creature twisted and slapped the Shardblade away. The assassin was grinning. He didn't speak, though Stormlight leaked between his teeth.

Adolin tried Smokestance, attacking with a quick sequence of jabs. The assassin silently battered them away, unfazed. Adolin focused, dueling the best he could, but he was a *child* before this thing.

Roion, still screaming, plummeted from the sky and hit nearby with a sickening wet crunch. A quick glance at his corpse told Adolin that the highprince would never rise again.

Adolin cursed and lunged for the assassin, but a fluttering tarp – brushed by the assassin in passing – leaped toward Adolin. The monster could command inanimate objects! Adolin sliced through the tarp and then jumped forward to swing for the assassin.

He found nothing to fight.

Duck.

He threw himself to the ground as something passed over his head, the assassin flying through the air. Szeth's hissing Shardblade missed Adolin's head by inches.

Adolin rolled and came to his knees, puffing.

How . . . What could he do . . . ?

You can't beat it, Adolin thought. *Nothing can beat it.*

The assassin landed lightly. Adolin climbed back to his feet, and found himself in company. A dozen of the bridgemen formed up around him. Skar, at their head, looked to Adolin and nodded. Good men. They'd seen Roion's fall, and still they joined him. Adolin hefted his Shardblade and noticed that a short distance away, his father had managed to regain his feet. Another small group of bridgemen moved in around him, and he allowed it. He and Adolin had dueled and lost. Their only chance now was a mad rush.

Nearby, shouts arose. General Khal and a large strike force of soldiers, judging by the banner approaching. There wasn't time. The assassin stood on the wet plateau between Dalinar's small troop and Adolin's, head bowed. Fallen blue lanterns gave light. The sky had gone as black as night, except when broken by that red lightning.

Charge and mob a Shardbearer. Hope for a lucky blow. It was the only way. Adolin nodded to Dalinar. His father nodded back, grim. He knew. He *knew* there was no beating this thing.

Lead them, Adolin.

Unite them.

Adolin screamed, charging forward, sword out, men running with him. Dalinar advanced too, more slowly, one arm across his chest. Storms, the man could barely walk.

Szeth snapped his head up, face devoid of all emotion. As they arrived, he leaped, shooting into the air.

Adolin's eyes followed him up. Surely they hadn't chased him off . . .

The assassin twisted in the air, then crashed back down to the ground, glowing like a comet. Adolin barely parried a blow from the Blade; the *force* of it was incredible. It tossed him backward. The assassin spun, and a pair of bridgemen fell with burning eyes. Others lost spearheads as they tried to stab at him.

The assassin ripped free from the press of bodies, trailing blood from a couple of wounds. Those wounds *closed* as Adolin watched, the blood stopping. It was as Kaladin had said. With a horrible sinking feeling, Adolin realized just how *little* a chance they'd ever had.

The assassin dashed for Dalinar, who brought up the rear of the attack. The aging soldier raised his Blade, as if in respect, then thrust once.

An attack. That was the way to go.

'Father . . .' Adolin whispered.

The assassin parried the thrust, then placed his hand against Dalinar's chest.

The highprince, suddenly glowing, lurched up into the dark sky. He didn't scream.

The plateau fell silent. Some bridgemen propped up wounded fellows. Others turned toward the assassin, pulling into a spear formation, looking frantic.

The assassin lowered his Blade, then started to walk away.

'Bastard!' Adolin spat, dashing after him. 'Bastard!' He could barely see for the tears.

The assassin stopped, then leveled his weapon toward Adolin.

Adolin stumbled to a halt. Storms, his head hurt.

'It is finished,' the assassin whispered. 'I am done.' He turned from Adolin and continued to walk away.

Like Damnation itself, you are! Adolin raised his Shardblade overhead.

The assassin spun and slapped the weapon so hard with his own Blade that Adolin distinctly heard something *snap* in his wrist. His Blade tumbled from his fingers, vanishing. The assassin's hand slapped out, knuckles striking Adolin in the chest, and he gasped, his breath suddenly gone from his throat.

Stunned, he sank to his knees.

'I suppose,' the assassin snarled, 'I can kill one more, on my own time.' Then he grinned, a terrible smile with teeth clenched, eyes wide. As if he were in enormous pain.

Gasping, Adolin awaited the blow. He looked toward the sky. *Father, I'm sorry. I . . .*

I . . .

What was that?

He blinked as he made out something glowing in the air, drifting down, like a leaf. A figure. A man.

Dalinar.

The highprince fell slowly, as if he were no more weighty than a cloud. White Light streamed from his body in glowing wisps. Nearby bridgemen murmured, soldiers shouted, pointing.

Adolin blinked, certain he was delusional. But no, that *was* Dalinar. Like . . . one of the Heralds themselves, coming down from the Tranquiline Halls.

The assassin looked, then stumbled back, mouth open in horror. 'No . . . *No!*'

And then, like a falling star, a blazing fireball of light and motion shot down in front of Dalinar. It crashed into the ground, sending out a ring of Stormlight like white smoke. At the center, a figure in blue crouched with one hand on the stones, the other clutching a glowing Shardblade.

His eyes afire with a light that somehow made the assassin's seem *dull* by comparison, he wore the uniform of a bridgeman, and bore the glyphs of slavery on his forehead.

The expanding ring of smoky light faded, save for a large glyph – a swordlike shape – which remained for a brief moment before puffing away.

'You sent him to the sky to die, assassin,' Kaladin said, Stormlight puffing from his lips, 'but the sky and the winds are mine. I claim them, as I now claim your life.'

One is almost certainly a traitor to the others.

—From the Diagram, Book of the 2nd Desk Drawer: paragraph 27

Kaladin let the Stormlight evaporate before him. He was running low – his frantic flight across the Plains had drained him. How shocked he had been when the flare of light rising into the darkening sky above a lit plateau had turned out to be Dalinar himself. Lashed to the sky by Szeth.

Kaladin had caught him quickly and sent him back to the ground with a careful Lashing of his own. Ahead, Szeth stumbled away from the princeling, holding out his sword wardingly toward Kaladin, eyes wide and lips trembling. Szeth looked horrified.

Good.

Dalinar finally landed on the plateau with a soft step, and Kaladin's Lashing ran out.

'Seek shelter,' Kaladin said, the tempest in his veins dampening further. 'I flew over a storm on my way here . . . a big one. Coming from the west.'

'We're in the process of withdrawing.'

'Hurry,' Kaladin said. 'I will deal with our friend.'

'Kaladin?'

Kaladin turned, glancing at the highprince, who stood tall, despite cradling one arm against his chest. Dalinar met his eyes. 'You *are* what I've been looking for.'

'Yes. Finally.'

Kaladin turned and strode toward the assassin. He passed Bridge Four in a tight formation, and the men – at a barked command from Teft – threw something down before Kaladin. Blue lanterns, lit by oversized gems that had lasted the Weeping.

Bless them. Stormlight streamed up as he passed, filling him. With a sinking feeling, however, he noticed two corpses with burned-out eyes at their feet. Pedin and Mart. Eth clutched his brother's body, weeping. Other bridgemen had lost limbs.

Kaladin snarled. No more. He would lose no further men to this monster.

'You ready?' he whispered.

Of course, Syl said in his head. *I'm not the one we've been waiting on.*

Burning with Stormlight, enraged and alight, Kaladin launched himself at the assassin and met him Blade against Blade.

⁘

'We're dead . . .' Renarin muttered.

'Someone shut him up,' Shallan snapped. 'Gag him if you have to.' She pointedly turned around, ignoring the raving prince. She still stood in the center of the muraled chamber. The pattern. What was the pattern?

A circular room. A thing on one side that adapted to fit different Shardblades. Depictions of Knights on the floor, glowing with Stormlight, pointing at a tower city, just as the myths described. Ten lamps on the walls. The lock hung over what she thought was a depiction of Natanatan, the kingdom of the Shattered Plains. It—

Ten lamps. With gems in them. Latticework of metal enclosing each one.

Shallan blinked, a shock running through her.

'It's a fabrial.'

⁘

The assassin hurtled into the air. Captain Kaladin flew upward, chasing him, trailing Light.

'Status of the retreat!' Dalinar bellowed, crossing the plateau, his ribs smarting like nothing else, his wound from before little better. Storms. That one had faded as he fought, but now it ached something fierce. 'Someone get me information!'

Scribes and ardents appeared from the nearby wreckage of tents. Shouts rose from around the plateau. The wind started to pick up – their period of reprieve, the short calm, was over. They needed to escape these plateaus. *Now.*

Dalinar reached Adolin and helped the young man to his feet. He looked quite a bit worse for wear, bruised, battered, dizzy. He flexed his right hand and winced in pain, then gingerly let it relax.

'Damnation,' Adolin said. 'That bridgeboy is really one of them? The Knights Radiant?'

'Yes.'

Oddly, Adolin smiled, seeming satisfied. 'Ha! I *knew* there was something wrong with that man.'

'Go,' Dalinar said, pushing Adolin along. 'We need to get the army to move two plateaus over, that direction, where Shallan waits. Get over there and organize what you can.' He looked westward as the wind whipped up further, with bursts of rain. 'Time is short.'

Adolin shouted for the bridgemen to join him, which they did, helping their wounded – though they were unfortunately forced to leave their dead. Several of them carried Adolin's Shardplate as well, which was apparently spent.

Dalinar limped eastward across the plateau as fast as he could manage in his condition, searching for . . .

Yes. The place where he'd left Gallant. The horse snorted, shaking a wet mane. 'Bless you, old friend,' Dalinar said, reaching the Ryshadium. Through the thunder and the chaos, the horse had not fled.

Dalinar moved much more easily once in the saddle, and eventually found Roion's army pouring southward toward Shallan's plateau, in organized ranks. He allowed himself a sigh of relief at their orderly march; the majority of the army had already crossed to the southern plateau, only one away from Shallan's round one. That was wonderful. He couldn't remember where Captain Khal had been sent, but with Roion himself fallen, Dalinar had assumed he'd left this army in chaos.

'Dalinar!' a voice called.

He turned to find the utterly incongruous sight of Sebarial and his mistress sitting beneath a canopy, eating dried sellafruit off a plate held by an awkward-looking soldier.

Sebarial raised a cup of wine toward Dalinar. 'Hope you don't mind,' Sebarial said. 'We liberated your stores. They were blowing past at the time, headed for certain doom.'

Dalinar stared at them. Palona even had a *novel* out and was *reading*.

'You did this?' Dalinar asked, nodding toward Roion's army.

'They were making a racket,' Sebarial said. 'Wandering around, shouting at one another, weeping and wailing. Very poetic. Figured someone should get them moving. My army is already off on that other plateau. It's getting *rather* cramped there, you realize.'

Palona flipped the page in her novel, barely paying attention.

'Have you seen Aladar?' Dalinar asked.

Sebarial gestured with his wine. 'He should be about finished crossing as well. You'll find him that direction. Downwind, happily.'

'Don't dally,' Dalinar said. 'You remain here, and you're a dead man.'

'Like Roion?' Sebarial asked.

'Unfortunately.'

'So it *is* true,' Sebarial said, standing up, brushing off his trousers – which were somehow still dry. 'Who am I going to make fun of now?' He shook his head sadly.

Dalinar rode off in the direction indicated. He noticed that, incredibly, a pair of bridgemen were still tailing him, only now catching up to where he'd found Sebarial. They saluted as Dalinar noticed them.

He told them where he was going, then sped up. Storms. In terms of pain, riding with broken ribs wasn't much better than walking with them. Worse, actually.

He did find Aladar on the next plateau over, supervising his army as it seeped onto the perfectly round plateau that Shallan had indicated. Rust Elthal was there as well, wearing his Plate – one of the suits Adolin had won – and guiding one of Dalinar's large, mechanical bridges. It settled down next to two others that spanned the chasm here, crossing in places the smaller bridges wouldn't have been able to.

The plateau everyone was crowding onto was relatively small, by the scale of the Shattered Plains – but it was still several hundred yards across. It would fit the armies, hopefully.

'Dalinar?' Aladar asked, trotting his horse over. Lit by a large diamond – stolen from one of Navani's fabrial lights, it seemed – hanging from his saddle, Aladar sported a soaked uniform and a bandage on his forehead, but appeared otherwise unharmed. 'What in Kelek's tongue is going on out here? I can't get a straight answer from anyone.'

'Roion is dead,' Dalinar said wearily, reining in Gallant. 'He fell with honor, attacking the assassin. The assassin, hopefully, has been distracted for a time.'

'We won the day,' Aladar said. 'I scattered those Parshendi. We left well over half of them dead on that plateau, perhaps even three quarters. Adolin did even better on his plateau, and from reports, the ones on Roion's plateau have fled. The Vengeance Pact is fulfilled! Gavilar is avenged, and the war is over!'

So proud. Dalinar had difficulty finding the words to deflate him, so he just stared at the other man. Feeling numb.

Can't afford that, Dalinar thought, sagging in his saddle. *Have to lead.*

'It doesn't matter, does it?' Aladar asked more softly. 'That we won?'

'Of course it matters.'

'But . . . shouldn't it feel different?'

'Exhaustion,' Dalinar said, 'pain, suffering. This is what victory usually feels like, Aladar. We've won, yes, but now we have to survive with our victory. Your men are almost across?'

He nodded.

'Get everyone onto that plateau,' Dalinar said. 'Force them up against one another if you have to. We need to be ready to move through the portal as quickly as possible, once it is opened.'

If it opened.

Dalinar urged Gallant forward, crossing one of the bridges to the packed ranks on the other side. From there, he forced his way – with difficulty – toward the center, where he hoped to find salvation.

·:·

Kaladin shot into the air after the assassin.

The Shattered Plains fell away beneath him. Fallen gemstones twinkled across the plateau, abandoned where tents had blown down or soldiers had fallen. They illuminated not only the central plateau, but three others around it and one more beyond, one that looked oddly circular from above.

The armies gathered on that one. Small lumps dotted the others like freckles. Corpses. So many.

Kaladin looked toward the sky. He was free once again. Winds *surged* beneath him, seeming to lift him, propel him. Carry him. His Shardblade shattered into mist and Syl zipped out, becoming a ribbon of light that spun around him as he flew.

Syl lived. Syl *lived*. He still felt euphoric about that. Shouldn't she be dead? When he'd asked on their flight out, her response had been simple.

I was only as dead as your oaths, Kaladin.

Kaladin continued upward, out of the path of the oncoming storms. He could see those distinctly from this vantage. Two of them, one rolling from the west and bursting with red lightning, the other approaching more quickly from the east with a dark grey stormwall. They were going to *collide*.

'A highstorm,' Kaladin said, shooting up through the sky after Szeth. 'The red storm is from the Parshendi, but why is there a *highstorm* coming? This isn't the time for one.'

'My father,' Syl said, voice growing solemn. 'He brought the storm, rushing its pace. He's ... broken, Kaladin. He doesn't think any of this should be happening. He wants to end it all, wash everyone away, and try to hide from the future.'

Her father ... did that mean the *Stormfather* wanted them dead? Great.

The assassin disappeared above, vanishing into the dark clouds. Kaladin gritted his teeth, Lashing himself upward again for more acceleration. He shot into the clouds, and all around him became featureless grey.

He kept watch for glimmers of light to announce the assassin coming for him. He might not have much warning.

The area around him lightened. Was that the assassin? Kaladin extended his hand to the side, and Syl formed into the Blade immediately.

'Not ten heartbeats?' he asked.

Not when I'm here with you, ready. The delay is primarily something of the dead. They need to be revived each time.

Kaladin burst out of the clouds and into sunlight.

He gasped. He'd forgotten that it was still daytime. Here, far above the earthy darkness of war, the sunlight beat upon the cover of clouds, making them glow with pale beauty. The thin air was frigid, but raging Stormlight inside him made that easy to ignore.

The assassin hovered nearby, toes pointed downward, head bowed, silvery Shardblade held to the side. Kaladin Lashed himself so that he stopped, then sank level with the assassin.

'I am Szeth-son-son-Vallano,' the man said. 'Truthless . . . Truthless.' He looked up, eyes wide, teeth clenched. 'You have stolen Honorblades. It is the only explanation.'

Storms. Kaladin had always imagined the Assassin in White as a calm, cold killer. This was something different.

'I possess no such weapon,' Kaladin said. 'And I don't know why it would matter if I did.'

'I hear your lies. I know them.' Szeth shot forward, sword out.

Kaladin Lashed himself to the side, jerking out of the way. He swiped with his Blade, but didn't come close to connecting. 'I should have practiced more with the sword,' he muttered.

Oh. That's right. You probably want me to be a spear, don't you?

The weapon fuzzed to mist, then elongated and grew into the shape of a silvery spear, with glowing, swirling glyphs along the sharpened sides of the spearhead.

Szeth twisted in the air, Lashing himself back into a hovering position. He looked at the spear, then seemed to tremble. 'No. Truthless. I am Truthless. No questions.'

Stormlight streaming from his mouth, Szeth threw his head back and screamed; a futile, human sound that dissipated in the infinite expanse of sky.

Beneath them, thunder rumbled and the clouds shivered with color.

⁂

Shallan dashed from lamp to lamp in the circular chamber, infusing each one with Stormlight. She glowed brightly, having drawn the Light from the ardents' lanterns. There wasn't time for explanation.

So much for keeping her nature as a Surgebinder hidden.

This room was a giant fabrial, powered by the Stormlight of those lamps. She should have seen it. She passed Inadara, who stared at her. 'How . . . how are you doing this, Brightness?'

Several of the scholars had settled onto the ground where they hurriedly sketched glyphward prayers onto cloths, using chalk because of the moisture. Shallan didn't know if those prayers were a request for safety from the storms or from Shallan herself. She did hear the words 'Lost Radiant' murmured by one.

Two more lanterns. She infused a ruby with Stormlight, bringing it to life, but then ran out of Light.

'Gemstones!' she said, spinning on the room. 'I need more Stormlight.'

The people inside looked to one another, all but Renarin, who continued to scratch identical glyphs on the rocks as he wept. Stormfather. She'd bled them all dry. One of the scholars had dug an oil lantern from her pack, and it paled beside the lamps on the walls.

Shallan ducked out of the opening in the door, looking at the mass of soldiers who gathered there. Thousands upon thousands shuffled in the darkness. Fortunately, some of them carried lanterns.

'I need your Stormlight!' she said. 'It—'

Was that *Adolin*? Shallan gasped, other thoughts fleeing for the moment as she spotted him in the front of the crowd, leaning on a bridgeman for support. Adolin was a mess, the left side of his face a patchwork of blood and bruises, his uniform ripped and bloodied. Shallan ran to him, pulling him close.

'Good to see you too,' he said, burying his face in her hair. 'I hear you're going to get us out of this mess.'

'Mess?' she asked.

Thunder rumbled and cracked without pause as red lightning blasted down not in streaks but in sheets. Storms! She hadn't realized it was so close!

'Mmm . . .' Pattern said. She looked left. A stormwall was approaching. The storms were like two hands, closing in to crush the armies between them.

Shallan breathed in sharply, and Stormlight entered her, bringing her to life. Adolin had a gemstone or two on him, apparently. He pulled back, looking her over.

'You *too*?' he said.

'Um . . .' She bit her lip. 'Yeah. Sorry.'

'Sorry? Storms, woman! Can you fly like he does?'

'Fly?'

Thunder cracked. Impending doom. Right.

'Make sure everyone is ready to move!' she said, dashing back into the chamber.

⁜

Storms crashed together beneath Kaladin. The clouds broke apart, black, red, and grey mingling in enormous swirls, lightning arcing among them. It seemed to be Aharietiam again, the ending of all things.

Above all this, atop the world, Kaladin fought for his life.

Szeth flew by in a sweeping flash of silvery metal. Kaladin deflected the blow, the spear in his hand vibrating with a plangent *ding*. Szeth continued on, passing him, and Kaladin Lashed himself in that direction.

They fell westward, skimming the tops of the clouds – though to Kaladin's eyes, that direction was down. He fell with his spear aimed, point straight toward the murderous Shin.

Szeth jerked left, and Kaladin followed, quickly Lashing himself that way. Violent, churning, angry clouds mixed beneath him. The two storms seemed to be fighting; the lightning that lit them was like thrown punches. Crashes sounded, and not all of them thunder. Near Kaladin a large stone churned up through the clouds, spinning vapors across its length. It breached in the light like a leviathan, then sank back into the clouds.

Stormfather . . . He was hundreds, perhaps thousands of feet in the air. What kind of violence was happening below if boulders were thrown this high?

Kaladin Lashed himself toward Szeth, picking up speed, moving along the top surface of the storms. He drew close, then eased back, letting his acceleration match that of Szeth so they flew side by side.

Kaladin drove his spear toward the assassin. Szeth parried deftly, Shardblade held in one hand while supporting the Blade from behind with the other, diverting Kaladin's thrust to the side.

'The Knights Radiant,' Szeth screamed, 'cannot have returned.'

'They have,' Kaladin said, yanking his spear back. 'And they're going to kill you.' He Lashed himself slightly to the side as he swung, twisting in the air and sweeping toward Szeth.

Szeth jerked upward, however, passing over Kaladin's spear. As they continued to fall through the air, clouds just beside them, Szeth dove inward and struck. Kaladin cursed, barely Lashing himself away in time.

Szeth dove past him, disappearing into the clouds below, becoming just a shadow. Kaladin tried to trace that shadow, but failed.

Szeth burst up beside Kaladin a second later, striking with three quick blows. One took Kaladin in the arm, and he dropped Syl.

Damnation. He Lashed himself back away from Szeth, then forced Stormlight into his greying, lifeless hand. With an effort, he made the color return, but Szeth was already upon him with an airborne lunge.

Mist formed in Kaladin's left hand as he raised it to ward, and a silvery shield appeared, glowing with a soft light. Szeth's Blade deflected away, causing the man to grunt in surprise.

Strength returned to Kaladin's right hand, the severing healed, but forcing that much Stormlight through it left him feeling drained. He fell away from Szeth, trying to keep his distance, but the assassin kept on him, jerking each direction that Kaladin did as he tried to escape.

'You are new at this,' Szeth called. 'You cannot fight me. I will win.'

Szeth zipped forward, and Syl formed into a spear in Kaladin's hands again. She seemed to be able to anticipate the weapon he wanted. Szeth slammed his weapon against Syl. It brought them face-to-face and they tumbled, eye to eye, their Lashings pulling them along the clouds.

'I *always* win,' Szeth said. He said it in a strange way, as if *angry*.

'You're wrong,' Kaladin said. 'About me. I'm not new to this.'

'You only just acquired your abilities.'

'No. The wind is mine. The sky is mine. They have been mine since childhood. You are the trespasser here. Not me.'

They broke apart, Kaladin throwing the assassin backward. He stopped thinking so much about his Lashings, about what he should be doing.

Instead, he let himself *be*.

He dove for Szeth, coat flapping, spear pointed for the man's heart. Szeth got out of the way, but Kaladin dropped the spear and swung his hand in a great arc. Syl formed an axehead halberd. It came within inches of Szeth's face.

The assassin cursed, but responded with his Blade. A shield was in Kaladin's hand a split second later, and he slammed away the attack. Syl shattered even as he did so, forming back into a sword as Kaladin thrust forward with empty hands. The sword appeared, and the weapon bit deeply into Szeth's shoulder.

The assassin's eyes widened. Kaladin twisted his Blade, pulling it out of the assassin's flesh, then tried a backhand to end the man permanently. Szeth was too fast. He Lashed himself backward, forcing Kaladin to follow, piling on Lashing after Lashing.

Szeth's hand still worked. Damnation. The strike to the shoulder hadn't fully severed the soul leading to the arm. And Kaladin's Stormlight was running out.

Szeth's looked even lower, fortunately. The assassin seemed to be using it up at a much faster rate than Kaladin, judging by the decreased glow around him. Indeed, he didn't try to heal his shoulder – which would have required a lot of Light – but continued to flee, jerking back and forth, trying to outrun Kaladin.

The shadowy battle continued below, a tangle of lightning, winds, and spinning clouds. As Kaladin chased Szeth, something gargantuan moved beneath the clouds, a shadow the size of a city. A second later, the top of an entire *plateau* broke through the dark clouds, twisting slowly, as if it had been thrown upward from below.

Szeth almost ran into it. Instead, he Lashed upward enough to crest it, then landed on the surface. He ran along it as it turned lethargically in the air, its momentum running out.

Kaladin landed behind him, though he retained most of a Lashing upward, keeping himself light. He ran up the side of the plateau, heading almost directly upward toward the sky, dodging to the side as Szeth suddenly twisted and cut through a rock formation, sending boulders tumbling downward.

Rocks clattered along the surface of the plateau, which itself began to tumble back down toward the ground. Szeth reached the peak and threw himself off, and Kaladin followed shortly thereafter, launching from the stone surface, which sank like a dying ship into the roiling clouds.

They continued their chase, but Szeth did it falling backward along the stormtop, his eyes on Kaladin. Wild eyes. 'You're trying to convince me!' he shouted. 'You can't be one of them!'

'You've seen that I am,' Kaladin shouted back.

'The Voidbringers!'

'Are back,' Kaladin shouted.

'THEY CAN'T BE. I AM TRUTHLESS!' The assassin panted. 'I

need not fight you. You are not my target. I have . . . I have work to do. I *obey!*'

He turned and Lashed himself downward.

Into the clouds, down toward the plateau where Dalinar had gone.

⁘

Shallan rushed into the room as the storms crashed together outside.

What was she doing? There wasn't time. Even if she could open a portal, those storms were *here*. She wouldn't have time to get people through.

They were dead. All of them. Thousands had probably already been swept to their deaths by the stormwall.

She ran to the last lamp anyway, infusing its spheres.

The floor started to glow.

Ardents jumped to their feet in surprise and Inadara yelped. Adolin stumbled in through the doorway, a crashing wind and a spray of angry rain trailing him.

Beneath them, the intricate design shone from within. It looked almost like stained glass. Gesturing frantically for Adolin to join her, Shallan ran across to the lock on the wall.

'Sword,' she shouted at Adolin over the sounds of storms outside. 'In there!' Renarin had long since dismissed his.

Adolin obeyed, scrambling forward, summoning his Shardblade. He rammed it into the slot, which again flowed to fit the weapon.

Nothing happened.

'It's not working,' Adolin shouted.

Only one answer.

Shallan grabbed the hilt of his sword and whipped it out – ignoring the scream in her mind that came from touching it – then tossed it aside. Adolin's sword vanished to mist.

A deep truth.

'There is something wrong with your Blade, and with all Blades.' She hesitated for just a second. 'All but mine. Pattern!'

He formed in her hands, the Blade she'd used to kill. The hidden soul. Shallan rammed it into the slot, and the weapon vibrated in her hands and glowed. Something deep within the plateau *unlocked*.

Outside, lightning fell and men screamed.

Now the mechanism's operation became clear to her. Shallan threw her weight against the sword, pushing it before her like the spoke on a mill. The inner wall of the building was like a ring inside a tube – it could rotate, while the outer wall remained in place. The sword moved the inner wall as she pushed on it, though it stuck at first, the fallen blocks of the cut doorway getting in the way. Adolin threw his weight against the sword with her, and together they pushed it around the circle until they were above the picture of Urithiru, half the circumference from Natanatan where she'd begun. She pulled her Blade free.

The ten lamps faded like closing eyes.

．＊．

Kaladin followed Szeth into the storm, diving into the blackness, falling amid the churning winds and the blasting lightning. Wind attacked him, tossing him about, and no Lashings could prevent this. He might be master of the winds, but storms were another thing.

Take care, Syl sent. *My father hates you. This is his domain. And it is mixed with something even more terrible, another storm. Their storm.*

Nevertheless, the highstorms were the source of Stormlight – and being in here *energized* Kaladin. His reserves of Stormlight burst alight, as they obviously did for Szeth. The assassin suddenly reappeared as a stark white explosion that zoomed through the maelstrom toward the plateaus.

Kaladin growled, Lashing himself after Szeth. Lightning of a dozen colors flashed around him, red, violet, white, yellow. Rain soaked him. Rocks spun past him, some colliding, but the Stormlight healed him as quickly as the debris did damage.

Szeth moved along the plateaus, coursing just above them, and Kaladin followed with difficulty. This churning wind was tough to navigate, and the darkness was near absolute. Flashes lit the Plains in fitful bursts. Fortunately, Szeth's glow could not be hidden, and Kaladin kept his attention on that blazing beacon.

Faster.

Just as Zahel had taught weeks ago, Szeth didn't need to defeat Kaladin to win. He just had to get to those Kaladin protected.

Faster.

A burst of lightning illuminated the battle plateaus. And beyond them, Kaladin caught a glimpse of the army. Thousands of men huddled on the large circular plateau. Many hunkered down. Others panicked.

The lightning was gone in a moment, and the land became dark again, though Kaladin had seen enough to know this was a disaster. A cataclysm. Men being blown off the edge, others crushed by falling rocks. In minutes, the army would be gone. Storms, Kaladin wasn't even certain if *he* could survive this nexus of destruction.

Szeth crashed down among them, a glowing light amid the blackness. As Kaladin Lashed himself down in that direction, lightning struck again.

Its light revealed Szeth standing on an empty plateau, baffled. The army was gone.

❖

The sounds of the raging storm outside vanished. Shallan shivered, wet and cold.

'Almighty above . . .' Adolin breathed. 'I'm almost scared of what we'll find.'

Rotating the inside wall of the building had moved their doorway opposite hardened crem. Perhaps there had been a natural doorway here before; Adolin summoned his Blade to cut a hole.

Pattern . . . her Shardblade . . . vanished back to mist, and the room's mechanisms settled down. She didn't hear anything outside, no crashing of winds, no thunder.

Emotions fought inside of her. She'd saved herself and Adolin, it appeared. But the rest of the army . . . Adolin cut a doorway; sunlight spilled through it. Shallan walked to the opening, nervous, passing Inadara, who sat in the corner, looking overwhelmed.

At the doorway, Shallan looked out at the same plateau as before, only now it was sunlit and calm. Four armies' worth of men and women crouched, soggy and wet, many holding their heads and hunkering down against wind that no longer blew. Nearby, two figures stood beside a massive Ryshadium stallion. Dalinar and Navani, who had apparently been on their way to the central building.

Beyond them spread the peaks of an unfamiliar mountain range. It was the same plateau, and here was in a ring with nine others. To Shallan's left, an enormous ribbed tower – shaped like cups of increasingly smaller sizes stacked atop one another – broke the peaks. Urithiru.

The plateau hadn't contained the portal.

The plateau *was* the portal.

⁂

Szeth screamed words at Kaladin, but those were lost in the tempest. Rocks crashed down around them, ripped from somewhere distant. Kaladin was sure he heard terrible screams over the winds, as red spren he'd never seen before – like small meteors, trailing light behind them – zipped around him.

Szeth screamed again. Kaladin caught the word this time. 'How!'

Kaladin's answer was to strike with his Blade. Szeth parried violently, and they clashed, two glowing figures in the blackness.

'I know this column!' Szeth screamed. 'I have seen its like before! They went to the city, didn't they!'

The assassin launched himself into the air. Kaladin was all too eager to follow. He wanted out of this tempest.

Szeth screamed away, heading westward, away from the storm with the red lightning – following the path of the common highstorm. That alone was dangerous enough.

Kaladin gave chase, but that proved difficult in the buffeting winds. It wasn't that they served Szeth more than Kaladin; the tempest was simply unpredictable. They'd shove him one way and Szeth another.

What happened if Szeth lost him?

He knows where Dalinar went, Kaladin thought, gritting his teeth as a flash of sudden whiteness blinded him from one side. *I don't.*

He couldn't protect Dalinar if he couldn't find the man. Unfortunately, a chase through this darkness favored the person who was trying to escape. Slowly, Szeth pulled ahead.

Kaladin tried to follow, but a surge of wind drove him in the wrong direction. Lashings didn't really let him fly. He couldn't resist such unpredictable winds; they controlled him.

No! Szeth's glowing form dwindled. Kaladin shouted into the darkness, blinking eyes against the rain. He'd almost lost sight . . .

Syl spun into the air in front of him. But he was still carrying the spear. What?

Another one, then another. Ribbons of light, occasionally taking the shapes of young women or men, laughing. Windspren. A dozen or more spun around him, leaving trails of light, their laughter somehow strong over the sounds of the storm.

There! Kaladin thought.

Szeth was ahead. Kaladin Lashed himself through the tempest toward him, jerking one way, then the other. Dodging blitzes of lightning, ducking under hurled boulders, blinking away the sheets of driven rain.

A whirlwind of chaos. And ahead . . . light?

The stormwall.

Szeth burst free of the storm's very front. Through the mess of water and debris, Kaladin could just barely make out the assassin turning around to look backward, his posture confident.

He thinks he's lost me.

Kaladin exploded out of the stormwall, surrounded by windspren that spiraled away in a pattern of light. He shouted, driving his spear toward Szeth, who parried hastily, his eyes wide. 'Impossible!'

Kaladin spun around and slashed his spear – which became a sword – through Szeth's foot.

The assassin lurched away along the length of the stormwall. Both Szeth and Kaladin continued to fall westward, just in front of the wall of water and debris.

Beneath them, the land passed in a blur. The two storms had finally separated, and the highstorm was moving along its normal path, east to west. The Shattered Plains were soon left behind, giving way to rolling hills.

As Kaladin chased, Szeth spun and fell backward, attacking, though Syl became a shield to block. Kaladin swung down and a hammer appeared in his hand, crashing against Szeth's shoulder, breaking bones. As Stormlight tried to heal the assassin, Kaladin pulled in close and slammed his hand against Szeth's stomach, a knife appearing there and digging deeply into the skin. He sought the spine.

Szeth gasped and frantically Lashed himself farther backward, pulling out of Kaladin's grip.

Kaladin followed. Boulders churned in the stormwall – which was now the ground from Kaladin's perspective. He had to repeatedly adjust his Lashing to stay in the right place, just ahead of the storm.

Kaladin leaped on churning boulders as they appeared, pursuing Szeth, who fell wildly, his clothing flapping. Windspren formed a halo around

Kaladin, zipping in and out, spiraling, spinning around his arms and legs. The proximity of the storm kept his Stormlight stoked, never letting it grow dim.

Szeth slowed, his wounds healing. He hung in front of the crashing stormwall, holding his sword before him. He took a breath, meeting Kaladin's eyes.

An ending, then.

Kaladin drove forward, Syl forming a spear in his fingers, the most familiar weapon.

Szeth attacked in a sequence, a relentless blur of strikes.

Kaladin blocked each one. He ended with his spear against the hilt of Szeth's Blade, pressing the two together, mere inches from the assassin's face.

'It is actually true,' Szeth whispered.

'Yes.'

Szeth nodded, and the edge of tension seemed to fade from him, replaced by an emptiness in his eyes. 'Then I was right all along. I was never Truthless. I could have stopped the murders at any time.'

'I don't know what that means,' Kaladin said. 'But you never *had* to kill.'

'My orders—'

'Excuses! If that was why you murdered, then you're not the evil man I assumed. You're a coward instead.'

Szeth looked him in the eyes, then nodded. He pushed Kaladin back, then moved to swing.

Kaladin drove his hands forward, forming Syl into a sword. He expected a parry. The move was intended to draw Szeth out of his attack pattern.

Szeth did not parry. He just closed his eyes to accept the attack.

In that instant, for reasons he could not have articulated – pity, perhaps? – Kaladin diverted his blow, driving the Blade through Szeth's wrist. The skin greyed. Flashing with reflected lightning, the sword tumbled from the assassin's fingers, then *dulled* as it plummeted.

The glow fled the assassin's form. All his Stormlight vanished in a puff, all Lashings banished.

Szeth started to fall.

Get that sword! Syl sent to Kaladin, a mental shout. *Grab it.*

'The assassin!'

He has released the bond. He's nothing without that sword! It must not be lost!

Kaladin dove after the Blade, passing Szeth, who tumbled through the air like a rag doll, buffeted by winds towards the stormwall.

Kaladin furiously Lashed himself downward, snatching the Blade just before the storm consumed it. Nearby, the assassin dropped past him into the storm and was swallowed up, leaving Kaladin with the haunting image of Szeth's limp silhouette being driven into a plateau below with all the tempest's force.

Raising the assassin's Blade, Kaladin Lashed himself back upward, passing along the stormwall, the windspren he'd attracted spiraling about him and laughing with pure joy. As he crested the top of the storm, they burst around him and zipped away, moving off to dance in front of the still-advancing storm.

That left him with only one. Syl – in the form of a young woman in a fluttering dress, full-sized this time – hovered before him. She smiled as the storm moved beneath them.

'I didn't kill him,' Kaladin said.

'Did you want to?'

'No,' Kaladin said, surprised that it was the truth. 'But I should have anyway.'

'You have his Blade,' she replied. 'The Stormfather likely took him. And if not . . . well, he is no longer the weapon he once was. I must say, that was very nicely done. Perhaps I'll keep you around this time.'

'Thank you.'

'You almost killed me, you realize.'

'I realize. I thought I had.'

'And?'

'And . . . um . . . you are intelligent and articulate?'

'You forgot the compliment.'

'But I just said—'

'Those were simple statements of fact.'

'You're wonderful,' he said. 'Truly, Syl. You are.'

'Also a fact,' she said, grinning. 'But I'll let it slide so long as you're willing to present me with a sufficiently sincere smile.'

He did.

And it felt very, very good.

Chaos in Alethkar is, of course, inevitable. Watch carefully, and do not let power in the kingdom solidify. The Blackthorn could become an ally or our greatest foe, depending on whether he takes the path of the warlord or not. If he seems likely to sue for peace, assassinate him expeditiously. The risk of competition is too great.

—From the Diagram, Writings upon the Bedstand Lamp: paragraph 4 (Adrotagia's 3rd translation from the original hieroglyphics)

The Shattered Plains had been shattered again.

Kaladin strolled across them with Szeth's Shardblade on his shoulder. He passed heaps of rock and fresh cracks in the ground. Enormous puddles like small lakes shimmered amid huge chunks of broken stone. Just to his left, an entire plateau had crumbled into the chasms around it. The jagged, ripped-up base of the plateau had a black, charred cast to it.

He found no sign of Szeth's corpse. That could mean the man had survived somehow, or it could just mean the storm had buried the body in rubble or blown it away, leaving it in some forgotten chasm to rot until the bones were finally picked over by an unfortunate salvage crew.

For now, the fact that Szeth had not summoned his Blade back to him was enough. Either he was dead, or – as Syl had said – the strange weapon was no longer bound to him. Kaladin didn't know how to tell. This Shardblade had no gemstone at the pommel to indicate.

Kaladin stopped at a high point of the plateau and surveyed the wreckage. Then he glanced toward Syl, who sat on his shoulder. 'This is going to happen again?' he said. 'That other storm is still out there?'

'Yes,' Syl said, 'A new storm. It's not of us, but of *him*.'

'Will it be this bad every time it passes?' Of the plateaus he could see, only the one had been destroyed completely. But if the storm could do that to pure rock, what would it do to a city? Particularly since it blew the *wrong way*.

Stormfather . . . Laits would no longer be laits. Buildings that had been constructed to face away from the storms would suddenly be exposed.

'I don't know,' Syl said softly. 'This is a new thing, Kaladin. Not from before. I don't know how it happened or what it means. Hopefully, it won't be this bad except when a highstorm and an everstorm crash into each other.'

Kaladin grunted, picking his way over to the edge of his current plateau. He breathed in a little Stormlight, then Lashed himself upward to offset the natural pull of the ground. He became weightless. He pushed off lightly with his foot and drifted across the chasm to the next plateau.

'So how did the army vanish like that?' he asked, removing his Lashing and settling down on the rock.

'Uh . . . how should I know?' Syl said. 'I was *kind of* distracted.'

He grunted. Well, this was the plateau where everyone had been. Perfectly round. Odd, that. On a nearby plateau, what had once been a large hill had been cracked wide open, exposing the remnants of a building inside. This perfectly circular one was far more flat, though it looked like there was a hill or something at the center. He strode in that direction.

'So they're all spren,' he said. 'Shardblades.'

Syl grew solemn.

'Dead spren,' Kaladin added.

'Dead,' Syl agreed. 'Then they live again a little when someone summons them, syncing a heartbeat to their essence.'

'How can something be "a little" alive?'

'We're spren,' Syl said. 'We're *forces*. You can't kill us completely. Just . . . sort of.'

'That's perfectly clear.'

'It's perfectly clear to us,' Syl said. 'You're the strange ones. Break a rock, and it's still there. Break a spren, and she's still there. Sort of. Break a person, and something leaves. Something changes. What's left is just meat. You're weird.'

'I'm glad we established that,' he said, stopping. He couldn't see any evidence of the Alethi. Had they really escaped? Or had a sudden surge of the storm swept them all into the chasms? It seemed unlikely such a disaster would have left *nothing* behind.

Please let it not be so. He lifted Szeth's sword off his shoulder and set it down, point first, in front of him. It sank a few inches into the rock.

'What about this?' he asked, looking over the thin, silvery weapon. An unornamented Blade. That was supposed to be odd. 'It doesn't scream when I hold it.'

'That's because it's not a spren,' Syl said softly.

'What is it, then?'

'Dangerous.'

She stood up from his shoulder, then walked as if down a flight of steps toward the sword. She rarely flew when she had a human form. She flew as a ribbon of light, or as a group of leaves, or as a small cloud. He'd never noticed before how odd, yet normal, it was that she stuck to the nature of the form she used.

She stopped just before the sword. 'I think this is one of the Honorblades, the swords of the Heralds.'

Kaladin grunted. He'd heard of those.

'Any man who holds this weapon will become a Windrunner,' Syl explained, looking back at Kaladin. 'The Honorblades are what we are based on, Kaladin. Honor gave these to men, and those men gained powers from them. Spren figured out what He'd done, and we imitated it. We're bits of His power, after all, like this sword. Be careful with it. It is a treasure.'

'So the assassin wasn't a Radiant.'

'No. But Kaladin, you have to understand. With this sword, someone can do what you can, but without the ... checks a spren requires.' She touched it, then shivered visibly, her form blurring for a second. 'This sword gave the assassin power to use Lashings, but it also fed upon his Stormlight. A person who uses this will need far, far more Light than you will. Dangerous levels of it.'

Kaladin reached out and took the sword by the hilt, and Syl flitted away, becoming a ribbon of light. He hefted the weapon and set it back on his shoulder before continuing on his way. Yes, there was a hill up ahead, probably a crem-covered building. As he drew closer, blessedly, he saw motion around it.

'Hello?' he called.

The figures near it stopped and turned. 'Kaladin?' a familiar voice called. 'Storms, is that you?'

He grinned, the figures resolving into men in blue uniforms. Teft scrambled across the rock like a madman to meet him. Others came after, shouting and laughing. Drehy, Peet, Bisig, and Sigzil, Rock towering over them all.

'Another one?' Rock asked, eyeing Kaladin's Shardblade. 'Or is he yours?'

'No,' Kaladin said. 'I took this from the assassin.'

'He is dead, then?' Teft asked.

'Near enough.'

'You *defeated* the Assassin in White,' Bisig breathed. 'It's truly over then.'

'I suspect that it is just beginning,' Kaladin said, nodding toward the building. 'What is this place?'

'Oh!' Bisig said. 'Come on! We need to show you the tower – that Radiant girl taught us how to summon the plateau back, so long as we have you.'

'Radiant girl?' Kaladin asked. 'Shallan?'

'You don't sound surprised,' Teft said with a grunt.

'She has a Shardblade,' Kaladin said. One that didn't scream in his mind. Either she was a Radiant or she had another of these Honorblades. As he stepped up to the building, he noticed a bridge in the shadows nearby.

'It's not ours,' Kaladin said.

'No,' Leyten said. 'That belongs to Bridge Seventeen. We had to leave ours behind in the storm.'

Rock nodded. 'We were too busy stopping lighteyed heads from becoming too friendly with swords of enemies. Ha! But we needed bridge here. Way platform works, we had to get off him for Shallan Davar to transport herself back.'

Kaladin poked his head into the chamber inside the hill, then paused at the beauty he found inside. Other members of Bridge Four waited here, including a tall man Kaladin didn't immediately recognize. Was that one of Lopen's cousins? The man turned around, and Kaladin realized what he'd mistaken for a cap was a reddish skullplate.

Parshendi. Kaladin tensed as the Parshendi man *saluted*. He was wearing a Bridge Four uniform.

And he had the tattoo.

'Rlain?' Kaladin said.

'Sir,' Rlain said. His features were no longer rounded and plump, but instead sharp, muscular, with a thick neck and a stronger jaw, now lined by a red and black beard.

'It appears you are more than you seemed,' Kaladin said.

'Pardon, sir,' he said. 'But I would suggest that applies to both of us.' When he spoke now, his voice had a certain musicality to it – an odd rhythm to his words.

'Brightlord Dalinar has pardoned Rlain,' Sigzil explained, walking around Kaladin and entering the chamber.

'For being Parshendi?' Kaladin asked.

'For being a spy,' Rlain said. 'A spy for a people who, it appears, no longer exist.' He said this to a different beat, and Kaladin thought he could sense pain in that voice. Rock walked over and put a hand on Rlain's shoulder.

'We can give you the story once we get back to the city,' Teft said.

'We figured you'd come back here,' Sigzil added. 'To this plateau, and so we needed to be here to greet you, for all Brightness Davar grumbled. Anyway, there's a lot to tell – a lot is happening. I think that you're kind of going to be at the center of it.'

Kaladin took a deep breath, but nodded. What else did he expect? No more hiding. He had made his decision.

What do I tell them about Moash? he wondered as the members of Bridge Four piled into the room around him, chattering about how he needed to infuse the spheres in the lanterns. A couple of the men bore wounds from the fighting, including Bisig, who kept his right hand in his coat pocket. Grey skin peeked out from the cuff. He'd lost the hand to the Assassin in White.

Kaladin pulled Teft aside. 'Did we lose anyone else?' Kaladin asked. 'I saw Mart and Pedin.'

'Rod,' Teft said with a grunt. 'Dead to the Parshendi.'

Kaladin closed his eyes, breathing out in a hiss. Rod had been one of Lopen's cousins, a jovial Herdazian who hardly spoke Alethi. Kaladin had barely known him, but the man had still been Bridge Four. Kaladin's responsibility.

'You can't protect us all, son,' Teft said. 'You can't stop people from feeling pain, can't stop men from dying.'

Kaladin opened his eyes, but did not challenge those statements. Not vocally, at least.

'Kal,' Teft said, voice getting even softer. 'At the end there, right before you arrived ... Storms, son, I swear I saw a couple of the lads glowing. Faintly, with Stormlight.'

'What?'

'I've been listening to readings of those visions Brightlord Dalinar sees,' Teft continued. 'I think you should do the same. From what I can guess, it seems that the orders of the Knights Radiant were made up of more than just the knights themselves.'

Kaladin looked over the men of Bridge Four, and found himself smiling. He shoved down the pain at his losses, at least for the time being. 'I wonder,' he said softly, 'what it will do to Alethi social structure when an entire *group* of former slaves starts going about with glowing skin.'

'Not to mention those eyes of yours,' Teft said with a grunt.

'Eyes?' Kaladin said.

'Haven't you seen?' Teft said. 'What am I saying? Ain't no mirrors out on the Plains. Your eyes, son. Pale blue, like glassy water. Lighter than that of any king.'

Kaladin turned away. He'd hoped his eyes wouldn't change. The truth, that they had, made him uncomfortable. It said worrisome things. He didn't want to believe that lighteyes had any grounds upon which to build the oppression.

They still don't, he thought, infusing the gemstones in the lanterns as Sigzil instructed him. *Perhaps the lighteyes rule because of the memory, buried deeply, of the Radiants. But just because they* look *a little like Radiants doesn't mean they should have been able to oppress everyone.*

Storming lighteyes. He ...

He was one of them now.

Storm it!

He summoned Syl as a Blade, following Sigzil's instructions, and used her as a key to work the fabrial.

.·.

Shallan stood at the front gates of Urithiru, looking up, trying to comprehend.

Inside, voices echoed in the grand hall and lights bobbed as people explored. Adolin had taken command of that endeavor, while Navani set up a camp to see to the wounded and to measure supplies. Unfortunately, they'd left most of their food and gear behind on the Shattered Plains. In addition, the travel through the Oathgate had not been as cheap as Shallan had first assumed. Somehow, the trip had drained the majority of the gemstones held by the men and women on the plateau – including Navani's fabrials, clutched in the hands of engineers and scholars.

They had run a few tests. The more people you moved, the more Light was required. It seemed that Stormlight, and not just the gemstones that contained it, would become a valuable resource. Already, they had to ration their gemstones and lanterns to explore the building.

Several scribes passed by, bringing paper to draw out maps of Adolin's exploration. They bobbed quick, uncomfortable bows to Shallan and called her 'Brightness Radiant.' She still hadn't talked at length with Adolin about what had happened to her.

'Is it true?' Shallan asked, tilting her head all the way back, looking up the side of the enormous tower toward the blue sky high above. 'Am I one of them?'

'Mmm ...' Pattern said from her skirt. 'Almost you are. Still a few Words to say.'

'What kind of words? An oath?'

'Lightweavers make no oaths beyond the first,' Pattern said. 'You must speak truths.'

Shallan stared up at the heights for a time longer, then turned and walked back down toward their improvised camp. It was not the Weeping here. She wasn't certain if that was because they were actually *above* the rainclouds, or if the weather patterns had simply been thrown off by the arrival of the strange highstorms.

In camp, men sat on the stone, divided by ranks, shivering in their wet coats. Shallan's breath puffed before her, though she had taken in Stormlight – just a dash – to keep herself from noticing the cold. Unfortunately, there wasn't much to use for fires. The large stone field in front of the tower city bore very few rockbuds, and the ones that did grow were tiny, smaller than a fist. They would provide little wood for fires.

The field was ringed by ten columnar plateaus, with steps winding around their bases. The Oathgates. Beyond that extended the mountain range.

Crem did cover some of the steps here, and dripped over the sides of the open field. There wasn't nearly as much as there had been on the Shattered Plains. Less rain must fall up here.

Shallan stepped up to one edge of the stone field. A sheer drop. If Nohadon really *had* walked to this city, as *The Way of Kings* claimed, then his path would have included scaling cliff faces. So far, they had found no way down other than through the Oathgates – and even if there were such a way, one would still be stranded in the middle of the mountains, weeks from civilization. Judging from the sun height, the scholars placed them near the center of Roshar, somewhere in the mountains near Tu Bayla or maybe Emul.

The remote location made the city incredibly defensible, or so Dalinar said. It also left them isolated, potentially cut off. And that, in turn, explained why everyone looked at Shallan as they did. They'd tried other Shardblades; none were effective at making the ancient fabrial work. Shallan was literally their only way out of these mountains.

One of the soldiers nearby cleared his throat. 'You certain you should be that close to the edge, Brightness Radiant?'

She gave the man a droll look. 'I could survive that drop and stroll away, soldier.'

'Um, yes, Brightness,' he said, blushing.

She left the edge and continued on to find Dalinar. Eyes followed her as she walked: soldiers, scribes, lighteyes, and highlords alike. Well, let them see Shallan the Radiant. She could always find freedom later, wearing another face.

Dalinar and Navani supervised a group of women near the center of the army. 'Any luck?' Shallan asked, approaching.

Dalinar glanced at her. The scribes wrote letters using every spanreed they had, delivering messages of warning to the warcamps and to the relay room in Tashikk. *A new storm might come, blowing in from the west, not the east. Prepare.*

New Natanan, on the very eastern coast of Roshar, would be struck today after the everstorm left the Shattered Plains. Then it would enter the eastern ocean and move toward the Origin.

None of them knew what would happen next. Would it round the world and come crashing into the western coast? Were the highstorms all one storm that rounded the planet, or did a new one start at the Origin each time, as mythology claimed?

Scholars and stormwardens thought the former, these days. Their calculations said that, assuming the everstorm moved at the same speed as a highstorm this time of year, they'd have a few days before it returned and hit Shinovar and Iri, then blew across the continent, laying waste to cities thought protected.

'No news,' Dalinar said, voice tense. 'The king seems to have vanished. What's more, Kholinar appears to be in a state of riot. I haven't been able to get straight answers on either question.'

'I'm sure the king is somewhere safe,' Shallan said, glancing at Navani. The woman maintained a composed face, but as she gave instructions to a scribe, her voice was terse and clipped.

One of the pillarlike plateaus nearby flashed. It happened with a wall of light revolving around its perimeter, leaving streaks of blurred afterimage to fade. Someone had activated the Oathgate.

Dalinar stepped up beside her and they waited tensely, until a group of figures in blue appeared at the plateau edge and started down the steps. Bridge Four.

'Oh, thank the *Almighty*,' Shallan whispered. It was him, not the assassin.

One of the figures pointed down toward where Dalinar and the rest of them stood. Kaladin separated from his men, dropping *off* the steps and floating over the army. He landed on the stones in stride, carrying a Shardblade on his shoulder, his long officer's coat unbuttoned and coming down to his knees.

He still has the slave brands, she thought, though his long hair obscured them. His eyes had become a pale blue. They glowed softly.

'Stormblessed,' Dalinar called.

'Highprince,' Kaladin said.

'The assassin?'

'Dead,' Kaladin said, hefting the Blade and sticking it down into the rock before Dalinar. 'We need to talk. This—'

'My son, bridgeman,' Navani asked from behind. She stepped up and took Kaladin by the arm, as if completely unconcerned by the Stormlight that drifted from his skin like smoke. 'What happened to my son?'

'There was an assassination attempt,' Kaladin said. 'I stopped it, but the king was wounded. I put him someplace safe before coming to help Dalinar.'

'Where?' Navani demanded. 'We've had our people in the warcamps search monasteries, mansions, the barracks . . .'

'Those places were too obvious,' Kaladin said. 'If you could think to look there, so might the assassins. I needed someplace nobody would think of.'

'Where, then?' Dalinar asked.

Kaladin smiled.

⁂

The Lopen made a fist with his hand, clutching the sphere inside. In the next room over, his mother scolded a king.

'No, no, Your Majesty,' she said, words thickly accented, using the same stern tone she used with the axehounds. 'You roll the whole thing up and eat it. You can't pick it apart like that.'

'I don't feel so hungry, nanha,' Elhokar said. His voice was weak, but he'd awoken from his drunken stupor, which was a good sign.

'You'll eat anyway!' Mother said. 'I know what to do when I see a man that pale in the face, and pardon, Your Majesty, but you are pale as a sheet hung out for the sun to bleach! And that's the truth of it. You're going to eat. No complaints.'

'I'm the king. I don't take orders from—'

'You're in my home now!' she said, and Lopen mouthed along with the words. 'In a Herdazian woman's home, nobody's station means nothing beside her own. I'm not going to have them come and get you and find you not properly fed! I'll not have people saying that, Your Brightship, no I won't! Eat up. I've got soup cooking.'

The Lopen smiled, and though he heard the king grumble, he *also* heard the sound of spoon against plate. Two of Lopen's strongest cousins sat out front of the hovel in Little Herdaz – which was technically in Highprince Sebarial's warcamp, though the Herdazians didn't pay much attention to that. Four more cousins sat at the end of the street, idly sewing some boots, watching for anything suspicious.

'All right,' Lopen whispered, 'you really need to work this time.' He focused on that sphere in his hand. Just like he did every day, and had done every day since Captain Kaladin had started glowing. He'd figure it out sooner or later. He was as sure of it as he was sure of his name.

'Lopen.' A wide face ducked in one of the windows, distracting him. Chilinko, his uncle. 'Get the king man dressed up like a Herdazian again. We might need to move.'

'Move?' Lopen said, standing.

'Word has come in to all the warcamps from Highprince Sebarial,' Chilinko said in Herdazian. 'They found something out there, on the Plains. Be ready. Just in case. Everyone's talking. I can't make sense of it.' He shook his head. 'First that highstorm nobody knew about, then the rains stop early, then the storming *king man of Alethkar* on my doorstep. Now this. I think we might be abandoning camp, even though nightfall's around the corner. Makes no sense to me, but get the king man taken care of.'

The Lopen nodded. 'I'll get to it. Just a sec.'

Chilinko ducked away. Lopen opened his palm and stared at the sphere. He didn't want to miss a day practicing with his sphere, just in case. After all, sooner or later, he was going to look at one of these and—

The Lopen sucked in Light.

It happened in an eyeblink, and then there he sat, Stormlight streaming from his skin.

'Ha!' he shouted, leaping to his feet. '*Ha!* Hey, Chilinko, come back here. I need to stick you to the wall!'

The Light winked out. The Lopen stopped, frowning, and held his hand up in front of him. Gone so fast? What had happened? He hesitated. That tingling . . .

He felt at his shoulder, the one where he'd lost his arm so long ago. There, his fingers prodded a new nub of flesh that had begun sprouting from his scar.

'Oh, *storms* yes! Everybody, give the Lopen your spheres! I have glowing that needs to be done.'

Moash sat on the back of the cart as it rattled and wound its way out of the warcamps. He could have ridden in front, but he didn't want to be far from his armor, which they'd wrapped up in packages and stacked back here. Hidden. The Blade and Plate might be his in name, but he had no illusions as to what would happen if the Alethi elite noticed him trying to flee with it.

His wagon crested the rise just outside of the warcamps. Behind them, enormous lines of people snaked out onto the Shattered Plains. Highprince Dalinar's orders had been clear, though baffling. The warcamps were being abandoned. All parshmen were to be left behind, and everyone was to make their way toward the center of the Shattered Plains.

Some of the highprinces obeyed. Others did not. Curiously, Sadeas was one of those who obeyed, his warcamp emptying almost as quickly as those of Sebarial, Roion, and Aladar. It seemed like everyone was going, even the children.

Moash's cart rolled to a stop. Graves stepped up beside the back a few moments later. 'We needn't have worried about hiding,' he mumbled, looking over the exodus. 'They're too busy to pay attention to us. Look there.'

Some groups of merchants gathered outside of Dalinar's warcamps. They pretended to be packing to leave, but weren't making any obvious progress.

'Scavengers,' Graves said. 'They'll head into the abandoned warcamps to loot. Storming fools. They deserve what is coming.'

'What *is* coming?' Moash said. He felt as if he had been tossed into a roiling river, one that had burst its banks following a highstorm. He swam with the current, but could barely keep his head above water.

He'd tried to kill Kaladin. *Kaladin.* It had all fallen apart. The king survived, Kaladin's powers were back, and Moash . . . Moash was a traitor. Twice over.

'Everstorm,' Graves said. He didn't look nearly so refined, now that he wore the patchwork overalls and shirt of a poor darkeyes. He'd used some strange eyedrops to change his eyes dark, then had instructed Moash to do the same.

'And that is?'

'The Diagram is vague,' Graves said. 'We only knew the term because of old Gavilar's visions. The Diagram says this will probably return the Voidbringers, though. Those have turned out to be the parshmen, it seems.' He shook his head. 'Damnation. That woman was right.'

'Woman?'

'Jasnah Kholin.'

Moash shook his head. He didn't understand *any* of what was happening. Graves's sentences felt like strings of words that shouldn't go together. Parshmen, Voidbringers? Jasnah Kholin? That was the king's sister. Hadn't she died at sea? What did Graves know of her?

'Who are you really?' Moash asked.

'A patriot,' Graves said. 'Just like I told you. We're allowed to pursue our own interests and goals until we're called up.' He shook his head. 'I thought for sure my interpretation was correct, that if we removed Elhokar, Dalinar would become our ally in what is to come. . . . Well, it appears I was wrong. Either that, or I was too slow.'

Moash felt sick.

Graves gripped him on the arm. 'Head up, Moash. Bringing a Shardbearer back with me will mean that my mission wasn't a *complete* loss. Besides, you can tell us about this new Radiant. I'll introduce you to the Diagram. We have an important work.'

'Which is?'

'The salvation of the entire world, my friend.' Graves patted him, then walked toward the front of the cart, where the others rode.

The salvation of the entire world.

I've been played for one of the ten fools, Moash thought, chin to his chest. *And I don't even know how.*

The wagon started rolling again.

88

THE MAN WHO OWNED THE WINDS

1173090605   1173090801   1173090901   1173091001   1173091004
1173100105   1173100205   1173100401   1173100603   1173100804

—From the Diagram, North Wall Coda,
Windowsill region: paragraph 2
(This appears to be a sequence of dates,
but their relevance is as yet unknown.)

They soon began to move into the tower.

There was nothing else they could do, though Adolin's explorations were far from finished. Night was approaching, and the temperature was dropping outside. Beyond that, the highstorm that had hit the Shattered Plains would be raging across the land currently, and would eventually hit these mountains. It took over a day for one to cross the entire continent, and they were probably somewhere near the center, so it would be growing close.

An unscheduled highstorm, Shallan thought, walking through the dark hallways with her guards. *And something* else *coming from the other direction.*

She could tell that this tower – its contents, every hallway – was a majestic wonder. It spoke worlds about how tired she was that she didn't want to draw any of it. She just wanted to sleep.

Their spherelight revealed something odd on the wall ahead. Shallan frowned, shaking off her fatigue and stepping up to it. A small folded piece of paper, like a card. She glanced back at her guards, who looked equally confused.

She pulled the card off the wall; it had been stuck in place with some weevilwax on the back. Inside was the triangle symbol of the Ghost-bloods. Beneath it, Shallan's name. Not Veil's name.

Shallan's.

Panic. Alertness. In a moment, she had sucked in the Light of their lantern, plunging the corridor into darkness. Light shone from a doorway nearby, however.

She stared at it. Gaz moved to investigate, but Shallan stopped him with a gesture.

Run or fight?

Run where? she thought. Hesitant, she stepped up to the doorway, again motioning her guards back.

Mraize stood inside, gazing out a large, glassless window that over-looked another section of the innards of this tower. He turned toward her, twisted and scarred, yet somehow refined in his gentleman's clothing.

So. She had been found out.

I am no longer a child who hides in her room when the shouting comes, she thought firmly to herself, walking into the room. *If I run from this man, he will see me as something to be hunted.*

She stepped right up to him, ready to summon Pattern. He wasn't like other Shardblades; she acknowledged that now. He could come more quickly than the ten requisite heartbeats.

He'd done that before. She hadn't been willing to admit that he was capable of it. Admitting that would have meant too much.

How many more of my lies, she thought, *hold me back from things I could accomplish?*

But she needed those lies. *Needed* them.

'You led me on a grand hunt, Veil,' Mraize said. 'If your abilities had not been manifest during the course of saving the army, I perhaps never would have located your false identity.'

'Veil is the false identity, Mraize,' Shallan said. 'I am me.'

He inspected her. 'I think not.'

527

She met that gaze, but shivered inside.

'A curious position you are in,' Mraize said. 'Will you hide the true nature of your powers? I was able to guess what they are, but others will not be so knowledgeable. They might see only the Blade, and not ask what else you can do.'

'I don't see how it's a concern of yours.'

'You are one of us,' Mraize said. 'We look after our own.'

Shallan frowned. 'But you've seen through the lie.'

'Are you saying you don't want to be one of the Ghostbloods?' His tone was not threatening, but those eyes . . . storms, those eyes could have drilled through stone. 'We do not offer the invitation to just anyone.'

'You killed Jasnah,' Shallan hissed.

'Yes. After she, in turn, had assassinated a number of our members. You didn't think her hands were clean of blood, did you, Veil?'

She looked away, breaking his gaze.

'I should have guessed that you would turn out to be Shallan Davar,' Mraize continued. 'I feel a fool for not seeing it earlier. Your family has a long history of involvement in these events.'

'I will not help you,' Shallan said.

'Curious. You should know that I have your brothers.'

She looked to him sharply.

'Your house is no more,' Mraize said. 'Your family's grounds seized by a passing army. I rescued your brothers from the chaos of the succession war, and am bringing them here. Your family, however, does owe me a debt. One Soulcaster. Broken.'

He met her eyes. 'How convenient that you, by my estimations, *are* one, little knife.'

She summoned Pattern. 'I will kill you before I let you use them as blackmail—'

'No blackmail,' Mraize said. 'They will arrive safe. A gift to you. You may wait upon my words and see. I mention your debt only so that it has a chance to find . . . purchase in your mind.'

She frowned, holding her Shardblade, wavering. 'Why?' she finally asked.

'Because, you are ignorant.' Mraize stepped closer to her, towering over her. 'You don't know who we are. You don't know what we're trying to accomplish. You don't know much of anything at all, Veil. Why did your father join us? Why did your brother seek out the Skybreakers? I have done some research, you see. I have answers for you.' Surprisingly, he turned from her and walked toward the doorway. 'I will give you time to consider. You seem to think that your newfound place among the Radiants makes you unfit for our numbers, but I see it differently, as does my *babsk*. Let Shallan Davar be a Radiant, conformist and noble. Let Veil come to us.' He stopped by the doorway. 'And let her find truth.'

He disappeared into the hallway. Shallan found herself feeling even more drained than before. She dismissed Pattern and leaned back against the wall. Of *course* Mraize would have found his way here – he'd likely been among the armies, somewhere. Getting to Urithiru had been one of the Ghostbloods' primary goals. Despite her determination not to help them, she'd transported them – along with the army – right where they wanted to go.

Her brothers? Would they actually be safe? What of her family servants, her brother's betrothed?

She sighed, walking to the doorway and collecting her guards. *Let her find truth.* What if she didn't want to find the truth? Pattern hummed softly.

After walking through the tower's ground floor – using her own glow for light – she found Adolin in the hallway beside a room, where he'd said he'd be. He had his wrist wrapped, and the bruises on his face were starting to purple. They made him look *slightly* less intoxicatingly handsome, though there was a rugged 'I punched a lot of people today' quality to that, which was fetching in its own right.

'You look exhausted,' he said, giving her a peck of a kiss.

'And you look like you let someone play sticks with your face,' she said, but smiled at him. 'You should get some sleep too.'

'I will,' he said. 'Soon.' He touched her face. 'You're amazing, you realize. You saved everything. Everyone.'

'No need to treat me like I'm glass, Adolin.'

'You're a Radiant,' he said. 'I mean . . .' He ran his hand through his persistently messy hair. 'Shallan. You're something greater than even a lighteyes.'

'Was that a wisecrack about my girth?'

'What? No. I mean . . .' He blushed.

'I will *not* let this be awkward, Adolin.'

'But—'

She grabbed him in an embrace and forced him into a kiss, a deep and passionate one. He tried to mumble something, but she kept on kissing, pressing her lips against his, letting him feel her desire. He melted into the kiss, then grabbed her by the torso and pulled her close.

After a moment, he pulled back. 'Storms, that smarts!'

'Oh!' Shallan raised a hand to her mouth, remembering the bruises on his face. 'Sorry.'

He grinned, then winced again, as apparently that hurt too. 'Worth it. Anyway, I'll promise to avoid being awkward if you avoid being too irresistible. At least until I'm healed up. Deal?'

'Deal.'

He looked to her guards. 'Nobody disturbs the Lady Radiant, understand?'

They nodded.

'Sleep well,' he said, pushing open a door into the room. Many of the rooms still had wooden doors, despite their long abandonment. 'Hopefully, the room is suitable. Your spren chose it.'

Her spren? Shallan frowned, then stepped into the room. Adolin closed the door.

Shallan studied the windowless stone chamber. Why had Pattern chosen this particular place for her? The room didn't seem distinctive. Adolin had left a Stormlight lantern for her – that was extravagant, considering how few lit gemstones they had – and it showed a small square chamber with a stone bench in the corner. There were a few blankets on it. Where had Adolin found blankets?

She frowned at the wall. The rock here was faded in a square, as if someone had once hung a picture there. Actually, that looked oddly familiar. Not that she'd been here before, but the place that square hung on the wall . . .

It was exactly in the same place where the picture had hung on her father's wall back in Jah Keved.

Her mind started to fuzz.

'Mmm . . .' Pattern said from the floor beside her. 'It is time.'

'No.'

'It is time,' he repeated. 'The Ghostbloods circle you. The people need a Radiant.'

'They have one. The bridgeboy.'

'Not enough. They need you.'

Shallan blinked out tears. Against her will, the room started to change. White carpet appeared. A picture on the wall. Furniture. Walls painted light blue.

Two corpses.

Shallan stepped over one, though it was just an illusion, and walked to the wall. A painting had appeared, part of the illusion, and it was outlined with a white glow. Something was hidden behind it. She pulled aside the picture, or tried to. Her fingers only made the illusion blur.

This was nothing. Just a re-creation of a memory she wished she didn't have.

'Mmm ... A better lie, Shallan.'

She blinked away tears. Her fingers lifted, and she pressed them against the wall again. This time, she could *feel* the painting's frame. It wasn't real. For the moment, she pretended that it was, and let the image capture her.

'Can't I just keep pretending?'

'No.'

She was there, in her father's room. Trembling, she pulled aside the picture, revealing the strongbox in the wall beyond. She raised the key, and hesitated. 'Mother's soul is inside.'

'Mmm ... No. Not her soul. That which took her soul.'

Shallan unlocked the safe, then tugged it open, revealing the contents. A small Shardblade. Thrust into the strongbox hastily, tip piercing through the back, hilt toward her.

'This was you,' she whispered.

'Mmm ... Yes.'

'Father took you from me,' Shallan said, 'and tried to hide you in here. Of course, that was useless. You vanished as soon as he closed the strongbox. Faded to mist. He wasn't thinking clearly. Neither of us were.'

She turned.

Red carpet. Once white. Her mother's friend lay on the floor, bleeding from the arm, though that wound hadn't killed him. Shallan walked to the other corpse, the one facedown in the beautiful dress of blue and gold. Red hair spilled out in a pattern around the head.

Shallan knelt and rolled over her mother's corpse, confronting a skull with burned-out eyes.

531

'Why did she try to kill me, Pattern?' Shallan whispered.

'Mmm . . .'

'It started when she found out what I could do.'

She remembered it now. Her mother's arrival, with a friend Shallan didn't recognize, to confront her father. Her mother's shouts, arguing with her father.

Mother calling Shallan one of *them*.

Her father barging in. Mother's friend with a knife, the two struggling, the friend getting cut in the arm. Blood spilled on the carpet. The friend had won that fight, eventually holding Father down, pinned on the ground. Mother took the knife and came for Shallan.

And then . . .

And then a sword in Shallan's hands.

'He let everyone believe that *he'd* killed her,' Shallan whispered. 'That he'd murdered his wife and her lover in a rage, when I was the one who had actually killed them. He lied to protect me.'

'I know.'

'That secret destroyed him. It destroyed our entire family.'

'I know.'

'I hate you,' she whispered, staring into her mother's dead eyes.

'I know.' Pattern buzzed softly. 'Eventually, you will kill me, and you will have your revenge.'

'I don't want revenge. I want my family.'

Shallan wrapped her arms around herself and buried her head in them, weeping as the illusion bled white smoke, then vanished, leaving her in an empty room.

⁘

I can only conclude, Amaram wrote hurriedly, the glyphs a mess of sloppy ink, *that we have been successful, Restares. The reports from Dalinar's army indicate that Voidbringers were not only spotted, but fought. Red eyes, ancient powers. They have apparently unleashed a new storm upon this world.*

He looked up from his pad and peeked out the window. His carriage rattled down the roadway in Dalinar's warcamp. All of his soldiers were away, and his remaining guards had gone to oversee the exodus. Even with Amaram's reputation, he'd been able to pass into the camp with ease.

He turned back to his paper. *I do not exult in this success,* he wrote. *Lives will be lost. It has ever been our burden as the Sons of Honor. To return the Heralds, to return the dominance of the Church, we had to put the world into a crisis.*

That crisis we now have, a terrible one. The Heralds will return. How can they not, with the problems we now face? But many will die. So very many. Nalan send that it is worth the loss. Regardless, I will have more information soon. When I next write you, I hope to do so from Urithiru.

The coach pulled to a stop and Amaram pushed open the door. He handed the letter to the carriage driver, Pama. She took it and began digging in her satchel for the spanreed to send the communication to Restares. He would have done it himself, but you could not use a spanreed while moving.

She would destroy the papers when done. Amaram spared a glance for the trunks on the back of the coach; they contained a precious cargo, including all of his maps, notes, and theories. Should he have left those with his soldiers? Bringing the force of fifty into Dalinar's warcamp would have drawn attention for certain, even with the chaos here, so he'd ordered them to meet him on the Plains.

He needed to keep moving. He strode away from the coach, pulling up the hood on his cloak. The grounds of Dalinar's temple complex were even more frenzied than most of the warcamps, as many people had come to the ardents in this time of stress. He passed a mother begging for one of them to burn a prayer for her husband, who fought with Dalinar's army. The ardent kept repeating that she should gather her things and join the caravans heading out across the Plains.

It was happening. It was *really* happening. The Sons of Honor had, at long last, achieved their goal. Gavilar would be proud. Amaram hastened his pace, turning as another ardent bustled up to him, to ask if he needed anything. Before she could look in his hood and recognize him, however, her attention was drawn by a pair of frightened youths who complained that their father was too old to make the trip, and begged for the ardents to help them carry him somehow.

He made it to the corner of the monastery building where they kept the insane and rounded to the back wall, out of sight, near the rim of the warcamp itself. He looked about, then summoned his Blade. A few swift slices would—

What was that?

He spun, certain he'd seen someone approach. But it was nothing. Shadows playing tricks on him. He made his slices in the wall and then carefully pushed open the hole he'd made. The Great One – Talenelat'Elin, Herald of War himself – sat in the dark room, in much the same posture he'd borne before. Perched on the end of his bed, slumped forward, head bowed.

'Why must they keep you in such darkness?' Amaram said, dismissing his Blade. 'This is not fit for the lowliest of men, let alone one such as yourself. I will have words with Dalinar about the way the insane are—'

No, he would not. Dalinar thought him a murderer. Amaram drew in a long, deep breath. Prices would need to be paid to see the Heralds return, but by Jezerezeh himself, the loss of Dalinar's friendship would be a stiff one indeed. Would that mercy had not stayed his hand, all those months ago, when he could have executed that spearman.

He hastened to the Herald's side. 'Great Prince,' Amaram whispered. 'We must go.'

Talenelat did not move. He was whispering again, though. The same things as before. Amaram could not help being reminded of the last time he had visited this place, in the company of someone who had been playing him for one of the ten fools all along. Who knew that Dalinar had grown so crafty in his old age? Time had changed both of them.

'Please, Great Prince,' Amaram said, getting the Herald to his feet with some difficulty. The man was enormous, as tall as Amaram but built like a wall. The dark brown skin had surprised him the first time he'd seen the man – Amaram had, somewhat foolishly, expected that all of the Heralds would look Alethi.

The Herald's dark eyes were, of course, some kind of disguise.

'The Desolation . . .' Talenelat whispered.

'Yes. It comes. And with it, your return to glory.' Amaram began to walk the Herald toward his opening. 'We must get you to—'

The Herald's hand snapped up in front of him.

Amaram started, freezing in place, as he saw something in the Herald's fingers. A small dart, the tip dripping with some clear liquid.

Amaram glanced at the opening, which spilled sunlight into the room. A small figure there made a puffing sound, a blowgun held to lips beneath a half mask that covered the upper face.

The Herald's other hand shot out, quick as an eyeblink, and snatched the dart from the air mere inches from Amaram's face. The Ghostbloods. They weren't trying to kill the Herald.

They were trying to kill Amaram.

He cried out, reaching his hand to the side, summoning his Blade. Too slow. The figure looked from him to the Herald, then scuttled away with a soft curse. Amaram chased after, leaping the rubble of the wall and breaking out into light, but the figure was moving too quickly.

Heart thumping in his chest, he looked back toward Talenelat, worried for the Herald's safety. Amaram started as he found the Herald standing tall, straight-backed, head up. Dark brown eyes, startlingly lucid, reflected the light of the opening. Talenelat raised one dart before himself and inspected it.

Then he dropped both darts and sat back down on his bed. His strange, unchanging mantra started over again, muttered. Amaram felt a chill run down his spine, but when he returned to the Herald, he could not get the man to respond.

With effort, he made the Herald rise again and ushered him to the coach.

⁘

Szeth opened his eyes.

He immediately squeezed them closed again. 'No. I died. I died!'

He felt rock beneath him. Blasphemy. He heard water dripping and felt the sun on his face. 'Why am I not dead?' he whispered. 'I released my bond to the Shardblade. I fell into the storm without Lashings. Why didn't I die?'

'You *did* die.'

Szeth opened his eyes again. He lay on an empty rock expanse, his clothing a wet mess. The Frostlands? He felt cold, despite the heat of the sun.

A man stood before him, wearing a crisp black and silver uniform. He had dark brown skin like a man from the Makabaki region, but had a pale mark on his right cheek in the shape of a small hooked crescent. He held one hand behind his back, while his other hand tucked something away into his coat pocket. A fabrial of some sort? Glowing brightly?

'I recognize you,' Szeth realized. 'I've seen you somewhere before.'

'You have.'

Szeth struggled to rise. He managed to make it to his knees, then knelt back on them. 'How?' he asked.

'I waited until you crashed to the ground,' the man said, 'until you were broken and mangled, your soul cut through, dead for certain. Then, I restored you.'

'Impossible.'

'Not if it is done before the brain dies. Like a drowned man restored to life with the proper ministrations, you could be restored with the right Surgebinding. If I had waited seconds longer, of course, it would have been too late. But surely you know this. Two of the Blades held by your people allow Regrowth. I suspect you have already seen the newly dead restored to life.'

He spoke the words calmly, without emotion.

'Who are you?' Szeth asked.

'You spend this long obeying the precepts of your people and religion, yet you fail to recognize one of your gods?'

'My gods are the spirits of the stones,' Szeth whispered. 'The sun and the stars. Not men.'

'Nonsense. Your people revere the spren of stone, but *you* do not worship them.'

That crescent ... He recognized it, didn't he?

'You, Szeth,' the man said, 'worship order, do you not? You follow the laws of your society to perfection. This attracted me, though I worry that emotion has clouded your ability to discern. Your ability to ... judge.'

Judgment.

'Nin,' he whispered. 'The one they call Nalan, or Nale, here. Herald of Justice.'

Nin nodded.

'Why save me?' Szeth said. 'Is my torment not enough?'

'Those words are foolishness,' Nin said. 'Unbecoming of one who would study beneath me.'

'I don't want to study,' Szeth said, curling up on the stone. 'I want to be dead.'

'Is that it? Truly, that is what you wish most? I will give it to you, if it is your honest desire.'

Szeth squeezed his eyes shut. The screams awaited him in that darkness. The screams of those he'd killed.

I was not wrong, he thought. *I was never Truthless.*

'No,' Szeth whispered. 'The Voidbringers *have* returned. I was right, and my people . . . *they* were wrong.'

'You were banished by petty men with no vision. I will teach you the path of one uncorrupted by sentiment. You will bring this back to your people, and you will carry with you justice for the leaders of the Shin.'

Szeth opened his eyes and looked up. 'I am not worthy.'

Nin cocked his head. 'You? Not worthy? I watched you destroy yourself in the name of order, watched you obey your personal code when others would have fled or crumbled. Szeth-son-Neturo, I watched you keep your word with perfection. This is a thing lost to most people – it is the only genuine beauty in the world. I doubt I have ever found a man more worthy of the Skybreakers than you.'

The Skybreakers? But that was an order of the Knights Radiant.

'I have destroyed myself,' Szeth whispered.

'You did, and you died. Your bond to your Blade severed, all ties – both spiritual and physical – undone. You are reborn. Come along. It is time to visit your people. Your training begins immediately.' Nin began to walk away, revealing that the thing he held behind his back was a sheathed sword.

You are reborn. Could he . . . could Szeth be reborn? Could he make the screams in the shadows go away?

You are a coward, the Radiant had said, the man who owned the winds. A small piece of Szeth thought it true. But Nin offered more. Something different.

Still kneeling, Szeth looked up after the man. 'You are right. My people have the other Honorblades, and have kept them safe for millennia. If I am to bring judgment to them, I will face enemies with Shards and with power.'

'This is not a problem,' Nin said, looking back. 'I have brought a replacement Shardblade for you. One that is a perfect match for your task and temperament.' He tossed his large sword to the ground. It skidded on stone and came to a rest before Szeth.

He had not seen a sword with a metal sheath before. And who sheathed a Shardblade? And the Blade itself . . . was it black? An inch or so of it had emerged from the sheath as it slid on the rocks.

Szeth swore he could see a small trail of black smoke coming off the metal. Like Stormlight, only dark.

Hello, a cheerful voice said in his mind. *Would you like to destroy some evil today?*

Therehastobeananswer Whatistheanswer Stop TheParshendi Oneofthem Yestheyarethemissingpiece PushfortheAlethitodestroy themoutrightbeforethisoneobtainstheirpowerItwillformabridge

—From the Diagram, Floorboard 17: paragraph 2, every second letter starting with the second

D alinar stood in darkness.

He turned about, trying to remember how he'd come to this place. In the shadows, he saw furniture. Tables, a rug, drapes from Azir with wild colors. His mother had always been proud of those drapes.

My home, he thought. *As it was when I was a child.* Back before conquest, back before Gavilar . . .

Gavilar . . . hadn't Gavilar died? No, Dalinar could hear his brother laughing in the next room. He was a child. They both were.

Dalinar crossed the shadowed room, feeling the fuzzy joy of familiarity. Of things being as they *should* be. He'd left his wooden swords out. He had a collection, each carved like a Shardblade. He was too old for those now, of course, but he still liked having them. As a collection.

He stepped to the balcony doors and pushed them open.

Warm light bathed him. A deep, enveloping, *piercing* warmth. A warmth that soaked down deep through his skin, into his very self. He stared at that light, and was not blinded. The source was distant, but he knew it. Knew it well.

He smiled.

Then he awoke. Alone in his new rooms in Urithiru, a temporary location for him to stay while they scouted the entire tower. A week had passed since they had arrived at this place, and the people of the warcamps had finally started to arrive, bearing spheres recharged during the unexpected highstorm. They needed those badly to make the Oathgate function.

Those from the warcamps arrived none too soon. The Everstorm had not yet returned, but if it moved like a regular highstorm, it should be striking any day now.

Dalinar sat in the darkness for a short time, contemplating that *warmth* he had felt. What had that been? It had been an odd time to get one of the visions. They always came during highstorms. Before, when he'd felt one coming on while sleeping, it had awakened him.

He checked with his guards. No highstorm was blowing. Contemplative, he started to dress. He wanted to see if he could get out onto the roof of the tower today.

⁘

As Adolin walked the dark halls of Urithiru, he tried not to show how overwhelmed he felt. The world had just *shifted*, like a door on its hinges. A few days ago, his causal betrothal had been that of a powerful man to a relatively minor scion of a distant house. Now, Shallan might be the most important person in the world, and he was . . .

What was he?

He raised his lantern, then made a few marks in chalk on the wall to indicate he'd been here. This tower was *huge*. How did the entire thing stay up? They could probably explore in here for months without opening every door. He had thrown himself into the duty of exploration because it seemed like something he could do. It also, unfortunately, gave him time to think. He didn't like how few answers he came up with.

He turned around, realizing he'd gotten far from the rest of his scouting party. He was doing that more and more often. The first groups from the Shattered Plains had started arriving, and they needed to decide where to house everyone.

Were those voices ahead? Adolin frowned, then continued down the corridor, leaving his lantern behind so it wouldn't give him away. He was surprised when he recognized one of the speakers down the hallway. Was that *Sadeas*?

It was. The highprince stood with a scouting party of his own. Silently, Adolin cursed the wind that had persuaded Sadeas – of all people – to heed the call to come to Urithiru. Everything would have been so much easier if he'd just stayed behind.

Sadeas gestured for a few of his soldiers to go down one branch of the tunnel-like corridor. His wife and a few of her scribes went the other way, two soldiers trailing. Adolin watched for a moment as the highprince himself raised a lantern, inspecting a faded painting on the wall. A fanciful picture, with animals from mythology. He recognized a few from children's stories, like the enormous, minklike creature with the mane of hair that burst out around and behind its head. What was it called again?

Adolin turned to go, but his boot scraped stone.

Sadeas spun, raising his lantern. 'Ah, Prince Adolin.' He wore white, which really didn't help his complexion – the pale color made his ruddy features seem downright bloody by comparison.

'Sadeas,' Adolin said, turning back. 'I wasn't aware that you had arrived.' Storming man. He'd ignored Father all those months, and *now* he decided to obey?

The highprince strolled up the hallway, passing Adolin. 'This place is remarkable. Remarkable indeed.'

'So you acknowledge that my father was right,' Adolin said. 'That his visions are true. The Voidbringers have returned, and you are made a fool.'

'I will admit,' Sadeas said, 'there is more fight left to your father than I'd once feared. A remarkable plan. Contacting the Parshendi, working out this deal with them. They put on quite a show, I hear. It certainly convinced Aladar.'

'You can't possibly believe it was all a show.'

'Oh please. You deny that he had a Parshendi among his *own guard*? Isn't it convenient that these new "Radiants" include the head of Dalinar's guard and your own betrothed?'

Sadeas smiled, and Adolin saw the truth. No, he didn't believe this, but it was the lie he would tell. He would start the whisperings again, trying to undermine Dalinar.

'Why?' Adolin asked, stepping up to him. '*Why* are you like this, Sadeas?'

'Because,' Sadeas said with a sigh, 'it has to happen. You can't have an army with two generals, son. Your father and I, we're two old whitespines who both want a kingdom. It's him or me. We've been pointed that way since Gavilar died.'

'It doesn't have to be that way.'

'It does. Your father will never trust me again, Adolin, and you know it.' Sadeas's face darkened. 'I will take this from him. This city, these discoveries. It's just a setback.'

Adolin stood for a moment, staring Sadeas in the eyes, and then something finally snapped.

That's it.

Adolin grabbed Sadeas by the throat with his unwounded hand, slamming the highprince back against the wall. The look of utter shock on Sadeas's face amused a part of Adolin, the very small part that wasn't completely, totally, and *irrevocably* enraged.

He squeezed, choking off a cry for help as he moved to pin Sadeas back against the wall, grabbing the man's arm with his own. But Sadeas was a trained soldier. He tried to break the hold, taking Adolin by the arm and twisting.

Adolin kept hold, but lost his balance. The two of them fell in a jumble, twisting, rolling. This wasn't the calculated intensity of the dueling grounds, or even the methodical butchery of the battlefield.

This was two sweating, straining men, both on the edge of panic. Adolin was younger, but he was still bruised from the fight with the Assassin in White.

He managed to come up on top, and as Sadeas struggled to yell, Adolin slammed the man's head down against the stone floor to daze him. Breathing in gasps, Adolin grabbed his side knife. He plunged the knife toward Sadeas's face, though the man managed to get his hands up to grab Adolin by the wrist.

Adolin grunted, forcing the knife closer, clutched in his off hand. He brought the right in anyway, the wrist flaring with pain, as he leaned it against the crossguard. Sweat prickled on Sadeas's brow, the knife's tip touching the end of his left nostril.

'My father,' Adolin said with a grunt, sweat from his nose dripping down onto the blade of the knife, 'thinks I'm a better man than he is.' He strained, and felt Sadeas's grip weaken. 'Unfortunately for you, he's wrong.'

Sadeas whimpered.

With a surge, Adolin forced the blade up past Sadeas's nose and into the eye socket – piercing the eye like a ripe berry – then rammed it home into the brain.

Sadeas shook for a moment, blood pooling around the blade as Adolin worked it to be certain.

A second later, a Shardblade appeared beside Sadeas – his father's Shardblade. Sadeas was dead.

Adolin stumbled back to not get blood on his clothing, though his cuffs were already stained. Storms. Had he just done that? Had he just *murdered* a *highprince*?

Dazed, he stared at that weapon. Neither man had summoned his Blade for the fight. The weapons might be worth a fortune, but they'd do less good than a rock in such a close-quarters fight.

Thoughts coming more clearly, Adolin picked up the weapon and stumbled away. He ditched the Blade out a window, dropping it down into one of the planterlike outcroppings of the terrace below. It might be safe there.

After that, he had the presence of mind to cut off his cuffs, remove his chalk mark on the wall by scraping it free with his own Blade, and walk as far away as he could before finding one of his scouting parties and pretending he'd been in that area all along.

❖

Dalinar finally figured out the locking mechanism, then pushed on the metal door at the end of the stairwell. The door was set into the ceiling here, the steps running straight up to it.

The trapdoor refused to open, despite being unlocked. He'd oiled the parts. Why wasn't it moving?

Crem, of course, he thought. He summoned his Shardblade and made a series of quick cuts around the trapdoor. Then, with an effort, he was able to force it to open. The ancient trapdoor swung upward and let him out onto the very top of the tower city.

He smiled, stepping onto the roof. Five days of exploration had sent Adolin and Navani into the depths of the city-tower. Dalinar, however, had been driven to seek the top.

For such an enormous tower, the roof was actually relatively small, and not that encrusted with crem. This high, less rain likely dropped during highstorms – and everyone knew crem was thicker in the east than it was in the west.

Storms, this place was high. His ears had popped several times while riding to the top, using the fabrial lift that Navani had discovered. She spoke of counterweights and conjoined gemstones, sounding awed by the technology of the ancients. All he knew was that her discovery had let him avoid climbing up some hundred flights of steps.

He stepped up to the edge and looked down. Below, each ring of the tower expanded out a little farther than the one above it. *Shallan is right*, he thought. *They're gardens. Each outer ring is dedicated to planting food.* He did not know why the eastern face of the tower was straight and sheer, facing the Origin. No balconies along that side.

He leaned out. Distant, so far down it made him queasy, he picked out the ten pillars that held the Oathgates. The one to the Shattered Plains flashed, and a large group of people appeared on it. They flew Hatham's flag. With the maps Dalinar's scholars had sent, it had only taken Hatham and the others about a week of quick marching to reach the Oathgate. When Dalinar's army had crossed that same distance, they'd done so very cautiously, wary of Parshendi attacks.

Now that he saw those pillars from this perspective, he recognized that there was one of them in Kholinar. It made up the dais upon which the palace and royal temple had been built. Shallan suspected that Jasnah had tried to open the Oathgate there; the woman's notes said that Oathgates to each of the cities were locked tight. Only the one in the Shattered Plains had been left open.

Shallan hoped to figure out how to use the others, though their tests right now showed them to be locked somehow. If she managed to make them work, the world would become a much, much smaller place. Assuming there was anything left of it.

Dalinar turned and looked upward, regarding the sky. He took a deep breath. This was why he had come to the top.

'You sent that storm to destroy us!' he shouted toward the clouds. 'You sent it to cover up what Shallan, and then Kaladin, were becoming! You tried to end this before it could begin!'

Silence.

'Why send me visions and tell me to prepare!' Dalinar shouted. 'Then try to destroy us when we listen to them?'

I WAS REQUIRED TO SEND THOSE VISIONS ONCE THE TIME ARRIVED. THE ALMIGHTY DEMANDED IT OF ME. I COULD NO MORE DISOBEY THAN I COULD REFUSE TO BLOW THE WINDS.

Dalinar breathed in deeply. The Stormfather had replied. Blessedly, he had replied.

'The visions were his, then,' Dalinar said, 'and you the vehicle for choosing who received them?'

YES.

'Why did you pick me?' Dalinar demanded.

IT DOES NOT MATTER. YOU WERE TOO SLOW. YOU FAILED. THE EVERSTORM IS HERE, AND THE SPREN OF THE ENEMY COME TO IN-HABIT THE ANCIENT ONES. IT IS OVER. YOU HAVE LOST.

'You said that you were a fragment of the Almighty.'

I AM HIS ... SPREN, YOU MIGHT SAY. NOT HIS SOUL. I AM THE MEMORY MEN CREATE FOR HIM, NOW THAT HE IS GONE. THE PERSON-IFICATION OF STORMS AND OF THE DIVINE. I AM NO GOD. I AM BUT A SHADOW OF ONE.

'I'll take what I can get.'

HE WISHED FOR ME TO FIND YOU, BUT YOUR KIND HAVE BROUGHT ONLY DEATH TO MINE.

'What do you know of this storm that the Parshendi unleashed?'

THE EVERSTORM. IT IS A NEW THING, BUT OLD OF DESIGN. IT ROUNDS THE WORLD NOW, AND CARRIES WITH IT HIS SPREN. ANY OF THE OLD PEOPLE IT TOUCHES WILL TAKE ON THEIR NEW FORMS.

'Voidbringers.'

THAT IS ONE TERM FOR THEM.

'This Everstorm *will* come again, for certain?'

REGULARLY, LIKE HIGHSTORMS, THOUGH LESS FREQUENT. YOU ARE DOOMED.

'And it will transform the parshmen. Is there no way to stop it?'

No.

Dalinar closed his eyes. It was as he had feared. His army had defeated the Parshendi, yes, but they were only a fraction of what was coming. Soon he would face hundreds of thousands of them.

The other lands weren't listening. He'd managed to speak, via spanreed, with the emperor of Azir himself – a new emperor, as Szeth had visited the last one. There had been no succession war in Azir, of course. Those required too much paperwork.

The new emperor had invited Dalinar to visit, but obviously considered his words to be ravings. Dalinar hadn't realized that rumors of his madness had traveled so far. Even without that, however, he suspected his warnings would be ignored, as the things he spoke of were insane. A storm that blew the wrong way? Parshmen turning into Voidbringers?

Only Taravangian of Kharbranth – and now, apparently, Jah Keved – had seemed willing to listen. Heralds bless that man; hopefully he could bring some peace to that tortured land. Dalinar had asked for more information about how he'd obtained that throne; initial reports indicated he'd stumbled into the position unexpectedly. But he was too new, and Jah Keved too broken, for him to be able to do much.

Beyond that, there were sudden and unexpected reports, coming via spanreed, of Kholinar rioting. No straight answers there yet, either. And what was this he heard of a plague in the Purelake? Storms, what a mess this all had become.

He would need to do something about it. All of it.

Dalinar looked to the sky again. 'I have been commanded to refound the Knights Radiant. I will need to join their number if I am to lead them.'

Distant thunder rumbled in the sky, though there were no clouds.

'Life before death!' Dalinar shouted. 'Strength before weakness! Journey before destination!'

I AM THE SLIVER OF THE ALMIGHTY HIMSELF! the voice said, sounding angry. I AM THE STORMFATHER. I WILL NOT LET MYSELF BE BOUND IN SUCH A WAY AS TO KILL ME!

'I need you,' Dalinar said. 'Despite what you did. The bridgeman spoke of oaths given, and of each order of knights being different. The First Ideal is the same. After that, each order is unique, requiring different Words.'

The thunder rumbled. It sounded . . . like a challenge. Could Dalinar interpret thunder now?

This was a dangerous gambit. He confronted something primal, something unknowable. Something that had actively tried to murder him and his entire army.

'Fortunately,' Dalinar said, 'I know the second oath I am to make. I don't need to be told it. I *will* unite instead of divide, Stormfather. I will bring men together.'

The thunder silenced. Dalinar stood alone, staring at the sky, waiting.

VERY WELL, the Stormfather finally said. THESE WORDS ARE ACCEPTED.

Dalinar smiled.

I WILL NOT BE A SIMPLE SWORD TO YOU, the Stormfather warned. I WILL NOT COME AS YOU CALL, AND YOU WILL HAVE TO DIVEST YOURSELF OF THAT ... MONSTROSITY THAT YOU CARRY. YOU WILL BE A RADIANT WITH NO SHARDS.

'It will be what it must,' Dalinar said, summoning his Shardblade. As soon as it appeared, screams sounded in his head. He dropped the weapon as if it were an eel that had snapped at him. The screams vanished immediately.

The Blade clanged to the ground. Unbonding a Shardblade was supposed to be a difficult process, requiring concentration and touching its stone. Yet this one was severed from him in an instant. He could feel it.

'What was the meaning of the last vision I received?' Dalinar said. 'The one this morning, that came with no highstorm.'

NO VISION WAS SENT THIS MORNING.

'Yes it was. I saw light and warmth.'

A SIMPLE DREAM. NOT OF ME, NOR OF GODS.

Curious. Dalinar could have sworn it felt the same way as the visions, if not stronger.

GO, BONDSMITH, the Stormfather said. LEAD YOUR DYING PEOPLE TO FAILURE. ODIUM DESTROYED THE ALMIGHTY HIMSELF. YOU ARE NOTHING TO HIM.

'The Almighty could die,' Dalinar said. 'If that is true, then this Odium can be killed. I will find a way to do it. The visions mentioned a challenge, a champion. Do you know anything of this?'

The sky gave no reply beyond a simple rumble. Well, there would be time for more questions later.

Dalinar walked down off the top of Urithiru and entered the stairwell again. The flight of steps opened into a room that encompassed nearly the entire top floor of the tower city, and it shone with light through glass windows. Glass with no shutters or support, some of it facing east. How it survived highstorms Dalinar did not know, though lines of crem did streak it in places.

Ten short pillars ringed this room, with another at the center. 'Well?' Kaladin asked, turning away from an inspection of one of them. Shallan rounded another; she looked far less ragged than she had when they'd first come to the city. Though their days here in Urithiru had been frantic, some good nights' sleep had served them all quite well.

In response to the question, Dalinar took a sphere from his pocket and held it up. Then he sucked in the Stormlight.

He knew to expect the feeling of a storm raging inside, as both Kaladin and Shallan had described it to him. It urged him to act, to move, to not stand still. It did not, however, feel like the Thrill of battle – which was what he had anticipated.

He felt his wounds healing in a familiar way. He'd done this before, he sensed. On the battlefield earlier? His arm felt fine now, and the cut on his side barely ached anymore.

'It's horribly unfair you managed that on your first try,' Kaladin noted. 'It took me forever.'

'I had instruction,' Dalinar said, walking into the room and tucking the sphere away. 'The Stormfather called me Bondsmith.'

'It was the name of one of the orders,' Shallan said, resting her fingers on one of the pillars. 'That makes three of us. Windrunner, Bondsmith, Lightweaver.'

'Four,' a voice said from the shadows of the stairwell. Renarin stepped up into the lit room. He looked at them, then shrank back.

'Son?' Dalinar asked.

Renarin remained in the darkness, looking down.

'No spectacles . . .' Dalinar whispered. 'You stopped wearing them. I thought you were trying to look like a warrior, but no. Stormlight healed your eyes.'

Renarin nodded.

'And the Shardblade,' Dalinar said, stepping over and taking his son by the shoulder. 'You hear screams. That's what happened to you in the arena. You couldn't fight because of those shouts in your head from summoning the Blade. Why? Why didn't you say anything?'

'I thought it was me,' Renarin whispered. 'My mind. But Glys, he says
. . .' Renarin blinked. 'Truthwatcher.'

'Truthwatcher?' Kaladin said, glancing at Shallan. She shook her head.
'I walk the winds. She weaves light. Brightlord Dalinar forges bonds.
What do you do?'

Renarin met Kaladin's eyes across the room. 'I *see*.'

'Four orders,' Dalinar said, squeezing Renarin's shoulder with pride.
Storms, the lad was trembling. What made him so worried? Dalinar
turned to the others. 'The other orders must be returning as well. We
need to find those whom the spren have chosen. Quickly, for the Everstorm is upon us, and it is worse than we feared.'

'How?' Shallan asked.

'It will change the parshmen,' Dalinar said. 'The Stormfather confirmed
it to me. When that storm hits it will bring back the Voidbringers.'

'Damnation,' Kaladin said. 'I need to get to Alethkar, to Hearthstone.'
He strode toward the exit.

'Soldier?' Dalinar called. 'I've done what I can to warn our people.'

'My *parents* are back there,' Kaladin said. 'And the citylord of my town
has parshmen. I'm going.'

'How?' Shallan asked. 'You'll fly the entire distance?'

'Fall,' Kaladin said. 'But yes.' He paused at the doorway out.

'How much Light will that take, son?' Dalinar asked.

'I don't know,' Kaladin admitted. 'A lot, probably.'

Shallan looked to Dalinar. They didn't have Stormlight to spare.
Though those from the warcamps brought recharged spheres, activat-
ing the Oathgate took a great deal of Stormlight, depending on how
many people were brought. Lighting the lamps in the room at the center
of the Oathgate was merely the minimum amount needed to start the
device – bringing many people partially drained the infused gemstones
they carried as well.

'I will get you what I can, lad,' Dalinar said. 'Go with my blessing.
Perhaps you will have enough left over to get to the capital afterward and
help the people there.'

Kaladin nodded. 'I'll put together a pack. I need to leave within the
hour.' He ducked from the room into the stairwell down.

Dalinar sucked in more Stormlight, and felt the last of his wounds retreat. This seemed a thing a man could easily grow accustomed to having.

He sent Renarin with orders to speak with the king and requisition some emerald broams that Kaladin could borrow for his trip. Elhokar had finally arrived, in the company of a group of Herdazians, of all things. One claiming his name needed to be added to the lists of Alethi kings . . .

Renarin went eagerly to obey the order. He seemed to want something he could do.

He's one of the Knights Radiant, Dalinar thought, watching him go. *I'll probably need to stop sending him on errands.*

Storms. It was really happening.

Shallan had walked to the windows. Dalinar stepped up beside her. This was the eastern face of the tower, the flat edge that looked directly toward the Origin.

'Kaladin will only have time to save a few,' Shallan said. 'If that many. There are four of us, Brightlord. Only four against a storm full of destruction . . .'

'It is what it is.'

'So many will die.'

'And we will save the ones we can,' Dalinar said. He turned to her. 'Life before death, Radiant. It is the task to which we are now sworn.'

She pursed her lips, still looking eastward, but nodded. 'Life before death, Radiant.'

ART AND EXPECTATION

'A blind man awaited the era of endings,' Wit said, 'contemplating the beauty of nature.'

Silence.

'That man is me,' Wit noted. 'I'm not physically blind, just spiritually. And that other statement was actually *very* clever, if you think about it.'

Silence.

'This is a lot more satisfying,' he said, 'when I have intelligent life whom I can render awed, rapt with attention for my clever verbosity.'

The ugly lizard-crab-thing on the next rock over clicked its claw, an almost hesitant sound.

'You're right, of course,' Wit said. 'My usual audience isn't *particularly* intelligent. That was also the obvious joke, however, so shame on you.'

The ugly lizard-crab-thing scuttled across its rock, moving onto the other side. Wit sighed. It was night, which was normally a good time for dramatic arrivals and meaningful philosophy. Unfortunately for him, there was nobody here upon which to philosophize or visit, dramatically or otherwise. A small river gurgled nearby, one of the few permanent waterways in this strange land. Extending in all directions were rolling hills, furrowed by passing water and grown over in the valleys with an odd kind of briar. Very few trees here, though farther west a true forest sprouted on the slopes down from the heights.

A couple of songlings made rattling sounds nearby, and he took out his pipes and tried to imitate them. He couldn't, not exactly. The singing sounds were too like percussion, a zipping rattle – musical, but not flutelike.

Still, the creatures seemed to alternate with him, responding to his music. Who knew? Maybe the things had a rudimentary intelligence. Those horses, the Ryshadium ... those had surprised him. He was glad that there were still some things that could do that.

He finally set down his pipes and contemplated. An audience of ugly lizard-crab-things and songlings was *some* audience, at least.

'Art,' he said, 'is fundamentally unfair.'

One songling continued to creak.

'You see, we pretend that art is eternal, that there is some kind of *persistence* to it. A Truth, you might say. Art is art because it is *art* and not because we say that it is art. I'm not going too quickly for you, am I?'

Creak.

'Good. But if art is eternal and meaningful and independent, why does it depend so damn much upon the audience? You've heard the story about the farmer visiting court during the Festival of Depiction, right?'

Creak?

'Oh, it's not that great a story. Utterly disposable. Standard beginning, the farmer who visits the big city, does something embarrassing, stumbles into the princess and – completely by accident – saves her from getting trampled. Princesses in these stories never do seem to be able to look where they are going. I think perhaps more of them should inquire with a reputable lensmaker and procure a suitable set of spectacles before attempting any further traversal of thoroughfares.

'Anyway, as this story is a comedy, the man is invited to the palace for a reward. Various nonsense follows, ending with the poor farmer wiping himself in the privy with one of the finest paintings ever painted, then strolling out to find all of the lighteyes staring at an empty frame and commenting on how beautiful the work is. Mirth and guffaws. Flourish and bow. Exit before anyone thinks too much about the tale.'

He waited.

Creak?

'Well, don't you see?' Wit said. 'The farmer found the painting near the privy, so assumed it was to be used for such a purpose. The lighteyes found the empty frame in the hall of art, and assumed it to be a masterwork. You may call this a silly story. It is. That does not depreciate its truthfulness. After all, I am frequently quite silly – but I am almost always truthful. Force of habit.

'Expectation. *That* is the true soul of art. If you can give a man more than he expects, then he will laud you his entire life. If you can create an air of anticipation and feed it properly, you will succeed.

'Conversely, if you gain a reputation for being *too* good, *too* skilled ... beware. The better art will be in their heads, and if you give them an ounce less than they imagined, suddenly you have failed. Suddenly you are useless. A man will find a single coin in the mud and talk about it for days, but when his inheritance comes and is accounted one percent less than he expected, then he will declare himself cheated.'

Wit shook his head, standing up and dusting off his coat. 'Give me an audience who have come to be entertained, but who expect nothing special. To them, I will be a god. That is the best truth I know.'

Silence.

'I could use a little music,' he said. 'For dramatic effect, you see. Someone is coming, and I want to be prepared to welcome them.'

The songling, obligingly, started its music again. Wit took a deep breath, then struck the appropriate pose – lazy expectation, calculated knowingness, insufferable conceit. After all, he did have a reputation, so he might as well *try* to live up to it.

The air in front of him blurred, as if heated in a ring near the ground. A streak of light spun about the ring, forming a wall five or six feet high. It faded immediately – really, it was just an afterimage, as if something glowing had spun in the circle very quickly.

In the center of it appeared Jasnah Kholin, standing tall.

Her clothing was ragged, her hair formed into a single utilitarian braid, her face lashed with burns. She'd once worn a fine dress, but that was tattered. She'd hemmed it at the knees and had sewn herself a glove out of something improvised. Curiously, she wore a kind of leather bandolier and a backpack. He doubted she'd had either one when her journey had begun.

She groaned a long groan, then looked to the side, where Wit stood.

He grinned at her.

She stabbed her hand out in the blink of an eye, mist twisting around her arm and snapping into the form of a long, thin sword pointed at Wit's neck.

He cocked an eyebrow.

'How did you find me?' she asked.

'You've been making quite a disturbance on the other side,' Wit said. 'It's been a long time since the spren had to deal with someone alive, particularly someone so demanding as yourself.'

She hissed out a breath, then pushed the Shardblade closer. 'Tell me what you know, Wit.'

'I once spent the better part of a year inside of a large stomach, being digested.'

She frowned at him.

'That *is* a thing that I know. You really should be more specific in your threats.' He looked down as she twisted her Shardblade, rotating the tip, still pointed at him. 'I'd be surprised if that little knife of yours poses me any real threat, Kholin. You can keep waving it about if you want, though. Perhaps it makes you feel more important.'

She studied him. Then the sword burst to mist, vaporizing. She lowered her arm. 'I don't have time for you. A storm is coming, a terrible storm. It will bring the Voidbringers to—'

'Already here.'

'Damnation. We need to find Urithiru and—'

'Already found.'

She hesitated. 'The Knights—'

'Refounded,' Wit said. 'In part by your apprentice who, I might add, is exactly seventy-seven percent more agreeable than you are. I took a poll.'

'You're lying.'

'Okay, so it was a rather *informal* poll. But the ugly lizard-crab-thing gave you really poor marks for—'

'About the *other* things.'

'I don't tell those kinds of lies, Jasnah. You know that. It's what you find so annoying about me.'

She inspected him, then sighed. 'It is *part* of what I find so annoying about you, Wit. Only a very small part of a vast, vast river.'

'You only say that because you don't know me very well.'

'Doubtful.'

'No, really. If you *did* know me, that river of annoyance would be an ocean, obviously. Regardless. I know things that you do not, and I think you might *actually* know some that I do not. That gives us what is called synergy. If you can contain your annoyance, we might both learn something.'

She looked him up and down, then drew her lips to a line and nodded. She started walking directly toward the nearest town. She had a good sense of direction, this woman.

Wit strolled up beside her. 'You realize we're at *least* a week away from civilization. Did you need to Elsecall this far out in the middle of nowhere?'

'I was somewhat pressed at the time of my escape. I'm lucky to be here at all.'

'Lucky? I don't know if I'd say that.'

'Why?'

'You'd likely be better off on the other side, Jasnah Kholin. The Desolation has come, and with it, the end of this land.' He looked at her. 'I'm sorry.'

'Don't be sorry,' she said, 'until we see how much I can salvage. The storm has come already? The parshmen have transformed?'

'Yes and no,' Wit said. 'The storm should hit Shinovar tonight, then work its way across the land. I believe that the storm will *bring* the transformation.'

Jasnah stopped in place. 'That's not how it happened in the past. I have learned things on the other side.'

'You are correct. It is different this time.'

She licked her lips, but otherwise did a good job containing her anxiety. 'If it's not happening as it did before, then everything I know could be false. The words of the highspren could be inaccurate. The records I seek could be meaningless.'

He nodded.

'We can't depend upon the ancient writings,' she said. 'And the supposed god of men is a fabrication. So we can't look to the heavens for salvation, but apparently we can't look toward the past either. So where *can* we look?'

'You're so convinced that there is no God.'

'The Almighty is—'

'Oh,' Wit said, 'I don't mean the Almighty. Tanavast was a fine enough fellow – bought me drinks once – but he was *not* God. I'll admit, Jasnah, that I empathize with your skepticism, but I don't agree with it. I just think you've been looking for God in the wrong places.'

'I suppose that you're going to tell me where you think I *should* look.'

'You'll find God in the same place you're going to find salvation from this mess,' Wit said. 'Inside the hearts of men.'

'Curiously,' Jasnah said, 'I believe I can actually agree with that, though I suspect for different reasons than you imply. Perhaps this walk won't be as bad as I had feared.'

'Perhaps,' he said, looking up toward the stars. 'Whatever else might be said, at least the world chose a nice night upon which to end. . . .'

THE END OF

Book Two of

THE STORMLIGHT ARCHIVE

ENDNOTE

Alight, winds approach deadly approaching winds alight.

This ketek, written on Lightday, Jeseses 1174, adorns the cover of Navani Kholin's personal journal. Inside, she describes first-hand the events leading to the arrival of the Everstorm.

The glyphs of the ketek were drawn in the shape of two storms crashing into one another.

—Nazh

ARS ARCANUM

THE TEN ESSENCES AND THEIR HISTORICAL ASSOCIATIONS

NUMBER	GEMSTONE	ESSENCE	BODY FOCUS	SOULCASTING PROPERTIES	PRIMARY / SECONDARY DIVINE ATTRIBUTES
1 Jes	Sapphire	Zephyr	Inhalation	Translucent gas, air	Protecting / Leading
2 Nan	Smokestone	Vapor	Exhalation	Opaque gas, smoke, fog	Just / Confident
3 Chach	Ruby	Spark	The Soul	Fire	Brave / Obedient
4 Vev	Diamond	Lucentia	The Eyes	Quartz, glass, crystal	Loving / Healing
5 Palah	Emerald	Pulp	The Hair	Wood, plants, moss	Learned / Giving
6 Shash	Garnet	Blood	The Blood	Blood, all non-oil liquid	Creative / Honest
7 Betab	Zircon	Tallow	Oil	All kinds of oil	Wise / Careful
8 Kak	Amethyst	Foil	The Nails	Metal	Resolute / Builder
9 Tanat	Topaz	Talus	The Bone	Rock and stone	Dependable / Resourceful
10 Ishi	Heliodor	Sinew	Flesh	Meats, flesh	Pious / Guiding

The preceding list is an imperfect gathering of traditional Vorin symbolism associated with the Ten Essences. Bound together, these form the Double Eye of the Almighty, an eye with two pupils representing the creation of plants and creatures. This is also the basis for the hourglass shape that was often associated with the Knights Radiant.

Ancient scholars also placed the ten orders of Knights Radiant on this list, alongside the Heralds themselves, who each had a classical association with one of the numbers and Essences.

I'm not certain yet how the ten levels of Voidbinding or its cousin the Old Magic fit into this paradigm, if indeed they can. My research suggests that, indeed, there should be another series of abilities that is even more esoteric than the Voidbindings. Perhaps the Old Magic fits into those, though I am beginning to suspect that it is something entirely different.

Note that I currently believe the concept of the 'Body Focus' to be more a matter of philosophical interpretation than an actual attribute of this Investiture and its manifestations.

THE TEN SURGES

As a complement to the Essences, the classical elements celebrated on Roshar, are found the Ten Surges. These – thought to be the fundamental forces by which the world operates – are more accurately a representation of the ten basic abilities offered to the Heralds, and then the Knights Radiant, by their bonds.

Adhesion: The Surge of Pressure and Vacuum
Gravitation: The Surge of Gravity
Division: The Surge of Destruction and Decay
Abrasion: The Surge of Friction
Progression: The Surge of Growth and Healing, or Regrowth
Illumination: The Surge of Light, Sound, and Various Waveforms
Transformation: The Surge of Soulcasting
Transportation: The Surge of Motion and Realmatic Transition
Cohesion: The Surge of Strong Axial Interconnection
Tension: The Surge of Soft Axial Interconnection

ON THE CREATION OF FABRIALS

Five groupings of fabrial have been discovered so far. The methods of their creation are carefully guarded by the artifabrian community, but they appear to be the work of dedicated scientists, as opposed to the more mystical Surgebindings once performed by the Knights Radiant. I am more and more convinced that the creation of these devices requires forced enslavement of transformative cognitive entities, known as 'spren' to the local communities.

ALTERING FABRIALS

Augmenters: These fabrials are crafted to enhance something. They can create heat, pain, or even a calm wind, for instance. They are powered – like all fabrials – by Stormlight. They seem to work best with forces, emotions, or sensations.

The so-called half-shards of Jah Keved are created with this type of fabrial attached to a sheet of metal, enhancing its durability. I have seen fabrials of this type crafted using many different kinds of gemstone; I am guessing that any one of the ten Polestones will work.

Diminishers: These fabrials do the opposite of what augmenters do, and generally seem to fall under the same restrictions as their cousins. Those artifabrians who have taken me into confidence seem to believe that even greater fabrials are possible than what have been created so far, particularly in regard to augmenters and diminishers.

PAIRING FABRIALS

Conjoiners: By infusing a ruby and using methodology that has not been revealed to me (though I have my suspicions), you can create a conjoined pair of gemstones. The process requires splitting the original ruby. The two halves will then create parallel reactions across a distance. Spanreeds are one of the most common forms of this type of fabrial.

Conservation of force is maintained; for instance, if one is attached to a heavy stone, you will need the same strength to lift the conjoined fabrial that you would need to lift the stone itself. There appears to be some sort of process used during the creation of the fabrial that influences how far apart the two halves can go and still produce an effect.

Reversers: Using an amethyst instead of a ruby also creates conjoined halves of a gemstone, but these two work in creating *opposite* reactions. Raise one, and the other will be pressed downward, for instance.

These fabrials have only just been discovered, and already the possibilities for exploitation are being conjectured. There appear to be some unexpected limitations to this form of fabrial, though I have not been able to discover what they are.

WARNING FABRIALS

There is only one type of fabrial in this set, informally known as the Alerter. An Alerter can warn one of a nearby object, feeling, sensation, or phenomenon. These fabrials use a heliodor stone as their focus. I do not know whether this is the only type of gemstone that will work, or if there is another reason heliodor is used.

In the case of this kind of fabrial, the amount of Stormlight you can infuse into it affects its range. Hence the size of gemstone used is very important.

WINDRUNNING AND LASHINGS

Reports of the Assassin in White's odd abilities have led me to some sources of information that, I believe, are generally unknown. The Windrunners were an order of the Knights Radiant, and they made use of two primary types of Surgebinding. The effects of these Surgebindings were known – colloquially among the members of the order – as the Three Lashings.

BASIC LASHING: GRAVITATIONAL CHANGE

This type of Lashing was one of the most commonly used Lashings among the order, though it was not the easiest to use. (That distinction belongs to the Full Lashing below.) A Basic Lashing involved revoking a being's or object's spiritual gravitational bond to the planet below, instead temporarily linking that being or object to a different object or direction.

Effectively, this creates a change in gravitational pull, twisting the energies of the planet itself. A Basic Lashing allowed a Windrunner to run up walls, to send objects or people flying off into the air, or to create similar effects. Advanced uses of this type of Lashing would allow a Windrunner to make himself or herself lighter by binding part of his or her mass upward. (Mathematically, binding a quarter of one's mass upward would halve a person's effective weight. Binding half of one's mass upward would create weightlessness.)

Multiple Basic Lashings could also pull an object or a person's body downward at double, triple, or other multiples of its weight.

FULL LASHING: BINDING OBJECTS TOGETHER

A Full Lashing might seem very similar to a Basic Lashing, but they worked on very different principles. While one had to do with gravitation, the other had to do with the force (or Surge, as the Radiants called them) of Adhesion – binding objects together as if they were one. I believe this Surge may have had something to do with atmospheric pressure.

To create a Full Lashing, a Windrunner would infuse an object with Stormlight, then press another object to it. The two objects would become bound together with an extremely powerful bond, nearly impossible to break. In fact, most materials would themselves break before the bond holding them together would.

REVERSE LASHING: GIVING AN OBJECT
A GRAVITATIONAL PULL

I believe this may actually be a specialized version of the Basic Lashing. This type of Lashing required the least amount of Stormlight of any of the three Lashings. The Windrunner would infuse something, give a mental command, and create a *pull* to the object that yanked other objects toward it.

At its heart, this Lashing created a bubble around the object that imitated its spiritual link to the ground beneath it. As such, it was much harder for the Lashing to affect objects touching the ground, where their link to the planet was strongest. Objects falling or in flight were the easiest to influence. Other objects could be affected, but the Stormlight and skill required were much more substantial.

LIGHTWEAVING

A second form of Surgebinding involves the manipulation of light and sound in illusory tactics common throughout the cosmere. Unlike the variations present on Sel, however, this method has a powerful Spiritual element, requiring not just a full mental picture of the intended creation, but some level of connection to it as well. The illusion is based not simply upon what the Lightweaver imagines, but upon what they *desire* to create. In many ways, this is the most similar ability to the original Yolish variant, which excites me. I wish to delve more into this ability, with the hope to gain a full understanding of how it relates to Cognitive and Spiritual attributes.